The Short Novels of

JOHN STEINBECK

"*A blessed companion is a book*"—JERROLD

BY JOHN STEINBECK

A RUSSIAN JOURNAL
THE PEARL
THE WAYWARD BUS
CANNERY ROW
BOMBS AWAY
THE MOON IS DOWN (*novel*)
THE MOON IS DOWN (*play*)
SEA OF CORTEZ (*In collaboration with Edward F. Ricketts*)
THE GRAPES OF WRATH
THE FORGOTTEN VILLAGE
THE LONG VALLEY
THE RED PONY
OF MICE AND MEN (*novel*)
OF MICE AND MEN (*play*)
SAINT KATY THE VIRGIN
IN DUBIOUS BATTLE
TORTILLA FLAT
TO A GOD UNKNOWN
THE PASTURES OF HEAVEN
CUP OF GOLD
BURNING BRIGHT
EAST OF EDEN
SWEET THURSDAY

The Short Novels of
JOHN STEINBECK

★

Tortilla Flat

The Red Pony

Of Mice and Men

The Moon is Down

Cannery Row

The Pearl

Sweet Thursday

★

THE COMPANION BOOK CLUB

LONDON

THIS edition, issued in 1956, is for members of The Companion Book Club, 8 Long Acre, London, W.C.2, from which address particulars of membership may be obtained. The original edition, published by William Heinemann Ltd., contained six novels by John Steinbeck; the present edition, by special arrangement with William Heinemann Ltd., also includes his subsequent novel *Sweet Thursday*.

Made and printed in Great Britain
for The Companion Book Club (Odhams Press Ltd.)
by Wyman & Sons Ltd., London, Reading and Fakenham

S. 756 T.

Contents

★

TORTILLA FLAT
page 9

THE RED PONY
page 131

OF MICE AND MEN
page 181

THE MOON IS DOWN
page 249

CANNERY ROW
page 325

THE PEARL
page 433

SWEET THURSDAY
page 487

TORTILLA FLAT

To Susan Gregory *of Monterey*

PREFACE

THIS IS the story of Danny and of Danny's friends and of Danny's house. It is a story of how these three became one thing, so that in Tortilla Flat if you speak of Danny's house you do not mean a structure of wood flaked with old whitewash, overgrown with an ancient untrimmed rose of Castile. No, when you speak of Danny's house you are understood to mean a unit of which the parts are men, from which came sweetness and joy, philanthropy and, in the end, a mystic sorrow. For Danny's house was not unlike the Round Table, and Danny's friends were not unlike the knights of it. And this is the story of how that group came into being, of how it flourished and grew to be an organization beautiful and wise. This story deals with the adventuring of Danny's friends, with the good they did, with their thoughts and their endeavours. In the end, this story tells how the talisman was lost and how the group disintegrated.

In Monterey, that old city on the coast of California, these things are well known, and they are repeated and sometimes elaborated. It is well that this cycle be put down on paper so that in a future time scholars, hearing the legends, may not say as they say of Arthur and of Roland and of Robin Hood—"There was no Danny, nor any group of Danny's friends, nor any house. Danny is a nature god and his friends primitive symbols of the wind, the sky, the sun." This history is designed now and ever to keep the sneers from the lips of sour scholars.

Monterey sits on the slope of a hill, with a blue bay below it and with a forest of tall dark pine trees at its back. The lower parts of the town are inhabited by Americans, Italians, catchers and canners of fish. But on the hill where the forest and the town intermingle, where the streets are innocent of asphalt and the corners free of street lights, the old inhabitants of Monterey are embattled as the Ancient Britons are embattled in Wales. These are the paisanos.

They live in old wooden houses set in weedy yards, and the pine trees from the forest are about the houses. The paisanos are clean of commercialism, free of the complicated systems of American business, and, having nothing that can be stolen, exploited, or mortgaged, that system has not attacked them very vigorously.

What is a paisano? He is a mixture of Spanish, Indian, Mexican, and assorted Caucasian bloods. His ancestors have lived in California for a hundred or two years. He speaks English with a paisano accent and Spanish with a paisano accent. When questioned concerning his race, he indignantly claims pure Spanish blood and rolls up his sleeve to show that the soft inside of his arm is nearly white. His colour, like that of a well-browned meerschaum pipe, he ascribes to sunburn. He is a paisano, and he lives in that uphill district above the town of Monterey called Tortilla Flat, although it isn't a flat at all.

Danny was a paisano, and he grew up in Tortilla Flat and everyone liked him, but he did not stand out particularly from the screeching children of Tortilla Flat. He was related to nearly everyone in the Flat by blood or romance. His grandfather was an important man who owned two small houses in Tortilla Flat and was respected for his wealth. If the growing Danny preferred to sleep in the forest, to work on ranches, and to wrest his food and wine from an unwilling world, it was not because he did not have influential relatives. Danny was small and dark and intent. At twenty-five his legs were bent to the exact curves of a horse's sides.

Now, when Danny was twenty-five years old, the war with Germany was declared. Danny and his friend Pilon (Pilon, by the way, is something thrown in when a trade is conducted—a boot) had two gallons of wine when they heard about the war. Big Joe Portagee saw the glitter of the bottles among the pines and he joined Danny and Pilon.

As the wine went down in the bottles, patriotism arose in the three men. And when the wine was gone they went down the hill arm-in-arm for comradeship and safety, and they walked into Monterey. In front of an enlistment station they cheered loudly for America and dared Germany to do her worst. They howled menaces at the German Empire until the enlistment sergeant awakened and put on his uniform and came into the street to silence them. He remained to enlist them.

The sergeant lined them up in front of his desk. They passed everything but the sobriety test and then the sergeant began his questions with Pilon.

"What branch do you want to go in?"

"I don' give a god-damn," said Pilon jauntily.

"I guess we need men like you in the infantry." And Pilon was written so.

He turned then to Big Joe, and the Portagee was getting sober. "Where do you want to go?"

"I want to go home," Big Joe said miserably.

The sergeant put him in the infantry too. Finally he confronted Danny, who was sleeping on his feet. "Where do you want to go?"

"Huh?"

"I say, what branch?"

"What do you mean, 'branch'?"

"What can you do?"

"Me? I can do anything."

"What did you do before?"

"Me? I'm a mule skinner."

"Oh, you are? How many mules can you drive?"

Danny leaned forward, vaguely and professionally. "How many you got?"

"About thirty thousand," said the sergeant.

Danny waved his hand. "String 'em up!" he said.

And so Danny went to Texas and broke mules for the duration of the war. And Pilon marched about Oregon with the infantry, and Big Joe, as shall be later made clear, went to jail.

CHAPTER I

How Danny, home from the wars, found himself an heir, and how he swore to protect the helpless

When Danny came home from the army he learned that he was an heir and an owner of property. The *viejo*, that is, the grandfather, had died, leaving Danny the two small houses on Tortilla Flat.

When Danny heard about it he was a little weighed down with the responsibility of ownership. Before he ever went to look at his property he bought a gallon of red wine and drank most of it himself. The weight of responsibility left him then, and his very worst nature came to the surface. He shouted; he broke a few chairs in a pool-room on Alvarado Street; he had two short but glorious fights. No one paid much attention to Danny. At last his wavering bow-legs took him towards the wharf, where, at this early hour in the morning, the Italian fishermen were walking down in rubber boots to go out to sea.

Race antipathy overcame Danny's good sense. He menaced the fishermen. "Sicilian bastards," he called them, and "Scum from the prison island," and "Dogs of dogs of dogs." He cried, "*Chinga tu madre, Piojo*." He thumbed his nose and made obscene gestures below his waist. The fishermen only grinned and shifted their oars and said, "Hello, Danny. When'd you get home? Come around to-night. We got new wine."

Danny was outraged. He screamed, "*Pon un condo a la cabeza*."

They called, "Good-bye, Danny. See you to-night." And they climbed into their little boats and rowed out to the lampara launches and started their engines and chugged away.

Danny was insulted. He walked back up Alvarado Street, breaking windows as he went, and in the second block a policeman took him in hand. Danny's great respect for the law caused him to go quietly. If he had not just been discharged from the army after the victory over Germany, he would have been sentenced to six months. As it was, the judge gave him only thirty days.

And so for one month Danny sat on his cot in the Monterey city jail. Sometimes he drew obscene pictures on the walls, and sometimes he thought over his army career. Time hung heavy on Danny's hands there in his cell in the city jail. Now and then a drunk was put in for the night, but for the most part crime in Monterey was stagnant, and Danny was lonely. The bed-bugs bothered him a little at first, but as they got used to the taste of him and he grew accustomed to their bites, they got along peacefully.

He started playing a satiric game. He caught a bed-bug, squashed it against the wall, drew a circle around it with a pencil and named it "Mayor Clough". Then he caught others and named them after the City Council. In a little while he had one wall decorated with squashed bed-bugs, each named after a local dignitary. He drew ears and tails on them, gave them big noses and moustaches. Tito Ralph, the jailer, was scandalized; but he made no complaint because Danny had not included either the justice of the peace who had sentenced him or any of the police force. He had a vast respect for the law.

One night when the jail was lonely, Tito Ralph came into Danny's cell bearing two bottles of wine. An hour later he went out for more wine, and Danny went with him. It was cheerless in the jail. They stayed at Torrelli's, where they bought the wine, until Torrelli threw them out. After that Danny went up among the pines and fell asleep, while Tito Ralph staggered back and reported his escape.

When the brilliant sun awakened Danny about noon, he determined to hide all day to escape pursuit. He ran and dodged behind bushes. He peered out of the undergrowth like a hunted fox. And at evening, the rules having been satisfied, he came out and went about his business.

Danny's business was fairly direct. He went to the back door of a restaurant. "Got any old bread I can give my dog?" he asked the cook. And while that gullible man was wrapping up the food, Danny stole two slices of ham, four eggs, a lamb chop, and a fly swatter.

"I will pay you sometime," he said.

"No need to pay for scraps. I throw them away if you don't take them."

Danny felt better about the theft then. If that was the way they felt, on the surface he was guiltless. He went back to Torrelli's, traded the four eggs, the lamb chop, and the fly swatter for a water glass of grappa and retired towards the woods to cook his supper.

The night was dark and damp. The fog hung like limp gauze among the black pines that guard the landward limits of Monterey. Danny put his head down and hurried for the shelter of the woods. Ahead of him he made out another hurrying figure; and as he narrowed the distance, he recognized the scuttling walk of his old friend Pilon. Danny was a generous man, but he recalled that he had sold all his food except the two slices of ham and the bag of stale bread.

"I will pass Pilon by," he decided. "He walks like a man who is full of roast turkey and things like that."

Then suddenly Danny noticed that Pilon clutched his coat lovingly across his bosom.

"Ai, Pilon, *amigo!*" Danny cried.

Pilon scuttled on faster. Danny broke into a trot. "Pilon, my little friend! Where goest thou so fast?"

Pilon resigned himself to the inevitable and waited. Danny approached warily, but his tone was enthusiastic. "I looked for thee, dearest of little angelic friends, for see, I have here two great steaks from God's own pig, and a sack of sweet white bread. Share my bounty, Pilon, little dumpling."

Pilon shrugged his shoulders. "As you say," he muttered savagely. They walked on together into the woods. Pilon was puzzled. At length he stopped and faced his friend. "Danny," he asked sadly. "how knewest thou I had a bottle of brandy under my coat?"

"Brandy?" Danny cried. "Thou hast brandy? Perhaps it is for some sick old mother," he said naïvely. "Perhaps thou keepest it for Our Lord Jesus when He comes again. Who am I, thy friend, to judge the destination of this brandy? I am not even sure thou hast it. Besides, I am not thirsty. I would not touch this brandy. Thou art welcome to this big roast of pork I have, but as for thy brandy, that is thine own."

Pilon answered him sternly. "Danny, I do not mind sharing my brandy with you, half and half. It is my duty to see you do not drink it all."

Danny dropped the subject then. "Here in the clearing I will cook this pig, and you will toast the sugar cakes in this bag here. Put thy brandy here, Pilon. It is better here, where we can see it, and each other."

They built a fire and broiled the ham and ate the stale bread. The brandy receded quickly down the bottle. After they had eaten, they huddled near the fire and sipped delicately at the bottle like effete bees. And the fog came down upon them and greyed their coats with moisture. The wind sighed sadly in the pines about them.

And after a time a loneliness fell upon Danny and Pilon. Danny thought of his lost friends.

"Where is Arthur Morales?" Danny asked, turning his palms up and thrusting his arms forward. "Dead in France," he answered himself, turning the palms down and dropping his arms in despair. "Dead for his country. Dead in a foreign land. Strangers walk near his grave and they do not know Arthur Morales lies there." He raised his hands palms upward again. "Where is Pablo, that good man?"

"In jail," said Pilon. "Pablo stole a goose and hid in the brush; and that goose bit Pablo and Pablo cried out and so was caught. Now he lies in jail for six months."

Danny sighed and changed the subject, for he realized that he had prodigally used up the only acquaintance in any way fit for oratory. But the loneliness was still on him and demanded an outlet. "Here we sit," he began at last.

"——broken-hearted," Pilon added rhythmically.

"No, this is not a poem," Danny said. "Here we sit, homeless. We gave our lives for our country, and now we have no roof over our head."

"We never did have," Pilon added helpfully.

Danny drank dreamily until Pilon touched his elbow and took the bottle. "That reminds me," Danny said, "of a story of a man who owned two whore-houses——" His mouth dropped open. "Pilon!" he cried. "Pilon! my little fat duck of a baby friend. I had forgotten! I am an heir! I own two houses."

"Whore-houses?" Pilon asked hopefully. "Thou art a drunken liar," he continued.

"No, Pilon. I tell the truth. The *viejo* died. I am the heir. I, the favourite grandson."

"Thou art the only grandson," said the realist Pilon. "Where are these houses?"

"You know the *viejo's* house on Tortilla Flat, Pilon?"

"Here in Monterey?"

"Yes, here in Tortilla Flat."

"Are they any good, these houses?"

Danny sank back, exhausted with emotion. "I do not know. I forgot I owned them."

Pilon was silent and absorbed. His face grew mournful. He threw a handful of pine needles on the fire, watched the flames climb frantically among them and die. For a long time he looked into Danny's face with deep anxiety, and then Pilon sighed noisily, and again he sighed. "Now it is over," he said sadly. "Now the great times are done. Thy friends will mourn, but nothing will come of their mourning."

Danny put down the bottle, and Pilon picked it up and set it in his own lap.

"Now what is over?" Danny demanded. "What do you mean?"

"It is not the first time," Pilon went on. "When one is poor, one thinks, 'If I had money I would share it with my good friends.' But let that money come and charity flies away. So it is with thee, my once-friend. Thou art lifted above thy friends. Thou art a man of property. Thou wilt forget thy friends who shared everything with thee, even their brandy."

His words upset Danny. "Not I," he cried. "I will never forget thee, Pilon."

"So you think now," said Pilon coldly. "But when you have two houses to sleep in, then you will see. Pilon will be a poor paisano, while you eat with the mayor."

Danny arose unsteadily and held himself upright against a tree. "Pilon, I swear, what I have is thine. While I have a house, thou hast a house. Give me a drink."

"I must see this to believe it," Pilon said in a discouraged voice. "It would be a world wonder if it were so. Men would come a thousand miles to look upon it. And besides, the bottle is empty."

CHAPTER II

How Pilon was lured by greed of position to forsake Danny's hospitality

THE LAWYER left them at the gate of the second house and climbed into his Ford and stuttered down the hill into Monterey.

Danny and Pilon stood in front of the paintless picket fence and looked with admiration at the property, a low house streaked with old whitewash, uncurtained windows blank and blind. But a great pink rose of Castile was on the porch, and grandfather geraniums grew among the weeds in the front yard.

"This is the best of the two," said Pilon. "It is bigger than the other."

Danny held a new skeleton key in his hand. He tiptoed over the rickety porch and unlocked the front door. The main room was just as it had been when the *viejo* had lived there. The red rose calendar for 1906, the silk banner on the wall, with Fighting Bob Evans looking between the superstructures of a battleship, the bunch of red paper roses tacked up, the strings of dusty red peppers and garlic, the airtight stove, the battered rocking-chairs.

Pilon looked in the door. "Three rooms," he said breathlessly, "and a bed and a stove. We will be happy here, Danny."

Danny moved cautiously into the house. He had bitter memories of the *viejo*. Pilon darted ahead of him and into the kitchen. "A sink with a faucet," he cried. He turned the handle. "No water. Danny, you must have the company turn on the water."

They stood and smiled at each other. Pilon noticed that the worry of property was settling on Danny's face. No more in life would that face be free of care. No more would Danny break windows now that he had windows of his own to break. Pilon had been right—he had been raised among his fellows. His shoulders had straightened to withstand the complexity of life. But one cry of pain escaped him before he left for all time his old and simple existence.

"Pilon," he said sadly, "I wish you owned it and I could come to live with you."

While Danny went to Monterey to have the water turned on, Pilon wandered into the weed-tangled back yard. Fruit trees were there, bony and black with age, and gnarled and broken from neglect. A few tent-like chicken coops lay among the weeds. A pile of rusty barrel hoops, a heap of ashes, and a sodden mattress. Pilon looked over the fence into Mrs. Morales' chicken-yard, and after a moment of consideration he opened a few small holes in the fence for the hens. "They will like to make nests in the tall weeds," he thought kindly. He considered how he could make a figure-four trap in case the roosters came in too and bothered the hens and kept them from the nests. "We will live happily," he thought again.

Danny came back indignant from Monterey. "That company wants a deposit," he said.

"Deposit?"

"Yes. They want three dollars before they will turn on the water."

"Three dollars," Pilon said severely, "is three gallons of wine. And when that is gone, we will borrow a bucket of water from Mrs. Morales, next door."

"But we haven't three dollars for wine."

"I know," Pilon said. "Maybe we can borrow a little wine from Mrs. Morales."

The afternoon passed. "To-morrow we will settle down," Danny announced. "To-morrow we will clean and scrub. And you, Pilon, will cut the weeds and throw the trash into the gulch."

"The weeds?" Pilon cried in horror. "Not *those* weeds." He explained his theory of Mrs. Morales' chickens.

Danny agreed immediately. "My friend," he said, "I am glad you have come to live with me. Now, while I collect a little wood, you must get something for dinner."

Pilon, remembering his brandy, thought this unfair. "I am getting in debt to him," he thought bitterly. "My freedom will be cut off. Soon I shall be a slave because of this Jew's house." But he did go out to look for some dinner.

Two blocks away, near the edge of the pine wood, he came upon a half-grown Plymouth Rock rooster scratching in the road. It had come to that adolescent age when its voice cracked, when its legs and neck and breast were naked. Perhaps because he had been thinking of Mrs. Morales' hens in a charitable vein, this little rooster engaged Pilon's sympathy. He walked slowly on towards the dark pine woods, and the chicken ran ahead of him.

Pilon mused. "Poor little bare fowl. How cold it must be for you in the early morning, when the dew falls and the air grows cold with the dawn. The good God is not always so good to little beasts." And he thought, "Here you play in the streets, little chicken. Some day an automobile will run over you; and if it kills you, that will be the best that can happen. It may only break your leg or your wing. Then all of your life you will drag along in misery. Life is too hard for you, little bird."

He moved slowly and cautiously. Now and then the chicken

tried to double back, but always there was Pilon in the place it chose to go. At last it disappeared into the pine forest, and Pilon sauntered after it.

To the glory of his soul be it said that no cry of pain came from that thicket. That chicken, which Pilon had prophesied might live painfully, died peacefully, or at least quietly. And this is no little tribute to Pilon's technique.

Ten minutes later he emerged from the woods and walked back towards Danny's house. The little rooster, picked and dismembered, was distributed in his pockets. If there was one rule of conduct more strong than any other to Pilon, it was this: Never under any circumstances bring feathers, head or feet home, for without these a chicken cannot be identified.

In the evening they had a fire of cones in the airtight stove. The flames growled in the chimney. Danny and Pilon, well-fed, warm, and happy, sat in the rocking-chairs and gently teetered back and forth. At dinner they had used a piece of candle, but now only the light from the stove cracks dispelled the darkness of the room. To make it perfect, rain began to patter on the roof. Only a little leaked through, and that in places where no one wanted to sit anyway.

"It is good, this," Pilon said. "Think of the nights when we slept in the cold. This is the way to live."

"Yes, and it is strange," Danny said. "For years I had no house. Now I have two. I cannot sleep in two houses."

Pilon hated waste. "This very thing has been bothering me. Why don't you rent the other house?" he suggested.

Danny's feet crashed down on the floor. "Pilon," he cried. "Why didn't I think of it?" The idea grew more familiar. "But who will rent it, Pilon?"

"I will rent it," said Pilon. "I will pay ten dollars a month in rent."

"Fifteen," Danny insisted. "It's a good house. It is worth fifteen."

Pilon agreed, grumbling. But he would have agreed to much more, for he saw the elevation that came to a man who lived in his own house; and Pilon longed to feel that elevation.

"It is agreed, then," Danny concluded. "You will rent my house. Oh, I will be a good landlord, Pilon. I will not bother you."

Pilon, except for his year in the army, had never possessed fifteen dollars in his life. But, he thought, it would be a month before the rent was due, and who could tell what might happen in a month?

They teetered contentedly by the fire. After a while Danny went out for a few moments and returned with some apples. "The rain would have spoiled them anyway," he apologized.

Pilon, not to be outdone, got up and lighted the candle; he went into the bedroom and in a moment returned with a wash-bowl and pitcher, two red glass vases and a bouquet of ostrich plumes. "It is not good to have so many breakable things around," he said. "When they are broken you become sad. It is much better never to have had them." He picked the paper roses from the wall. "A compliment for Señora Torrelli," he explained as he went out of the door.

Shortly afterwards he returned, wet through from the rain, but triumphant in manner, for he had a gallon jug of red wine in his hand.

They argued bitterly later, but neither cared who won, for they were tired with the excitements of the day. The wine made them drowsy, and they went to sleep on the floor. The fire died down; the stove cricked as it cooled. The candle tipped over and expired in its own grease, with little blue protesting flares. The house was dark and quiet and peaceful.

CHAPTER III

How the poison of possessions wrought with Pilon, and how evil temporarily triumphed in him

THE NEXT day Pilon went to live in the other house. It was exactly like Danny's house, only smaller. It had its pink rose of Castile over the porch, its weed-grown yard, its ancient, barren fruit trees, its red geraniums—and Mrs. Soto's chicken-yard was next door.

Danny became a great man, having a house to rent, and Pilon went up the social scale by renting a house.

It is impossible to say whether Danny expected any rent, or whether Pilon expected to pay any. If they did, both were disappointed. Danny never asked for it, and Pilon never offered it.

The two friends were often together. Let Pilon come by a jug of wine or a piece of meat and Danny was sure to drop in to visit. And if Danny were lucky or astute in the same way, Pilon spent a riotous night with him. Poor Pilon would have paid the money if he ever had any, but he never did have—not long enough to locate Danny. Pilon was an honest man. It worried him sometimes to think of Danny's goodness and his own poverty.

One night he had a dollar, acquired in a manner so astounding that he tried to forget it immediately for fear the memory might make him mad. A man in front of the San Carlos hotel had put the dollar in his hand, saying, "Run down and get four bottles of ginger ale. The hotel is out." Such things were almost miracles, Pilon thought. One should take them on faith, not worry and question them. He took the dollar up the road to give to Danny, but on the way he bought a gallon of wine, and with the wine he lured two plump girls into his house.

Danny, walking by, heard the noise and joyfully went in. Pilon fell into his arms and placed everything at Danny's disposal. And later, after Danny had helped to dispose of one of the girls and half of the wine, there was a really fine fight. Danny lost a tooth, and Pilon had his shirt torn off. The girls stood shrieking by and kicked whichever man happened to be down. At last Danny got up off the floor and butted one of the girls in the stomach, and she went out the door croaking like a frog. The other girl stole two cooking pots and followed her.

For a little while Danny and Pilon wept over the perfidy of women.

"Thou knowest not what bitches women are," Danny said wisely.

"I do know," said Pilon.

"Thou knowest not."

"I do know."

"Liar."

There was another fight, but not a very good one.

After that Pilon felt better about the unpaid rent. Had he not been host to his landlord?

A number of months passed. Pilon began again to worry about the rent. And as time went by the worry grew intolerable. At last in desperation he worked a whole day cleaning squids for Chin Kee and made two dollars. In the evening he tied his red handkerchief around his neck, put on his father's revered hat, and started up the hill to pay Danny the two dollars on account.

But on the way he bought two gallons of wine. "It is better so," he thought. "If I give him hard money, it does not express how warmly I feel towards my friend. But a present, now. And I will tell him the two gallons cost five dollars." This was silly, and Pilon knew it, but he indulged himself. No one in Monterey better knew the price of wine than Danny.

Pilon was proceeding happily. His mind was made up; his nose pointed straight towards Danny's house. His feet moved, not quickly, but steadily, in the proper direction. Under each arm he carried a paper bag, and a gallon of wine was in each bag.

It was purple dusk, that sweet time when the day's sleeping is over and the evening of pleasure and conversation has not begun. The pine trees were very black against the sky and all objects on the ground were obscured with dark; but the sky was as mournfully bright as memory. The gulls flew lazily home to the sea rocks after a day's visit to the fish canneries of Monterey.

Pilon was a lover of beauty and a mystic. He raised his face into the sky and his soul arose out of him into the sun's afterglow. That not too perfect Pilon, who plotted and fought, who drank and cursed, trudged slowly on; but a wistful and shining Pilon went up to the seagulls where they bathed on sensitive wings in the evening. That Pilon was beautiful, and his thoughts were unstained with selfishness and lust. And his thoughts are good to know.

"Our Father is in the evening," he thought. "These birds are flying across the forehead of the Father. Dear birds, dear seagulls, how I love you all. Your slow wings stroke my heart as the hand of a gentle master strokes the full stomach of a sleeping dog, as the hand of Christ stroked the heads of little children. Dear birds," he thought, "fly to our Lady of Sweet Sorrows with my open heart." And then he said the loveliest words he knew, "*Ave Maria, gratia plena*——"

The feet of the bad Pilon had stopped moving. In truth the bad Pilon for the moment had ceased to exist. (Hear this, recording angel!) There was, nor is, nor ever has been a purer soul than Pilon's at that moment. Galvez' bad bulldog came to Pilon's deserted legs standing alone in the dark. And Galvez' bulldog sniffed and went away without harming the legs.

A soul washed and saved is a soul doubly in danger, for everything in the world conspires against such a soul. "Even the straws under my knees," says Saint Augustine, "shout to distract me from prayer."

Pilon's soul was not even proof against his own memories; for, as he watched the birds, he remembered that Mrs. Pastano used seagulls sometimes in her tamales, and that memory made him hungry, and hunger tumbled his soul out of the sky. Pilon moved on, once more a cunning mixture of good and evil. Galvez' bad bulldog turned snarling and stalked back, sorry now that he had let go such a perfect chance at Pilon's legs.

Pilon hunched his arms to ease the weight of the bottles.

It is a fact verified and recorded in many histories that the soul capable of the greatest good is also capable of the greatest evil. Who is there more impious than a backsliding priest? Who more carnal than a recent virgin? This, however, may be a matter of appearance.

Pilon, just back from Heaven, was, although he did not know it, singularly receptive of every bitter wind, toward every evil influence that crowded the night about him. True, his feet still moved towards Danny's house, but there was neither intention nor conviction in them. They awaited the littlest signal to turn about. Already Pilon was thinking how stupendously drunk he could get on two gallons of wine, and more, how long he could stay drunk.

It was almost dark now. The dirt road was no longer visible, nor the ditches on either side. No moral conclusion is drawn from the fact that at this moment, when Pilon's impulses were balanced as precariously as a feather between generosity and selfishness, at this very moment Pablo Sanchez happened to be sitting in the ditch at the side of the road wishing he had a cigarette and a glass of wine.

Ah, the prayers of the millions, how they must fight and destroy each other on their way to the throne of God.

Pablo first heard footsteps, then saw a blurred figure, and then recognized Pilon. "Ai, *amigo*," he called enthusiastically. "What great burden is it thou carriest?"

Pilon stopped dead and faced the ditch. "I thought you were in jail," he said severely. "I heard about a goose."

"So I was, Pilon," Pablo said jocularly. "But I was not well received. The judge said the sentence did me no good, and the police said I ate more than the allowance for three men. And so," he finished proudly, "I am on parole."

Pilon was saved from selfishness. True, he did not take the wine to Danny's house, but instantly he invited Pablo to share it at the rented house. If two generous paths branch from the high-road of life and only one can be followed, who is to judge which is best?

Pilon and Pablo entered the little house joyfully. Pilon lighted a candle and produced two fruit jars for glasses.

"Health!" said Pablo.

"*Salud!*" said Pilon.

And in a few moments, "*Salud!*" said Pablo.

"Mud in your eye!" said Pilon.

They rested a little while. "*Su servidor*," said Pilon.

"Down the rat-hole," said Pablo.

Two gallons is a great deal of wine, even for two paisanos. Spiritually the jugs may be graduated thus: Just below the shoulder of the first bottle, serious and concentrated conversation. Two inches farther down, sweetly sad memory. Three inches more, thoughts of old and satisfactory loves. An inch, thoughts of old bitter loves. Bottom of the first jug, general and undirected sadness. Shoulder of the second jug, black, unholy despondency. Two fingers down, a song of death or longing. A thumb, every other song each one knows. The graduations stop here, for the trail splits and there is no certainty. From this point on, anything can happen.

But let us go back to the first mark, which says serious and concentrated conversation, for it was at that place that Pilon made his coup. "Pablo," he said, "dost thou never get tired of sleeping in ditches, wet and homeless, friendless and alone?"

"No," said Pablo.

Pilon mellowed his voice persuasively. "So *I* thought, my friend, when I was a dirty gutter-dog. I too was content, for I did not know how sweet a little house is, and a roof, and a garden. Ah, Pablo, this is indeed living."

"It's pretty nice," Pablo agreed.

Pilon pounced. "See, Pablo, how would you like to rent part of my house? There would never be the cold ground for you any more. Never the hard sand under the wharf with crabs getting in your shoes. How would you like to live here with me?"

"Sure," said Pablo.

"Look, you will pay only fifteen dollars a month! And you may use all the house except my bed, and all the garden. Think of it, Pablo! And if someone should write you a letter, he will have some place to send it to."

"Sure," said Pablo. "That's swell."

Pilon sighed with relief. He had not realized how the debt to Danny rode on his shoulders. The fact that he was fairly sure Pablo would never pay any rent did not mitigate his triumph. If Danny should ever ask for money, Pilon would say, "I will pay when Pablo pays."

They moved on to the next graduation, and Pilon remembered how happy he had been when he was a little boy. "No care then, Pablo. I knew not sin. I was very happy."

"We have never been happy since," Pablo agreed sadly.

CHAPTER IV

How Jesus Maria Corcoran, a good man, became an unwilling vehicle of evil

Life passed smoothly on for Pilon and Pablo. In the morning when the sun was up clear of the pine trees, when the blue bay rippled and sparkled below them, they arose slowly and thoughtfully from their beds.

It is a time of quiet joy, the sunny morning. When the glittery dew is on the mallow weeds, each leaf holds a jewel which is beautiful if not valuable. This is no time for hurry or for bustle. Thoughts are slow and deep and golden in the morning.

Pablo and Pilon in their blue jeans and blue shirts walked in comradeship into the gulch behind the house, and after a little time they returned to sit in the sun on the front porch, to listen to the fish horns on the streets of Monterey, to discuss in wandering, sleepy tones the doings of Tortilla Flat; for there are a thousand climaxes on Tortilla Flat for every day the world wheels through.

They were at peace there on the porch. Only their toes wriggled on the warm boards when the flies landed on them.

"If all the dew were diamonds," Pablo said, "we would be very rich. We would be drunk all our lives."

But Pilon, on whom the curse of realism lay uneasily, added,

"Everybody would have too many diamonds. There would be no price for them, but wine always costs money. If only it would rain wine for a day, now, and we had a tank to catch it in."

"But good wine," interjected Pablo. "Not rotgut swill like the last you got."

"I didn't pay for it," said Pilon. "Someone hid it in the grass by the dance hall. What can you expect of wine you find?"

They sat and waved their hands listlessly at the flies. "Cornelia Ruiz cut up the black Mexican yesterday," Pilon observed.

Pablo raised his eyes in mild interest. "Fight?" he asked.

"Oh, no, the black one did not know Cornelia got a new man yesterday, and he tried to come in. So Cornelia cut him."

"He should have known," Pablo said virtuously.

"Well, he was down in the town when Cornelia got her new man. The black one just tried to go in through the window when she locked the door."

"The black one is a fool," said Pablo. "Is he dead?"

"Oh, no. She just cut him up a little bit on the arms. Cornelia was not angry. She just didn't want the black one to come in."

"Cornelia is not a very steady woman," said Pablo. "But still she has masses sung for her father, ten years dead."

"He will need them," Pilon observed. "He was a bad man and never went to jail for it, and he never went to confession. When old Ruiz was dying, the priest came to give him solace, and Ruiz confessed. Cornelia says that priest was white as buckskin when he came out of the sick-room. But afterwards that priest said he didn't believe half what Ruiz confessed."

Pablo, with a cat-like stroke, killed a fly that landed on his knee. "Ruiz was always a liar," he said. "That soul will need plenty of masses. But do you think a mass has virtue when the money for that mass comes out of men's pockets while they sleep in wine at Cornelia's house?"

"A mass is a mass," said Pilon. "Where you get two-bits is of no interest to the man who sells you a glass of wine. And where a mass comes from is of no interest to God. He just likes them, the same as you like wine. Father Murphy used to go fishing all the time, and for months the Holy Sacrament tasted like mackerel, but that did not make it less holy. These things are for priests to explain. They are nothing for us to worry about. I wonder where we could get some eggs to eat. It would be good to eat an egg now."

Pablo tilted his hat down over his eyes to keep the sun from bothering him. "Charlie Meeler told me that Danny is with Rosa Martin, that Portagee girl."

Pilon sat upright in alarm. "Maybe that girl will want to marry Danny. Those Portagees always want to marry, and they love money. Maybe when they are married Danny will bother us about the rent. That Rosa will want new dresses. All women do. I know them."

Pablo, too, looked annoyed. "Maybe if we went and talked to Danny——" he suggested.

"Maybe Danny has some eggs," said Pilon. "Those chickens of Mrs. Morales are good layers."

They put on their shoes and walked slowly towards Danny's house.

Pilon stooped and picked up a beer-bottle cap and cursed and threw it down. "Some evil man has left it there to deceive people," he said.

"I tried it last night," said Pablo. He looked into a yard where the green corn was ripe and made a mental note of its ripeness.

They found Danny sitting on his front porch, behind the rose bush, wriggling his toes to keep the flies off.

"Ai, *amigos*," he greeted them listlessly.

They sat down beside him and took off their shoes. Danny took out a sack of tobacco and some papers and passed them to Pilon. Pilon looked mildly shocked, but made no comment.

"Cornelia Ruiz cut up the black Mexican," he said.

"I heard about it," said Danny.

Pablo spoke acidly. "These women, there is no virtue in them any more."

"It is dangerous to lie with them," said Pilon. "I have heard that there is one young Portagee girl here on the Flat who can give a man something to remember her by, if he goes to the trouble to get it."

Pablo made disapproving clucking noises with his tongue. He spread his hands in front of him. "What is a man to do?" he asked. "Is there no one to trust?"

They watched Danny's face and saw no alarm appear there.

"This girl's name is Rosa," said Pilon. "I would not say her last name."

"Oh, you mean Rosa Martin," Danny observed with very little interest. "Well, what çan you expect of a Portagee?"

Pablo and Pilon sighed with relief.

"How are Mrs. Morales' chickens getting along?" Pilon asked casually.

Danny shook his head sadly. "Every one of those chickens is dead. Mrs. Morales put up some string beans in jars, and the jars blew up, and she fed the beans to the chickens, and those chickens all died, every one."

"Where are those chickens now?" Pablo demanded.

Danny waved two fingers back and forth in negation. "Someone told Mrs. Morales not to eat those chickens or she would be sick, but we scraped the insides good and sold them to the butcher."

"Has anybody died?" Pablo asked.

"No. I guess those chickens would have been all right."

"Perhaps you bought a little wine with the money from those chickens?" Pilon suggested.

Danny smiled cynically at him. "Mrs. Morales did, and I went to her house last night. That is a pretty woman in some lights, and not so old either."

The alarm came back to Pablo and Pilon.

"My cousin Weelie says she is fifty years old," Pilon said excitedly.

Danny spread his hands. "What is it how old in years she is?" he observed philosophically. "She is lively, that one. She owns her house and has two hundred dollars in the bank." Then Danny became a little embarrassed. "I would like to make a little present to Mrs. Morales."

Pilon and Pablo regarded their feet and tried by strenuous mental effort to ward off what was coming. But their effort had no value.

"If I had a little money," said Danny, "I would buy her a box of big candy." He looked meaningly at his tenants, but neither one answered him. "I would need only a dollar or two," he suggested.

"Chin Kee is drying squids," Pilon observed. "Perhaps you could cut squids for half a day."

Danny spoke pointedly. "It would not look well for a man who owns two houses to cut squids. But perhaps if a little rent were ever paid——"

Pilon arose angrily. "Always the rent," he cried. "You would force us into the streets—into the gutters, while you sleep in your soft bed. Come, Pablo," Pilon said angrily, "we will get money for this miser, this Jew."

The two of them stalked off.

"Where will we get money?" Pablo asked.

"I don't know," said Pilon. "Maybe he won't ask again." But the inhuman demand had cut deep into their mental peace. "We will call him 'Old Jew' when we see him," said Pilon. "We have been his friends for years. When he was in need, we fed him. When he was cold, we clothed him."

"When was that?" Pablo asked.

"Well, we would have, if he needed anything and we had it. That is the kind of friends we were to him. And now he crushes our friendship into the ground for a box of big candy to give to an old fat woman."

"Candy is not good for people," said Pablo.

So much emotion had exhausted Pilon. He sat down in the ditch beside the road and put his chin in his hands and was disconsolate.

Pablo sat down too, but he only did it to rest, for his friendship with Danny was not as old and beautiful as Pilon's was.

The bottom of the ditch was choked with dry grass and bushes. Pilon, staring downward in his sorrow and resentment, saw a human arm sticking out from under a bush. And then, beside the arm, a half-full gallon of wine. He clutched Pablo's arm and pointed.

Pablo stared. "Maybe he is dead, Pilon."

Pilon had got his breath and his fine clear vision again. "If he is dead, the wine will do him no good. He can't be buried with it."

The arm stirred, swept back the bushes, and disclosed the frowsy face and red stubble beard of Jesus Maria Corcoran. "Ai, Pilon. Ai, Pablo," he said hazily. "*Que tomas?*"

Pilon leaped down the bank on him. "*Amigo*, Jesus Maria! you are not well!"

Jesus Maria smiled sweetly. "Just drunk," he murmured. He rose to his knees. "Come have a drink, my friends. Drink deep. There is plenty more."

Pilon tilted the bottle over his elbow. He swallowed four times and over a pint left the jug. Then Pablo took the bottle from him, and Pablo played with it as a cat plays with a feather. He polished the mouth with his sleeve. He smelled the wine. He took three or four preliminary sips and let a few drops run all around his mouth, to tantalize himself. At last, "*Madre de Dios, que vino!*" he said. He raised the jug and the red wine gurgled happily down his throat.

Pilon's hand was out long before Pablo had to breathe again. Pilon turned a soft and admiring countenance to his friend Jesus Maria. "Hast thou discovered a treasure in the woods?" he asked. "Has some great man died and named thee in his will, my little friend?"

Jesus Maria was a humanitarian, and kindness was always in him. He cleared his throat and spat. "Give me a drink," he said. "My throat is dry. I will tell you how it was." He drank dreamily, like a man who has so much wine that he can take his time in drinking it, can even spill a little without remorse. "I was sleeping on the beach two nights ago," he said. "Out on the beach near Seaside. In the night the little waves washed a rowboat to the shore. Oh, a nice little rowboat, and the oars were there. I got in and rowed it down to Monterey. It was easily worth twenty dollars, but trade was slow, and I only got seven."

"Thou has money left?" Pilon put in excitedly.

"I am telling you how it was," Jesus Maria said with some dignity. "I bought two gallons of wine and brought them up here to the woods, and then I went to walk with Arabella Gross. For her I bought one pair of silk drawers in Monterey. She liked them—so soft they were, and so pink. And then I bought a pint of whisky for Arabella, and then after a while we met some soldiers and she went away with them."

"Oh, the thief of a good man's money!" Pilon cried in horror.

"No," said Jesus Maria dreamily. "It was time she went anyway. And then I came here and went to sleep."

"Then thou hast no more money?"

"I don't know," said Jesus Maria. "I will see." He fished in his pocket and brought out three crumpled dollar bills and a dime. "To-night," he said, "I will buy for Arabella Gross one of those little things that goes around higher up."

"You mean the little silk pockets on a string?"

"Yes," said Jesus Maria, "and not so little as you might think either." He coughed to clear his throat.

Instantly Pilon was filled with solicitude. "It is the night air," he said. "It is not good to sleep out in the open. Come, Pablo, we will take him to our house and cure this cold of his. The malady of the lungs has a good start, but we will cure it."

"What are you talking about?" said Jesus Maria. "I'm all right."

"So you think," said Pilon. "So Rudolfo Kelling thought. And you yourself went to his funeral a month ago. So Angelina Vasquez thought. She died last week."

Jesus Maria was frightened. "What do you think is the matter?"

"It is sleeping in this night air," Pilon said sagely. "Your lungs will not stand it."

Pablo wrapped the wine jug in a big weed, so disguising it that anyone passing would have been consumed with curiosity until he knew what that weed contained.

Pilon walked beside Jesus Maria, touching him now and then under the elbow to remind him that he was not a well man. They took him to their house and laid him on a cot, and although the day was warm, they covered him with an old comforter. Pablo spoke movingly of those poor ones who writhed and suffered with tuberculosis. And then Pilon pitched his voice to sweetness. He spoke with reverence of the joy of living in a little house. When the night was far gone, and all the talk of wine was gone, and outside the deadly mists clung to the ground like the ghosts of giant leeches, then one did not go out to lie in the sickly damp of a gulch. No, one got into a deep, soft, warm bed, and slept like a little child.

Jesus Maria went to sleep at this point. Pilon and Pablo had to wake him up and give him a drink. Then Pilon spoke movingly of the morning when one lay in one's warm nest until the sun was high enough to be of some use. One did not go shivering about in the dawn, beating one's hands to keep them from freezing.

At last Pilon and Pablo moved in on Jesus Maria as two silent hunting Airedales converge on their prey. They rented the use of their house to Jesus for fifteen dollars a month. He accepted happily. They shook hands all around. The jug came out of its weed. Pilon drank deeply, for he knew his hardest task was before him. He said it very gently and casually, while Jesus Maria was drinking out of the bottle.

"And you will pay only three dollars on account now."

Jesus Maria put down the bottle and looked at him in horror. "No," he exploded. "I made a promise to Arabella Gross to buy one of those little things. I will pay the rent when it is time."

Pilon knew he had blundered. "When you lay on that beach at Seaside, God floated the little rowboat to you. Do you think the good God did it so you could buy silk drawers for a cannery slut? No! God did it so you would not die from sleeping on the ground in the cold. Do you think God is interested in Arabella's breasts? And besides, we will take a two dollar deposit," he went on. "For one dollar you can get one of those things big enough to hold the udders of a cow."

Still Jesus Maria protested.

"I will tell you," Pilon went on, "unless we pay Danny two dollars we shall all be turned into the street, and it will be your fault. You will have it on your soul that we sleep in ditches."

Under so many shots coming from so many directions, Jesus Maria Corcoran succumbed. He passed two of the crumpled bills to Pilon.

And now the tense feeling went out of the room, and peace and quiet and a warm deep comradeship took its place. Pilon relaxed. Pablo took the comforter back to his own bed, and conversation sprang up.

"We must take this money to Danny."

Their first appetite over, they were sipping the wine out of fruit jars now.

"What is this great need Danny has for two dollars?" Jesus Maria asked.

Pilon grew confidential. His hands came into play like twin moths, restrained only by his wrists and arms from flying out the door. "Danny, our friend, is taking up with Mrs. Morales. Oh, don't think Danny is a fool. Mrs. Morales has two hundred dollars in the bank. Danny wants to buy a box of big candy for Mrs. Morales."

"Candy is not good for people," Pablo observed. "It makes their teeth ache."

"That is up to Danny," said Jesus Maria. "If he wants to ache Mrs. Morales' teeth, that is his business. What do we care for Mrs. Morales' teeth?"

A cloud of anxiety had settled on Pilon's face. "But," he interposed sternly, "if our friend Danny takes big candy to Mrs. Morales, he will eat some too. So it is the teeth of our friend that will ache."

Pablo shook his head anxiously. "It would be a bad thing if Danny's friends, on whom he depends, should bring about the aching of his teeth."

"What shall we do, then?" asked Jesus Maria, although he and everyone else knew exactly what they would do. They waited politely, each one for another to make the inevitable suggestion. The silence ran on. Pilon and Pablo felt that the suggestion should not come from them, since, by some lines of reasoning, they might be considered interested parties. Jesus Maria kept silence in duty to his hosts, but when their silence made him aware of what was required of him, he came instantly into the breach.

"A gallon of wine makes a nice present for a lady," he suggested in a musing tone.

Pilon and Pablo were astonished at his brilliance. "We can tell Danny it would be better for his teeth to get wine."

"But maybe Danny will pay no heed to our warning. If you give money to that Danny you can't tell what he will do with it. He might buy candy anyway, and then all our time and worry are wasted."

They had made of Jesus Maria their feeder of lines, their opener of uneasy situations. "Maybe if we buy the wine ourselves and then give it to Danny there is no danger," he suggested.

"That is the thing," cried Pilon. "Now you have it."

Jesus Maria smiled modestly at being given credit for this. He felt that sooner or later this principle would have been promulgated by someone in the room.

Pablo poured the last little bit of wine into the fruit jars and they drank tiredly after their effort. It was a matter of pride to them that the idea had been arrived at so logically, and in such a philanthropic cause.

"Now I am hungry," said Pablo.

Pilon got up and went to the door and looked at the sun. "It is after noon," he said. "Pablo and I will go to Torrelli's to get the wine, while you, Jesus Maria, go into Monterey for something to eat. Maybe Mrs. Bruno, on the wharf, will give you a fish. Maybe you can get a little bread someplace."

"I would rather go with you," said Jesus Maria, for he suspected that another sequence, just as logical, and just as inevitable, was beginning to grow in the heads of his friends.

"No, Jesus Maria," they said firmly. "It is now two o'clock, or about that. In an hour it will be three o'clock. Then we will meet you here and have something to eat. And maybe a little glass of wine to go with it."

Jesus Maria started for Monterey very reluctantly, but Pablo and Pilon walked happily down the hill towards Torrelli's house.

CHAPTER V

How Saint Francis turned the tide and put a gentle punishment on Pilon and Pablo and Jesus Maria

THE AFTERNOON came down as imperceptibly as age comes to a happy man. A little gold entered into the sunlight. The bay became bluer and dimpled with shore-wind ripples. Those lonely fishermen who believe that the fish bite at high tide left their rocks, and their places were taken by others, who were convinced that the fish bite at low tide.

At three o'clock the wind veered around and blew softly in from the bay, bringing all manner of fine kelp odours. The menders of nets in the vacant lots of Monterey put down their spindles and rolled cigarettes. Through the streets of the town, fat ladies, in whose eyes lay the weariness and the wisdom one sees so often in the eyes of pigs, were trundled in over-powered motor-cars towards tea and gin fizzes at the Hotel del Monte. On Alvarado Street, Hugo Machador, the tailor, put a sign in his shop door, "Back in Five Minutes", and went home for the day. The pines waved slowly and voluptuously. The hens in a hundred hen yards complained in placid voices of their evil lot.

Pilon and Pablo sat under a pink rose of Castile in Torrelli's yard and quietly drank wine and let the afternoon grow on them as gradually as hair grows.

"It is just as well that we do not take two gallons of wine to Danny," said Pilon. "He is a man who knows little restraint in drinking."

Pablo agreed. "Danny looks healthy," he said, "but it is just such people that you hear of dying every day. Look at Rudolfo Kelling. Look at Angelina Vasquez."

Pilon's realism arose mildly to the surface. "Rudolfo fell into the quarry above Pacific Grove," he observed in mild reproof. "Angelina ate a bad can of fish. But," he continued kindly, "I know what you mean. And there are plenty of people who die through abuse of wine."

All Monterey began to make gradual instinctive preparations against the night. Mrs. Guttierez cut little chiles into her enchilada sauce. Rupert Hogan, the seller of spirits, added water to his gin and put it away to be served after midnight. And he shook a little pepper into his early evening whisky. At El Paseo dancing pavilion Bullet Rosendale opened a carton of pretzels and arranged them like coarse brown lace on the big courtesy plates. The Palace Drug Company wound up its awnings. A little group of men who had spent the afternoon in front of the post office, greeting their friends, moved towards the station to see the Del Monte Express from San Francisco come in. The seagulls arose glutted from the fish cannery beaches and flew towards the sea rocks. Lines of pelicans pounded doggedly over the water wherever they go to spend the night. On the purse-seine fishing-boats the Italian men folded their nets over the big rollers. Little Miss Alma Alvarez, who was ninety years old, took her daily bouquet of pink geraniums to the Virgin on the outer wall of the church of San Carlos. In the neighbouring and Methodist village of Pacific Grove the W.C.T.U. met for tea and discussion, listened while a little lady described the vice and prostitution of Monterey with energy and colour. She thought a committee should visit these resorts to see exactly how terrible conditions really were. They had gone over the situation so often, and they needed new facts.

The sun went westering and took on an orange blush. Under the rose bush in Torrelli's yard Pablo and Pilon finished the first gallon of wine. Torrelli came out of his house and passed out of the yard without seeing his erstwhile customers. They waited until he was out of sight on the way to Monterey; whereupon Pablo and Pilon went into the house, and, with a conscious knowledge of their art, cozened their supper out of Mrs. Torrelli. They slapped her on the buttocks and called her a "Butter Duck" and took little courteous liberties with her person, and finally left her, flattered and slightly tousled.

Now it was evening in Monterey, and the lights went on. The windows glowed softly. The Monterey Theatre began to spell "Children of Hell—Children of Hell" over and over with its lights. A small but fanatic group of men who believe that the fish bite in the evening took their places on the cold sea rocks. A little fog drifted through the streets and hung about the chimneys, and a fine smell of burning pine wood filled the air.

Pablo and Pilon went back to their rose bush and sat on the ground, but they were not as contented as they had been. "It is cool here," said Pilon, and he took a drink of wine to warm himself.

"We should go to our own house, where it is warm," said Pablo

"But there is no wood for the stove."

"Well," said Pablo, "if you will take the wine, I will meet you at the corner of the street." And he did, in about half an hour.

Pilon waited patiently, for he knew there are some things even one's friends cannot help with. While he waited, Pilon kept a watchful eye aimed down the street in the direction Torrelli had taken, for Torrelli was a forceful man to whom explanations, no matter how carefully considered nor how beautifully phrased, were as chaff. Moreover, Torrelli had, Pilon knew, the Italian's exaggerated and wholly quixotic ideal of marital relations. But Pilon watched in vain. No Torrelli came brutally home. In a little while Pablo joined him, and Pilon noticed with admiration and satisfaction that he carried an armful of pine sticks from Torrelli's wood pile.

Pablo made no comment on his recent adventure until they arrived at their house. Then he echoed Danny's words. "A lively one, that Butter Duck."

Pilon nodded his head in the dark and spoke with a quiet philosophy. "It is seldom that one finds all things at one market—wine, food, love and firewood. We must remember Torrelli, Pablo my friend. There is a man to know. We must take him a little present sometime."

Pilon built a roaring fire in the cast-iron stove. The two friends drew their chairs close and held their fruit jars to the heat to warm the wine a little. This night the light was holy, for Pablo had bought a candle to burn for San Francisco. Something had distracted his attention before that sacred plan had been consummated. Now the little wax taper burned beautifully in an abalone shell, and it threw the shadows of Pablo and Pilon on the wall and made them dance.

"I wonder where that Jesus Maria has gone," Pilon observed.

"He promised he would come back long ago," said Pablo. "I do not know whether that is a man to trust or not."

"Perhaps some little thing happened to detain him, Pablo. Jesus Maria, with that red beard and that kind heart, is nearly always in some kind of trouble with ladies."

"His is a grasshopper brain," said Pablo. "He sings and plays and jumps. There is no seriousness in him."

They had no great time to wait. They had barely started their second fruit jar of wine when Jesus Maria staggered in. He held each side of the door to steady himself. His shirt was torn and his face was bloody. One eye showed dark and ominous in the dancing candlelight.

Pablo and Pilon rushed to him. "Our friend! He is hurt. He has fallen from a cliff. He has been run over by a train!" There was not the slightest tone of satire, but Jesus Maria knew it for the most deadly kind of satire. He glared at them out of the eye which still had some volition in such matters.

"Both thy mothers were udderless cows," he remarked.

They fell back from him in horror at the vulgarity of the curse. "Our friend is wandering in his mind."

"The bone of his head has been broken."

"Pour him a little wine, Pablo."

Jesus Maria sat morosely by the fire and caressed his fruit jar, while his friends waited patiently for an explanation of the tragedy. But Jesus Maria seemed content to leave his friends in ignorance of the mishap. Although Pilon cleared his throat several times, and although Pablo looked at Jesus Maria with eyes which offered sympathy and understanding, Jesus Maria sat sullenly and glared at the stove and at the wine and at the blessed candle, until at length his discourteous reticence drove Pilon to an equal discourtesy. Afterwards he did not see how he could have done it.

"Those soldiers again?" he asked.

"Yes," Jesus Maria growled. "This time they came too soon."

"There must have been twenty of them to have used thee so," Pablo observed for the good of his friend's spirit. "Everyone knows thou art a bad man in a fight."

And Jesus Maria did look a little happier then.

"They were four," he said. "Arabella Gross helped too. She hit me on the head with a rock."

Pilon felt a wave of moral resentment rising within him. "I would not remind thee," he said severely, "how thy friends warned thee against this cannery slob." He wondered whether he had warned Jesus Maria, and seemed to remember that he had.

"These cheap white girls are vicious, my friend," Pablo broke in. "But did you give her that little thing that goes around?"

Jesus Maria reached into his pocket and brought out a crumpled pink rayon brassière. "The time had not come," he said. "I was just getting to that point; and besides, we had not come into the woods yet."

Pilon sniffed the air and shook his head, but not without a certain sad tolerance. "Thou hast been drinking whisky."

Jesus Maria nodded.

"Where did this whisky come from?"

"From those soldiers," said Jesus Maria. "They hid it under a culvert. Arabella knew it was there, and she told me. But those soldiers saw us with the bottle."

The story was gradually taking shape. Pilon liked it this way. It ruined a story to have it all come out quickly. The good story lay in half-told things which must be filled in out of the hearer's own experience. He took the pink brassière from Jesus Maria's lap and ran his fingers over it, and his eyes went to musing. But in a moment they shone with a joyous light.

"I know," he cried. "We'll give this to Danny as a gift to Mrs. Morales."

Everyone except Jesus Maria applauded the idea, and he felt

himself hopelessly outnumbered. Pablo, with a delicate understanding of the defeat, filled up Jesus Maria's fruit jar.

When a little time had passed, all three men began to smile. Pilon told a very funny story of a thing that had happened to his father. Good spirits returned to the company. They sang. Jesus Maria did a shuffling dance to prove he was not badly hurt. The wine went down and down in the jug, but before it was gone the three friends grew sleepy. Pilon and Pablo staggered off to bed, and Jesus Maria lay comfortably on the floor, beside the stove.

The fire died down. The house was filled with the deep sounds of slumber. In the front room only one thing moved. The blessed candle darted its little spear-pointed flame up and down with incredible rapidity.

Later, this little candle gave Pilon and Pablo and Jesus Maria some ethical things to think about. Simple small rod of wax with a string through it. Such a thing, you would say, is answerable to certain physical laws, and to none other. Its conduct, you would think, was guaranteed by certain principles of heat and combustion. You light the wick, ; the wax is caught and drawn up the wick; the candle burns a number of hours, goes out, and that is all. The incident is finished. In a little while the candle is forgotten, and then, of course, it has never existed.

Have you forgotten that this candle was blessed? That in a moment of conscience, or perhaps pure religious exaltation, it was designed by Pablo for San Francisco? Here is the principle which takes the waxen rod outside the jurisdiction of physics.

The candle aimed its spear of light at heaven, like an artist who consumes himself to become divine. The candle grew shorter and shorter. A wind sprang up outside and sifted through the cracks in the wall. The candle sagged sideways. A silken calendar, bearing the face of a lovely girl looking out of the heart of an American Beauty rose, floated out a little distance from the wall. It came into the spear of flame. The fire licked up the silk and raced towards the ceiling. A loose piece of wallpaper caught fire and fell flaming into a bundle of newspapers.

In the sky, saints and martyrs looked on with set and unforgiving faces. The candle was blessed. It belonged to Saint Francis. Saint Francis will have a big candle in its place to-night.

If it were possible to judge depth of sleep, it could be said with justice that Pablo, whose culpable action was responsible for the fire, slept even more soundly than his two friends. But since there is no gauge, it can only be said that he slept very very soundly.

The flames ran up the walls and found little holes in the roof, and leaked through into the night. The house filled with the roar of fire. Jesus Maria turned over uneasily and began, in his sleep, to take off his coat. Then a flaming shingle dropped in his face. He leaped up with a cry, and stood shocked at the fire that raged about him.

"Pilon!" he shrieked. "Pablo!" He ran into the other room, pulled his friends out of bed and pushed them out of the house. Pilon still grasped the pink brassière in his fingers.

They stood outside the burning house and looked in the open fire-curtained door. They could see the jug standing on the table with a good two inches of wine in it.

Pilon sensed the savage incipient heroism of Jesus Maria. "Do not do it," he shouted. "It must be lost in the fire as a punishment on us for leaving it."

The cry of sirens came to them, and the roar of trucks climbing the hill in second gear from the fire house in Monterey. The big red fire vehicles drew near and their searchlights played among the pine trunks.

Pilon turned hastily to Jesus Maria. "Run and tell Danny his house is burning. Run quickly, Jesus Maria."

"Why don't you go?"

"Listen," said Pilon. "Danny does not know you are one who rents his house. He may be a little bit angry with Pablo and me."

Jesus Maria grasped this logic and raced towards Danny's house. The house was dark. "Danny," Jesus Maria cried. "Danny, your house is on fire!" There was no answer. "Danny!" he cried again.

A window went up in Mrs. Morales' house next door. Danny sounded irritable. "What the hell do you want?"

"Your other house is on fire, the one Pablo and Pilon live in."

For a moment Danny did not answer. Then he demanded, "Is the fire department there?"

"Yes," cried Jesus Maria.

The whole sky was lighted up by now. The crackling of burning timbers could be heard. "Well," said Danny, "if the fire department can't do anything about it, what does Pilon expect me to do?"

Jesus Maria heard the window bang shut, and he turned and trotted back towards the fire. It was a bad time to call Danny, he knew, but then how could one tell? If Danny had missed the fire, he might have been angry. Jesus Maria was glad he had told him about it anyway. Now the responsibility lay on Mrs. Morales.

It was a little house, there was plenty of draught, the walls were perfectly dry. Perhaps not since old Chinatown had burned had there been such a quick and thorough fire. The men of the fire department took a look at the blazing walls and then began wetting the brush and the trees and the neighbouring houses. In less than an hour the house was completely gone. Only then did the hoses play on the heap of ashes to put out the coals and the sparks.

Pilon and Pablo and Jesus Maria stood shoulder to shoulder and watched the whole thing. Half the population of Monterey and all the population of Tortilla Flat except Danny and Mrs. Morales stood happily about and watched the fire. At last, when it was all over, when only a cloud of steam arose from the black heap, Pilon turned silently away.

"Where goest thou?" Pablo called.

"I go," said Pilon, "to the woods to have out my sleep. I counsel you to come too. It will be well if Danny does not see us for a little while." They nodded gravely and followed him into the pine forest. "It is a lesson to us," said Pilon. "By this we learn never to leave wine in a house overnight."

"Next time," Pablo said hopelessly, "you will take it outside and someone will steal it."

CHAPTER VI

How three sinful men, through contrition, attained peace. How Danny's Friends swore comradeship

When the sun was clear of the pines, and the ground was warm, and the night's dew was drying on the geranium leaves, Danny came out on his porch to sit in the sunshine and to muse warmly of certain happenings. He slipped off his shoes and wriggled his toes on the sun-warmed boards of the porch. He had walked down earlier in the morning and viewed the square black ashes and twisted plumbing which had been his other house. He had indulged in a little conventional anger against careless friends, had mourned for a moment over that transitory quality of earthly property which made spiritual property so much more valuable. He had thought over the ruin of his status as a man with a house to rent; and, all this clutter of necessary and decent emotion having been satisfied and swept away, he finally slipped into his true emotion, one of relief that at least one of his burdens was removed.

"If it were still there, I would be covetous of the rent," he thought. "My friends have been cool toward me because they owed me money. Now we can be free and happy again."

But Danny knew he must discipline his friends a little, or they would consider him soft. Therefore, as he sat on his porch, warding off flies with a moving hand which conveyed more warning than threat to the flies, he went over the things he must say to his friends before he allowed them back into the corral of his affection. He must show them that he was not a man to be imposed upon. But he yearned to get it over and to be once more that Danny whom everyone loved, that Danny whom people sought out when they had a gallon of wine or a piece of meat. As the owner of two houses he had been considered rich, and he had missed a great many tidbits.

Pilon and Pablo and Jesus Maria Corcoran slept a long time on the pine needles in the forest. It had been a night of terrible excitement, and they were tired. But at length the sun shone into their faces with noonday ardour and the ants walked on them, and two blue jays stood on the ground near-by, calling them all manner of sharp names.

What finished their sleep, though, was a picnic party which settled just on the other side of the bush from them and opened a big lunch basket from which moving smells drifted to Pilon and Pablo and Jesus Maria. They awakened; they sat up; and then the enormity of their situation burst upon them.

"How did the fire start?" asked Pablo plaintively, and no one knew.

"Perhaps," said Jesus Maria, "we had better go to another town for a while—to Watsonville or to Salinas; those are nice towns."

Pilon pulled the brassière from his pocket and ran his fingers over its pink smoothness. And he held it to the sunlight and looked through it.

"That would only delay matters," he decided. "I think it would be better to go to Danny and confess our fault, like little children to a father. Then he can't say anything without being sorry. And besides, have we not this present for Mrs. Morales?"

His friends nodded agreement. Pilon's eyes strayed through the thick brush to the picnic party, and particularly to that huge lunch basket from which came the penetrating odours of devilled eggs. Pilon's nose wrinkled a little, like a rabbit's. He smiled in a quiet reverie. "I am going to walk, my friends. In a little while I will meet you at the quarry. Do not bring the basket if you can help it."

They watched sadly as Pilon got up and walked away, through the trees, in a direction at right-angles to the picnic and the basket. Pablo and Jesus Maria were not surprised, a few moments later, to hear a dog bark, a rooster crow, high shrill laughter, the snarl of a wild cat, a little short scream and a cry for help; but the picnic party was surprised and fascinated. The two men and two women left their basket and trotted away towards these versatile sounds.

Pablo and Jesus Maria obeyed Pilon. They did not take the basket, but always afterwards their hats and their shirts were stained with devilled eggs.

At about three o'clock in the afternoon the three penitents walked slowly towards Danny's house. Their arms were loaded with offerings of reconciliation: oranges and apples and bananas, bottles of olives and pickles, sandwiches of pressed ham, egg sandwiches, bottles of soda pop, a paper carton of potato salad, and a copy of the *Saturday Evening Post*.

Danny saw them coming, and he stood up and tried to remember the things he had to say. They lined up in front of him and hung their heads.

"Dog of dogs," Danny called them, and "Thieves of decent folks' other house," and "Spawn of cuttlefish." He named their mothers cows and their fathers ancient sheep.

Pilon opened the bag he held and exposed the ham sandwiches. And Danny said he had no more trust in friends, that his faith had been frost-bitten and his friendship trampled upon. And then he began to have a little trouble remembering, for Pablo had taken two devilled eggs out of his bosom. But Danny went back to the grand generation and criticized the virtue of its women and the potency of its men.

Pilon pulled the pink brassière from his pocket and let it dangle listlessly from his fingers.

Danny forgot everything then. He sat down on the porch and his friends sat down, and the packages came open. They ate to a point of discomfort. It was an hour later, when they reclined at ease on the porch, giving attention to little besides digestion, when Danny asked casually, as about some far-off object, "How did the fire start?"

"We don't know," Pilon explained. "We went to sleep, and then it started. Perhaps we have enemies."

"Perhaps," said Pablo devoutly, "perhaps God had a finger in it."

"Who can say what makes the good God act the way He does?" added Jesus Maria.

When Pilon handed over the brassière and explained how it was a present for Mrs. Morales, Danny was reticent. He eyed the brassière with some scepticism. His friends, he felt, were flattering Mrs. Morales. "That is not a woman to give presents to," he said finally. "Too often we are tied to women by the silk stockings we give them." He could not explain to his friends the coolness that had come to his relationship with Mrs. Morales since he was the owner of only one house; nor could he, in courtesy to Mrs. Morales, describe his own pleasure at that coolness. "I will put this little thing away," he said. "Some day it may be of use to someone."

When the evening came, and it was dark, they went into the house and built a fire of cones in the air-tight stove. Danny, in proof of his forgiveness, brought out a quart of grappa and shared its fire with his friends.

They settled easily into the new life. "It is too bad Mrs. Morales' chickens are all dead," Pilon observed.

But even here was no bar to happiness. "She is going to buy two dozen new ones on Monday," said Danny.

Pilon smiled contentedly. "Those hens of Mrs. Soto's were no good," he said. "I told Mrs. Soto they needed oyster shells, but she paid no attention to me."

They drank the quart of grappa, and there was just enough to promote the sweetness of comradeship.

"It is good to have friends," said Danny. "How lonely it is in the world if there are no friends to sit with one and to share one's grappa."

"Or one's sandwiches," Pilon added quickly.

Pablo was not quite over his remorse, for he suspected the true state of celestial politics which had caused the burning of the house. "In all the world there are few friends like thee, Danny. It is not given to many to have such solace."

Before Danny sank completely under the waves of his friends, he sounded one warning. "I want all of you to keep out of my bed," he ordered. "That is one thing I must have to myself."

Although no one had mentioned it, each of the four knew they were all going to live in Danny's house.

Pilon sighed with pleasure. Gone was the worry of the rent; gone the responsibility of owing money. No longer was he a tenant, but a guest. In his mind he gave thanks for the burning of the other house.

"We will all be happy here, Danny," he said. "In the evenings we will sit by the fire and our friends will come in to visit. And sometimes maybe we will have a glass of wine to drink for friendship's sake."

Then Jesus Maria, in a frenzy of gratefulness, made a rash promise. It was the grappa that did it, and the night of the fire, and all the devilled eggs. He felt that he had received great gifts, and he wanted to distribute a gift. "It shall be our burden and our duty to see that there is always food in the house for Danny," he declaimed. "Never shall our friend go hungry."

Pilon and Pablo looked up in alarm, but the thing was said; a beautiful and generous thing. No man could with impunity destroy it. Even Jesus Maria understood, after it was said, the magnitude of his statement. They could only hope that Danny would forget it.

"For," Pilon mused to himself, "if this promise were enforced, it would be worse than rent. It would be slavery."

"We swear it, Danny!" he said.

They sat about the stove with tears in their eyes, and their love for one another was almost unbearable.

Pablo wiped his wet eyes with the back of his hand, and he echoed Pilon's remark. "We shall be very happy living here," he said.

CHAPTER VII

How Danny's Friends became a force for Good.
How they succoured the poor Pirate.

A GREAT many people saw the Pirate every day, and some laughed at him, and some pitied him, but no one knew him very well, and no one interfered with him. He was a huge, broad man, with a tremendous black and bushy beard. He wore jeans and a blue shirt, and he had no hat. In town he wore shoes. There was a shrinking in the Pirate's eyes when he confronted any grown person, the secret look of an animal that would like to run away if it dared turn its back long enough. Because of this expression, the paisanos of Monterey knew that his head had not grown up with the rest of his body. They called him the Pirate because of his beard. Every day people saw him wheeling his barrow of pitchwood about the streets until he sold the load. And always in a cluster at his heels walked his five dogs.

Enrique was rather houndish in appearance, although his tail was bushy. Pajarito was brown and curly, and these were the only two things you could see about him. Rudolph was a dog of whom passers-by said, "He is an American dog." Fluff was a Pug and Señor Alec Thompson seemed to be a kind of an Airedale. They walked in a squad behind the Pirate, very respectful towards him, and very solicitous for his happiness. When he sat down to rest from wheeling his barrow, they all tried to sit on his lap and have their ears scratched.

Some people had seen the Pirate early in the morning on Alvarado Street; some had seen him cutting pitchwood; some knew he sold kindling; but no one except Pilon knew everything the Pirate did. Pilon knew everybody and everything about everybody.

The Pirate lived in a deserted chicken-house in the yard of a deserted house on Tortilla Flat. He would have thought it presumptuous to live in the house itself. The dogs lived around and on top of him, and the Pirate liked this, for his dogs kept him warm on the coldest nights. If his feet were cold, he had only to put them against the belly of Señor Alec Thompson. The chicken-house was so low that the Pirate had to crawl in on his hands and knees.

Early every morning, well before daylight, the Pirate crawled out of his chicken-house, and the dogs followed him, roughing their coats and sneezing in the cold air. Then the party went down to Monterey and worked along an alley. Four or five restaurants had their back doors on this alley. The Pirate entered each one, into a restaurant kitchen, warm and smelling of food. Grumbling cooks put packages of scraps in his hands at each place.. They didn't know why they did it.

When the Pirate had visited each back door and had his arms full of parcels, he walked back up the hill to Munroe Street and entered a vacant lot, and the dogs excitedly swarmed about him. Then he opened the parcels and fed the dogs. For himself, he took bread or a piece of meat out of each package, but he did not pick the best for himself. The dogs sat down about him, licking their lips nervously and shifting their feet while they waited for food. They never fought over it, and that was a surprising thing. The Pirate's dogs never fought each other, but they fought everything else that wandered the streets of Monterey on four legs. It was a fine thing to see the pack of five hunting fox-terriers and Pomeranians like rabbits.

Daylight had come by the time the meal was over. The Pirate sat on the ground and watched the sky turn blue with the morning. Below him he saw the schooners put out to sea with deckloads of lumber. He heard the bell buoy ringing sweetly off China Point. The dogs sat about him and gnawed at the bones. The Pirate seemed to be listening to the day rather than seeing it, for while his eyes did not move about, there was an air of attentiveness in him. His big hands strayed to the dogs and his fingers worked soothingly in the coarse hair. After about half an hour the Pirate went to the corner of the vacant lot, threw the covering of sacks from his wheelbarrow, and dug up his axe out of the ground where he buried it every evening. Then up the hill he pushed the barrow, and into the woods, until he found a dead tree, full of pitch. By noon he had a load of fine kindling; and then, still followed by his dogs, he walked the streets until he had sold the load for twenty-five cents.

It was possible to observe all this, but what he did with the quarter, no one could tell. He never spent it. In the night, guarded from danger by his dogs, he went into the woods and hid the day's quarter with hundreds of others. Somewhere he had a great hoard of money.

Pilon, that acute man, from whom no details of the life of his fellows escaped, and who was doubly delighted to come upon those secrets that nestled deep in the brains of his acquaintances, discovered the Pirate's hoard by a logical process. Pilon reasoned thus: "Every day that Pirate has a quarter. If it is two dimes and a nickel, he takes it to a store and gets a twenty-five cent piece.

He never spends any money at all. Therefore, he must be hiding it."

Pilon tried to compute the amount of the treasure. For years the Pirate had been living in this way. Six days a week he cut pitchwood, and on Sundays he went to church. His clothes he got from the back doors of houses, his food at the back doors of restaurants. Pilon puzzled with the great numbers for a while, and then gave it up. "The Pirate must have at least a hundred dollars," he thought.

For a long time Pilon had considered these things. But it was only after the foolish and enthusiastic promise to feed Danny that the thought of the Pirate's hoard gained any personal significance to Pilon.

Before he approached the subject at all, Pilon put his mind through a long and stunning preparation. He felt very sorry for the Pirate. "Poor little half-formed one," he said to himself. "God did not give him all the brain he should have. That poor little Pirate cannot look after himself. For see, he lives in filth in an old chicken-house. He feeds upon scraps fit only for his dogs. His clothes are thin and ragged. And because his brain is not a good one, he hides his money."

Now, with his groundwork of pity laid, Pilon moved on to his solution. "Would it not be a thing of merit," he thought, "to do those things for him which he cannot do for himself? To buy him warm clothes, to feed him food fit for a human? But," he reminded himself, "I have no money to do these things, although they lie squirming in my heart. How can these charitable things be accomplished?"

Now he was getting somewhere. Like the cat which during a long hour closes in on a sparrow, Pilon was ready for his pounce. "I have it!" his brain cried. "It is like this: The Pirate has money, but he has not the brain to use it. I have the brain! I will offer my brain to his use. I will give freely of my mind. That shall be my charity toward this poor little half-made man."

It was one of the finest structures Pilon had ever built. The urge of the artist to show his work to an audience came upon him. "I will tell it to Pablo," he thought. But he wondered whether he would dare do such a thing. Was Pablo strictly honest? Would he not want to divert some of this money to his own ends? Pilon decided not to take the chance, right then, anyway.

It is astounding to find that the belly of every black and evil thing is as white as snow. And it is saddening to discover how the concealed parts of angels are leprous. Honour and peace to Pilon, for he had discovered how to uncover and to disclose to the world the good that lay in every evil thing. Nor was he blind, as so many saints are, to the evil of good things. It must be admitted with sadness that Pilon had neither the stupidity, the self-righteousness, nor the greediness for reward ever to become a saint. Enough for Pilon to do good and to be rewarded by the glow of human brotherhood accomplished.

That very night he paid a visit to the chicken-house where the Pirate lived with his dogs. Danny, Pablo, and Jesus Maria, sitting by the stove, saw him go and said nothing. For, they thought delicately, either a vapour of love had been wafted to Pilon or else he knew where he could get a little wine. In either case it was none of their business until he told them about it.

It was well after dark, but Pilon had a candle in his pocket, for it might be a good thing to watch the expression on the Pirate's face while he talked. And Pilon had a big round sugar cookie in a bag, that Susie Francisco, who worked in a bakery, had given him in return for a formula for getting the love of Charlie Guzman. Charlie was a Postal Telegraph messenger and rode a motor-cycle; and Susie had a man's cap to put on backwards in case Charlie should ever ask her to ride with him. Pilon thought the Pirate might like the sugar cookie.

The night was very dark. Pilon picked his way along a narrow street bordered with vacant lots and with weed-grown, neglected gardens.

Galvez' bad bulldog came snarling out of Galvez' yard, and Pilon spoke soothing compliments to him. "Nice dog," he said gently, and "Pretty dog," both of them palpable lies. They impressed the bulldog, however, for he retired into Galvez' yard.

Pilon came at last to the vacant property where the Pirate lived. And now he knew he must be careful, for the Pirate's dogs, if they suspected ill of anyone towards their master, where known to become defending furies. As Pilon stepped into the yard, he heard deep and threatening growls from the chicken-house.

"Pirate," he called, "it is thy good friend Pilon, come to talk with thee."

There was silence. The dogs stopped growling.

"Pirate, it is only Pilon."

A deep surly voice answered him. "Go away. I am sleeping now. The dogs are sleeping. It is dark, Pilon. Go to bed."

"I have a candle in my pocket," Pilon called. "It will make a light as bright as day in thy dark house. I have a big sugar cookie for thee too."

A faint scuffling sounded in the chicken-house. "Come, then," the Pirate said. "I will tell the dogs it is all right."

As he advanced through the weeds, Pilon could hear the Pirate talking softly to his dogs, explaining to them that it was only Pilon, who would do no harm. Pilon bent over in front of the dark doorway and scratched a match and lighted his candle.

The Pirate was seated on the dirt floor, and his dogs were all about him. Enrique growled and had to be reassured again. "That one is not so wise as the others," the Pirate said pleasantly. His eyes were the pleased eyes of an amused child. When he smiled his big white teeth glistened in the candlelight.

Pilon held out the bag. "It is a fine cake for you," he said.

The Pirate took the bag and looked into it; then he smiled delightedly and brought out the cookie. The dogs all grinned and faced him, and moved their feet and licked their lips. The Pirate broke his cookie into seven pieces. The first he gave to Pilon, who was his guest. "Now, Enrique," he said. "Now, Fluff. Now, Señor Alec Thompson." Each dog received his piece and gulped it and looked for more. Last, the Pirate ate his and held up his hands to the dogs. "No more, you see," he told them. Immediately the dogs lay down about him.

Pilon sat on the floor and stood the candle on the ground in front of him. The Pirate questioned him self-consciously with his eyes. Pilon sat silently, to let many questions pass through the Pirate's head. At length he said, "Thou art a worry to thy friends."

The Pirate's eyes filled with astonishment. "I? To my friends? What friends?"

Pilon softened his voice. "Thou hast many friends who think of thee. They do not come to see thee because thou art proud. They think it might hurt thy pride to have them see thee living in this chicken-house, clothed in rags, eating garbage with thy dogs. But these friends of thine worry for fear the bad life may make thee ill."

The Pirate was following his words with breathless astonishment, and his brain tried to realize these new things he was hearing. It did not occur to him to doubt them, since Pilon was saying them. "I have all these friends?" he said in wonder. "And I did not know it. And I am a worry to those friends. I did not know, Pilon. I would not have worried them if I had known." He swallowed to clear his throat of emotion. "You see, Pilon, the dogs like it here. And I like it because of them. I did not think I was a worry to my friends." Tears came into the Pirate's eyes.

"Nevertheless," Pilon said, "thy mode of living keeps all thy friends uneasy."

The Pirate looked down at the ground and tried to think clearly, but, as always when he attempted to cope with a problem, his brain grew grey and no help came from it, but only a feeling of helplessness. He looked to his dogs for protection, but they had gone back to sleep, for it was none of their business. And then he looked earnestly into Pilon's eyes. "You must tell me what to do, Pilon. I did not know these things."

It was too easy. Pilon was a little ashamed that it should be so easy. He hesitated; nearly gave it up; but then he knew he would be angry with himself if he did. "Thy friends are poor," he said. "They would like to help thee, but they have no money. If thou has money hidden, bring it out into the open. Buy thyself some clothes. Eat food that is not cast out by other people. Bring thy money out of its hiding place, Pirate."

Pilon had been looking closely at the Pirate's face while he spoke. He saw the eyes droop with suspicion and then with sullenness. In a moment Pilon knew two things certainly: first, that the Pirate had money hidden; and second, that it was not going to be easy to get at it. He was pleased at the latter fact. The Pirate had become a problem in tactics such as Pilon enjoyed.

Now the Pirate was looking at him again, and in his eyes was cunning, and on top of that, a studied ingenuousness. "I have no money anywhere," he said.

"But every day, my friend, I have seen thee get a quarter for thy wood, and never have I seen thee spend it."

This time the Pirate's brain came to his rescue. "I give it to a poor old woman," he said. "I have no money anywhere." And with this tone he closed a door tightly on the subject.

"So it must be guile," Pilon thought. So those gifts, that in him were so sharpened, must be called into play. He stood up and lifted his candle. "I only thought to tell thee how thy friends worry," he said critically. "If thou wilt not try to help, I can do nothing for thee."

The sweetness came back into the Pirate's eyes. "Tell them I am healthy," he begged. "Tell my friends to come and see me. I will not be too proud. I will be glad to see them any time. Will thou tell them for me, Pilon?"

"I will tell them," Pilon said ungraciously. "But thy friends will not be pleased when they see thou dost nothing to relieve their minds." Pilon blew out his candle and went away into the darkness. He knew that the Pirate would never tell where his hoard was. It must be found by stealth, taken by force, and then all the good things given to the Pirate. It was the only way.

And so Pilon set himself to watch the Pirate. He followed him into the forest when he went to cut kindlings. He lay in wait outside the chicken-house at night. He talked to him long and earnestly, and nothing came of it. The treasure was as far from discovery as ever. Either it lay buried in the chicken-house or it was hidden deep in the forest and was visited only at night.

The long and fruitless vigils wore out the patience of Pilon. He knew he must have help and advice. And who could better give it than those comrades, Danny, Pablo, and Jesus Maria? Who could be so stealthy, so guileful? Who would melt to kindness with more ease?

Pilon took them into his confidence; but first he prepared them, as he had prepared himself. The Pirate's poverty, his helplessness, and finally—the solution. When he came to the solution, his friends were in a philanthropic frenzy. They applauded him. Their faces shone with kindness. Pablo thought there might be well over a hundred dollars in the hoard.

When their joy had settled to a working enthusiasm, they came to plans.

"We must watch him," Pablo said.

"But I have watched him," Pilon argued. "It must be that he creeps off in the night, and then one cannot follow too close, for his dogs guard him like devils. It is not going to be so easy."

"You've used every argument?" Danny asked.

"Yes. Every one."

In the end it was Jesus Maria, that humane man, who found the way out. "It is difficult while he lives in that chicken-house," he said. "But suppose he lived here, with us? Either his silence would break under our kindness, or else it would be easier to know when he goes out at night."

The friends gave a good deal of thought to this suggestion. "Sometimes the things he gets out of restaurants are nearly new," mused Pablo. "I have seen him with a steak out of which only a little was missing."

"It might be as much as two hundred dollars," said Pilon.

Danny offered an objection. "But those dogs—he would bring his dogs with him."

"They are good dogs," said Pilon. "They obey him exactly. You may draw a line around a corner and say, 'Keep thy dogs within this line.' He will tell them, and those dogs will stay."

"I saw the Pirate one morning, and he had nearly half a cake, just a little bit damp with coffee," said Pablo.

The question settled itself. The house resolved itself into a committee, and the committee visited the Pirate.

It was a crowded place, that chicken-house, when they all got inside. The Pirate tried to disguise his happiness with a gruff tone. "The weather has been bad," he said socially. And, "You wouldn't believe, maybe, that I found a tick as big as a pigeon's egg on Rudolph's neck." And he spoke disparagingly of his home, as a host should. "It is too small," he said. "It is not a fit place for one's friends to come. But it is warm and snug, especially for the dogs."

Then Pilon spoke. He told the Pirate that worry was killing his friends; but if he would go to live with them, then they could sleep again, with their minds at rest.

It was a very great shock to the Pirate. He looked at his hands. And he looked to his dogs for comfort, but they would not meet his glance. At last he wiped the happiness from his eyes with the back of his hand, and he wiped his hand on his big black beard.

"And the dogs?" he asked softly. "You want the dogs too? Are you friends of the dogs?"

Pilon nodded. "Yes, the dogs too. There will be a whole corner set aside for the dogs."

The Pirate had a great deal of pride. He was afraid he might not conduct himself well. "Go away now," he said pleadingly. "Go home now. To-morrow I will come."

His friends knew how he felt. They crawled out of the door and left him alone.

"He will be happy with us, that one," said Jesus Maria.

"Poor little lonely man," Danny added. "If I had known, I would have asked him long ago, even if he had no treasure."

A flame of joy burned in all of them.

They settled soon into the new relationship. Danny, with a piece of blue chalk, drew a segment of a circle, enclosing a corner of the living-room, and that was where the dogs must stay when they were in the house. The Pirate slept in that corner too, with the dogs.

The house was beginning to be a little crowded, with five men and five dogs; but from the first Danny and his friends realized that their invitation to the Pirate had been inspired by that weary and anxious angel who guarded their destinies and protected them from evil.

Every morning, long before his friends were awake, the Pirate arose from his corner and, followed by his dogs, he made the rounds of the restaurant and the wharves. He was one of those for whom everyone feels a kindliness. His packages grew larger. The paisanos received his bounty and made use of it: fresh fish, half pies, untouched loaves of stale bread, meat that required only a little soda to take the green out. They began really to live.

And their acceptance of his gifts touched the Pirate more deeply than anything they could have done for him. There was a light of worship in his eyes as he watched them eat the food he brought.

In the evening, when they sat about the stove and discussed the doings of Tortilla Flat with the lazy voices of fed gods, the Pirate's eyes darted from mouth to mouth, and his own lips moved, whispering again the words his friends said. The dogs pressed in about him jealously.

These were his friends, he told himself in the night, when the house was dark, when the dogs snuggled close to him so that all might be warm. These men loved him so much that it worried them to have him live alone. The Pirate had often to repeat this to himself, for it was an astounding thing, an unbelievable thing, His wheelbarrow stood in Danny's yard now, and every day he cut his pitchwood and sold it. But so afraid was the Pirate that he might miss some word his friends said in the evening, might not be there to absorb some stream of the warm companionship, that he had not visited his hoard for several days to put the new coins there.

His friends were kind to him. They treated him with a sweet courtesy; but always there was some eye open and upon him. When he wheeled his barrow into the woods, one of the friends walked with him, and sat on a log while he worked. When he went into the gulch, the last thing at night, Danny or Pablo or Pilon or Jesus Maria kept him company. And in the night he must have been very quiet to have crept out without a shadow behind him.

For a week the friends merely watched the Pirate. But at last the inactivity tired them. Direct action was out of the question, they knew. And so one evening the subject of the desirability of hiding one's money came up for discussion.

Pilon began it. "I had an uncle, a regular miser, and he hid his gold in the woods. And one time he went to look at it, and it was gone. Someone had found it and stolen it. He was an old man then, and all his money was gone, and he hanged himself." Pilon noticed with some satisfaction, the look of apprehension that came upon the Pirate's face.

Danny noticed it, too; and he continued, "The *viejo*, my grandfather, who owned this house, also buried money. I do not know how much, but he was reputed a rich man, so there must have been three or four hundred dollars. The *viejo* dug a deep hole and put his money in it, and then he covered it up, and then he strewed pine needles over the ground until he thought no one could see that anything had been done there. But when he went back, the hole was open, and the money was gone."

The Pirate's lips followed the words. A look of terror came into his face. His fingers picked among the neck hairs of Señor Alec Thompson. The friends exchanged a glance and dropped the subject for the time being. They turned to the love life of Cornelia Ruiz.

In the night the Pirate crept out of the house, and the dogs crept after him; and Pilon crept after all of them. The Pirate went swiftly into the forest, leaping with sure feet over logs and brush. Pilon floundered behind him. But when they had gone at least two miles, Pilon was winded, and torn by vines. He paused to rest a moment; and then he realized that all sounds ahead of him had ceased. He waited and listened and crept about, but the Pirate had disappeared.

After two hours Pilon went back again, slowly and tiredly. There was the Pirate in the house, fast asleep among his dogs. The dogs lifted their heads when Pilon entered, and Pilon thought they smiled satirically at him for a moment.

A conference took place in the gulch the next morning.

"It is not possible to follow him," Pilon reported. "He vanished. He sees in the dark. He knows every tree in the forest. We must find some other way."

"Perhaps one is not enough," Pablo suggested. "If all of us should follow him, then one might not lose track of him."

"We will talk again to-night," said Jesus Maria, "only worse. A lady I know is going to give me a little wine," he added modestly. "Maybe if the Pirate has a little wine in him, he will not disappear so easily." So it was left.

Jesus Maria's lady gave him a whole gallon of wine. What could compare with the Pirate's delight that evening when a fruit jar of wine was put into his hand, when he sat with his friends and sipped his wine and listened to the talk? Such joy had come rarely into the Pirate's life. He wished he might clasp these dear people to his breast and tell them how much he loved them. But that was not a thing he could do, for they might think he was drunk. He wished he could do some tremendous thing to show them his love.

"We spoke last night of burying money," said Pilon. "To-day I remembered a cousin of mine, a clever man. If anyone in the world could hide money where it would never be found, he could do it. So he took his money and hid it. Perhaps you have seen him, that poor little one who crawls about the wharf and begs fish-heads to make soup of. That is my cousin. Someone stole his buried money."

The worry came back into the Pirate's face.

Story topped story, and in each one all manner of evil dogged the footsteps of those who hid their money.

"It is better to keep one's money close, to spend some now and then, to give a little to one's friends," Danny finished.

They had been watching the Pirate narrowly, and in the middle of the worst story they had seen the worry go from his face, and a smile of relief take its place. Now he sipped his wine and his eyes glittered with joy.

The friends were in despair. All their plans had failed. They were sick at heart. After all their goodness and their charity, this had happened. The Pirate had in some way escaped the good they had intended to confer upon him. They finished their wine and went moodily to bed.

Few things could happen in the night without Pilon's knowledge. His ears remained open while the rest of him slept. He heard the stealthy exit of the Pirate and his dogs from the house. He leaped to awaken his friends; and in a moment the four were following the Pirate in the direction of the forest. The four friends ran into trees, tripped on berry vines; but for a long time they could hear the Pirate marching on ahead of them. They followed as far as Pilon had followed the night before, and then, suddenly, silence, and the whispering forest and the vague night winds. They combed the woods and the brush patches, but the Pirate had disappeared again.

At last, cold and disconsolate, they came together and trudged wearily back towards Monterey. The dawn came before they got back. The sun was already shining on the bay. The smoke of the morning fires arose to them out of Monterey.

The Pirate walked out on the porch to greet them, and his face was happy. They passed him sullenly and filed into the living-room. There on the table lay a large canvas bag.

The Pirate followed them in. "I lied to thee, Pilon," he said. "I told thee I had no money, for I was afraid. I did not know about my friends then. You have told how hidden money is so often stolen, and I am afraid again. Only last night did a way out come to me. My money will be safe with my friends. No one can steal it if my friends guard it for me."

The four men stared at him in horror. "Take thy money back to the woods and hide it," Danny said savagely. "We do not want to watch it."

"No," said the Pirate. "I would not feel safe to hide it. But I will be happy knowing my friends guard it for me. You would not believe it, but the last two nights someone followed me into the forest to steal my money."

Terrible as the blow was, Pilon, that clever man, tried to escape it. "Before this money is put into our hands, maybe you would like to take some out," he suggested smoothly.

The Pirate shook his head. "No. I cannot do that. It is promised. I have nearly a thousand two-bitses. When I have a thousand I will buy a gold candlestick for San Francisco de Assisi.

"Once I had a nice dog, and that dog was sick; and I promised a gold candlestick of one thousand dimes if that dog would get well. And," he spread his great hands, "that dog got well."

"Is it one of these dogs?" Pilon demanded.

"No," said the Pirate. "A truck ran over him a little later."

So it was over, all hope of diverting the money. Danny and Pablo morosely lifted the heavy bag of silver quarters, took it in the other room, and put it under the pillow of Danny's bed. In time they would take a certain pleasure in the knowledge that this money lay under the pillow, but now their defeat was bitter. There was nothing in the world they could do about it. Their chance had come, and it had gone.

The Pirate stood before them, and there were tears of happiness in his eyes, for he had proved his love for his friends.

"To think," he said, "all those years I lay in that chicken-house, and I did not know any pleasure. But now," he added, "oh, now I am very happy."

CHAPTER VIII

How Danny's Friends sought mystic treasure on Saint Andrew's Eve. How Pilon found it and later how a pair of serge trousers changed ownership twice.

If he had been a hero, the Portagee would have spent a miserable time in the army. The fact that he was Big Joe Portagee, with a decent training in the Monterey jail, not only saved him the misery of patriotism thwarted, but solidified his conviction that as a man's days are rightly devoted half to sleeping and half to waking, so a man's years are rightly spent half in jail and half out. Of the duration of the war, Joe Portagee spent considerably more time in jail than out.

In civilian life one is punished for things one does; but army codes add a new principle to this—they punish a man for things he does not do. Joe Portagee never did figure this out. He didn't clean his rifle; he didn't shave; and once or twice, on leave, he didn't come back. Coupled with these shortcomings was a propensity Big Joe had for genial argument when he was taken to task.

Ordinarily he spent half his time in jail; of two years in the army he spent eighteen months in jail. And he was far from satisfied with prison life in the army. In the Monterey jail he was accustomed to ease and companionship. In the army he found only work. In Monterey only one charge was ever brought against him: Drunk and Disorderly Conduct. The charges in the army bewildered him so completely that the effect on his mind was probably permanent.

When the war was over, and all the troops were disbanded, Big Joe still had six months' sentence to serve. The charge had been: Being drunk on duty. Striking a sergeant with a kerosene can. Denying his identity (he couldn't remember it, so he denied everything). Stealing two gallons of cooked beans. And going A.W.O.L. on the major's horse.

If the Armistice had not already been signed, Big Joe would probably have been shot. He came home to Monterey long after the other veterans had arrived and had eaten up all the sweets of victory.

When Big Joe swung down from the train, he was dressed in an army overcoat and tunic and a pair of blue serge trousers.

The town hadn't changed much, except for prohibition; and

prohibition hadn't changed Torrelli's. Joe traded his overcoat for a gallon of wine and went out to find his friends.

True friends he found none that night, but in Monterey he found no lack of those vile and false harpies and pimps who are ever ready to lead men into the pit. Joe, who was not very moral, had no revulsion for the pit; he liked it.

Before very many hours had passed, his wine was gone, and he had no money; and then the harpies tried to get Joe out of the pit, and he wouldn't go. He was comfortable there.

When they tried to eject him by force, Big Joe, with a just and terrible resentment, broke all the furniture and all the windows, sent half-clothed girls screaming into the night; and then, as an afterthought, set fire to the house. It was not a safe thing to lead Joe into temptation; he had no resistance to it at all.

A policeman finally interfered and took him in hand. The Portagee sighed happily. He was home again.

After a short and juryless trial, in which he was sentenced to thirty days, Joe lay luxuriously on his leather cot and slept heavily for one-tenth of his sentence.

The Portagee liked the Monterey jail. It was a place to meet people. If he stayed there long enough, all his friends were in and out. The time passed quickly. He was a little sad when he had to go, but his sadness was tempered with the knowledge that it was very easy to get back again.

He would have liked to go into the pit again, but he had no money and no wine. He combed the streets for his old friends, Pilon and Danny and Pablo, and could not find them. The police sergeant said he hadn't booked them for a long time.

"They must be dead," said the Portagee.

He wandered sadly to Torrelli's, but Torrelli was not friendly toward the man who had neither money nor barterable property, and he gave Big Joe little solace; but Torrelli did say that Danny had inherited a house on Tortilla Flat, and that all his friends lived there with him.

Affection and a desire to see his friends came to Big Joe. In the evening he wandered up towards Tortilla Flat to find Danny and Pilon. It was dusk as he walked up the street, and on the way he met Pilon, hurrying by in a businesslike way.

"Ai, Pilon. I was just coming to see you."

"Hello, Joe Portagee," Pilon was brusque. "Where you been?"

"In the army," said Joe.

Pilon's mind was not on the meeting. "I have to go on."

"I will go with you," said Joe.

Pilon stopped and surveyed him. "Don't you remember what night it is?" he asked.

"No. What is it?"

"It is Saint Andrew's Eve."

Then the Portagee knew; for this was the night when every paisano who wasn't in jail wandered restlessly through the forest. This was the night when all buried treasure sent up a faint phosphorescent glow through the ground. There was plenty of treasure in the woods too. Monterey had been invaded many times in two hundred years, and each time valuables had been hidden in the earth.

The night was clear. Pilon had emerged from his hard daily shell, as he did now and then. He was the idealist to-night, the giver of gifts. This night he was engaged in a mission of kindness.

"You may come with me, Big Joe Portagee, but if we find any treasure I must decide what to do with it. If you do not agree, you can go by yourself and look for your own treasure."

Big Joe was not an expert at directing his own efforts. "I will go with you, Pilon," he said. "I don't care about the treasure."

The night came down as they walked into the forest. Their feet found the pine-needle beds. Now Pilon knew it for a perfect night. A high fog covered the sky, and behind it the moon shone, so that the forest was filled with a gauze-like light. There was none of the sharp outline we think of as reality. The tree trunks were not black columns of wood, but soft and unsubstantial shadows. The patches of brush were formless and shifting in the queer light. Ghosts could walk freely to-night, without fear of the disbelief of men; for this night was haunted, and it would be an insensitive man who did not know it.

Now and then Pilon and Big Joe passed other searchers who wandered restlessly, zigzagging among the pines. Their heads were down, and they moved silently and passed no greeting. Who could say whether all of them were really living men? Joe and Pilon knew that some were shades of those old folk who had buried the treasures; and who, on Saint Andrew's Eve, wandered back to the earth to see that their gold was undisturbed. Pilon wore his saint's medallion hung around his neck, outside his clothes; so he had no fear of the spirits. Big Joe walked with his fingers crossed in the Holy Sign. Although they might be frightened, they knew they had protection more than adequate to cope with the unearthly night.

The wind arose as they walked, and drove the fog across the pale moon like a thin wash of grey water-colour. The moving fog gave shifting form to the forest, so that every tree crept stealthily along and the bushes moved soundlessly, like great dark cats. The tree-tops in the wind talked huskily, told fortunes and foretold deaths. Pilon knew it was not good to listen to the talking of the trees. No good ever came of knowing the future; and besides, this whispering was unholy. He turned the attention of his ears from the trees' talking.

He began a zigzag path through the forest, and Big Joe walked beside him like a great alert dog. Lone silent men passed them and went on without a greeting; and the dead passed them noiselessly, and went on without a greeting.

The fog siren began its screaming on the Point, far below them; and it wailed its sorrow for all the good ships that had drowned on the iron reef, and for all those others that would sometime die there.

Pilon shuddered and felt cold, although the night was warm. He whispered a Hail Mary under his breath.

They passed a grey man who walked with his head down and who gave them no greeting.

An hour went by, and still Pilon and Big Joe wandered as restlessly as the dead who crowded the night.

Suddenly Pilon stopped. His hand found Big Joe's arm. "Do you see?" he whispered.

"Where?"

"Right ahead there."

"Yes—I think so."

It seemed to Pilon that he could see a soft pillar of blue light that shone out of the ground ten yards ahead of him.

"Big Joe," he whispered, "find two sticks about three or four feet long. I do not want to look away. I might lose it."

He stood like a pointing dog while Big Joe scurried off to find the sticks. Pilon heard him break two small dead limbs from a pine tree. And he heard the snaps as Big Joe broke the twigs from his sticks. And still Pilon stared at the pale shaft of nebulous light. So faint it was that sometimes it seemed to disappear altogether. Sometimes he was not sure he saw it at all. He did not move his eyes when Big Joe put the sticks in his hands. Pilon crossed the sticks at right angles and advanced slowly, holding the cross in front of him. As he came close, the light seemed to fade away, but he saw where it had come from, a perfectly round depression in the pine needles.

Pilon laid his cross over the depression, and he said, "All that lies here is mine by discovery. Go away, all evil spirits. Go away, spirits of men who buried this treasure, *In Nomine Patris et Filii et Spiritus Sancti*," and then he heaved a great sigh and sat down on the ground.

"We have found it, oh my friend, Big Joe," he cried. "For many years I have looked, and now I have found it."

"Let's dig," said Big Joe.

But Pilon shook his head impatiently. "When all the spirits are free? When even to be here is dangerous? You are a fool, Big Joe. We will sit here until morning; and then we will mark the place, and to-morrow night we will dig. No one else can see the light now that we have covered it with the cross. To-morrow night there will be no danger."

The night seemed more fearful now that they sat in the pine needles, but the cross sent out a warmth of holiness and safety, like a little bonfire on the ground. Like a fire, however, it only warmed the front of them. Their backs were to the cold and evil things that wandered about in the forest.

Pilon got up and drew a big circle around the whole place, and he was inside when he closed the circle. "Let no evil thing cross this line, in the Name of the Most Holy Jesus," he chanted. Then he sat down again. Both he and Big Joe felt better. They could hear the muffled footsteps of the weary, wandering ghosts; they could see the little lights that glowed from the transparent forms as they walked by; but their protecting line was impregnable. Nothing bad from this world or from any other world could cross into the circle.

"What are you going to do with the money?" Big Joe asked.

Pilon looked at him with contempt. "You have never looked for treasure, Big Joe Portagee, for you do not know how to go about it. I cannot keep this treasure for myself. If I go after it intending to keep it, then the treasure will dig itself down and down like a clam in the sand, and I shall never find it. No, that is not the way. I am digging this treasure for Danny."

All the idealism in Pilon came out then. He told Big Joe how good Danny was to his friends.

"And we do nothing for him," he said. "We pay no rent. Sometimes we get drunk and break the furniture. We fight with Danny when we are angry with him, and we call him names. Oh, we are very bad, Big Joe. And so all of us, Pablo and Jesus Maria and the Pirate and I, talked and planned. We are all in the woods to-night, looking for treasure. And the treasure is to be for Danny. He is so good, Big Joe. He is so kind; and we are so bad. But if we take a great sack of treasure to him, then he will be glad. It is because my heart is clean of selfishness that I can find this treasure."

"Won't you keep any of it?" Big Joe asked incredulously. "Not even for a gallon of wine?"

Pilon had no speck of the Bad Pilon in him this night. "No, not one scrap of gold! Not one little brown penny! It is all for Danny, every bit."

Joe was disappointed. "I walked all this way and I won't even get a glass of wine for it," he mourned.

"When Danny has the money," Pilon said delicately, "it may

be that he will buy a little wine. Of course I shall not suggest it, for this treasure is Danny's. But I think maybe he might buy a little wine. And then if you were good to him, you might get a glass."

Big Joe was comforted, for he had known Danny a long time. He thought it possible that Danny might buy a great deal of wine.

The night passed on over them. The moon went down and left the forest in muffled darkness. The fog siren screamed and screamed. During the whole night Pilon remained unspotted. He preached a little to Big Joe as recent converts are likely to do.

"It is worth while to be kind and generous," he said. "Not only do such actions pile up a house of joy in Heaven; but there is, too, a quick reward here on earth. One feels a golden warmth glowing like a hot enchilada in one's stomach. The Spirit of God clothes one in a coat as soft as camel's hair. I have not always been a good man, Big Joe Portagee. I confess it freely."

Big Joe knew it perfectly well.

"I have been bad," Pilon continued ecstatically. He was enjoying himself thoroughly. "I have lied and stolen. I have been lecherous. I have committed adultery and taken God's name in vain."

"Me too," said Big Joe happily.

"And what was the result, Big Joe Portagee? I have had a mean feeling. I have known I would go to Hell. But now I see that the sinner is never so bad that he cannot be forgiven. Although I have not yet been to confession, I can feel that the change in me is pleasing to God, for His grace is upon me. If you too would change your ways, Big Joe, if you would give up drunkenness and fighting and those girls down at Dora Williams' House, you too might feel as I do."

But Big Joe had gone to sleep. He never stayed awake very long when he was not moving about.

The grace was not quite so sharp to Pilon when he could not tell Big Joe about it, but he sat and watched the treasure place while the sky greyed and the dawn came behind the fog. He saw the pine trees take shape and emerge out of obscurity. The wind died down and the little blue rabbits came out of the brush and hopped about on the pine needles. Pilon was heavy-eyed but happy.

When it was light he stirred Big Joe Portagee with his foot. "It is time to go to Danny's house. The day has come." Pilon threw the cross away, for it was no longer needed, and he erased the circle. "Now," he said, "we must make no mark, but we must remember this by trees and rocks."

"Why don't we dig now?" Big Joe asked.

"And everybody in Tortilla Flat would come to help us," Pilon said sarcastically.

They looked hard at the surroundings, saying. "Now there are three trees together on the right, and two on the left. That patch of brush is down there, and here is a rock." At last they walked away from the treasure, memorizing the way as they went.

At Danny's house they found tired friends. "Did you find any?" the friends demanded.

"No," said Pilon quickly, to forestall Joe's confession.

"Well, Pablo thought he saw the light, but it disappeared before he got to it. And the Pirate saw the ghost of an old woman, and she had his dog with her."

The Pirate broke into a smile. "That old woman told me my dog was happy now," he said.

"Here is Big Joe Portagee, back from the army," announced Pilon.

"Hello, Joe."

"You got a nice place here," said the Portagee, and let himself down easily into a chair.

"You keep out of my bed," said Danny, for he knew that Joe Portagee had come to stay. The way he sat in a chair and crossed his knees had an appearance of permanence.

The Pirate went out and took his wheelbarrow and started into the forest to cut his kindlings; but the other five men lay down in the sunshine that broke through the fog, and in a little while they were asleep.

It was mid-afternoon before any of them awakened. At last they stretched their arms and sat up and looked listlessly down at the bay below, where a brown oil tanker moved slowly out to sea. The Pirate had left the bags on the table and the friends opened them and brought out the food the Pirate had collected.

Big Joe walked down the path towards the sagging gate. "See you later," he called to Pilon.

Pilon anxiously watched him until he saw that Big Joe was headed down the hill to Monterey, not up towards the pine forest. The four friends sat down and dreamily watched the evening come.

At dusk Joe Portagee returned. He and Pilon conferred in the yard, out of earshot of the house.

"We will borrow tools from Mrs. Morales," Pilon said. "A shovel and a pick-axe stand by her chicken-house."

When it was quite dark they started. "We go to see some girls, friends of Joe Portagee's," Pilon explained. They crept into Mrs. Morales' yard and borrowed the tools. And then, from the weeds beside the road, Big Joe lifted out a gallon jug of wine.

"Thou hast sold the treasure," Pilon cried fiercely. "Thou art a traitor, oh, dog of a dog."

Big Joe quietened him firmly. "I did not tell where the treasure was," he said, with some dignity. "I told like this, 'We found a treasure,' I said, 'but it is for Danny. When Danny has it, I will borrow a dollar and pay for the wine.'"

Pilon was overwhelmed. "And they believed, and let you take the wine?" he demanded.

"Well——" Big Joe hesitated. "I left something to prove I would bring the dollar."

Pilon turned like lightning and took him by the throat. "What did you leave?"

"Only one little blanket, Pilon," Joe Portagee wailed. "Only one."

Pilon shook him, but Big Joe was so heavy that Pilon only succeeded in shaking himself. "What blanket?" he cried. "Say what blanket it was you stole."

Big Joe blubbered. "Only one of Danny's. Only one. He has two. I took only the little tiny one. Do not hurt me, Pilon. The other one was bigger. Danny will get it back when we find the treasure."

Pilon whirled him around and kicked him with accuracy and fire. "Pig," he said. "Dirty thieving cow. You will get the blanket back or I will beat you to ribbons."

Big Joe tried to placate him. "I thought how we are working for Danny," he whispered. "I thought, 'Danny will be so glad, he can buy a hundred new blankets.'"

"Be still," said Pilon. "You will get that same blanket back or I will beat you with a rock." He took up the jug and uncorked it and drank a little to soothe his frayed sensibilities; moreover, he drove the cork back and refused the Portagee even a drop. "For this theft you must do all the digging. Pick up those tools and come with me."

Big Joe whined like a puppy and obeyed. He could not stand against the righteous fury of Pilon.

They tried to find the treasure for a long time. It was late when Pilon pointed to three trees in a row. "There!" he said.

They searched about until they found the depression in the ground. There was a little moonlight to guide them, for this night the sky was free of fog.

Now that he was not going to dig, Pilon developed a new theory for uncovering treasure. "Sometimes the money is in sacks," he said, "and the sacks are rotted. If you dig straight down you might lose some." He drew a generous circle around the hollow. "Now, dig a deep trench around, and then we will come *up* on the treasure."

"Aren't you going to dig?" Big Joe asked.

Pilon broke into a fury. "Am I a thief of blankets?" he cried. "Do I steal from the bed of my friend who shelters me?"

"Well, I ain't going to do all the digging," Big Joe said.

Pilon picked up one of the pine limbs that only the night before had served as part of the cross. He advanced ominously towards Big Joe Portagee. "Thief," he snarled. "Dirty pig of an untrue friend. Take up that shovel."

Big Joe's courage flowed away, and he stooped for the shovel on the ground. If Joe Portagee's conscience had not been bad, he might have remonstrated; but his fear of Pilon, armed with a righteous cause and a stick of pine wood, was great.

Big Joe abhorred the whole principle of shovelling. The line of the moving shovel was unattractive. The end to be gained, that of taking dirt from one place and putting it in another was, to one who held the larger vision, silly and gainless. A whole lifetime of shovelling could accomplish practically nothing. Big Joe's reaction was a little more simple than this. He didn't like to shovel. He had joined the army to fight and had done nothing but dig.

But Pilon stood over him, and the trench stretched around the treasure place. It did no good to profess sickness, hunger, or weakness. Pilon was inexorable, and Joe's crime of the blanket was held against him. Although he whined, complained, held up his hands to show how they were hurt, Pilon stood over him and forced the digging.

Midnight came, and the trench was three feet down. The roosters of Monterey crowed. The moon sank behind the trees. At last Pilon gave the word to move in on the treasure. The bursts of dirt came slowly now; Big Joe was exhausted. Just before daylight his shovel struck something hard.

"Ai," he cried. "We have it, Pilon."

The find was large and square. Frantically they dug at it in the dark, and they could not see it.

"Careful," Pilon cautioned. "Do not hurt it."

The daylight came before they had it out. Pilon felt metal and leaned down in the grey light to see. It was a good-sized square of concrete. On the top was a round brown plate. Pilon spelled out the words on it:

UNITED STATES
GEODETIC SURVEY
+ 1915 +
ELEVATION 600 FEET

Pilon sat down in the pit and his shoulders sagged in defeat.

"No treasure?" Big Joe asked plaintively.

Pilon did not answer him. The Portagee inspected the cement post and his brow wrinkled with thought. He turned to the sorrowing Pilon. "Maybe we can take this good piece of metal and sell it."

Pilon peered up out of his dejection. "Johnny Pom-pom found one," he said with quietness of great disappointment. "Johnny Pom-pom took the metal piece and tried to sell it. It is a year in jail to dig one of these up," Pilon mourned. "A year in jail and two thousand dollars' fine." In his pain Pilon wanted only to get away from this tragic place. He stood up, found a weed in which to wrap the wine bottle, and started down the hill.

Big Joe trotted after him solicitously. "Where are we going?" he asked.

"I don't know," said Pilon.

The day was bright when they arrived at the beach, but even there Pilon did not stop. He trudged along the hard sand by the water's edge until Monterey was far behind and only the sand dunes of Seaside and the rippling waves of the bay were there to see his sorrow. At last he sat in the dry sand, with the sun warming him. Big Joe sat beside him, and he felt that in some way he was responsible for Pilon's silent pain.

Pilon took the jug out of its weed and uncorked it and drank deeply, and because sorrow is the mother of a general compassion, he passed Joe's wine to the miscreant Joe.

"How we build," Pilon cried. "How our dreams lead us. I had thought how we could carry bags of gold to Danny. I could see how his face would look. He would be surprised. For a long time he would not believe it." He took the bottle from Joe Portagee and drank colossally. "All this is gone, blown away in the night."

The sun was warming the beach now. In spite of his disappointment, Pilon felt a traitorous comfort stealing over him, a treacherous impulse to discover some good points in the situation.

Big Joe, in his quiet way, was drinking more than his share of the wine. Pilon took it indignantly and drank again and again.

"But after all," he said philosophically, "maybe if we had found gold, it might not have been good for Danny. He has always been a poor man. Riches might make him crazy."

Big Joe nodded solemnly. The wine went down and down in the bottle.

"Happiness is better than riches," said Pilon. "If we try to make Danny happy, it will be a better thing than to give him money."

Big Joe nodded again and took off his shoes. "Make him happy. That's the stuff."

Pilon turned sadly upon him. "You are only a pig and not fit to live with men," he said gently. "You who stole Danny's blanket should be kept in a sty and fed potato peelings."

They were getting very sleepy in the warm sun. The little waves whispered along the beach. Pilon took off his shoes.

"Even Stephen," said Big Joe, and they drained the jug to the last drop.

The beach was swaying gently, heaving and falling with a movement like a ground-swell.

"You aren't a bad man," Pilon said. But Big Joe Portagee was already asleep. Pilon took off his coat and laid it over his face. In a few moments he, too, was sleeping sweetly.

The sun wheeled over the sky. The tide spread up the beach and then retreated. A squad of scampering kildeers inspected the sleeping men. A wandering dog sniffed them. Two elderly ladies, collecting sea-shells, saw the bodies and hurried past lest these men should awaken in passion, pursue and criminally assault them. It was a shame, they agreed, that the police did nothing to control such matters. "They are drunk," one said.

And the other stared back up the beach at the sleeping men. "Drunken beasts," she agreed.

When at last the sun went behind the pines of the hill behind Monterey, Pilon awakened. His mouth was as dry as alum; his head ached and he was stiff from the hard sand. Big Joe snored on.

"Joe," Pilon cried, but the Portagee was beyond call. Pilon rested on his elbow and stared out to sea. "A little wine would be good for my dry mouth," he thought. He tipped up the jug and got not a single drop to soothe his dry tongue. Then he turned out his pockets in the hope that while he slept some miracle had taken place there; but none had. There was a broken pocket-knife for which he had been refused a glass of wine at least twenty times. There was a fish-hook in a cork, a piece of dirty string, a dog's tooth, and several keys that fit nothing Pilon knew of. In the whole lot was not a thing Torrelli would consider as worth having, even in a moment of insanity.

Pilon looked speculatively at Big Joe. "Poor fellow," he thought. "When Joe Portagee wakes up he will fell as dry as I do. He will like it if I have a little wine for him." He pushed Big Joe roughly several times; and when the Portagee only mumbled, and then snored again, Pilon looked through his pockets. He found a brass pants button, a little metal disc which said "Good Eats at the Dutchman", four or five headless matches, and a little piece of chewing-tobacco.

Pilon sat back on his heels. So it was no use. He must wither here on the beach while his throat called lustily for wine.

He noticed the serge trousers the Portagee was wearing and stroked them with his fingers. "Nice cloth," he thought. "Why should this dirty Portagee wear such good cloth when all his friends go about in jeans?" Then he remembered how badly the trousers fitted Big Joe, how tight the waist was even with two fly-buttons undone, how the cuffs missed the shoe tops by inches. "Someone of a decent size would be happy in those pants."

Pilon remembered Big Joe's crime against Danny, and he became an avenging angel. How did this big black Portagee dare to insult Danny so! "When he wakes up I will beat him! But," the more subtle Pilon argued, "his crime was theft. Would it not teach him a lesson to know how it feels to have something stolen? What good is punishment unless something is learned?" It was a triumphant position for Pilon. If, with one action, he could avenge Danny, discipline Big Joe, teach an ethical lesson, and get a little wine, who in the world could criticize him?

He pushed the Portagee vigorously, and Big Joe brushed at him as though he were a fly. Pilon deftly removed the trousers, rolled them up, and sauntered away into the sand dunes.

Torrelli was out, but Mrs. Torrelli opened the door to Pilon. He was mysterious in his manner, but at last he held up the trousers for her inspection.

She shook her head decisively.

"But look," said Pilon, "you are seeing only the spots and the dirt. Look at this fine cloth underneath. Think, señora! You have cleaned the spots off and pressed the trousers! Torrelli comes in! He is silent; he is glum. And then you bring him these fine pants! See how his eyes grow bright! See how happy he is! He takes you on his lap! Look how he smiles at you, señora! Is so much happiness too high at one gallon of red wine?"

"The seat of the pants is thin," she said.

He held them up to the light. "Can you see through them? No! The stiffness, the discomfort is taken out of them. They are in prime condition."

"No," she said firmly.

"You are cruel to your husband, señora. You deny him happiness. I should not be surprised to see him going to other women, who are not so heartless. For a quart, then?"

Finally her resistance was beaten down and she gave him the quart. Pilon drank it off immediately. "You try to break down the price of pleasure," he warned her. "I should have half a gallon."

Mrs. Torelli was hard as stone. Not a drop more could Pilon get. He sat there brooding in the kitchen. "Jewess, that's what she is. She cheats me out of Big Joe's pants."

Pilon thought sadly of his friend out there on the beach. What could he do? If he came into town he would be arrested. And what had this harpy done to deserve the pants? She had tried to buy Pilon's friend's pants for a miserable quart of miserable wine. Pilon felt himself dissolving into anger at her.

"I am going away in a moment," he told Mrs. Torrelli. The trousers were hung in a little alcove off the kitchen.

"Good-bye," said Mrs. Torrelli over her shoulder. She went into her little pantry to prepare dinner.

On his way out, Pilon passed the alcove and lifted down not only the trousers, but Danny's blanket.

Pilon walked back down the beach, towards the place where he had left Big Joe. He could see a bonfire burning brightly on the sand, and as he drew nearer a number of small dark figures passed in front of the flame. It was very dark now; he guided himself by the fire. As he came close, he saw that it was a Girl Scout wienie bake. He approached warily.

For a while he could not see Big Joe, but at last he discovered him, lying half covered with sand, speechless with cold and agony. Pilon walked firmly up to him and held up the trousers.

"Take them, Big Joe, and be glad you have them back."

Joe's teeth were chattering. "Who stole my pants, Pilon? I have been lying here for hours, and I could not go away because of those girls."

Pilon obligingly stood between Big Joe and the little girls who were running about the bonfire. The Portagee brushed the cold damp sand from his legs and put on his trousers. They walked side by side along the dark beach towards Monterey, where the lights hung, necklace above necklace against the hill. The sand dunes crouched along the back of the beach like tired hounds, resting; and the waves gently practised at striking and hissed a little. The night was cold and aloof, and its warm life was withdrawn, so that it was full of bitter warnings to man that he is alone in the world, and alone among his fellows; that he has no comfort owing him from anywhere.

Pilon was still brooding, and Joe Portagee sensed the depth of his feeling. At last Pilon turned his head towards his friend. "We learn by this that it is great foolishness to trust a woman," he said.

"Did some woman take my pants?" Big Joe demanded excitedly. "Who was it? I'll kick the hell out of her!"

But Pilon shook his head as sadly as old Jehovah, resting on the seventh day, sees that his world is tiresome. "She is punished," Pilon said. "You might say she punished herself, and that is the best way. She had thy pants; she bought them with greed; and now she has them not."

These things were beyond Big Joe. They were mysteries it was better to let alone; and this was as Pilon wished it. Big Joe said humbly, "Thanks for getting my pants back, Pilon." But Pilon was so sunk in philosophy that even thanks were valueless.

"It was nothing," he said. "In the whole matter only the lesson we learn has any value."

They climbed up from the beach and passed the great silver tower of the gas works.

Big Joe Portagee was happy to be with Pilon. "Here is one who takes care of his friends," he thought. "Even when they sleep he is alert to see that no harm comes to them." He resolved to do something nice for Pilon sometime.

CHAPTER IX

How Danny was ensnared by a vacuum-cleaner and how Danny's Friends rescued him

DOLORES ENGRACIA RAMIREZ lived in her own little house on the upper edge of Tortilla Flat. She did housework for some of the ladies in Monterey, and she belonged to the Native Daughters of the Golden West. She was not pretty, this lean-faced paisana, but there was in her figure a certain voluptuousness of movement; there was in her voice a throatiness some men found indicative. Her eyes could burn behind a mist with a sleepy passion which those men to whom the flesh is important found attractive and downright inviting.

In her brusque moments she was not desirable, but an amorous combination came about within her often enough so that she was called Sweets Ramirez on Tortilla Flat.

It was a pleasant thing to see her when the beast in her was prowling. How she leaned over her front gate! How her voice purred drowsily! How her hips moved gently about, now pressing against the fence, now swelling back like a summer beach-wave, and then pressing the fence again! Who in the world could put so much husky meaning in "*Ai, amigo, a' onde vas?*"

It is true that ordinarily her voice was shrill, her face hard and sharp as a hatchet, her figure lumpy, and her intentions selfish. The softer self came into possession only once or twice a week, and then, ordinarily, in the evening.

When Sweets heard that Danny was an heir, she was glad for him. She dreamed of being his lady, as did every other female on Tortilla Flat. In the evenings she leaned over the front gate waiting for the time when he would pass by and fall into her trap. But for a long time her baited trap caught nothing but poor Indians and paisanos who owned no houses, and whose clothes were sometimes fugitive from better wardrobes.

Sweets was not content. Her house was up the hill from Danny's house, in a direction he did not often take. Sweets could not go looking for him. She was a lady, and her conduct was governed by very strict rules of propriety. If Danny should walk by, now, if they should talk, like the old friends they were, if he should come in for a social glass of wine; and then, if nature proved too strong, and her feminine resistance too weak, there was no grave breach of propriety. But it was unthinkable to leave her web on the front gate.

For many months of evenings she waited in vain, and took such gifts as walked by in jeans. But there are only a limited number of pathways on Tortilla Flat. It was inevitable that Danny should, sooner or later, pass the gate of Dolores Engracia Ramirez; and so he did.

In all the time they had known each other, there had never been an occasion when it was more to Sweets' advantage to have him walk by; for Danny had only that morning found a keg of copper shingle nails, lost by the Central Supply Company. He had judged them jetsam because no member of the company was anywhere near. Danny removed the copper nails from the keg and put them in a sack. Then, borrowing the Pirate's wheel-barrow, and the Pirate to push it, he took his salvage to the Western Supply Company, where he sold the copper for three dollars. The keg he gave to the Pirate.

"You can keep things in it," he said. That made the Pirate very happy.

And now Danny came down the hill, aimed with a fine accuracy towards the house of Torrelli, and the three dollars were in his pocket.

Dolores' voice sounded as huskily sweet as the drone of a bumblebee. "*Ai, amigo, a' onde vas?*"

Danny stopped. A revolution took place in his plans. "How are you, Sweets?"

"What difference is it how I am? None of my friends are interested," she said archly. And her hips floated in a graceful and circular undulation.

"What do you mean?" he demanded.

"Well, does my friend Danny ever come to see me?"

"I am here to see thee now," he said gallantly.

She opened the gate a little. "Wilt thou come in for a tiny glass of wine in friendship's name?" Danny went into her house. "What hast thou been doing in the forest?" she cooed.

Then he made an error. He told vaingloriously of his transaction up the hill, and he boasted of his three dollars.

"Of course I have only enough wine to fill two thimbles," she said.

They sat in Sweets' kitchen and drank a glass of wine. In a little while Danny assaulted her virtue with true gallantry and vigour. He found to his amazement a resistance out of all proportion to her size and reputation. The ugly beast of lust was awakened in him. He was angry. Only when he was leaving was the way made clear to him.

The husky voice said, "Maybe you would like to come and see me this evening, Danny." Sweets' eyes swam in a mist of drowsy invitation. "One has neighbours," she suggested with delicacy.

Then he understood. "I will come back," he promised.

It was mid-afternoon. Danny walked down the street, reaimed at Torrelli's, and the beast in him had changed. From a savage and snarling wolf it had become a great, shaggy, sentimental bear. "I will take wine to that nice Sweets," he thought.

On the way down, whom should he meet but Pablo, and Pablo had two sticks of gum. He gave one to Danny and fell into step. "Where goest thou?"

"It is no time for friendship," Danny said tartly. "First I go to buy a little wine to take to a lady. You may come with me, and have one glass only. I am tired of buying wine for ladies only to have my friends drink it all up."

Pablo agreed that such a practice was unendurable. For himself, he didn't want Danny's wine, but only his companionship.

They went to Torrelli's. They had a glass of wine out of the new-bought gallon. Danny confessed that it was shabby treatment to give his friend only one little glass. Over Pablo's passionate protest they had another. Ladies, Danny thought, should not drink too much wine. They were apt to become silly; and besides, it dulled some of those senses one liked to find alert in a lady. They had a few more glasses. Half a gallon of wine was a bountiful present, especially as Danny was about to go down to buy another present. They measured down half a gallon and drank what was over. Then Danny hid the jug in the weeds in a ditch.

"I would like you to come with me to buy the present, Pablo," he said.

Pablo knew the reason for the invitation. Half of it was a desire for Pablo's company, and half was fear of leaving the wine while Pablo was at large. They walked with studied dignity and straightness down the hill of Monterey.

Mr. Simon, of Simon's Investment, Jewellery, and Loan Company, welcomed them into his store. The name of the store defined the outward limits of the merchandise the company sold; for there were saxophones, radios, rifles, knives, fishing-rods, and old coins on the counter; all second-hand, but all really better than new because they were just well broken-in.

"Something you would like to see?" Mr. Simon asked.

"Yes," said Danny.

The proprietor named over a tentative list and then stopped in the middle of a word, for he saw that Danny was looking at a large aluminium vacuum-cleaner. The dust-bag was blue and yellow checks. The electric cord was long and black and slick. Mr. Simon went to it and rubbed it with his hand and stood off and admired it. "Something in a vacuum-cleaner?" he asked.

"How much?"

"For this one, fourteen dollars." It was not a price so much as an endeavour to find out how much Danny had. And Danny wanted it, for it was large and shiny. No woman of Tortilla Flat had one. In this moment he forgot there was no electricity on Tortilla Flat. He laid his two dollars on the counter and waited while the explosion took place; the fury, the rage, the sadness, the poverty, the ruin, the cheating. The polish was invoked, the colour of the bag, the extra-long cord, the value of the metal alone. And when it was all over, Danny went out carrying the vacuum-cleaner.

Often as a *pasatiempo* in the afternoon, Sweets brought out the vacuum-cleaner and leaned it against a chair. While her friends looked on, she pushed it back and forth to show how easily it rolled. And she made a humming with her voice to imitate a motor.

"My friend is a rich man," she said. "I think pretty soon there will be wires full of electricity coming right into the house, and then zip and zip and zip! And you have the house clean!"

Her friends tried to belittle the present, saying, "It is too bad you can't run this machine." And, "I have always held that a broom and dust-pan, *properly* used, are more thorough."

But their envy could do nothing against the vacuum. Through its possession Sweets climbed to the peak of the social scale of Tortilla Flat. People who did not remember her name referred to her as "that one with the sweeping-machine". Often when her enemies passed the house, Sweets could be seen through the window, pushing the cleaner back and forth, while a loud humming came from her throat. Indeed, after she had swept her house every day, she pushed the cleaner about on the theory that of course it would clean better with electricity but one could not have everything.

She excited envy in many houses. Her manner became dignified and gracious, and she held her chin high as befitted one who had a sweeping-machine. In her conversation she included it. "Ramon passed this morning while I was pushing the sweeping-machine"; "Louise Meater cut her hand this morning, not three hours after I had been pushing the sweeping-machine."

But in her elevation she did not neglect Danny. Her voice growled with emotion when he was about. She swayed like a pine tree in the wind. And he spent every evening at the house of Sweets.

At first his friends ignored his absence, for it is the right of every man to have these little affairs. But as the weeks went on, and as a rather violent domestic life began to make Danny listless and pale, his friends became convinced that Sweets' gratitude for the sweeping-machine was not to Danny's best physical interests. They were jealous of a situation that was holding his attention so long.

Pilon and Pablo and Jesus Maria Corcoran in turn assaulted the nest of his affections during his absence; but Sweets, while she was sensible of the compliment, remained true to the man who had raised her position to such a gratifying level. She tried to keep their friendship for a future time of need, for she knew how fickle fortune is; but she stoutly refused to share with Danny's friends that which was dedicated for the time being to Danny.

Wherefore the friends, in despair, organized a group, formed for and dedicated to her destruction.

It may be that Danny, deep in his soul, was beginning to tire of Sweets' affection and the duty of attendance it demanded. If such a change were taking place, he did not admit it to himself.

At three o'clock one afternoon, Pilon and Pablo and Jesus Maria, followed vaguely by Big Joe Portagee, returned triumphant from three-quarters of a day of strenuous effort. Their campaign had called into play and taxed to the limit the pitiless logic of Pilon, the artistic ingenuousness of Pablo, and the gentleness and humanity of Jesus Maria Corcoran. Big Joe had contributed nothing.

But now, like four hunters, they returned from the chase more happy because their victory had been a difficult one. And in Monterey a poor puzzled Indian came gradually to the conviction that he had been swindled.

Pilon carried a gallon jug of wine concealed in a bundle of ivy. They marched joyfully into Danny's house, and Pilon set the gallon on the table.

Danny, awakened out of a sound sleep, smiled quietly, got up from bed, and laid out the fruit jars. He poured the wine. His four friends fell into chairs, for it had been an exhausting day.

They drank quietly in the late afternoon, that time of curious intermission. Nearly everyone in Tortilla Flat stops then and considers those things that have taken place in the day just past, and thinks over the possibilities of the evening. There are many things to discuss in an afternoon.

"Cornelia Ruiz got a new man this morning," Pilon observed. "He has a bald head. His name is Kilpatrick. Cornelia says her other man didn't come home three nights last week. She didn't like that."

"Cornelia is a woman who changes her mind too quickly," said Danny. He thought complacently of his own sure establishment, built on the rock of the vacuum-cleaner.

"Cornelia's father was worse," said Pablo. "He could not tell the truth. Once he borrowed a dollar from me. I have told Cornelia about it, and she does nothing."

"Two of one blood. 'Know the breed and know the dog,'" Pilon quoted virtuously.

Danny poured the jars full of wine again, and the gallon was exhausted. He looked ruefully at it.

Jesus Maria, that lover of the humanities, spoke up quietly. "I saw Susie Francisco, Pilon. She said the recipe worked fine. She has been out riding with Charlie Guzman on his motor-cycle three times. The first two times she gave him the love medicine it made him sick. She thought it was no good. But now Susie says you can have some cookies any time."

"What was in that potion?" Pablo asked.

Pilon became secretive. "I cannot tell all of it. I guess it must have been the poison oak in it that made Charlie Guzman sick."

The gallon of wine had gone too quickly. Each of the six friends was conscious of a thirst so sharp that it was a pain of desire. Pilon looked at his friends with drooped eyes, and they looked back at him. The conspiracy was ready.

Pilon cleared his throat. "What hast thou done, Danny, to set the whole town laughing at thee?"

Danny looked worried. "What do you mean?"

Pilon chuckled. "It is said by many that you bought a sweeping-machine for a lady, and that machine will not work unless wires are put into the house. Those wires cost a great deal of money. Some people find this present very funny."

Danny grew uncomfortable. "That lady likes the sweeping-machine," he said defensively.

"Why not?" Pablo agreed. "She has told some people that you have promised to put wires into her house so the sweeping-machine will work."

Danny looked even more perturbed. "Did she say that?"

"So I was told."

"Well, I will not," Danny cried.

"If I did not think it funny, I should be angry to hear my friend laughed at," Pilon observed.

"What will you do when she asks for those wires?" Jesus Maria asked.

"I will tell her 'no'," said Danny.

Pilon laughed. "I wish I could be there. It is not such a simple thing to tell that lady 'no'."

Danny felt that his friends were turning against him. "What shall I do?" he asked helplessly.

Pilon gave the matter his grave consideration and brought his realism to bear on the subject. "If that lady did not have the sweeping-machine, she would not want those wires," he said.

The friends nodded in agreement. "Therefore," Pilon continued, "the thing to do is to remove the sweeping-machine."

"Oh, she wouldn't let me take it," Danny protested.

"Then we will help you," said Pilon. "I will take the machine, and in return you can take the lady a present of a gallon of wine. She will not even know where the sweeping-machine has gone."

"Some neighbour will see you take it."

"Oh no," said Pilon. "You stay here, Danny. I will get the machine."

Danny sighed with relief that his problem was assumed by his good friends.

There were few things going on in Tortilla Flat that Pilon did not know. His mind made sharp little notes of everything that his eyes saw or his ears heard. He knew that Sweets went to the store at four-thirty every afternoon. He depended upon this almost invariable habit to put his plan into effect.

"It is better that you do not know anything about it," he told Danny.

In the yard Pilon had a gunny sack in readiness. With his knife he cut a generous branch from the rose bush and pushed it into the sack.

At Sweets' house he found her absent, as he had expected and hoped she would be. "It is really Danny's machine," he told himself.

It was a moment's work to enter the house, to put the vacuum-cleaner in the sack, and to arrange the rose bush artistically in the sack's mouth.

As he came out of the yard, he met Sweets. Pilon took off his hat politely. "I stepped in to pass the time," he said.

"Will you stop now, Pilon?"

"No. I have business down in Monterey. It is late."

"Where do you go with this rose bush?"

"A man in Monterey is to buy it. A very fine rose bush. See how strong it is."

"Stop in some other time, Pilon."

He heard no cry of anger as he walked sedately down the street. "Perhaps she will not miss it for a while," he thought.

Half the problem was solved, but half was yet to be approached. "What can Danny do with this sweeping-machine?" Pilon asked himself. "If he has it, Sweets will know he has taken it. Can I throw it away? No, for it is valuable. The thing to do would be to get rid of it and still to reap the benefit of its value."

Now the whole problem was solved. Pilon headed down the hill towards Torrelli's house.

It was a large and shining vacuum-cleaner. When Pilon came again up the hill, he had a gallon of wine in each hand.

The friends received him in silence when he entered Danny's house. He set one jug on the table and the other on the floor.

"I have brought you a present to take to the lady," he told Danny. "And here is a little wine for us."

They gathered happily, for their thirst was a raging fire. When the first gallon was far gone, Pilon held his glass to the candlelight and looked through it. "Things that happen are of no importance," he said. "But from everything that happens there is a lesson to be learned. By this we learn that a present, especially to a lady, should have no quality that will require a further present. Also we learn that it is sinful to give presents of too great value, for they may excite greed."

The first gallon was gone. The friends looked at Danny to see how he felt about it. He had been very quiet, but now he saw that his friends were waiting on him.

"That lady was lively," he said judiciously. "That lady had a very sympathetic nature. But God damn it!" he said. "I'm sick of it!" He went to the second jug and drew the cork.

The Pirate, sitting in the corner among his dogs, smiled to himself and whispered in admiration, " 'God damn it, I'm sick of it.' " That, thought the Pirate, was very fine.

They had not more than half finished the second jug, indeed they had sung only two songs, when young Johnny Pom-pom came in. "I was at Torrelli's," Johnny said. "Oh, that Torrelli is mad! He is shouting! He is beating on the table with his fists."

The friends looked up with mild interest. "Something has happened. It is probable Torrelli deserves it."

"Often he has refused his good customers a little glass of wine."

"What is the matter with Torrelli?" Pablo asked.

Johnny Pom-pom accepted a jar of wine. "Torelli says he bought a sweeping-machine from Pilon, and when he hooked it up to his light wire, it would not work. So he looked on the inside, and it had no motor. He says he will kill Pilon."

Pilon looked shocked. "I did not know this machine was at fault," he said. "But did I not say Torrelli deserved what was the matter with him? That machine was worth three or four gallons of wine, but that miser Torrelli would give no more than two."

Danny still felt a glow of gratitude towards Pilon. He smacked his lips on his wine. "This stuff of Torrelli's is getting worse and worse," he said. "At his best it is swill the pigs leave, but lately it is so bad that Charlie Marsh even would not drink it."

They all felt a little bit revenged on Torrelli then.

"I think," said Danny, "that we will buy our wine someplace else, if Torrelli does not look out."

CHAPTER X

How the Friends solaced a corporal and in return received a lesson in paternal ethics

Jesus Maria Corcoran was a pathway for the humanities. Suffering he tried to relieve; sorrow he tried to assuage; happiness he shared. No hard nor haunted Jesus Maria existed. His heart was free for the use of anyone who had a use for it. His resources and wits were at the disposal of anyone who had less of either than had Jesus Maria.

He it was who carried José de la Nariz four miles when José's leg was broken. When Mrs. Palochico lost the goat of her heart, the good goat of milk and cheese, it was Jesus Maria who tracked that goat to Big Joe Portagee and halted the murder and made Big Joe give it back. It was Jesus Maria who once picked Charlie Marsh out of a ditch where he lay in his own filth, a deed which required not only a warm heart, but a strong stomach.

Together with his capacity for doing good, Jesus Maria had a gift for coming in contact with situations where good wanted doing.

Such was his reputation that Pilon had once said, "If that Jesus Maria had gone into the Church, Monterey would have had a saint for the calendar, I tell you."

Out of some deep pouch in his soul, Jesus Maria drew kindness that renewed itself by withdrawal.

It was Jesus Maria's practice to go to the post office every day, first because there he could see many people whom he knew, and second because on that windy post-office corner he could look at the legs of a great many girls. It must not be supposed that in this latter interest there was any vulgarity. As soon criticize a man who goes to art galleries or to concerts. Jesus Maria liked to look at girls' legs.

One day when he had leaned against the post office for two hours with very little success, he was witness to a pitiful scene. A policeman came along the sidewalk leading a young boy of about sixteen, and the boy carried a little baby wrapped in a piece of grey blanket.

The policeman was saying, "I don't care if I can't understand you. You can't sit in the gutter all day. We'll find out about you."

And the boy in Spanish with a peculiar inflection, said, "But, señor, I do nothing wrong. Why do you take me away?"

The policeman saw Jesus Maria. "Hey, paisano," he called. "What's this *cholo* talking about?"

Jesus Maria stepped out and addressed the boy. "Can I be of service to you?"

The boy broke into a relieved flood. "I came here to work. Some Mexican men said there would be work here, and there was none. I was sitting down resting when this man came to me and dragged me away."

Jesus Maria nodded and turned back to the policeman. "Has he done some crime, this little one?"

"No, but he's been sitting in the gutter on Alvarado Street for about three hours."

"He is a friend of mine," Jesus Maria said. "I will take care of him."

"Well, keep him out of the gutter."

Jesus Maria and his new friend walked up the hill. "I will take you to the house where I live. There you will have something to eat. What baby is this?"

"It is my baby," said the boy. "I am a *caporál*, and he is my baby. He is sick now; but when he grows up he is going to be a *generál*."

"What is he sick from, Señor Caporál?"

"I don't know. He is just sick." He showed the baby's face, and it looked very ill indeed.

The sympathies of Jesus Maria mounted. "The house where I live is owned by my friend Danny, and there is a good man, Señor Caporál. There is one to appeal to when trouble is upon one. Look, we will go there, and that Danny will give us shelter. My friend Mrs. Palochico has a goat. We will borrow a little milk for the baby."

The corporal's face for the first time wore a smile of comfort. "It is good to have friends," he said. "In Torreón I have many friends who would make themselves beggars to help me." He boasted a little to Jesus Maria. "I have rich friends, but of course they do not know my need."

Jesus Maria pushed open the gate of Danny's yard, and they entered together. Danny and Pablo and Big Joe were sitting in the living-room, waiting for the daily miracle of food. Jesus Maria pushed the boy into the room.

"Here is a young soldier, a *caporál*," he explained. "He has a baby here with him, and that baby is sick."

The friends arose with alacrity. The corporal threw back the grey blanket from the baby's face.

"He is sick, all right," Danny said. "Maybe we should get a doctor."

But the soldier shook his head. "No doctors. I do not like doctors This baby does not cry, and he will not eat much. Maybe when he rests, then he will be well again."

At this moment Pilon entered and inspected the child. "This baby is sick," he said.

Pilon immediately took control. Jesus Maria he sent to Mrs. Palochico's house to borrow goat milk; Big Joe and Pablo to get an apple-box, pad it with dry grass, and line it with a sheepskin coat. Danny offered his bed, but it was refused. The corporal stood in the living-room and smiled gently on these good people. At last the baby lay in its box, but its eyes were listless and it refused the milk.

The Pirate came in, bearing a bag of mackerels. The friends cooked the fish and had their dinner. The baby would not even eat mackerel. Every now and then one of the friends jumped up and ran to look at the baby. When supper was over, they sat about the stove and prepared for a quiet evening.

The corporal had been silent, had given no account of himself. The friends were a little hurt at this, but they knew he would tell them in time. Pilon, to whom knowledge was as gold to be mined, made a few tentative drills into the corporal's reticence.

"It is not often that one sees a young soldier with a baby," he suggested delicately.

The corporal grinned with pride.

Pablo added, "This baby was probably found in the garden of love. And that is the best kind of babies, for only good things are in it."

"We too have been soldiers," said Danny. "When we die, we will go to the grave on a gun-carriage, and a firing squad will shoot over us."

They waited to see whether the corporal would improve upon the opportunity they had offered. The corporal looked his appreciation. "You have been good to me," he said. "You have been as good and kind as my friends in Torreón would be. This is my baby, the baby of my wife."

"And where is your wife?" Pilon asked.

The corporal lost his smile. "She is in Mexico," he said. Then he grew vivacious again. "I met a man, and he told me a curious thing. He said we can make of babies what we will. He said, 'You tell the baby often what you want him to do, and when he grows up he will do that.' Over and over I tell this baby, 'You will be a *generál*.' Do you think it will be so?"

The friends nodded politely. "It may be," said Pilon. "I have not heard of this practice."

"I say twenty times a day, 'Manuel, you will be a *generál* some day. You will have big epaulettes and a sash. Your sword will be gold. You will ride a palomino horse. What a life for you, Manuel!' The man said he surely will be a *generál* if I say it so."

Danny got up and went to the apple-box. "You will be a *generál*," he said to the baby. "When you grow up you will be a great *generál*."

The others trooped over to see whether the formula had had any effect.

The Pirate whispered, "You will be a *generál*," and he wondered whether the same method would work on a dog.

"This baby is sick all right," Danny said. "We must keep him warm."

They went back to their seats.

"Your wife is in Mexico——" Pilon suggested.

The corporal wrinkled his brows and thought for a while, and then he smiled brilliantly. "I will tell you. It is not a thing to tell to strangers, but you are my friends. I was a soldier in Chihuahua, and I was diligent, and clean and kept oil in my rifle, so that I became a *caporál*. And then I was married to a beautiful girl. I do not say that it was not because of the chevrons that she married me. But she was very beautiful and young. Her eyes were bright, she had good white teeth, and her hair was long and shining. So pretty soon this baby was born."

"That is good," said Danny. "I should like to be you. There is nothing so good as a baby."

"Yes," said the corporal, "I was glad. And we went in to the baptism, and I wore a sash, although the book of the army did not mention it. And when we came out of that church, a *capitán* with epaulettes and a sash and a silver sword saw my wife. Pretty soon my wife went away. Then I went to that *capitán* and I said, 'Give me back my wife,' and he said, 'You do not value your life, to talk this way to your superior.' " The corporal spread his hands and lifted his shoulders in a gesture of caged resignation.

"Oh, that thief!" cried Jesus Maria.

"You gathered your friends. You killed that *capitán*," Pablo anticipated.

The corporal looked self-conscious. "No. There was nothing to do. The first night, someone shot at me through the window. The second day a field-gun went off by mistake and it came so close to me that the wind knocked me down. So I went away from there, and I took the baby with me."

There was fierceness in the faces of the friends, and their eyes were dangerous. The Pirate, in his corner, snarled, and all the dogs growled.

"We should have been there," Pilon cried. "We would have made that *capitán* wish he had never lived. My grandfather suffered at the hands of a priest, and he tied that priest naked to a post in a corral and turned a little calf in with him. Oh, there are ways."

"I was only a *caporál*," said the boy. "I had to run away." Tears of shame were in his eyes. "There is no help for a *caporál* when a *capitán* is against him; so I ran away, with the baby Manuel. In Fresno I met this wise man, and he told me I could make Manuel be what I wished. I tell that baby twenty times every day, 'You will be a *generál*. You will wear epaulettes and carry a golden sword.' "

Here was drama that made the experiments of Cornelia Ruiz seem uninteresting and vain. Here was a situation which demanded the action of the friends. But its scene was so remote that action was impossible. They looked in admiration at the corporal. He was so young to have had such an adventure!

"I wish," Danny said wickedly, "that we were in Torreón now. Pilon would make a plan for us. It is too bad we cannot go there."

Big Joe Portagee had stayed awake, a tribute to the fascination of the corporal's story. He went to the apple-box and looked in. "You going to be a general," he said. And then, "Look! This baby is moving funny." The friends crowded around. The spasm had already started. The little feet kicked down and then drew up. The hands clawed about helplessly, and then the baby scrabbled and shuddered.

"A doctor," Danny cried. "We must have a doctor." But he and everyone knew it was no use. Approaching death wears a cloak no one ever mistakes. While they watched, the baby stiffened and the struggle ended. The mouth dropped open, and the baby was dead. In kindness, Danny covered the apple-box with a piece of blanket. The corporal stood very straight and stared before him, so shocked that he could not speak nor think.

Jesus Maria laid a hand on his shoulder and led him to a chair. "You are so young," he said. "You will have many more babies."

The corporal moaned, "Now he is dead. Now he will never be a *generál* with that sash and that sword."

There were tears in the eyes of the friends. In the corner all the dogs whined miserably. The Pirate buried his big head in the fur of Señor Alec Thompson.

In a soft tone, almost a benediction, Pilon said, "Now you yourself must kill the *capitán*. We honour you for a noble plan of revenge; but that is over and you must take your own vengeance, and we will help you, if we can."

The corporal turned dull eyes to him. "Revenge?" he asked. "Kill the *capitán*? What do you mean?"

"Why, it was plain what your plan was," Pilon said. "This baby would grow up, and he would be a *generál;* and in time he would find that *capitán,* and he would kill him slowly. It was a good plan. The long waiting, and then the stroke. We, your friends, honour you for it."

The corporal was looking bewilderedly at Pilon. "What is this?" he demanded. "I have nothing to do with this *capitán.* He is the *capitán.*"

The friends sat forward.

Pilon cried, "Then what was this plan to make the baby be a *generál*? Why was that?"

The corporal was a little embarrassed then. "It is the duty of a father to do well by his child. I wanted Manuel to have more good things than I had."

"Is that all?" Danny cried.

"Well," said the corporal, "my wife was so pretty, and she was not any *puta,* either. She was a good woman, and that *capitán* took her. He had little epaulettes, and a little sash, and his sword was only of a silver colour. Consider," said the corporal, and he spread out his hands, "if that *capitán,* with the little epaulettes and the little sash, could take my wife, imagine what a *generál* with a big sash and a gold sword could take!"

There was a long silence while Danny and Pilon and Pablo and Jesus Maria and the Pirate and Big Joe Portagee digested the principle. And when it was digested, they waited for Danny to speak.

"It is to be pitied," said Danny at last, "that so few parents have the well-being of their children at heart. Now we are more sorry than ever that the baby is gone, for, with such a father, what a happy life he has missed."

All of the friends nodded solemnly.

"What will you do now?" asked Jesus Maria, the discoverer.

"I will go back to Mexico," said the corporal. "I am a soldier in my heart. It may be, if I keep oiling my rifle, I myself may be an officer some day. Who can tell?"

The six friends looked at him admiringly. They were proud to have known such a man.

CHAPTER XI

How, under the most adverse circumstances, love came to Big Joe Portagee

For Big Joe Portagee, to feel love was to do something about it. And this is the history of one of his love affairs.

It had been raining in Monterey; from the tall pines the water dripped all day. The paisanos of Tortilla Flat did not come out of their houses, but from every chimney a blue column of pinewood smoke drifted so that the air smelled clean and fresh and perfumed.

At five o'clock in the afternoon the rain stopped for a few moments, and Big Joe Portagee, who had been under a rowboat on the beach for most of the day, came out and started up the hill towards Danny's house. He was cold and hungry.

When he came to the very edge of Tortilla Flat, the skies opened and the rain poured down. In an instant Big Joe was soaked through. He ran into the nearest house to get out of the rain, and that house was inhabited by Tia Ignacia.

The lady was about forty-five, a widow of long standing and some success. Ordinarily she was taciturn and harsh, for there was in her veins more Indian blood than is considered decent in Tortilla Flat.

When Big Joe entered she had just opened a gallon of red wine and was pouring out a glass for her stomach's sake. Her attempt to push the jug under a chair was unsuccessful. Big Joe stood in her doorway, dripping water on the floor.

"Come in and get dry," said Tia Ignacia. Big Joe, watching the bottle as a terrier watches a bug, entered the room. The rain roared down on the roof. Tia Ignacia poked up a blaze in her airtight stove.

"Would you care for a glass of wine?"

"Yes," said Big Joe. Before he had finished his first glass, Big Joe's eyes had refastened themselves on the jug. He drank three glasses before he consented to say a word, and before the wolfishness went out of his eyes.

Tia Ignacia had given her new jug of wine up for lost. She drank with him as the only means to preserve a little of it to her own use. It was only when the fourth glass of wine was in his hand that Big Joe relaxed and began to enjoy himself.

"This is not Torrelli's wine," he said.

"No, I get it from an Italian lady who is my friend." She poured out another glass.

The early evening came. Tia Ignacia lighted a kerosene lamp and put some wood in the fire. As long as the wine must go it must go, she thought. Her eyes dwelt on the huge frame of Big Joe Portagee with critical appraisal. A little flush warmed her chest.

"You have been working out in the rain, poor man," she said. "Here, take off your coat and let it dry."

Big Joe rarely told a lie. His mind didn't work quickly enough. "I been on the beach under a rowboat asleep," he said.

"But you are all wet, poor fellow." She inspected him for some response to her kindness, but on Big Joe's face nothing showed except gratification at being out of the rain and drinking wine. He put out his glass to be filled again. Having eaten nothing all day, the wine was having a profound effect on him.

Tia Ignacia addressed herself anew to the problem. "It is not good to sit in a wet coat. You will be ill with cold. me help you to take off your coat."

Big Joe wedged himself comfortably into his chair. "I'm all right," he said stubbornly.

Tia Ignacia poured herself another glass. The fire made a rushing sound to counteract with comfort the drumming of water on the roof.

Big Joe made absolutely no move to be friendly, to be gallant, even to recognize the presence of his hostess. He drank his wine in big swallows. He smiled stupidly at the stove. He rocked himself a little in the chair.

Anger and despair arose in Tia Ignacia. "This pig," she thought, "this big and dirty animal. It would be better for me if I brought some cow in the house out of the rain. Another man would say some little friendly word at least."

Big Joe stuck out his glass to be filled again.

Now Tia Ignacia strove heroically. "In a little warm house there is happiness on such a night," she said. "When the rain is dripping, and the stove burns sweetly, then is a time for people to feel friendly. Don't you feel friendly?"

"Sure," said Big Joe.

"Perhaps the light is too bright in your eyes," she said coyly. "Would you like me to blow out the light?"

"It don't bother me none," said Big Joe. "If you want to save oil, go ahead."

She blew down the lamp chimney, and the room leaped to darkness. Then she went back to her chair and waited for his gallantry to awaken. She could hear the gentle rocking of his chair. A little light came from the cracks of the stove and struck the shiny corners of the furniture. The room was nearly luminous with warmth. Tia Ignacia heard his chair stop rocking and braced herself to repel him. Nothing happened.

"To think," she said, "you might be out in this storm, shivering in a shed or lying on the cold sand under a boat. But no; you are sitting in a good chair, drinking good wine, in the company of a lady who is your friend."

There was no answer from Big Joe. She could neither hear him nor see him. Tia Ignacia drank off her glass. She threw virtue to the winds. "My friend Cornelia Ruiz has told me that some of her best friends came to her out of the rain and cold. She comforted them, and they were her good friends."

The sound of a little crash came from the direction of Big Joe.

She knew he had dropped his glass, but no movement followed the crash. "Perhaps he is ill," she thought. "Maybe he has fainted." She jumped up, lighted a match and set it to the lamp wick. And then she turned to her guest.

Big Joe was mountainously asleep. His feet stuck out ahead of him. His head was back, and his mouth wide open. While she looked, amazed and shocked, a tremendous rattling snore came from his mouth. Big Joe simply could not be warm and comfortable without going to sleep.

It was a moment before Tia Ignacia could move all her crowding emotions into line. She inherited a great deal of Indian blood. She did not cry out. No, shivering with rage though she was, she walked to her wood basket, picked out a likely stick, weighed it, put it down, and picked out another one. And then she turned slowly on Big Joe Portagee. The first blow caught him on the shoulder and knocked him out of the chair.

"Pig!" Tia Ignacia screamed. "Big dirty garbage! Out in the mud with you!"

Joe rolled over on the floor. The next blow made a muddy indentation on the seat of his trousers. Big Joe was waking up rapidly now.

"Huh?" he said. "What's the matter? What you doing?"

"I'll show you," she screamed. She flung open her door and ran back to him. Big Joe staggered to his feet under the beating. The stick hammered at his back and shoulders and head. He ran out of the door, protecting his head with his hands.

"Don't," he pleaded. "Now don't do that. What's the matter?"

The fury followed him like a hornet, down the garden path and into the muddy street. Her rage was terrible. She followed him along the street, still beating him.

"Hey," he cried. "Now don't." He grabbed her and held her while her arms struggled violently to be free to continue the beating.

"Oh, great garbage pig!" she cried. "Oh, cow!"

He could not let her go without more beating, so he held her tightly; and as he stood there, love came to Big Joe Portagee. It sang in his head; it roared through his body like a great freshet; it shook him as a tropical storm shakes a forest of palms. He held her tightly for a moment, until her anger relaxed.

In the night, in Monterey, a policeman patrols the streets on a motor-cycle to see that good things come to no evil. Jake Lake rode about now, his slicker shining dully, like basalt. He was unhappy and uncomfortable. It was not so bad on the paved streets, but part of his route lay through the mud paths of Tortilla Flat, and there the yellow mud splashed nastily. His little light flashed about. The motor coughed with effort.

All of a sudden Jake cried out in astonishment and stopped his motor. "What the devil! Say, what the hell is this?"

Big Joe twisted his neck. "Oh, is that you, Jake? Say, Jake, as long as you're going to take us to jail anyway, can't you just wait a minute?"

The policeman turned his motor around. "You get out of the street," he said. "Somebody'll come along and run over you."

His motor roared in the mud, and the flicker of his little headlight disappeared around the corner. The rain pattered gently among the trees of Tortilla Flat.

CHAPTER XII

How Danny's Friends assisted the Pirate to keep a vow, and how as a reward for merit the Pirate's dogs saw a holy vision

EVERY AFTERNOON the Pirate pushed his empty wheel-barrow up the hill and into Danny's yard. He leaned it against the fence and covered it with a sack; then he buried his axe in the ground, for, as everyone knows, it makes steel much harder to be buried. Last, he went into the house, reached into a Bull Durham bag which hung around his neck on a string, took out the day's quarter dollar, and gave it to Danny. Then Danny and the Pirate and any other of the friends who happened to be in the house went solemnly into the bedroom, stepping over the bedding that littered the floor. While the paisanos looked on, Danny reached under his pillow, brought out the canvas bag, and deposited the new quarter. This practice had continued for a long time.

The bag of money had become the symbolic centre of the friendship, the point of trust about which the fraternity revolved. They were proud of the money, proud that they had never tampered with it. About the guardianship of the Pirate's money there had grown a structure of self-respect and not a little complacency. It is a fine thing for a man to be trusted. This money had long ceased, in the minds of the friends, to be currency. It is true that for a time they had dreamed of how much wine it would buy, but after a while they lost the conception of it as legal tender. The hoard was aimed at a gold candlestick, and this potential candlestick was the property of San Francisco de Assisi. It is far worse to defraud a saint than it is to take liberties with the law.

One evening, by that quick and accurate telegraph no one understands, news came in that a coastguard cutter had gone on the rocks near Carmel. Big Joe Portagee was away on business of his own, but Danny and Pablo and Pilon and Jesus Maria and the Pirate and his dogs joyfully started over the ridge; for if there was anything they loved, it was to pick up usable articles on the beach. This they thought the most exciting thing in the world. Although they arrived a little late, they made up for lost time. All night the friends scurried about the beach, and they accumulated a good pile of flotsam, a five-pound can of butter, several cases of canned goods, a water-soaked Bowditch, two pea-jackets, a water-barrel from a lifeboat, and a machine-gun. When daylight came they had a goodly pile under guard.

They accepted a lump sum of five dollars for the lot from one of the spectators, for it was out of the question to carry all those heavy things over six miles of steep hillside to Tortilla Flat.

Because he had not cut his day's wood, the Pirate received a quarter from Danny, and he put it in his Bull Durham bag. Then they started tiredly, but with a warm and expectant happiness, straight over the hills to Monterey.

It was afternoon when they got back to Danny's house. The Pirate ritualistically opened his bag and gave the quarter to Danny. The whole squad trooped into the other room. Danny reached under the pillow—and his hand came out empty. He threw the pillow back, threw the mattress back, and then he turned slowly to his friends, and his eyes had become as fierce as a tiger's eyes. He looked from face to face, and on every one saw horror and indignation that could not be simulated.

"Well," he said, ". . . well." The Pirate began to cry; Danny put his arm around his shoulder. "Do not cry, little friend," he said ominously. "Thou wilt have thy money again."

The paisanos went silently out of the room. Danny walked out into the yard and found a heavy pine stick three feet long, and swung it experimentally. Pablo went into the kitchen and returned bearing an ancient can-opener with a vicious blade. Jesus Maria from under the house pulled out a broken pick handle. The Pirate watched them, bewildered. They all came back to the house and sat quietly down.

The Pirate aimed down the hill with his thumb. "Him?" he asked.

Danny nodded slowly. His eyes were veiled and deadly. His chin stuck out, and as he sat in the chair his whole body weaved a little, like a rattlesnake aiming to strike.

The Pirate went into the yard and dug up his axe.

For a long time they sat in the house. No words were spoken, but a wave of cold fury washed and crouched in the room. The feeling in the house was the feeling of a rock when the fuse is burning in towards the dynamite.

The afternoon waned; the sun went behind the hill. The whole of Tortilla Flat seemed hushed and expectant.

They heard his footsteps on the street and their hands tightened on their sticks. Joe Portagee walked uncertainly up on the porch and in at the front door. He had a gallon of wine in his hand. His eyes went uneasily from face to face, but the friends sat still and did not look directly at him.

"Hello," said Big Joe.

"Hello," said Danny. He stood up and stretched lazily. He did not look at Big Joe; he did not walk directly towards him, but at an angle as though to pass him. When he was abreast, he struck with the speed of a striking snake. Fair on the back of Big Joe's head the stick crashed, and Big Joe went down, completely out.

Danny thoughtfully took a string of rawhide from his pocket and tied the Portagee's thumbs together. "Now water," he said.

Pablo threw a bucket of water in Big Joe's face. He turned his head and stretched his neck like a chicken, and then he opened his eyes and looked dazedly at his friends. They did not speak to him at all. Danny measured his distance carefully, like a golfer addressing the ball. His stick smashed on Big Joe's shoulder; then the friends went about the business in a cold and methodical manner. Jesus Maria took the legs, Danny the shoulders and chest. Big Joe howled and rolled on the floor. They covered his body from the neck down. Each blow found a new space and welted it. The shrieks were deafening. The Pirate stood helplessly by, holding his axe.

At last, when the whole front of the body was one bruise, they stopped. Pablo knelt at Big Joe's head with his can-opener. Pilon took off the Portagee's shoes and picked up his stick again.

Then Big Joe squalled with fear. "It's buried out by the front gate," he cried. "For the love of Christ, don't kill me!"

Danny and Pilon went out the front door and in a few minutes they came back, carrying the canvas bag. "How much did you take out?" Danny asked. There was no inflection in his voice at all.

"Only four, honest to God. I only took four, and I'll work and put them back."

Danny leaned down, took him by the shoulder, and rolled him over on his face. Then the friends went over his back with the same deadly precision. The cries grew weaker, but the work stopped only when Big Joe was beaten into unconsciousness. Then Pilon tore off the blue shirt and exposed the pulpy raw back. With the can-opener he cross-hatched the skin so deftly that a little blood ran from each line. Pablo brought the salt to him and helped him to rub it in all over the torn back. At last Danny threw a blanket over the unconscious man.

"I think he will be honest now," said Danny.

"We should count the money," Pilon observed. "We have not

counted it for a long time." They opened Big Joe's gallon of wine and poured the fruit jars full, for they were tired from their work, and their emotions were exhausted.

Then they counted the quarters out in piles of ten, and excitedly counted again. "Pirate," Danny cried, "there are seven over a thousand! Thy time is done! The day is come for thee to buy thy candlestick for San Francisco!"

The day had been too full for the Pirate. He went into the corner with his dogs, and he put his head down on Fluff, and burst into hysterical sobs. The dogs moved uneasily about, and they licked his ears and pushed at his head with their noses; but Fluff, sensible of the honour of being chosen, lay quietly and nuzzled the thick hair on Pirate's neck.

Danny put all the money back in the bag, and the bag under his pillow again.

Now Big Joe came to and groaned, for the salt was working into his back. The paisanos paid no attention to him until at last Jesus Maria, that prey to the humanities, untied Big Joe's thumbs and gave him a jar of wine. "Even the enemies of our Saviour gave him a little comfort," he excused himself.

That action broke up the punishment. The friends gathered tenderly about Big Joe. They laid him on Danny's bed and washed the salt out of his wounds. They put cold cloths on his head and kept his jar full of wine. Big Joe moaned whenever they touched him. His morals were probably untouched, but it would have been safe to prophesy that never again would he steal from the paisanos of Danny's house.

The Pirate's hysteria was over. He drank his wine and his face shone with pleasure while he listened to Danny make plans for him. "If we take all this money into town, to the bank, they will think we have stolen it from a slot machine. We must take this money to Father Ramon and tell him about it. Then he will buy the gold candlestick, and he will bless it, and the Pirate will go into the church. Maybe Father Ramon will say a word about him on Sunday. The Pirate must be there to hear."

Pilon looked distastefully at the Pirate's dirty, ragged clothes. "To-morrow," he said sternly, "you must take the seven extra two-bitses and buy some decent clothes. For ordinary times these may be all right, but on such an occasion as this you cannot go into the church looking like a gutter rat. It will not be a compliment to your friends."

The Pirate beamed at him. "To-morrow I will do it," he promised.

The next morning, true to his promise, he went down to Monterey. He shopped carefully and bargained with an astuteness that seemed to belie the fact that he had bought nothing in over two years. He came back to Danny's house in triumph, bearing a huge silk handkerchief in purple and green and also a broad belt studded profusely with coloured glass jewels. His friends admired his purchases.

"But what are you going to wear?" Danny asked despairingly. "Two toes are out of your shoes where you cut holes to ease your bunions. You have only ragged overalls and no hat."

"We will have to lend him clothes," said Jesus Maria. "I have a coat and vest. Pilon has his father's good hat. You, Danny, have a shirt, and Big Joe has those fine blue pants."

"But then we can't go," Pilon protested.

"It is not our candlestick," said Jesus Maria. "Father Ramon is not likely to say anything nice about us."

That afternoon they convoyed the treasure to the priest's house. He listened to the story of the sick dog, and his eyes softened. ". . . And then, Father," said the Pirate, "there was that good little dog, and his nose was dry, and his eyes were like the glass of bottles out of the sea, and he groaned because he hurt inside. And then, Father, I promised the gold candlestick of one thousand days to San Francisco. He is really my patron, Father. And then there was a miracle! For that dog wagged his tail three times, and right away he started to get well. It was a miracle from San Francisco, Father, wasn't it?"

The priest nodded his head gravely. "Yes," he said. "It was a miracle sent by our good Saint Francis. I will buy the candlestick for thee."

The Pirate was very glad, for it is no little thing to have one's prayer answered with a true miracle. If it were noised about, the Pirate would have a higher station on Tortilla Flat. Already his friends looked at him with a new respect. They thought no more of his intelligence than they had before, but they knew now that his meagre wits were supplemented with all the power of Heaven and all the strength of the saints.

They walked back up to Danny's house, and the dogs walked behind them. The Pirate felt that he had been washed in a golden fluid of beatitude. Little chills and fevers of pleasure chased one another through his body. The paisanos were glad they had guarded his money, for even they took a little holiness from the act. Pilon was relieved that he had not stolen the money in the first place. What terrible things might not have happened if he had taken the two-bitses belonging to a saint! All of the friends were as subdued as though they were in church.

The five dollars from the salvage had lain like fire in Danny's pocket, but now he knew what to do with it. He and Pilon went to the market and bought seven pounds of hamburger and a bag of onions and bread and a big paper of candy. Pablo and Jesus Maria went to Torrelli's for two gallons of wine, and not a drop did they drink on the way home either.

That night when the fire was lighted and two candles burned on the table, the friends feasted themselves to repletion. It was a party in the Pirate's honour. He behaved himself with a great deal of dignity. He smiled and smiled when he should have been grave though. But he couldn't help that.

After they had eaten enormously, they sat back and sipped wine out of the fruit jars. "Our little friend," they called the Pirate.

Jesus Maria asked, "How did you feel when it happened? When you promised the candlestick and the dog began to get well, how did you feel? Did you see any holy vision?"

The Pirate tried to remember. "I don't think so—— Maybe I saw a little vision—maybe I saw San Francisco in the air and he was shining like the sun——"

"Wouldn't you remember that?" Pilon demanded.

"Yes—I think I remember—San Francisco looked on me—and he smiled, like the good saint he is. Then I knew the miracle was done. He said, 'Be good to little doggies, you dirty man.' "

"He called you that?"

"Well, I was, and he is not a saint to be telling lies."

"I don't think you remember that at all," said Pablo.

"Well—maybe not. I think I do, though." The Pirate was drunk with happiness from the honour and the attention.

"My grandmother saw the Holy Virgin," said Jesus Maria. "She was sick to death, and I myself heard her cry out. She said. 'Ohee. I see the Mother of God. Ohee. My dear Mary, full of grace.' "

"It is given to some to see these things," said Danny. "My father was not a very good man, but he sometimes saw saints, and sometimes he saw bad things. It depended on whether he was good or bad when he saw them. Have you ever seen any other visions, Pirate?"

"No," said the Pirate. "I would be afraid to see any more."

It was a decorous party for a long time. The friends knew that they were not alone this night. Through the walls and the windows and the roof they could feel the eyes of the holy saints looking down upon them.

"On Sunday your candlestick will be there," said Pilon. "We cannot go, for you will be wearing our clothes. I do not say Father Ramon will mention you by name, but maybe he will say something about the candlestick. You must try to remember what he says, Pirate, so you can tell us."

Then Pilon grew stern. "To-day, my friend, there were dogs all over Father Ramon's house. That was all right for to-day, but you must remember not to take them to church on Sunday. It is not fitting that dogs should be in the church. Leave the dogs at home."

The Pirate looked disappointed. "They want to go," he cried. "How can I leave them? Where can I leave them?"

Pablo was shocked. "In this affair so far thou hast conducted thyself with merit, little Pirate. Right at the last do you wish to commit sacrilege?"

"No," said the Pirate humbly.

"Then leave thy dogs here, and we will take care of them. It will be a sacrilege to take them into the church."

It was curious how soberly they drank that night. It was three hours before they sang even an obscene song. And it was late before their thoughts strayed to light women. And by the time their minds turned to fighting they were almost too sleepy to fight. This evening was a great good marker in their lives.

On Sunday morning the preparation was violent. They washed the Pirate and inspected his ears and his nostrils. Big Joe, wrapped in a blanket, watched the Pirate put on his blue serge trousers. Pilon brought out his father's hat. They persuaded the Pirate not to wear his jewel-studded belt outside his coat and showed him how he could leave his coat open so that the jewels flashed now and then. The item of shoes gave the most trouble. Big Joe had the only shoes big enough for the Pirate, and his were worse even than the Pirate's. The difficulty lay in the holes cut for the comfort of his bunions, where the toes showed through. Pilon solved it finally with a little soot from the inside of the stove. Well rubbed into the skin, the soot made it quite difficult to see the bunion holes.

At last he was ready; Pilon's father's hat rakishly on his head, Danny's shirt, Big Joe's trousers, the huge handkerchief around his neck, and, at intervals, the flashing of the jewelled belt. He walked, for the friends to inspect him, and they looked on critically.

"Pick up your feet, Pirate."

"Don't drag your heels."

"Stop picking at your handkerchief."

"Those people who see you will think you are not in the habit of wearing good clothes."

At last the Pirate turned to his friends. "If those dogs could only come with me," he complained. "I would tell them they must not come in the church."

But the paisanos were firm. "No," said Danny. "They might get in some way. We will keep them here in the house for you."

"They won't like it," said the Pirate helplessly. "They will be lonely, maybe." He turned to the dogs in the corner. "You must stay here," he said. "It would not be good for you to go to church. Stay with my friends until I come back again." And then he slipped out and closed the door behind him. Instantly a wild clamour of barking and howling broke out in the house. Only his faith in the judgment of his friends prevented the Pirate's relenting.

As he walked down the street, he felt naked and unprotected without his dogs. It was as though one of his senses were gone. He was frightened to be out alone. Anyone might attack him. But he walked bravely on, through the town and out to the Church of San Carlos.

Now, before the service began, the swinging doors were open. The Pirate dipped Holy Water out of the marble font, crossed himself, genuflected before the Virgin, went into the church, did his duty to the altar, and sat down. The long church was rather dark, but the high altar was on fire with candles. And in front of the images at the sides the votive lights were burning. The old and sweet incense perfumed the church.

For a time the Pirate sat looking at the altar, but it was too remote, too holy to think about very much, too unapproachable by a poor man. His eyes sought something warmer, something that would not frighten him. And there, in front of the figure of Saint Francis, was a beautiful golden candlestick, and in it a tall candle was burning.

The Pirate sighed with excitement. And although the people came in and the swinging doors were shut, and the service began and the Pirate went through the form, he could not stop looking at his saint and at the candlestick. It was so beautiful. He could not believe that he, the Pirate, had given it. He searched the face of the saint to see whether Saint Francis liked the candlestick. He was sure the image smiled a little now and then, the recurring smile of one who thinks of pleasant things.

At last the sermon began. "There is a new beauty in the church," Father Ramon said, "One of the children of the church has given a golden candlestick to the glory of Saint Francis." He told the story of the dog then, told it rather badly on purpose. His eyes searched the faces of the parishioners until he saw little smiles appear there. "It is not a thing to be considered funny," he said. "Saint Francis loved the beasts so much that he preached to them." Then Father Ramon told the story of the bad wolf of Gubbio and he told of the wild turtle-doves and of the sister larks. The Pirate looked at him in wonder as the sermon went on.

Suddenly a rushing sound came from the door. A furious barking and scratching broke out. The doors swung wildly and in rushed Fluff and Rudolph, Enrique, Pajarito, and Señor Alec Thompson. They raised their noses, and then darted in a struggling squad to the Pirate. They leaped upon him with little cries and whinings. They swarmed over him.

The priest stopped talking and looked down towards the commotion. The Pirate looked back helplessly in agony. So it was in vain, and the sacrilege was committed.

Then Father Ramon laughed, and the congregation laughed. "Take the dogs outside," he said. "Let them wait until we are through."

The Pirate, with embarrassed, apologetic gestures, conducted his dogs outside. "It is wrong," he said to them. "I am angry with you. Oh, I am ashamed of you." The dogs cringed to the ground and whined piteously. "I know what you did," said the Pirate. "You bit my friends, you broke a window, and you came. Now stay here and wait, oh wicked dogs; oh dogs of sacrilege."

He left them stricken with grief and repentance and went back into the church. The people, still laughing, turned and looked at him, until he sank into his seat and tried to efface himself.

"Do not be ashamed," Father Ramon said. "It is no sin to be loved by your dogs, and no sin to love them. See how Saint Francis loved the beasts." Then he told more stories of that good saint.

The embarrassment left the Pirate. His lips moved. "Oh," he thought, "if the dogs could only hear this. They would be glad if they could know all this." When the sermon was over, his ears still rang with the stories. Automatically he followed the ritual, but he did not hear the service. And when it was over he rushed for the door. He was the first out of the church. The dogs, still sad and diffident, crowded about him.

"Come," he cried. "I have some things to tell you."

He started at a trot up the hill towards the pine forest, and the dogs galloped and bounced about him. He came at last to the shelter of the woods and still he went on, until he found a long aisle among the pines, where the branches met overhead, where the tree trunks were near together. For a moment he looked helplessly about.

"I want it to be the way it was," he said. "If only you could have been there and heard Father say it." He laid one big stone on top of another. "Now here is the image," he told the dogs. He stuck a little stick in the ground. "Right here is the candlestick, with a candle in it."

It was dusky in the glade and the air was sweet with pine resin. The trees whispered softly in the breeze. The Pirate said with authority, "Now, Enrique, you sit here. And you, Rudolph, here. I want Fluff here because he is the littlest. Pajarito, thou great fool, sit here and make no trouble. Señor Alec Thompson, you may *not* lie down."

Thus he arranged them in two rows, two in the front line and three in the back.

"I want to tell you how it was," he said. "You are forgiven for breaking into the church. Father Ramon said it was no sacrilege this time. Now, attention. I have things to tell."

The dogs sat in their places and watched him earnestly. Señor Alec Thompson flapped his tail, until the Pirate turned to him. "Here is no place for that," he said. "Saint Francis would not mind, but I do not like you to wag your tail while you listen. Now, I am going to tell you about Saint Francis."

That day his memory was inspired. The sun found interstices in the foliage and threw brilliant patterns on the pine-needle carpet. The dogs sat patiently, their eyes on the Pirate's lips. He told everything the priest had told, all the stories, all the observations. Hardly a word was out of its place.

When he was done, he regarded the dogs solemnly. "Saint Francis did all that," he said.

The trees hushed their whispering. The forest was silent and enchanted.

Suddenly there was a tiny sound behind the Pirate. All the dogs looked up. The Pirate was afraid to turn his head. A long moment passed.

And then the moment was over. The dogs lowered their eyes. The tree-tops stirred to life again and the sunlight patterns moved bewilderingly.

The Pirate was so happy that his heart pained him. "Did you see him?" he cried. "Was it San Francisco? Oh! What good dogs you must be to see a vision."

The dogs leaped up at his tone. Their mouths opened and their tails threshed joyfully.

CHAPTER XIII

How Danny's Friends threw themselves to the aid of a distressed lady

Senora Teresina Cortez and her eight children and her ancient mother lived in a pleasant cottage on the edge of the deep gulch that defines the southern frontier of Tortilla Flat. Teresina was a good figure of a mature woman, nearing thirty. Her mother, that ancient, dried, toothless one, relic of a past generation, was nearly fifty. It was long since anyone had remembered that her name was Angelica.

During the week work was ready to this *vieja's* hand, for it was her duty to feed, punish, cajole, dress, and bed down seven of the eight children. Teresina was busy with the eighth, and with making certain preparations for the ninth.

On Sunday, however, the *vieja*, clad in black satin more ancient even than she, hatted in a grim and durable affair of black straw, on which were fastened two true cherries of enamelled plaster, threw duty to the wind and went firmly to church, where she sat as motionless as the saints in their niches. Once a month, in the afternoon she went to confession. It would be interesting to know what sins she confessed, and where she found the time to commit them, for in Teresina's house there were creepers, crawlers, stumblers, shriekers, cat-killers, fallers-out-of-trees; and each one of these charges could be trusted to be ravenous every two hours.

Is it any wonder that the *vieja* had a remote soul and nerves of steel? Any other kind would have gone screaming out of her body like little skyrockets.

Teresina was a mildly puzzled woman, as far as her mind was concerned. Her body was one of those perfect retorts for the distillation of children. The first baby, conceived when she was fourteen, had been a shock to her; such a shock, that she delivered it in the ball park at night, wrapped it in a newspaper, and left it for the night watchman to find. This is a secret. Even now Teresina might get into trouble if it were known.

When she was sixteen, Mr. Alfred Cortez married her and gave her his name and the two foundations of her family, Alfredo and Ernie. Mr. Cortez gave her that name gladly. He was only using it temporarily anyway. His name, before he came to Monterey and after he left, was Gugliemo. He went away after Ernie was born. Perhaps he foresaw that being married to Teresina was not going to be a quiet life.

The regularity with which she became a mother always astonished Teresina. It occurred sometimes that she could not remember who the father of the impending baby was; and occasionally she almost grew convinced that no lover was necessary. In the time when she had been under quanratine as a diphtheria carrier she conceived just the same. However, when a question became too complicated for her mind to unravel, she usually laid that problem in the arms of the Mother of Jesus, who, she knew, had more knowledge of, interest in, and time for such things than she.

Teresina went often to confession. She was the despair of Father Ramon. Indeed he had seen that while her knees, her hands, and her lips did penance for an old sin, her modest and provocative eyes, flashing under drawn lashes, laid the foundation for a new one.

During the time I have been telling this, Teresina's ninth child was born, and for the moment she was unengaged. The *vieja* received another charge; Alfredo entered his third year in the first grade, Ernie his second, and Panchito went to school for the first time.

At about this time in California it became the stylish thing for school nurses to visit the classes and to catechize the children on intimate details of their home life. In the first grade, Alfredo was called to the principal's office, for it was thought that he looked thin.

The visiting nurse, trained in child psychology, said kindly, "Freddie, do you get enough to eat?"

"Sure," said Alfredo.

"Well, now. Tell me what you had for breakfast?"

"Tortillas and beans," said Alfredo.

The nurse nodded her head dismally to the principal. "What do you have when you go home for lunch?"

"I don't go home."

"Don't you eat at noon?"

"Sure. I bring some beans wrapped up in a tortilla."

Actual alarm showed in the nurse's eyes, but she controlled herself. "At night what do you have to eat?"

"Tortillas and beans."

Her psychology deserted her. "Do you mean to stand there and tell me you eat nothing but tortillas and beans?"

Alfredo was astonished. "Jesus Christ," he said, "what more do you want?"

In due course the school doctor listened to the nurse's horrified report. One day he drove up to Teresina's house to look into the matter. As he walked through the yard the creepers, the crawlers, and the stumblers were shrieking one terrible symphony. The doctor stood in the open kitchen door. With his open eyes he saw the *vieja* go to the stove, dip a great spoon into a kettle, and sow the floor with boiled beans. Instantly the noise ceased. Creepers, crawlers, and stumblers went to work with silent industry, moving from bean to bean, pausing only to eat them. The *vieja* went back to her chair for a few moments of peace. Under the bed, under the chairs, under the stove the children crawled with the intentness of little bugs. The doctor stayed two hours, for his scientific interest was piqued. He went away shaking his head.

He shook his head incredulously while he made his report. "I gave them every test I know of," he said, "teeth, skin, blood, skeleton, eyes, co-ordination. Gentlemen, they are living on what constitutes a slow poison, and they have from birth. Gentlemen, I tell you I have never seen healthier children in my life!" His emotion overcame him. "The little beasts," he cried. "I never saw such teeth in my life. I *never* saw such teeth!"

You will wonder how Teresina procured food for her family. When the bean threshers have passed, you will see, where they have stopped, big piles of bean chaff. If you will spread a blanket on the ground, and, on a windy afternoon, toss the chaff in the air over the blanket, you will understand that the threshers are not infallible. For an afternoon of work you may collect twenty or more pounds of beans.

In the autumn the *vieja* and those children who could walk went into the fields and winnowed the chaff. The landowners did not mind, for she did no harm. It was a bad year when the *vieja* did not collect three or four hundred pounds of beans.

When you have four hundred pounds of beans in the house, you need have no fear of starvation. Other things, delicacies such as sugar, tomatoes, peppers, coffee, fish, or meat, may come sometimes miraculously, through the intercession of the Virgin, sometimes through industry or cleverness; but your beans are there, and you are safe. Beans are a roof over your stomach. Beans are a warm cloak against economic cold.

Only one thing could threaten the lives and happiness of the family of the Señora Teresina Cortez; that was a failure of the bean crop.

When the beans are ripe, the little bushes are pulled and gathered into piles, to dry crisp for the threshers. Then is the time to pray that the rain may hold off. When the little piles of beans lie in lines, yellow against the dark fields, you will see the farmers watching the sky, scowling with dread at every cloud that sails over; for if a rain comes, the bean piles must be turned over to dry again. And if more rain falls before they are dry, they must be turned again. If a third shower falls, mildew and rot set in, and the crop is lost.

When the beans were drying, it was the *vieja's* custom to burn a candle to the Virgin.

In the year of which I speak, the beans were piled and the candle had been burned. At Teresina's house the gunny sacks were laid out in readiness.

The threshing machines were oiled and cleaned.

A shower fell.

Extra hands rushed to the fields and turned the sodden hummocks of beans. The *vieja* burned another candle.

More rain fell.

Then the *vieja* bought two candles with a little gold piece she had kept for many years. The field hands turned over the beans to the sun again; and then came a downpour of cold, streaking rain. Not a bean was harvested in all Monterey County. The soggy lumps were turned under by the ploughs.

Oh, then distress entered the house of Señora Teresina Cortez. The staff of life was broken; the little roof destroyed. Gone was that eternal verity, beans. At night the children cried with terror at the approaching starvation. They were not told, but they knew. The *vieja* sat in church, as always, but her lips drew back in a sneer when she looked at the Virgin. "You took my candles," she thought. "Ohee, yes. Greedy you are for candles. Oh, thoughtless one." And sullenly she transferred her allegiance to Santa Clara. She told Santa Clara of the injustice that had been done. She permitted herself a little malicious thought at the Virgin Birth. "You know, sometimes Teresina can't remember either," she told Santa Clara viciously.

It has been said that Jesus Maria Corcoran was a great-hearted man. He had also that gift some humanitarians possess of being inevitably drawn toward those spheres where his instinct was needed. How many times had he not come upon young ladies when they needed comforting. Toward any pain or sorrow he was irresistibly drawn. He had not been to Teresina's house for many months. If there is no mystical attraction between pain and humanitarianism, how did it happen that he went there to call on the very day when the last of the old year's beans was put in the pot?

He sat in Teresina's kitchen, gently brushing children off his legs. And he looked at Teresina with polite and pained eyes while she told of the calamity. He watched, fascinated, when she turned the last bean sack inside out to show that not one single bean was left. He nodded sympathetically when she pointed out the children, so soon to be skeletons, so soon to die of starvation.

Then the *vieja* told bitterly how she had been tricked by the Virgin. But upon this point, Jesus Maria was not sympathetic.

"What do you know, old one?" he said sternly. "Maybe the Blessed Virgin had business someplace else."

"But four candles I burned," the *vieja* insisted shrilly.

Jesus Maria regarded her coldly. "What are four candles to Her?" he said. "I have seen one church where She had hundreds. She is no miser of candles."

But his mind burned with Teresina's trouble. That evening he talked mightily and piteously to the friends at Danny's house. Out of his great heart he drew a compelling oratory, a passionate plea for those little children who had no beans. And so telling was his speech that the fire in his heart ignited the hearts of his friends. They leaped up. Their eyes glowed.

"The children shall not starve," they cried. "It shall be our trust!"

"We live in luxury," Pilon said.

"We shall give of our substance," Danny agreed. "And if they needed a house, they could live here."

"To-morrow we shall start," Pablo exclaimed. "No more laziness! To work! There are things to be done!"

Jesus Maria felt the gratification of a leader with followers.

Theirs was no idle boast. Fish they collected. The vegetable patch of the Hotel Del Monte they raided. It was a glorious game. Theft robbed of the stigma of theft, crime altruistically committed—what is more gratifying?

The Pirate raised the price of kindlings to thirty cents and went to three new restaurants every morning. Big Joe stole Mrs. Palochio's goat over and over again, and each time it went home.

Now food began to accumulate in the house of Teresina. Boxes of lettuce lay on her porch, spoiled mackerel filled the neighbourhood with a strong odour. And still the flame of charity burned in the friends.

If you could see the complaint book at the Monterey Police Department, you would notice that during this time there was a minor crime wave in Monterey. The police car hurried from place to place. Here a chicken was taken, there a whole patch of pumpkins. Paladini Company reported the loss of two one-hundred-pound cases of albalone steaks.

Teresina's house was growing crowded. The kitchen was stacked high with food. The back porch overflowed with vegetables. Odours like those of a packing house permeated Tortilla Flat. Breathlessly the friends dashed about at their larcenies, and long they talked and planned with Teresina.

At first Teresina was maddened with joy at so much food, and her head was turned by the compliment. After a week of it, she was not so sure. The baby was down with colic. Ernie had some kind of bowel trouble. Alfredo's face was flushed. The creepers and crawlers cried all the time. Teresina was ashamed to tell the friends what she must tell them. It took her several days to get her courage up; and during that time there arrived fifty pounds of celery and a crate of cantaloupes. At last she had to tell them. The neighbours were beginning to look at her with lifted brows.

She asked all of Danny's friends into her kitchen, and then she informed them of the trouble, modestly and carefully, that their feelings might not be hurt.

"Green things and fruit are not good for children," she explained. "Milk is constipating to a baby after it is weaned." She pointed to the flushed and irritable children. See, they were all sick. They were not getting the proper food.

"What is the proper food?" Pilon demanded.

"Beans," she said. "There you have something to trust, something that will not go right through you."

The friends went silently away. They pretended to themselves to be disheartened, but they knew that the first fire of their enthusiasm had been lacking for several days.

At Danny's house they held a conference.

This must not be told in some circles, for the charge might be serious.

Long after midnight four dark forms who shall be nameless moved like shadows through the town. Four indistinct shapes crept up on the Western Warehouse Company platform. The watchman said afterwards that he heard sounds, investigated, and saw nothing. He could not say how the thing was done, how a lock was broken and the door forced. Only four men know that the watchman was sound asleep, and they will never tell on him.

A little later four shadows left the warehouse, and now they were bent under tremendous loads. Pantings and snortings came from the shadows.

At three o'clock in the morning Teresina was awakened by hearing her back door open. "Who is there?" she cried.

There was no answer, but she heard four great thumps that shook the house. She lighted a candle and went to the kitchen in her bare feet. There, against the wall, stood four one-hundred-pound sacks of pink beans.

Teresina rushed in and awakened the *vieja.* "A miracle!" she cried. "Come look in the kitchen."

The *vieja* regarded with shame the plump full sacks. "Oh, miserable dirty sinner am I," she moaned. "Oh, Holy Mother, look with pity on an old fool. Every month thou shalt have a candle, as long as I live."

At Danny's house four friends were lying happily in their blankets. What pillow can one have like a good conscience? They slept well into the afternoon, for their work was done.

And Teresina discovered, by a method she had found to be infallible, that she was going to have a baby. As she poured a quart of the new beans into the kettle, she wondered idly which one of Danny's friends was responsible.

CHAPTER XIV

Of the good life at Danny's House, of a gift pig, of the pain of Tall Bob, and of the thwarted love of the Viejo Ravanno

CLOCKS AND watches were not used by the paisanos of Tortilla Flat. Now and then one of the friends acquired a watch in some extraordinary manner, but he kept it only long enough to trade it for something he really wanted. Watches were in good repute at Danny's house, but only as media of exchange. For practical purposes, there was the great golden watch of the sun. It was better than a watch, and safer, for there was no way of diverting it to Torrelli.

In the summer when the hands of a clock point to seven, it is a nice time to get up, but in winter the same time is of no value whatever. How much better is the sun! When he clears the pine tops and clings to the front porch, be it summer or winter, that is the sensible time to get up. That is a time when one's hands do not quiver nor one's belly quake with emptiness.

The Pirate and his dogs slept in the living-room, secure and warm in their corner. Pilon and Pablo and Jesus Maria and Danny and Big Joe Portagee slept in the bedroom. For all his kindness, his generosity, Danny never allowed his bed to be occupied by anyone but himself. Big Joe tried it twice, and was smacked across the soles of his feet with a stick; so that even he learned the inviolable quality of Danny's bed.

The friends slept on the floor, and their bedding was unusual. Pablo had three sheepskins stitched together. Jesus Maria retired by putting his arms through the sleeves of one old overcoat and his legs through the sleeves of another. Pilon wrapped himself in a big strip of carpet. Most of the time Big Joe simply curled up like a dog and slept in his clothes. Big Joe, while he had no ability to keep any possession for very long, had a well-developed genius for trading everything that came into his hands for some little measure of wine. Thus they slept, noisily sometimes, but always comfortably. On one cold night Big Joe tried to borrow a dog for his feet, and got well bitten, for the Pirate's dogs were not lendable.

No curtains covered the windows, but a generous Nature had obscured the glass with cobwebs, with dust, and with the neat marks of raindrops.

"It would be nice to clean that window with soap and water," Danny said one time.

Pilon's sharp mind leaped to the problem with energy, but it was too easy for him. It did not require a decent quota of his powers. "More light would get in," he said. "We would not spend so much time out in the air if it were light in here. And at night, when the air is poisonous, we have no need for light."

Danny retired from the field, for if one little mention brought such clear and quick refutation of his project, what crushing logic would insistence bring forth? The window remained as it was; and as time passed, as fly after fly went to feed the spider family with his blood and left his huskish body in the webs against the glass, as dust adhered to dust, the bedroom took on a pleasant obscurity which made it possible to sleep in a dusky light even at noon-day.

They slept peacefully, the friends; but when the sun struck the window in the morning and, failing to get in, turned the dust to silver and shone on the iridescence of the bluebottle flies, then the friends awakened and stretched and looked about for their shoes.

They knew the front porch was warm when the sun was on the window.

They did not awaken quickly, nor fling about nor shock their systems with any sudden movement. No, they arose from slumber as gently as a soap bubble floats out from its pipe. Down into the gulch they trudged, still only half awake. Gradually their wills coagulated. They built a fire and boiled some tea and drank it from the fruit jars, and at last they settled in the sun on the front porch. The flaming flies made haloes about their heads. Life took shape about them, the shape of yesterday and of to-morrow.

Discussion began slowly, for each man treasured the little sleep he still possessed. From this time until well after noon, intellectual comradeship came into being. Then roofs were lifted, houses peered into, motives inspected, adventures recounted. Ordinarily their thoughts went first to Cornelia Ruiz, for it was a rare day and night during which Cornelia had not some curious and interesting adventure. And it was an unusual adventure from which no moral lesson could be drawn.

The sun glistened in the pine needles. The earth smelled dry and good. The rose of Castile perfumed the world with its flowers. This was one of the best of times for the friends of Danny. The struggle for existence was remote. They sat in judgment on their fellows, judging not for morals, but for interest. Anyone having a good thing to tell saved it for recounting at this time. The big brown butterflies came to the rose and sat on the flowers and waved their wings slowly, as though they pumped honey out by wing power.

"I saw Albert Rasmussen," said Danny. "He came from Cornelia's house. What trouble that Cornelia has. Every day some trouble."

"It is her way of life," said Pablo. "I am not one to cast stones, but sometimes I think Cornelia is a little too lively. Two things only occur to Cornelia, love and fighting."

"Well," said Pilon, "what do you want?"

"She never has any peace," Jesus Maria said sadly.

"She doesn't want any," said Pilon. "Give peace to that Cornelia, and she will die. Love and fighting. That is good, what you said, Pablo. Love and fighting, and a little wine. Then you are always young, always happy. What happened to Cornelia yesterday?"

Danny looked in triumph at Pilon. It was an unusual thing for Pilon not to know everything that happened. And now Danny could tell by the hurt and piqued look on Pilon's face that he did not know this one.

"All of you know, Cornelia," he began. "Sometimes men take presents to Cornelia, a chicken or a rabbit or a cabbage. Just little things, and Cornelia likes those things. Well, yesterday Emilio Murietta took to Cornelia a little pig, only so long; a nice little pink pig. Emilio found that pig in the gulch. The sow chased him when he picked it up, but he ran fast, and he came to Cornelia's house with that pig.

"This Emilio is a great talker. He said to Cornelia. 'There is nothing nicer to have than a pig. He will eat anything. He is a nice pet. You get to love that little pig. But then that pig grows up and his character changes. That pig becomes mean and evil-tempered, so that you do not love him any more. Then one day that pig bites you, and you are angry. And so you kill that pig and eat him.' "

The friends nodded gravely, and Pilon said, "In some ways Emilio is not a dull man. See how many satisfactions he has made with his pig—affection, love, revenge, and food. I must go to talk with Emilio sometime." But the friends could see that Pilon was jealous of a rival logician.

"Go on with this pig," said Pablo.

"Well," said Danny, "Cornelia took that little pig, and she was nice to Emilio. She said that when the time came, and she was angry at that pig, Emilio could have some of it to eat. Well, then Emilio went away. Cornelia made a little box for that pig to sleep in, by the stove.

"Some ladies came in to see her then, and Cornelia let them hold the little pig and pet it. After a while Sweets Ramirez stepped on that pig's tail. Oh! It squealed like a steam whistle. The front door was open. That big sow she came in for her little pig again. All the tables and all the dishes were smashed. All the chairs, they were broken. And that big sow bit Sweets Ramirez and pulled off Cornelia's skirt, and then, when those ladies were in the kitchen and the door locked, the sow went away, and that little pig went too. Now Cornelia is furious. She says she will beat Emilio."

"There it is," said Pablo. "That is the way life goes, never the way you planned. It was that way when Tall Bob Smoke went to kill himself."

The faces of the friends swung appreciatively towards Pablo.

"You will know Bob Smoke," Pablo began. "He looks the way a vaquero should look, long legs, thin body; but he cannot ride very well. At the rodeo he is often in the dust. Now this Bob is one who wants to be admired. When there is a parade he likes to carry the flag. When there is a fight he wants to be referee. At the show he is always the first one to say 'Down in front!' Yes, there is a man who wants to be a great man, and to have people see him, and admire him. And something you do not know, perhaps, he wants people to love him too.

"Poor unfortunate one, he is a man born to be laughed at. Some people pity him, but most of them just laugh at him. And laughter stabs that Tall Bob Smoke.

"Maybe you remember that time in the parade when he carried the flag. Very straight Bob sat, on a big white horse. Right in front of the place where the judges sat that big stupid horse fainted from the heat. Bob went flying right over that horse's head, and the flag sailed through the air like a spear and stuck in the ground, upside down.

"That is how it is with him. Whenever he tries to be a great man, something happens and everybody laughs. You remember when he was poundmaster he tried all afternoon to lasso a dog. Everybody in town came to see. He threw the rope and the dog squatted down and the rope slipped off and the dog ran away. Oh, the people laughed. Bob was so ashamed that he thought, 'I will kill myself, and then people will be sad. They will be sorry they laughed.' And then he thought, 'But I will be dead. I will not know how sorry they are.' So he made this plan, 'I will wait until I hear someone coming to my room. I will point a pistol at my head. Then that friend will argue with me. He will make me promise not to shoot myself. The people will be sorry then that they drove me to kill myself.' That is the way he thought it.

"So he walked home to his little house, and everybody he passed called out, 'Did you catch the dog, Bob?' He was very sad when he got home. He took a pistol and put cartridges in it, and then he sat down and waited for someone to come.

"He planned how it would be, and he practised it with a pistol. The friend would say, 'Ai, what you doing? Don't shoot yourself, poor fellow.' Then Bob would say how he didn't want to live any more because everyone was so mean.

"He thought about it over and over, but no one came. And the next day he waited, and no one came. But that next night Charlie Meeler came. Bob heard him on the porch and put the pistol to his head. And he cocked it to make it look more real. "Now he will argue with me, and I will let him persuade me," Bob thought.

"Charlie Meeler opened the door. He saw Bob holding that pistol to his head. But he did not shout; no, Charlie Meeler jumped and grabbed that gun and that gun went off and shot away the end of Bob's nose. And then the people laughed even more. There were pieces in the paper about it. The whole town laughed.

"You have all seen Bob's nose, with the end shot off. The people laughed; but it was a hard kind of laughing, and they felt bad to laugh. And ever since then they let Tall Bob carry the flag in every parade there is. And the city bought him a net to catch dogs with.

"But he is not a happy man, with his nose like that." Pablo fell silent and picked up a stick from the porch and whipped his leg a little.

"I remember his nose, how it was," said Danny. "He is not a bad one, that Bob. The Pirate can tell you when he gets back. Sometimes the Pirate puts all his dogs in Bob's wagon and then the people think Bob has caught them, and the people say, 'There is a poundman for you.' It is not so easy to catch dogs when it is your business to catch dogs."

Jesus Maria had been brooding, with his head back against the wall. He observed, "It is worse than whipping to be laughed at. Old Tomas, the rag sucker, was laughed right into his grave. And afterward the people were sorry they laughed.

"And," said Jesus Maria, "there is another kind of laughing too. That story of Tall Bob is funny; but when you open your mouth to laugh, something like a hand squeezes your heart. I know about old Mr. Ravanno who hanged himself last year. And there is a funny story too, but it is not pleasant to laugh at."

"I heard something about it," said Pilon, "but I do not know that story."

"Well," said Jesus Maria. "I will tell you that story, and you will see if you can laugh. When I was a little boy, I played games with Petey Ravanno. A good quick little boy, that Petey, but always in trouble. He had two brothers and four sisters, and there was his father, Old Pete. All that family is gone now. One brother is in San Quentin, the other was killed by a Japanese gardener for stealing a wagon-load of water-melons. And the girls, well, you know how girls are; they went away. Susy is in Old Jenny's house in Salinas right now.

"So there was only Petey and the old man left. Petey grew up, and always he was in trouble. He went to reform school for a while, then he came back. Every Saturday he was drunk, and every time he went to jail until Monday. His father was a kind of a friendly man. He got drunk every week with Petey. Nearly always they were in jail together. Old man Ravanno was lonely when Petey was not there with him. He liked that boy Petey. Whatever Petey did, that old man did, even when he was sixty years old.

"Maybe you remember that Gracie Montez?" Jesus Maria asked. "She was not a very good girl. When she was only twelve years old the fleet came to Monterey, and Gracie had her first baby, so young as that. She was pretty, you see, and quick, and her tongue was sharp. Always she seemed to run away from men, and men ran fast after her. And sometimes they caught her. But you could not get close to her. Always that Gracie seemed to have something nice that she did not give to you, something in back of her eyes that said, 'If I really wanted to, I would be different to you from any woman you ever knew.'

"I know about that," said Jesus Maria, "for I ran after Gracie too. And Petey ran after her. Only Petey was different." Jesus Maria looked sharply into his friends' eyes to emphasize his point.

"Petey wanted what Gracie had so much that he grew thin, and his eyes were as wide and pained as the eyes of one who smokes marihuana. Petey could not eat, and he was sick. Old Man Ravanno went over and talked to Gracie. He said, 'If you are not nice to Petey, he will die.' But she only laughed. She was not a very good one. And then her little sister 'Tonia came into the room. 'Tonia was fourteen years old. The old man looked at her and his breath stopped. 'Tonia was like Gracie, with that funny thing that she kept away from men. Old Man Ravanno could not help it. He said, 'Come to me, little girl.' But 'Tonia was not a little girl. She knew. So she laughed and ran out of the room.

"Old Man Ravanno went home then. Petey said, 'Something is the matter with thee, my father.'

" 'No, Petey,' the old man said, 'only I worry that you do not get this Gracie, so you can be well again.'

"Hot-blooded, all those Ravannos were!

"And then what do you think?" Jesus Maria continued. "Petey went to cut squids for Chin Kee, and he made presents to Gracie, big bottles of Agua Florida and ribbons and garters. He paid to have her picture taken, with colours on the picture too.

"Gracie took all the presents and she ran away from him and laughed. You should have heard how she laughed. It made you want to choke her and pet her at the same time. It made you want to cut her open and get that thing that was inside of her. I know how it was. I ran after her, and Petey told me too. But it made Petey crazy. He could not sleep any more. He said to me, 'If that Gracie will marry me in the church, then she will not dare to run away any more, because she will be married, and it will be a sin to run away.' So he asked her. She laughed that high laugh that made you want to choke her.

"Oh! Petey was crazy. He went home and put a rope over a rafter and he stood on a box and put the rope around his neck and then he kicked out the box. Well, Petey's father came in then. He cut the rope and called the doctor. But it was two hours before Petey opened his eyes, and it was four days before he could talk."

Jesus Maria paused. He saw with pride that his friends were leaning in towards the story. "That was the way of it," he said.

"But Gracie Montez married that Petey Ravanno," Pilon cried excitedly. "I know her. She is a good woman. She never misses mass, and she goes once a month to confession."

"So it is now," Jesus Maria agreed. "Old Man Ravanno was angry. He ran to Gracie's house, and he cried, 'See how you murder my boy with your foolishness. He tried to kill himself for you, dung-heap chicken.'

"Gracie was afraid, but she was pleased too, because it is not many women who can make a man go so far. She went to see Petey where he was in bed with a crooked neck. After a little while they were married.

"It turned out the way Petey thought it would, too. When the church told her to be a good wife, she was a good wife. She didn't laugh to men any more. And she didn't run away so they chased her. Petey went on cutting squids, and pretty soon Chin Kee let him empty the squid boxes. And not long after that he was mayor-domo of the squid yard. You see," said Jesus Maria, "there is a good story. It would be a story for a priest to tell, if it stopped there."

"Oh, yes," said Pilon gravely. "There are things to be learned in this story."

The friends nodded appreciatively, for they liked a story with a meaning.

"I knew a girl in Texas like that," said Danny. "Only she didn't change. They called her the wife of the second platoon. 'Mrs. Second Platoon,' they said."

Pablo held up his hand. "There is more to this story," he said. "Let Jesus Maria tell the rest."

"Yes, there is more. And it is not such a good story, in the ending. There was the *viejo*, over sixty. And Petey and Gracie went to live in another house. The Viejo Ravanno was lonely, for he had always been with Petey. He didn't know how to take up his time. He just sat and looked sad, until one day he saw 'Tonia again. 'Tonia was fifteen, and she was prettier, even, than Gracie. Half the soldiers from the Presidio followed her around like little dogs.

"Now as it had been with Petey, so it was with the old man. His desire made him ache all over. He could not eat or sleep. His cheeks sunk in, and his eyes stared like the eyes of a marihuana smoker. He carried candy to 'Tonia, and she grabbed the candy out of his hands and laughed at him. He said, 'Come to me, little dear one, for I am thy friend.' She laughed again.

"Then the *viejo* told Petey about it. And Petey laughed too. 'You old fool,' Petey said. 'You've had enough women in your life. Don't run after babies.' But it did no good. Old Man Ravanno grew sick with longing. They are hot-blooded, those Ravannos. He hid in the grass and watched her pass by. His heart ached in his breast.

"He needed money to buy presents, so he got a job in the Standard Service Station. He raked the gravel and watered the flowers at that station. He put water in the radiators and cleaned the windshields. With every cent he bought presents for 'Tonia, candy and ribbons and dresses. He paid to have her picture taken with colours.

"She only laughed more, and the *viejo* was nearly crazy. So he thought, 'If marriage in the church made Gracie a good woman, it will make 'Tonia a good woman too.' He asked her to marry him.

Then she laughed more than ever. She flung up her skirts at him to worry him. Oh, she was a devil, that 'Tonia."

"He was a fool," said Pilon smugly. "Old men should not run after babies. They should sit in the sun."

Jesus Maria went on irritably. "Those Ravannos are different," he said, "so hot-blooded."

"Well, it was not a decent thing," said Pilon. "It was a shame on Petey."

Pablo turned to him. "Let Jesus Maria go on. It is his story, Pilon, not thine. Sometime we will listen to thee."

Jesus Maria looked gratefully at Pablo. "I was telling.

"The *viejo* could not stand it any more. But he was not a man to invent anything. He was not like Pilon. He could not think of anything new. The Viejo Ravanno thought like this: 'Gracie married Petey because he hanged himself. I will hang myself, and maybe 'Tonia will marry me.' And then he thought, 'If no one finds me soon enough, I will be dead. Someone must find me.'

"You must know," said Jesus Maria, "at that service station there is a tool-house. Early in the morning, the *viejo* went down and unlocked the tool-house and raked the gravel and watered the flowers before the station opened. The other men came to work at eight o'clock. So, one morning, the *viejo* went into the tool-house and put up a rope. Then he waited until it was eight o'clock. He saw the men coming. He put the rope around his neck and stepped off a work bench. And just when he did that, the door of the tool-shed blew shut."

Broad smiles broke out on the faces of the friends. Sometimes, they thought, life was very, very humorous.

"Those men did not miss him right away," Jesus Maria went on. "They said, 'He is probably drunk, that old one.' It was an hour later when they opened the door of that tool-shed." He looked around.

The smiles were still on the faces of the friends, but they were changed smiles. "You see," Jesus Maria said, "it is funny. But it squeezes in you too."

"What did 'Tonia say?" Pilon demanded. "Did she read a lesson and change her living?"

"No. She did not. Petey told her, and she laughed. Petey laughed, too. But he was ashamed. 'Tonia said, 'What an old fool he was,' and 'Tonia looked at Petey that way she had.

"Then Petey said, 'It is good to have a little sister like thee. Some night I will walk in the woods with thee.' Then 'Tonia laughed again and ran away a little. And she said, 'Do you think I am as pretty as Gracie?' So Petey followed her into the house."

Pilon complained, "It is not a good story. There are too many meanings and too many lessons in it. Some of those lessons are opposite. There is not a story to take into your head. It proves nothing."

"I like it," said Pablo. "I like it because it hasn't any meaning you can see, and still it does seem to mean something, I can't tell what."

The sun had turned across noon and the air was hot.

"I wonder what the Pirate will bring to eat," said Danny.

"There is a mackerel run in the bay," Pablo observed.

Pilon's eyes brightened. "I have a plan that I thought out," he said. ' When I was a little boy, we lived by the railroad. Every day when the train went by, my brothers and I threw rocks at the engine, and the firemen threw coal at us. Sometimes we picked up a big bucketful of coal and took it in to our mother. Now I thought maybe we could take rocks down on the pier. When the boats come near, we will call names, we will throw rocks. How can those fishermen get back at us? Can they throw oars, or nets? No. They can only throw mackerel."

Danny stood up joyfully. "Now there is a plan!" he cried. "How this little Pilon of ours is our friend. What would we do without our Pilon? Come, I know where there is a great pile of rocks."

"I like mackerel better than any other fish," said Pablo.

CHAPTER XV

How Danny brooded and became mad. How the devil in the shape of Torrelli assaulted Danny's House.

There is a changeless quality about Monterey. Nearly every day in the morning the sun shines in the windows on the west sides of the streets; and, in the afternoons, on the east sides of the streets. Every day the red bus clangs back and forth between Monterey and Pacific Grove. Every day the canneries send a stink of reducing fish into the air. Every afternoon the wind blows in from the bay and sways the pines on the hills. The rock fishermen sit on the rocks holding their poles, and their faces are graven with patience and with cynicism.

On Tortilla Flat, above Monterey, the routine is changeless too; for there is only a given number of adventures that Cornelia Ruiz can have with her slowly changing procession of sweethearts. She has been known to take again a man long since discarded.

In Danny's house there was even less change. The friends had sunk into a routine which might have been monotonous for anyone but a paisano—up in the morning, to sit in the sun and wonder what the Pirate would bring. The Pirate still cut pitchwood and sold it in the streets of Monterey, but now he bought food with the quarter he earned every day. Occasionally the friends procured some wine, and then there was singing and fighting.

Time is more complex near the sea than in any other place, for in addition to the circling of the sun and the turning of the seasons, the waves beat out the passage of time on the rocks and the tides rise and fall as a great clepsydra.

Danny began to feel the beating of time. He looked at his friends and saw how with them every day was the same. When he got out of his bed in the night and stepped over the sleeping paisanos, he was angry with them for being there. Gradually, sitting on the front porch, in the sun, Danny began to dream of the days of his freedom. He had slept in the woods in summer, and in the warm hay of barns when the winter cold was in. The weight of property was not upon him. He remembered that the name of Danny was a name of storm. Oh, the fights! The flights through the woods with an outraged chicken under his arm! The hiding places in the gulch when an outraged husband proclaimed feud! Storm and violence, sweet violence! When Danny thought of the old lost time, he could taste again how good the stolen food was, and he longed for that old time again. Since his inheritance had lifted him, he had not fought often. He had been drunk, but not adventurously so. Always the weight of the house was upon him; always the responsibility of his friends.

Danny began to mope on the front porch, so that his friends thought him ill.

"Tea made from yerba buena will be good," Pilon suggested. "If you will go to bed, Danny, we will put hot rocks to your feet."

It was not coddling that Danny wanted, it was freedom. For a month he brooded, stared at the ground, looked with sullen eyes at his ubiquitous friends, kicked the friendly dogs out of his way.

In the end he gave up to his longing. One night he ran away. He went into the pine woods and disappeared.

When in the morning the friends awakened and found him missing, Pilon said, "It is some lady. He is in love."

They left it there, for every man has a right to love. The friends went on living as they had. But when a week passed with no sign of Danny, they began to worry. In a body they went to the woods to look for him.

"Love is nice," said Pilon. "We cannot blame any man for following a girl, but a week is a week. It must be a lively girl to keep Danny away for a week."

Pablo said, "A little love is like a little wine. Too much of either will make a man sick. Maybe Danny is already sick. Maybe this girl is too lively."

Jesus Maria was worried too. "It is not like the Danny we know to be gone so long. Some bad thing has happened."

The Pirate took his dogs into the woods. The friends advised the dogs. "Find Danny. He may be sick. Somewhere he may be dead, that good Danny who lets you sleep in his house."

The Pirate whispered to them, "Oh, evil, ungrateful dogs, find our friend." But the dogs waved their tails happily and sought out a rabbit and went kyoodling after it.

The paisanos ranged all day through the woods, calling Danny's name, looking in places they themselves might have chosen to sleep in, the good hollows between the roots of trees, the thick needled beds encircled by bushes. They knew where a man would sleep, but they found no sign of Danny.

"Perhaps he is mad," Pilon suggested. "Some secret worry may have turned his wit."

In the evening they went back to Danny's house and opened the door and went in. Instantly they became intense. A thief had been busy. Danny's blankets were gone. All the food was stolen. Two pots were missing.

Pilon looked quickly at Big Joe Portagee, and then he shook his head. "No, you were with us. You didn't do it."

"Danny did it," Pablo said excitedly. "Truly he is mad. He is running through the woods like an animal."

Great care and worry settled on Danny's house. "We must find him," the friends assured one another. "Some harm will fall upon our friend in his craziness. We must search through the whole world until we find him."

They threw off their laziness. Every day they looked for him, and they began to hear curious rumours. "Yes, Danny was here last night. Oh, that drunk one! Oh, that thief! For see, Danny knocked down the *viejo* with a fence picket and he stole a bottle of grappa. What kind of friends are these who let their friend do such things?"

"Yes, we saw Danny. His eye was closed, and he was singing, 'Come into the woods and we will dance, little girls,' but we would not go. We were afraid. That Danny did not look very quiet."

At the wharf they found more evidence of their friend. "He was here," the fishermen said. "He wanted to fight everybody. Benito broke an oar on Danny's head. Then Danny broke some windows, and then a policeman took him to jail."

Hot on the path of their wayward friend, they continued. "McNear brought him in last night," the sergeant said. "Some way he got loose before morning. When we catch him, we'll give him six months."

The friends were tired of the chase. They went home, and to their horror they found that the new sack of potatoes that Pilon had found only that morning had gone.

"Now it is too much," Pilon cried. "Danny is crazy, and he is in danger. Some terrible thing will happen to him if we do not save him."

"We will search," said Jesus Maria.

"We will look behind every tree and every shed," Pablo guaranteed.

"Under the boats on the beach," Big Joe suggested.

"The dogs will help," the Pirate said.

Pilon shook his head. "That is not the way. Every time we come to a place after Danny has gone. We must wait in some place where he will come. We must act as wise men, not as fools."

"But where will he come?"

The light struck all of them at once. "Torrelli's. Sooner or later Danny will go to Torrelli's. We must go there to catch him, to restrain him in the madness that has fallen upon him."

"Yes," they agreed. "We must save Danny."

In a body they visited Torrelli, and Torrelli would not let them in. "Ask me," he cried through the door, "have I seen Danny? Danny brought three blankets and two cooking pots, and I gave him a gallon of wine. What did the devil do then? My wife he insulted and me he called bad names. My baby he spanked, my dog he kicked! He stole the hammock from my porch." Torrelli gasped with emotion. "I chased him to get my hammock back, and when I returned, he was with my wife! Seducer, thief, drunkard! That is your friend, Danny! I myself will see that he goes to penitentiary."

The eyes of the friends glinted. "Oh, Corsican pig," Pilon said evenly. "You speak of our friend. Our friend is not well."

Torrelli locked the door. They could hear the bolt slide, but Pilon continued to speak through the door. "Oh, Jew," he said, "if thou wert a little more charitable with thy wine, these things would not happen. See that thou keepest that cold frog which is thy tongue from dirtying our friend. See thou treatest him gently, for his friends are many. We will tear thy stomach out if thou art not nice to him."

Torrelli made no sound inside the locked house, but he trembled with rage and fear at the ferocity of the tones. He was relieved when he heard the footsteps of the friends receding up the path.

That night, after the friends had gone to bed, they heard a stealthy step in the kitchen. They knew it was Danny, but he escaped before they could catch him. They wandered about in the dark, calling disconsolately, "Come, Danny, our little sugar friend, we need thee with us."

There was no reply, but a thrown rock struck Big Joe in the

stomach and doubled him up on the ground. Oh, how the friends were dismayed, and how their hearts were heavy!

"Danny is running to his death," they said sadly. "Our little friend is in need, and we cannot help him."

It was difficult to keep house now, for Danny had stolen nearly everything in it. A chair turned up at a bootlegger's. All the food was taken, and once, when they were searching for Danny in the woods, he stole the air-tight stove; but it was heavy, he abandoned it in the gulch. Money there was none, for Danny stole the Pirate's wheelbarrow and traded it to Joe Ortiz for a bottle of whisky. Now all peace had gone from Danny's house, and there was only worry and sadness.

"Where is our happiness gone?" Pablo mourned. "Somewhere we have sinned. It is a judgment. We should go to confession."

No more did they discuss the marital parade of Cornelia Ruiz. Gone were the moralities, lost were the humanities. Truly the good life lay in ruins. And into the desolation came the rumours.

"Danny committed partial rape last night."

"Danny has been milking Mrs. Palochico's goat."

"Danny was in a fight with some soldiers the night before last."

Sad as they were at his moral decay, the friends were not a little jealous of the good time Danny was having.

"If he is not crazy, he will be punished," said Pilon. "Be sure of that. Danny is sinning in a way which, sin for sin, beats any record I ever heard of. Oh, the penances when he wants to be decent again! In a few weeks Danny has piled up more sins than Old Ruiz did in a lifetime."

That night, Danny, unhindered by the friendly dogs, crept into the house as silently as the moving shadow of a limb under a street light, and wantonly he stole Pilon's shoes. In the morning it did not take Pilon long to understand what had happened. He went firmly to the porch and sat down in the sun and regarded his feet.

"Now he has gone too far," Pilon said. "Pranks he has played, and we were patient. But now he turns to crime. This is not the Danny we know. This is another man, a bad man. We must capture this bad man."

Pablo looked complacently down at his shoes. "Maybe this is only a prank too," he suggested.

"No," Pilon said severely. "This is crime. They were not very good shoes, but it is a crime against friendship to take them. And that is the worst kind of crime. If Danny will steal the shoes of his friends, there is no crime he will stop at."

The friends nodded in agreement. "Yes, we must catch him," said Jesus Maria of the humanities. "We know he is sick. We will tie him to his bed and try to cure him of the sickness. We must try to wipe the darkness from his brain."

"But now," said Pablo, "before we catch him, we must remember to put our shoes under our pillows when we sleep."

The house was in a state of siege. All about it raged Danny, and Danny was having a wonderful time.

Seldom did the face of Torrelli show any emotions but suspicion and anger. In his capacity as bootlegger, and in his dealings with the people of Tortilla Flat, those two emotions were often called into his heart, and their line was written on his face. Moreover, Torrelli had never visited anyone. He had only to stay at home to have everyone visit him. Consequently, when Torrelli walked up the road towards Danny's house in the morning, his face suffused with a ferocious smile of pleasure and anticipation, the children ran into their yards and peeked through the pickets at him; the dogs caressed their stomachs with their tails and fled with backward, fearful looks; men meeting him stepped out of his path, and clenched their fists to repel a madman.

This morning the fog covered the sky. The sun, after a number of unsuccessful skirmishes, gave up and retired behind the grey folds. The pine trees dripped dusty dew on the ground; and in the faces of the few people who were about, the day was reflected with sombre looks and grey skins. There were no hearty greetings. There was none of that human idealism which blandly hopes this day will be better than all other days.

Old Roca, seeing Torrelli smiling, went home and told his wife, "That one has just killed and eaten his children. You will see!"

Torrelli was happy, for in his pocket there was a folded, precious paper. His fingers sought his coat again and again, and pressed until a little crackling sound assured Torrelli that the paper was still there. As he walked through the grey morning, he muttered to himself.

"Nest of snakes," he said. "I will wipe out this pestilence of Danny's friends. No more will I give wine for goods, and have the goods stolen again. Each man alone is not so bad, but the nest of them! Madonna, look down how I will cast them out into the street! The toads, the lice, the stinging flies! When they sleep in the woods again, they will not be so proud.

"I would have them know that Torrelli has triumphed. They thought to cheat me, despoil my house of furniture and my wife of virtue! They will see that Torrelli, the great sufferer, can strike back. Oh, yes, they will see!"

Thus he muttered as he walked, and his fingers crackled the paper in his pocket. The trees dripped mournful drops into the dust. The seagulls circled in the air, screaming tragically. Torrelli moved like grey Fate on Danny's house.

In Danny's house there was gloom. The friends could not sit on the porch in the sunshine, for there was no sunshine. No one can produce a better reason for gloom. They had brought back the stolen stove from the gulch and set it up. They clustered to it now, and Johnny Pom-pom, who had come to call, told the news he had.

"Tito Ralph," he said, "is no longer the jailer down at the city jail. No, this morning, the police judge sent him away."

"I liked Tito Ralph," said Pilon. "When a man was in jail, Tito Ralph would bring him a little wine. And he knew more stories than a hundred other men. Why did he lose his job. Johnny Pom-pom?"

"That is what I came to tell. Tito Ralph, you know, was often in jail, and he was a good prisoner. He knew how a jail should be run. After a while he knew more about the jail than anyone. Then Daddy Marks the old jailer died, and Tito Ralph took his place. Never has there been such a good jailer as Tito Ralph. Everything he did just right. But he has one little fault. When he drinks wine, he forgets he is the jailer. He escapes, and they have to catch him."

The friends nodded. "I know," said Pablo. "I have heard he is hard to catch too. He hides."

"Yes," continued Johnny Pom-pom, "except for that, he is the best jailer they ever had. Well, this is the thing that I came to tell. Last night Danny had enough wine for ten men, and he drank it. Then he drew pictures on windows. He was very rich, he bought eggs to throw at a Chinaman. And one of those eggs missed the Chinaman and hit a policeman. So, Danny was in jail."

"But he was rich. He sent Tito Ralph out to get some wine, and then some more wine. There were four men in the jail. They all drank wine. And at last that fault of Tito Ralph's came out. So he escaped, and all the others escaped with him. They caught Tito Ralph this morning and told him he could not be jailer any more. He was so sad that he broke a window, and now he is in jail again."

"But Danny," Pilon cried. "What about Danny?"

"Oh, Danny," said Johnny Pom-pom, "he escaped too. They did not catch him."

The friends sighed in dismay.

"Danny is getting bad," Pilon said seriously. "He will not come to a good end. I wonder where he got the money."

It was at this moment that the triumphant Torrelli opened the gate and strode up the path. The Pirate's dogs got up nervously from their corner and moved towards the door, snarling. The friends looked up and questioned one another with their eyes. Big Joe picked up the pick handle that had so lately been used on him. The heavy confident step of Torrelli pounded on the porch. The door flew open, and there stood Torrelli, smiling. He did not bluster at them. No, he approached as delicately as a house cat. He patted them kindly, as a house cat pats a cockroach.

"Ah, my friends," he said gently, at their looks of alarm. "My dear good friends and customers. My heart is torn that I must be a carrier of bad news to those whom I love."

Pilon leaped up. "It is Danny. He is sick, he is hurt. Tell us."

Torrelli shook his head daintily. "No, my little ones, it is not Danny. My heart bleeds, but I must tell you that you cannot live here any more." His eyes gloated at the amazement his words wrought. Every mouth dropped open, every eye went blank with astonishment.

"That is foolish," Pablo cried. "Why can't we live here any more?"

Torrelli's hand went lovingly into his breast pocket, and his fingers brought out the precious paper and waved it in the air. "Imagine my suffering," Torrelli went on. "Danny does not own this house any more."

"What!" they cried. "What do you mean? How does not Danny own this house any more? Speak, O Corsican pig."

Torrelli giggled, a thing so terrible that the paisanos stepped back from him. "Because," he said, "the house belongs to me. Danny came to me and sold me his house for twenty-five dollars last night." Fiendishly he watched the thoughts crowd on their faces.

"It is a lie," their faces said. "Danny would not do such a thing." And then, "But Danny has been doing many bad things lately. He has been stealing from us. Maybe he has sold the house over our heads."

"It is a lie," Pilon cried aloud. "It is a dirty wop lie."

Torrelli smiled on and waved the paper. "Here I have proof," he said. "Here is the paper Danny signed. It is what we of business call a bill of sale."

Pablo came to him furiously. "You got him drunk. He did not know what he did."

Torrelli opened the paper a little bit. "The law will not be interested in that," he said. "And so, my dear little friends, it is my terrible duty to tell you that you must leave my house. I have plans for it." His face lost its smile then, and all the cruelty came back into it. "If you are not out by noon, I will send a policeman."

Pilon moved gently towards him. Oh, beware, Torrelli, when Pilon moves smiling on you! Run, hide yourself in some iron room and weld up the door. "I do not understand these things," Pilon said gently. "Of course I am sad that Danny should do a thing like this."

Torrelli giggled again.

"I never had a house to sell," Pilon continued. "Danny signed this paper, is that it?"

"Yes," Torrelli mimicked him, "Danny signed this paper. That is it."

Pilon blundered on, stupidly. "That is the thing that proves you own this house?"

"Yes, O little fool. This is the paper that proves it."

Pilon looked puzzled. "I thought you must take it down and have some record made."

Torrelli laughed scornfully. Oh, beware, Torrelli! Do you not see how quietly these snakes are moving? There is Jesus Maria in front of the door. There is Pablo by the kitchen door. See Big Joe's knuckles white on the pick handle.

Torrelli said, "You know nothing of business, little hobos and tramps. When I leave here I shall take this paper down and——"

It happened so quickly that the last words belched out explosively. His feet flew up in the air. He landed with a great thump on the floor and clawed at the air with his fat hands. He heard the stove lid clang.

"Thieves," he screamed. The blood pressed up his neck and into his face. "Thieves, O rats and dogs, give me my paper!"

Pilon standing in front of him, looked amazed.

"Paper?" he asked politely. "What is this paper you speak of so passionately?"

"My bill of sale, my ownership. Oh, the police will hear of this!

"I do not recall a paper," said Pilon. "Pablo, do you know what is this paper he talks about?"

"Paper?" said Pablo. "Does he mean a newspaper or a cigarette paper?"

Pilon continued with the roll. "Johnny Pom-pom.?"

"He is dreaming, maybe, that one," said Johnny Pom-pom.

"Jesus Maria? Do you know of a paper?"

"I think he is drunk," Jesus Maria said in a scandalized voice. "It is too early in the morning to be drunk."

"Joe Portagee?"

"I wasn't here," Joe insisted. "I just come in now."

"Pirate?"

"He don't have no paper"—the Pirate turned to his dogs—"do he?"

Pilon turned back to the apoplectic Torrelli. "You are mistaken, my friend. It is possible that I might have been wrong about this paper, but you can see for yourself that no one but you saw this paper. Do you blame me when I think that maybe there was no paper? Maybe you should go to bed and rest a little."

Torrelli was too stunned to shout any more. They turned him about and helped him out of the door and sped him on his way, sunk in the awfulness of his defeat.

And then they looked at the sky and were glad; for the sun had fought again, and this time won a pathway through the fog. The friends did not go back into the house. They sat happily down on the front porch.

"Twenty-five dollars," said Pilon. "I wonder what he did with the money."

The sun, once its first skirmish was won, drove the fog headlong from the sky. The porch boards warmed up, and the flies sang in the light. Exhaustion had settled on the friends.

"It was a close thing," Pablo said wearily. "Danny should not do such things."

"We will get all our wine from Torrelli to make it up to him," said Jesus Maria.

A bird hopped into the rose bush and flirted its tail. Mrs. Morales' new chickens sang a casual hymn to the sun. The dogs, in the front yard, thoughtfully scratched all over and gnawed their tails.

At the sound of footsteps from the road, the friends looked up, and then stood up with welcoming smiles. Danny and Tito Ralph walked in the gate, and each of them carried two heavy bags. Jesus Maria darted into the house and brought out the fruit jars. The friends noticed that Danny looked a little tired when he set his jugs on the porch.

"It is hot climbing that hill," Danny said.

"Tito Ralph," cried Johnny Pom-pom, "I heard you were put in jail."

"I escaped again," Tito Ralph said wanly. "I still had the keys."

The fruit jars gurgled full. A great sigh escaped from the men, a sigh of relief that everything was over.

Pilon took a big drink. "Danny," he said, "that big Torrelli came up here this morning with lies. He had a paper he said you signed."

Danny looked startled. "Where is that paper?" he demanded.

"Well," Pilon continued, "we knew it was a lie, so we burned that paper. You didn't sign it, did you?"

"No," said Danny, and he drained his jar.

"It would be nice to have something to eat," observed Jesus Maria.

Danny smiled sweetly. "I forgot. In one of those bags are three chickens and some bread."

So great was Pilon's pleasure and relief that he stood up and made a little speech. "Where is there a friend like our friend?" he exclaimed. "He takes us into his house out of the cold. He shares his good food with us, and his wine. Ohee, the good man, the dear friend."

Danny was embarrassed. He looked at the floor. "It is nothing," he murmured. "It has no merit."

But Pilon's joy was so great that it encompassed the world, and even the evil things of the world. "We must do something nice some time for Torrelli," he said.

CHAPTER XVI

Of the sadness of Danny. How through sacrifice Danny's Friends gave a party. How Danny was Translated.

WHEN DANNY came back to his house and to his friends after his amok, he was not conscience-stricken, but he was very tired. The rough fingers of violent experience had harped upon his soul. He began to live listlessly, arising from bed only to sit on the porch, under the rose of Castile; arising from the porch only to eat; arising from the table only to go to bed. The talk flowed about him and he listened, but he did not care. Cornelia Ruiz had a quick and superb run of husbands, and no emotion was aroused in Danny. When Big Joe got in his bed one evening, so apathetic was Danny that Pilon and Pablo had to beat Big Joe for him. When Sammy Rasper, celebrating a belated New Year with a shotgun and a gallon of whisky, killed a cow and went to jail, Danny could not even be drawn into a discussion of the ethics of the case, although the arguments raged about him and although his judgment was passionately appealed to.

After a while it came about that the friends began to worry about Danny. "He is changed," said Pilon. "He is old."

Jesus Maria suggested, "This Danny has crowded the good times of a life into a little three weeks. He is sick of fun."

In vain the friends tried to draw him from the cavern of his apathy. In the mornings, on the porch, they told their funniest stories. They reported details of the love life of Tortilla Flat so penetratingly that they would have been of interest to a dissection class. Pilon winnowed the Flat for news and brought home every seedling of interest to Danny; but there was age in Danny's eyes and weariness.

"Thou art not well," Jesus Maria insisted in vain. "There is some bitter secret in thine heart."

"No," said Danny.

It was noticed that he let flies crawl on his feet a long time, and that when he did slap them off there was no art in his stroke. Gradually the high spirits, the ready laughter, went out of Danny's house and tumbled into the dark pool of Danny's quietness.

Oh, it was a pity to see him, that Danny who had fought for lost causes, or any other kind; that Danny who could drink glass for glass with any man in the world; that Danny who responded to the look of love like an aroused tiger. Now he sat on his front porch in the sunlight, his blue-jeaned knees drawn up against his chest, his arms hanging over, his hands dangling from limp wrists, his head bent forward as though by a heavy black thought. His eyes had no light of desire nor displeasure nor joy nor pain.

Poor Danny, how has life left thee! Here thou sittest like the first man before the world grew up around him; and like the last man, after the world has eroded away. But see, Danny! Thou art not alone. Thy friends are caught in this state of thine. They look at thee from their eye-corners. They wait like expectant little dogs for the first waking movement of their master. One joyful word from thee, Danny, one joyful look, and they will bark and chase their tails. Thy life is not thine own to govern, Danny, for it controls other lives. See how thy friends suffer! Spring to life, Danny, that thy friends may live again!

This, in effect, although not in words so beautiful, was what Pilon said. Pilon held out a jar of wine to Danny. "Come on," he said. "Get up off your can."

Danny took the jar and drained it. And then he settled back and tried to find again his emotional Nirvana.

"Do you hurt anyplace?" Pilon asked.

"No," said Danny.

Pilon poured him another jar of wine and watched his face while the wine disappeared. The eyes lost their lack-lustre. Somewhere in the depths, the old Danny stirred to life for a moment. He killed a fly with a stroke that would have done justice to a master.

Slowly a smile spread over Pilon's face. And later he gathered all the friends, Pablo and Jesus Maria and Big Joe and the Pirate and Johnny Pom-pom, and Tito Ralph.

Pilon led them all into the gulch behind the house. "I gave Danny the last of the wine, and it did him good. What Danny needs is lots of wine, and maybe a party. Where can we get wine?"

Their minds combed the possibilities of Monterey like rat terriers in a barn, but there were no rats. These friends were urged on by altruism more pure than most men can conceive. They loved Danny.

Jesus Maria said, finally, "Chin Kee is packing squids."

Their minds bolted, turned with curiosity and looked at the thing, crept stealthily back and sniffed it. It was several moments before their shocked imaginations could become used to the thing. "But after all, why not?" they argued silently. "One day would not be so bad—only one day."

Their faces showed the progress of the battle, and how they were defeating their fears in the interest of Danny's welfare.

"We will do it," Pilon said. "To-morrow we will all go down and cut squid, and to-morrow night we will give a party for Danny."

When Danny awakened the next morning, the house was deserted.

He got up from his bed and looked through the silent rooms. But Danny was not a man to brood very long. He gave it up as a problem, and then as a thought. He went to the front porch and listlessly sat down.

Is it premonition, Danny? Do you fear the fate that is closing in on you? Are there no pleasures left? No. Danny is as sunk in himself as he has been for a week.

Not so Tortilla Flat. Early the rumour flew about. "Danny's friends are cutting squids for Chin Kee." It was a portent, like the overthrow of a government, or even of the solar system. It was spoken of in the street, called over back fences to ladies who were just then hurrying to tell it. "All of Danny's friends are down cutting squids."

The morning was electric with the news. There must be some reason, some secret. Mothers instructed their children and sent them running towards Chin Kee's squid yard. Young matrons waited anxiously behind their curtains for later news. And news came.

"Pablo has cut his hand with a squid knife."

"Chin Kee has kicked the Pirate's dogs."

Riot.

"The dogs are back."

"Pilon looks grim."

A few small bets were laid. For months nothing so exciting had happened. During one whole morning not a single person spoke of Cornelia Ruiz. It was not until the noon hour that the real news leaked out, but then it came with a rush.

"They are going to give a big party for Danny."

"Everyone is going."

Instructions began to emerge from the squid yard. Mrs. Morales dusted her gramophone and picked out her loudest records. Some spark flared, and Tortilla Flat was tinder. Seven friends, indeed, to give a party for Danny! It is as though to say Danny had only seven friends! Mrs. Soto descended upon her chicken yard with a cleaver. Mrs. Palochico poured a bag of sugar into her largest cooking pot to make dulces. A delegation of girls went into the Woolworth store in Monterey and bought the complete stock of coloured crêpe paper. Guitars and accordions cried experimentally through the Flat.

News! More news from the squid yard. They are going to make it. They are firm. They will have at least fourteen dollars. See that fourteen gallons of wine are ready.

Torrelli was overwhelmed with business. Everyone wanted to buy a gallon to take to Danny's house. Torrelli himself, caught in the fury of the movement, said to his wife, "Maybe we will go to Danny's house. I will take a few gallons for my friends."

As the afternoon passed, waves of excitement poured over the

Flat. Dresses unworn in a lifetime were unpacked and hung to air. Shawls the moths had yearned for during two hundred years hung from porch railings and exuded the odour of moth-balls.

And Danny? He sat like a half-melted man. He moved only when the sun moved. If he realized that every inhabitant of Tortilla Fla had passed his gate that afternoon, he gave no sign. Poor Danny! At least two dozen pairs of eyes watched his front gate. At about four o'clock he stood up, stretched, and sauntered out of his yard, towards Monterey.

Why, they hardly waited until he was out of sight. Oh, the twisting and stringing of green and yellow and red crêpe paper! Oh, the candles shaved, and the shavings thrown on the floor! Oh, the mad children who skated the wax in evenly!

Food appeared. Basins of rice, pots of steaming chicken, dumplings to startle you! And the wine came, gallons and gallons of it. Martinez dug up a keg of potato whisky from his manure pile and carried it to Danny's house.

At five-thirty the friends marched up the hill, tired and bloody, but triumphant. So must the Old Guard have looked when they returned to Paris after Austerlitz. They saw the house bristling with colour. They laughed, and their weariness fell from them. They were so happy that tears came into their eyes.

Mama Chipo walked into the yard followed by her two sons who carried a wash-tub of salsa pura between them. Paulito, that rich scamp, rushed the fire under a big kettle of beans and chili. Shouts, songs broken off, shrieks of women, the general turmoil of excited children.

A carful of apprehensive policemen drove up from Monterey. "Oh, it is only a party. Sure, we'll have a glass of wine. Don't kill anybody."

Where is Danny? Lonely as smoke on a clear cold night, he drifts through Monterey in the evening. To the post office he goes, to the station, to the pool-rooms on Alvarado Street, to the wharf, where the black water mourns among the piles. What is it, Danny? What makes you feel this way? Danny didn't know. There was an ache in his heart like the farewell to a dear woman; there was vague sorrow in him like the despair of autumn. He walked past the restaurants he used to smell with interest, and no appetite was aroused in him. He walked by Madam Zuca's great establishment, and exchanged no obscene jests with the girls in the windows. Back to the wharf he went. He leaned over the rail and looked into the deep, deep water. Do you know, Danny, how the wine of your life is pouring into the fruit jars of the gods? Do you see the procession of your days in the oily water among the piles? He remained motionless, staring down.

They were worried about him at Danny's house when it began to get dark. The friends left the party and trotted down the hill into Monterey. They asked, "Have you seen Danny?"

"Yes, Danny walked by here an hour ago. He walked slow."

Pilon and Pablo hunted together. They traced their friend over the route he had followed, and at last they saw him, on the end of the dark pier. He was lighted by a dim electric wharf light. They hurried out to him.

Pablo did not mention it then, but ever afterward it was his custom, when Danny was mentioned, to describe what he saw as he and Pilon walked out on the wharf towards Danny. "There he stood," Pablo always said. "I could just see him, leaning on the rail. I looked at him, and then I saw something else. At first it looked like a black cloud in the air over Danny's head. And then I saw it was a big black bird, as big as a man. It hung in the air like a hawk over a rabbit hole. I crossed myself and said two Hail Marys. The bird was gone when we came to Danny."

Pilon did not see it. Moreover, Pilon did not remember Pablo crossing himself and saying the Hail Marys. But he never interfered with the story, for it was Pablo's story.

They walked rapidly towards Danny; the wharf boards drummed hollowly under their feet. Danny did not turn. They took him by the arm and turned him about.

"Danny! What is wrong?"

"Nothing. I'm all right."

"Are you sick, Danny?"

"No."

"Then what is it that makes you so sad?"

"I don't know," said Danny. "I just feel this way. I don't want to do anything."

"Maybe a doctor could do something for you, Danny."

"I tell you I am not sick."

"Then look," Pilon cried. "We are having a party for you at your house. Everybody in Tortilla Flat is there, and music and wine and chicken! There are maybe twenty or thirty gallons of wine. And bright paper hanging up. Don't you want to come?"

Danny breathed deeply. For a moment he turned back to the deep black water. Perhaps he whispered to the gods a promise or a defiance.

He swung around again to his friends. His eyes were feverish.

"You're goddam right I want to go. Hurry up. I am thirsty. Any girls there?"

"Lots of girls. All the girls."

"Come on, then. Hurry up."

He led them, running up the hill. Long before they arrived they could hear the sweetness of the music through the pines, and the shrill notes of excited happy voices. The three belated ones arrived at a dead run. Danny lifted his head and howled like a coyote. Jars of wine were held out to him. He took a gulp from each one.

That was a party for you! Always afterwards when a man spoke of a party with enthusiasm, someone was sure to say with reverence, "Did you go to that party at Danny's house?" And, unless the first speaker were a newcomer, he had been there. That was a party for you! No one ever tried to give a better one. Such a thing was unthinkable, for within two days Danny's party was lifted out of possible comparison with all other parties that ever were. What man came out of that night without some glorious cuts and bruises? Never had there been so many fights; not fights between two men, but roaring battles that raged through whole clots of men, each one for himself.

Oh, the laughter of women! Thin and high and brittle as spun glass. Oh, the ladylike shrieks of protest from the gulch. Father Ramon was absolutely astounded and incredulous at the confessions the next week. The whole happy soul of Tortilla Flat tore itself from restraint and arose into the air, one ecstatic unit. They danced so hard that the floor gave way in one corner. The accordions played so loudly that always afterwards they were wind-broken, like foundered horses.

And Danny—just as this party knew no comparison, so Danny defied emulation as a celebrant. In the future let some squirt say with excitement, "Did you see me? Did you see me ask that nigger wench for a dance? Did you seen us go 'round and 'round like tom cats?" and some old, wise, and baleful eye would be turned on him. Some voice, sated with having known the limit of possibilities, would ask quietly, "Did you see Danny the night of the party?"

Some time a historian may write a cold, dry, fungus-like history of The Party. He may refer to the moment when Danny defied and attacked the whole party, men, women and children, with a table-leg. He may conclude, "A dying organism is often observed to be capable of extraordinary endurance and strength." Referring to Danny's superhuman amorous activity that night, this same historian may write with unshaking hand: "When any living organism is attacked, its whole function seems to aim toward reproduction."

But I say, and the people of Tortilla Flat would say, "To hell with it. That Danny was a man for you!" No one kept actual count, and afterwards, naturally, no lady would willingly admit that she had been ignored; so that the reputed prowess of Danny may be somewhat overstated. One tenth of it would be an overstatement for anyone in the world.

Where Danny went, a magnificent madness followed. It is passionately averred in Tortilla Flat that Danny alone drank three gallons of wine. It must be remembered, however, that Danny is now a god. In a few years it may be thirty gallons. In twenty years it may be plainly remembered that the clouds flamed and spelled DANNY in tremendous letters; that the moon dripped blood; that the wolf of the world bayed prophetically from the mountains of the Milky Way.

Gradually a few of those whose stuff was less stern than Danny's began to wilt, to sag, to creep out from under foot. Those who were left, feeling the lack, shouted the louder, fought the more viciously, danced the harder. In Monterey the motors of the fire trucks were kept running, and the firemen, in their red tin hats and raincoats, silently sat in their places and waited.

The night passed quickly, and still Danny roared through the party.

What happened is attested by many witnesses, both men and women. And although their value as witnesses is sometimes attacked on the ground that they had drunk thirty gallons of wine and a keg of potato whisky, those people are sullenly sure of the major points. It took some weeks to get the story into line; some said one thing, some another. But gradually the account clarified into the reasonable form it now has and always will have.

Danny, say the people of Tortilla Flat, had been rapidly changing his form. He had grown huge and terrible. His eyes flared like the headlights of an automobile. There was something fearsome about him. There he stood, in the room of his own house. He held the pine table-leg in his right hand, and even it had grown. Danny challenged the world.

"Who will fight?" he cried. "Is there no one left in the world who is not afraid?" The people were afraid; that table-leg, so hideous and so alive, had become a terror to them all. Danny swung it back and forth. The accordions wheezed to silence. The dancing stopped. The room grew chill, and a silence seemed to roar in the air like an ocean.

"No one?" Danny cried again. "Am I alone in the world? Will no one fight with me?" The men shuddered before his terrible eyes, and watched, fascinated, the slashing path of the table-leg through the air. And no one answered the challenge.

Danny drew himself up. It is said that his head just missed touching the ceiling. "Then I will go out to The One who can fight. I will find The Enemy who is worthy of Danny!" He stalked to the door, staggering a little as he went. The terrified people made a broad path for him. He bent to get out of the door. The people stood still and listened.

Outside the house they heard his roaring challenge. They heard the table-leg whistle like a meteor through the air. They heard his footsteps charging down the yard. And then, behind the house, in the gulch, they heard an answering challenge so fearful and so chill that their spines wilted like nasturtium stems under frost. Even now, when the people speak of Danny's Opponent, they lower their voices and look furtively about. They heard Danny charge to the fray. They heard his last shrill cry of defiance, and then a thump. And then silence.

For a long moment the people waited, holding their breaths lest the harsh rush of air from their lungs should obscure some sound. But they listened in vain. The night was hushed, and the grey dawn was coming.

Pilon broke the silence. "Something is wrong," he said. And Pilon it was who first rushed out of the door. Brave man, no terror could restrain him. The people followed him. Back of the house they went, where Danny's footsteps had sounded, and there was no Danny. They came to the edge of the gulch, where a sharp zigzag led down to the bottom of that ancient water-course wherein no stream had flowed for many generations. The following people saw Pilon dart down the path. They went after him, slowly. And they found Pilon at the bottom of the gulch leaning over a broken and twisted Danny. He had fallen forty feet. Pilon lighted a match. "I think he is alive," he shrieked. "Run for a doctor. Run for Father Ramon."

The people scattered. Within fifteen minutes, four doctors were awakened, dragged from their beds by frantic paisanos. They were not allowed that slow deliberateness by which doctors love to show that they are no slaves to emotion. No! They were hustled, rushed, pushed, their instrument cases were shoved into their hands by men hopelessly incapable of saying what they wanted. Father Ramon, dragged from his bed, came panting up the hill, uncertain whether it was a devil to drive out, a newborn baby to baptize before it died, or a lynching to attend. Meanwhile Pilon and Pablo and Jesus Maria carried Danny up the hill and laid him on his bed. They stood candles all about him. Danny was breathing heavily.

First the doctors arrived. They glanced suspiciously at one another, considered precedence; but the moment of delay brought threatening looks into the eyes of the people. It did not take long to look Danny over. They were all through by the time Father Ramon arrived.

I shall not go into the bedroom with Father Ramon, for Pilon and Pablo and Jesus Maria and Big Joe and Johnny Pom-pom and Tito Ralph and the Pirate and the dogs were there; and they were Danny's family. The door was, and is, closed. For after all there is pride in men, and some things cannot decently be pried into.

But in the big room, crowded to suffocation with the people of Tortilla Flat, there was tenseness and a waiting silence. Priests and doctors have developed a subtle means of communication. When

Father Ramon came out of the bedroom his face had not changed, but at sight of him the women broke into a high and terrible wail. The men shifted their feet like horses in a box stall, and then went outside into the dawning. And the bedroom door remained closed.

CHAPTER XVII

How Danny's sorrowing Friends defied the conventions. How the Talismanic Bond was burned. How each Friend departed alone.

DEATH IS a personal matter, arousing sorrow, despair, fervour, or dry-hearted philosophy. Funerals, on the other hand, are social functions. Imagine going to a funeral without first polishing the automobile. Imagine standing at a graveside not dressed in your best dark suit and your best black shoes, polished delightfully. Imagine sending flowers to a funeral with no attached card to prove you had done the correct thing. In no social institution is the codified ritual of behaviour more rigid than in funerals. Imagine the indignation if the minister altered his sermon or experimented with facial expression. Consider the shock if, at the funeral parlours, any chairs were used but those little folding yellow torture chairs with the hard seats. No, dying, a man may be loved, hated, mourned, missed; but once dead he becomes the chief ornament of a complicated and formal social celebration.

Danny was dead, two days dead; and already he had ceased to be Danny. Although the faces of the people were decently and mournfully veiled with gloom, there was excitement in their hearts. The government has promised a military funeral to all of its ex-soldier sons who wish it. Danny was the first of Tortilla Flat to go, and Tortilla Flat was ready critically to test the government promises. Already news had been sent to the Presidio and Danny's body had been embalmed at government expense. Already a caisson was newly painted and waiting in the artillery shed with a neat new flag folded on top of it. Already orders of the day for Friday were made out:

TEN TO ELEVEN A.M., FUNERAL ESCORT, SQUADRON A, 11TH CAVALRY BAND, AND FIRING SQUAD.

Were these not things to set every woman in Tortilla Flat window-shopping at the National Dollar Store in Monterey? During the day dark children walked the streets of Monterey, begging flowers from the gardens for Danny's funeral. And at night the same children visited the same gardens to augment their bouquets.

At the party the finest clothes had been worn. During the two-day interval those clothes had to be cleaned, washed, starched, mended, and ironed. The activity was frantic. The excitement was decently intense.

On the evening of the second day, Danny's friends were gathered in Danny's house. The shock and the wine had worn off, and now they were horror-stricken, for in all Tortilla Flat they, who had loved Danny most, who had received the most from his hands, they, the paisanos, were the only ones who could not attend Danny's funeral. Through the murk of the headaches they had been conscious of this appalling tragedy, but only on this evening had the situation become so concrete that it must be faced. Ordinarily their clothes were unspeakable. The party had aged their jeans and blue shirts by years. Where was the trouser-knee unburst? Where the shirt unripped? If anyone else had died, they could have borrowed clothes; but there was no person in Tortilla Flat who was not going to wear his good clothes to the funeral. Only Cocky Riordan was not going, but Cocky was in quarantine for smallpox, and so were his clothes. Money might be begged or stolen to buy one good suit, but money for six suits was simply impossible to get.

You may say, did they not love Danny enough to go to his funeral in rags? Would you go in rags when your neighbours were dressed in finery? Would not the disrespect to Danny be more if they went in rags than if they did not go at all?

The despair that lay in their hearts was incalculable. They cursed their fate. Through the front door they could see Galvez parading by. Galvez had bought a new suit for the funeral, and he had it on twenty-four hours in advance. The friends sat, chin in hand, crushed by their ill fortune. Every possibility had been discussed.

Pilon, for once in his life, descended to absurdity. "We might go out to-night and each one steal a suit," he suggested. He knew that was silly, for every suit would be laid on a chair beside a bed that night. It would be death to steal a suit.

"The Salvation Army sometimes gives suits," said Jesus Maria.

"I have been there," Pablo said. "They have fourteen dresses this time, but no suits."

On every side Fate was against them. Tito Ralph came in with his new green handkerchief sticking out of his breast pocket, but the hostility he aroused made him back apologetically out of the room.

"If we had a week, we could cut squids," Pilon said heroically. "The funeral is to-morrow. We must look in the eye at this thing. Of course we can go to the funeral all right."

"How?" the friends demanded.

"We can go on the sidewalk, while the band and the people march in the street. It is all grass around the cemetery fence. We can lie there in the grass and see everything."

The friends looked at Pilon gratefully. They knew how his sharp wits had been digging over possibilities. But it was only half, less than half, to see the funeral. Being seen at the funeral was the more important half. This was the best that could be done.

"In this we learn a lesson," said Pilon. "We must take it to heart that we should always have a good suit of clothes laid by. We can never tell what may happen."

There they left it, but they felt that they had failed. All through the night they wandered in the town. What yard then was not plundered of its finest blooms? What flowering tree remained standing? In the morning the hole in the cemetery that was to receive Danny's body was almost hidden by a mound of the finest flowers from the best gardens in Monterey.

It is not always that Nature arranges her effects with good taste. Truly it rained before Waterloo; forty feet of snow fell in the path of the Donner Party. But Friday turned out a nice day. The sun arose as though this were a day for a picnic. The gulls flew in across a smiling bay to the sardine canneries. The rock fishermen took their places on the rocks for the ebbing tide. The Palace Drug Company ran down its awnings to protect the red hot-water bottles in its windows from the chemical action of the sun. Mr. Machado, the tailor, put a sign in his window, "Back in Ten Minutes", and went home to dress for the funeral. Three purse seiners came in, loaded with sardines. Louie Duarte painted his boat, and changed its name from Lolita to The Three Cousins. Jake Lake, the cop, arrested a roadster from Del Monte and turned it loose and bought a cigar.

It is a puzzle. How can life go on its stupid course on such a day? How can Mamie Jackson hose off her front sidewalk? How can George W. Merk write his fourth and angriest letter to the water company? How can Charlie Marsh be as dirtily drunk as usual? It is sacrilege. It is outrage.

Danny's friends awakened sadly and got up off the floor. Danny's bed was empty. It was like the riderless charger of an officer which follows its master to his grave. Even Big Joe Portagee had cast no covetous glance at Danny's bed. The sun shone enthusiastically through the window and cast the delicate shadows of spider webs on the floor.

"Danny was glad on mornings like this," said Pilon.

After their trip to the gulch the friends sat for a while on the front porch and celebrated the memory of their friend. Loyally they remembered and proclaimed Danny's virtues. Loyally they forgot his faults.

"And strong," said Pablo. "He was as strong as a mule! He could lift a bale of hay."

They told little stories of Danny, of his goodness, his courage, his piety.

All too soon it was time to go to the church, to stand across the street in their ragged clothes. They blushed inwardly when luckier people went into the church, dressed so beautifully, smelling so prodigally of Agua Florida. The friends could hear the music and the shrill drone of the service. From their vantage point they saw the cavalry arrive, and the band with muffled drums, and the firing squad, and the caisson with its three pairs of horses, and a cavalryman on the near horse of each pair. The mournful clop-clop of shod horses on asphalt put despair in the hearts of the friends. Helplessly they watched the casket carried out and laid on the caisson, and the flag draped over it. The officer blew his whistle, raised his hand and threw it forward. The squadron moved, the firing squad dropped its rifles. The drums thundered their heart-breaking, slow rhythm. The band played its sodden march. The caisson moved. The people walked majestically behind, men straight and stern, women daintily holding their skirts up out of the indelible trail of the cavalry. Everyone was there, Cornelia Ruiz, Mrs. Morales, Galvez, Torrelli and his plump wife, Mrs. Palochico, Tito Ralph the traitor, Sweets Ramirez, Mr. Machado, everyone who amounted to anything on Tortilla Flat, and everyone else, was there.

Is it any wonder that the friends could not stand the shame and misery of it? For a little while they slunk along the sidewalk, bolstered with heroism.

Jesus Maria broke down first. He sobbed with shame, for his father had been a rich and respected prize-fighter. Jesus Maria put down his head and bolted; and the five other friends followed, and the five dogs bounded behind them.

Before the procession was in sight, Danny's friends were lying in the tall grass that edged the cemetery. The service was short and military. The casket was lowered; the rifles cracked; the bugle sang taps, and at the sound, Enrique and Fluff, Pajarito and Rudolph and Señor Alec Thompson laid back their heads and howled. The Pirate was proud of them then!

It was over too soon; the friends walked hurriedly away so that the people would not see them.

They had to pass Torrelli's deserted house anyway, on the way home. Pilon went in through a window and brought out two gallons of wine. And then they walked slowly back to Danny's quiet house. Ceremoniously they filled the fruit jars and drank.

"Danny liked wine," they said. "Danny was happy when he had a little wine."

The afternoon passed, and the evening came. Each man, as he sipped his wine, roved through the past. At seven o'clock a shamed Tito Ralph came in with a box of cigars he had won on a punchboard. The friends lighted the cigars and spat, and opened the second gallon. Pablo tried a few notes of the song "Tuli Pan", to see whether his voice was gone for good.

"Cornelia Ruiz was alone to-day," Pilon said speculatively.

"Maybe it would be all right to sing a few sad songs," said Jesus Maria.

"But Danny did not like sad songs," Pablo insisted. "He liked the quick ones, about lively women."

They all nodded gravely. "Yes, Danny was a great one for women."

Pablo tried the second verse to "Tuli Pan", and Pilon helped a little, and the others joined in towards the end.

When the song was done, Pilon puffed at his cigar, but it had gone out. "Tito Ralph," he said, "why don't you get your guitar so we can sing a little better?" He lighted his cigar and flipped the match.

The little burning stick landed on an old newspaper against the wall. Each man started up to stamp it out; and each man was struck with a celestial thought, and settled back. They found one another's eyes and smiled the wise smiles of the deathless and hopeless ones. In a reverie they watched the flame flicker and nearly die, and sprout to life again. They saw it bloom on the paper. Thus do the gods speak with tiny causes. And the men smiled on as the paper burned and the dry wooden wall caught.

Thus must it be, O wise friends of Danny. The cord that bound you together is cut. The magnet that drew you has lost its virtue. Some stranger will own the house, some joyless relative of Danny's. Better that this symbol of holy friendship, this good house of parties and fights, of love and comfort, should die as Danny died, in one last glorious hopeless assault on the gods.

They sat and smiled. And the flame climbed like a snake to the ceiling and broke through the roof and roared. Only then did the friends get up from their chairs and walk like dreaming men out of the door.

Pilon, who profited by every lesson, took what was left of the wine with him.

The sirens screamed from Monterey. The trucks roared up the hill in second gear. The searchlights played among the trees. When the Department arrived, the house was one great blunt spear of flame. The hoses wet the trees and brush to keep the flames from spreading.

Among the crowding people of Tortilla Flat, Danny's friends stood entranced and watched until at last the house was a mound of black, steaming cinders. Then the fire trucks turned and coasted away down the hill.

The people of the Flat melted into the darkness. Danny's friends still stood looking at the smoking ruin. They looked at one another strangely, and then back at the burned house. And after a while they turned and walked slowly away, and no two walked together.

THE RED PONY

I

THE GIFT

II

THE GREAT MOUNTAINS

III

THE PROMISE

I

THE GIFT

AT DAYBREAK Billy Buck emerged from the bunk-house and stood for a moment on the porch looking up at the sky. He was a broad, bandy-legged little man with a walrus moustache, with square hands, puffed and muscled on the palms. His eyes were a contemplative, watery grey and the hair which protruded from under his Stetson hat was spiky and weathered. Billy was still stuffing his shirt into his blue jeans as he stood on the porch. He unbuckled his belt and tightened it again. The belt showed, by the worn, shiny places opposite each hole, the gradual increase of Billy's middle over a period of years. When he had seen to the weather, Billy cleared each nostril by holding its mate closed with his forefinger and blowing fiercely. Then he walked down to the barn, rubbing his hands together. He curried and brushed two saddle horses in the stalls, talking quietly to them all the time; and he had hardly finished when the iron triangle started ringing at the ranch-house. Billy stuck the brush and currycomb together and laid them on the rail and went up to breakfast. His action had been so deliberate and yet so wasteless of time that he came to the house while Mrs. Tiflin was still ringing the triangle. She nodded her grey head to him and withdrew into the kitchen. Billy Buck sat down on the steps, because he was a cow-hand, and it wouldn't be fitting that he should go first into the dining-room. He heard Mr. Tiflin in the house, stamping his feet into his boots.

The high jangling note of the triangle put the boy Jody in motion. He was only a little boy, ten years old, with hair like dusty yellow grass and with shy polite grey eyes, and with a mouth that worked when he thought. The triangle picked him up out of sleep. It didn't occur to him to disobey the harsh note. He never had; no one he knew ever had. He brushed the tangled hair out of his eyes and skinned his nightgown off. In a moment he was dressed—blue chambray shirt and overalls. It was late in the summer, so of course there were no shoes to bother with. In the kitchen he waited until his mother got from in front of the sink and went back to the stove. Then he washed himself and brushed back his wet hair with his fingers. His mother turned sharply on him as he left the sink. Jody looked shyly away.

"I've got to cut your hair before long," his mother said. "Breakfast's on the table. Go on in, so Billy can come."

Jody sat at the long table which was covered with white oilcloth washed through to the fabric in some places. The fried eggs lay in rows on their platter. Jody took three eggs on his plate and followed with three thick slices of crisp bacon. He carefully scraped a spot of blood from one of the egg yolks.

Billy Buck clumped in. "That won't hurt you," Billy explained. "That's only a sign the rooster leaves."

Jody's tall stern father came in then and Jody knew from the noise on the floor that he was wearing boots, but he looked under the table anyway, to make sure. His father turned off the oil lamp over the table, for plenty of morning light now came through the windows.

Jody did not ask where his father and Billy Buck were riding that day, but he wished he might go along. His father was a disciplinarian. Jody obeyed him in everything without questions of any kind. Now Carl Tiflin sat down and reached for the egg platter.

"Got the cows ready to go, Billy?" he asked.

"In the lower corral," Billy said. "I could just as well take them in alone."

"Sure you could. But a man needs company. Besides, your throat gets pretty dry." Carl Tiflin was jovial this morning.

Jody's mother put her head in the door. "What time do you think to be back, Carl?"

"I can't tell. I've got to see some men in Salinas. Might be gone till dark."

The eggs and coffee and big biscuits disappeared rapidly. Jody followed the two men out of the house. He watched them mount their horses and drive six old milk cows out of the corral and start over the hill towards Salinas. They were going to sell the old cows to the butcher.

When they had disappeared over the crown of the ridge Jody walked up the hill behind the house. The dogs trotted around the house corner hunching their shoulders and grinning horribly with pleasure. Jody patted their heads—Doubletree Mutt with the big thick tail and yellow eyes, and Smasher, the shepherd, who had killed a coyote and lost an ear doing it. Smasher's one good ear stood up higher than a collie's ear should. Billy Buck said that always happened. After the frenzied greeting the dogs lowered their noses to the ground in a business-like way and went ahead, looking back now and then to make sure that the boy was coming. They walked up through the chicken-yard and saw the quail eating with the chickens. Smasher chased the chickens a little to keep in practice in case there should ever be sheep to herd. Jody continued on through the large vegetable patch where the green corn was higher than his head. The cow-pumpkins were green and small yet. He went on to the sagebrush line where the cold spring ran out of its pipe and fell into a round wooden tub. He leaned over and drank close to the green mossy wood where the water tasted best. Then he turned and looked back on the ranch, on the low, whitewashed house girded with red geraniums, and on the long bunk-house by the cypress tree where Billy Buck lived alone. Jody could see the great black kettle under the cypress tree. That was where the pigs were scalded. The sun was coming over the ridge now, glaring on the whitewash of the houses and barns, making the wet grass blaze softly. Behind him, in the tall sagebrush, the birds were scampering on the ground, making a great noise among the dry leaves; the squirrels piped shrilly on the side-hills. Jody looked along at the farm buildings. He felt an uncertainty in the air, a feeling of change and of loss and of the gain of new and unfamiliar things. Over the hillside, two big black buzzards sailed low to the ground and their shadows slipped smoothly and quickly ahead of them. Some animal had died in the vicinity. Jody knew it. It might be a cow or it might be the remains of a rabbit. The buzzards overlooked nothing. Jody hated them as all decent things hate them, but they could not be hurt because they made away with carrion.

After a while the boy sauntered downhill again. The dogs had long ago given him up and gone into the brush to do things in their own way. Back through the vegetable garden he went, and he paused for a moment to smash a green musk-melon with his heel, but he was not happy about it. It was a bad thing to do, he knew perfectly well. He kicked dirt over the ruined melon to conceal it.

Back at the house his mother bent over his rough hands, inspecting his fingers and nails. It did little good to start him clean to school, for too many things could happen on the way. She sighed over the black cracks on his fingers, and then gave him his books and his lunch and started him on the mile walk to school. She noticed that his mouth was working a good deal this morning.

Jody started his journey. He filled his pockets with little pieces of white quartz that lay in the road, and every so often he took a shot at a bird or at some rabbit that had stayed sunning itself in the road too long. At the crossroads over the bridge he met two friends and the three of them walked to school together, making ridiculous strides and being rather silly. School had just opened two weeks before. There was still a spirit of revolt among the pupils.

It was four o'clock in the afternoon when Jody topped the hill and looked down on the ranch again. He looked for the saddle horses, but the corral was empty. His father was not back yet. He went slowly then towards the afternoon chores. At the ranch-house he found his mother sitting on the porch, mending socks.

"There's two doughnuts in the kitchen for you," she said. Jody slid to the kitchen, and returned with half of one of the doughnuts already eaten and his mouth full. His mother asked him what he had learned in school that day, but she didn't listen to his doughnut-muffled answer. She interrupted: "Jody, to-night see you fill the wood-box clear full. Last night you crossed the sticks and it wasn't only about half full. Lay the sticks flat to-night. And Jody, some of the hens are hiding eggs, or else the dogs are eating them. Look about in the grass and see if you can find any nests."

Jody, still eating, went out and did his chores. He saw the quail come down to eat with the chickens when he threw out the grain. For some reason his father was proud to have them come. He never allowed any shooting near the house for fear the quail might go away.

When the wood-box was full, Jody took his twenty-two rifle up to the cold spring at the brush line. He drank again and then aimed the gun at all manner of things, at rocks, at birds on the wing, at the big black pig kettle under the cypress tree, but he didn't shoot, for he had no cartridges and wouldn't have until he was twelve. If his father had seen him aim the rifle in the direction of the house he would have put the cartridges off another year. Jody remembered this and did not point the rifle down the hill again. Two years was enough to wait for cartridges. Nearly all of his father's presents were given with reservations which hampered their value somewhat. It was good discipline.

The supper waited until dark for his father to return. When at last he came in with Billy Buck, Jody could smell the delicious brandy on their breaths. Inwardly he rejoiced, for his father sometimes talked to him when he smelled of brandy, sometimes even told things he had done in the wild days when he was a boy.

After supper Jody sat by the fireplace and his shy, polite eyes sought the room corners, and he waited for his father to tell what it was he contained, for Jody knew he had news of some sort. But he was disappointed. His father pointed a stern finger at him.

"You'd better go to bed, Jody. I'm going to need you in the morning."

That wasn't so bad. Jody liked to do the things he had to do as long as they weren't routine things. He looked at the floor and his mouth worked out a question before he spoke it. "What are we going to do in the morning, kill a pig?" he asked softly.

"Never you mind. You better get to bed."

When the door was closed behind him, Jody heard his father and Billy Buck chuckling and he knew it was a joke of some kind. And later, when he lay in bed, trying to make words out of the murmurs in the other room, he heard his father protest, "But, Ruth, I didn't give much for him."

Jody heard the hoot-owls hunting mice down by the barn, and he heard a fruit-tree limb tap-tapping against the house. A cow was lowing when he went to sleep.

When the triangle sounded in the morning, Jody dressed more quickly even than usual. In the kitchen, while he washed his face and combed back his hair, his mother addressed him irritably. "Don't you go out until you get a good breakfast in you."

He went into the dining-room and sat at the long white table. He took a steaming hotcake from the platter, arranged two fried eggs on it, covered them with another hotcake and squashed the whole thing with his fork.

His father and Billy Buck came in. Jody knew from the sound on the floor that both of them were wearing flat-heeled shoes, but he peered under the table to make sure. His father turned off the oil lamp, for the day had arrived, and he looked stern and disciplinary, but Billy Buck didn't look at Jody at all. He avoided the shy questioning eyes of the boy and soaked a whole piece of toast in his coffee.

Carl Tiffin said crossly, "You come with us after breakfast!"

Jody had trouble with his food then, for he felt a kind of doom in the air. After Billy had tilted his saucer and drained the coffee which had slopped into it, and had wiped his hands on his jeans, the two men stood up from the table and went out into the morning light together, and Jody respectfully followed a little behind them. He tried to keep his mind from running ahead, tried to keep it absolutely motionless.

His mother called, "Carl! Don't you let it keep him from school."

They marched past the cypress, where a single-tree hung from a limb to butcher the pigs on, and past the black iron kettle, so it was not a pig-killing. The sun shone over the hill and threw long, dark shadows of the trees and buildings. They crossed a stubble-field to short-cut to the barn. Jody's father unhooked the door and they went in. They had been walking toward the sun on the way down. The barn was black as night in contrast and warm from the hay and from the beasts. Jody's father moved over toward the one box stall. "Come here!" he ordered. Jody could begin to see things now. He looked into the box stall and then stepped back quickly.

A red pony colt was looking at him out of the stall. Its tense ears were forward and a light of disobedience was in its eyes. Its coat was rough and thick as an Airedale's fur and its mane was long and tangled. Jody's throat collapsed in on itself and cut his breath short.

"He needs a good currying," his father said, "and if I ever hear of you not feeding him or leaving his stall dirty, I'll sell him off in a minute."

Jody couldn't bear to look at the pony's eyes any more. He gazed down at his hands for a moment, and he asked very shyly: "Mine?" No one answered him. He put his hand out toward the pony. Its grey nose came close, sniffing loudly, and then the lip drew back and the strong teeth closed on Jody's fingers. The pony shook its head up and down and seemed to laugh with amusement. Jody regarded his bruised fingers. "Well," he said with pride—"well, I guess he can bite all right." The two men laughed, somewhat in relief. Carl Tiflin went out of the barn and walked up a side-hill to be by himself, for he was embarrassed, but Billy Buck stayed. It was easier to talk to Billy Buck. Jody asked again—"Mine?"

Billy became professional in tone. "Sure! That is, if you look out for him and break him right. I'll show you how. He's just a colt. You can't ride him for some time."

Jody put out his bruised hand again, and this time the red pony let his nose be rubbed. "It ought to have a carrot," Jody said. "Where'd we get him, Billy?"

"Bought him at a sheriff's auction," Billy explained. "A show went broke in Salinas and had debts. The sheriff was selling off their stuff."

The pony stretched out his nose and shook the forelock from his wild eyes. Jody stroked the nose a little. He said softly, "There isn't a—saddle?"

Billy Buck laughed. "I'd forgot. Come along."

In the harness room he lifted down a little saddle of red morocco leather. "It's just a show saddle," Billy Buck said disparagingly. "It isn't practical for the brush, but it was cheap at the sale."

Jody couldn't trust himself to look at the saddle either, and he couldn't speak at all. He brushed the shining red leather with his finger-tips, and after a long while he said, "It'll look pretty on him, though." He thought of the grandest and prettiest things he knew. "If he hasn't a name already, I think I'll call him Gabilan Mountains," he said.

Billy Buck knew how he felt. "It's a pretty long name. Why don't you call him Gabilan? That means hawk. That would be a fine name for him." Billy felt glad. "If you will collect tail hair, I might be able to make a hair rope for you sometime. You could use it for a hackamore."

Jody wanted to go back to the box stall. "Could I lead him to school, do you think—to show the kids?"

But Billy shook his head. "He's not even halter-broke yet. We had a time getting him here. Had to almost drag him. You better be starting for school, though."

"I'll bring the kids to see him here this afternoon," Jody said.

Six boys came over the hill half an hour early that afternoon, running hard, their heads down, their forearms working, their breath whistling. They swept by the house and cut across the stubble-field to the barn. And then they stood self-consciously before the pony, and then they looked at Jody with eyes in which there was a new admiration and a new respect. Before to-day Jody had been a boy, dressed in overalls and a blue shirt—quieter than most, even suspected of being a little cowardly. And now he was different. Out of a thousand centuries they drew the ancient admiration of the footman for the horseman. They knew instinctively that a man on a horse is spiritually as well as physically bigger than a man on foot. They knew that Jody had been miraculously lifted out of equality with them, and had been placed over them. Gabilan put his head out of the stall and sniffed them.

"Why'n't you ride him?" the boys cried. "Why'n't you braid his tail with ribbons like in the fair?" "When you going to ride him?"

Jody's courage was up. He too felt the superiority of the horseman. "He's not old enough. Nobody can ride him for a long time. I'm going to train him on the long halter. Billy Buck is going to show me how."

"Well, can't we even lead him around a little?"

"He isn't even halter-broke," Jody said. He wanted to be completely alone when he took the pony out for the first time. "Come and see the saddle."

They were speechless at the red morocco saddle, completely shocked out of comment. "It isn't much use in the brush," Jody explained. "It'll look pretty on him, though. Maybe I'll ride bareback when I go into the brush."

"How you going to rope a cow without a saddle horn?"

"Maybe I'll get another saddle for every day. My father might want me to help him with the stock." He let them feel the red saddle, and showed them the brass chain throat-latch on the bridle and the big brass buttons at each temple where the headstall and brow band crossed. The whole thing was too wonderful. They had to go away after a little while, and each boy, in his mind, searched among his possessions for a bribe worthy of offering in return for a ride on the red pony when the time should come.

Jody was glad when they had gone. He took brush and currycomb from the wall, took down the barrier of the box stall and stepped cautiously in. The pony's eyes glittered, and he edged around into kicking position. But Jody touched him on the shoulder and rubbed his high arched neck as he had always seen Billy Buck do, and he crooned, "So-o-o, Boy," in a deep voice. The pony gradually relaxed his tenseness. Jody curried and brushed until a pile of dead hair lay in the stall and until the pony's coat had taken on a deep red shine. Each time he finished he thought it might have been done better. He braided the mane into a dozen little pigtails, and he braided the forelock, and then he undid them and brushed the hair out straight again.

Jody did not hear his mother enter the barn. She was angry when she came, but when she looked in at the pony and at Jody working over him, she felt a curious pride rise up in her. "Have you forgot the wood-box?" she asked gently. "It's not far off from dark and there's not a stick of wood in the house, and the chickens aren't fed."

Jody quickly put up his tools. "I forgot, ma'am."

"Well, after this do your chores first. Then you won't forget. I expect you'll forget lots of things now if I don't keep an eye on you."

"Can I have carrots from the garden for him, ma'am?"

She had to think about that. "Oh—I guess so, if you only take the big tough ones."

"Carrots keep the coat good," he said, and again she felt the curious rush of pride.

Jody never waited for the triangle to get him out of bed after the coming of the pony. It became his habit to creep out of bed even before his mother was awake, to slip into his clothes and to go quietly down to the barn to see Gabilan. In the grey quiet mornings when the land and the brush and the houses and the trees were silver-grey and black like a photograph negative, he stole toward the barn, past the sleeping stones and the sleeping cypress tree. The turkeys, roosting in the tree out of coyotes' reach, clicked drowsily. The fields glowed with a grey frost-like light and in the dew the tracks of rabbits and of fieldmice stood out sharply. The good dogs came stiffly out of their little houses, hackles up and deep growls in their throats. Then they caught Jody's scent, and their stiff tails rose up and waved a greeting—Doubletree Mutt with the big thick tail, and Smasher, the incipient shepherd—then went lazily back to their warm beds.

It was a strange time and a mysterious journey, to Jody—an extension of a dream. When he first had the pony he liked to torture himself during the trip by thinking Gabilan would not be in his stall, and worse, would never have been there. And he had other delicious little self-induced pains. He thought how the rats had gnawed ragged holes in the red saddle, and how the mice had nibbled Gabilan's tail until it was stringy and thin. He usually ran the last little way to the barn. He unlatched the rusty hasp of the barn door and stepped in, and, no matter how quietly he opened the door, Gabilan was always looking at him over the barrier of the box stall and Gabilan whinnied softly and stamped his front foot, and his eyes had big sparks of red fire in them like oakwood embers.

Sometimes, if the work-horses were to be used that day, Jody found Billy Buck in the barn harnessing and currying. Billy stood with him and looked long at Gabilan and he told Jody a great many things about horses. He explained that they were terribly afraid for their feet, so that one must make a practice of lifting the legs and patting the hooves and ankles to remove their terror. He told Jody how horses love conversation. He must talk to the pony all the time, and tell him the reasons for everything. Billy wasn't sure a horse could understand everything that was said to him, but it was impossible to say how much was understood. A horse never kicked up a fuss if someone he liked explained things to him. Billy could give examples, too. He had known, for instance, a horse nearly dead-beat with fatigue to perk up when told it was only a little farther to his destination. And he had known a horse paralysed with fright to come out of it when his rider told him what it was that was frightening him. While he talked in the mornings, Billy Buck cut twenty or thirty straws into neat three-inch lengths and stuck them into his hat-band. Then, during the whole day, if he wanted to pick his teeth or merely to chew on something, he had only to reach up for one of them.

Jody listened carefully, for he knew and the whole country knew that Billy Buck was a fine hand with horses. Billy's own horse was a stringy cayuse with a hammer head, but he nearly always won the first prizes at the stock trials. Billy could rope a steer, take a double half-hitch about the horn with his riata, and dismount, and his horse would play the steer as an angler plays a fish, keeping a tight rope until the steer was down or beaten.

Every morning, after Jody had curried and brushed the pony, he let down the barrier of the stall, and Gabilan thrust past him and raced down the barn and into the corral. Around and around he galloped, and sometimes he jumped forward and landed on stiff legs. He stood quivering, stiff ears forward, eyes rolling so that the whites showed, pretending to be frightened. At last he walked snorting to the water-trough and buried his nose in the water up to the nostrils. Jody was proud then, for he knew that was the way to judge a horse. Poor horses only touched their lips to the water, but a fine spirited beast put his whole nose and mouth under, and only left room to breathe.

Then Jody stood and watched the pony, and he saw things he had never noticed about any other horse, the sleek, sliding flank muscles and the cords of the buttocks, which flexed like a closing fist, and the shine the sun put on the red coat. Having seen horses all his life, Jody had never looked at them very closely before. But now he noticed the moving ears which gave expression and even inflection of expression to the face. The pony talked with his ears. You could tell exactly how he felt about everything by the way his ears pointed. Sometimes they were stiff and upright and sometimes lax and sagging. They went back when he was angry or fearful, and forward when he was anxious and curious and pleased; and their exact position indicated which emotion he had.

Billy Buck kept his word. In the early fall the training began. First there was the halter-breaking, and that was the hardest because it was the first thing. Jody held a carrot and coaxed and promised and pulled on the rope. The pony set his feet like a burro when he felt the strain. But before long he learned. Jody walked all over the ranch leading him. Gradually he took to dropping the rope until the pony followed him unled wherever he went.

And then came the training on the long halter. That was slower work. Jody stood in the middle of the circle, holding the long halter. He clucked with his tongue and the pony started to walk in a big circle, held in by the long rope. He clucked again to make the pony trot, and again to make him gallop. Around and around Gabilan went thundering and enjoying it immensely. Then he called "Whoa," and the pony stopped. It was not long until Gabilan was perfect at it. But in many ways he was a bad pony. He bit Jody in the legs and stomped on Jody's feet. Now and then his ears went back and he aimed a tremendous kick at the boy. Every time he did one of these bad things, Gabilan settled back and seemed to laugh at himself.

Billy Buck worked at the hair rope in the evenings before the fireplace. Jody collected tail hair in a bag, and he sat and watched Billy slowly constructing the rope, twisting a few hairs to make a string and rolling two strings together for a cord, and then braiding a number of cords to make the rope. Billy rolled the finished rope on the floor under his foot to make it round and hard.

The long halter work rapidly approached perfection. Jody's father, watching the pony stop and start and trot and gallop, was a little bothered by it.

"He's getting to be almost a trick pony," he complained. "I don't like trick horses. It takes all the—dignity out of a horse to make him do tricks. Why, a trick horse is kind of like an actor—no dignity, no character of his own." And his father said, "I guess you better be getting him used to the saddle pretty soon."

Jody rushed for the harness-room. For some time he had been riding the saddle on a saw-horse. He changed the stirrup length over and over, and could never get it just right. Sometimes, mounted on the saw-horse in the harness-room, with collars and hames and tugs hung all about him, Jody rode out beyond the room. He carried his rifle across the pommel. He saw the fields go flying by, and he heard the beat of the galloping hoofs.

. . . .

It was a ticklish job, saddling the pony the first time. Gabilan hunched and reared and threw the saddle off before the cinch could be tightened. It had to be replaced again and again until at last the pony let it stay. And the cinching was difficult, too. Day by day Jody tightened the girth a little more until at last the pony didn't mind the saddle at all.

Then there was the bridle. Billy explained how to use a stick of licorice for a bit until Gabilan was used to having something in his mouth. Billy explained, "Of course we could force-break him to everything, but he wouldn't be as good a horse if we did. He'd always be a little bit afraid, and he wouldn't mind because he wanted to."

The first time the pony wore the bridle he whipped his head about and worked his tongue against the bit until the blood oozed from the corners of his mouth. He tried to rub the headstall off on the manger. His ears pivoted about and his eyes turned red with fear and with general devilishness. Jody rejoiced, for he knew that only a mean-souled horse does not resent training.

And Jody trembled when he thought of the time when he would first sit in the saddle. The pony would probably throw him off. There was no disgrace in that. The disgrace would come if he did not get right up and mount again. Sometimes he dreamed that he lay in the dirt and cried and couldn't make himself mount again. The shame of the dream lasted until the middle of the day.

Gabilan was growing fast. Already he had lost the long-leggedness of the colt; his mane was getting longer and blacker. Under the constant currying and brushing his coat lay as smooth and gleaming as orange-red lacquer. Jody oiled the hoofs and kept them carefully trimmed so they would not crack.

The hair rope was nearly finished. Jody's father gave him an old pair of spurs and bent in the side bars and cut down the strap and took up the chainlets until they fitted. And then one day Carl Tiflin said:

"The pony's growing faster than I thought. I guess you can ride him by Thanksgiving. Think you can stick on?"

"I don't know," said Jody shyly. Thanksgiving was only three weeks off. He hoped it wouldn't rain, for rain would spot the red saddle.

Gabilan knew and liked Jody by now. He nickered when Jody came across the stubble-field, and in the pasture he came running when his master whistled for him. There was always a carrot for him every time.

Billy Buck gave him riding instructions over and over. "Now when you get up there, just grab tight with your knees and keep your hands away from the saddle, and if you get throwed, don't let that stop you. No matter how good a man is, there's always some horse can pitch him. You just climb up again before he gets to feeling smart about it. Pretty soon, he won't throw you no more, and pretty soon he can't throw you no more. That's the way to do it."

"I hope it don't rain before," Jody said.

"Why not? Don't want to get throwed in the mud?"

That was partly it, and also he was afraid that in the flurry of bucking Gabilan might slip and fall on him and break his leg or his hip. He had seen that happen to men before, had seen how they writhed on the ground like squashed bugs, and he was afraid of it.

He practised on the saw-horse how he would hold the reins in his left hand and a hat in his right hand. If he kept his hands thus busy, he couldn't grab the horn if he felt himself going off. He didn't like to think of what would happen if he did grab the horn. Perhaps his father and Billy Buck would never speak to him again, they would be so ashamed. The news would get about and his mother would be ashamed too. And in the school yard—it was too awful to contemplate.

He began putting his weight in a stirrup when Gabilan was saddled, but he didn't throw his leg over the pony's back. That was forbidden until Thanksgiving.

Every afternoon he put the red saddle on the pony and cinched it tight. The pony was learning already to fill his stomach out unnaturally large while the cinching was going on, and then to let it down when the straps were fixed. Sometimes Jody led him up to the brush line and let him drink from the round green tub, and sometimes he led him up through the stubble-field to the hill-top from which it was possible to see the white town of Salinas and the geometric fields of the great valley, and the oak trees clipped by the sheep. Now and then they broke through the brush and came to little cleared circles so hedged in that the world was gone and only the sky and the circle of brush were left from the old life. Gabilan liked these trips and showed it by keeping his head very high and by quivering his nostrils with interest. When the two came back from an expedition they smelled of the sweet sage they had forced through.

Time dragged on toward Thanksgiving, but winter came fast. The clouds swept down and hung all day over the land and brushed the hilltops, and the winds blew shrilly at night. All day the dry oak-leaves drifted down from the trees until they covered the ground and yet the trees were unchanged.

Jody had wished it might not rain before Thanksgiving, but it did. The brown earth turned dark and the trees glistened. The cut ends of the stubble turned black with mildew; the haystacks greyed from exposure to the damp, and on the roofs the moss, which had been all summer as grey as lizards, turned a brilliant yellow-green. During the week of rain Jody kept the pony in the box stall out of the dampness, except for a little time after school when he took him out for exercise and to drink at the water-trough in the upper corral. Not once did Gabilan get wet.

The wet weather continued until little new grass appeared. Jody walked to school dressed in a slicker and short rubber boots. At length one morning the sun came out brightly. Jody, at his work in the box stall, said to Billy Buck, "Maybe I'll leave Gabilan in the corral when I go to school to-day."

"Be good for him out in the sun," Billy assured him. "No animal likes to be cooped up too long. Your father and me are going back on the hill to clean the leaves out of the spring." Billy nodded and picked his teeth with one of his little straws.

"If the rain comes, though——" Jody suggested.

"Not likely to rain to-day. She's rained herself out." Billy pulled up his sleeves and snapped his arm bands. "If it comes on to rain—why, a little rain don't hurt a horse."

"Well, if it does come on to rain, you put him in, will you, Billy? I'm scared he might get cold so I couldn't ride him when the time comes."

"Oh, sure! I'll watch out for him if we get back in time. But it won't rain to-day."

And so Jody, when he went to school, left Gabilan standing out in the corral.

Billy Buck wasn't wrong about many things. He couldn't be. But he was wrong about the weather that day, for a little after noon the clouds pushed over the hills and the rain began to pour down. Jody heard it start on the school-house roof. He considered holding up one finger for permission to go to the outhouse and, once outside, running for home to put the pony in. Punishment would be prompt both at school and at home. He gave it up and took ease from Billy's assurance that rain couldn't hurt a horse. When school was finally out, he hurried home through the dark rain. The banks at the sides of the road spouted little jets of muddy water. The rain slanted and swirled under a cold and gusty wind. Jody dog-trotted home, slopping through the gravelly mud of the road.

From the top of the ridge he could see Gabilan standing miserably in the corral. The red coat was almost black, and streaked with water. He stood head down with his rump to the rain and wind. Jody arrived running and threw open the barn door and led the wet pony in by his forelock. Then he found a gunny sack and rubbed the soaked hair and rubbed the legs and ankles. Gabilan stood patiently, but he trembled in gusts like the wind.

When he had dried the pony as well as he could, Jody went up to the house and brought hot water down to the barn and soaked the grain in it. Gabilan was not very hungry. He nibbled at the hot mash, but he was not very much interested in it, and he still shivered now and then. A little steam rose from his damp back.

It was almost dark when Billy Buck and Carl Tiflin came home. "When the rain started we put up at Ben Herche's place, and the rain never let up all afternoon," Carl Tiflin explained. Jody looked reproachfully at Billy Buck and Billy felt guilty.

"You said it wouldn't rain," Jody accused him.

Billy looked away. "It's hard to tell, this time of year," he said, but his excuse was lame. He had no right to be fallible, and he knew it.

"The pony got wet, got soaked through."

"Did you dry him off?"

"I rubbed him with a sack and I gave him hot grain."

Billy nodded in agreement.

"Do you think he'll take cold, Billy?"

"A little rain never hurt anything," Billy assured him.

Jody's father joined the conversation then and lectured the boy a little. "A horse," he said, "isn't any lap-dog kind of thing." Carl Tiflin hated weakness and sickness, and he held a violent contempt for helplessness.

Jody's mother put a platter of steaks on the table and boiled potatoes and boiled squash, which clouded the room with their steam. They sat down to eat. Carl Tiflin still grumbled about weakness put into animals and men by too much coddling.

Billy Buck felt bad about his mistake. "Did you blanket him?" he asked.

"No. I couldn't find any blanket. I laid some sacks over his back."

"We'll go down and cover him up after we eat, then." Billy felt better about it then. When Jody's father had gone in to the fire and his mother was washing dishes, Billy found and lighted a lantern. He and Jody walked through the mud to the barn. The barn was dark and warm and sweet. The horses still munched their evening hay. "You hold the lantern!" Billy ordered. And he felt the pony's legs and tested the heat of the flanks. He put his cheek against the pony's grey muzzle and then he rolled up the eyelids to look at the eyeballs and he lifted the lips to see the gums, and he put his fingers inside the ears. "He don't seem so chipper," Billy said. "I'll give him a rub-down."

Then Billy found a sack and rubbed the pony's legs violently and he rubbed the chest and the withers. Gabilan was strangely spiritless. He submitted patiently to the rubbing. At last Billy brought an old cotton comforter from the saddle-room, and threw it over the pony's back and tied it at neck and chest with string.

"Now he'll be all right in the morning," Billy said.

Jody's mother looked up when he got back to the house. "You're late up from bed," she said. She held his chin in her hard hand and brushed the tangled hair out of his eyes and she said, "Don't worry about the pony. He'll be all right. Billy's as good as any horse-doctor in the country."

Jody hadn't known she could see his worry. He pulled gently away from her and knelt down in front of the fireplace until it burned his stomach. He scorched himself through and then went in to bed, but it was a hard thing to go to sleep. He awakened after what seemed a long time. The room was dark, but there was a greyness in the window like that which precedes the dawn. He got up and found his overalls and searched for the legs, and then the clock in the other room struck two. He laid his clothes down and got back into bed. It was broad daylight when he awakened again. For the first time he had slept through the ringing of the triangle. He leaped up, flung on his clothes and went out of the door still buttoning his shirt. His mother looked after him for a moment and then went quietly back to her work. Her eyes were brooding and kind. Now and then her mouth smiled a little, but without changing her eyes at all.

Jody ran on toward the barn. Half-way there he heard the sound he dreaded, the hollow rasping cough of a horse. He broke into a sprint then. In the barn he found Billy Buck with the pony, Billy was rubbing its legs with his strong thick hands. He looked up and smiled gaily. "He just took a little cold," Billy said. "We'll have him out of it in a couple of days."

Jody looked at the pony's face. The eyes were half closed and the lids thick and dry. In the eye corners a crust of hard mucus stuck. Gabilan's ears hung loosely sideways and his head was low. Jody put out his hand, but the pony did not move close to it. He coughed again and his whole body constricted with the effort. A little stream of thin fluid ran from his nostrils.

Jody looked back at Billy Buck. "He's awful sick, Billy."

"Just a little cold, like I said," Billy insisted. "You go get some breakfast and then go back to school. I'll take care of him."

"But you might have to do something else. You might leave him."

"No, I won't. I won't leave him at all. To-morrow's Saturday. Then you can stay with him all day." Billy had failed again, and he felt badly about it. He had to cure the pony now.

Jody walked up to the house and took his place listlessly at the table. The eggs and bacon were cold and greasy, but he didn't notice it. He ate his usual amount. He didn't even ask to stay home from school. His mother pushed his hair back when she took his plate. "Billy'll take care of the pony," she assured him.

He moped through the whole day at school. He couldn't answer any questions nor read any words. He couldn't even tell anyone the pony was sick, for that might make him sicker. And when school was finally out he started home in dread. He walked slowly and let the other boys leave him. He wished he might continue walking and never arrive at the ranch.

Billy was in the barn, as he had promised, and the pony was worse. His eyes were almost closed now, and his breath whistled shrilly past an obstruction in his nose. A film covered that part of the eyes that was visible at all. It was doubtful whether the pony could see any more. Now and then he snorted, to clear his nose, and by the action seemed to plug it tighter. Jody looked dispiritedly at the pony's coat. The hair lay rough and unkempt and seemed to have lost all of its old lustre. Billy stood quietly beside the stall. Jody hated to ask, but he had to know.

"Billy, is he—is he going to get well?"

Billy put his fingers between the bars under the pony's jaw and felt about. "Feel there," he said and he guided Jody's fingers to a large lump under the jaw. "When that gets bigger, I'll open it up and then he'll get better."

Jody looked quickly away, for he had heard about that lump. "What is it the matter with him?"

Billy didn't want to answer, but he had to. He couldn't be wrong three times. "Strangles," he said shortly, "but don't you worry about that. I'll pull him out of it. I've seen them get well when they were worse than Gabilan is. I'm going to steam him now. You can help."

"Yes," Jody said miserably. He followed Billy into the grain-room and watched him make the steaming bag ready. It was a long canvas nose-bag with straps to go over a horse's ears. Billy filled it one-third full of bran and then he added a couple of handfuls of dried hops. On top of the dry substance he poured a little carbolic acid and a little turpentine. "I'll be mixing it all up while you run to the house for a kettle of boiling water," Billy said.

When Jody came back with the steaming kettle, Billy buckled the straps over Gabilan's head and fitted the bag tightly around his nose. Then through a little hole in the side of the bag he poured the boiling water on the mixture. The pony started away as a cloud of strong steam rose up, but then the soothing fumes crept through his nose and into his lungs, and the sharp steam began to clear out the nasal passages. He breathed loudly. His legs trembled in an ague, and his eyes closed against the biting cloud. Billy poured in more water and kept the steam rising for fifteen minutes. At last he set down the kettle and took the bag from Gabilan's nose. The pony looked better. He breathed freely, and his eyes were open wider than they had been.

"See how good it makes him feel," Billy said. "Now we'll wrap him up in the blanket again. Maybe he'll be nearly well by morning."

"I'll stay with him to-night," Jody suggested.

"No. Don't you do it. I'll bring my blankets down here and put them in the hay. You can stay to-morrow and steam him if he needs it."

The evening was falling when they went to the house for their supper. Jody didn't even realize that someone else had fed the chickens and filled the wood-box. He walked up past the house to the dark brush line and took a drink of water from the tub. The spring water was so cold that it stung his mouth and drove a shiver through him. The sky above the hills was still light. He saw a hawk flying so high that it caught the sun on its breast and shone like a spark. Two blackbirds were driving him down the sky, glittering as they attacked their enemy. In the west the clouds were moving in to rain again.

Jody's father didn't speak at all while the family ate supper, but after Billy Buck had taken his blankets and gone to sleep in the barn, Carl Tiflin built a high fire in the fireplace and told stories. He told about the wild man who ran naked through the country and had a tail and ears like a horse, and he told about the rabbit-cats of Moro Cojo that hopped into the trees for birds. He revived the famous Maxwell brothers who found a vein of gold and hid the traces of it so carefully that they could never find it again.

Jody sat with his chin in his hands; his mouth worked nervously, and his father gradually became aware that he wasn't listening very carefully. "Isn't that funny?" he asked.

Jody laughed politely and said, "Yes, sir." His father was angry and hurt then. He didn't tell any more stories. After a while, Jody took a lantern and went down to the barn. Billy Buck was asleep in the hay, and, except that his breath rasped a little in his lungs, the pony seemed to be much better. Jody stayed a little while, running his fingers over the red rough coat, and then he took up the lantern and went back to the house. When he was in bed, his mother came into the room.

"Have you enough covers on? It's getting winter."

"Yes, ma'am."

"Well, get some rest to-night." She hesitated to go out, stood uncertainly. "The pony will be all right," she said.

Jody was tired. He went to sleep quickly and didn't awaken until dawn. The triangle sounded, and Billy Buck came up from the barn before Jody could get out of the house.

"How is he?" Jody demanded.

Billy always wolfed his breakfast. "Pretty good. I'm going to open that lump this morning. Then he'll be better maybe."

After breakfast Billy got out his best knife, one with a needle point. He whetted the shining blade a long time on a little carborundum stone. He tried the point and the blade again and again on his calloused thumb-ball, and at last he tried it on his upper lip.

On the way to the barn, Jody noticed how the young grass was up and how the stubble was melting day by day into the new green crop of volunteer. It was a cold sunny morning.

As soon as he saw the pony, Jody knew he was worse. His eyes were closed and sealed shut with dried mucus. His head hung so low that his nose almost touched the straw of his bed. There was a little groan in each breath, a deep-seated patient groan.

Billy lifted the weak head and made a quick slash with the knife. Jody saw the yellow pus run out. He held up the head while Billy swabbed out the wound with weak carbolic acid salve.

"Now he'll feel better," Billy assured him. "That yellow poison is what makes him sick."

Jody looked unbelievingly at Billy Buck. "He's awful sick."

Billy thought a long time what to say. He nearly tossed off a careless assurance, but he saved himself in time. "Yes, he's pretty sick," he said at last. "I've seen worse ones get well. If he doesn't get pneumonia, we'll pull him through. You stay with him. If he gets worse, you can come and get me."

For a long time after Billy went away, Jody stood beside the pony stroking him behind the ears. The pony didn't flip his head the way he had done when he was well. The groaning in his breathing was becoming more hollow.

Doubletree Mutt looked into the barn, his big tail waving provocatively, and Jody was so incensed at his health that he found a hard black clod on the floor and deliberately threw it. Doubletree Mutt went yelping away to nurse a bruised paw.

In the middle of the morning Billy Buck came back and made another steam-bag. Jody watched to see whether the pony improved this time as he had before. His breathing eased a little, but he did not raise his head.

The Saturday dragged on. Late in the afternoon Jody went to the house and brought his bedding down and made up a place to sleep in the hay. He didn't ask permission. He knew from the way his mother looked at him that she would let him do almost anything. That night he left a lantern burning on a wire over the box stall. Billy had told him to rub the pony's legs every little while.

At nine o'clock the wind sprang up and howled around the barn. And in spite of his worry, Jody grew sleepy. He got into his blankets and went to sleep, but the breathy groans of the pony sounded in his dreams. And in his sleep he heard a crashing noise which went on and on until it awakened him. The wind was rushing through the barn. He sprang up and looked down the lane of stalls. The barn door had blown open, and the pony was gone.

He caught the lantern and ran outside into the gale, and he saw Gabilan weakly shambling away into the darkness, head down, legs working slowly and mechanically. When Jody ran up and caught him by the forelock, he allowed himself to be led back and put into his stall. His groans were louder, and a fierce whistling came from his nose. Jody didn't sleep any more then. The hissing of the pony's breath grew louder and sharper.

He was glad when Billy Buck came in at dawn. Billy looked for a time at the pony as though he had never seen him before. He felt the ears and flanks. "Jody," he said, "I've got to do something you won't want to see. You run up to the house for a while."

Jody grabbed him fiercely by the forearm. "You're not going to shoot him?"

Billy patted his hand. "No. I'm going to open a little hole in his windpipe so he can breathe. His nose is filled up. When he gets well, we'll put a little brass button in the hole for him to breathe through."

Jody couldn't have gone away if he had wanted to. It was awful to see the red hide cut, but infinitely more terrible to know it was being cut and not to see it. "I'll stay right here," he said bitterly. "You sure you got to?"

"Yes. I'm sure. If you stay, you can hold his head. If it doesn't make you sick, that is."

The fine knife came out again and was whetted again just as carefully as it had been the first time. Jody held the pony's head up and the throat taut, while Billy felt up and down for the right place. Jody sobbed once as the bright knife-point disappeared into the throat. The pony plunged weakly away and then stood still, trembling violently. The blood ran thickly out and up the knife and across Billy's hand and into his shirt-sleeve. The sure square hand sawed out a round hole in the flesh, and the breath came bursting out of the hole, throwing a fine spray of blood. With the rush of oxygen, the pony took a sudden strength. He lashed out with his hind feet and tried to rear, but Jody held his head down while Billy mopped the new wound with carbolic salve. It was a good job. The blood stopped flowing and the air puffed out the hole and sucked it in regularly with a little bubbling noise.

The rain brought in by the night wind began to fall on the barn roof. Then the triangle rang for breakfast. "You go up and eat while I wait," Billy said. "We've got to keep this hole from plugging up."

Jody walked slowly out of the barn. He was too dispirited to tell Billy the barn door had blown open and let the pony out. He emerged into the wet gloomy morning and sloshed up to the house, taking perverse pleasure in splashing through all the puddles. His mother fed him and put dry clothes on. She didn't question him. She seemed to know he couldn't answer questions. But when he was ready to go back to the barn she brought him a pan of steaming meal. "Give him this," she said.

But Jody did not take the pan. He said, "He won't eat anything," and ran out of the house. At the barn, Billy showed him how to fix a ball of cotton on a stick, with which to swab out the breathing-hole when it became clogged with mucus.

Jody's father walked into the barn and stood with them in front of the stall. At length he turned to the boy. "Hadn't you better come with me? I'm going to drive over the hill." Jody shook his head. "You better come on, out of this," his father insisted.

Billy turned on him angrily. "Let him alone. It's his pony, isn't it?"

Carl Tiflin walked away without saying another word. His feelings were badly hurt.

All morning, Jody kept the wound open and the air passing in and out freely. At noon the pony lay wearily down on his side and stretched his nose out.

Billy came back. "If you're going to stay with him to-night, you had better take a little nap," he said. Jody went absently out of the barn. The sky had cleared to a hard thin blue. Everywhere the birds were busy with worms that had come to the damp surface of the ground.

Jody walked to the brush line and sat on the edge of the mossy tub. He looked down at the house and at the old bunk-house and at the dark cypress tree. The place was familiar, but curiously changed. It wasn't itself any more, but a frame for things that were happening. A cold wind blew out of the east now, signifying that the rain was over for a little while. At his feet Jody could see the little arms of new weeds spreading out over the ground. In the mud about the spring were thousands of quail tracks.

Doubletree Mutt came sideways and embarrassed up through the vegetable patch, and Jody, remembering how he had thrown the clod, put his arm about the dog's neck and kissed him on his wide black nose. Doubletree Mutt sat still, as though he knew some solemn thing was happening. His big tail slapped the ground gravely. Jody pulled a swollen tick out of Mutt's neck and popped it dead between his thumb-nails. It was a nasty thing. He washed his hands in the cold spring water.

Except for the steady swish of the wind, the farm was very quiet. Jody knew his mother wouldn't mind if he didn't go in to eat his lunch. After a little while he went slowly back to the barn. Mutt crept into his own little house and whined softly to himself for a long time.

Billy Buck stood up from the box and surrendered the cotton swab. The pony still lay on his side and the wound in his throat bellowed in and out. When Jody saw how dry and dead the hair looked, he knew at last that there was no hope for the pony. He had seen the dead hair before on dogs and on cows, and it was a sure sign. He sat heavily on the box and let down the barrier of the box stall. For a long time he kept his eyes on the moving wound, and at last he dozed, and the afternoon passed quickly. Just before dark his mother brought a deep dish of stew and left it for him and went away. Jody ate a little of it, and when it was dark he set the lantern on the floor by the pony's head, so he could watch the wound and keep it open. And he dozed again until the night chill awakened him. The wind was blowing fiercely, bringing the north cold with it. Jody brought a blanket from his bed in the hay and wrapped himself in it. Gabilan's breathing was quiet at last; the hole in his throat moved gently. The owls flew through the hayloft, shrieking and looking for mice. Jody put his head down on his hands and slept. In his sleep he was aware that the wind had increased. He heard it slamming about the barn.

It was daylight when he awakened. The barn door had swung open. The pony was gone. He sprang up and ran out into the morning light.

The pony's tracks were plain enough, dragging through the frost-like dew on the young grass, tired tracks with little lines between them where the hoofs had dragged. They headed for the brush line half-way up the ridge. Jody broke into a run and followed them. The sun shone on the sharp white quartz that stuck through the ground here and there. As he followed the plain trail, a shadow cut across in front of him. He looked up and saw a high circle of black buzzards, and the slowly revolving circle dropped lower and lower. The solemn birds soon disappeared over the ridge. Jody ran faster then, forced on by panic and rage. The trail entered the brush at last and followed a winding route among the tall sage bushes.

At the top of the ridge Jody was winded. He paused, puffing noisily. The blood pounded in his ears. Then he saw what he was looking for. Below, in one of the little clearings in the brush, lay the red pony. In the distance, Jody could see the legs moving slowly and convulsively. And in a circle around him stood the buzzards, waiting for the moment of death they know so well.

Jody leaped forward and plunged down the hill. The wet ground muffled his steps and the brush hid him. When he arrived, it was all over. The first buzzard sat on the pony's head and its beak had just risen dripping with dark eye fluid. Jody plunged into the circle like a cat. The black brotherhood arose in a cloud, but the big one on the pony's head was too late. As it hopped along to take off, Jody caught its wing tip and pulled it down. It was nearly as big as he was. The free wing crashed into his face with the force of a club, but he hung on. The claws fastened on his leg and the wing elbows battered his head on either side. Jody groped blindly with his free hand. His fingers found the neck of the struggling bird. The red eyes looked into his face, calm and fearless and fierce; the naked head turned from side to side. Then the beak opened and vomited a stream of putrefied fluid. Jody brought up his knee and fell on the great bird. He held the neck to the ground with one hand while his other found a piece of sharp white quartz. The first blow broke the beak sideways and black blood spurted from the twisted, leathery mouth-corners. He struck again and missed. The red fearless eyes still looked at him, impersonal and unafraid and detached. He struck again and again, until the buzzard lay dead, until its head was a red pulp. He was still beating the dead bird when Billy Buck pulled him off and held him tightly to calm his shaking.

Carl Tiflin wiped the blood from the boy's face with a red bandana. Jody was limp and quiet now. His father moved the buzzard with his toe. "Jody," he explained, "the buzzard didn't kill the pony. Don't you know that?"

"I know it," Jody said wearily.

It was Billy Buck who was angry. He had lifted Jody in his arms, and had turned to carry him home. But he turned back on Carl Tiflin. " 'Course he knows it," Billy said furiously. "Jesus Christ! man, can't you see how he'd feel about it?"

II

THE GREAT MOUNTAINS

IN THE humming heat of a midsummer afternoon the little boy, Jody, listlessly looked about the ranch for something to do. He had been to the barn, had thrown rocks at the swallows' nests under the eaves until every one of the little mud houses broke open and dropped its lining of straw and dirty feathers. Then at the ranch-house he baited a rat-trap with the stale cheese and set it where Doubletree Mutt, that good big dog, would get his nose snapped. Jody was not moved by an impulse of cruelty; he was bored with the long hot afternoon. Doubletree Mutt put his stupid nose in the trap and got it smacked, and shrieked with agony and limped away with blood on his nostrils. No matter where he was hurt, Mutt limped. It was just a way he had. Once when he was young, Mutt got caught in a coyote trap, and always after that he limped, even when he was scolded.

When Mutt yelped, Jody's mother called from inside the house, "Jody! Stop torturing that dog and find something to do."

Jody felt mean then, so he threw a rock at Mutt. Then he took his slingshot from the porch and walked up toward the brush line to try to kill a bird. It was a good slingshot, with store-bought rubbers, but while Jody had often shot at birds, he had never hit one. He walked up through the vegetable patch, kicking his bare toes into the dust. And on the way he found the perfect sling-shot stone, round and slightly flattened and heavy enough to carry through the air. He fitted it into the leather pouch of his weapon and proceeded to the brush line. His eyes narrowed, his mouth worked strenuously; for the first time that afternoon he was intent. In the shade of the sagebrush the little birds were working, scratching in the leaves, flying restlessly a few feet and scratching again. Jody pulled back the rubbers of the sling and advanced cautiously. One little thrush paused and looked at him and crouched, ready to fly. Jody sidled nearer, moving one foot slowly after the other. When he was twenty feet away, he carefully raised the sling and aimed. The stone whizzed; the thrush started up and flew right into it. And down the little bird went with a broken head. Jody ran to it and picked it up.

"Well, I got you," he said.

The bird looked much smaller dead than it had alive. Jody felt a little mean pain in his stomach, so he took out his pocket-knife and cut off the bird's head. Then he disembowelled it, and took off its wings; and finally he threw all the pieces into the brush. He didn't care about the bird, or its life, but he knew what older people would say if they had seen him kill it; he was ashamed because of their potential opinion. He decided to forget the whole thing as quickly as he could, and never to mention it.

The hills were dry at this season, and the wild grass was golden, but where the spring-pipe filled the round tub and the tub spilled over, there lay a stretch of fine green grass, deep and sweet and moist. Jody drank from the mossy tub and washed the bird's blood from his hands in cold water. Then he lay on his back in the grass and looked up at the dumpling summer clouds. By closing one eye and destroying perspective he brought them down within reach so that he could put up his fingers and stroke them. He helped the gentle wind push them down the sky; it seemed to him that they went faster for his help. One fat white cloud he helped clear to the mountain rims and pressed it firmly over, out of sight. Jody wondered what it was seeing then. He sat up the better to look at the great mountains where they went piling back, growing darker and more savage until they finished with one jagged ridge, high up against the west. Curious secret mountains; he thought of the little he knew about them.

"What's on the other side?" he asked his father once.

"More mountains, I guess. Why?"

"And on the other side of them?"

"More mountains. Why?"

"More mountains on and on?"

"Well, no. At last you come to the ocean."

"But what's in the mountains?"

"Just cliffs and brush and rocks and dryness."

"Were you ever there?"

"No."

"Has anybody ever been there?"

"A few people, I guess. It's dangerous, with cliffs and things. Why, I've read there's more unexplored country in the mountains of Monterey County than any place in the United States." His father seemed proud that this should be so.

"And at last the ocean?"

"At last the ocean."

"But," the boy insisted, "but in between? No one knows?"

"Oh, a few people do, I guess. But there's nothing there to get. And not much water. Just rocks and cliffs and greasewood. Why?"

"It would be good to go."

"What for? There's nothing there."

Jody knew something was there, something very wonderful because it wasn't known, something secret and mysterious. He could feel within himself that this was so. He said to his mother, "Do you know what's in the big mountains?"

She looked at him and then back at the ferocious range, and she said, "Only the bear, I guess."

"What bear?"

"Why, the one that went over the mountain to see what he could see."

Jody questioned Billy Buck, the ranch hand, about the possibility of ancient cities lost in the mountains, but Billy agreed with Jody's father.

"It ain't likely," Billy said. "There'd be nothing to eat unless a kind of people that can eat rocks live there."

That was all the information Jody ever got, and it made the mountains dear to him, and terrible. He thought often of the miles of ridge after ridge until at last there was the sea. When the peaks were pink in the morning they invited him among them: and when the sun had gone over the edge in the evening, and the mountains were a purple-like despair, then Jody was afraid of them; then they were so impersonal and aloof, that their very imperturbability was a threat.

Now he turned his head toward the mountains of the east, the Gabilans, and they were jolly mountains, with hill ranches in their creases, and with pine trees growing on the crests. People lived there, and battles had been fought against the Mexicans on the slopes. He looked back for an instant at the Great Ones and shivered a little at the contrast. The foot-hill cup of the home ranch below him was sunny and safe. The house gleamed with white light and the barn was brown and warm. The red cows on the farther hill ate their way slowly towards the north. Even the dark cypress tree by the bunk-house was usual and safe. The chickens scratched about in the dust of the farmyard with quick waltzing steps.

Then a moving figure caught Jody's eye. A man walked slowly over the brow of the hill, on the road from Salinas, and he was headed toward the house. Jody stood up and moved down towards the house, too, for if someone was coming he wanted to be there to see. By the time the boy had got to the house the walking man was only half-way down the road, a lean man, very straight in the shoulders. Jody could tell he was old only because his heels struck the ground with hard jerks. As he approached nearer, Jody saw that he was dressed in blue jeans and in a coat of the same material. He wore clodhopper shoes and an old flat-brimmed Stetson hat. Over his shoulder he carried a gunny sack, lumpy and full. In a few moments he had trudged close enough so that his face could be seen. And his face was as dark as dried beef. A moustache, blue-white against the dark skin, hovered over his mouth, and his hair was white, too, where it showed at his neck. The skin of his face had shrunk back against the skull until it defined bone, not flesh, and made the nose and chin seem sharp and fragile. The eyes were large and deep and dark, with eyelids stretched tightly over them. Irises and pupils were one, and very black, but the eyeballs were brown. There were no wrinkles in the face at all. This old man wore a blue denim coat buttoned to the throat with brass buttons, as all men do who wear no shirts. Out of the sleeves came strong bony wrists and hands gnarled and knotted and hard as peach branches. The nails were flat and blunt and shiny.

The old man drew close to the gate and swung down his sack when he confronted Jody. His lips fluttered a little and a soft impersonal voice came from between them.

"Do you live here?"

Jody was embarrassed. He turned and looked at the house, and he turned back and looked toward the barn where his father and Billy Buck were. "Yes," he said, when no help came from either direction.

"I have come back," the old man said. "I am Gitano, and I have come back."

Jody could not take all this responsibility. He turned abruptly, and ran into the house for help, and the screen door banged after him. His mother was in the kitchen poking out the clogged holes on a colander with a hairpin, and biting her lower lip with concentration.

"It's an old man," Jody cried excitedly. "It's an old paisano man, and he says he's come back."

His mother put down the colander and stuck the hairpin behind the sink board. "What's the matter now?" she asked patiently.

"It's an old man outside. Come on out."

"Well, what does he want?" She untied the strings of her apron and smoothed her hair with her fingers.

"I don't know. He came walking."

His mother smoothed down her dress and went out, and Jody followed her. Gitano had not moved.

"Yes?" Mrs. Tiflin asked.

Gitano took off his old black hat and held it with both hands in front of him. He repeated, "I am Gitano, and I have come back."

"Come back? Back where?"

Gitano's whole straight body leaned forward a little. His right hand described the circle of the hills, the sloping fields and the mountains, and ended at his hat again. "Back to the rancho. I was born here, and my father, too."

"Here?" she demanded. "This isn't an old place."

"No, there," he said, pointing to the western ridge. "On the other side there, in a house that is gone."

At last she understood. "The old 'dobe that's washed almost away, you mean?"

"Yes, señora. When the rancho broke up they put no more lime on the 'dobe, and the rains washed it down."

Jody's mother was silent for a little, and curious home-sick thoughts ran through her mind, but quickly she cleared them out. "And what do you want here now, Gitano?"

"I will stay here," he said quietly, "until I die."

"But we don't need an extra man here."

"I cannot work hard any more, señora. I can milk a cow, feed chickens, cut a little wood, no more. I will stay here." He indicated the sack on the ground beside him. "Here are my things."

She turned to Jody. "Run down to the barn and call your father."

Jody dashed away, and he returned with Carl Tiflin and Billy

Buck behind him. The old man was standing as he had been, but he was resting now. His whole body had sagged into a timeless repose.

"What is it?" Carl Tiflin asked. "What's Jody so excited about?"

Mrs. Tiflin motioned to the old man. "He wants to stay here. He wants to do a little work and stay here."

"Well, we can't have him. We don't need any more men. He's too old. Billy does everything we need."

They had been talking over him as though he did not exist, and now, suddenly, they both hesitated and looked at Gitano and were embarrassed.

He cleared his throat. "I am too old to work. I come back where I was born."

"You weren't born here," Carl said sharply.

"No. In the 'dobe house over the hill. It was all one rancho before you came."

"In the mud house that's all melted down?"

"Yes. I and my father. I will stay here now on the rancho."

"I tell you you won't stay," Carl said angrily. "I don't need an old man. This isn't a big ranch. I can't afford food and doctor bills for an old man. You must have relatives and friends. Go to them. It is like begging to come to strangers."

"I was born here," Gitano said patiently and inflexibly.

Carl Tiflin didn't like to be cruel, but he felt he must. "You can eat here to-night," he said. "You can sleep in the little room of the old bunk-house. We'll give you your breakfast in the morning, and then you'll have to go along. Go to your friends. Don't come to die with strangers."

Gitano put on his black hat and stooped for the sack. "Here are my things," he said.

Carl turned away. "Come on, Billy, we'll finish down at the barn. Jody, show him the little room in the bunk-house."

He and Billy turned back toward the barn. Mrs. Tiflin went into the house, saying over her shoulder, "I'll send some blankets down."

Gitano looked questioningly at Jody. "I'll show you where it is," Jody said.

There was a cot with a shuck mattress, an apple-box holding a tin lantern, and a backless rocking-chair in the little room of the bunk-house. Gitano laid his sack carefully on the floor and sat down on the bed. Jody stood shyly in the room, hesitating to go. At last he said:

"Did you come out of the big mountains?"

Gitano shook his head slowly. "No, I worked down the Salinas Valley."

The afternoon thought would not let Jody go. "Did you ever go into the big mountains back there?"

The old dark eyes grew fixed, and their light turned inward on the years that were living in Gitano's head. "Once—when I was a little boy. I went with my father."

"Way back, clear into the mountains?"

"Yes."

"What was there?" Jody cried. "Did you see any people or any houses?"

"No."

"Well, what was there?"

Gitano's eyes remained inward. A little wrinkled strain came between his brows.

"What did you see in there?" Jody repeated.

"I don't know," Gitano said. "I don't remember."

"Was it terrible and dry?"

"I don't remember."

In his excitement, Jody had lost his shyness. "Don't you remember anything about it?"

Gitano's mouth opened for a word, and remained open while his brain sought the word. "I think it was quiet—I think it was nice."

Gitano's eyes seemed to have found something back in the years, for they grew soft and a little smile seemed to come and go in them.

"Didn't you ever go back in the mountains again?" Jody insisted.

"No."

"Didn't you ever want to?"

But now Gitano's face became impatient. "No," he said in a tone that told Jody he didn't want to talk about it any more. The boy was held by a curious fascination. He didn't want to go away from Gitano. His shyness returned.

"Would you like to come down to the barn and see the stock?" he asked.

Gitano stood up and put on his hat and prepared to follow.

It was almost evening now. They stood near the watering trough while the horses sauntered in from the hillsides for an evening drink. Gitano rested his big twisted hands on the top rail of the fence. Five horses came down and drank, and then stood about, nibbling at the dirt or rubbing their sides against the polished wood of the fence. Long after they had finished drinking an old horse appeared over the brow of the hill and came painfully down. It had long yellow teeth; its hoofs were flat and sharp as spades, and its ribs and hip-bones jutted out under its skin. It hobbled up to the trough and drank water with a loud sucking noise.

"That's old Easter," Jody explained. "That's the first horse my father ever had. He's thirty years old." He looked up into Gitano's old eyes for some response.

"No good any more," Gitano said.

Jody's father and Billy Buck came out of the barn and walked over.

"Too old to work," Gitano repeated. "Just eats and pretty soon dies."

Carl Tiflin caught the last words. He hated his brutality toward old Gitano, and so he became brutal again.

"It's a shame not to shoot old Easter," he said. "It'd save him a lot of pains and rheumatism." He looked secretly at Gitano, to see whether he noticed the parallel, but the big bony hands did not move, nor did the dark eyes turn from the horse. "Old things ought to be put out of their misery," Jody's father went on. "One shot, a big noise, one big pain in the head maybe, and that's all. That's better than stiffness and sore teeth."

Billy Buck broke in, "They got a right to rest after they worked all of their life. Maybe they like to just walk around."

Carl had been looking steadily at the skinny horse. "You can't imagine now what Easter used to look like," he said softly. "High neck, deep chest, fine barrel. He could jump a five-bar gate in stride. I won a flat race on him when I was fifteen years old. I could of got two hundred dollars for him any time. You wouldn't think how pretty he was." He checked himself, for he hated softness. "But he ought to be shot now," he said.

"He's got a right to rest," Billy Buck insisted.

Jody's father had a humorous thought. He turned to Gitano. "If ham and eggs grew on a side-hill I'd turn you out to pasture too," he said. "But I can't afford to pasture you in my kitchen."

He laughed to Billy Buck about it as they went on toward the house. "Be a good thing for all of us if ham and eggs grew on the side-hills."

Jody knew how his father was probing for a place to hurt in Gitano. He had been probed often. His father knew every place in the boy where a word would fester.

"He's only talking," Jody said. "He didn't meant it about shooting Easter. He likes Easter. That was the first horse he ever owned."

The sun sank behind the high mountains as they stood there, and the ranch was hushed. Gitano seemed to be more at home in the evening. He made a curious sharp sound with his lips and stretched one of his hands over the fence. Old Easter moved stiffly to him, and Gitano rubbed the lean neck under the mane.

"You like him?" Jody asked softly.

"Yes—but he's no damn good."

The triangle sounded at the ranch-house. "That's supper," Jody cried "Come on up to supper."

As they walked up toward the house Jody noticed again that Gitano's body was as straight as that of a young man. Only by a jerkiness in his movements and by the scuffling of his heels could it be seen that he was old.

The turkeys were flying heavily into the lower branches of the cypress tree by the bunk-house. A fat sleek ranch cat walked across the road carrying a rat so large that its tail dragged on the ground. The quail on the side-hills were still sounding the clear water call.

Jody and Gitano came to the back steps and Mrs. Tiflin looked out through the screen door at them.

"Come running, Jody. Come in to supper, Gitano."

Carl and Billy Buck had started to eat at the long oilcloth-covered table. Jody slipped into his chair without moving it, but Gitano stood holding his hat until Carl looked up and said, "Sit down, sit down. You might as well get your belly full before you go on." Carl was afraid he might relent and let the old man stay, and so he continued to remind himself that this couldn't be.

Gitano laid his hat on the floor and diffidently sat down. He wouldn't reach for food. Carl had to pass it to him. "Here, fill yourself up." Gitano ate very slowly, cutting tiny pieces of meat and arranging little pats of mashed potato on his plate.

The situation would not stop worrying Carl Tiflin. "Haven't you got any relatives in this part of the country?" he asked.

Gitano answered with some pride. "My brother-in-law's in Monterey. I have cousins, there, too."

"Well, you can go and live there, then."

"I was born here," Gitano said in gentle rebuke.

Jody's mother came in from the kitchen, carrying a large bowl of tapioca pudding.

Carl chuckled to her, "Did I tell you what I said to him? I said if ham and eggs grew on the side-hills I'd put him out to pasture, like old Easter."

Gitano stared unmoved at his plate.

"It's too bad he can't stay," said Mrs. Tiflin.

"Now don't you start anything," Carl said crossly.

When they had finished eating, Carl and Billy Buck and Jody went into the living-room to sit for a while, but Gitano, without a word of farewell or thanks, walked through the kitchen and out the back door. Jody sat and secretly watched his father. He knew how mean his father felt.

"This country's full of these old paisanos," Carl said to Billy Buck.

"They're damn good men," Billy defended them. "They can work older than white men. I saw one of them a hundred and five years old, and he could still ride a horse. You don't see any white men as old as Gitano walking twenty or thirty miles."

"Oh, they're tough, all right," Carl agreed. "Say, are you standing up for him, too? Listen, Billy," he explained, "I'm having a hard enough time keeping this ranch out of the Bank of Italy without taking on anybody else to feed. You know that, Billy."

"Sure I know," said Billy. "If you was rich, it'd be different."

"That's right, and it isn't like he didn't have relatives to go to. A brother-in-law and cousins right in Monterey. Why should I worry about him?"

Jody sat quietly listening, and he seemed to hear Gitano's gentle voice and its unanswerable, "But I was born here." Gitano was mysterious like the mountains. There were ranges back as far as you could see, but behind the last range piled up against the sky there was a great unknown country. And Gitano was an old man, until you got to the dull, dark eyes. And in behind them was some unknown thing. He didn't ever say enough to let you guess what was inside, under the eyes. Jody felt himself irresistibly drawn toward the bunk-house. He slipped from his chair while his father was talking and he went out the door without making a sound.

The night was very dark and far-off noises carried in clearly. The hamebells of a wood team sounded from way over the hill on the county road. Jody picked his way across the dark yard. He could see a light through the window of the little room of the bunk-house. Because the night was secret he walked quietly up to the window and peered in. Gitano sat in the rocking-chair and his back was toward the window. His right arm moved slowly back and forth in front of him. Jody pushed the door open and walked in. Gitano jerked upright and, seizing a piece of deerskin, he tried to throw it over the thing in his lap, but the skin slipped away. Jody stood overwhelmed by the thing in Gitano's hand, a lean and lovely rapier with a golden basket hilt. The blade was like a thin ray of dark light. The hilt was pierced and intricately carved.

"What is it?" Jody demanded.

Gitano only looked at him with resentful eyes, and he picked up the fallen deerskin and firmly wrapped the beautiful blade in it.

Jody put out his hand. "Can't I see it?"

Gitano's eyes smouldered angrily and he shook his head.

"Where'd you get it? Where'd it come from?"

Now Gitano regarded him profoundly, as though he pondered. "I got it from my father."

"Well, where'd he get it?"

Gitano looked down at the long deerskin parcel in his hand. "I don't know."

"Didn't he ever tell you?"

"No."

"What do you do with it?"

Gitano looked slightly surprised. "Nothing. I just keep it."

"Can't I see it again?"

The old man slowly unwrapped the shining blade and let the lamplight slip along it for a moment. Then he wrapped it up again. "You go now. I want to go to bed." He blew out the lamp almost before Jody had closed the door.

As he went back towards the house, Jody knew one thing more sharply than he had ever known anything. He must never tell anyone about the rapier. It would be a dreadful thing to tell anyone about it, for it would destroy some fragile structure of truth. It was a truth that might be shattered by division.

On the way across the dark yard Jody passed Billy Buck. "They're wondering where you are," Billy said.

Jody slipped into the living-room, and his father turned to him. "Where have you been?"

"I just went out to see if I caught any rats in my new trap."

"It's time you went to bed," his father said.

. . . . .

Jody was first at the breakfast table in the morning. Then his father came in, and last, Billy Buck. Mrs. Tiflin looked in from the kitchen.

"Where's the old man, Billy?" she asked.

"I guess he's out walking," Billy said. "I looked in his room and he wasn't there."

"Maybe he started early to Monterey," said Carl. "It's a long walk."

"No," Billy explained. "His sack is in the little room."

After breakfast Jody walked down to the bunk-house. Flies were flashing about in the sunshine. The ranch seemed especially quiet this morning. When he was sure no one was watching him, Jody went into the little room, and looked into Gitano's sack. An extra pair of long cotton underwear was there, an extra pair of jeans and three pairs of worn socks. Nothing else was in the sack. A sharp loneliness fell on Jody. He walked slowly back towards the house. His father stood on the porch talking to Mrs. Tiflin.

"I guess old Easter's dead at last," he said. "I didn't see him come down to water with the other horses."

In the middle of the morning, Jess Taylor from the ridge ranch rode down.

"You didn't sell that old grey crowbait of yours, did you, Carl?"

"No, of course not. Why?"

"Well," Jess said, "I was out this morning early, and I saw a funny thing. I saw an old man on an old horse, no saddle, only a piece of rope for a bridle. He wasn't on the road at all. He was cutting right up straight through the brush. I think he had a gun. At least I saw something shine in his hand."

"That's old Gitano," Carl Tiflin said. "I'll see if any of my guns are missing." He stepped into the house for a second. "Nope, all here. Which way was he heading, Jess?"

"Well, that's the funny thing. He was heading straight back into the mountains."

Carl laughed. "They never get too old to steal," he said. "I guess he just stole old Easter."

"Want to go after him, Carl?"

"Hell no, just save me burying that horse. I wonder where he got the gun. I wonder what he wants back there."

Jody walked up through the vegetable patch, toward the brush line. He looked searchingly at the towering mountains—ridge after ridge after ridge until at last there was the ocean. For a moment he thought he could see a black speck crawling up the farthest ridge. Jody thought of the rapier and of Gitano. And he thought of the great mountains. A longing caressed him, and it was so sharp that he wanted to cry to get it out of his breast. He lay down in the green grass near the round tub at the brush line. He covered his eyes with his crossed arms and lay there a long time, and he was full of a nameless sorrow.

III

THE PROMISE

In a mid-afternoon of spring, the little boy Jody walked martially along the brush-lined road toward his home ranch. Banging his knee against the golden lard bucket he used for school lunch, he contrived a good bass drum, while his tongue fluttered sharply against his teeth to fill in snare drums and occasional trumpets. Some time back the other members of the squad that walked so smartly from the school had turned into the various little canyons and taken the wagon roads to their own home ranches. Now Jody marched seemingly alone, with high-lifted knees and pounding feet; but behind him there was a phantom army with great flags and swords, silent but deadly.

The afternoon was green and gold with spring. Underneath the spread branches of the oaks the plants grew pale and tall and on the hills the feed was smooth and thick. The sagebrushes shone with new silver leaves and the oaks wore hoods of golden green. Over the hills there hung such a green odour that the horses on the flats galloped madly, and then stopped; wondering lambs, and even old sheep, jumped in the air unexpectedly and landed on stiff legs, and went on eating; young clumsy calves butted their heads together and drew back and butted again.

As the grey and silent army marched past, led by Jody, the animals stopped their feeding and their play and watched it go by.

Suddenly Jody stopped. The grey army halted, bewildered and nervous. Jody went down on his knees. The army stood in long uneasy ranks for a moment, and then, with a soft sigh of sorrow, rose up in a faint grey mist and disappeared. Jody had seen the thorny crown of a horny-toad moving under the dust of the road. His grimy hand went out and grasped the spiked halo and held firmly while the little beast struggled. Then Jody turned the horny-toad over, exposing its pale gold stomach. With a gentle forefinger he stroked the throat and chest until the horny-toad relaxed, until its eyes closed and it lay languorous and asleep.

Jody opened his lunch pail and deposited the first game inside. He moved on now, his knees bent slightly, his shoulders crouched; his bare feet were wise and silent. In his right hand there was a long grey rifle. The brush along the road stirred restively under a new and unexpected population of grey tigers and grey bears. The hunting was very good, for by the time Jody reached the fork of the road where the mail box stood on a post, he had captured two more horny-toads, four little grass lizards, a blue snake, sixteen yellow-winged grasshoppers and a brown damp newt from under a rock. This assortment scrabbled unhappily against the tin of the lunch bucket.

At the road fork the rifle evaporated and the tigers and bears melted from the hillsides. Even the moist and uncomfortable creatures in the lunch pail ceased to exist, for the little red metal flag was up on the mail box, signifying that some postal matter was inside. Jody set his pail on the ground and opened the letter box. There was a Montgomery Ward catalogue and a copy of the *Salinas Weekly Journal*. He slammed the box, picked up his lunch pail and trotted over the ridge and down into the cup of the ranch. Past the barn he ran, and past the used-up haystack and the bunk-house and the cypress tree. He banged through the front screen door of the ranch house calling: "Ma'am, ma'am, there's a catalogue."

Mrs. Tiflin was in the kitchen spooning clabbered milk into a cotton bag. She put down her work and rinsed her hands under the tap. "Here in the kitchen, Jody. Here I am."

He ran in and clattered his lunch pail on the sink. "Here it is. Can I open the catalogue, ma'am?"

Mrs. Tiflin took up the spoon again and went back to her cottage cheese. "Don't lose it, Jody. Your father will want to see it." She scraped the last of the milk into the bag. "Oh, Jody, your father wants to see you before you go to your chores." She waved a cruising fly from the cheese bag.

Jody closed the new catalogue in alarm. "Ma'am?"

"Why don't you ever listen? I say your father wants to see you."

The boy laid the catalogue gently on the sink board. "Do you—is it something I did?"

Mrs. Tiflin laughed. "Always a bad conscience. What did you do?"

"Nothing, ma'am," he said lamely. But he couldn't remember, and besides it was impossible to know what action might later be construed as a crime.

His mother hung the full bag on a nail where it could drip into the sink. "He just said he wanted to see you when you got home. He's somewhere down by the barn."

Jody turned and went out the back door. Hearing his mother open the lunch pail and then gasp with rage, a memory stabbed him and he trotted away toward the barn, conscientiously not hearing an angry voice that called him from the house.

Carl Tiflin and Billy Buck, the ranch hand, stood against the lower pasture fence. Each man rested one foot on the lowest bar and both elbows on the top bar. They were talking slowly and aimlessly. In the pasture half-a-dozen horses nibbled contentedly at the sweet grass. The mare, Nellie, stood backed up against the gate, rubbing her buttocks on the heavy post.

Jody sidled uneasily near. He dragged one foot to give an impression of great innocence and nonchalance. When he arrived beside the men he put one foot on the lowest fence-rail, rested his elbows on the second bar and looked into the pasture too. The two men glanced sideways at him.

"I wanted to see you," Carl said in the stern tone he reserved for children and animals.

"Yes, sir," said Jody guiltily.

"Billy, here, says you took good care of the pony before it died."

No punishment was in the air. Jody grew bolder. "Yes, sir, I did."

"Billy says you have a good patient hand with horses."

Jody felt a sudden warm friendliness for the ranch hand.

Billy put in, "He trained that pony as good as anybody I ever seen."

Then Carl Tiflin came gradually to the point. "If you could have another horse would you work for it?"

Jody shivered. "Yes, sir."

"Well, look here, then. Billy says the best way for you to be a good hand with horses is to raise a colt."

"It's the *only* good way," Billy interrupted.

"Now, look here, Jody," continued Carl. "Jess Taylor, up to the ridge ranch, has a fair stallion, but it'll cost five dollars. I'll put up the money, but you'll have to work it out all summer. Will you do that?"

Jody felt his insides were shrivelling. "Yes, sir," he said softly.

"And no complaining? And no forgetting when you're told to do something?"

"Yes, sir."

"Well, all right, then. To-morrow morning you take Nellie up to the ridge ranch and get her bred. You'll have to take care of her, too, till she throws the colt."

"Yes, sir."

"You better get to the chickens and the wood now."

Jody slid away. In passing behind Billy Buck he very nearly put out his hands to touch the blue-jeaned legs. His shoulders swayed a little with maturity and importance.

He went to his work with unprecedented seriousness. This night he did not dump the can of grain to the chickens so that they had to leap over each other and struggle to get it. No, he spread the wheat so far and so carefully that the hens couldn't find some of it at all. And in the house, after listening to his mother's despair over boys who filled their lunch pails with slimy, suffocated reptiles, and bugs, he promised never to do it again. Indeed, Jody felt that all such foolishness was lost in the past. He was far too grown up ever to put horn-toads in his lunch pail any more. He carried in so much wood and built such a high structure with it that his mother walked in fear of an avalanche of oak. When he was done, when he had gathered eggs that had remained hidden for weeks, Jody walked down again past the cypress tree, and past the bunk-house toward the pasture. A fat warty toad that looked out at him from under the watering trough had no emotional effect on him at all.

Carl Tiflin and Billy Buck were not in sight, but from a metallic ringing on the other side of the barn Jody knew that Billy Buck was just starting to milk a cow.

The other horses were eating toward the upper end of the pasture, but Nellie continued to rub herself nervously against the post. Jody walked slowly near, saying, "So, girl, so-o, Nellie." The mare's ears went back naughtily and her lips drew away from her yellow teeth. She turned her head around; her eyes were glazed and mad. Jody climbed to the top of the fence and hung his feet over and looked paternally down on the mare.

The evening hovered while he sat there. Bats and night-hawks flicked about. Billy Buck, walking toward the house carrying a full milk bucket, saw Jody and stopped. "It's a long time to wait," he said gently. "You'll get awful tired waiting."

"No I won't, Billy. How long will it be?"

"Nearly a year."

"Well, I won't get tired."

The triangle at the house rang stridently. Jody climbed down from the fence and walked to supper beside Billy Buck. He even put out his hand and took hold of the milk bucket to help carry it.

The next morning after breakfast Carl Tiflin folded a five-dollar bill in a piece of newspaper and pinned the package in the bib pocket of Jody's overalls. Billy Buck haltered the mare, Nellie, and led her out of the pasture.

"Be careful now," he warned. "Hold her up short here so she can't bite you. She's crazy as a coot."

Jody took hold of the halter leather itself and started up the hill toward the ridge ranch with Nellie skittering and jerking behind him. In the pasturage along the road the wild oat heads were just clearing their scabbards. The warm morning sun shone on Jody's back so sweetly that he was forced to take a serious stiff-legged hop now and then in spite of his maturity. On the fences the shiny blackbirds with red epaulettes clicked their dry call. The meadowlarks sang like water, and the wild doves, concealed among the bursting leaves of the oaks, made a sound of restrained grieving. In the fields the rabbits sat sunning themselves, with only their forked ears showing above the grass heads.

After an hour of steady uphill walking, Jody turned into a narrow road that led up a steeper hill to the ridge ranch. He could see the red roof of the barn sticking up above the oak trees, and he could hear a dog barking unemotionally near the house.

Suddenly Nellie jerked back and nearly freed herself. From the direction of the barn Jody heard a shrill whistling scream and a splintering of wood, and then a man's voice shouting. Nellie reared and whinnied. When Jody held to the halter rope she ran at him with bared teeth. He dropped his hold and scuttled out of the way, into the brush. The high scream came from the oaks again, and Nellie answered it. With hoofs battering the ground the stallion appeared and charged down the hill trailing a broken halter rope. His eyes glittered feverishly. His stiff, erected nostrils were as red as flame. His black, sleek hide shone in the sunlight. The stallion came on so fast that he couldn't stop when he reached the mare. Nellie's ears went back; she whirled and kicked at him as he went by. The stallion spun around and reared. He struck the mare with his front hoof, and while she staggered under the blow, his teeth raked her neck and drew an ooze of blood.

Instantly Nellie's mood changed. She became coquettishly feminine. She nibbled his arched neck with her lips. She edged around and rubbed her shoulder against his shoulder. Jody stood half-hidden in the brush and watched. He heard the step of a horse behind him, but before he could turn, a hand caught him by the overall straps and lifted him off the ground. Jess Taylor sat the boy behind him on the horse.

"You might have got killed," he said. "Sundog's a mean devil sometimes. He busted his rope and went right through a gate."

Jody sat quietly, but in a moment he cried, "He'll hurt her, he'll kill her. Get him away!"

Jess chuckled. "She'll be all right. Maybe you'd better climb off and go up to the house for a little. You could get maybe a piece of pie up there."

But Jody shook his head. "She's mine, and the colt's going to be mine. I'm going to raise it up."

Jess nodded. "Yes, that's a good thing. Carl has good sense sometimes."

In a little while the danger was over. Jess lifted Jody down and then caught the stallion by its broken halter rope. And he rode ahead, while Jody followed, leading Nellie.

It was only after he had unpinned and handed over the five dollars, and after he had eaten two pieces of pie, that Jody started for home again. And Nellie followed docilely after him. She was so quiet that Jody climbed on a stump and rode her most of the way home.

The five dollars his father had advanced reduced Jody to peonage for the whole late spring and summer. When the hay was cut he drove a rake. He led the horse that pulled on the Jackson-fork tackle, and when the baler came he drove the circling horse that put pressure on the bales. In addition, Carl Tiflin taught him to milk and put a cow under his care, so that a new chore was added night and morning.

The bay mare, Nellie, quickly grew complacent. As she walked about the yellowing hillsides or worked at easy tasks, her lips were curled in a perpetual fatuous smile. She moved slowly, with the calm importance of an empress. When she was put to a team, she pulled steadily and unemotionally. Jody went to see her every day. He studied her with critical eyes and saw no change whatever.

One afternoon Billy Buck leaned the many-tined manure fork against the barn wall. He loosened his belt and tucked in his shirt-tail and tightened the belt again. He picked one of the little straws from his hatband and put it in the corner of his mouth. Jody, who was helping Doubletree Mutt, the big serious dog, to dig out a gopher, straightened up as the ranch hand sauntered out of the barn.

"Let's go up and have a look at Nellie," Billy suggested.

Instantly Jody fell into step with him. Doubletree Mutt watched them over his shoulder; then he dug furiously, growled, sounded little sharp yelps to indicate that the gopher was practically caught. When he looked over his shoulder again, and saw that neither Jody nor Billy was interested, he climbed reluctantly out of the hole and followed them up the hill.

The wild oats were ripening. Every head bent sharply under its load of grain, and the grass was dry enough so that it made a swishing sound as Jody and Billy stepped through it. Halfway up the hill they could see Nellie and the iron-grey gelding, Pete, nibbling the heads from the wild oats. When they approached, Nellie looked at them and backed her ears and bobbed her head up and down rebelliously. Billy walked to her and put his hand under her mane and patted her neck, until her ears came forward again and she nibbled delicately at his shirt.

Jody asked, "Do you think she's really going to have a colt?"

Billy rolled the lids back from the mare's eyes with his thumb and forefinger. He felt the lower lip and fingered the black, leathery teats. "I wouldn't be surprised," he said.

"Well, she isn't changed at all. It's three months gone."

Billy rubbed the mare's flat forehead with his knuckle while she grunted with pleasure. "I told you you'd get tired waiting. It'll be five months more before you can even see a sign, and it'll be at least eight months more before she throws the colt, about next January."

Jody sighed deeply. "It's a long time, isn't it?"

"And then it'll be about two years more before you can ride."

Jody cried out in despair, "I'll be grown up."

"Yep, you'll be an old man," said Billy.

"What colour do you think the colt'll be?"

"Why, you can't ever tell. The stud is black and the dam is bay. Colt might be black or bay or grey or dappled. You can't tell. Sometimes a black dam might have a white colt."

"Well, I hope it's black, and a stallion."

"If it's a stallion, we'll have to geld it. Your father wouldn't let you have a stallion."

"Maybe he would," Jody said. "I could train him not to be mean."

Billy pursed his lips, and the little straw that had been in the corner of his mouth rolled down to the centre. "You can't ever trust a stallion," he said critically. "They're mostly fighting and making trouble. Sometimes when they're feeling funny they won't work. They make the mares uneasy and kick hell out of the geldings. Your father wouldn't let you keep a stallion."

Nellie sauntered away, nibbling the drying grass. Jody skinned the grain from a grass stem and threw the handful into the air, so that each pointed, feathered seed sailed out like a dart. "Tell me how it'll be, Billy. Is it like when the cows have calves?"

"Just about. Mares are a little more sensitive. Sometimes you have to be there to help the mare. And sometimes if it's wrong, you have to——" he paused.

"Have to what, Billy?"

"Have to tear the colt to pieces to get it out, or the mare'll die."

"But it won't be that way this time, will it, Billy?"

"Oh, no. Nellie's thrown good colts."

"Can I be there, Billy? Will you be certain to call me? It's my colt."

"Sure, I'll call you. Of course I will."

"Tell me how it'll be."

"Why, you've seen the cows calving. It's almost the same. The mare starts groaning and stretching, and then, if it's a good right birth, the head and forefeet come out, and the front hoofs kick a hole just the way the calves do. And the colt starts to breathe. It's good to be there, 'cause if its feet aren't right maybe he can't break the sack, and then he might smother."

Jody whipped his leg with a bunch of grass. "We'll have to be there, then, won't we?"

"Oh, we'll be there all right."

They turned and walked slowly down the hill toward the barn. Jody was tortured with a thing he had to say, although he didn't want to. "Billy," he began miserably, "Billy, you won't let anything happen to the colt, will you?"

And Billy knew he was thinking of the red pony, Gabilan, and of how it had died of strangles. Billy knew he had been infallible before that, and now he was capable of failure. This knowledge made Billy much less sure of himself than he had been. "I can't tell," he said roughly. "All sorts of things might happen, and they wouldn't be my fault. I can't do everything." He felt badly about his lost prestige, and so he said, meanly, "I'll do everything I know, but I won't promise anything. Nellie's a good mare. She's thrown good colts before. She ought to this time." And he walked away from Jody and went into the saddle-room beside the barn, for his feelings were hurt.

Jody travelled often to the brush line behind the house. A rusty iron pipe ran a thin stream of spring water into an old green tub. Where the water spilled over and sank into the ground there was a patch of perpetually green grass. Even when the hills were brown and baked in the summer that little patch was green. The water whined softly into the trough all the year round. This place had grown to be a centre-point for Jody. When he had been punished the cool green grass and the singing water soothed him. When he had been mean the biting acid of meanness left him at the brush line. When he sat in the grass and listened to the purling stream, the barriers set up in his mind by the stern day went down to ruin.

On the other hand, the black cypress tree by the bunk-house was as repulsive as the water-tub was dear; for to this tree all the pigs came, sooner or later to be slaughtered. Pig-killing was fascinating, with the screaming and the blood, but it made Jody's heart beat so fast that it hurt him. After the pigs were scalded in the big iron tripod kettle and their skins were scraped and white, Jody had to go to the water-tub to sit in the grass until his heart grew quiet. The water-tub and the black cypress were opposites and enemies.

When Billy left him and walked angrily away, Jody turned up toward the house. He thought of Nellie as he walked, and of the little colt. Then suddenly he saw that he was under the black cypress, under the very single-tree where the pigs were hung. He brushed his dry-grass hair off his forehead and hurried on. It seemed to him an unlucky thing to be thinking of his colt in the very slaughter place, especially after what Billy had said. To counteract any evil result of that bad conjunction he walked quickly past the ranch house, through the chicken yard, through the vegetable patch, until he came at last to the brush line.

He sat down in the green grass. The trilling water sounded in his ears. He looked over the farm buildings and across at the round hills, rich and yellow with grain. He could see Nellie feeding on the slope. As usual the water place eliminated time and distance. Jody saw a black, long-legged colt, butting against Nellie's flanks, demanding milk. And then he saw himself breaking a large colt to halter. All in a few moments the colt grew to be a magnificent animal, deep of chest, with a neck as high and arched as a sea-horse's neck, with a tail that tongued and rippled like black flame. This horse was terrible to everyone but Jody. In the school yard the boys begged rides, and Jody smilingly agreed. But no sooner were they mounted than the black demon pitched them off. Why, that was his name. Black Demon! For a moment the trilling water and the grass and the sunshine came back, and then . . .

Sometimes in the night the ranch people, safe in their beds, heard a roar of hoofs go by. They said, "It's Jody, on Demon. He's helping out the sheriff again." And then . . .

The golden dust filled the air in the arena at Salinas Rodeo. The announcer called the roping contests. When Jody rode the black horse to the starting chute the other contestants shrugged and gave up first place, for it was well known that Jody and Demon could rope and throw and tie a steer a great deal quicker than any roping team of two men could. Jody was not a boy any more, and Demon was not a horse. The two together were one glorious individual. And then . . .

The President wrote a letter and asked them to help catch a bandit in Washington. Jody settled himself comfortably in the grass. The little stream of water whined into the mossy tub.

The year passed slowly on. Time after time Jody gave up his

colt for lost. No change had taken place in Nellie. Carl Tiflin still drove her to a light cart, and she pulled on a hay rake and worked the Jackson-fork tackle when the hay was being put into the barn.

The summer passed, and the warm bright autumn. And then the frantic morning winds began to twist along the ground, and a chill came into the air, and the poison oak turned red. One morning in September, when he had finished his breakfast, Jody's mother called him into the kitchen. She was pouring boiling water into a bucket full of dry middlings, and stirring the materials to a steaming paste.

"Yes, ma'am?" Jody asked.

"Watch how I do it. You'll have to do it after this every other morning."

"Well, what is it?"

"Why, it's warm mash for Nellie. It'll keep her in good shape."

Jody rubbed his forehead with a knuckle. "Is she all right?" he asked timidly.

Mrs. Tiflin put down the kettle and stirred the mash with a wooden paddle. "Of course she's all right, only you've got to take better care of her from now on. Here, take this breakfast out to her!"

Jody seized the bucket and ran, down past the bunk-house, past the barn, with the heavy bucket banging against his knees. He found Nellie playing with the water in the trough, pushing waves and tossing her head so that the water slopped out on the ground.

Jody climbed the fence and set the bucket of steaming mash beside her. Then he stepped back to look at her. And she was changed. Her stomach was swollen. When she moved, her feet touched the ground gently. She buried her nose in the bucket and gobbled the hot breakfast. And when she had finished and had pushed the bucket around the ground with her nose a little, she stepped quietly over to Jody and rubbed her cheek against him.

Billy Buck came out of the saddle-room and walked over. "Starts fast when it starts, doesn't it?"

"Did it come all at once?"

"Oh, no, you just stopped looking for a while." He pulled her head around toward Jody. "She's goin' to be nice, too. See how nice her eyes are! Some mares turn mean, but when they turn nice, they just love everything." Nellie slipped her head under Billy's arm and rubbed her neck up and down between his arm and his side. "You better treat her awful nice now," Billy said.

"How long will it be?" Jody demanded breathlessly.

The man counted in whispers on his fingers. "About three months," he said aloud. "You can't tell exactly. Sometimes it's eleven months to the day, but it might be two weeks early, or a month late, without hurting anything."

Jody looked hard at the ground. "Billy," he began nervously, "Billy, you'll call me when it's getting born, won't you? You'll let me be there, won't you?"

Billy bit the tip of Nellie's ear with his front teeth. "Carl says he wants you to start right at the start. That's the only way to learn. Nobody can tell you anything. Like my old man did with me about the saddle blanket. He was a government packer when I was your size, and I helped him some. One day I left a wrinkle in my saddle blanket and made a saddle-sore. My old man didn't give me hell at all. But the next morning he saddled me up with a forty-pound stock saddle. I had to lead my horse and carry that saddle over a whole damn mountain in the sun. It darn near killed me, but I never left no wrinkles in a blanket again. I couldn't. I never in my life since then put on a blanket but I felt that saddle on my back."

Jody reached up a hand and took hold of Nellie's mane. "You'll tell me what to do about everything, won't you? I guess you know everything about horses, don't you?"

Billy laughed. "Why I'm half horse myself, you see," he said. "My ma died when I was born, and being my old man was a government packer in the mountains, and no cows around most of the time, why he just gave me mostly mare's milk." He continued seriously, "and horses know that. Don't you know it, Nellie?"

The mare turned her head and looked full into his eyes for a moment, and this is a thing horses practically never do. Billy was proud and sure of himself now. He boasted a little. "I'll see you get a good colt. I'll start you right. And if you do like I say, you'll have the best horse in the country."

That made Jody feel warm and proud, too; so proud that when he went back to the house he bowed his legs and swayed his shoulders as horsemen do. And he whispered, "Whoa, you Black Demon, you! Steady down there and keep your feet on the ground."

The winter fell sharply. A few preliminary gusty showers, and then a strong steady rain. The hills lost their straw colour and blackened under the water, and the winter streams scrambled noisily down the canyons. The mushrooms and puffballs popped up and the new grass started before Christmas.

But this year Christmas was not the central day to Jody. Some undetermined time in January had become the axis day around which the months swung. When the rains fell, he put Nellie in a box stall and fed her warm food every morning and curried her and brushed her.

The mare was swelling so greatly that Jody became alarmed. "She'll pop wide open," he said to Billy.

Billy laid his strong square hand against Nellie's swollen abdomen.

"Feel here," he said quietly. "You can feel it move. I guess it would surprise you if there were twin colts."

"You don't think so?" Jody cried. "You don't think it will be twins, do you, Billy?"

"No, I don't, but it does happen, sometimes."

During the first two weeks of January it rained steadily. Jody spent most of his time, when he wasn't in school, in the box stall with Nellie. Twenty times a day he put his hand on her stomach to feel the colt move. Nellie became more and more gentle and friendly to him. She rubbed her nose on him. She whinnied softly when he walked into the barn.

Carl Tiflin came to the barn with Jody one day. He looked admiringly at the groomed bay coat, and he felt the firm flesh over ribs and shoulders. "You've done a good job," he said to Jody. And this was the greatest praise he knew how to give. Jody was tight with pride for hours afterward.

The fifteenth of January came, and the colt was not born. And the twentieth came; a lump of fear began to form in Jody's stomach. "Is it all right?" he demanded of Billy.

"Oh, sure."

And again: "Are you sure it's going to be all right?"

Billy stroked the mare's neck. She swayed her head uneasily. "I told you it wasn't always the same time, Jody. You just have to wait."

When the end of the month arrived with no birth, Jody grew frantic. Nellie was so big that her breath came heavily, and her ears were close together and straight up, as though her head ached. Jody's sleep grew restless and his dreams confused.

On the night of the second of February he awakened crying. His mother called to him, "Jody, you're dreaming. Wake up and start over again."

But Jody was filled with terror and desolation. He lay quietly a few moments, waiting for his mother to go back to sleep, and then he slipped his clothes on, and crept out in his bare feet.

The night was black and thick. A little misting rain fell. The cypress tree and the bunk-house loomed and then dropped back into the mist. The barn door screeched as he opened it, a thing it never did in the daytime. Jody went to the rack and found a lantern and a tin box of matches. He lighted the wick and walked down the long straw-covered aisle to Nellie's stall. She was standing up. Her whole body weaved from side to side. Jody called to her, "So, Nellie, so-o, Nellie," but she did not stop her swaying nor look around. When he stepped into the stall and touched her on the shoulder she shivered under his hand. Then Billy Buck's voice came from the hayloft right above the stall.

"Jody, what are you doing?"

Jody started back and turned miserable eyes up toward the nest where Billy was lying in the hay. "Is she all right, do you think?"

"Why sure, I think so."

"You won't let anything happen, Billy, you're sure you won't?"

Billy growled down at him, "I told you I'd call you, and I will. Now you get back to bed and stop worrying that mare. She's got enough to do without you worrying her."

Jody cringed, for he had never heard Billy speak in such a tone. "I only thought I'd come and see," he said. "I woke up."

Billy softened a little then. "Well, you get to bed. I don't want you bothering her. I told you I'd get you a good colt. Get along now."

Jody walked slowly out of the barn. He blew out the lantern and set it in the rack. The blackness of the night, and the chilled mist struck him and enfolded him. He wished he believed everything Billy said as he had before the pony died. It was a moment before his eyes, blinded by the feeble lantern-flame, could make any form of the darkness. The damp ground chilled his bare feet. At the cypress tree the roosting turkeys chattered a little in alarm, and the two good dogs responded to their duty and came charging out, barking to frighten away the coyotes they thought were prowling under the tree.

As he crept through the kitchen, Jody stumbled over a chair. Carl called from his bedroom, "Who's there? What's the matter there?"

And Mrs. Tiflin said sleepily, "What's the matter, Carl?"

The next second Carl came out of the bedroom carrying a candle, and found Jody before he could get into bed. "What are you doing out?"

Jody turned shyly away. "I was down to see the mare."

For a moment anger at being awakened fought with approval in Jody's father. "Listen," he said, finally. "there's not a man in this country that knows more about colts than Billy. You leave it to him."

Words burst out of Jody's mouth, "But the pony died——"

"Don't you go blaming that on him," Carl said sternly. "If Billy can't save a horse, it can't be saved."

Mrs. Tiflin called, "Make him clean his feet and go to bed, Carl. He'll be sleepy all day to-morrow."

It seemed to Jody that he had just closed his eyes to try to go to sleep when he was shaken violently by the shoulder. Billy Buck stood beside him, holding a lantern in his hand. "Get up," he said. "Hurry up." He turned and walked quickly out of the room.

Mrs. Tiflin called, "What's the matter? Is that you, Billy?"

"Yes, ma'am."

"Is Nellie ready?"

"Yes, ma'am."

"All right, I'll get up and heat some water in case you need it."

Jody jumped into his clothes so quickly that he was out the back door before Billy's swinging lantern was halfway to the barn. There was a rim of dawn on the mountain-tops, but no light had penetrated into the cup of the ranch yet. Jody ran frantically after the lantern and caught up to Billy just as he reached the barn. Billy hung the lantern to a nail on the stall-side and took off his blue denim coat. Jody saw that he wore only a sleeveless shirt under it.

Nellie was standing rigid and stiff. While they watched, she crouched. Her whole body was wrung with a spasm. The spasm passed. But in a few moments it started over again, and passed.

Billy muttered nervously, "There's something wrong." His bare hand disappeared. "Oh, Jesus," he said. "It's wrong."

The spasm came again, and this time Billy strained, and the muscles stood out on his arm and shoulder. He heaved strongly, his forehead beaded with perspiration. Nellie cried with pain. Billy was muttering, "It's wrong. I can't turn it. It's way wrong. It's turned all around wrong."

He glared wildly toward Jody. And then his fingers made a careful, careful diagnosis. His cheeks were growing tight and grey. He looked for a long questioning minute at Jody standing back of the stall. Then Billy stepped to the rack under the manure window and picked up a horseshoe hammer with his wet right hand.

"Go outside, Jody," he said.

The boy stood still and stared dully at him.

"Go outside, I tell you. It'll be too late."

Jody didn't move.

Then Billy walked quickly to Nellie's head. He cried, "Turn your face away, damn you, turn your face."

This time Jody obeyed. His head turned sideways. He heard Billy whispering hoarsely in the stall. And then he heard a hollow crunch of bone. Nellie chuckled shrilly. Jody looked back in time to see the hammer rise and fall again on the flat forehead. Then Nellie fell heavily to her side and quivered for a moment.

Billy jumped to the swollen stomach; his big pocket-knife was in his hand. He lifted the skin and drove the knife in. He sawed and ripped at the tough belly. The air filled with the sick odour of warm living entrails. The other horses reared back against their halter chains and squealed and kicked.

Billy dropped the knife. Both of his arms plunged into the terrible ragged hole and dragged out a big, white, dripping bundle. His teeth tore a hole in the covering. A little black head appeared through the tear, and little slick, wet ears. A gurgling breath was drawn, and then another. Billy shucked off the sac and found his knife and cut the string. For a moment he held the little black colt in his arms and looked at it. And then he walked slowly over and laid it in the straw at Jody's feet.

Billy's face and arms and chest were dripping red. His body shivered and his teeth chattered. His voice was gone; he spoke in a throaty whisper: "There's your colt. I promised. And there it is. I had to do it—had to." He stopped and looked over his shoulder into the box stall. "Go get hot water and a sponge," he whispered. "Wash him and dry him the way his mother would. You'll have to feed him by hand. But there's your colt, the way I promised."

Jody stared stupidly at the wet, panting foal. It stretched out its chin and tried to raise its head. Its blank eyes were navy-blue.

"God damn you," Billy shouted, "will you go now for the water? *Will* you go?"

Then Jody turned and trotted out of the barn into the dawn. He ached from his throat to his stomach. His legs were stiff and heavy. He tried to be glad because of the colt, but the bloody face and the haunted, tired eyes of Billy Buck hung in the air ahead of him.

OF MICE AND MEN

CHAPTER I

A FEW miles south of Soledad, the Salinas River drops in close to the hill-side bank and runs deep and green. The water is warm too, for it has slipped twinkling over the yellow sands in the sunlight before reaching the narrow pool. On one side of the river the golden foot-hill slopes curve up to the strong and rocky Gabilan mountains, but on the valley side the water is lined with trees—willows fresh and green with every spring, carrying in their lower leaf-junctures the debris of the winter's flooding; and sycamores with mottled, white, recumbent limbs and branches that arch over the pool. On the sandy bank under the trees the leaves lie deep and so crisp that a lizard makes a great skittering if he runs among them. Rabbits come out of the brush to sit on the sand in the evening, and the damp flats are covered with the night tracks of 'coons, and with the spread pads of dogs from the ranches, and with the split-wedge tracks of deer that come to drink in the dark.

There is a path through the willows and among the sycamores, a path beaten hard by boys coming down from the ranches to swim in the deep pool, and beaten hard by tramps who come wearily down from the highway in the evening to jungle-up near water. In front of the low horizontal limb of a giant sycamore there is an ash pile made by many fires; the limb is worn smooth by men who have sat on it.

Evening of a hot day started the little wind to moving among the leaves. The shade climbed up the hills toward the top. On the sand-banks the rabbits sat as quietly as little grey, sculptured stones. And then from the direction of the state highway came the sound of footsteps on crisp sycamore leaves. The rabbits hurried noiselessly for cover. A stilted heron laboured up into the air and pounded down-river. For a moment the place was lifeless, and then two men emerged from the path and came into the opening by the green pool. They had walked in single file down the path, and even in the open one stayed behind the other. Both were dressed in denim trousers and in denim coats with brass buttons. Both wore black, shapeless hats and both carried tight blanket rolls slung over their shoulders. The first man was small and quick, dark of face, with restless eyes and sharp, strong features. Every part of him was defined: small, strong hands, slender arms, a thin and bony nose. Behind him walked his opposite, a huge man, shapeless of face, with large, pale eyes, with wide, sloping shoulders; and he walked heavily, dragging his feet a little, the way a bear drags his paws. His arms did not swing at his sides, but hung loosely and only moved because the heavy hands were pendula.

The first man stopped short in the clearing, and the follower nearly ran over him. He took off his hat and wiped the sweat-band with his forefinger and snapped the moisture off. His huge companion dropped his blankets and flung himself down and drank from the surface of the green pool; drank with long gulps, snorting into the water like a horse. The small man stepped nervously beside him.

"Lennie!" he said sharply. "Lennie, for God's sake don't drink so much." Lennie continued to snort into the pool. The small man leaned over and shook him by the shoulder. "Lennie. You gonna be sick like you was last night."

Lennie dipped his whole head under, hat and all, and then he sat up on the bank and his hat dripped down on his blue coat and ran down his back. "Tha's good," he said. "You drink some, George. You take a good big drink." He smiled happily.

George unslung his bindle and dropped it gently on the bank. "I ain't sure it's good water," he said. "Looks kinda scummy."

Lennie dabbled his big paw in the water and wiggled his fingers so the water arose in little splashes; rings widened across the pool to the other side and came back again. Lennie watched them go. "Look, George. Look what I done."

George knelt beside the pool and drank from his hand with quick scoops. "Tastes all right," he admitted. "Don't really seem to be running, though. You never oughta drink water when it ain't running, Lennie," he said hopelessly. "You'd drink out of a gutter if you was thirsty." He threw a scoop of water into his face and rubbed it about with his hand, under his chin and around the back of his neck. Then he replaced his hat, pushed himself back from the river, drew up his knees and embraced them. Lennie, who had been watching, imitated George exactly. He pushed himself back, drew up his knees, embraced them, looked over to George to see whether he had it just right. He pulled his hat down a little more over his eyes, the way George's hat was.

George stared morosely at the water. The rims of his eyes were red with sun glare. He said angrily, "We could just as well of rode clear to the ranch if that bastard bus-driver knew what he was talkin' about. 'Jes' a little stretch down the highway,' he says. 'Jes' a little stretch.' God-damn near four miles, that's what it was! Didn't want to stop at the ranch gate, that's what. Too god-damn lazy to pull up. Wonder he isn't too damn good to stop in Soledad at all. Kicks us out and says, 'Jes' a little stretch down the road.' I bet it was *more* than four miles. Damn hot day."

Lennie looked timidly over to him. "George?"

"Yeah, what ya want?"

"Where we goin', George?"

The little man jerked down the brim of his hat and scowled over at Lennie. "So you forgot that awready, did you? I gotta tell you again, do I? Jesus Christ, you're a crazy bastard!"

"I forgot," Lennie said softly. "I tried not to forget. Honest to God I did, George."

"O.K.—O.K. I'll tell ya again. I ain't got nothing to do. Might jus' as well spen' all my time tellin' you things and then you forget 'em, and I tell you again."

"Tried and tried," said Lennie, "but it didn't do no good. I remember about the rabbits, George."

"The hell with the rabbits. That's all you ever can remember is them rabbits. O.K.! Now you listen and this time you got to remember so we don't get in no trouble. You remember settin' in that gutter on Howard Street and watchin' that blackboard?"

Lennie's face broke into a delighted smile. "Why sure, George. I remember that . . . but . . . what'd we do then? I remember some girls come by and you says . . . you says . . ."

"The hell with what I says. You remember about us goin' into Murray and Ready's, and they give us work cards and bus tickets?"

"Oh, sure, George. I remember that now." His hands went quickly into his side coat pockets. He said gently, "George . . . I ain't got mine. I musta lost it." He looked down at the ground in despair.

"You never had none, you crazy bastard. I got both of 'em here. Think I'd let you carry your own work card?"

Lennie grinned with relief. "I . . . I thought I put it in my side pocket." His hand went into the pocket again.

George looked sharply at him. "What'd you take outa that pocket?"

"Ain't a thing in my pocket," Lennie said cleverly.

"I know there ain't. You got it in your hand. What you got in your hand—hidin' it?"

"I ain't got nothin', George. Honest."

"Come on, give it here."

Lennie held his closed hand away from George's direction. "It's on'y a mouse, George."

"A mouse? A live mouse?"

"Uh-uh. Jus' a dead mouse, George. I didn't kill it. Honest! I found it. I found it dead."

"Give it here," said George.

"Aw, leave me have it, George."

"*Give it here!*"

Lennie's closed hand slowly obeyed. George took the mouse and threw it across the pool to the other side, among the brush. "What you want of a dead mouse, anyways?"

"I could pet it with my thumb while we walked along," said Lennie.

"Well, you ain't petting no mice while you walk with me. You remember where we're goin' now?"

Lennie looked startled and then in embarrassment hid his face against his knees. "I forgot again."

"Jesus Christ," George said resignedly. "Well—look, we're gonna work on a ranch like the one we come from up north."

"Up north?"

"In Weed."

"Oh, sure. I remember. In Weed."

"That ranch we're goin' to is right down there about a quarter mile. We're gonna go in an' see the boss. Now, look—I'll give him the work tickets, but you ain't gonna say a word. You jus' stand there and don't say nothing. If he finds out what a crazy bastard you are, we won't get no job, but if he sees ya work before he hears ya talk, we're set. Ya got that?"

"Sure, George. Sure I got it."

"O.K. Now when we go in to see the boss, what you gonna do?"

"I . . . I . . ." Lennie thought. His face grew tight with thought. "I . . . ain't gonna say nothin'. Jus' gonna stan' there."

"Good boy. That's swell. You say that over two, three times so you won't forget it."

Lennie droned to himself softly, "I ain't gonna say nothin' . . . I ain't gonna say nothin' . . . I ain't gonna say nothin'."

"O.K.," said George. "An' you ain't gonna do no bad things like you done in Weed, neither."

Lennie looked puzzled. "Like I done in Weed?"

"Oh, so ya forgot that too, did ya? Well, I ain't gonna remind ya, fear ya do it again."

A light of understanding broke on Lennie's face. "They run us outa Weed," he exploded triumphantly.

"Run us out, hell," said George disgustedly. "We run. They was lookin' for us, but they didn't catch us."

Lennie giggled happily. "I didn't forget that, you bet."

George lay back on the sand and crossed his hands under his head, and Lennie imitated him, raising his head to see whether he were doing it right. "God, you're a lot of trouble," said George. "I could get along so easy and so nice if I didn't have you on my tail. I could live so easy and maybe have a girl."

For a moment Lennie lay quiet, and then he said hopefully, "We gonna work on a ranch, George."

"Awright. You got that. But we're gonna sleep here because I got a reason."

The day was going fast now. Only the tops of the Gabilan mountains flamed with the light of the sun that had gone from the valley. A water-snake slipped along on the pool, its head held up like a little periscope. The reeds jerked slightly in the current. Far off toward the highway a man shouted something, and another man shouted back. The sycamore limbs rustled under a little wind that died immediately.

"George—why ain't we goin' on to the ranch and get some supper? They got supper at the ranch."

George rolled on his side. "No reason at all for you. I like it here. To-morra we're gonna go to work. I seen thrashin' machines on the way down. That means we'll be bucking grain-bags, bustin' a gut. To-night I'm gonna lay right here and look up. I like it."

Lennie got up on his knees and looked down at George. "Ain't we gonna have no supper?"

"Sure we are, if you gather up some dead willow sticks. I got three cans of beans in my bindle. You get a fire ready. I'll give you a match when you get the sticks together. Then we'll heat the beans and have supper."

Lennie said, "I like beans with ketchup."

"Well, we ain't got no ketchup. You go get wood. An' don't you fool around. It'll be dark before long."

Lennie lumbered to his feet and disappeared in the brush. George lay where he was and whistled softly to himself. There were sounds of splashing down the river in the direction Lennie had taken. George stopped whistling and listened. "Poor bastard," he said softly, and then went on whistling again.

In a moment Lennie came crashing back through the brush. He carried one small willow stick in his hand. George sat up. "Aw right," he said brusquely. "Gi'me that mouse!"

But Lennie made an elaborate pantomime of innocence. "What mouse, George? I ain't got no mouse."

George held out his hand. "Come on. Give it to me. You ain't puttin' nothing over."

Lennie hesitated, backed away, looked wildly at the brush line as though he contemplated running for his freedom. George said coldly. "You gonna give me that mouse or do I have to sock you?"

"Give you what, George?"

"You know god-damn well what. I want that mouse."

Lennie reluctantly reached into his pocket. His voice broke a little. "I don't know why I can't keep it. It ain't nobody's mouse. I didn't steal it. I found it lyin' right beside the road."

George's hand remained outstretched imperiously. Slowly, like a terrier who doesn't want to bring a ball to its master, Lennie approached, drew back, approached again. George snapped his fingers sharply, and at the sound Lennie laid the mouse in his hand.

"I wasn't doin' nothing bad with it, George. Jus' strokin' it."

George stood up and threw the mouse as far as he could into the darkening brush, and then he stepped to the pool and washed his hands. "You crazy fool. Don't you think I could see your feet was wet where you went acrost the river to get it?" He heard Lennie's whimpering cry and wheeled about. "Blubberin' like a baby! Jesus Christ! A big guy like you." Lennie's lip quivered and tears started in his eyes. "Aw, Lennie!" George put his hand on Lennie's shoulder. "I ain't takin' it away jus' for meanness. That mouse ain't fresh, Lennie; and besides, you've broke it pettin' it. You get another mouse that's fresh and I'll let you keep it a little while."

Lennie sat down on the ground and hung his head dejectedly. "I don't know where there is no other mouse. I remember a lady used to give 'em to me—ever' one she got. But that lady ain't here."

George scoffed. "Lady, huh? Don't even remember who that lady was. That was your own Aunt Clara. An' she stopped givin' 'em to ya. You always killed 'em."

Lennie looked sadly up at him. "They was so little," he said apologetically. "I'd pet 'em, and pretty soon they bit my fingers and I pinched their heads a little and then they was dead—because they was so little.

"I wish't we'd get the rabbits pretty soon, George. They ain't so little."

"The hell with the rabbits. An' you ain't to be trusted with no live mice. Your Aunt Clara give you a rubber mouse and you wouldn't have nothing to do with it."

"It wasn't no good to pet," said Lennie.

The flame of the sunset lifted from the mountain-tops and dusk came into the valley, and a half-darkness came in among the willows and the sycamores. A big carp rose to the surface of the pool, gulped air and then sank mysteriously into the dark water again, leaving widening rings on the water. Overhead the leaves whisked again and little puffs of willow cotton blew down and landed on the pool's surface.

"You gonna get that wood?" George demanded. "There's plenty right up against the back of that sycamore. Flood-water wood. Now you get it."

Lennie went behind the tree and brought out a litter of dried leaves and twigs. He threw them in a heap on the old ash-pile and went back for more and more. It was almost night now. A dove's wings whistled over the water. George walked to the fire pile and lighted the dry leaves. The flame cracked up among the twigs and fell to work. George undid his bindle and brought out three cans of beans. He stood them about the fire, close in against the blaze, but not quite touching the flame.

"There's enough beans for four men," George said.

Lennie watched him from over the fire. He said patiently, "I like 'em with ketchup."

"Well, we ain't got any," George exploded. "Whatever we ain't got, that's what you want. God a'mighty, if I was alone I could live so easy. I could go get a job an' work, an' no trouble. No mess at all, and when the end of the month come I could take my fifty bucks and go into town and get whatever I want. Why, I could stay in a cat-house all night. I could eat any place I want, hotel or any place, and order any damn thing I could think of. An' I could do all that every damn month. Get a gallon of whisky, or set in a pool-room and play cards or shoot pool." Lennie knelt and looked over the fire at the angry George. And Lennie's face was drawn with terror. "An' whatta I got?" George went on furiously. "I got you! You can't keep a job and you lose me ever' job I get. Jus' keep me shovin' all over the country all the time. An' that ain't the worst. You get in trouble. You do bad things and I got to get you out." His voice rose nearly to a shout. "You crazy son-of-a-bitch. You keep me in hot water all the time." He took on the elaborate manner of little girls when they are mimicking one another. "Jus' wanted to feel that little girl's dress—jus' wanted to pet it like it was a mouse—— Well, how the hell did she know you jus' wanted to feel her dress? She jerks back and you hold on like it was a mouse. She yells and we got to hide in a irrigation ditch all day with guys lookin' for us, and we got to sneak out in the dark and get outta the country. All the time somethin' like that—all the time. I wisht I could put you in a cage with about a million mice and let you have fun." His anger left him suddenly. He looked across the fire at Lennie's anguished face, and then he looked ashamedly at the flames.

It was quite dark now, but the fire lighted the trunks of the trees and the curving branches overhead. Lennie crawled slowly and cautiously around the fire until he was close to George. He sat back on his heels. George turned the bean-cans so that another side faced the fire. He pretended to be unaware of Lennie so close beside him.

"George," very softly. No answer. "George!"

"Whatta you want?"

"I was only foolin', George. I don't want no ketchup. I wouldn't eat no ketchup if it was right here beside me."

"If it was here, you could have some."

"But I wouldn't eat none, George. I'd leave it all for you. You could cover your beans with it and I wouldn't touch none of it."

George still stared morosely at the fire. "When I think of the swell time I could have without you, I go nuts. I never get no peace."

Lennie still knelt. He looked off into the darkness across the river. "George, you want I should go away and leave you alone?"

"Where the hell could you go?"

"Well, I could. I could go off in the hills there. Someplace I'd find a cave."

"Yeah? How'd you eat? You ain't got sense enough to find nothing to eat."

"I'd find things, George. I don't need no nice food with ketchup. I'd lay out in the sun and nobody'd hurt me. An' if I foun' a mouse, I could keep it. Nobody'd take it away from me."

George looked quickly and searchingly at him. "I been mean, ain't I?"

"If you don' want me I can go off in the hills an' find a cave. I can go away any time."

"No—look! I was jus' foolin', Lennie. 'Cause I want you to stay with me. Trouble with mice is you always kill 'em." He paused. "Tell you what I'll do, Lennie. First chance I get I'll give you a pup. Maybe you wouldn't kill *it*. That'd be better than mice. And you could pet it harder."

Lennie avoided the bait. He had sensed his advantage. "If you don't want me, you only jus' got to say so, and I'll go off in those hills right there—right up in those hills and live by myself. An' I won't get no mice stole from me."

George said, "I want you to stay with me, Lennie. Jesus Christ, somebody'd shoot you for a coyote if you was by yourself. No, you stay with me. Your Aunt Clara wouldn't like you running off by yourself, even if she is dead."

Lennie spoke craftily: "Tell me—like you done before."

"Tell you what?"

"About the rabbits."

George snapped, "You ain't gonna put nothing over on me."

Lennie pleaded, "Come on, George. Tell me. Please, George. Like you done before."

"You get a kick outta that, don't you. A'right, I'll tell you, and then we'll eat our supper. . . ."

George's voice became deeper. He repeated his words rhythmically as though he had said them many times before. "Guys like us, that work on ranches, are the loneliest guys in the world. They got no family. They don't belong no place. They come to a ranch an' work up a stake and then they go inta town and blow their stake, and the first thing you know they're poundin' their tail on some other ranch. They ain't got nothing to look ahead to."

Lennie was delighted. "That's it—that's it. Now tell how it is with us."

George went on. "With us it ain't like that. We got a future. We got somebody to talk to that gives a damn about us. We don't have to sit in no bar-room blowin' in our jack jus' because we got no place else to go. If them other guys gets in jail they can rot for all anybody gives a damn. But not us."

Lennie broke in. "*But not us! An' why? Because . . . because I got you to look after me, and you got me to look after you, and that's why.*" He laughed delightedly. "Go on now, George."

"You got it by heart. You can do it yourself."

"No, you. I forget some a' the things. Tell about how it's gonna be."

"O.K. Some day—we're gonna get the jack together and we're gonna have a little house and a couple of acres an' a cow and some pigs and——"

"*An' live off the fatta the lan'*," Lennie shouted. "An' have *rabbits*. Go on, George! Tell about what we're gonna have in the garden and about the rabbits in the cages and about the rain in the winter and the stove, and how thick the cream is on the milk like you can hardly cut it. Tell about that, George."

"Why'n't you do it yourself. You know all of it."

"No . . . you tell it. It ain't the same if I tell it. Go on . . . George. How I get to tend the rabbits."

"Well," said George. "We'll have a big vegetable patch and a rabbit-hutch and chickens. And when it rains in the winter, we'll just say the hell with goin' to work, and we'll build up a fire in the stove and set around it an' listen to the rain comin' down on the roof—Nuts!" He took out his pocket-knife. "I ain't got time for no more." He drove his knife through the top of one of the bean-cans, sawed out the top and passed the can to Lennie. Then he opened a second can. From his side pocket he brought out two spoons and passed one of them to Lennie.

They sat by the fire and filled their mouths with beans and chewed mightily. A few beans slipped out of the side of Lennie's mouth. George gestured with his spoon. "What you gonna say to-morrow when the boss asks you questions?"

Lennie stopped chewing and swallowed. His face was concentrated. "I . . . I ain't gonna . . . say a word."

"Good boy! That's fine, Lennie! Maybe you're gettin' better. When we get the coupla acres I can let you tend the rabbits all right. 'Specially if you remember as good as that."

Lennie choked with pride. "I can remember," he said.

George motioned with his spoon again.

"Look, Lennie. I want you to look around here. You can remember this place, can't you? The ranch is about a quarter-mile up that way. Just follow the river."

"Sure," said Lennie. "I can remember this. Di'n't I remember about not gonna say a word?"

" 'Course you did. Well, look. Lennie—if you jus' happen to get in trouble like you always done before, I want you to come right here an' hide in the brush."

"Hide in the brush," said Lennie slowly.

"Hide in the brush till I come for you. Can you remember that?"

"Sure I can, George. Hide in the brush till you come."

"But you ain't gonna get in no trouble, because if you do, I won't let you tend the rabbits." He threw his empty bean can off into the brush.

"I won't get in no trouble, George. I ain't gonna say a word."

"O.K. Bring your bindle over here by the fire. It's gonna be nice sleepin' here. Lookin' up, and the leaves. Don't build up no more fire. We'll let her die down."

They made their beds on the sand, and as the blaze dropped from the fire the sphere of light grew smaller; the curling branches disappeared and only a faint glimmer showed where the tree-trunks were. From the darkness Lennie called, "George—you asleep?"

"No. Whatta you want?"

"Let's have different colour rabbits, George."

"Sure we will," George said sleepily. "Red and blue and green rabbits, Lennie. Millions of 'em."

"Furry ones, George, like I seen in the fair in Sacramento."

"Sure, furry ones."

" 'Cause I can jus' as well go away, George, an' live in a cave."

"You can jus' as well go to hell," said George. "Shut up now."

The red light dimmed on the coals. Up the hill from the river a coyote yammered, and a dog answered from the other side of the stream. The sycamore leaves whispered in a little night breeze.

CHAPTER II

THE BUNK-HOUSE was a long, rectangular building. Inside, the walls were whitewashed and the floor unpainted. In three walls there were small, square windows, and in the fourth a solid door with a wooden latch. Against the walls were eight bunks, five of them made up with blankets and the other three showing their burlap ticking. Over each bunk there was nailed an apple-box with the opening forward so that it made two shelves for the personal belongings of the occupant of the bunk. And these shelves were loaded with little articles, soap and talcum-powder, razors and those Western magazines ranch-men love to read and scoff at and secretly believe. And there were medicines on the shelves, and little vials, combs; and, from nails on the box sides, a few neckties. Near one wall there was a black cast-iron stove, its stove-pipe going straight up through the ceiling. In the middle of the room stood a big square table littered with playing-cards, and around it were grouped boxes for the players to sit on.

At about ten o'clock in the morning the sun threw a bright dust-laden bar through one of the side windows, and in and out of the beam flies shot like rushing stars.

The wooden latch raised. The door opened and a tall, stoop-shouldered old man came in. He was dressed in blue jeans and he carried a big push-broom in his left hand. Behind him came George, and behind George, Lennie.

"The boss was expectin' you last night," the old man said. "He was sore as hell when you wasn't here to go out this morning." He pointed with his right arm, and out of the sleeve came a round stick-like wrist, but no hand. "You can have them two beds there," he said, indicating two bunks near the stove.

George stepped over and threw his blankets down on the burlap sack of straw that was a mattress. He looked into the box shelf and then picked a small yellow can from it. "Say. What the hell's this?"

"I don't know," said the old man.

"Says 'positively kills lice, roaches and other scourges.' What the hell kind of bed you giving us, anyways? We don't want no pants rabbits."

The old swamper shifted his broom and held it between his elbow and his side while he held out his hand for the can. He studied the label carefully. "Tell you what——" he said finally, "last guy that had this bed was a blacksmith—hell of a nice fella and as clean a guy as you want to meet. Used to wash his hands even *after* he ate."

"Then how come he got grey-backs?" George was working up a slow anger. Lennie put his bindle on the neighbouring bunk and sat down. He watched George with open mouth.

"Tell you what," said the old swamper. "This here blacksmith—name of Whitey—was the kind of guy that would put that stuff around even if there wasn't no bugs—just to make sure, see? Tell you what he used to do—— At meals he'd peel his boil' potatoes, an' he'd take out ever' little spot, no matter what kind, before he'd eat it. And if there was a red splotch on an egg, he'd scrape it off. Finally quit about the food. That's the kinda guy he was—clean. Used ta dress up Sundays even when he wasn't going no place, put on a necktie even, and then set in the bunk-house."

"I ain't so sure," said George sceptically. "What did you say he quit for?"

The old man put the yellow can in his pocket, and he rubbed his bristly white whiskers with his knuckles. "Why . . . he . . . just quit, the way a guy will. Says it was the food. Just wanted to move. Didn't give no other reason but the food. Just says 'Gimme my time' one night, the way any guy would."

George lifted his tick and looked underneath it. He leaned over and inspected the sacking closely. Immediately Lennie got up and did the same with his bed. Finally George seemed satisfied. He unrolled his bindle and put things on the shelf, his razor and bar of soap, his comb and bottle of pills, his liniment and leather wristband. Then he made his bed up neatly with blankets. The old man said, "I guess the boss'll be out here in a minute. He was sure burned when you wasn't here this morning. Come right in when we was eatin' breakfast and says, 'Where the hell's them new men?' An' he give the stable buck hell, too."

George patted a wrinkle out of his bed, and then sat down. "Give the stable buck hell?" he asked.

"Sure. Ya see, the stable buck's a nigger."

"Nigger, huh?"

"Yeah. Nice fella, too. Got a crooked back where a horse kicked him. The boss gives him hell when he's mad. But the stable buck don't give a damn about that. He reads a lot. Got books in his room."

"What kind of a guy is the boss?" George asked.

"Well, he's a pretty nice fellow. Gets pretty mad sometimes, but he's pretty nice. Tell ya what—know what he done Christmas? Brang a gallon of whisky right in here and says: 'Drink hearty, boys. Christmas comes but once a year.'"

"The hell he did! Whole gallon?"

"Yes, sir. Jesus, we had fun. They let the nigger come in that night. Little skinner name of Smitty took after the nigger. Done pretty good, too. The guys wouldn't let him use his feet, so the nigger got him. If he coulda used his feet, Smitty says he woulda killed the nigger. The guys said on account of the nigger's got a crooked back, Smitty can't use his feet." He paused in relish of the memory. "After that the guys went into Soledad and raised hell. I didn't go in there. I ain't got the poop no more."

Lennie was just finishing making his bed. The wooden latch raised again and the door opened. A little stocky man stood in the open doorway. He wore blue jean trousers, a flannel shirt, a black, unbuttoned vest and a black coat. His thumbs were stuck in his belt, on each side of a square steel buckle. On his head was a soiled brown Stetson hat, and he wore high-heeled boots and spurs to prove he was not a labouring man.

The old swamper looked quickly at him, and then shuffled to the door rubbing his whiskers with his knuckles as he went. "Them guys just come," he said, and shuffled past the boss and out the door.

The boss stepped into the room with the short, quick steps of a fat-legged man. "I wrote Murray and Ready I wanted two men this morning. You got your work slips?" George reached into his pocket and produced the slips and handed them to the boss. "It wasn't Murray and Ready's fault. Says right here on the slip that you was to be here for work this morning."

George looked down at his feet. "Bus-driver give us a bum steer," he said. "We hadda walk ten miles. Says we was here when we wasn't. We couldn't get no rides in the morning."

The boss squinted his eyes. "Well, I had to send out the grain teams short two buckers. Won't do any good to go out now till after dinner." He pulled his time-book out of his pocket and opened it where a pencil was stuck between the leaves. George scowled meaningfully at Lennie, and Lennie nodded to show that he understood. The boss licked his pencil. "What's your name?"

"George Milton."

"And what's yours?"

George said, "His name's Lennie Small."

The names were entered in the book. "Le's see, this is the twentieth, noon the twentieth." He closed the book. "Where you boys been working?"

"Up around Weed," said George.

"You too?" to Lennie.

"Yeah, him too," said George.

The boss pointed a playful finger at Lennie. "He ain't much of a talker, is he?"

"No, he ain't, but he's sure a hell of a good worker. Strong as a bull."

Lennie smiled to himself. "Strong as a bull," he repeated.

George scowled at him, and Lennie dropped his head in shame at having forgotten.

The boss said suddenly, "Listen, Small!" Lennie raised his head. "What can you do?"

In a panic, Lennie looked at George for help. "He can do anything you tell him," said George. "He's a good skinner. He can rassel grain-bags, drive a cultivator. He can do anything. Just give him a try."

The boss turned to George. "Then why don't you let him answer? What you trying to put over?"

George broke in loudly, "Oh! I ain't saying he's bright. He ain't. But I say he's a god-damn good worker. He can put up a four-hundred-pound bale."

The boss deliberately put the little book in his pocket. He hooked his thumbs in his belt and squinted one eye nearly closed. "Say—what you sellin'?"

"Huh?"

"I said what stake you got in this guy? You takin' his pay away from him?"

"No, 'course I ain't. Why ya think I'm sellin' him out?"

"Well, I never seen one guy take so much trouble for another guy. I just like to know what your interest is."

George said, "He's my . . . cousin. I told his old lady I'd take care of him. He got kicked in the head by a horse when he was a kid. He's awright. Just ain't bright. But he can do anything you tell him."

The boss turned half away. "Well, God knows he don't need any brains to buck barley bags. But don't you try to put nothing over, Milton. I got my eye on you. Why'd you quit in Weed?"

"Job was done," said George promptly.

"What kinda job?"

"We . . . we was diggin' a cesspool."

"All right. But don't try to put nothing over, 'cause you can't get away with nothing. I seen wise guys before. Go on out with the grain teams after dinner. They're pickin' up barley at the threshing machine. Go out with Slim's team."

"Slim?"

"Yeah. Big tall skinner. You'll see him at dinner." He turned abruptly and went to the door, but before he went out he turned and looked for a long moment at the two men.

When the sound of his footsteps had died away, George turned on Lennie. "So you wasn't gonna say a word. You was gonna leave your big flapper shut and leave me do the talkin'. Damn near lost us the job."

Lennie stared hopelessly at his hands. "I forgot, George."

"Yeah, you forgot. You always forget, an' I got to talk you out of it." He sat down heavily on the bunk. "Now he's got his eye on us. Now we got to be careful and not make no slips. You keep your big flapper shut after this." He fell morosely silent.

"George."

"What you want now?"

"I wasn't kicked in the head with no horse, was I, George?"

"Be a damn good thing if you was," George said viciously. "Save ever'body a hell of a lot of trouble."

"You said I was your cousin, George."

"Well, that was a lie. An' I'm damn glad it was. If I was a relative of yours I'd shoot myself." He stopped suddenly, stepped to the open front door and peered out. "Say, what the hell you doin' listenin'?"

The old man came slowly into the room. He had his broom in his hand. And at his heels there walked a drag-footed sheep-dog, grey of muzzle, and with pale, blind old eyes. The dog struggled lamely to the side of the room and lay down, grunting softly to himself and licking his grizzled, moth-eaten coat. The swamper watched him until he was settled. "I wasn't listenin'. I was jus' standin' in the shade a minute scratchin' my dog. I jus' now finished swampin' out the wash-house."

"You was pokin' your big ears into our business," George said. "I don't like nobody to get nosey."

The old man looked uneasily from George to Lennie, and then back. "I jus' come there," he said. "I didn't hear nothing you guys was sayin'. I ain't interested in nothing you was sayin'. A guy on a ranch don't never listen nor he don't ast no questions."

"Damn right he don't," said George, slightly mollified, "not if he wants to stay workin' long." But he was reassured by the swamper's defence. "Come on in and set down a minute," he said. "That's a hell of an old dog."

"Yeah. I had 'im ever since he was a pup. God, he was a good sheep-dog when he was younger." He stood his broom against the wall and he rubbed his white bristled cheek with his knuckles. "How'd you like the boss?" he asked.

"Pretty good. Seemed awright."

"He's a nice fella," the swamper agreed. "You got to take him right."

At that moment a young man came into the bunk-house; a thin young man with a brown face, with brown eyes and a head of tightly curled hair. He wore a work glove on his left hand, and, like the boss, he wore high-heeled boots. "Seen my old man?" he asked.

The swamper said, "He was here jus' a minute ago, Curley. Went over to the cookhouse, I think."

"I'll try to catch him," said Curley. His eyes passed over the new men and he stopped. He glanced coldly at George, and then at Lennie. His arms gradually bent at the elbows and his hands closed into fists. He stiffened and went into a slight crouch. His glance was at once calculating and pugnacious. Lennie squirmed under the look and shifted his feet nervously. Curley stepped gingerly close to him. "You the new guys the old man was waitin' for?"

"We just come in," said George.

"Let the big guy talk."

Lennie twisted with embarrassment.

George said, "S'pose he don't want to talk?"

Curley lashed his body around. "By Christ, he's gotta talk when he's spoke to. What the hell are you gettin' into it for?"

"We travel together," said George coldly.

"Oh, so it's that way."

George was tense and motionless. "Yeah, it's that way."

Lennie was looking helplessly to George for instruction.

"An' you won't let the big guy talk, is that it?"

"He can talk if he wants to tell you anything." He nodded slightly to Lennie.

"We jus' come in," said Lennie softly.

Curley stared levelly at him. "Well, nex' time you answer when you're spoke to." He turned toward the door and walked out, and his elbows were still bent out a little.

George watched him out, and then he turned back to the swamper. "Say, what the hell's he got on his shoulder? Lennie didn't do nothing to him."

The old man looked cautiously at the door to make sure no one was listening. "That's the boss's son," he said quietly. "Curley's pretty handy. He done quite a bit in the ring. He's a lightweight, and he's handy."

"Well, let him be handy," said George. "He don't have to take after Lennie. Lennie didn't do nothing to him. What's he got against Lennie?"

The swamper considered: "—Well—tell you what. Curley's like a lot of little guys. He hates big guys. He's alla time picking scraps with big guys. Kind of like he's mad at 'em because he ain't a big guy. You seen little guys like that, ain't you—always scrappy?"

"Sure," said George. "I seen plenty tough little guys. But this Curley better not make no mistakes about Lennie. Lennie ain't handy, but this Curley punk is gonna get hurt if he messes around with Lennie."

"Well, Curley's pretty handy," the swamper said sceptically. "Never did seem right to me. S'pose Curley jumps a big guy an' licks him. Ever'body says what a game guy Charley is. And s'pose he does the same thing and gets licked. Then ever'body says the big guy oughtta pick somebody his own size, and maybe they gang up on the big guy. Never did seem right to me. Seems like Curley ain't givin' nobody a chance."

George was watching the door. He said ominously. "Well, he better watch out for Lennie. Lennie ain't no fighter, but Lennie's strong and quick and Lennie don't know no rules." He walked to the square table and sat down on one of the boxes. He gathered some of the cards together and shuffled them.

The old man sat down on another box. "Don't tell Curley I said none of this. He'd slough me. He just don't give a damn. Won't ever get canned 'cause his old man's the boss."

George cut the cards and began turning them over, looking at each one and throwing it down on a pile. He said, "This guy Curley sounds like a son-of-a-bitch to me. I don't like mean little guys."

"Seems to me like he's worse lately," said the swamper. "He got married a couple of weeks ago. Wife lives over in the boss's house Seems like Curley is cockier'n ever since he got married."

George grunted. "Maybe he's showin' off for his wife."

The swamper warmed to his gossip. "You seen that glove on his left hand?"

"Yeah. I seen it."

"Well, that glove's fulla vaseline."

"Vaseline? What the hell for?"

"Well, I tell ya what, Curley says he's keepin that hand soft for his wife."

George studied the cards absorbedly. "That's a dirty thing to tell around," he said.

The old man was reassured. He had drawn a derogatory statement from George. He felt safe now, and he spoke more confidently. "Wait'll you see Curley's wife."

George cut the cards again and put out a solitaire lay, slowly and deliberately. "Purty?" he asked casually.

"Yeah. Purty . . . but——"

George studied his cards. "But what?"

"Well—she got the eye."

"Yeah? Married two weeks and got the eye? Maybe that's why Curley's pants is full of ants."

"I seen her give Slim the eye. Slim's a jerkline skinner. Hell of a nice fella. Slim don't need to wear no high-heeled boots on a grain team. I seen her give Slim the eye. Curley never seen it. An' I seen her give Carlson the eye."

George pretended a lack of interest. "Looks like we was gonna have fun."

The swamper stood up from his box. "Know what I think?" George did not answer. "Well, I think Curley's married . . . a tart."

"He ain't the first," said George. "There's plenty done that."

The old man moved towards the door, and his ancient dog lifted his head and peered about, and then got painfully to his feet to follow. "I gotta be settin' out the wash-basins for the guys. The teams'll be in before long. You guys gonna buck barley?"

"Yeah."

"You won't tell Curley nothing I said?"

"Hell, no."

"Well, you look her over, mister. You see if she ain't a tart." He stepped out the door into the brilliant sunshine.

George laid down his cards thoughtfully, turned his piles of three. He built four clubs on his ace pile. The sun square was on the floor now, and the flies whipped through it like sparks. A sound of jingling harness and the croak of heavy-laden axles sounded from outside.

From the distance came a clear call. "Stable Buck—ooh, Sta-able Buck!" And then: "Where the hell is that god-damn nigger?"

George stared at his solitaire lay, and then flounced the cards together and turned around to Lennie. Lennie was lying down on the bunk watching him.

"Look, Lennie! This here ain't no set-up. I'm scared. You gonna have trouble with that Curley guy. I seen that kind before. He was kinda feeling you out. He figures he's got you scared and he's gonna take a sock at you the first chance he gets."

Lennie's eyes were frightened. "I don't want no trouble," he said plaintively. "Don't let him sock me, George."

George got up and went over to Lennie's bunk and sat down on it. "I hate that kinda bastard," he said. "I seen plenty of 'em. Like the old guy says, Curley don't take no chances. He always wins." He thought for a moment. "If he tangles with you, Lennie, we're gonna get the can. Don't make no mistake about that. He's the boss's son. Look, Lennie. You try to keep away from him, will you? Don't never speak to him. If he comes in here you move clear to the other side of the room. Will you do that, Lennie?"

"I don't want no trouble," Lennie mourned. "I never done nothing to him."

"Well, that won't do you no good if Curley wants to plug himself up for a fighter. Just don't have anything to do with him. Will you remember?"

"Sure, George. I ain't gonna say a word."

The sound of the approaching grain teams was louder, thud of big hooves on hard ground, drag of brakes and the jingle of trace chains. Men were calling back and forth from the teams. George, sitting on the bunk beside Lennie, frowned as he thought. Lennie asked timidly, "You ain't mad, George?"

"I ain't mad at you. I'm mad at this here Curley bastard. I hoped we was gonna get a little stake together—maybe a hundred dollars." His tone grew decisive. "You keep away from Curley, Lennie."

"Sure I will, George. I won't say a word."

"Don't let him pull you in—but—if the son-of-a-bitch socks you —let 'im have it."

"Let 'im have what, George?"

"Never mind, never mind. I'll tell you when. I hate that kind of a guy. Look, Lennie, if you get in any kind of trouble, you remember what I told you to do?"

Lennie raised up on his elbow. His face contorted with thought. Then his eyes moved sadly to George's face. "If I get in any trouble, you ain't gonna let me tend the rabbits."

"That's not what I meant. You remember where we slep' last night? Down by the river?"

"Yeah. I remember. Oh, sure I remember! I go there an' hide in the brush."

"Hide till I come for you. Don't let nobody see you. Hide in the brush by the river. Say that over."

"Hide in the brush by the river, down in the brush by the river."

"If you get in trouble."

"If I get in trouble."

A brake screeched outside. A call came: "Stable—Buck. Oh! Sta-able Buck."

George said. "Say it over to yourself, Lennie, so you won't forget it."

Both men glanced up, for the rectangle of sunshine in the doorway was cut off. A girl was standing there looking in. She had full, rouged lips and wide-spaced eyes, heavily made up. Her finger-nails were red. Her hair hung in little rolled clusters, like sausages. She wore a cotton house dress and red mules, on the insteps of which were little bouquets of red ostrich feathers. "I'm looking for Curley," she said. Her voice had a nasal, brittle quality.

George looked away from her and then back. "He was in here a minute ago, but he went."

"Oh!" She put her hand behind her back and leaned against the door-frame so that her body was thrown forward. "You're the new fellas that just come, ain't ya?"

"Yeah."

Lennie's eyes moved down over her body, and although she did not seem to be looking at Lennie, she bridled a little. She looked down at her finger-nails. "Sometimes Curley's in here," she explained.

George said brusquely, "Well, he ain't now."

"If he ain't, I guess I better look someplace else," she said playfully.

Lennie watched her, fascinated. George said, "If I see him, I'll pass word you was looking for him."

She smiled archly and twitched her body. "Nobody can't blame a person for lookin'," she said. There were footsteps behind her, going by. She turned her head. "Hi, Slim," she said.

Slim's voice came through the door. "Hi, Good-lookin'."

"I'm tryin' to find Curley, Slim."

"Well, you ain't tryin' very hard. I seen him goin' in your house."

She was suddenly apprehensive. " 'Bye, boys," she called into the bunk-house, and she hurried away.

George looked around at Lennie. "Jesus, what a tramp," he said. "So that's what Curley picks for a wife."

"She's purty," said Lennie defensively.

"Yeah, and she's sure hidin' it. Curley got his work ahead of him. Bet she'd clear out for twenty bucks."

Lennie still stared at the doorway where she had been. "Gosh, she was purty." He smiled admiringly. George looked quickly down at him and then he took him by an ear and shook him.

"Listen to me, you crazy bastard," he said fiercely. "Don't you even take a look at that bitch. I don't care what she says and what she does. I seen 'em poison before, but I never seen no piece of jail-bait worse than her. You leave her be."

Lennie tried to disengage his ear. "I never done nothing, George."

"No, you never. But when she was standin' in the doorway showin' her legs, you wasn't looking the other way, neither."

"I never meant no harm, George. Honest I never."

"Well, you keep away from her, 'cause she's a rat-trap if I ever seen one. You let Curley take the rap. He let himself in for it. Glove fulla vaseline," George said disgustedly. "An' I bet he's eatin' raw eggs and writin' to the patent medicine houses."

Lennie cried out suddenly, "I don' like this place, George. This ain't no good place. I wanna get outa here."

"We gotta keep it till we get a stake. We can't help it, Lennie. We'll get out jus' as soon as we can. I don't like it no better than you do." He went back to the table and set out a new solitaire hand. "No, I don't like it," he said. "For two bits I'd shove out of here. If we can get jus' a few dollars in the poke we'll shove off and go up the American River and pan gold. We can make maybe a couple of dollars a day there, and we might hit a pocket."

Lennie leaned eagerly toward him. "Le's go, George. Le's get outa here. It's mean here."

"We gotta stay," George said shortly. "Shut up now. The guys'll be comin' in."

From the wash-room near-by came the sound of running water and rattling basins. George studied the cards. "Maybe we oughtta wash up," he said. "But we ain't done nothing to get dirty."

A tall man stood in the doorway. He held a crushed Stetson hat under his arm while he combed his long, black, damp hair straight back. Like the others, he wore blue jeans and a short denim jacket. When he had finished combing his hair he moved into the room, and he moved with a majesty only achieved by royalty and master craftsmen. He was a jerkline skinner, the prince of the ranch, capable of driving ten, sixteen, even twenty mules with a single line to the leaders. He was capable of killing a fly on the wheeler's butt with a bull whip without touching the mule. There was a gravity in his manner and a quiet so profound that all talk stopped when he spoke. His authority was so great that his word was taken on any subject, be it politics or love. This was Slim, the jerkline skinner. His hatchet face was ageless. He might have been thirty-five or fifty. His ear heard more than was said to him, and his slow speech had overtones not of thought, but of understanding beyond thought. His hands, large and lean, were as delicate in their action as those of a temple dancer.

He smoothed out his crushed hat, creased it in the middle and put it on. He looked kindly at the two in the bunk-house. "It's brighter'n a bitch outside," he said gently. "Can't hardly see nothing in here. You the new guys?"

"Just come," said George.

"Gonna buck barley?"

"That's what the boss says."

Slim sat down on a box across the table from George. He studied the solitaire hand that was upside-down to him. "Hope you get on my team," he said. His voice was very gentle. "I gotta pair of punks on my team that don't know a barley bag from a blue ball. You guys ever bucked any barley?"

"Hell, yes," said George. "I ain't nothing to scream about, but that big bastard there can put up more grain alone than most pairs can."

Lennie, who had been following the conversation back and forth with his eyes, smiled complacently at the compliment. Slim looked approvingly at George for having given the compliment. He leaned over the table and snapped the corner of a loose card. "You guys travel around together?" His tone was friendly. It invited confidence without demanding it.

"Sure," said George. "We kinda look after each other." He indicated Lennie with his thumb. "He ain't bright. Hell of a good worker, though. Hell of a nice fella, but he ain't bright. I've knew him for a long time."

Slim looked through George and beyond him. "Ain't many guys travel around together," he mused. "I don't know why. Maybe ever'body in the whole damn world is scared of each other."

"It's a lot nicer to go around with a guy you know," said George.

A powerful, big-stomached man came into the bunk-house. His head still dripped water from the scrubbing and dousing. "Hi, Slim," he said, and then stopped and stared at George and Lennie.

"These guys jus' come," said Slim by way of introduction.

"Glad ta meet ya," the big man said. "My name's Carlson."

"I'm George Milton. This here's Lennie Small."

"Glad ta meet ya," Carlson said again. "He ain't very small." He chuckled softly at his joke. "Ain't small at all," he repeated. "Meant to ask you, Slim—how's your bitch? I seen she wasn't under your wagon this morning."

"She slang her pups last night," said Slim. "Nine of 'em. I drowned four of 'em right off. She couldn't feed that many."

"Got five left, huh?"

"Yeah, five. I kept the biggest."

"What kinda dogs you think they're gonna be?"

"I dunno," said Slim. "Some kinda shepherds, I guess. That's the most kind I seen around here when she was in heat."

Carlson went on, "Got five pups, huh. Gonna keep all of 'em?"

"I dunno. Have to keep 'em a while so they can drink Lulu's milk."

Carlson said thoughtfully, "Well, looka here, Slim. I been thinkin'. That dog of Candy's is so god-damn old he can't hardly walk. Stinks like hell, too. Ever' time he comes into the bunk-house I can smell him for two, three days. Why'n't you get Candy to shoot his old dog and give him one of the pups to raise up. I can smell that dog a mile away. Got no teeth, damn near blind, can't eat. Candy feeds him milk. He can't chew nothing else."

George had been staring intently at Slim. Suddenly a triangle began to ring outside, slowly at first, and then faster and faster until the beat of it disappeared into one ringing sound. It stopped as suddenly as it had started.

"There she goes," said Carlson.

Outside, there was a burst of voices as a group of men went by.

Slim stood up slowly and with dignity. "You guys better come on while they's still something to eat. Won't be nothing left in a couple of minutes."

Carlson stepped back to let Slim precede him, and then the two of them went out the door.

Lennie was watching George excitedly. George rumpled his cards into a messy pile. "Yeah!" George said, "I heard him, Lennie. I'll ask him."

"A brown and white one," Lennie cried excitedly.

"Come on. Le's get dinner. I don't know whether he got a brown and white one."

Lennie didn't move from his bunk. "You ask him right away, George, so he won't kill no more of 'em."

"Sure. Come on now, get up on your feet."

Lennie rolled off his bunk and stood up, and the two of them started for the door. Just as they reached it, Curley bounced in.

"You seen a girl around here?" he demanded angrily.

George said coldly, " 'Bout half an hour ago maybe."

"Well, what the hell was she doin'?"

George stood still, watching the angry little man. He said insultingly, "She said—she was lookin' for you."

Curley seemed really to see George for the first time. His eyes flashed over George, took in his height, measured his reach, looked at his trim middle. "Well, which way'd she go?" he demanded at last.

"I dunno," said George. "I didn' watch her go."

Curley scowled at him and, turning, hurried out the door.

George said, "Ya know, Lennie, I'm scared I'm gonna tangle with that bastard myself. I hate his guts. Jesus Christ! Come on. They won't be a damn thing left to eat."

They went out the door. The sunshine lay in a thin line under the window. From a distance there could be heard a rattle of dishes.

After a moment the ancient dog walked lamely in through the open door. He gazed about with mild, half-blind eyes. He sniffed, and then lay down and put his head between his paws. Curley popped into the doorway again and stood looking into the room. The dog raised his head, but when Curley jerked out, the grizzled head sank to the floor again.

CHAPTER III

ALTHOUGH THERE was evening brightness showing through the windows of the bunk-house, inside it was dusk. Through the open door came the thuds and occasional clangs of a horse-shoe game, and now and then the sound of voices raised in approval or derision.

Slim and George came into the darkening bunk-house together. Slim reached up over the card-table, and turned on the tin-shaded electric light. Instantly the table was brilliant with light, and the cone of the shade threw its brightness straight downward, leaving the corners of the bunk-house still in dusk. Slim sat down on a box and George took his place opposite.

"It wasn't nothing," said Slim. "I would of had to drowned most of 'em, anyways. No need to thank me about that."

George said, "It wasn't much to you, maybe, but it was a hell of a lot to him. Jesus Christ, I don't know how we're gonna get him to sleep in here. He'll want to sleep right out in the barn with 'em. We'll have trouble keepin' him from getting right in the box with them pups."

"It wasn't nothing," Slim repeated. "Say, you sure was right about him. Maybe he ain't bright, but I never seen such a worker. He damn near killed his partner buckin' barley. There ain't nobody can keep up with him. God Awmighty, I never seen such a strong guy."

George spoke proudly. "Jus' tell Lennie what to do and he'll do it if it don't take no figuring. He can't think of nothing to do himself, but he sure can take orders."

There was a clang of horse-shoe on iron stake outside and a little cheer of voices.

Slim moved back slightly so the light was not on his face. "Funny how you an' him string along together." It was Slim's calm invitation to confidence.

"What's funny about it?" George demanded defensively.

"Oh, I dunno. Hardly none of the guys ever travel together. I hardly never seen two guys travel together. You know how the hands are, they just come in and get their bunk and work a month, and then they quit and go out alone. Never seem to give a damn about nobody. It jus' seems kinda funny a cuckoo like him and a smart little guy like you travellin' together."

"He ain't no cuckoo," said George. "He's dumb as hell, but he ain't crazy. An' I ain't so bright neither, or I wouldn't be buckin' barley for my fifty and found. If I was bright, if I was even a little bit smart, I'd have my own little place, an' I'd be bringin' in my own crops, 'stead of doin' all the work and not getting what comes up outa the ground." George fell silent. He wanted to talk. Slim neither encouraged nor discouraged him. He just sat back quiet and receptive.

"It ain't so funny, him an' me goin' aroun' together," George said at last. "Him and me was both born in Auburn. I knowed his Aunt Clara. She took him when he was a baby and raised him up. When his Aunt Clara died, Lennie just come along with me out workin'. Got kinda used to each other after a little while."

"Umm," said Slim.

George looked over at Slim and saw the calm, god-like eyes fastened on him. "Funny," said George. "I used to have a hell of a lot of fun with 'im. Used to play jokes on 'im 'cause he was too dumb to take care of 'imself. But he was too dumb even to know he had a joke played on him. I had fun. Made me seem god-damn smart alongside of him. Why, he'd do any damn thing I tol' him. If I tol' him to walk over a cliff, over he'd go. That wasn't so damn much fun after a while. He never got mad about it, neither. I've beat the hell outa him, and he coulda bust every bone in my body jus' with his han's, but he never lifted a finger against me." George's voice was taking on the tone of confession. "Tell you what made me stop that. One day a bunch of guys was standin' around up on the Sacramento River. I was feelin' pretty smart. I turns to Lennie and says: 'Jump in.' An' he jumps. Couldn't swim a stroke. He damn near drowned before we could get him. An' he was so damn nice to me for pullin' him out. Clean forgot I told him to jump in. Well, I ain't done nothing like that no more."

"He's a nice fella," said Slim. "Guy don't need no sense to be a nice fella. Seems to me sometimes it jus' works the other way around. Take a real smart guy and he ain't hardly ever a nice fella."

George stacked the scattered cards and began to lay out his solitaire hand. The shoes thudded on the ground outside. At the windows the light of the evening still made the window squares bright.

"I ain't got no people," George said. "I seen the guys that go around on the ranches alone. That ain't no good. They don't have no fun. After a long time they get mean. They get wantin' to fight all the time."

"Yeah, they get mean," Slim agreed. "They get so they don't want to talk to nobody."

" 'Course Lennie's a god-damn nuisance most of the time," said George. "But you get used to goin' around with a guy an' you can't get rid of him."

"He ain't mean," said Slim. "I can see Lennie ain't a bit mean."

" 'Course he ain't mean. But he gets in trouble alla time because he's so god-damn dumb. Like what happened in Weed——" He stopped, stopped in the middle of turning over a card. He looked alarmed and peered over at Slim. "You wouldn't tell nobody."

"What'd he do in Weed?" Slim asked calmly.

"You wouldn' tell?—no, 'course you wouldn'."

"What'd he do in Weed?" Slim asked again.

"Well, he seen this girl in a red dress. Dumb bastard like he is, he wants to touch ever'thing he likes. Just wants to feel it. So he reaches out to feel this red dress an' the girl lets out a squawk, and that gets Lennie all mixed up, and he holds on 'cause that's the only thing he can think to do. Well, this girl squawks and squawks. I was jus' a little bit off, and I heard all the yellin', so I comes running, an' by that time Lennie's so scared all he can think to do is jus' hold on. I socked him over the head with a fence picket to make him let go. He was so scairt he couldn't let go of that dress. And he's so god-damn strong, you know."

Slim's eyes were level and unwinking. He nodded very slowly. "So what happens?"

George carefully built his line of solitaire cards. "Well, that girl rabbits in an' tells the law she been raped. The guys in Weed start a party out to lynch Lennie. So we sit in a irrigation ditch under water all the rest of that day. Got on'y our heads sticking outa water, an' up under the grass that sticks out from the side of the ditch. An' that night we scrammed outa there."

Slim sat in silence for a moment. "Didn't hurt the girl none, huh?" he asked finally.

"Hell, no. He just scared her. I'd be scared too if he grabbed me.

But he never hurt her. He jus' wanted to touch that red dress, like he wants to pet them pups all the time."

"He ain't mean," said Slim. "I can tell a mean guy a mile off."

" 'Course he ain't, and he'll do any damn thing I——"

Lennie came in through the door. He wore his blue denim coat over his shoulders like a cape, and he walked hunched way over.

"Hi, Lennie," said George. "How do you like the pup now?"

Lennie said breathlessly, "He's brown an' white jus' like I wanted." He went directly to his bunk and lay down and turned his face to the wall and drew up his knees.

George put down his cards very deliberately. "Lennie," he said sharply.

Lennie twisted his neck and looked over his shoulder. "Huh? What you want, George?"

"I tol' you you couldn't bring that pup in here."

"What pup, George? I ain't got no pup."

George went quickly to him, grabbed him by the shoulder and rolled him over. He reached down and picked the tiny puppy from where Lennie had been concealing it against his stomach.

Lennie sat up quickly. "Give 'um to me, George."

George said, "You get right up an' take this pup back to the nest. He's gotta sleep with his mother. You want to kill him? Just born last night an' you take him out of the nest. You take him back or I'll tell Slim not to let you have him."

Lennie held out his hands pleadingly. "Give 'um to me, George. I'll take 'um back. I didn't mean no harm, George. Honest I didn't. I jus' wanted to pet 'um a little."

George handed the pup to him. "Awright. You get him back there quick, and don't you take him out no more. You'll kill him, the first thing you know." Lennie fairly scuttled out of the room.

Slim had not moved. His calm eyes followed Lennie out the door. "Jesus," he said. "He's jes' like a kid, ain't he?"

"Sure he's jes' like a kid. There ain't no more harm in him than a kid neither, except he's so strong. I bet he won't come in here to sleep to-night. He'd sleep right alongside that box in the barn. Well—let 'im. He ain't doin' no harm out there."

It was almost dark outside now. Old Candy, the swamper, came in and went to his bunk, and behind him struggled his old dog. "Hello, Slim. Hello, George. Didn't neither of you play horse-shoes?"

"I don't like to play ever' night," said Slim.

Candy went on, "Either you guys got a slug of whisky? I gotta gut ache."

"I ain't," said Slim. "I'd drink it myself if I had, an' I ain't got a gut ache neither."

"Gotta bad gut ache," said Candy. "Them god-damn turnips give it to me. I knowed they was going to before I ever eat 'em."

The thick-bodied Carlson came in out of the darkening yard. He walked to the other end of the bunk-house and turned on the second shaded light. "Darker'n'hell in here," he said. "Jesus, how that nigger can pitch shoes."

"He's plenty good," said Slim.

"Damn right he is," said Carlson. "He don't give nobody else a chance to win——" He stopped and sniffed the air, and, still sniffing, looked down at the old dog. "God Almighty, that dog stinks. Get him outa here, Candy! I don't know nothing that stinks so bad as an old dog. You gotta get him out."

Candy rolled to the edge of his bunk. He reached over and patted the ancient dog, and he apologized, "I been around him so much I never notice how he stinks."

"Well, I can't stand him in here," said Carlson. "That stink hangs around even after he's gone." He walked over with his heavy-legged stride and looked down at the dog. "Got no teeth," he said. "He's all stiff with rheumatism. He ain't no good to you, Candy. An' he ain't no good to himself. Why'n't you shoot him, Candy?"

The old man squirmed uncomfortably. "Well—hell! I had him so long. Had him since he was a pup. I herded sheep with him." He said proudly, "You wouldn't think it to look at him now, but he was the best damn sheep dog I ever seen."

George said, "I seen a guy in Weed that had an Airedale could herd sheep. Learned it from the other dogs."

Carlson was not to be put off. "Look, Candy. This o'l dog jus' suffers hisself all the time. If you was to take him out and shoot him right in the back of the head"—he leaned over and pointed—"right there, why, he'd never know what hit him."

Candy looked about him unhappily. "No," he said softly. "No, I couldn' do that. I had 'im too long."

"He don't have no fun," Carlson insisted. "And he stinks to beat hell. Tell you what. I'll shoot him for you. Then it won't be you that does it."

Candy threw his legs off his bunk. He scratched the white stubble whiskers on his cheek nervously. "I'm so used to him," he said softly. "I had him from a pup."

"Well, you ain't bein' kind to him keepin' him alive," said Carlson. "Look, Slim's bitch got a litter right now. I bet Slim would give you one of them pups to raise up, wouldn't you, Slim?"

The skinner had been studying the old dog with his calm eyes. "Yeah," he said. "You can have a pup if you want to." He seemed to shake himself free for speech. "Carl's right, Candy. That dog ain't no good to himself. I wisht somebody'd shoot me if I get old an' a cripple."

Candy looked helplessly at him, for Slim's opinions were law. "Maybe it'd hurt him," he suggested. "I don't mind takin' care of him."

Carlson said, "The way I'd shoot him, he wouldn't feel nothing. I'd put the gun right there." He pointed with his toe. "Right back of the head. He wouldn't even quiver."

Candy looked for help from face to face. It was quite dark outside by now. A young labouring man came in. His sloping shoulders were bent forward and he walked heavily on his heels, as though he carried the invisible grain bag. He went to his bunk and put his hat on the shelf. Then he picked a pulp magazine from his shelf and brought it to the light over the table. "Did I show you this, Slim?" he asked.

"Show me what?"

The young man turned to the back of the magazine, put it down on the table and pointed with his finger. "Right there, read that," Slim bent over it. "Go on," said the young man. "Read it out loud."

" 'Dear Editor,' " Slim read slowly: " 'I read your mag for six years and I think it's the best on the market. I like stories by Peter Rand. I think he is a whing-ding. Give us more like the "Dark Rider". I don't write many letters. Just thought I would tell you I think your mag is the best dime's worth I ever spent.' "

Slim looked up questioningly. "What you want me to read that for?"

Whit said, "Go on. Read the name at the bottom."

Slim read: " 'Yours for success, William Tenner.' " He glanced up at Whit again. "What you want me to read that for?"

Whit closed the magazine impressively. "Don't you remember Bill Tenner? Worked here about three months ago?"

Slim thought. . . . "Little guy?" he asked. "Drove a cultivator?"

"That's him," Whit cried. "That's the guy!"

"You think he's the guy wrote this letter?"

"I know it. Bill and me was in here one day. Bill had one of them books that just come. He was lookin' in it and he says: 'I wrote a letter. Wonder if they put it in the book!' But it wasn't there. Bill says: 'Maybe they're savin' it for later.' An' that's just what they done. There it is."

"Guess you're right," said Slim. "Got it right in the book."

George held out his hand for the magazine. "Let's look at it?"

Whit found the place again, but he did not surrender his hold on it. He pointed out the letter with his forefinger. And then he went to his box shelf and laid the magazine carefully in. "I wonder if Bill seen it," he said. "Bill and me worked in that patch of field peas. Run cultivators, both of us. Bill was a hell of a nice fella."

During the conversation Carlson had refused to be drawn in.

He continued to look down at the old dog. Candy watched him uneasily. At last Carlson said, "If you want me to, I'll put the old devil out of his misery right now and get it over with. Ain't nothing left for him. Can't eat, can't see, can't even walk without hurtin'."

Candy said hopefully, "You ain't got no gun."

"The hell I ain't. Got a Luger. It won't hurt him none at all."

Candy said, "Maybe to-morra. Le's wait till to-morra."

"I don't see no reason for it," said Carlson. He went to his bunk, pulled his bag from underneath it, and took out a Luger pistol. "Le's get it over with," he said. "We can't sleep with him stinkin' around in here." He put the pistol in his hip pocket.

Candy looked a long time at Slim to try to find some reversal. And Slim gave him none. At last Candy said softly and hopelessly, "Awright—take 'im." He did not look down at the dog at all. He lay back on his bunk and crossed his arms behind his head and stared at the ceiling.

From his pocket, Carlson took a little leather thong. He stooped over and tied it around the old dog's neck. All the men except Candy watched him. "Come, boy. Come on, boy," he said gently. And he said apologetically to Candy, "He won't even feel it." Candy did not move nor answer him. He twitched the thong. "Come on, boy." The old dog got slowly and stiffly to his feet and followed the gently-pulling leash.

Slim said, "Carlson."

"Yeah?"

"You know what to do."

"What ya mean, Slim?"

"Take a shovel," said Slim shortly.

"Oh, sure! I get you." He led the dog out into the darkness.

George followed to the door and shut the door and set the latch gently in its place. Candy lay rigidly on his bed staring at the ceiling.

Slim said loudly, "One of my lead mules got a bad hoof. Got to get some tar on it." His voice trailed off. It was silent outside. Carlson's footsteps died away. The silence come into the room. And the silence lasted.

George chuckled, "I bet Lennie's right out there in the barn with his pup. He won't want to come in here no more now he's got a pup."

Slim said, "Candy, you can have any one of them pups you want."

Candy did not answer. The silence fell on the room again. It came out of the night and invaded the room. George said, "Anybody like to play a little euchre?"

"I'll play out a few with you," said Whit.

They took places opposite each other at the table under the light, but George did not shuffle the cards. He rippled the edge of the deck nervously, and the little snapping noise drew the eyes of all the men in the room, so that he stopped doing it. The silence fell on the room again. A minute passed, and another minute. Candy lay still, staring at the ceiling. Slim gazed at him for a moment and then looked down at his hands; he subdued one hand with the other, and held it down. There came a little gnawing sound from under the floor and all the men looked down toward it gratefully. Only Candy continued to stare at the ceiling.

"Sounds like there was a rat under there," said George. "We ought to get a trap down there."

Whit broke out, "What the hell's takin' him so long? Lay out some cards, why don't you? We ain't going to get no euchre played this way."

George brought the cards together tightly and studied the backs of them. The silence was in the room again.

A shot sounded in the distance. The men looked quickly at the old man. Every head turned toward him.

For a moment he continued to stare at the ceiling. Then he rolled slowly over and faced the wall and lay silent.

George shuffled the cards noisily and dealt them. Whit drew a scoring board to him and set the pegs to start. Whit said, "I guess you guys really come here to work."

"How do ya mean?" George asked.

Whit laughed. "Well, ya come on a Friday. You got two days to work till Sunday."

"I don't see how you figure," said George.

Whit laughed again. "You do if you been around these big ranches much. Guy that wants to look over a ranch comes in Sat'day afternoon. He gets Sat'day night supper an' three meals on Sunday, and he can quit Monday mornin' after breakfast without turning his hand. But you come to work Friday noon. You got to put in a day an' a half no matter how you figure."

George looked at him levelly. "We're gonna stick aroun' a while," he said. "Me an' Lennie's gonna roll up a stake."

The door opened quietly and the stable buck put in his head; a lean negro head, lined with pain, the eye patient. "Mr. Slim."

Slim took his eyes from old Candy. "Huh? Oh! Hello, Crooks. What's a' matter?"

"You told me to warm up tar for that mule's foot. I got it warm."

"Oh! Sure, Crooks. I'll come right out an' put it on."

"I can do it if you want, Mr. Slim."

"No. I'll come do it myself." He stood up.

Crooks said, "Mr. Slim."

"Yeah."

"That big new guy's messin' around your pups out in the barn."

"Well, he ain't doin' no harm. I give him one of them pups."

"Just thought I'd tell ya," said Crooks. "He's takin' 'em outa nest and handlin' them. That won't do them no good."

"He won't hurt 'em," said Slim. "I'll come along with you now."

George looked up. "If that crazy bastard's foolin' around too much, jus' kick him out, Slim."

Slim followed the stable buck out of the room.

George dealt and Whit picked up his cards and examined them. "Seen the new kid yet?" he asked.

"What kid?" George asked.

"Why, Curley's new wife."

"Yeah, I see her."

"Well, ain't she a looloo?"

"I ain't seen that much of her," said George.

Whit laid down his cards impressively. "Well, stick around an' keep your eyes open. You'll see plenty. She ain't concealin' nothing. I never seen nobody like her. She got the eye goin' all the time on everybody. I bet she even gives the stable buck the eye. I don't know what the hell she wants."

George asked casually, "Been any trouble since she got here?"

It was obvious that Whit was not interested in his cards. He laid his hand down and George scooped it in. George laid out his deliberate solitaire hand—seven cards, and six on top, and five on top of those.

Whit said, "I see what you mean. No, they ain't been nothing yet. Curley's got yella-jacket in his drawers, but that's all so far. Ever' time the guys is around she shows up. She's lookin' for Curley, or she thought she lef' somethin' layin' around and she's lookin' for it. Seems like she can't keep away from guys. An' Curley's pants is just crawlin' with ants, but they ain't nothing come of it yet."

George said, "She's gonna make a mess. They's gonna be a bad mess about her. She's a jail-bait all set on the trigger. That Curley got his work cut out for him. Ranch with a bunch of guys on it ain't no place for a girl, specially like her."

Whit said, "If you got idears, you ought to come in town with us guys to-morra night."

"Why? What's doin'?"

"Jus' the usual thing. We go in to old Susy's place. Hell of a nice place. Old Susy's a laugh—always crackin' jokes. Like she says when we come up on the front porch las' Sat'day night. Susy opens the door and then she yells over her shoulder, 'Get yor coats on, girls, here comes the sheriff.' She never talks dirty, neither. Got five girls there."

"What's it set you back?" George asked.

"Two an' a half. You can get a shot for two bits. Susy got nice chairs to set in, too. If a guy don't want a flop, why he can jest set in the chairs and have a couple or three shots and pass the time of day and Susy don't give a damn. She ain't rushin' guys through and kickin' 'em out if they don't want a flop."

"Might go in and look the joint over," said George.

"Sure. Come along. It's a hell of a lot of fun—her crackin' jokes all the time. Like she says one time, she says, 'I've knew people that if they got a rag rug on the floor an' a kewpie doll lamp on the phonograph, they think they're running a parlour house.' That's Clara's house she's talkin' about. An' Susy says, 'I know what you boys want,' she says. 'My girls is clean,' she says, 'an' there ain't no water in my whisky,' she says. 'If any you guys wanta look at a kewpie doll lamp an' take your own chance gettin' burned, why you know where to go.' An' she says, 'There's guys around here walkin' bow-legged 'cause they like to look at a kewpie doll lamp.' "

George asked, "Clara runs the other house, huh?"

"Yeah," said Whit. "We don't never go there. Clara gets three bucks a crack and thirty-five cents a shot, and she don't crack no jokes. But Susy's place is clean and she got nice chairs. Don't let no goo-goos in, neither."

"Me an' Lennie's rollin' up a stake," said George. "I might go in an' set and have a shot, but I ain't puttin' out no two and a half."

"Well, a guy got to have some fun sometime," said Whit.

The door opened and Lennie and Carlson came in together. Lennie crept to his bunk and sat down, trying not to attract attention. Carlson reached under his bunk and brought out his bag. He didn't look at old Candy, who still faced the wall. Carlson found a little cleaning rod in the bag and a can of oil. He laid them on his bed and then brought out the pistol, took out the magazine and snapped the loaded shell from the chamber. Then he fell to cleaning the barrel with the little rod. When the ejector snapped, Candy turned over and looked for a moment at the gun before he turned back to the wall again.

Carlson said casually, "Curley been in yet?"

"No," said Whit. "What's eatin' on Curley?"

Carlson squinted down the barrel of his gun. "Lookin' for his old lady. I seen him going round and round outside."

Whit said sarcastically, "He spends half his time lookin' for her, and the rest of the time she's lookin' for him."

Curley burst into the room excitedly. "Any you guys seen my wife?" he demanded.

"She ain't been here," said Whit.

Curley looked threateningly about the room. "Where the hell's Slim?"

"Went out in the barn," said George. "He was gonna put some tar on a split hoof."

Curley's shoulders dropped and squared. "How long ago'd he go?"

"Five—ten minutes."

Curley jumped out the door and banged it after him.

Whit stood up. "I guess maybe I'd like to see this," he said. "Curley's just spoilin' or he wouldn't start for Slim. An' Curley's handy, god-damn handy. Got in the finals for the Golden Gloves. He got newspaper clippings about it." He considered. "But jus' the same, he better leave Slim alone. Nobody knows what Slim can do."

"Thinks Slim's with his wife, don't he?" said George.

"Looks like it," Whit said. " 'Course Slim ain't. Least I don't think Slim is. But I like to see the fuss if it comes off. Come on, le's go."

George said, "I'm stayin' right here. I don't want to get mixed up in nothing. Lennie and me got to make a stake."

Carlson finished the cleaning of the gun and put it in the bag and pushed the bag under the bunk. "I guess I'll go out and look her over," he said. Old Candy lay still, and Lennie, from his bunk, watched George cautiously.

When Whit and Carlson were gone, and the door closed after them, George turned to Lennie. "What you got on your mind?"

"I ain't done nothing, George. Slim says I better not pet them pups so much for a while. Slim says it ain't good for them; so I come right in. I been good, George."

"I coulda told you that," said George.

"Well, I wasn't hurtin' 'em none. I jus' had mine in my lap pettin' it."

George asked, "Did you see Slim out in the barn?"

"Sure I did. He tol' me I better not pet that pup no more."

"Did you see that girl?"

"You mean Curley's girl?"

"Yeah. Did she come in the barn?"

"No. Anyways I never seen her."

"You never seen Slim talkin' to her?"

"Uh-uh. She ain't been in the barn."

"O.K.," said George. "I guess them guys ain't gonna see no fight. If there's any fightin', Lennie, you keep out of it."

"I don't want no fights," said Lennie. He got up from his bunk and sat down at the table, across from George. Almost automatically George shuffled the cards and laid out his solitaire hand. He used a deliberate, thoughtful slowness.

Lennie reached for a face card and studied it, then turned it upside down and studied it. "Both ends the same," he said. "George why is it both end's the same?"

"I don't know," said George. "That's jus' the way they make 'em. What was Slim doin' in the barn when you seen him?"

"Slim?"

"Sure. You seen him in the barn, an' he tol' you not to pet the pups so much."

"Oh, yeah. He had a can a' tar an' a paint-brush. I don't know what for."

"You sure that girl didn't come in like she come in here to-day?"

"No. She never come."

George sighed. "You give me a good whore-house every time," he said. "A guy can go in an' get drunk and get ever'thing outa his system all at once, an' no messes. And he knows how much it's gonna set him back. These here jail-baits is just set on the trigger of the hoosegow."

Lennie followed his words admiringly, and moved his lips a little to keep up. George continued, "You remember Andy Cushman, Lennie? Went to grammar school?"

"The one that his old lady used to make hot cakes for the kids?" Lennie asked.

"Yeah. That's the one. You can remember anything if there's anything to eat in it." George looked carefully at the solitaire hand. He put an ace up on his scoring rack and piled a two, three and four of diamonds on it. "Andy's in San Quentin right now on account of a tart," said George.

Lennie drummed on the table with his fingers. "George?"

"Huh?"

"George, how long's it gonna be till we get that little place an' live on the fatta the lan'—an' rabbits?"

"I don't know," said George. "We gotta get a big stake together. I know a little place we can get cheap, but they ain't givin' it away." Old Candy turned slowly over. His eyes were wide open. He watched George carefully.

Lennie said, "Tell about that place, George."

"I jus' tol' you jus' las' night."

"Go on—tell again, George."

"Well, it's ten acres," said George. "Got a little win'mill. Got a little shack on it, an' a chicken run. Got a kitchen, orchard, cherries, apples, peaches, 'cots, nuts, got a few berries. They's a place for alfalfa and plenty water to flood it. They's a pig pen——"

"An' rabbits, George."

"No place for rabbits now, but I could easy build a few hutches and you could feed alfalfa to the rabbits."

"Damn right, I could," said Lennie. "You god-damn right I could."

George's hands stopped working with the cards. His voice was growing warmer. "An' we could have a few pigs. I could build a smoke-house like the one gran'pa had, an' when we kill a pig we can smoke the bacon and the hams, and make sausage an' all like that. An' when the salmon run up the river we could catch a hundred of 'em an' salt 'em down or smoke 'em. We could have them for breakfast. They ain't nothing so nice as smoked salmon. When the fruit come in we could can it—and tomatoes, they're easy to can. Ever' Sunday we'd kill a chicken or a rabbit. Maybe, we'd have a cow or a goat, and the cream is so god-damn thick you got to cut it with a knife and take it out with a spoon."

Lennie watched him with wide eyes, and old Candy watched him too. Lennie said softly, "We could live offa the fatta the lan'."

"Sure," said George. "All kin's a vegetables in the garden, and if we want a little whisky we can sell a few eggs or something, or some milk. We'd jus' live there. We'd belong there. There wouldn't be no more runnin' round the country and gettin' fed by a Jap cook. No, sir, we'd have our own place where we belonged and not sleep in no bunk-house."

"Tell about the house, George," Lennie begged.

"Sure, we'd have a little house an' a room to ourself. Little fat iron stove, an' in the winter we'd keep a fire goin' in it. It ain't enough land so we'd have to work too hard. Maybe six, seven hours a day. We wouldn't have to buck no barley eleven hours a day. An' when we put in a crop, why, we'd be there to take the crop up. We'd know what come of our planting."

"An' rabbits," Lennie said eagerly. "An' I'd take care of 'em. Tell how I'd do that, George."

"Sure, you'd go out in the alfalfa patch an' you'd have a sack. You'd fill up the sack and bring it in an' put in the rabbit cages."

"They'd nibble an' they'd nibble," said Lennie, "the way they do. I seen 'em."

"Ever' six weeks or so," George continued, "them does would throw a litter, so we'd have plenty rabbits to eat an' to sell. An' we'd keep a few pigeons to go flyin' around the win'mill like they done when I was a kid." He looked raptly at the wall over Lennie's head. "An' it'd be our own, an' nobody could can us. If we don't like a guy we can say, 'Get the hell out,' and by God he's got to do it. An' if a fren' come along, why we'd have an extra bunk, and we'd say, 'Why don't you spen' the night?' an' by God he would. We'd have a setter dog and a couple stripe cats, but you gotta watch out them cats don't get the little rabbits."

Lennie breathed hard. "You jus' let 'em try to get the rabbits. I'll break their god-damn necks. I'll . . . I'll smash 'em with a stick."

He subsided, grumbling to himself, threatening the future cats which might dare to disturb the future rabbits.

George sat entranced with his own picture.

When Candy spoke they both jumped as though they had been caught doing something reprehensible. Candy said, "You know where's a place like that?"

George was on guard immediately. "S'pose I do," he said. "What's that to you?"

"You don't need to tell me where it's at. Might be any place."

"Sure," said George. "That's right. You couldn't find it in a hundred years."

Candy went on excitedly, "How much they want for a place like that?"

George watched him suspiciously. "Well—I could get it for six hundred bucks. The ol' people that owns it is flat bust an' the ol' lady needs an operation. Say—what's it to you? You got nothing to do with us."

Candy said, "I ain't much good with on'y one hand. I lost my hand right here on this ranch. That's why they give me a job swampin'. An' they give me two hundred an' fifty dollars 'cause I los' my hand. An' I got fifty more saved up right in the bank, right now. Tha's three hundred, and I got fifty more comin' the enda the month. Tell you what——" He leaned forward eagerly. "S'spose I went in with you guys. Tha's three hundred an' fifty bucks I'd put in. I ain't much good, but I could cook and tend the chickens and hoe the garden some. How'd that be?"

George half-closed his eyes. "I gotta think about that. We was always gonna do it by ourself."

Candy interrupted him, "I'd make a will an' leave my share to you guys in case I kicked off, 'cause I ain't got no relatives nor nothing. You guys got any money? Maybe we could do her right now?"

George spat on the floor disgustedly. "We got ten bucks between us." Then he said thoughtfully, "Look, if me an' Lennie work a month an' don't spen' nothing, we'll have a hundred bucks. That'd be four fifty. I bet we could swing her for that. Then you an' Lennie could go get her started an' I'd get a job an' make up the res', an' you could sell eggs an' stuff like that."

They fell into a silence. They looked at one another, amazed. This thing they had never really believed in was coming true. George said reverently, "Jesus Christ! I bet we could swing her." His eyes were full of wonder. "I bet we could swing her," he repeated softly.

Candy sat on the edge of his bunk. He scratched the stump of his wrist nervously. "I got hurt four years ago," he said. "They'll can me purty soon. Jus' as soon as I can't swamp out no bunkhouses they'll out me on the county. Maybe if I give you guys my money, you'll let me hoe in the garden even after I ain't no good at it. An' I'll wash dishes an' little chicken stuff like that. But I'll be on our own place, an' I'll be let to work on our own place." He said miserably, "You seen what they done to my dog to-night? They says he wasn't no good to himself nor nobody else. When they can me here I wish somebody'd shoot me. But they won't do nothing like that. I won't have no place to go, an' I can't get no more jobs. I'll have thirty dollars more comin', time you guys is ready to quit."

George stood up. "We'll do her," he said. "We'll fix up that little old place an' we'll go live there." He sat down again. They all sat still, all bemused by the beauty of the thing, each mind was popped into the future when this lovely thing should come about.

George said wanderingly, "S'pose they was a carnival or a circus come to town, or a ball game, or any damn thing." Old Candy nodded in appreciation of the idea. "We'd just go to her," George said. "We wouldn't ask nobody if we could. Jus' say, 'We'll go to her,' an' we would. Jus' milk the cow and sling some grain to the chickens an' go to her."

"An' put some grass to the rabbits." Lennie broke in. "I wouldn't never forget to feed them. When we gon'ta do it, George?"

"In one month. Right squack in one month. Know what I'm gon'ta do? I'm gon'ta write to them old people that owns the place that we'll take it. An' Candy'll send a hunderd dollars to bind her."

"Sure will," said Candy. "They got a good stove there?"

"Sure, got a nice stove, burns coal or wood."

"I'm gonna take my pup," said Lennie. "I bet by Christ he likes it there, by Jesus."

Voices were approaching from outside. George said quickly, "Don't tell nobody about it. Jus' us three an' nobody else. They li'ble to can us so we can't make no stake. Jus' go on like we was gonna buck barley the rest of our lives, then all of a sudden some day we'll go get our pay an' scram outa here."

Lennie and Candy nodded, and they were grinning with delight. "Don't tell nobody," Lennie said to himself.

Candy said, "George."

"Huh?"

"I ought to of shot that dog myself, George. I shouldn't ought to of let no stranger shoot my dog."

The door opened. Slim came in, followed by Curley and Carlson and Whit. Slim's hands were black with tar and he was scowling. Curley hung close to his elbow.

Curley said, "Well, I didn't mean nothing, Slim. I just ast you."

Slim said, "Well, you been askin' me too often. I'm gettin' god-damn sick of it. If you can't look after your own god-damn wife, what you expect me to do about it? You lay offa me."

"I'm jus' tryin' to tell you I didn't mean nothing," said Curley. "I jus' thought you might of saw her."

"Why'n't you tell her to stay the hell home where she belongs?" said Carlson. "You let her hang around bunk-houses and pretty soon you're gonna have som'pin on your hands and you won't be able to do nothing about it."

Curley whirled on Carlson. "You keep outa this les' you wanta step outside."

Carlson laughed. "You god-damn punk," he said. "You tried to throw a scare into Slim, an' you couldn't make it stick. Slim throwed a scare into you. You're yella as a frog belly. I don't care if you're the best welter in the country. You come for me, an' I'll kick your god-damn head off."

Candy joined the attack with joy. "Glove fulla vaseline," he said disgustedly. Curley glared at him. His eyes slipped on past and lighted on Lennie; and Lennie was still smiling with delight at the memory of the ranch.

Curley stepped over to Lennie like a terrier. "What the hell you laughin' at?"

Lennie looked blankly at him. "Huh?"

Then Curley's rage exploded. "Come on, ya big bastard. Get up on your feet. No big son-of-a-bitch is gonna laugh at me. I'll show ya who's yella."

Lennie looked helplessly at George, and then he got up and tried to retreat. Curley was balanced and poised. He slashed at Lennie with his left, and then smashed down his nose with a right. Lennie gave a cry of terror. Blood welled from his nose. "George," he cried. "Make 'um let me alone, George." He backed until he was against the wall, and Curley followed, slugging him in the face. Lennie's hands remained at his sides; he was too frightened to defend himself.

George was on his feet yelling, "Get him, Lennie. Don't let him do it."

Lennie covered his face with his huge paws and bleated with terror. He cried, "Make 'um stop, George." Then Curley attacked his stomach and cut off his wind.

Slim jumped up. "The dirty little rat," he cried, "I'll get 'um myself."

George put out his hand and grabbed Slim. "Wait a minute," he shouted. He cupped his hands around his mouth and yelled, "Get 'im, Lennie!"

Lennie took his hands away from his face and looked about for

George, and Curley slashed at his eyes. The big face was covered with blood. George yelled again, "I said get him."

Curley's fist was swinging when Lennie reached for it. The next minute Curley was flopping like a fish on a line, and his closed fist was lost in Lennie's big hand. George ran down the room. "Leggo of him, Lennie. Let go."

But Lennie watched in terror the flopping little man whom he held. Blood ran down Lennie's face, one of his eyes was cut and closed. George slapped him on the face again and again, and still Lennie held on to the closed fist. Curley was white and shrunken by now, and his struggling had become weak. He stood crying, his fist lost in Lennie's paw.

George shouted over and over, "Leggo his hand, Lennie. Leggo. Slim, come help me while the guy got any hand left."

Suddenly Lennie let go his hold. He crouched cowering against the wall. "You tol' me to, George," he said miserably.

Curley sat down on the floor, looking in wonder at his crushed hand. Slim and Carlson bent over him. Then Slim straightened up and regarded Lennie with horror. "We got to get him in to a doctor," he said. "Looks to me like ever' bone in his han' is bust."

"I didn't wanta," Lennie cried. "I didn't wanta hurt him."

Slim said, "Carlson, you get the candy wagon hitched up. We'll take 'um into Soledad an' get 'um fixed up." Carlson hurried out. Slim turned to the whimpering Lennie. "It ain't your fault," he said. "This punk sure had it comin' to him. But—Jesus! He ain't hardly got no han' left." Slim hurried out, and in a moment returned with a tin cup of water. He held it to Curley's lips.

George said, "Slim, will we get canned now? We need the stake. Will Curley's old man can us now?"

Slim smiled wryly. He knelt down beside Curley. "You got your senses in hand enough to listen?" he asked. Curley nodded. "Well then, listen," Slim went on. "I think you got your han' caught in a machine. If you don't tell nobody what happened, we ain't going to. But you jus' tell an' try to get this guy canned and we'll tell ever'-body, an' then will you get the laugh."

"I won't tell," said Curley. He avoided looking at Lennie.

Buggy wheels sounded outside. Slim helped Curley up. "Come on now. Carlson's gonna take you to a doctor." He helped Curley out the door. The sound of wheels drew away. In a moment Slim came back into the bunk-house. He looked at Lennie, still crouched fearfully against the wall. "Let's see your hands," he asked.

Lennie stuck out his hands.

"Christ awmighty, I hate to have you get mad at me," Slim said.

George broke in, "Lennie was jus' scairt," he explained. "He didn't know what to do. I told you nobody ought never to fight him. No, I guess it was Candy I told."

Candy nodded solemnly. "That's jus' what you done," he said. "Right this morning when Curley first lit intil your fren', you says, 'He better not fool with Lennie if he knows what's good for 'um.' That's just what you says to me."

George turned to Lennie. "It ain't your fault," he said. "You don't need to be scairt no more. You done just what I tol' you to. Maybe you better go in the wash-room an' clean up your face. You look like hell."

Lennie smiled with his bruised mouth. "I didn't want no trouble," he said. He walked toward the door, but just before he came to it he turned back. "George?"

"What do you want?"

"I can still tend the rabbits, George?"

"Sure. You ain't done nothing wrong."

"I didn't mean no harm, George."

"Well, get the hell out and wash your face."

CHAPTER IV

Crooks the negro stable buck, had his bunk in the harness-room; a little shed that leaned off the wall of the barn. On one side of the little room there was a square four-paned window, and on the other a narrow plank door leading into the barn. Crook's bunk was a long box filled with straw, on which his blankets were flung. On the wall by the window there were pegs on which hung broken harness in process of being mended, strips of new leather; and under the window itself a little bench for leather-working tools, curved knives and needles and balls of linen thread, and a small hand-riveter. On pegs were also pieces of harness, a split collar with the horsehair stuffing sticking out, a broken hame, and a trace chain with its leather covering split. Crooks had his apple-box over his bunk, and in it a range of medicine bottles, both for himself and for the horses. There were cans of saddle soap and a drippy can of tar with its paint-brush sticking over the edge. And scattered about the floor were a number of personal possessions; for, being alone, Crooks could leave his things about, and being a stable buck and a cripple, he was more permanent than the other men, and he had accumulated more possessions than he could carry on his back.

Crooks possessed several pairs of shoes, a pair of rubber boots, a big alarm clock and a single-barrelled shotgun. And he had books, too; a tattered dictionary and a mauled copy of the California civil code for 1905. There were battered magazines and a few dirty books on a special shelf over his bunk. A pair of large gold-rimmed spectacles hung from a nail on the wall above his bed.

This room was swept and fairly neat, for Crooks was a proud, aloof man. He kept his distance and demanded that other people keep theirs. His body was bent over to the left by his crooked spine, and his eyes lay deep in his head, and because of their depth seemed to glitter with intensity. His lean face was lined with deep black wrinkles, and he had thin, pain-tightened lips which were lighter than his face.

It was Saturday night. Through the open door that led into the barn came the sound of moving horses, of feet stirring, of teeth champing on hay, of the rattle of halter chains. In the stable buck's room a small electric globe threw a meagre yellow light.

Crooks sat on his bunk. His shirt was out of his jeans at the back. In one hand he held a bottle of liniment, with the other he rubbed his spine. Now and then he poured a few drops of the liniment into his pink-palmed hand and reached up under his shirt to rub again. He flexed his muscles against his back and shivered.

Noiselessly, Lennie appeared in the open doorway and stood there looking in, his big shoulders nearly filling the opening. For a moment Crooks did not see him, but on raising his eyes he stiffened and a scowl came on his face. His hand came out from under his shirt.

Lennie smiled helplessly in an attempt to make friends.

Crooks said sharply, "You got no right to come in my room. This here's my room. Nobody got any right in here but me."

Lennie gulped and his smile grew more fawning. "I ain't doing nothing," he said. "Just come to look at my puppy. And I seen your light," he explained.

"Well, I got a right to have a light. You go on get outa my room. I ain't wanted in the bunk-house, and you ain't wanted in my room."

"Why ain't you wanted?" Lennie asked.

" 'Cause I'm black. They play cards in there, but I can't play because I'm black. They say I stink. Well, I tell you, you all of you stink to me."

Lennie flapped his big hands helplessly. "Ever'body went into town," he said. "Slim an' George an' ever'body. George says I gotta stay here an' not get in no trouble. I seen your light."

"Well, what do you want?"

"Nothing—I seen your light. I thought I could jus' come in an' set."

Crooks stared at Lennie, and he reached behind him and took

down the spectacles and adjusted them over his pink ears and stared again. "I don't know what you're doin' in the barn anyway," he complained. "You ain't no skinner. They's no call for a bucker to come into the barn at all. You ain't no skinner. You ain't got nothing to do with the horses."

"The pup," Lennie repeated. "I come to see my pup."

"Well, go see your pup, then. Don't come in a place where you're not wanted."

Lennie lost his smile. He advanced a step into the room, then remembered and backed to the door again. "I looked at 'em a little. Slim says I ain't to pet 'em very much."

Crooks said, "Well, you been takin' 'em out of the nest all the time. I wonder the old lady don't move 'em someplace else."

"Oh, she don't care. She lets me." Lennie had moved into the room again.

Crooks scowled, but Lennie's disarming smile defeated him. "Come on in and set a while," Crooks said. " 'Long as you won't get out and leave me alone, you might as well set down." His tone was a little more friendly. "All the boys gone into town, huh?"

"All but old Candy. He just sets in the bunk-house sharpening his pencil and sharpening and figuring."

Crooks adjusted his glasses. "Figuring? What's Candy figuring about?"

Lennie almost shouted, " 'Bout the rabbits."

"You're nuts," said Crooks. "You're crazy as a wedge. What rabbits you talkin' about?"

"The rabbits we're gonna get, and I get to tend 'em, cut grass. an' give 'em water, an' like that."

"Jus' nuts," said Crooks. "I don't blame the guy you travel with for keepin' you outa sight."

Lennie said quietly, "It ain't no lie. We're gonna do it. Gonna get a little place an' live on the fatta the lan'."

Crooks settled himself more comfortably on his bunk. "Set down," he invited. "Set down on the nail-keg."

Lennie hunched down on the little barrel. "You think it's a lie," Lennie said, "but it ain't no lie. Ever' word's the truth, an' you can ast George."

Crooks put his dark chin into his pink palm. "You travel aroun' with George, don't ya?"

"Sure. Me an' him goes ever' place together."

Crooks continued, "Sometimes he talks, and you don't know what the hell he's talkin' about. Ain't that so?" He leaned forward, boring Lennie with his deep eyes. "Ain't that so?"

"Yeah . . . sometimes."

"Jus' talks on, an' you don't know what the hell it's all about?"

"Yeah . . . sometimes. But . . . not always."

Crooks leaned forward over the edge of the bunk. "I ain't a southern negro," he said. "I was born right here in California. My old man had a chicken ranch, 'bout ten acres. The white kids come to play at our place, an' sometimes I went to play with them, and some of them was pretty nice. My ol' man didn't like that. I never knew till long later why he didn't like that. But I know now." He hesitated, and when he spoke again his voice was softer. "There wasn't another coloured family for miles around. And now there ain't a coloured man on this ranch an' there's jus' one family in Soledad." He laughed. "If I say something, why' it's just a nigger sayin' it."

Lennie asked, "How long you think it'll be before them pups will be old enough to pet?"

Crooks laughed again. "A guy can talk to you an' be sure you won't go blabbin'. Couple of weeks' an' them pups'll be all right. George knows what he's about. Jus' talks, an' you don't understand nothing." He leaned forward excitedly. "This is just a nigger talkin' an' a busted-back nigger. So it don't mean nothing, see? You couldn't remember it anyways. I seen it over an' over an' over—a guy talkin' to another guy and it don't make no difference if he don't hear or understand. The thing is, they're talkin', or they're settin' still not talkin'. It don't make no difference, no difference." His excitement had increased until he pounded his knee with his hand. "George can tell you screwy things, and it don't matter. It's just the talking. It's just bein' with another guy. That's all." He paused.

His voice grew soft and persuasive. "S'pose George don't come back no more. S'pose he took a powder and just ain't coming back. What'll you do then?"

Lennie's attention came gradually to what had been said. "What?" he demanded.

"I said s'pose George went into town to-night and you never heard of him no more." Crooks pressed forward some kind of private victory. "Just s'pose that," he repeated.

"He won't do it," Lennie cried. "George wouldn't do nothing like that. I been with George a long time. He'll come back to-night——" But the doubt was too much for him. "Don't you think he will?"

Crooks' face lighted with pleasure in his torture. "Nobody can't tell what a guy'll do," he observed calmly. "Le's say he wants to come back and can't. S'pose he gets killed or hurt so he can't come back."

Lennie struggled to understand. "George won't do nothing like that," he repeated. "George is careful. He won't get hurt. He ain't never been hurt, 'cause he's careful."

"Well, s'pose, jus' s'pose he don't come back. What'll you do then?"

Lennie's face wrinkled with apprehension. "I don't know. Say, what you doin' anyways?" he cried. "This ain't true. George ain't got hurt."

Crooks bored in on him. "Want me ta tell ya what'll happen? They'll take ya to the booby hatch. They'll tie ya up with a collar, like a dog."

Suddenly Lennie's eyes centred and grew quiet and mad. He stood up and walked dangerously towards Crooks. "Who hurt George?" he demanded.

Crooks saw the danger as it approached him. He edged back on his bunk to get out of the way. "I was just supposin'," he said. "George ain't hurt. He's all right. He'll be back all right."

Lennie stood over him. "What you supposin' for? Ain't nobody goin' to suppose no hurt to George."

Crooks removed his glasses and wiped his eyes with his fingers. "Jus' set down," he said. "George ain't hurt."

Lennie growled back to his seat on the nail-keg. "Ain't nobody goin' to talk no hurt to George," he grumbled.

Crooks said gently, "Maybe you can see now. You got George. You *know* he's goin' to come back. S'pose you didn't have nobody. S'pose you couldn't go into the bunk-house and play rummy 'cause you was black. How'd you like that? S'pose you had to sit out here an' read books. Sure, you could play horse-shoes till it got dark, but then you got to read books. Books ain't no good. A guy needs somebody—to be near him." He whined, "A guy goes nuts if he ain't got nobody. Don't make no difference who the guy is, long's he's with you. I tell ya," he cried, "I tell ya a guy gets too lonely, and' he gets sick."

"George gonna come back," Lennie reassured himself in a frightened voice. "Maybe George come back already. Maybe I better go see."

Crooks said, "I didn't mean to scare you. He'll come back. I was talkin' about myself. A guy sets alone out here at night, maybe readin' books or thinkin' or stuff like that. Sometimes he gets thinkin', an' he got nothing to tell him what's so an' what ain't so. Maybe if he sees somethin', he don't know whether it's right or not. He can't turn to some other guy and ast him if he sees it too. He can't tell. He got nothing to measure by. I seen things out here. I wasn't drunk. I don't know if I was asleep. If some guy was with me, he could tell me I was asleep, an' then it would be all right. But I jus' don't know." Crooks was looking across the room now, looking toward the window.

Lennie said miserably, "George wun't go away and leave me. I know George wun't do that."

The stable buck went on dreamily, "I remember when I was a little kid on my old man's chicken ranch. Had two brothers. They was always near me, always there. Used to sleep right in the same room, right in the same bed—all three. Had a strawberry patch. Had an alfalfa patch. Used to turn the chickens out in the alfalfa on a sunny morning. My brothers'd set on a fence rail an' watch 'em—white chickens they was."

Gradually Lennie's interest came around to what was being said. "George says we're gonna have alfalfa for the rabbits."

"What rabbits?"

"We're gonna have rabbits an' a berry patch."

"You're nuts."

"We are too. You ast George."

"You're nuts." Crooks was scornful. "I seen hunderds of men come by on the road an' on the ranches with their bindles on their back an' that same damn thing in their heads. Hunderds of them. They come, an' they quit an' go on; an' every damn one of 'em's got a little piece of land in his head. An' never a god-damn one of 'em ever gets it. Just like heaven. Ever'body wants a little piece of lan'. I read plenty of books out here. Nobody never gets to heaven, and nobody gets no land. It's just in their head. They're all the time talking about it, but it's jus' in their head." He paused and looked toward the open door, for the horses were moving restlessly and the halter chains clinked. A horse whinnied. "I guess somebody's out there," Crooks said. "Maybe Slim. Slim comes in sometimes two, three times a night. Slim's a real skinner. He looks out for his team." He pulled himself painfully upright and moved towards the door. "That you, Slim?" he called.

Candy's voice answered. "Slim went in town. Say, you seen Lennie?"

"Ya mean the big guy?"

"Yeah. Seen him around anyplace?"

"He's in here," Crooks said shortly. He went back to his bunk and lay down.

Candy stood in the doorway scratching his bald wrist and looking blindly into the lighted room. He made no attempt to enter. "Tell ya what, Lennie. I been figuring out about them rabbits."

Crooks said irritably, "You can come in if you want."

Candy seemed embarrassed. "I do' know. 'Course, if ya want me to."

"Come on in. If ever'body's comin' in, you might just as well." It was difficult for Crooks to conceal his pleasure with anger.

Candy came in, but he was still embarrassed. "You got a nice cosy little place in here," he said to Crooks. "Must be nice to have a room all to yourse'f this way."

"Sure," said Crooks. "And a manure pile under the window. Sure it's swell."

Lennie broke in, "You said about them rabbits."

Candy leaned against the wall beside the broken collar while he scratched the wrist stump "I· been here a long time," he said. "An' Crooks been here a long time. This's the first time I ever been in his room."

Crooks said darkly, "Guys don't come into a coloured man's room very much. Nobody been here but Slim. Slim an' the boss."

Candy quickly changed the subject. "Slim's as good a skinner as I ever seen."

Lennie leaned toward the old swamper. "About them rabbits," he insisted.

Candy smiled. "I got it figured out. We can make some on them rabbits if we go about it right."

"But I tend 'em," Lennie broke in. "George says I get to tend 'em. He promised."

Crooks interrupted brutally. "You guys is just kiddin' yourself. You'll talk about it a hell of a lot, but you won't get no land. You'll be a swamper here till they take you out in a box. Hell, I seen too many guys. Lennie here'll quit an' be on the road in two, three weeks. Seems like ever' guy got land in his head."

Candy rubbed his cheek angrily. "You god-damn right we're gonna do it. George says we are. We got the money right now."

"Yeah?" said Crooks. "An' where's George now? In town in a whore-house. That's where your money's goin'. Jesus, I seen it happen too many times. I see too many guys with land in their head. They never get none under their hand."

Candy cried, "Sure they all want it. Everybody wants a little bit of land, not much. Jus' som'thin' that was his. Som'thin' he could live on and there couldn't nobody throw him off of it. I never had none. I planted crops for damn near ever'body in this state, but they wasn't my crops, and when I harvested 'em, it wasn't none of my harvest. But we gonna do it now, and don't you make no mistake about that. George ain't got the money in town. The money's in the bank. Me an' Lennie an' George. We gonna have a room to ourselves. We're gonna have a dog an' rabbits an' chickens. We're gonna have green corn an' maybe a cow or a goat." He stopped, overwhelmed with his picture.

Crooks asked, "You say you got the money?"

"Damn right. We got most of it. Just a little bit more to get. Have it all in one month. George got the land all picked out, too."

Crooks reached around and explored his spine with his hand.

"I never seen a guy really do it," he said. "I seen guys nearly crazy with loneliness for land, but ever' time a whore-house or a blackjack game took what it takes." He hesitated. ". . . If you . . . guys would want a hand to work for nothing—just his keep, why I'd come an' lend a hand. I ain't so crippled I can't work like a son-of-a-bitch if I want to."

"Any you boys seen Curley?"

They swung their heads toward the door. Looking in was Curley's wife. Her face was heavily made up. Her lips were slightly parted. She breathed strongly, as though she had been running.

"Curley ain't been here," Candy said sourly.

She stood still in the doorway, smiling a little at them, rubbing the nails of one hand with the thumb and forefinger of the other. And her eyes travelled from one face to another. "They left all the weak ones here," she said finally. "Think I don't know where they all went? Even Curley. I know where they all went."

Lennie watched her, fascinated; but Candy and Crooks were scowling down away from her eyes. Candy said, "Then if you know, why you want to ast us where Curley is at?"

She regarded them amusedly. "Funny thing," she said. "If I catch any one man, and he's alone, I get along fine with him. But just let two of the guys get together an' you won't talk. Jus' nothing but mad." She dropped her fingers and put her hands on her hips. "You're all scared of each other, that's what. Ever' one of you's scared the rest is goin' to get something on you."

After a pause Crooks said, "Maybe you better go along to your own house now. We don't want no trouble."

"Well, I ain't giving you no trouble. Think I don't like to talk to somebody ever' once in a while? Think I like to stick in that house alla time?"

Candy laid the stump of his wrist on his knee and rubbed it gently with his hand. He said accusingly: "You gotta husban'. You got no call foolin' around with other guys, causin' trouble."

The girl flared up. "Sure I've gotta husban'. You all seen him. Swell guy, ain't he? Spends all his time sayin' what he's gonna do to guys he don't like, and he don't like nobody. Think I'm gonna stay in that two-by-four house and listen how Curley's gonna lead with his left twice, and then bring in the ol' right cross? 'One-two,' he says. 'Jus' the ol' one-two an' he'll go down.' " She paused and her face lost its sullenness and grew interested. "Say—what happened to Curley's han'?"

There was an embarrassed silence. Candy stole a look at Lennie. Then he coughed. "Why . . . Curley . . . he got his han' caught in a machine, ma'am. Bust his han'."

She watched for a moment, and then she laughed. "Baloney!

What you think you're sellin' me? Curley started somep'in he didn't finish. Caught in a machine—baloney! Why, he ain't give nobody the good ol' one-two since he got his han' bust. Who bust him?"

Candy repeated sullenly, "Got it caught in a machine."

"Awright," she said contemptuously. "Awright, cover 'im up if ya wanta. Whatta I care? You bindle bums think you're so damn good. Whatta ya think I am, a kid? I tell you I could of went with shows. Not jus' one, neither. An' a guy tol' me he could put me in pitchers. . . ." She was breathless with indignation. "—Sat'iday night. Ever'body out doin' som'pin. Ever'body! An' what am I doin'? Standin' here talking to a bunch of bindle stiffs—a nigger an' a dum-dum and a lousy ol' sheep—an' likin' it because they ain't nobody else."

Lennie watched her, his mouth half open. Crooks had retired into the terrible protective dignity of the negro. But a change came over Candy. He stood up suddenly and knocked his nail-keg over backward. "I had enough," he said angrily. "You ain't wanted here. We told you you ain't. An' I tell ya, you got floosy idears about what us guys amounts to. You ain't got sense enough in that chicken head to even see that we ain't stiffs. S'pose you get us canned. S'pose you do. You think we'll hit the highway an' look for another lousy two-bit job like this. You don't know that we got our own ranch to go to, an' our own house. We ain't got to stay here. We gotta house and chickens an' fruit trees an' a place a hunderd times prettier than this. An' we got fren's, that's what we got. Maybe there was a time when we was scared of gettin' canned, but we ain't no more. We got our own lan', and it's ours, an' we c'n go to it."

Curley's wife laughed at him. "Baloney," she said. "I seen too many you guys. If you had two bits in the worl', why you'd be in gettin' two shots of corn with it and suckin' the bottom of the glass. I know you guys."

Candy's face had grown redder and redder, but before she was done speaking he had control of himself. He was master of the situation. "I might of knew," he said gently. "Maybe you just better go along an' roll your hoop. We ain't got nothing to say to you at all. We know what we got, and we don't care whether you know it or not. So maybe you better jus' scatter along now, 'cause Curley maybe ain't gonna like his wife out in the barn with us 'bindle stiffs'."

She looked from one face to another, and they were all closed against her. And she looked longest at Lennie, until he dropped his eyes in embarrassment. Suddenly she said, "Where'd you get them bruises on your face?"

Lennie looked up guiltily. "Who—me?"

"Yeah, you."

Lennie looked to Candy for help, and then he looked at his lap again. "He got his han' caught in a machine," he said.

Curley's wife laughed. "O.K., Machine. I'll talk to you later. I like machines."

Candy broke in. "You let this guy alone. Don't you do no messing aroun' with him. I'm gonna tell George what you says. George won't have you messin' with Lennie."

"Who's George?" she asked. "The little guy you come with?"

Lennie smiled happily. "That's him," he said. "That's the guy, an' he's gonna let me tend the rabbits."

"Well, if that's all you want, I might get a couple rabbits myself."

Crooks stood up from his bunk and faced her. "I had enough," he said coldly. "You got no rights comin' in a coloured man's room. You got no rights messing around in here at all. Now you jus' get out, an' get out quick. If you don't, I'm gonna ast the boss not to ever let you come in the barn no more."

She turned to him in scorn. "Listen, Nigger," she said. "You know what I can do if you open your trap?"

Crooks stared hopelessly at her, and then he sat down on his bunk and drew into himself.

She closed on him. "You know what I could do?"

Crooks seemed to grow smaller, and he pressed himself against the wall. "Yes, ma'am."

"Well, you keep your place, then, Nigger. I could get you strung up on a tree so easy it ain't even funny."

Crooks had reduced himself to nothing. There was no personality, no ego—nothing to arouse either like or dislike. He said, "Yes, ma'am," and his voice was toneless.

For a moment she stood over him as though waiting for him to move so that she could whip at him again; but Crooks sat perfectly still, his eyes averted, everything that might be hurt drawn in. She turned at last to the other two.

Old Candy was watching her, fascinated. "If you was to do that, we'd tell," he said quietly. "We'd tell about you framin' Crooks."

"Tell an' be damned," she cried. "Nobody'd listen to you, an' you know it. Nobody'd listen to you."

Candy subsided. "No," he agreed. "——Nobody'd listen to us."

Lennie whined, "I wisht George was here. I wisht George was here."

Candy stepped over to him. "Don't you worry none," he said. "I jus' heard the guys comin' in. George'll be in the bunk-house right now, I bet." He turned to Curley's wife. "You better go home now," he said quietly. "If you go right now, we won't tell Curley you was here."

She appraised him coolly. "I ain't sure you heard nothing."

"Better not take no chances," he said. "If you ain't sure, you better take the safe way."

She turned to Lennie. "I'm glad you bust up Curley a little bit. He got it comin' to him. Sometimes I'd like to bust him myself." She slipped out the door and disappeared into the dark barn. And while she went through the barn, the halter chains rattled, and some horses snorted and some stamped their feet.

Crooks seemed to come slowly out of the layers of protection he had put on. "Was that the truth what you said about the guys come back?" he asked.

"Sure. I heard 'em."

"Well, I didn't hear nothing."

"The gate banged," Candy said, and he went on, "Jesus Christ, Curley's wife can move quiet. I guess she had a lot of practice, though."

Crooks avoided the whole subject now. "Maybe you guys better go," he said. "I ain't sure I want you in here no more. A coloured man got to have some rights, even if he don't like 'em."

Candy said, "That bitch didn't ought to of said that to you."

"It wasn't nothing," Crooks said dully. "You guys comin' in an' settin' made me forget. What she says is true."

The horses snorted out in the barn and the chains rang and a voice called, "Lennie. Oh, Lennie. You in the barn?"

"It's George," Lennie cried. And he answered, "Here, George. I'm right in here."

In a second George stood framed in the door, and he looked disapprovingly about. "What you doin' in Crooks' room? You hadn't ought to be here."

Crooks nodded. "I tol' 'em, but they come in anyways."

"Well, why'n't you kick 'em out?"

"I di'n't care much," said Crooks. "Lennie's a nice fella."

Now Candy aroused himself. "Oh, George! I been figurin' and figurin'. I got it doped out how we can even make some money on them rabbits."

George scowled. "I thought I tol' you not to tell nobody about that."

Candy was crestfallen. "Didn't tell nobody but Crooks."

George said, "Well, you guys get outa here. Jesus, seems like I can't go away for a minute."

Candy and Lennie stood up and went toward the door. Crooks called, "Candy!"

"Huh?"

" 'Member what I said about hoein' and doin' odd jobs?"

"Yeah," said Candy. "I remember."

"Well, jus' forget it," said Crooks. "I didn' mean it. Jus' foolin'. I wouldn't want to go no place like that."

"Well, O.K., if you feel like that. Good night."

The three men went out of the door. As they went through the barn the horses snorted and the halter chains rattled.

Crooks sat on his bunk and looked at the door for a moment, and then he reached for the liniment bottle. He pulled out his shirt at the back, poured a little liniment in his pink palm and, reaching around, he fell slowly to rubbing his back.

CHAPTER V

ONE END of the great barn was piled high with new hay and over the pile hung the four-taloned Jackson fork suspended from its pulley. The hay came down like a mountain slope to the other end of the barn, and there was a level place as yet unfilled with the new crop. At the sides the feeding racks were visible, and between the slats the heads of horses could be seen.

It was Sunday afternoon. The resting horses nibbled the remaining wisps of hay, and they stamped their feet and they bit the wood of the mangers and rattled the halter chains. The afternoon sun sliced in through the cracks of the barn walls and lay in bright lines on the hay. There was the buzz of flies in the air, the lazy afternoon humming.

From outside came the clang of horse-shoes on the playing peg and the shouts of men, playing, encouraging, jeering. But in the barn it was quiet and humming and lazy and warm.

Only Lennie was in the barn, and Lennie sat in the hay beside a packing-case under a manger in the end of the barn that had not been filled with hay. Lennie sat in the hay and looked at a little dead puppy that lay in front of him. Lennie looked at it for a long time, and then he put out his huge hand and stroked it, stroked it clear from one end to the other.

And Lennie said softly to the puppy, "Why do you got to get killed? You ain't so little as mice. I didn't bounce you hard." He bent the pup's head up and looked in its face, and he said to it, "Now maybe George ain't gonna let me tend no rabbits, if he fin's out you got killed."

He scooped a little hollow and laid the puppy in it and covered it over with hay, out of sight; but he continued to stare at the mound he had made. He said, "This ain't no bad thing like I got to go hide in the brush. Oh no! This ain't. I'll tell George I foun' it dead."

He unburied the puppy and inspected it, and he stroked it from ears to tail. He went on sorrowfully, "But he'll know. George always knows. He'll say, 'You done it. Don't try to put nothing over on me.' An' he'll say, 'Now jus' for that you don' get to tend no rabbits!'"

Suddenly his anger rose. "God damn you," he cried. "Why do you got to get killed? You ain't so little as mice." He picked up the pup and hurled it from him. He turned his back on it. He sat bent over his knees and he whispered, "Now I won't get to tend the rabbits. Now he won't let me." He rocked himself back and forth in his sorrow.

From outside came the clang of horse-shoes on the iron stake, and then a little chorus of cries. Lennie got up and brought the puppy back and laid it on the hay and sat down. He stroked the pup again. "You wasn't big enough," he said. "They tol' me and tol' me you wasn't. I di'n't know you'd get killed so easy." He worked his fingers on the pup's limp ear. "Maybe George won't care," he said. "This here god-damn little son-of-a-bitch wasn't nothing to George."

Curley's wife came around the end of the last stall. She came very quietly, so that Lennie didn't see her. She wore her bright cotton dress and the mules with the red ostrich feathers. Her face was made up and the little sausage curls were all in place. She was quite near to him before Lennie looked up and saw her.

In a panic he shovelled hay over the puppy with his fingers. He looked sullenly up at her.

She said, "What you got there, sonny boy?"

Lennie glared at her. "George says I ain't to have nothing to do with you—talk to you or nothing."

She laughed. "George giving you orders about everything?"

Lennie looked down at the hay. "Says I can't tend no rabbits if I talk to you or anything."

She said quietly, "He's scared Curley'll get mad. Well, Curley got his arm in a sling—an' if Curley gets tough, you can break his other han'. You didn't put nothing over on me about gettin' it caught on no machine."

But Lennie was not to be drawn. "No, sir. I ain't gonna talk to you or nothing."

She knelt in the hay beside him. "Listen," she said. "All the guys got a horse-shoe tenement goin' on. It's on'y about four o'clock. None of them guys is goin' to leave that tenement. Why can't I talk to you? I never get to talk to nobody. I get awful lonely."

Lennie said, "Well, I ain't supposed to talk to you or nothing."

"I get lonely," she said. "You can talk to people, but I can't talk to nobody but Curley. Else he gets mad. How'd you like not to talk to anybody?"

Lennie said, "Well, I ain't supposed to. George's scared I'll get in trouble."

She changed the subject. "What you got covered up there?"

Then all of Lennie's woe came back on him. "Jus' my pup," he said sadly. "Jus' my little pup." And he swept the hay from on top of it.

"Why, he's dead," she cried.

"He was so little," said Lennie. "I was jus' playin' with him . . . an' he made like he's gonna bite me . . . an' I made like I was gonna smack him . . . an' . . . an' I done it. An' then he was dead."

She consoled him. "Don't you worry none. He was jus' a mutt. You can get another one easy. The whole country is fulla mutts."

"It ain't that so much," Lennie explained miserably. "George ain't gonna let me tend no rabbits now."

"Why don't he?"

"Well, he said if I done any more bad things he ain't gonna let me tend the rabbits."

She moved closer to him and she spoke soothing. "Don't you worry about talkin' to me. Listen to the guys yell out there. They got four dollars bet in that tenement. None of them ain't gonna leave till it's over."

"If George sees me talkin' to you he'll give me hell," Lennie said cautiously. "He tol' me so."

Her face grew angry.

"What's the matter with me?" she cried. "Ain't I got a right to talk to nobody? Whatta they think I am, anyways? You're a nice guy. I don't know why I can't talk to you. I ain't doin' no harm to you."

"Well, George says you'll get us in a mess."

"Aw, nuts!" she said. "What kinda harm am I doin' to you? Seems like they ain't none of them cares how I gotta live. I tell you I ain't used to livin' like this. I coulda made somethin' of myself." She said darkly, "Maybe I will yet." And then her words tumbled out in a passion of communication, as though she hurried before her listener could be taken away. "I live right in Salinas," she said. "Come there when I was a kid. Well, a show come through, an' I met one of the actors. He says I could go with that show. But my ol' lady wouldn' let me. She says because I was on'y fifteen. But the guy says I coulda. If I'd went, I wouldn't be livin' like this, you bet." Lennie stroked the pup back and forth. "We gonna have a little place—an' rabbits," he explained.

She went on with her story quickly, before she should be interrupted. " 'Nother time I met a guy, an' he was in pitchers. Went out to the Riverside Dance Palace with him. He says he was gonna put me in the movies. Says I was a natural. Soon's he got back to Hollywood he was gonna write to me about it." She looked closely at Lennie to see whether she was impressing him. "I never got that letter," she said. "I always thought my ol' lady stole it. Well, I wasn't gonna stay no place where I couldn't get nowhere or make something of myself, an' where they stole your letters. I ast her if she stole it, too, an' she says no. So I married Curley. Met him out to the Riverside Dance Palace that same night." She demanded, "You listenin'?"

"Me? Sure."

"Well, I ain't told this to nobody before. Maybe I oughtn't to. I don' *like* Curley. He ain't a nice fella." And because she had confided in him, she moved closer to Lennie and sat beside him. "Coulda been in the movies, an' had nice clothes—all them nice clothes like they wear. An' I coulda sat in them big hotels, an' had pitchers took of me. When they had them previews I coulda went to them, an' spoke in the radio, an' it wouldn' cost me a cent because I was in the pitcher. An' all them nice clothes like they wear. Because this guys says I was a natural." She looked up at Lennie, and she made a small grand gesture with her arm and hand to show that she could act. The fingers trailed after her leading wrist, and her little finger stuck out grandly from the rest.

Lennie sighed deeply. From outside came the clang of a horseshoe on metal, and then a chorus of cheers. "Somebody made a ringer," said Curley's wife.

Now the light was lifting as the sun went down, and the sun-streaks climbed up the wall and fell over the feeding-racks and over the heads of the horses.

Lennie said, "Maybe if I took this pup out and throwed him away, George wouldn't never know. An' then I could tend the rabbits without no trouble."

Curley's wife said angrily, "Don't you think of nothing but rabbits?"

"We gonna have a little place," Lennie explained patiently. "We gonna have a house an' a garden and a place for alfalfa, an' that alfalfa is for the rabbits, an' I take a sack and get it all fulla alfalfa and then I take it to the rabbits."

She asked, "What makes you so nuts about rabbits?"

Lennie had to think carefully before he could come to a conclusion. He moved cautiously close to her, until he was right against her. "I like to pet nice things. Once at a fair I seen some of them long-hair rabbits. An' they was nice, you bet. Sometimes I've even pet mice, but not when I could get nothing better."

Curley's wife moved away from him a little. "I think you're nuts," she said.

"No, I ain't," Lennie explained earnestly. "George says I ain't. I like to pet nice things with my fingers, sof' things."

She was a little bit reassured. "Well, who don't?" she said. "Ever'body like that. I like to feel silk an' velvet. Do you like to feel velvet?"

Lennie chuckled with pleasure. "You bet, by God," he cried happily. "An' I had some, too. A lady give me some, an' that lady was—my own Aunt Clara. She give it right to me—'bout this big a piece. I wisht I had that velvet right now." A frown came over his face. "I lost it," he said. "I ain't seen it for a long time."

Curley's wife laughed at him. "You're nuts," she said. "But you're a kinda nice fella. Jus' like a big baby. But a person can see kinda what you mean. When I'm doin' my hair sometimes I jus' set an' stroke it 'cause it's so soft." To show how she did it, she ran her fingers over the top of her head. "Some people got kinda coarse hair," she said complacently. "Take Curley. His hair is jus' like wire. But mine is soft and fine. 'Course I brush it a lot. That makes it fine. Here—feel right here." She took Lennie's hand and put it on her head. "Feel right aroun' there an' see how soft it is."

Lennie's big fingers fell to stroking her hair.

"Don't you muss it up," she said.

Lennie said, "Oh! That's nice," and he stroked harder. "Oh, that's nice."

"Look out, now, you'll muss it." And then she cried angrily, "You stop it now, you'll mess it all up." She jerked her head sideways, and Lennie's fingers closed on her hair and hung on. "Let go," she cried. "You let go."

Lennie was in a panic. His face was contorted. She screamed then, and Lennie's other hand closed over her mouth and nose. "Please don't," he begged. "Oh! Please don't do that. George'll be mad."

She struggled violently under his hands. Her feet battered on the hay and she writhed to be free; and from under Lennie's hand came a muffled screaming. Lennie began to cry with fright. "Oh! Please don't do none of that," he begged. "George gonna say I done a bad thing. He ain't gonna let me tend no rabbits." He moved his hand a little and her hoarse cry came out. Then Lennie grew angry. "Now don't," he said. "I don't want you to yell. You gonna get me in trouble jus' like George says you will. Now don't you do that." And she continued to struggle, and her eyes were wild with terror. He shook her then, and he was angry with her. "Don't you go yellin'," he said, and he shook her; and her body flopped like a fish. And then she was still, for Lennie had broken her neck.

He looked down at her, and carefully he removed his hand from over her mouth, and she lay still. "I don't want ta hurt you," he said, "but George'll be mad if you yell." When she didn't answer nor move he bent closely over her. He lifted her arm and let it drop. For a moment he seemed bewildered. And then he whispered in fright. "I done a bad thing. I done another bad thing."

He pawed up the hay until it partly covered her.

From outside the barn came a cry of men and the double clang of shoes on metal. For the first time Lennie became conscious of the outside. He crouched down in the hay and listened. "I done a real bad thing," he said. "I shouldn't of did that. George'll be mad. An' . . . he said . . . an' hide in the brush till he come. He's gonna be mad. In the brush till he come. Tha's what he said." Lennie went back and looked at the dead girl. The puppy lay close to her. Lennie picked it up. "I'll throw him away," he said. "It's bad enough like it is." He put the pup under his coat, and he crept to the barn wall and peered out between the cracks, toward the horse-shoe game. And then he crept around the end of the last manger and disappeared.

The sun-streaks were high on the wall by now, and the light was growing soft in the barn. Curley's wife lay on her back, and she was half covered with hay.

It was very quiet in the barn, and the quiet of the afternoon was on the ranch. Even the clang of the pitched shoes, even the voices of the men in the game seemed to grow more quiet. The air in the barn was dusky in advance of the outside day. A pigeon flew in through the open hay door and circled and flew out again. Around the last stall came a shepherd bitch, lean and long, with heavy, hanging dugs. Half-way to the packing-box where the puppies were, she caught the dead scent of Curley's wife, and the hair arose along her spine. She whimpered and cringed to the packing-box, and jumped in among the puppies.

Curley's wife lay with a half-covering of yellow hay. And the meanness and the plannings and the discontent and the ache for attention were all gone from her face. She was very pretty and simple, and her face was sweet and young. Now her rouged cheeks and her reddened lips made her seem alive and sleeping very lightly. The curls, tiny little sausages, were spread on the hay behind her head, and her lips were parted.

As happens sometimes, a moment settled and hovered and remained for much more than a moment. And sound stopped and movement stopped for much, much more than a moment.

Then gradually time awakened again and moved sluggishly on. The horses stamped on the other side of the feeding-racks and the halter chains clinked. Outside, the men's voices became louder and clearer.

From around the end of the last stall old Candy's voice came. "Lennie," he called. "Oh, Lennie! You in here? I been figuring some more. Tell you what we can do, Lennie." Old Candy appeared around the end of the last stall. "Oh, Lennie!" he called again; and then he stopped, and his body stiffened. He rubbed his smooth wrist on his white stubble whiskers. "I di'n't know you was here," he said to Curley's wife.

When she didn't answer, he stepped nearer. "You oughten to sleep out here," he said disapprovingly; and then he was beside her and—"Oh, Jesus Christ!" He looked about helplessly, and he rubbed his beard. And then he jumped up and went quickly out of the barn.

But the barn was alive now. The horses stamped and snorted, and they chewed the straw of their bedding and they clashed the chains of their halters. In a moment Candy came back, and George was with him.

George said, "What was it you wanted to see me about?"

Candy pointed at Curley's wife. George stared. "—What's the matter with her?" he asked. He stepped closer, and then he echoed Candy's words. "Oh, Jesus Christ!" he was down on his knees beside her. He put his hand over her heart. And finally, when he stood up, slowly and stiffly, his face was as hard and tight as wood, and his eyes were hard.

Candy said, "What done it?"

George looked coldly at him. "Ain't you got any idear?" he asked. And Candy was silent. "I should of knew," George said hopelessly. "I guess maybe way back in my head I did."

Candy asked, "What we gonna do now, George? What we gonna do now?"

George was a long time in answering. "Guess . . . we gotta tell the . . . guys. I guess we gotta get 'im an' lock 'im up. We can't let 'im get away. Why the poor bastard'd starve." And he tried to reassure himself. "Maybe they'll lock 'im up an' be nice to 'im."

But Candy said excitedly, "We oughtta let 'im get away. You don't know that Curley. Curley go'n'ta wanta get 'im lynched. Curley'll get 'im killed."

George watched Candy's lips. "Yeah," he said at last, "that's right, Curley will. An' the other guys will." And he looked back at Curley's wife.

Now Candy spoke his greatest fear. "You an' me can get that little place, can't we, George? You an' me can go there an' live nice, can't we, George? Can't we?"

Before George answered, Candy dropped his head and looked down at the hay. He knew.

George said softly, "—I think I knowed from the very first. I think I knowed we'd never do her. He usta like to hear about it so much I got to thinking maybe we would."

"Then—it's all off?" Candy asked sulkily.

George didn't answer his question. George said, "I'll work my month an' I'll take my fifty bucks an' I'll stay all night in some lousy cat-house. Or I'll set in some pool-room till ever'body goes home. An' then I'll come back an' work another month an' I'll have fifty bucks more."

Candy said, "He's such a nice fella. I didn't think he'd do nothing like this."

George still stared at Curley's wife. "Lennie never done it in meanness," he said. "All the time he done bad things, but he never done one of 'em mean." He straightened up and looked back at Candy. "Now listen. We gotta tell the guys. They got to bring him in, I guess. They ain't no way out. Maybe they won't hurt 'im." He said sharply, "I ain't gonna let 'em hurt Lennie. Now you listen. The guys might think I was in on it. I'm gonna go in the bunkhouse. Then in a minute you come out and tell the guys about her, and I'll come along and make like I never seen her. Will you do that? So the guys won't think I was in on it?"

Candy said, "Sure, George. Sure I'll do that."

"O.K. Give me a couple minutes, then, and you come runnin' out an' tell like you jus' found her. I'm going now." George turned and went quickly out of the barn.

Old Candy watched him go. He looked helplessly back at Curley's wife, and gradually his sorrow and his anger grew into words. "You god-damn tramp," he said viciously. "You done it, di'n't you? I s'pose you're glad. Ever'body knowed you'd mess things up. You wasn't no good. You ain't no good now, you lousy tart." He snivelled, and his voice shook. "I could of hoed in the garden and washed dishes for them guys." He paused, and then went on in a sing-song. And he repeated the old words: "If they was a circus or a baseball game . . . we would of went to her . . . jus' said 'Ta hell with work,' an' went to her. Never ast nobody's say-so. An' they'd of been a pig and chickens . . . an' in the winter . . . the little fat stove . . . an' the rain comin' . . . an' us jus' settin' there." His eyes blinded with tears and he turned and went weakly out of the barn, and he rubbed his bristly whiskers with his wrist stump.

Outside the noise of the game stopped. There was a rise of voices in question, a drum of running feet and the men burst into the barn. Slim and Carlson and young Whit and Curley, and Crooks keeping back out of attention range. Candy came after them, and last of all came George. George had put on his blue denim coat and buttoned it, and his black hat was pulled down low over his eyes. The men raced around the last stall. Their eyes found Curley's wife in the gloom, they stopped and stood still and looked.

Then Slim went quietly over to her, and he felt her wrist. One lean finger touched her cheek, and then his hand went under her slightly twisted neck and his fingers explored her neck. When he stood up the men crowded near and the spell was broken.

Curley came suddenly to life. "I know who done it," he cried. "That big son-of-a-bitch done it. I know he done it. Why—ever'-body else was out there playin' horse-shoes." He worked himself into a fury. "I'm gonna get him. I'm going for my shot-gun. I'll kill the big son-of-a-bitch myself. I'll shoot 'im in the guts. Come on, you guys." He ran furiously out of the barn. Carlson said, "I'll get my Luger," and he ran out, too.

Slim turned quietly to George. "I guess Lennie done it, all right," he said. "Her neck's bust. Lennie coulda did that."

George didn't answer, but he nodded slowly. His hat was so far down on his forehead that his eyes were covered.

Slim went on, "Maybe like that time in Weed you was tellin' about."

Again George nodded.

Slim sighed. "Well, I guess we got to get him. Where you think he might of went?"

It seemed to take George some time to free his words. "He—would of went south," he said. "We come from north so he would of went south."

"I guess we gotta get 'im," Slim repeated.

George stepped close. "Couldn't we maybe bring him in an' they'll lock him up? He's nuts, Slim. He never done this to be mean."

Slim nodded. "We might," he said. "If we could keep Curley in, we might. But Curley's gonna want to shoot 'im. Curley's still mad about his hand. An 's'pose they lock him up an' strap him down and put him in a cage. That ain't no good, George."

"I know," said George. "I know."

Carlson came running in. "The bastard's stole my Luger," he shouted. "It ain't in my bag." Curley followed him, and Curley carried a shotgun in his good hand. Curley was cold now.

"All right, you guys," he said. "The nigger's got a shotgun. You take it, Carlson. When you see 'im, don't give 'im no chance. Shoot for his guts. That'll double 'im over."

Whit said excitedly, "I ain't got a gun."

Curley said, "You go in Soledad an' get a cop. Get Al Wilts, he's deputy sheriff. Le's go now." He turned suspiciously on George. "You're comin' with us, fella."

"Yeah," said George. "I'll come. But listen, Curley. The poor bastard's nuts. Don't shoot 'im. He di'n't know what he was doin'."

"Don't shoot 'im?" Curley cried. "He got Carlson's Luger. 'Course we'll shoot 'im."

George said weakly, "Maybe Carlson lost his gun."

"I seen it this morning," said Carlson. "No, it's been took."

Slim stood looking down at Curley's wife. He said, "Curley—maybe you better stay here with your wife."

Curley's face reddened. "I'm goin'," he said. "I'm gonna shoot the guts outa that big bastard myself, even if I only got one hand. I'm gonna get 'im."

Slim turned to Candy. "You stay here with her, then, Candy. The rest of us better get goin'."

They moved away. George stopped a moment beside Candy and they both looked down at the dead girl until Curley called, "You, George! You stick with us so we don't think you had nothin' to do with this."

George moved slowly after them, and his feet dragged heavily. And when they were gone, Candy squatted down in the hay and watched the face of Curley's wife. "Poor bastard," he said softly.

The sound of the men grew fainter. The barn was darkening gradually, and in their stalls the horses shifted their feet and rattled the halter chains. Old Candy lay down in the hay and covered his eyes with his arm.

CHAPTER VI

THE DEEP green pool of the Salinas River was still in the late afternoon. Already the sun had left the valley to go climbing up the slopes of the Gabilan mountains, and the hill-tops were rosy in the sun. But by the pool among the mottled sycamores, a pleasant shade had fallen.

A water-snake glided smoothly up the pool, twisting its periscope head from side to side; and it swam the length of the pool and came to the legs of a motionless heron that stood in the shallows. A silent head and beak lanced down and plucked it out by the head, and the beak swallowed the little snake while its tail waved frantically.

A far rush of wind sounded and a gust drove through the tops of the trees like a wave. The sycamore leaves turned up their silver sides, the brown, dry leaves on the ground scudded a few feet. And row on row of tiny wind-waves flowed up the pool's green surface.

As quickly as it had come, the wind died, and the clearing was quiet again. The heron stood in the shallows, motionless and waiting. Another little water-snake swam up the pool, turning its periscope head from side to side.

Suddenly Lennie appeared out of the brush, and he came as

silently as a creeping bear moves. The heron pounded the air with its wings, jacked itself clear of the water and flew off down-river. The little snake slid in among the reeds at the pool's side.

Lennie came quietly to the pool's edge. He knelt down and drank, barely touching his lips to the water. When a little bird skittered over the dry leaves behind him, his head jerked up and he strained toward the sound with eyes and ears until he saw the bird, and then he dropped his head and drank again.

When he was finished, he sat down on the bank, with his side to the pool, so that he could watch the trail's entrance. He embraced his knees and laid his chin down on his knees.

The light climbed on out of the valley and, as it went, the tops of the mountains seemed to blaze with increasing brightness.

Lennie said softly, "I di'n't forget, you bet, god damn. Hide in the brush an' wait for George." He pulled his hat down low over his eyes. "George gonna give me hell," he said. "George gonna wish he was alone an' not have me botherin' him." He turned his head and looked at the bright mountain-tops. "I can go right off there an' find a cave," he said. And he continued sadly, "—an' never have no ketchup—but I won't care. If George don't want me . . . I'll go away. I'll go away."

And then from out of Lennie's head there came a little fat old woman. She wore thick bull's-eye glasses and she wore a huge gingham apron with pockets, and she was starched and clean. She stood in front of Lennie and put her hands on her hips, and she frowned disapprovingly at him.

And when she spoke, it was in Lennie's voice. "I tol' you an' tol' you," she said. "I tol' you, 'Min' George because he's such a nice fella an' good to you.' But you don't never take no care. You do bad things."

And Lennie answered her, "I tried, Aunt Clara, ma'am. I tried and tried. I couldn't help it."

"You never give a thought to George," she went on in Lennie's voice. "He been doin' nice things for you alla time. When he got a piece a pie you always got half or more'n half. An' if they was any ketchup, why, he'd give it all to you."

"I know," said Lennie miserably. "I tried, Aunt Clara, ma'am. I tried and tried."

She interrupted him. "All the time he coulda had such a good time if it wasn't for you. He woulda took his pay an' raised hell in a whore-house, and he coulda set in a pool-room an' played snooker. But he got to take care of you."

Lennie moaned with grief. "I know, Aunt Clara, ma'am. I'll go right off in the hills an' I'll fin' a cave an' I'll live there so I won't be no more trouble to George."

"You jus' say that," she said sharply. "You're always sayin' that, an' you know son-of-a-bitching well you ain't never gonna do it. You'll jus' stick around an' stew the b'Jesus outa George all the time."

Lennie said, "I might jus' as well go away. George ain't gonna let me tend no rabbits now."

Aunt Clara was gone, and from out of Lennie's head there came a gigantic rabbit. It sat on its haunches in front of him, and it waggled its ears and crinkled its nose at him. And it spoke in Lennie's voice, too.

"Tend rabbits," it said scornfully. "You crazy bastard. You ain't fit to lick the boots of no rabbit. You'd forget 'em and let 'em go hungry. That's what you'd do. An' then what would George think?"

"I would *not* forget," Lennie said loudly.

"The hell you wouldn'," said the rabbit. "You ain't worth a greased jack-pin to ram you into hell. Christ knows George done ever'thing he could to jack you outa the sewer, but it don't do no good. If you think George gonna let you tend rabbits, you're even crazier'n usual. He ain't. He's gonna beat hell outa you with a stick, that's what he's gonna do."

Now Lennie retorted belligerently, "He ain't neither. George won't do nothing like that. I've knew George since—I forget when—and he ain't never raised his han' to me with a stick. He's nice to me. He ain't gonna be mean."

"Well, he's sick of you," said the rabbit. "He's gonna beat hell outa you an' then go away an' leave you."

"He won't," Lennie cried frantically. "He won't do nothing like that. I know George. Me an' him travels together."

But the rabbit repeated softly over and over, "He gonna leave you, ya crazy bastard. He gonna leave ya all alone. He gonna leave ya, crazy bastard."

Lennie put his hands over his ears. "He ain't, I tell ya he ain't." And he cried: "Oh! George—George—George!"

George came quietly out of the brush and the rabbit scuttled back into Lennie's brain.

George said quietly, "What the hell you yellin' about?"

Lennie got up on his knees. "You ain't gonna leave me, are ya, George? I know you ain't."

George came stiffly near and sat down beside him. "No."

"I knowed it," Lennie cried. "You ain't that kind."

George was silent.

Lennie said, "George."

"Yeah?"

"I done another bad thing."

"It don't make no difference," George said, and he fell silent again.

Only the topmost ridges were in the sun now. The shadow in the valley was blue and soft. From the distance came the sound of men shouting to one another. George turned his head and listened to the shouts.

Lennie said, "George."

"Yeah?"

"Ain't you gonna give me hell?"

"Give ya hell?"

"Sure, like you always done before. Like: 'If I di'n't have you I'd take my fifty bucks——' "

"Jesus Christ, Lennie! You can't remember nothing that happens, but you remember ever' word I say."

"Well, ain't you gonna say it?"

George shook himself. He said woodenly, "If I was alone I could live so easy." His voice was monotonous, had no emphasis. "I could get a job an' not have no mess." He stopped.

"Go on," said Lennie. "An' when the enda the month come——"

"An' when the end of the month come I could take my fifty bucks an' go to a . . . cat-house. . . ." He stopped again.

Lennie looked eagerly at him. "Go on, George. Ain't you gonna give me no more hell?"

"No," said George.

"Well, I can go away," said Lennie. "I'll go right off in the hills an' find a cave if you don' want me."

George shook himself again. "No," he said. "I want you to stay with me here."

Lennie said craftily, "Tell me like you done before."

"Tell you what?"

" 'Bout the other guys an' about us."

George said, "Guys like us got no fambly. They make a little stake an' then they blow it in. They ain't got nobody in the worl' that gives a hoot in hell about 'em——"

"*But not us*," Lennie cried happily. "Tell about us now."

George was quiet for a moment. "But not us," he said.

"Because——"

"Because I got you an'——"

"An' I got you. We got each other, that's what, that gives a hoot in hell about us," Lennie cried in triumph.

The little evening breeze blew over the clearing and the leaves rustled and the wind waves flowed up the green pool. And the shouts of men sounded again, this time much closer than before.

George took off his hat. He said shakily, "Take off your hat, Lennie. The air feels fine."

Lennie removed his hat dutifully and laid it on the ground in front of him. The shadow in the valley was bluer, and the evening came fast. On the wind the sound of crashing in the brush came to them.

Lennie said, "Tell how it's gonna be."

George had been listening to the distant sounds. For a moment he was business-like. "Look acrost the river, Lennie, an' I'll tell you so you can almost see it."

Lennie turned his head and looked off across the pool and up the darkening slopes of the Gabilans. "We gonna get a little place," George began. He reached in his side pocket and brought out Carlson's Luger; he snapped off the safety, and the hand and gun lay on the ground behind Lennie's back. He looked at the back of Lennie's head, at the place where the spine and skull were joined.

A man's voice called from up the river, and another man answered.

"Go on," said Lennie.

George raised the gun and his hand shook, and he dropped his hand to the ground again.

"Go on," said Lennie. "How's it gonna be? We gonna get a little place."

"We'll have a cow," said George. "An' we'll have maybe a pig an' chickens . . . an' down the flat we'll have a . . . little piece alfalfa——"

"For the rabbits," Lennie shouted.

"For the rabbits," George repeated.

"And I get to tend the rabbits."

"An' you get to tend the rabbits."

Lennie giggled with happiness. "An' live on the fatta the lan'."

"Yes."

Lennie turned his head.

"No, Lennie. Look down there acrost the river, like you can almost see the place."

Lennie obeyed him. George looked down at the gun.

There were crashing footsteps in the brush now. George turned and looked toward them.

"Go on, George. When we gonna do it?"

"Gonna do it soon."

"Me an' you."

"You . . . an' me. Ever'body gonna be nice to you. Ain't gonna be no more trouble. Nobody gonna hurt nobody nor steal from 'em."

Lennie said, "I thought you was mad at me, George."

"No," said George. "No, Lennie. I ain't mad. I never been mad, an' I ain't now. That's a thing I want ya to know."

The voices came close now. George raised the gun and listened to the voices.

Lennie begged, "Le's do it now. Le's get that place now."

"Sure, right now. I gotta. We gotta."

And George raised the gun and steadied it, and he brought the muzzle of it close to the back of Lennie's head. The hand shook violently, but his face set and his hand steadied. He pulled the trigger. The crash of the shot rolled up the hills and rolled down again. Lennie jarred, and then settled forward to the sand, and he lay without quivering.

George shivered and looked at the gun, and then he threw it from him, back up on the bank, near the pile of old ashes.

The brush seemed filled with cries and with the sound of running feet. Slim's voice shouted, "George. Where you at, George?"

But George sat stiffly on the bank and looked at his right hand that had thrown the gun away. The group burst into the clearing, and Curley was ahead. He saw Lennie lying on the sand. "Got him, by God." He went over and looked down at Lennie, and then he looked back at George. "Right in the back of the head," he said softly.

Slim came directly to George and sat down beside him, sat very close to him. "Never you mind," said Slim. "A guy got to sometimes."

But Carlson was standing over George. "How'd you do it?" he asked.

"I just done it," George said tiredly.

"Did he have my gun?"

"Yeah. He had your gun."

"An' you got it away from him and you took it an' you killed him?"

"Yeah. Tha's how." George's voice was almost a whisper. He looked steadily at his right hand that had held the gun.

Slim twitched George's elbow. "Come on, George. Me an' you'll go in an' get a drink."

George let himself be helped to his feet. "Yeah, a drink."

Slim said, "You hadda, George. I swear you hadda. Come on with me." He led George into the entrance of the trail and up toward the highway.

Curley and Carlson looked after them. And Carlson said, "Now what the hell ya suppose is eatin' them two guys?"

THE MOON IS DOWN

CHAPTER I

By ten-forty-five it was all over. The town was occupied, the defenders defeated, and the war finished. The invader had prepared for this campaign as carefully as he had for larger ones. On this Sunday morning the postman and the policeman had gone fishing in the boat of Mr. Corell, the popular storekeeper. He had lent them his trim sail-boat for the day. The postman and the policeman were several miles at sea when they saw the small, dark transport, loaded with soldiers, go quietly past them. As officials of the town, this was definitely their business, and these two put about, but of course the battalion was in possession by the time they could make port. The policeman and the postman could not even get into their own offices in the Town Hall, and when they insisted on their rights they were taken prisoners of war and locked up in the town jail.

The local troops, all twelve of them, had been away, too, on this Sunday morning, for Mr. Corell, the popular storekeeper, had donated lunch, targets, cartridges, and prizes for a shooting competition to take place six miles back in the hills, in a lovely glade Mr. Corell owned. The local troops, big, loose-hung boys, heard the planes and in the distance saw the parachutes, and they came back to town at double-quick step. When they arrived, the invader had flanked the road with machine-guns. The loose-hung soldiers, having very little experience in war and none at all in defeat, opened fire with their rifles. The machine-guns clattered for a moment and six of the soldiers became dead riddled bundles, and three half-dead riddled bundles, and three of the soldiers escaped into the hills with their rifles.

By ten-thirty the brass band of the invader was playing beautiful and sentimental music in the town square while the townsmen, their mouths a little open and their eyes astonished, stood about listening to the music and staring at the grey-helmeted men who carried sub-machine-guns in their arms.

By ten-thirty-eight the riddled six were buried, the parachutes were folded, and the battalion was billeted in Mr. Corell's warehouse by the pier, which had on its shelves blankets and cots for a battalion.

By ten-forty-five old Mayor Orden had received the formal request that he grant an audience to Colonel Lanser of the invaders, an audience which was set for eleven sharp at the Mayor's five-room palace.

The drawing-room of the palace was very sweet and comfortable. The gilded chairs covered with their worn tapestry were set about stiffly like too many servants with nothing to do. An arched marble fireplace held its little basket of red flameless heat, and a hand-painted coal-scuttle stood on the hearth. On the mantel, flanked by fat vases, stood a large, curly porcelain clock which swarmed with tumbling cherubs. The wall-paper of the room was dark red with gold figures, and the woodwork was white, pretty and clean. The paintings on the wall were largely preoccupied with the amazing heroism of large dogs faced with imperilled children. Nor water nor fire nor earthquake could do in a child so long as a big dog was available.

Beside the fireplace old Doctor Winter sat, bearded and simple and benign, historian and physician to the town. He watched in amazement while his thumbs rolled over and over on his lap. Doctor Winter was a man so simple that only a profound man would know him as profound. He looked up at Joseph, the Mayor's serving-man, to see whether Joseph had observed the rolling wonders of his thumbs.

"Eleven o'clock?" Doctor Winter asked.

And Joseph answered abstractedly, "Yes, sir. The note said eleven."

"You read the note?"

"No, sir, His Excellency read the note to me."

And Joseph went about testing each of the gilded chairs to see whether it had moved since he had last placed it. Joseph habitually scowled at furniture, expecting it to be impertinent, mischievous, or dusty. In a world where Mayor Orden was the leader of men, Joseph was the leader of furniture, silver and dishes. Joseph was elderly and lean and serious, and his life was so complicated that only a profound man would know him to be simple. He saw nothing amazing about Doctor Winter's rolling thumbs; in fact he found them irritating. Joseph suspected that something pretty important was happening, what with foreign soldiers in the town and the local army killed or captured. Sooner or later Joseph would have to get an opinion about it all. He wanted no levity, no rolling thumbs, no nonsense from furniture. Doctor Winter moved his chair a few inches from its appointed place and Joseph waited impatiently for the moment when he could put it back again.

Doctor Winter repeated, "Eleven o'clock, and they'll be here then, too. A time-minded people, Joseph."

And Joseph said, without listening, "Yes, sir."

"A time-minded people," the doctor repeated.

"Yes, sir," said Joseph.

"Time and machines."

"Yes, sir."

"They hurry towards their destiny as though it would not wait. They push the rolling world along with their shoulders."

And Joseph said, "Quite right, sir," simply because he was getting tired of saying, "Yes, sir."

Joseph did not approve of this line of conversation, since it did not help him to have an opinion about anything. If Joseph remarked to the cook later in the day, "A time-minded people, Annie," it would not make any sense. Annie would ask, "Who?" and then "Why?" and finally say, "That's nonsense, Joseph." Joseph had tried carrying Doctor Winter's remarks below-stairs before and it had always ended the same; Annie always discovered them to be nonsense.

Doctor Winter looked up from his thumbs and watched Joseph disciplining the chairs. "What's the Mayor doing?"

"Dressing to receive the colonel, sir."

"And you aren't helping him? He will be ill-dressed by himself."

"Madame is helping him. Madame wants him to look his best. She"—Joseph blushed a little—"Madame is trimming the hair out of his ears, sir. It tickles. He won't let me do it."

"Of course it tickles," said Doctor Winter.

"Madame insists," said Joseph.

Doctor Winter laughed suddenly. He stood up and held his hands to the fire and Joseph skilfully darted behind him and replaced the chair where it should be.

"We are so wonderful," the doctor said. "Our country is falling, our town is conquered, the Mayor is about to receive the conqueror, and Madame is holding the struggling Mayor by the neck and trimming the hair out of his ears."

"He was getting very shaggy," said Joseph. "His eyebrows, too. His Excellency is even more upset about having his eyebrows trimmed than his ears. He says it hurts. I doubt if even Madame can do it."

"She will try," Doctor Winter said.

"She wants him to look his best, sir."

Through the glass window of the entrance door a helmeted face looked in and there was a rapping on the door. It seemed that some warm light went out of the room and a little greyness took its place.

Doctor Winter looked up at the clock and said, "They are early. Let them in, Joseph."

Joseph went to the door and opened it. A soldier stepped in, dressed in a long coat. He was helmeted and he carried a sub-machine-gun over his arm. He glanced quickly about and then stepped aside. Behind him an officer stood in the doorway. The officer's uniform was common and it had rank showing only on the shoulders.

The officer stepped inside and looked at Doctor Winter. He was rather like an overdrawn picture of an English gentleman. He had a slouch, his face was red, his nose long but rather pleasing; he seemed about as unhappy in his uniform as most British general officers are. He stood in the doorway, staring at Doctor Winter, and he said, "Are you Mayor Orden, sir?"

Doctor Winter smiled. "No, no, I am not."

"You are an official, then?"

"No, I am the town doctor and I am a friend of the Mayor."

The officer said, "Where is Mayor Orden?"

"Dressing to receive you. You are the colonel?"

"No, I am not. I am Captain Bentick." He bowed and Doctor Winter returned the bow slightly. Captain Bentick continued, as though a little embarrassed at what he had to say. "Our military regulations, sir, prescribe that we search for weapons before the commanding officer enters a room. We mean no disrespect, sir." And he called over his shoulder, "Sergeant!"

The sergeant moved quickly to Joseph, ran his hands over his pockets, and said, "Nothing, sir."

Captain Bentick said to Doctor Winter: "I hope you will pardon us." And the sergeant went to Doctor Winter and patted his pockets. His hands stopped at the inside coat pocket. He reached quickly in, brought out a little, flat, black leather case, and took it to Captain Bentick. Captain Bentick opened the case, and found there a few simple surgical instruments—two scalpels, some surgical needles, some clamps, a hypodermic needle. He closed the case again and handed it back to Doctor Winter.

Doctor Winter said, "You see, I am a country doctor. One time I had to perform an appendectomy with a kitchen knife. I have always carried these with me since then."

Captain Bentick said, "I believe there are some firearms here?" He opened a little leather book that he carried in his pocket.

Doctor Winter said, "You are thorough."

"Yes, our local man has been working here for some time."

Doctor Winter said, "I don't suppose you would tell who that man is?"

Bentick said, "His work is all done now. I don't suppose there would be any harm in telling. His name is Corell."

And Doctor Winter said in astonishment, "George Corell? Why, that seems impossible! He's done a lot for this town. Why, he even gave prizes for the shooting-match in the hill this morning." And as he said it his eyes began to understand what had happened and his mouth closed slowly, and he said, "I see, that is why he gave the shooting-match. Yes, I see. But George Corell—that sounds impossible!"

The door to the left opened and Mayor Orden came in; he was digging in his right ear with his little finger. He was dressed in his official morning coat, with his chain of office about his neck. He had a large, white, spraying moustache and two smaller ones, one over each eye. His white hair was so recently brushed that only now were the hairs struggling to be free, to stand up again. He had been Mayor so long that he was the Idea-Mayor in the town. Even grown people when they saw the word 'mayor', printed or written, saw Mayor Orden in their minds. He and his office were one. It had given him dignity and he had given it warmth.

From behind him Madame emerged, small and wrinkled and fierce. She considered that she had created this man out of whole cloth, had thought him up, and she was sure that she could do a better job if she had it to do again. Only once or twice in her life had she ever understood all of him, but the part of him which she knew, she knew intricately and well. No little appetite or pain, no meanness in him escaped her; no thought or dream or longing in him ever reached her. And yet several times in her life she had seen the stars.

She stepped around the Mayor and she took his hand and pulled his finger out of his outraged ear and pushed his hand to his side, the way she would take a baby's thumb away from his mouth.

"I don't believe for a moment it hurts as much as you say," she said, and to Doctor Winter, "He won't let me fix his eyebrows."

"It hurts," said Mayor Orden.

"Very well, if you want to look like that there is nothing I can do about it." She straightened his already straight tie. "I'm glad you're here, Doctor," she said. "How many do you think will come?" And then she looked up and saw Captain Bentick. "Oh," she said, "the colonel!"

Captain Bentick said, "No, ma'am, I am only preparing for the colonel. Sergeant!"

The sergeant, who had been turning over pillows, looking behind pictures, came quickly to Mayor Orden and ran his hands over his pockets.

Captain Bentick said, "Excuse him, sir, it's regulations."

He glanced again at the little book in his hand. "Your Excellency, I think you have firearms here. Two items, I believe?"

Mayor Orden said, "Firearms? Guns, you mean, I guess. Yes, I have a shotgun and a sporting-rifle." He said deprecatingly, "You know, I don't hunt very much any more. I always think I'm going to, and then the season opens and I don't get out. I don't take the pleasure in it I used to."

Captain Bentick insisted. "Where are these guns, Your Excellency?"

The Mayor rubbed his cheek and tried to think. "Why, I think——" He turned to Madame. "Weren't they in the back of that cabinet in the bedroom with the walking-sticks?"

Madame said, "Yes, and every stitch of clothing in that cabinet smells of oil. I wish you'd put them somewhere else."

Captain Bentick said, "Sergeant!" and the sergeant went quickly into the bedroom.

"It's an unpleasant duty. I'm sorry," said the captain.

The sergeant came back, carrying a double-barrelled shotgun and rather nice sporting-rifle with a shoulder strap. He leaned them against the side of the entrance door.

Captain Bentick said, "That's all, thank you, Your Excellency. Thank you, Madame."

He turned and bowed slightly to Doctor Winter. "Thank you, Doctor. Colonel Lanser will be here directly. Good morning!"

And he went out to the front door, followed by the sergeant with the two guns in one hand and the sub-machine-gun over his right arm.

Madame said, "For a moment I thought he was the colonel. He was a rather nice-looking young man."

Doctor Winter said sardonically, "No, he was just protecting the colonel."

Madame was thinking, "I wonder how many officers will come?" And she looked at Joseph and saw that he was shamelessly eavesdropping. She shook her head at him and frowned and he went back to the little things he had been doing. He began dusting all over again.

And Madame said. "How many do you think will come?"

Doctor Winter pulled out a chair outrageously and sat down again. "I don't know," he said.

"Well"—she frowned at Joseph—"we've been talking it over. Should we offer them tea or a glass of wine? If we do, I don't know how many there will be, and if we don't, what are we to do?"

Doctor Winter shook his head and smiled. "I don't know. It's been so long since we conquered anybody or anybody conquered us. I don't know what is proper."

Mayor Orden had his finger back in his itching ear. He said, "Well, I don't think we should. I don't think the people would like it. I don't want to drink wine with them. I don't know why."

Madame appealed to the doctor then. "Didn't people in the old days—the leaders, that is—compliment each other and take a glass of wine?"

Doctor Winter nodded. "Yes, indeed they did." He shook his

head slowly. "Maybe that was different. Kings and princes played at war the way Englishmen play at hunting. When the fox was dead they gathered at a hunt breakfast. But Mayor Orden is probably right: the people might not like him to drink wine with the invader."

Madame said, "The people are down listening to the music. Annie told me. If they can do that, why shouldn't we keep civilized procedure alive?"

The Mayor looked steadily at her for a moment and his voice was sharp. "Madame, I think with your permission we will not have wine. The people are confused now. They have lived at peace so long that they do not quite believe in war. They will learn and then they will not be confused any more. They elected me not to be confused. Six town boys were murdered this morning. I think we will have no hunt breakfast. The people do not fight wars for sport."

Madame bowed slightly. There had been a number of times in her life when her husband had become the Mayor. She had learned not to confuse the Mayor with her husband.

Mayor Orden looked at his watch and when Joseph came in, carrying a small cup of black coffee, he took it absent-mindedly. "Thank you," he said, and he sipped it. "I should be clear," he said apologetically to Doctor Winter. "I should be—do you know how many men the invader has?"

"Not many," the doctor said. "I don't think over two hundred and fifty; but all with those little machine-guns."

The Mayor sipped his coffee again and made a new start. "What about the rest of the country?"

The doctor raised his shoulders and dropped them again.

"Was there no resistance anywhere?" the Mayor went on hopelessly.

And again the doctor raised his shoulders. "I don't know. The wires are cut or captured. There is no news."

"And our boys, our soldiers?"

"I don't know," said the doctor.

Joseph interrupted. "I heard—that is, Annie heard——"

"What, Joseph?"

"Six men were killed, sir, by the machine-guns. Annie heard three were wounded and captured."

"But there were twelve."

"Annie heard that three escaped."

The Mayor turned sharply. "Which ones escaped?" he demanded.

"I don't know, sir. Annie didn't hear."

Madame inspected a table for dust with her finger. She said, "Joseph, when they come, stay close to your bell. We might want some little thing. And put on your other coat, Joseph, the one with the buttons." She thought for a moment, "And, Joseph, when you finish what you are told to do, go out of the room. It makes a bad impression when you just stand around listening. It's provincial, that's what it is."

"Yes, Madame," Joseph said.

"We won't serve wine, Joseph, but you might have some cigarettes handy in that little silver conserve box. And don't strike the match to light the colonel's cigarette on your shoe. Strike it on the match-box."

"Yes, Madame."

Mayor Orden unbuttoned his coat and took out his watch and looked at it and put it back and buttoned his coat again, one button too high. Madame went to him and rebuttoned it correctly.

Doctor Winter asked, "What time is it?"

"Five to eleven."

"A time-minded people," the doctor said. "They will be here on time. Do you want me to go away?"

Mayor Orden looked startled. "Go? No—no, stay." He laughed softly. "I'm a little afraid," he said apologetically. "Well, not afraid, but I'm nervous." And he said helplessly, "We have never been conquered, for a long time——" He stopped to listen. In the distance there was a sound of band music, a march. They all turned in its direction and listened.

Madame said, "Here they come. I hope not too many try to crowd in here at once. It isn't a very big room."

Doctor Winter said sardonically, "Madame would prefer the Hall of Mirrors at Versailles?"

She pinched her lips and looked about, already placing the conquerors with her mind. "It is a very small room," she said.

The band music swelled a little and then grew fainter. There came a gentle tap on the door.

"Now, who can that be? Joseph, if it is anyone, tell him to come back later. We are very busy."

The tap came again. Joseph went to the door and opened it a crack and then a little wider. A grey figure, helmeted and gauntleted, appeared.

"Colonel Lanser's compliments," the head said. "Colonel Lanser requests an audience with Your Excellency."

Joseph opened the door wide. The helmeted orderly stepped inside and looked quickly about the room and then stood aside. "Colonel Lanser!" he announced.

A second helmeted figure walked into the room, and his rank showed only on his shoulders. Behind him came a rather short man in a black business suit. The colonel was a middle-aged man, grey and hard and tired-looking. He had the square shoulders of a soldier, but his eyes lacked the blank look of the ordinary soldier. The little man beside him was bald and rosy-cheeked, with small black eyes and a sensual mouth.

Colonel Lanser took off his helmet. With a quick bow, he said, "Your Excellency!" He bowed to Madame. "Madame!" And he said, "Close the door, please, Corporal." Joseph quickly shut the door and stared in small triumph at the soldier.

Lanser looked questioningly at the doctor, and Mayor Orden said, "This is Doctor Winter."

"An official?" the colonel asked.

"A doctor, sir, and, I might say, the local historian."

Lanser bowed slightly. He said, "Doctor Winter, I do not mean to be impertinent, but there will be a page in your history, perhaps——"

And Doctor Winter smiled. "Many pages, perhaps."

Colonel Lanser turned slightly towards his companion. "I think you know Mr. Corell," he said.

The Mayor said, "George Corell? Of course I know him. How are you, George?"

Doctor Winter cut in sharply. He said, very formally, "Your Excellency, our friend, George Corell, prepared this town for the invasion. Our benefactor, George Corell, sent our soldiers into the hills. Our dinner guest, George Corell, has made a list of every firearm in the town. Our friend, George Corell!"

Corell said angrily, "I work for what I believe in! That is an honourable thing."

Orden's mouth hung a little open. He was bewildered. He looked helplessly from Winter to Corell. "This isn't true," he said. "George, this isn't true! You have sat at my table, you have drunk port with me. Why, you helped me plan the hospital! This isn't true!"

He was looking very steadily at Corell and Corell looked belligerently back at him. There was a long silence. Then the Mayor's face grew slowly tight and very formal and his whole body was rigid. He turned to Colonel Lanser and he said, "I do not wish to speak in this gentleman's company."

Corell said, "I have a right to be here! I am a soldier like the rest. I simply do not wear a uniform."

The Mayor repeated, "I do not wish to speak in this gentleman's presence."

Colonel Lanser said, "Will you leave us now, Mr. Corell?"

And Corell said, "I have a right to be here!"

Lanser repeated sharply, "Will you leave us now, Mr. Corell? Do you outrank me?"

"Well, no, sir."

"Please go, Mr. Corell," said Colonel Lanser.

And Corell looked at the Mayor angrily, and then he turned and went quickly out of the doorway. Doctor Winter chuckled and said, "That's good enough for a paragraph in my history." Colonel Lanser glanced sharply at him but he did not speak.

Now the door on the right opened, and straw-haired, red-eyed Annie put an angry face into the doorway. "There's soldiers on the back porch, Madame," she said. "Just standing there."

"They won't come in," Colonel Lanser said. "It's only military procedure."

Madame said icily, "Annie, if you have anything to say, let Joseph bring the message."

"I didn't know but they'd try to get in," Annie said. "They smelled the coffee."

"Annie!"

"Yes, Madame," and she withdrew.

The colonel said, "May I sit down?" And he explained, "We have been a long time without sleep."

The Mayor seemed to start out of sleep himself. "Yes," he said, "of course, sit down!"

The colonel looked at Madame and she seated herself and he settled tiredly into a chair. Mayor Orden stood, still half dreaming.

The colonel began, "We want to get along as well as we can. You see, sir, this is more like a business venture than anything else. We need the coal-mine here and the fishing. We will try to get along with just as little friction as possible."

The Mayor said, "I have had no news. What about the rest of the country?"

"All taken," said the colonel. "It was well planned."

"Was there no resistance anywhere?"

The colonel looked at him compassionately. "I wish there had not been. Yes, there was some resistance, but it only caused bloodshed. We had planned very carefully."

Orden stuck to his point. "But there was resistance?"

"Yes, but it was foolish to resist. Just as here, it was destroyed instantly. It was sad and foolish to resist."

Doctor Winter caught some of the Mayor's anxiousness about the point. "Yes," he said, "foolish, but they resisted."

And Colonel Lanser replied, "Only a few and they are gone. The people as a whole are quiet."

Doctor Winter said, "The people don't know yet what has happened."

"They are discovering," said Lanser. "They won't be foolish again." He cleared his throat and his voice became brisk. "Now, sir, I must get to business. I'm really very tired, but before I can sleep I must make my arrangements." He sat forward in his chair.

"I am more engineer than soldier. This whole thing is more an engineering job than conquest. The coal must come out of the ground and be shipped. We have technicians, but the local people will continue to work the mine. Is that clear? We do not wish to be harsh."

And Orden said, "Yes, that's clear enough. But suppose the people do not want to work the mine?"

The colonel said, "I hope they will want to, because they must. We must have the coal."

"But if they don't?"

"They must. They are an orderly people. They don't want trouble." He waited for the Mayor's reply and none came. "Is that not so, sir?" the colonel asked.

Mayor Orden twisted his chain. "I don't know, sir. They are orderly under their own government. I don't know how they would be under yours. It is untouched ground, you see. We have built our government over four hundred years."

The colonel said quickly, "We know that, and so we are going to keep your government. You will still be the Mayor, you will give the orders, you will penalize and reward. In that way they will not give trouble."

Mayor Orden looked at Doctor Winter. "What are you thinking about?"

"I don't know," said Doctor Winter. "It would be interesting to see. I'd expect trouble. This might be a bitter people."

Mayor Orden said, "I don't know, either." He turned to the colonel. "Sir, I am of this people, and yet I don't know what they will do. Perhaps you know. Or maybe it would be different from anything you know or we know. Some people accept appointed leaders and obey them. But my people have elected me. They made me and they can unmake me. Perhaps they will if they think I have gone over to you. I just don't know."

The colonel said, "You will be doing them a service if you keep them in order."

"A service?"

"Yes, a service. It is your duty to protect them from harm. They will be in danger if they are rebellious. We must get the coal, you see. Our leaders do not tell us how; they order us to get it. But you have your people to protect. You must make them do the work and thus keep them safe."

Mayor Orden asked, "But suppose they don't want to be safe?"

"Then you must think for them."

Orden said, a little proudly, "My people don't like to have others think for them. Maybe they are different from your people. I am confused, but that I am sure of."

Now Joseph came in quickly and he stood leaning forward, bursting to speak. Madame said, "What is it, Joseph? Get the silver box of cigarettes."

"Pardon Madame," said Joseph. "Pardon, Your Excellency."

"What do you want?" the Mayor asked.

"It's Annie," he said. "She's getting angry, sir."

"What is the matter?" Madame demanded.

"Annie don't like the soldiers on the back porch."

The colonel asked, "Are they causing trouble?"

"They are looking through the door at Annie," said Joseph. "She hates that."

The colonel said, "They are carrying out orders. They are doing no harm."

"Well, Annie hates to be stared at," said Joseph.

Madame said, "Joseph, tell Annie to take care."

"Yes, Madame," and Joseph went out.

The colonel's eyes dropped with tiredness. "There's another thing, Your Excellency," he said. "Would it be possible for me and my staff to stay here?"

Mayor Orden thought a moment and he said, "It's a small place. There are larger, more comfortable places."

Then Joseph came back with the silver box of cigarettes and he opened it and held it in front of the colonel. When the colonel took one, Joseph ostentatiously lighted it. The colonel puffed deeply.

"It isn't that," he said. "We have found that when a staff lives under the roof of the local authority, there is more tranquillity."

"You mean," said Orden, "the people feel there is collaboration involved?"

"Yes, I suppose that is it."

Mayor Orden looked hopelessly at Doctor Winter, and Winter could offer him nothing but a wry smile. Orden said softly, "Am I permitted to refuse this honour?"

"I'm sorry," the colonel said. "No. These are the orders of my leader."

"The people will not like it," Orden said.

"Always the people! The people are disarmed. The people have no say."

Mayor Orden shook his head. "You do not know, sir."

From the doorway came the sound of an angry woman's voice, and a thump and a man's cry. Joseph came scuttling through the door. "She's thrown boiling water," Joseph said. "She's very angry."

There were commands through the door and the clump of feet. Colonel Lanser got up heavily. "Have you no control over your servants, sir?" he asked.

Mayor Orden smiled. "Very little," he said. "She's a very good cook when she is happy. Was anyone hurt?" he asked Joseph.

"The water was boiling, sir."

Colonel Lanser said, "We just want to do our job. It's an engineering job. You will have to discipline your cook."

"I can't," said Orden. "She'll quit."

"This is an emergency. She can't quit."

"Then she'll throw water," said Doctor Winter.

The door opened and a soldier stood in the opening. "Shall I arrest this woman, sir?"

"Was anyone hurt?" Lanser asked.

"Yes, sir, scalded, and one man bitten. We are holding her, sir."

Lanser looked helpless, then he said, "Release her and go outside and off the porch."

"Yes, sir," and the door closed behind the soldier.

Lanser said, "I could have her shot; I could lock her up."

"Then we would have no cook," said Orden.

"Look," said the colonel. "We are instructed to get along with your people."

Madame said, "Excuse me, sir, I will just go and see if the soldiers hurt Annie," and she went out.

Now Lanser stood up. "I told you I'm very tired, sir. I must have some sleep. Please co-operate with us for the good of all." When Mayor Orden made no reply, "For the good of all," Lanser repeated. "Will you?"

Orden said, "This is a little town. I don't know. The people are confused and so am I."

"But will you try to co-operate?"

Orden shook his head. "I don't know. When the town makes up its mind what it wants to do, I'll probably do that."

"But you are the authority."

Orden smiled. "You won't believe this, but it is true: authority is in the town. I don't know how or why, but it is so. This means we cannot act as quickly as you can, but when a direction is set, we all act together. I am confused. I don't know yet."

Lanser said wearily, "I hope we can get along together. It will be so much easier for everyone. I hope we can trust you. I don't like to think of the means the military will take to keep order."

Mayor Orden was silent.

"I hope we can trust you," Lanser repeated.

Orden put his finger in his ear and wiggled his hand. "I don't know," he said.

Madame came through the door then. "Annie is furious," she said. "She is next door, talking to Christine. Christine is angry, too."

"Christine is even a better cook than Annie," said the Mayor.

CHAPTER II

UPSTAIRS IN the little palace of the Mayor, the staff of Colonel Lanser made its headquarters. There were five of them besides the colonel. There was Major Hunter, a haunted little man of figures, a little man who, being a dependable unit, considered all other men either as dependable units or as unfit to live. Major Hunter was an engineer, and except in case of war no one would have thought of giving him command of men. For Major Hunter set his men in rows like figures and he added and subtracted and multiplied them. He was an arithmetician rather than a mathematician. None of the humour, the music, or the mysticism of higher mathematics ever entered his head. Men might vary in height or weight or colour, just as six is different from eight, but there was little other difference. He had been married several times and he did not know why his wives became very nervous before they left him.

Captain Bentick was a family man, a lover of dogs and pink children and Christmas. He was too old to be a captain, but a curious lack of ambition had kept him in that rank. Before the war he had admired the British country gentleman very much, wore English clothes, kept English dogs, smoked in an English pipe a special pipe mixture sent him from London, and subscribed to those country magazines which extol gardening and continually argue about the relative merits of English and Gordon setters. Captain Bentick spent all his holidays in Sussex and liked to be mistaken for an Englishman in Budapest or Paris. The war changed all that outwardly, but he had sucked on a pipe too long, had carried a stick too long, to give them up too suddenly. Once, five years before, he had written a letter to *The Times* about grass dying in the Midlands and had signed it Edmund Twitchell, Esq., and, furthermore, *The Times* had printed it.

If Captain Bentick was too old to be a captain, Captain Loft was too young. Captain Loft was as much a captain as one can imagine. He lived and breathed his captaincy. He had no un-military moments. A driving ambition forced him up through the grades. He rose like cream to the top of milk. He clicked his heels as perfectly as a dancer does. He knew every kind of military courtesy and insisted on using it all. Generals were afraid of him because he knew more about the deportment of a soldier than they did. Captain Loft thought and believed that a soldier is the highest development of animal life. If he considered God at all, he thought of Him as an old and honoured general, retired and grey, living among remembered battles and putting wreaths on the graves of his lieutenants several times a year. Captain Loft believed that all women fall in love with a uniform and he did not see how it could be otherwise. In the normal course of events he would be a brigadier-general at forty-five and have his picture in the illustrated papers, flanked by tall, pale, masculine women wearing lacy picture hats.

Lieutenants Prackle and Tondor were snot-noses, undergraduates, lieutenants, trained in the politics of the day, believing the great new system invented by a genius so great that they never bothered to verify its results. They were sentimental young men, given to tears and to furies. Lieutenant Prackle carried a lock of hair in the back of his watch, wrapped in a bit of blue satin, and the hair was constantly getting loose and clogging the balance-wheel, so that he wore a wrist-watch for telling time. Prackle was a dancing-partner, a gay young man who nevertheless could scowl like the Leader, could brood like the Leader. He hated degenerate art and had destroyed several canvases with his own hands. In cabarets he sometimes made pencil sketches of his companions which were so good that he had often been told he should have been an artist. Prackle had several blonde sisters of whom he was so proud that he had on occasion caused a commotion when he thought they had been insulted. The sisters were a little disturbed about it because they were afraid someone might set out to prove the insults, which would not have been hard to do. Lieutenant Prackle spent nearly all his time off duty day-dreaming of seducing Lieutenant Tonder's blonde sister, a buxom girl who loved to be seduced by older men who did not muss her hair as Lieutenant Prackle did.

Lieutenant Tonder was a poet, a bitter poet, who dreamed of perfect, ideal love of elevated young men for poor girls. Tonder was a dark romantic with a vision as wide as his experience. He sometimes spoke blank verse under his breath to imaginary dark women. He longed for death on the battlefield, with weeping parents in the background, and the Leader, brave but sad in the presence of the dying youth. He imagined his death very often, lighted by a fair setting sun which glinted on broken military equipment, his men standing silently around him, with heads sunk low, as over a fat cloud galloped the Valkyries, big-breasted, mothers and mistresses in one, while Wagnerian thunder crashed in the background. And he even had his dying words ready.

These were the men of the staff, each one playing war as children play "Run, Sheep, Run". Major Hunter thought of war as an arithmetical job to be done so he could get back to his fireplace; Captain Loft as the proper career of a properly brought-up young man; and Lieutenants Prackle and Tonder as a dreamlike thing in which nothing was very real. And their war so far had been play—fine weapons and fine planning against unarmed, planless enemies. They had lost no fights and suffered little hurt. They were, under pressure, capable of cowardice or courage, as everyone is. Of them all, only Colonel Lanser knew what war really is in the long run.

Lanser had been in Belgium and France twenty years before and he tried not to think what he knew—that war is treachery and hatred, the muddling of incompetent generals, the torture and killing and sickness and tiredness, until at last it is over and nothing has changed except for new weariness and new hatreds. Lanser told himself he was a soldier, given orders to carry out. He was not expected to question or to think but only to carry out orders; and he tried to put aside the sick memories of the other war and the certainty that this would be the same. This one will be different, he said to himself fifty times a day; this one will be very different.

In marching, in mobs, in football games, and in war, outlines become vague; real things become unreal and a fog creeps over the mind. Tension and excitement, weariness, movement—all merge in one great grey dream, so that, when it is over, it is hard to remember how it was when you killed men or ordered them to be killed. Then other people who were not there tell you what it was like and you say vaguely, "Yes, I guess that's how it was."

This staff had taken three rooms on the upper floor of the Mayor's palace. In the bedrooms they had put their cots and blankets and equipment, and in the room next to them and directly over the little drawing-room on the ground floor they had made a kind of club, rather an uncomfortable club. There were a few chairs and a table. Here they wrote letters and read letters. They talked and ordered coffee and planned and rested. On the walls between the windows there were pictures of cows and lakes and little farmhouses, and from the windows they could look down over the town to the waterfront, to the docks where the shipping was tied up, to the docks where the coal barges pulled up and took their loads and went out to sea. They could look down over the little town that twisted past the square to the waterfront, and they could see the fishing-boats lying at anchor in the bay, the sails furled, and they could smell the drying fish on the beach, right through the window.

There was a large table in the centre of the room and Major Hunter sat beside it. He had his drawing-board in his lap and resting on the table, and with a T-square and triangle he worked at a design for a new railroad siding. The drawing-board was unsteady and the major was growing angry with its unsteadiness. He called over his shoulder, "Prackle!" And then, "Lieutenant Prackle!"

The bedroom door opened and the lieutenant came out, half his ace covered with shaving-cream. He held the brush in his hand. 'Yes?" he said.

Major Hunter jiggled his drawing-board. "Hasn't that tripod or my board turned up in the baggage?"

"I don't know, sir," said Prackle. "I didn't look."

"Well, look now, will you? It's bad enough to have to work in his light. I'll have to draw this again before I ink it."

Prackle said, "Just as soon as I finish shaving, I'll look."

Hunter said irritably, "This siding is more important than your ooks. See if there is a canvas case like a golf bag under that pile in here."

Prackle disappeared into the bedroom. The door to the right pened and Captain Loft came in. He wore his helmet, a pair of eld-glasses, side-arm, and various little leather cases strung all ver him. He began to remove his equipment as soon as he entered.

"You know, that Bentick's crazy," he said. "He was going out on luty in a fatigue cap, right down the street."

Loft put his field-glasses on the table and took off his helmet, then is gas-mask bag. A little pile of equipment began to heap up on the able.

Hunter said, "Don't leave that stuff there. I have to work here. Vhy shouldn't he wear a cap? There hasn't been any trouble. I get ick of these tin things. They're heavy and you can't see."

Loft said primly, "It's bad practice to leave it off. It's bad for the eople here. We must maintain a military standard, an alertness, nd never vary it. We'll just invite trouble if we don't."

"What makes you think so?" Hunter asked.

Loft drew himself up a little. His mouth thinned with certainty. ooner or later everyone wanted to punch Loft in the nose for his ureness about things. He said, "I don't think it. I was paraphrasing *Manual X*-12 on deportment in occupied countries. It is very carefully worked out." He began to say, "You——" and then changed t to, "Everybody should read *X*-12 very closely."

Hunter said, "I wonder whether the man who wrote it was ever n occupied country. These people are harmless enough. They seem o be good, obedient people."

Prackle came through the door, his face still half covered with having-soap. He carried a brown canvas tube, and behind him ame Lieutenant Tonder. "Is this it?" Prackle asked.

"Yes. Unpack it, will you, and set it up."

Prackle and Tonder went to work on the folding tripod and ested it and put it near Hunter. The major screwed his board to it, ilted it right and left, and finally settled gruntingly behind it.

Captain Loft said, "Do you know you have soap on your face, ieutenant?"

"Yes, sir," Prackle said. "I was shaving when the major asked m to get the tripod."

"Well, you had better get it off," Loft said. "The colonel migh see you."

"Oh, he wouldn't mind. He doesn't care about things like that.'

Tonder was looking over Hunter's shoulder as he worked.

Loft said, "Well, he may not, but it doesn't look right."

Prackle took a handkerchief and rubbed the soap from his chee Tonder pointed to a little drawing on the corner of the major board. "That's a nice-looking bridge, Major. But where in th world are we going to build a bridge?"

Hunter looked down at the drawing and then over his should at Tonder. "Huh? Oh, that isn't any bridge we're going to buil Up here is the work drawing."

"What are you doing with a bridge, then?"

Hunter seemed a little embarrassed. "Well, you know, in m back-yard at home I've got a model railroad line. I was going t bridge a little creek for it. Brought the line right down to the cree but I never did get the bridge built. I thought I'd kind of work out while I was away."

Lieutenant Prackle took from his pocket a folded rotogravu page and he unfolded it and held it up and looked at it. It was picture of a girl, all legs and dress and eyelashes, a well-develope blonde in black openwork stockings and a low bodice, and this pa ticular blonde peeped over a black lace fan. Lieutenant Prack held her up and said, "Isn't she something?" Lieutenant Tond looked critically at the picture and said, "I don't like her."

"What don't you like about her?"

"I just don't like her," said Tonder. "What do you want h picture for?"

Prackle said, "Because I do like her and I bet you do, too."

"I do not," said Tonder.

"You mean to say you wouldn't take a date with her if yo could?" Prackle asked.

Tonder said, "No."

"Well, you're just crazy," and Prackle went to one of the curtain He said, "I'm just going to stick her up here and let you broo about her for a while." He pinned the picture to the curtain.

Captain Loft was gathering his equipment into his arms now and he said, "I don't think it looks very well out here, Lieutenan You'd better take it down. It wouldn't make a good impression o the local people."

Hunter looked up from his board. "What wouldn't?" He fo lowed their eyes to the picture. "Who's that?" he asked.

"She's an actress," said Prackle.

Hunter looked at her carefully. "Oh, do you know her?"

Tonder said, "She's a tramp."

Hunter said, "Oh, then you know her?"

Prackle was looking steadily at Tonder. He said, "Say, how do you know she's a tramp?"

"She looks like a tramp," said Tonder.

"Do you know her?"

"No, and I don't want to."

Prackle began to say, "Then how do you know?" when Loft broke in. He said, "You'd better take the picture down. Put it up over your bed if you want to. This room's kind of official here."

Prackle looked at him mutinously and was about to speak when Captain Loft said, "That's an order, Lieutenant," and poor Prackle folded his paper and put it into his pocket again. He tried cheerily to change the subject. "There are some pretty girls in this town, all right," he said. "As soon as we get settled down and everything going smoothly, I'm going to get acquainted with a few."

Loft said, "You'd better read *X*-12. There's a section dealing with sexual matters." And he went out, carrying his duffel, glasses and equipment. Lieutenant Tonder, still looking over Hunter's shoulder, said, "That's clever—the coal cars come right through the mines to the ship."

Hunter came slowly out of his work and he said, "We have to speed it up; we've got to get that coal moving. It's a big job. I'm awful thankful that the people here are calm and sensible."

Loft came back into the room without his equipment. He stood by the window, looking out towards the harbour, towards the coal-mine, and he said, "They are calm and sensible because we are calm and sensible. I think we can take credit for that. That's why I keep harping on procedure. It is very carefully worked out."

The door opened and Colonel Lanser came in, removing his coat as he entered. His staff gave him military courtesy—not very rigid, but enough. Lanser said, "Captain Loft, will you go down and relieve Bentick? He isn't feeling well, says he's dizzy."

"Yes, sir," said Loft. "May I suggest, sir, that I only recently came off duty?"

Lanser inspected him closely. "I hope you don't mind going, Captain."

"Not at all, sir; I just mention it for the record."

Lanser relaxed and chuckled. "You like to be mentioned in the reports, don't you?"

"It does no harm, sir."

"And when you have enough mentions," Lanser went on, "there will be a little dangler on your chest."

"They are the milestones in a military career, sir."

Lanser sighed. "Yes, I guess they are. But they won't be the ones you'll remember, Captain."

"Sir?" Loft asked.

"You'll know what I mean later—perhaps."

Captain Loft put his equipment on rapidly. "Yes, sir," he said, and went out and his footsteps clattered down the wooden stairs, and Lanser watched him go with a little amusement. He said quietly, "There goes a born soldier." And Hunter looked up and poised his pencil and he said, "A born ass."

"No," said Lanser, "he's being a soldier the way a lot of men would be politicians. He'll be on the General Staff before long. He'll look down on war from above and so he'll always love it."

Lieutenant Prackle said, "When do you think the war will be over, sir?"

"Over? Over? What do you mean?"

Lieutenant Prackle continued, "How soon will we win?"

Lanser shook his head. "Oh, I don't know. The enemy is still in the world."

"But we will lick them," said Prackle.

Lanser said, "Yes?"

"Won't we?"

"Yes; yes, we always do."

Prackle said excitedly, "Well, if it's quiet around Christmas, do you think there will be some furloughs granted?"

"I don't know," said Lanser. "Such orders will have to come from home. Do you want to get home for Christmas?"

"Well, I'd kind of like to."

"Maybe you will," said Lanser, "maybe you will."

Lieutenant Tonder said, "We won't drop out of this occupation, will we, sir, after the war is over?"

"I don't know," said the colonel. "Why?"

"Well," said Tonder, "it's a nice country, nice people. Our men—some of them—might even settle here."

Lanser said jokingly, "You've seen some place you like, perhaps?"

"Well," said Tonder, "there are some beautiful farms here. If four or five of them were thrown together, it would be a nice place to settle, I think."

"You have no family land, then?" Lanser asked.

"No, sir, not any more. Inflation took it away."

Lanser was tired now of talking to children. He said, "Ah, well, we still have a war to fight. We still have coal to take out. Do you suppose we can wait until it is over before we build up these estates? Such orders will come from above. Captain Loft can tell you that."

His manner changed. He said, "Hunter, your steel will be in to-morrow. You can get your tracks started this week."

There was a knock at the door and a sentry put his head in. He said, "Mr. Corell wishes to see you, sir."

"Send him in," said the colonel. And he said to the others, "This is the man who did the preliminary work here. We might have some trouble with him."

"Did he do a good job?" Tonder asked.

"Yes, he did, and he won't be popular with the people here. I wonder whether he will be popular with us."

"He deserves credit, certainly," Tonder said.

"Yes," Lanser said, "and don't think he won't claim it."

Corell came in, rubbing his hands. He radiated good-will and good-fellowship. He was dressed still in his black business suit, but on his head there was a patch of white bandage, stuck to his hair with a cross of adhesive tape. He advanced to the centre of the room and said, "Good morning, Colonel. I should have called yesterday after the trouble downstairs, but I knew how busy you would be."

The colonel said, "Good morning." Then with a circular gesture of his hand. "This is my staff, Mr. Corell."

"Fine boys," said Corell. "They did a good job. Well, I tried to prepare for them well."

Hunter looked down at his board and he took out an inking-pen and dipped it and began to ink in his drawing.

Lanser said, "You did very well. I wish you hadn't killed those six men, though. I wish their soldiers hadn't come back."

Corell spread his hands and said comfortably, "Six men is a small loss for a town of this size, with a coal-mine, too."

Lanser said sternly, "I am not averse to killing people if that finishes it. But sometimes it is better not to."

Corell had been studying the officers. He looked sideways at the lieutenants, and he said, "Could we—perhaps—talk alone, Colonel?"

"Yes, if you wish. Lieutenant Prackle and Lieutenant Tonder, will you go to your room, please?" And the colonel said to Corell, "Major Hunter is working. He doesn't hear anything when he's working." Hunter looked up from his board and smiled quietly and looked down again. The young lieutenants left the room, and when they were gone Lanser said, "Well, here we are. Won't you sit down?"

"Thank you, sir," and Corell sat down behind the table.

Lanser looked at the bandage on Corell's head. He said bluntly, "Have they tried to kill you already?"

Corell felt the bandage with his fingers. "This? Oh, this was a stone that fell from a cliff in the hills this morning."

"You're sure it wasn't thrown?"

"What do you mean?" Corell asked. "These aren't fierce people. They haven't had a war for a hundred years. They've forgotten about fighting."

"Well, you've lived among them," said the colonel. "You ought to know." He stepped close to Corell. "But if you are safe, these people are different from any in the world. I've helped to occupy countries before. I was in Belgium twenty years ago and in France." He shook his head a little as though to clear it, and he said gruffly, "You did a good job. We should thank you. I mentioned your work in my report."

"Thank you, sir," said Corell. "I did my best."

Lanser said, a little wearily, "Well, sir, now what shall we do? Would you like to go back to the capital? We can put you on a coal barge if you're in a hurry, or on a destroyer if you want to wait."

Corell said, "But I don't want to go back. I'll stay here."

Lanser studied this for a moment and he said, "You know, I haven't a great many men. I can't give you a very adequate bodyguard."

"But I don't need a bodyguard. I tell you these aren't violent people."

Lanser looked at the bandage for a moment. Hunter glanced up from his board and remarked, "You'd better start wearing a helmet." He looked down at his work again.

Now Corell moved forward in his chair. "I wanted particularly to talk to you, Colonel. I thought I might help with the civil administration."

Lanser turned on his heel and walked to the window and looked out, and then he swung around and said quietly, "What have you in mind?"

"Well, you must have a civil authority you can trust. I thought perhaps that Mayor Orden might step down now and—well, if I were to take over his office, it and the military would work very nicely together."

Lanser's eyes seemed to grow large and bright. He came close to Corell and he spoke sharply. "Have you mentioned this in your report?"

Corell said, "Well, yes, naturally—in my analysis."

Lanser interrupted. "Have you talked to any of the town people since we arrived—outside of the Mayor, that is?"

"Well, no. You see, they are still a bit startled. They didn't expect it." He chuckled. "No, sir, they certainly didn't expect it."

But Lanser pressed his point. "So you don't really know what's going on in their minds?"

"Why, they're startled," said Corell. "They're—well, they're almost dreaming."

"You don't know what they think of you?" Lanser asked.

"I have many friends here. I know everyone."

"Did anyone buy anything in your store this morning?"

"Well, of course, business is at a standstill," Corell answered. "No one's buying anything."

Lanser relaxed suddenly. He went to a chair and sat down and crossed his legs. He said quietly, "Yours is a difficult and brave branch of the service. It should be greatly rewarded."

"Thank you, sir."

"You will have their hatred in time," said the colonel.

"I can stand that, sir. They are the enemy."

Now Lanser hesitated a long moment before he spoke, and then he said softly, "You will not even have *our* respect."

Corell jumped to his feet excitedly. "This is contrary to the Leader's words!" he said. "The Leader has said that all branches are equally honourable."

Lanser went on very quietly, "I hope the Leader knows. I hope he can read the minds of soldiers." And then almost compassionately he said: "You should be greatly rewarded." For a moment he sat quietly, and then he pulled himself together and said, "Now we must come to exactness. I am in charge here. My job is to get coal out. To do that I must maintain order and discipline, and to do that I must know what is in the minds of these people. I must anticipate revolt. Do you understand that?"

"Well, I can find out what you wish to know, sir. As Mayor here, I will be very effective," said Corell.

Lanser shook his head. "I have no orders about this. I must use my own judgment. I think you will never again know what is going on here. I think no one will speak to you; no one will be near to you except those people who will live on money, who can live on money. I think without a guard you will be in great danger. It will please me if you go back to the capital, there to be rewarded for your fine work."

"But my place is here, sir," said Corell. "I have made my place. It is all in my report."

Lanser went on as though he had not heard. "Mayor Orden is more than a mayor," he said. "He is his people. He knows what they are doing, thinking, without asking, because he will think what they think. By watching him I will know them. He must stay. That is my judgment."

Corell said, "My work, sir, merits better treatment than being sent away."

"Yes, it does," Lanser said slowly. "But to the larger work I think you are only a detriment now. If you are not hated yet, you will be. In any little revolt you will be the first to be killed. I think I will suggest that you go back."

Corell said stiffly, "You will, of course, permit me to wait for a reply to my report to the capital?"

"Yes, of course. But I shall recommend that you go back for your own safety. Frankly, Mr. Corell, you have no value here. But—well, there must be other plans and other countries. Perhaps you will go now to some new town in some new country. You will win new confidence in a new field. You may be given a larger town, even a city, a greater responsibility. I think I will recommend you highly for your work here."

Corell's eyes were shining with gratification. "Thank you, sir," he said. "I've worked hard. Perhaps you are right. But you must permit me to wait for the reply from the capital."

Lanser's voice was tight. His eyes were slitted. He said harshly, "Wear a helmet; keep indoors, do not go out at night, and, above all, do not drink. Trust no woman nor any man. Do you understand that?"

Corell looked pityingly at the colonel. "I don't think you understand. I have a little house. A pleasant country girl waits on me. I even think she's a little fond of me. These are simple, peaceful people. I know them."

Lanser said, "There are no peaceful people. When will you learn it? There are no friendly people. Can't you understand that? We have invaded this country—you, by what they call treachery, prepared for us." His face grew red and his voice rose. "Can't you understand that we are at war with these people?"

Corell said, a little smugly, "We have defeated them."

The colonel stood up and swung his arms helplessly, and Hunter looked up from his board and put his hand out to protect his board from being jiggled. Hunter said, "Careful now, sir. I'm inking in. I wouldn't want to do it all over again."

Lanser looked down at him and said, "Sorry," and went on as though he were instructing a class. He said, "Defeat is a momentary thing. A defeat doesn't last. We were defeated and now we attack. Defeat means nothing. Can't you understand that? Do you know what they are whispering behind doors?"

Corell asked, "Do you?"

"No, but I suspect."

Then Corell said insinuatingly, "Are you afraid, Colonel? Should the commander of this occupation be afraid?"

Lanser sat down heavily and said, "Maybe that's it." And he said disgustedly, "I'm tired of people who have not been at war who know all about it." He held his chin in his hand and said, "I remember a little old woman in Brussels—sweet face, white hair; she was only four feet eleven; delicate old hands. You could see the veins almost black against her skin. And her black shawl and her blue-white hair. She used to sing our national songs to us in a quivering, sweet voice. She always knew where to find a cigarette or a virgin." He dropped his hand from his chin, and he caught himself as though he had been asleep. "We didn't know her son had been executed," he said. "When we finally shot her, she had killed twelve men with a long, black hat-pin. I have it yet at home. It has an enamel button with a bird over it, red and blue."

Corell said, "But you shot her?"

"Of course we shot her."

"And the murders stopped?" asked Corell.

"No, the murders did not stop. And when we finally retreated, the people cut off stragglers and they burned some and they gouged the eyes from some, and some they even crucified."

Corell said loudly, "These are not good things to say, Colonel."

"They are not good things to remember," said Lanser.

Corell said, "You should not be in command if you are afraid."

And Lanser answered softly, "I know how to fight, you see. If you know, at least you do not make silly errors."

"Do you talk this way to the young officers?"

Lanser shook his head. "No, they wouldn't believe me."

"Why do you tell me, then?"

"Because, Mr. Corell, your work is done. I remember one time——" and as he spoke there was a tumble of feet on the stairs and the door burst open. A sentry looked in and Captain Loft brushed past him. Loft was rigid and cold and military; he said, "There's trouble, sir."

"Trouble?"

"I have to report, sir, that Captain Bentick has been killed."

Lanser said, "Oh—yes—Bentick!"

There was the sound of a number of footsteps on the stairs and two stretcher-bearers came in, carrying a figure covered with blankets.

Lanser said, "Are you sure he's dead?"

"Quite sure," Loft said stiffly.

The lieutenants came in from the bedroom, their mouths a little open, and they looked frightened. Lanser said, "Put him down there," and he pointed to the wall beside the windows. When the bearers had gone, Lanser knelt and lifted a corner of the blanket and then quickly put it down again. And still kneeling, he looked at Loft and said, "Who did this?"

"A miner," said Loft.

"Why?"

"I was there, sir."

"Well, make your report, then! Make your report, damn it, man!"

Loft drew himself up and said formally, "I had just relieved Captain Bentick, as the colonel ordered. Captain Bentick was about to leave to come here when I had some trouble about a recalcitrant miner who wanted to quit work. He shouted something about being a free man. When I ordered him to work, he rushed at me with his pick. Captain Bentick tried to interfere." He gestured slightly towards the body.

Lanser, still kneeling, nodded slowly. "Bentick was a curious man," he said. "He loved the English. He loved everything about them. I don't think he liked to fight very much. . . . You captured the man?"

"Yes, sir," Loft said.

Lanser stood up slowly and spoke as though to himself. "So it starts again. We will shoot this man and make twenty new enemies. It's the only thing we know, the only thing we know."

Prackle said, "What do you say, sir?"

Lanser answered, "Nothing, nothing at all. I was just thinking." He turned to Loft and said, "Please give my compliments to Mayor Orden and my request that he see me immediately. It is very important."

Major Hunter looked up, dried his inking-pen carefully, and put it away in a velvet-lined box.

CHAPTER III

In the town the people moved sullenly through the streets. Some of the light of astonishment was gone from their eyes, but still a light of anger had not taken its place. In the coal shaft the working-men pushed the coal cars sullenly. The small tradesmen stood behind their counters and served the people, but no one communicated with them. The people spoke to one another in monosyllables, and everyone was thinking of the war, thinking of himself, thinking of the past and how it had suddenly been changed.

In the drawing-room of the palace of Mayor Orden a small fire burned and the lights were on, for it was a grey day outside and there was frost in the air. The room was itself undergoing a change. The tapestry-covered chairs were pushed back, the little tables out of the way, and through the doorway to the right, Joseph and Annie were struggling to bring in a large, square dining-table.

They had it on its side. Joseph was in the drawing-room and Annie's red face showed through the door. Joseph manœuvred the legs around sideways, and he cried, "Don't push, Annie! Now!"

"I am 'now-ing'," said Annie the red-nosed, the red-eyed, the angry. Annie was always a little angry and these soldiers, this occupation, did not improve her temper. Indeed, what for years had been considered simply a bad disposition was suddenly become a patriotic emotion. Annie had gained some little reputation as an exponent of liberty by throwing hot water on the soldiers. She would have thrown it on anyone who cluttered up her porch, but it just happened that she had become a heroine; and since anger had been the beginning of her success, Annie went on to new successes by whipping herself into increased and constant anger.

"Don't scuff the bottom," Joseph said. The table wedged in the doorway. "Steady!" Joseph warned.

"I am steady," said Annie.

Joseph stood off and studied the table, and Annie crossed her arms and glared at him. He tested a leg. "Don't push," he said. "Don't push so hard." And by himself he got the table through while Annie followed with crossed arms. "Now, up she goes," said Joseph, and at last Annie helped him settle it on four legs and move it to the centre of the room. "There," Annie said. "If His Excellency hadn't told me to, I wouldn't have done it. What right have they got moving tables around?"

"What right coming in at all?" said Joseph.

"None," said Annie.

"None," repeated Joseph. "I see it like they have no right at all, but they do it, with their guns and their parachutes; they do it, Annie."

"They got no right," said Annie. "What do they want with a table in here, anyway? This isn't a dining-room."

Joseph moved a chair up to the table and he set it carefully at the right distance from the table, and he adjusted it. "They're going to hold a trial," he said. "They're going to try Alexander Morden."

"Molly Morden's husband?"

"Molly Morden's husband."

"For bashing that fellow with a pick?"

"That's right," said Joseph.

"But he's a nice man," Annie said. "They've got no right to try him. He gave Molly a big red dress for her birthday. What right have they got to try Alex?"

"Well," Joseph explained, "he killed this fellow."

"Suppose he did; the fellow ordered Alex around. I heard about it. Alex doesn't like to be ordered. Alex's been an alderman in his time, and his father, too. And Molly Morden makes a nice cake," Annie said charitably. "But her frosting gets too hard. What'll they do with Alex?"

"Shoot him," Joseph said gloomily.

"They can't do that."

"Bring up the chairs, Annie. Yes, they can. They'll just do it."

Annie shook a very rigid finger in his face. "You remember my words," she said angrily. "People aren't going to like it if they hurt Alex. People like Alex. Did he ever hurt anybody before? Answer me that!"

"No," said Joseph.

"Well, there, you see! If they hurt Alex, people are going to be mad and I'm going to be mad. I won't stand for it!"

"What will you do?" Joseph asked her.

"Why, I'll kill some of them myself," said Annie.

"And then they'll shoot you," said Joseph.

"Let them! I tell you, Joseph, things can go too far—tramping in and out all hours of the night, shooting people."

Joseph adjusted a chair at the head of the table, and he became in some curious way a conspirator. He said softly, "Annie."

She paused and, sensing his tone, walked nearer to him. He said, "Can you keep a secret?"

She looked at him with a little admiration, for he had never had a secret before. "Yes. What is it?"

"Well, William Deal and Walter Doggel got away last night."

"Got away? Where?"

"They got away to England, in a boat."

Annie sighed with pleasure and anticipation. "Does everybody know it?"

"Well, not everybody," said Joseph. "Everybody but——" and he pointed a quick thumb towards the ceiling.

"When did they go? Why didn't I hear about it?"

"You were busy." Joseph's voice and face were cold. "You know that Corell?"

"Yes."

Joseph came close to her. "I don't think he's going to live long."

"What do you mean?" Annie asked.

"Well, people are talking."

Annie sighed with tension. "Ah-h-h!"

Joseph at last had opinions. "People are getting together," he said. "They don't like to be conquered. Things are going to happen. You keep your eyes peeled, Annie. There're going to be things for you to do."

Annie asked, "How about His Excellency? What's he going to do? How does His Excellency stand?"

"Nobody knows," said Joseph. "He doesn't say anything."

"He wouldn't be against us," Annie said.

"He doesn't say," said Joseph.

The knob turned on the left-hand door, and Mayor Orden came in slowly. He looked tired and old. Behind him Doctor Winter walked. Orden said, "That's good, Joseph. Thank you, Annie. It looks very well."

They went out and Joseph looked back through the door for a moment before he closed it.

Mayor Orden walked to the fire and turned to warm his back. Doctor Winter pulled out the chair at the head of the table and sat down. "I wonder how much longer I can hold this position?" Orden said. "The people don't quite trust me and neither does the enemy. I wonder whether this is a good thing."

"I don't know," said Winter. "You trust yourself, don't you? There's no doubt in your own mind?"

"Doubt? No. I am the Mayor. I don't understand many things." He pointed to the table. "I don't know why they have to hold this trial in here. They're going to try Alex Morden here for murder. You remember Alex? He has that pretty little wife, Molly."

"I remember," said Winter. "She used to teach in the grammar school. Yes, I remember. She's so pretty, she hated to get glasses when she needed them. Well, I guess Alex killed an officer, all right. Nobody's questioned that."

Mayor Orden said bitterly, "Nobody questions it. But why do they try him? Why don't they shoot him? This is not a matter of doubt or certainty, justice or injustice. There's none of that here. Why must they try him—and in my house?"

Winter said, "I would guess it is for the show. There's an idea about it: if you go through the form of a thing, you have it, and sometimes people are satisfied with the form of a thing. We had an army—soldiers with guns—but it wasn't an army, you see. The invaders will have a trial and hope to convince the people that there is justice involved. Alex did kill the captain, you know."

"Yes, I see that," Orden said.

And Winter went on, "If it comes from your house, where the people expect justice——"

He was interrupted by the opening of the door to the right. A young woman entered. She was about thirty and quite pretty. She carried her glasses in her hand. She was dressed simply and neatly and she was very excited. She said quickly, "Annie told me to come right in, sir."

"Why, of course," said the Mayor. "You're Molly Morden."

"Yes, sir, I am. They say that Alex is to be tried and shot."

Orden looked down at the floor for a moment, and Molly went

on, "They say you will sentence him. It will be your words that send him out."

Orden looked up, startled. "What's this? Who says this?"

"The people in the town." She held herself very straight and she asked, half pleadingly, half demandingly, "You wouldn't do that, would you, sir?"

"How could the people know what I don't know?" he said.

"That is a great mystery," said Doctor Winter. "That is a mystery that has disturbed rulers all over the world—how the people know. It disturbs the invaders now, I am told, how news runs through censorships, how the truth of things fights free of control. It is a great mystery."

The girl looked up, for the room had suddenly darkened, and she seemed to be afraid. "It's a cloud," she said. "There's word snow is on the way, and it's early, too." Doctor Winter went to the window and squinted up at the sky, and he said, "Yes, it's a big cloud; maybe it will pass over."

Mayor Orden switched on a lamp that made only a little circle of light. He switched it off again and said, "A light in the daytime is a lonely thing."

Now Molly came near to him again. "Alex is not a murdering man," she said. "He's a quick-tempered man, but he's never broken a law. He's a respected man."

Orden rested his hand on her shoulder and he said, "I have known Alex since he was a little boy. I knew his father and his grandfather. His grandfather was a bear-hunter in the old days. Did you know that?"

Molly ignored him. "You wouldn't sentence Alex?"

"No," he said. "How could I sentence him?"

"The people said you would, for the sake of order."

Mayor Orden stood behind a chair and gripped its back with his hands. "Do the people want order, Molly?"

"I don't know," she said. "They want to be free."

"Well, do they know how to go about it? Do they know what method to use against an armed enemy?"

"No," Molly said, "I don't think so."

"You are a bright girl, Molly; do you know?"

"No, sir, but I think the people feel that they are beaten if they are docile. They want to show these soldiers they're unbeaten."

"They've had no chance to fight. It's no fight to go against machine-guns," Doctor Winter said.

Orden said, "When you know what they want to do, will you tell me, Molly?"

She looked at him suspiciously. "Yes——" she said.

"You mean 'no'. You don't trust me."

"But how about Alex?" she questioned.

"I'll not sentence him. He has committed no crime against our people," said the Mayor.

Molly was hesitant now. She said, "Will they—will they kill Alex?"

Orden stared at her and he said, "Dear child, my dear child."

She held herself rigid. "Thank you."

Orden came close to her and she said weakly, "Don't touch me. Please don't touch me. Please don't touch me." And his hand dropped. For a moment she stood still, then she turned stiffly and went out of the door.

She had just closed the door when Joseph entered. "Excuse me, sir, the colonel wants to see you. I said you were busy. I knew she was here. And Madame wants to see you, too."

Orden said, "Ask Madame to come in."

Joseph went out and Madame came in immediately.

"I don't know how I can run a house," she began; "it's more people than the house can stand. Annie's angry all the time."

"Hush!" Orden said.

Madame looked at him in amazement. "I don't know what——"

"Hush!" he said. "Sarah, I want you to go to Alex Morden's house. Do you understand? I want you to stay with Molly Morden while she needs you. Don't talk, just stay with her."

Madame said, "I've a hundred things——"

"Sarah, I want you to stay with Molly Morden. Don't leave her alone. Go now."

She comprehended slowly. "Yes," she said. "Yes, I will. When will it be over?"

"I don't know," he said. "I'll send Annie when it's time."

She kissed him lightly on the cheek and went out. Orden walked to the door and called, "Joseph, I'll see the colonel now."

Lanser came in. He had on a new pressed uniform with a little ornamental dagger at the belt. He said, "Good morning, Your Excellency. I wish to speak to you informally." He glanced at Doctor Winter. "I should like to speak to you alone."

Winter went slowly to the door and as he reached it Orden said, "Doctor!"

Winter turned. "Yes?"

"Will you come back this evening?"

"You will have work for me?" the doctor asked.

"No—no. I just won't like to be alone."

"I will be here," said the doctor.

"And, Doctor, do you think Molly looked all right?"

"Oh, I think so. Close to hysteria, I guess. But she's good stock. She's good, strong stock. She is a Kenderly, you know."

"I'd forgotten," Orden said. "Yes, she is a Kenderly, isn't she?"

Doctor Winter went out and shut the door gently behind him.

Lanser had waited courteously. He watched the door close. He looked at the table and the chairs about it. "I will not tell you, sir, how sorry I am about this. I wish it had not happened."

Mayor Orden bowed, and Lanser went on: "I like you, sir, and I respect you, but I have a job to do. You surely recognize that."

Orden did not answer. He looked straight into Lanser's eyes.

"We do not act alone or on our own judgment."

Between sentences Lanser waited for an answer, but he received none.

"There are rules laid down for us, rules made in the capital. This man has killed an officer."

At last Orden answered, "Why didn't you shoot him then? That was the time to do it?"

Lanser shook his head. "If I agreed with you, it would make no difference. You know as well as I that punishment is largely for the purpose of deterring the potential criminal. Thus, since punishment is for others than the punished, it must be publicized. It must even be dramatized." He thrust a finger in back of his belt and flipped his little dagger.

Orden turned away and looked out of the window at the dark sky. "It will snow to-night," he said.

"Mayor Orden, you know our orders are inexorable. We must get the coal. If your people are not orderly, we will have to restore that order by force." His voice grew stern. "We must shoot people if it is necessary. If you wish to save your people from hurt, you must help us to keep order. Now, it is considered wise by my government that punishment emanate from the local authority. It makes for a more orderly situation."

Orden said softly, "So the people did know. That is a mystery." And louder he said, "You wish me to pass sentence of death on Alexander Morden after a trial here?"

"Yes, and you will prevent much bloodshed later if you will do it."

Orden went to the table and pulled out the big chair at its head and sat down. And suddenly he seemed to be the judge, with Lanser the culprit. He drummed with his fingers on the table. He said, "You and your government do not understand. In all the world yours is the only government and people with a record of defeat after defeat for centuries and every time because you did not understand people." He paused. "This principle does not work. First, I am the Mayor. I have no right to pass sentence of death. There is no one in this community with that right. If I should do it, I would be breaking the law as much as you."

"Breaking the law?" said Lanser.

"You killed six men when you came in. Under our law you are guilty of murder, all of you. Why do you go into this nonsense of law, Colonel? There is no law between you and us. This is war. Don't you know you will have to kill all of us or we in time will kill all of you? You destroyed the law when you came in, and a new law took its place. Don't you know that?"

Lanser said, "May I sit down?"

"Why do you ask? That is another lie. You could make me stand if you wished."

Lanser said, "No; it is true, whether you believe it or not; personally, I have respect for you and your office, and"—he put his forehead in his hand for a moment—"you see, what I think, sir, I, a man of a certain age and certain memories, is of no importance. I might agree with you, but that would change nothing. The military, the political-pattern I work in has certain tendencies and practices which are invariable."

Orden said, "And these tendencies and practices have been proven wrong in every single case since the beginning of the world."

Lanser laughed bitterly. "I, an individual man with certain memories, might agree with you, might even add that one of the tendencies of the military mind and pattern is an inability to learn, an inability to see beyond the killing which is its job. But I am not a man subject to memories. The coal-miner must be shot publicly, because the theory is that others will then restrain themselves from killing our men."

Orden said, "We need not talk any more, then."

"Yes, we must talk. We want you to help."

Orden sat quietly for a while and then he said, "I'll tell you what I'll do. How many men were on the machine-guns which killed our soldiers?"

"Oh, not more than twenty, I guess," said Lanser.

"Very well. If you will shoot them, I will condemn Morden."

"You're not serious!" said the colonel.

"But I am serious."

"This can't be done. You know it."

"I know it," said Orden. "And what you ask cannot be done."

Lanser said, "I suppose I knew. Corell will have to be Mayor after all." He looked up quickly. "You will stay for the trial?"

"Yes, I'll stay. Then Alex won't be so lonely."

Lanser looked at him and smiled a little sadly. "We have taken on a job, haven't we?"

"Yes," said the Mayor, "the one impossible job in the world, the one thing that can't be done."

"And that is?"

"To break man's spirit permanently."

Orden's head sank a little towards the table, and he said, without looking up, "It's started to snow. It didn't wait for night. I like the sweet, cool smell of the snow."

CHAPTER IV

BY ELEVEN o'clock the snow was falling heavily in big, soft puffs and the sky was not visible at all. People were scurrying through the falling snow, and snow piled up in the doorways and it piled up on the statue in the public square and on the rails from the mine to the harbour. Snow piled up and the little cartwheels skidded as they were pushed along. And over the town there hung a blackness that was deeper than the cloud, and over the town there hung a sullenness and a dry, growing hatred. The people did not stand in the streets long, but they entered the doors and the doors closed and there seemed to be eyes looking from behind the curtains, and when the military went through the street or when the patrol walked down the main street, the eyes were on the patrol, cold and sullen. And in the shops people came to buy little things for lunch and they asked for the goods and got it and paid for it and exchanged no good-day with the seller.

In the little palace drawing-room the lights were on and the lights shone on the falling snow outside the window. The court was in session. Lanser sat at the head of the table with Hunter on his right, then Tonder, and, at the lower end, Captain Loft with a little pile of papers in front of him. On the opposite side, Mayor Orden sat on the colonel's left and Prackle was next to him—Prackle, who scribbled on his pad of paper. Beside the table two guards stood with bayonets fixed, with helmets on their heads, and they were little wooden images. Between them was Alex Morden a big young man with a wide, low forehead, with deep-set eyes and a long, sharp nose. His chin was firm and his mouth sensual and wide. He was wide of shoulder, narrow of hip, and in front of him his manacled hands clasped and unclasped. He was dressed in black trousers, a blue shirt open at the neck, and a dark coat shiny from wear.

Captain Loft read from the paper in front of him: " 'When ordered back to work, he refused to go, and when the order was repeated, the prisoner attacked Captain Loft with the pick-axe he carried. Captain Bentick interposed his body——' "

Mayor Orden coughed and, when Loft stopped reading, said,

"Sit down, Alex. One of you guards get him a chair." The guard turned and pulled up a chair unquestioningly.

Loft said, "It is customary for the prisoner to stand."

"Let him sit down," Orden said. "Only we will know. You can report that he stood."

"It is not customary to falsify reports," said Loft.

"Sit down, Alex," Orden repeated.

And the big young man sat down and his manacled hands were restless in his lap.

Loft began, "This is contrary to all——"

The colonel said, "Let him be seated."

Captain Loft cleared his throat. " 'Captain Bentick interposed his body and received a blow on the head which crushed his skull.' A medical report is appended. Do you wish me to read it?"

"No need," said Lanser. "Make it as quick as you can."

" 'These facts have been witnessed by several of our soldiers. whose statements are attached. This military court finds the prisoner is guilty of murder and recommends a death sentence.' Do you wish me to read the statements of the soldiers?"

Lanser sighed. "No." He turned to Alex. "You don't deny that you killed the captain, do you?"

Alex smiled sadly. "I hit him," he said. "I don't know that I killed him."

Orden said, "Good work, Alex!" And the two looked at each other as friends.

Loft said, "Do you mean to imply that he was killed by someone else?"

"I don't know," said Alex. "I only hit him, and then somebody hit me."

Colonel Lanser said, "Do you want to offer any explanation? I can't think of anything that will change the sentence, but we will listen."

Loft said, "I respectfully submit that the colonel should not have said that. It indicates that the court is not impartial."

Orden laughed dryly. The colonel looked at him and smiled a little. "Have you any explanation?" he repeated.

Alex lifted a hand to gesture and the other came with it. He looked embarrassed and put them in his lap again. "I was mad," he said. "I have a pretty bad temper. He said I must work. I am a free man. I got mad and I hit him. I guess I hit him hard. It was the wrong man." He pointed at Loft. "That's the man I wanted to hit, that one."

Lanser said, "It doesn't matter whom you wanted to hit. Anybody would have been the same. Are you sorry you did it?" He said aside to the table, "It would look well in the record if he were sorry."

"Sorry?" Alex asked. "I am not sorry. He told me to go to work—me, a free man! I used to be alderman. He said I had to work."

"But if the sentence is death, won't you be sorry then?"

Alex sank his head and really tried to think honestly. "No," he said. "You mean, would I do it again?"

"That's what I mean."

"No," Alex said thoughtfully, "I don't think I'm sorry."

Lanser said, "Put in the record that the prisoner was overcome with remorse. Sentence is automatic. Do you understand?" he said to Alex. "The court has no leeway. The courts finds you guilty and sentences you to be shot immediately. I do not see any reason to torture you with this any more. Captain Loft, is there anything I have forgotten?"

"You've forgotten me," said Orden. He stood up and pushed back his chair and stepped over to Alex. And Alex, from long habit, stood up respectfully. "Alexander, I am the elected Mayor."

"I know it, sir."

"Alex, these men are invaders. They have taken our country by surprise and treachery and force."

Captain Loft said, "Sir, this should not be permitted."

Lanser said, "Hush! Is it better to hear it, or would you rather it were whispered?"

Orden went on as though he had not been interrupted. "When they came, the people were confused and I was confused. We did not know what to do or think. Yours was the first clear act. Your private anger was the beginning of a public anger. I know it is said in town that I am acting with these men. I can show the town, but you—you are going to die. I want you to know."

Alex dropped his head and then raised it. "I know, sir."

Lanser said, "Is the squad ready?"

"Outside, sir."

"Who is commanding?"

"Lieutenant Tonder, sir."

Tonder raised his head and his chin was hard and he held his breath.

Orden said softly, "Are you afraid, Alex?"

And Alex said, "Yes, sir."

"I can't tell you not to be. I would be, too, and so would these young—gods of war."

Lanser said, "Call your squad." Tonder got up quickly and went to the door. "They're here, sir," He opened the door wide and the helmeted men could be seen.

Orden said, "Alex, go, knowing that these men will have no

rest, no rest at all until they are gone, or dead. You will make the people one. It's a sad knowledge and little enough gift to you, but it is so. No rest at all."

Alex shut his eyes tightly. Mayor Orden leaned close and kissed him on the cheek. "Good-bye, Alex," he said.

The guard took Alex by the arm and the young man kept his eyes tightly closed, and they guided him through the door. The squad faced about, and their feet marched away down out of the house and into the snow, and the snow muffled their footsteps.

The men about the table were silent. Orden looked towards the window and saw a little round spot being rubbed clear of snow by a quick hand. He stared at it, fascinated, and then he looked quickly away. He said to the colonel, "I hope you know what you are doing."

Captain Loft gathered his papers and Lanser asked, "In the square, Captain?"

"Yes, in the square. It must be public," Loft said.

And Orden said, "I hope you know."

"Man," said the colonel, "whether we know or not, it is what must be done."

Silence fell on the room and each man listened. And it was not long. From the distance there came a crash of firing. Lanser sighed deeply. Orden put his hand to his forehead and filled his lungs deeply. Then there was a shout outside. The glass of the window crashed inward and Lieutenant Prackle wheeled about. He brought his hand up to his shoulder and stared at it.

Lanser leaped up, crying, "So, it starts! Are you badly hurt, Lieutenant?"

"My shoulder," said Prackle.

Lanser took command. "Captain Loft, there will be tracks in the snow. Now, I want every house searched for firearms. I want every man who has one taken hostage. You, sir," he said to the Mayor, "are placed in protective custody. And understand this, please: we will shoot, five, ten, a hundred for one."

Orden said quietly, "A man of certain memories."

Lanser stopped in the middle of an order. He looked over slowly at the Mayor and for a moment they understood each other. And then Lanser straightened his shoulders. "A man of no memories!" he said sharply. And then: "I want every weapon in town gathered. Bring in everyone who resists. Hurry, before their tracks are filled."

The staff found their helmets and loosed their pistols and started out. And Orden went to the broken window. He said sadly, "The sweet, cool smell of the snow."

CHAPTER V

THE DAYS and the weeks dragged on, and the months dragged on. The snow fell and melted and fell and melted and finally fell and stuck. The dark buildings of the little town wore bells and hats and eyebrows of white and there were trenches through the snow to the doorways. In the harbour the coal barges came empty and went away loaded, but the coal did not come out of the ground easily. The good miners made mistakes. They were clumsy and slow. Machinery broke and took a long time to fix. The people of the conquered country settled in a slow, silent, waiting revenge. The men who had been traitors, who had helped the invaders—and many of them believed it was for a better state and an ideal way of life—found that the control they took was insecure, that the people they had known looked at them coldly and never spoke.

And there was death in the air, hovering and waiting. Accidents happened on the railway which clung to the mountains and connected the little town with the rest of the nation. Avalanches poured down on the tracks and rails were spread. No train could move unless the tracks were first inspected. People were shot in reprisal and it made no difference. Now and then a group of young men escaped and went to England. And the English bombed the coal-mine and did some damage and killed some of both their friends and their enemies. And it did no good. The cold hatred grew with the winter, the silent, sullen hatred, the waiting hatred. The food supply was controlled—issued to the obedient and withheld from the disobedient—so that the whole population turned coldly obedient. There was a point where food could not be withheld, for a starving man cannot mine coal, cannot lift and carry. And the hatred was deep in the eyes of the people, beneath the surface.

Now it was that the conqueror was surrounded, the men of the battalion alone among silent enemies, and no man might relax his guard for even a moment. If he did, he disappeared, and some snowdrift received his body. If he went alone to a woman, he disappeared, and some snowdrift received his body. If he drank, he disappeared. The men of the battalion could sing only together, could dance only together, and dancing gradually stopped and the singing expressed a longing for home. Their talk was of friends and relatives who loved them and their longings were for warmth and love, because a man can be a soldier for only so many hours a day and for only so many months in a year, and then he wants to be a man again, wants girls and drinks and music and laughter and ease, and when these are cut off, they become irresistibly desirable.

And the men thought always of home. The men of the battalion came to detest the place they had conquered, and they were curt with the people and the people were curt with them, and gradually a little fear began to grow in the conquerors, a fear that it would never be over, that they could never relax and go home, a fear that one day they would crack and be hunted through the mountains like rabbits, for the conquered never relaxed their hatred. The patrols, seeing lights, hearing laughter, would be drawn as to a fire, and when they came near, the laughter stopped, the warmth went out, and the people were cold and obedient. And the soldiers, smelling warm food from the little restaurants, went in and ordered the warm food and found that it was over-salted or over-peppered.

Then the soldiers read the news from home and from the other conquered countries, and the news was always good, and for a while they believed it, and then after a while they did not believe it any more. And every man carried in his heart the terror. "If home crumbled, they would not tell us, and then it would be too late. These people will not spare us. They will kill us all." They remembered stories of their men retreating through Belgium and retreating out of Russia. And the more literate remembered the frantic, tragic retreat from Moscow, when every peasant's pitchfork tasted blood and the snow was rotten with bodies.

And they knew when they cracked, or relaxed, or slept too long, it would be the same here, and their sleep was restless and their days were nervous. They asked questions their officers could not answer because they did not know. They were not told, either. They did not believe the reports from home, either.

Thus it came about that the conquerors grew afraid of the conquered and their nerves wore thin and they shot at shadows in the night. The cold, sullen silence was with them always. Then three soldiers went insane in a week and cried all night and all day until they were sent away home. And others might have gone insane if they had not heard that mercy deaths await the insane at home, and a mercy death is a terrible thing to think of. Fear crept in on the men in their billets and it made them sad, and it crept into the patrols and it made them cruel.

The year turned and the nights grew long. It was dark at three o'clock in the afternoon and not light again until nine in the morning. The jolly lights did not shine out on the snow, for by law every window must be black against the bombers. And yet when the English bombers came over, some light always appeared near the coal-mine. Sometimes the sentries shot a man with a lantern and once a girl with a flashlight. And it did no good. Nothing was cured by the shooting.

And the officers were a reflection of their men, more restrained because their training was more complete, more resourceful because they had more responsibility, but the same fears were a little deeper buried in them, the same longings were more tightly locked in their hearts. And they were under a double strain, for the conquered people watched them for mistakes and their own men watched them for weakness, so that their spirits were taut to the breaking-point. The conquerors were under the terrible spiritual siege and everyone knew, conquered and conquerors, what would happen when the first crack appeared.

From the upstairs room of the Mayor's palace the comfort seemed to have gone. Over the windows black paper was tacked tightly and there were little piles of precious equipment about the room—the instruments and equipment that could not be jeopardised, the glasses and masks and helmets. And discipline here at least was laxer, as though these officers knew there must be some laxness somewhere or the machine would break. On the table were two petrol lanterns which threw a hard, brilliant light and they made great shadows on the walls, and their hissing was an undercurrent in the room.

Major Hunter went on with his work. His drawing-board was permanently ready now, for the bombs tore out his work nearly as fast as he put it in. And he had little sorrow, for to Major Hunter building was life and here he had more building than he could project or accomplish. He sat at his drawing-board with a light behind him and his T-square moved up and down the board and his pencil was busy.

Lieutenant Prackle, his arm still in a sling, sat in a straight chair behind the centre table, reading an illustrated paper. At the end of the table Lieutenant Tonder was writing a letter. He held his pen pinched high and occasionally he looked up from his letter and gazed at the ceiling, to find words to put in his letter.

Prackle turned a page of the illustrated paper and he said, "I can close my eyes and see every shop on this street here." And Hunter went on with his work and Tonder wrote a few more words. Prackle continued, "There is a restaurant right behind here. You can see it in the picture. It's called Burdens."

Hunter did not look up. He said, "I know the place. They had good scallops."

"Sure, they did," Prackle said. "Everything was good there. Not a single bad thing did they serve. And their coffee——"

Tonder looked up from his letter and said, "They won't be serving coffee now—or scallops."

"Well, I don't know about that," said Prackle. "They did and they will again. And there was a waitress there." He described her figure with his hand, with the good hand. "Blonde, so and so." He looked down at the magazine. "She had the strangest eyes—has, I mean—always kind of moist-looking as though she had just been laughing or crying." He glanced at the ceiling and he spoke softly. "I was out with her. She was lovely. I wonder why I didn't go back oftener. I wonder if she's still there."

Tonder said gloomily, "Probably not. Working in a factory, maybe."

Prackle laughed. "I hope they aren't rationing girls at home."

"Why not?" said Tonder.

Prackle said playfully, "You don't care much for girls, do you? Not much, you don't!"

Tonder said, "I like them for what girls are for. I don't let them crawl around my other life."

And Prackle said tauntingly, "It seems to me that they crawl all over you all the time."

Tonder tried to change the subject. He said, "I hate these damn lanterns. Major, when are you going to get that dynamo fixed?"

Major Hunter looked up slowly from his board and said, "It should be done by now. I've got good men working on it. I'll double the guard on it from now on, I guess."

"Did you get the fellow that wrecked it?" Prackle said.

And Hunter said grimly, "It might be any one of five men. I got all five." He went on musingly, "It's so easy to wreck a dynamo if you know how. Just short it and it wrecks itself." He said, "The light ought to be on any time now."

Prackle still looked at his magazine. "I wonder when we will be relieved. I wonder when we will go home for a while, Major; wouldn't you like to go home for a rest?"

Hunter looked up from his work and his face was hopeless for a moment. "Yes, of course." He recovered himself. "I've built this siding four times. I don't know why a bomb always knocks out this particular siding. I'm getting tired of this piece of track. I have to change the route every time because of the craters. There's no time to fill them in. The ground is frozen too hard. It seems to be too much work."

Suddenly the electric lights came on and Tonder automatically reached out and turned off the two petrol lanterns. The hissing was gone from the room.

Tonder said, "Thank God for that! That hissing gets on my nerves. It makes me think there's whispering." He folded the letter he had been writing and he said, "It's strange more letters don't come through. I've only had one in two weeks."

Prackle said, "Maybe nobody writes to you."

"Maybe," said Tonder. He turned to the major. "If anything happened—at home, I mean—do you think they would let us know—anything bad, I mean, any deaths or anything like that?"

Hunter said, "I don't know."

"Well," Tonder went on, "I would like to get out of this god-forsaken hole!"

Prackle broke in, "I thought you were going to live here after the war?" And he imitated Tonder's voice. "Put four or five farms together. Make a nice place, a kind of family seat. Wasn't that it? Going to be a little lord of the valley, weren't you? Nice, pleasant people, beautiful lawns and deer and little children. Isn't that the way it was, Tonder?"

As Prackle spoke, Tonder's hand dropped. Then he clasped his temples with his hands and he spoke with emotion. "Be still! Don't talk like that! These people! These horrible people! These cold people! They never look at you." He shivered. "They never speak. They answer like dead men. They obey, these horrible people. And the girls are frozen!"

There was a light tap on the door and Joseph came in with a scuttle of coal. He moved silently through the room and set the scuttle down so softly that he made no noise, and he turned without looking up at anyone and went towards the door again. Prackle said loudly, "Joseph!" And Joseph turned without replying, without looking up, and he bowed very slightly. And Prackle said, still loudly, "Joseph, is there any wine or any brandy?" Joseph shook his head.

Tonder started up from the table, his face wild with anger, and he shouted. "Answer, you swine! Answer in words!"

Joseph did not look up. He spoke tonelessly, "No, sir; no, sir, there is no wine."

And Tonder said furiously, "And no brandy?"

Joseph looked down and spoke tonelessly again. "There is no brandy, sir." He stood perfectly still.

"What do you want?" Tonder said.

"I want to go, sir."

"Then go, god-damn it!"

Joseph turned and went silently out of the room and Tonder took a handkerchief out of his pocket and wiped his face. Hunter looked up at him and said, "You shouldn't let him beat you so easily."

Tonder sat down on his chair and put his hands to his temples and he said brokenly, "I want a girl. I want to go home. I want a girl. There's a girl in this town, a pretty girl. I see her all the time. She has blonde hair. She lives beside the old-iron store. I want that girl."

Prackle said, "Watch yourself. Watch your nerves."

At that moment the lights went out again and the room was in darkness. Hunter spoke while the matches were being struck and an attempt was being made to light the lanterns; he said, "I thought I had all of them. I must have missed one. But I can't be running down there all the time. I've got good men down there."

Tonder lighted the first lantern and then he lighted the other, and Hunter spoke sternly to Tonder. "Lieutenant, do your talking to us if you have to talk. Don't let the enemy hear you talk this way. There's nothing these people would like better than to know your nerves are getting thin. Don't let the enemy hear you."

Tonder sat down again. The light was sharp on his face and the hissing filled the room. He said, "That's it! The enemy's everywhere! Every man, every woman, even children! The enemy's everywhere. Their faces look out of doorways. The white faces behind the curtains, listening. We have beaten them, we have won everywhere, and they wait and obey, and they wait. Half the world is ours. Is it the same in other places, Major?"

And Hunter said, "I don't know."

"That's it," Tonder said. "We don't know. The reports—everything in hand. Conquered countries cheer our soldiers, cheer the new order." His voice changed and grew soft and still softer. "What do the reports say about us? Do they say we are cheered, loved, flowers in our paths? Oh, these horrible people waiting in the snow!"

And Hunter said, "Now that's off your chest, do you feel better?"

Prackle had been beating the table softly with his good fist, and he said, "He shouldn't talk that way. He should keep things to himself. He's a soldier, isn't he? Then let him be a soldier."

The door opened quietly and Captain Loft came in, and there was snow on his helmet and snow on his shoulders. His nose was pinched and red and his overcoat collar was high about his ears. He took off his helmet and the snow fell to the floor and he brushed his shoulders. "What a job!" he said.

"More trouble?" Hunter asked.

"Always trouble. I see they've got your dynamo again. Well, I think I fixed the mine for a while."

"What's your trouble?" Hunter asked.

"Oh, the usual thing with me—the slow-down and a wrecked dump car. I saw the wrecker, though. I shot him. I think I have a cure for it, Major, now. I just thought it up. I'll make each man take out a certain amount of coal. I can't starve the men or they can't work, but I've really got the answer. If the coal doesn't come out, no food for the families. We'll have the men eat at the mine, so there's no dividing at home. That ought to cure it. They work or their kids don't eat. I told them just now."

"What did they say?"

Loft's eyes narrowed fiercely. "Say? What do they ever say? Nothing! Nothing at all! But we'll see whether the coal comes out now." He took off his coat and shook it, and his eyes fell on the entrance door and he saw that it was open a crack. He moved silently to the door, jerked it open, then closed it. "I thought I had closed that door tight," he said.

"You did," said Hunter.

Prackle still turned the pages of his illustrated paper. His voice was normal again. "Those are monster guns we're using in the east. I never saw one of them. Did you, Captain?"

"Oh, yes," said Captain Loft. "I've seen them fired. They're wonderful. Nothing can stand up against them."

Tonder said, "Captain, do you get much news from home?"

"A certain amount," said Loft.

"Is everything well there?"

"Wonderful!" said Loft. "The armies move ahead everywhere."

"The British aren't defeated yet?"

"They are defeated in every engagement."

"But they fight on?"

"A few air-raids, no more."

"And the Russians?"

"It's all over."

Tonder said insistently, "But they fight on?"

"A little skirmishing, no more."

"Then we have just about won, haven't we, Captain?" Tonder asked.

"Yes, we have."

Tonder looked closely at him and said, "You believe this, don't you, Captain?"

Prackle broke in, "Don't let him start that again!"

Loft scowled at Tonder. "I don't know what you mean."

Tonder said, "I mean this: we'll be going home before long, won't we?"

"Well, the reorganization will take some time," Hunter said. "The new order can't be put into effect in a day, can it?"

Tonder said, "All our lives, perhaps?"

And Prackle said, "Don't let him start it again!"

Loft came very close to Tonder and he said, "Lieutenant, I don't like the tone of your questions. I don't like the tone of doubt."

Hunter looked up and said, "Don't be hard on him, Loft. He's tired. We're all tired."

"Well, I'm tired, too," said Loft, "but I don't let treasonable doubts get in."

Hunter said, "Don't bedevil him, I tell you! Where's the colonel, do you know?"

"He's making out his report. He's asking for reinforcements," said Loft. "It's a bigger job than we thought."

Prackle asked excitedly, "Will he get them—the reinforcements?"

"How would I know?"

Tonder smiled. "Reinforcements!" he said softly. "Or maybe replacements. Maybe we could go home for a while." And he said, smiling, "Maybe I could walk down the street and people would say 'Hello', and they'd say, 'There goes a soldier', and they'd be glad for me and they'd be glad of me. And there'd be friends about, and I could turn my back to a man without being afraid."

Prackle said, "Don't start that again! Don't let him get out of hand again!"

And Loft said disgustedly, "We have enough trouble now without having the staff go crazy."

But Tonder went on, "You really think replacements will come, Captain?"

"I didn't say so."

"But you said they might."

"I said I didn't know. Look, Lieutenant, we've conquered half the world. We must police it for a while. You know that."

"But the other half?" Tonder asked.

"They will fight on hopelessly for a while," said Loft.

"Then we must be spread out all over."

"For a while," said Loft.

Prackle said nervously, "I wish you'd make him shut up. I wish you would shut him up. Make him stop it."

Tonder got out his handkerchief and blew his nose, and he spoke a little like a man out of his head. He laughed embarrassedly. He said, "I had a funny dream. I guess it was a dream. Maybe it was a thought. Maybe a thought or a dream."

Prackle said, "Make him stop it, Captain!"

Tonder said, "Captain, is this place conquered?"

"Of course," said Loft.

A little note of hysteria crept into Tonder's laughter. He said, "Conquered and we're afraid; conquered and we're surrounded." His laughter grew shrill. "I had a dream—or a thought—out in the snow with the black shadows and the faces in the doorways, the cold faces behind curtains. I had a thought or a dream."

Prackle said, "Make him stop!"

Tonder said, "I dreamed the Leader was crazy."

And Loft and Hunter laughed together, and Loft said, "The enemy have found out how crazy. I'll have to write that one home.

The papers would print that one. The enemy have learned how crazy the Leader is."

And Tonder went on laughing. "Conquest after conquest, deeper and deeper into molasses." His laughter choked him and he coughed into his handkerchief. "Maybe the Leader is crazy. Flies conquer the flypaper! Flies captured two hundred miles of new flypaper." His laughter was growing more hysterical now.

Prackle leaned over and shook him with his good hand. "Stop it! You stop it! You have no right!"

And gradually Loft recognized that the laughter was hysterical and he stepped closer to Tonder and slapped him in the face. He said, "Lieutenant, stop it!"

Tonder's laughter went on and Loft slapped him again in the face and he said, "Stop it, Lieutenant! Do you hear me!"

Suddenly Tonder's laughter stopped and the room was quiet except for the hissing of the lanterns. Tonder looked in amazement at his hand and he felt his bruised face with his hand and he looked at his hand again and his head sank down towards the table. "I want to go home," he said.

CHAPTER VI

THERE WAS a little street not far from the town square where small peaked roofs and little shops were mixed up together. The snow was beaten down on the walks and in the street, but it piled high on the fences and it puffed on the roof peaks. It drifted against the shuttered windows of the little houses. And into the yards paths were shovelled. The night was dark and cold and no light showed from the windows to attract the bombers. And no one walked in the streets, for the curfew was strict. The houses were dark lumps against the snow. Every little while the patrol of six men walked down the street, peering about, and each man carried a long flashlight. The hushed tramp of their feet sounded in the street, the squeaks of their boots on the packed snow. They were muffled figures deep in thick coats; under their helmets were knitted caps which came down over their ears and covered their chins and mouths. A little snow fell, only a little, like rice.

The patrol talked as they walked, and they talked of things that they longed for—of meat and of hot soup and of the richness of butter, of the prettiness of girls and of their smiles and of their lips and their eyes. They talked of these things and sometimes they talked of their hatred of what they were doing and of their loneliness.

A small, peak-roofed house beside the iron shop was shaped like the others and wore its snow cap like the others. No light came from its shuttered windows and its storm doors were tightly closed. But inside a lamp burned in the small living-room and the door to the bedroom was open and the door to the kitchen was open. An iron stove was against the back wall with a little coal fire burning in it. It was a warm, poor, comfortable room, the floor covered with worn carpet, the walls papered in warm brown with an old-fashioned *fleur-de-lis* figure in gold. And on the back wall were two pictures, one of fish lying dead on a plate of ferns and the other of grouse lying dead on a fir bough. On the right wall there was a picture of Christ walking on the waves towards the despairing fishermen. Two straight chairs were in the room and a couch covered with a bright blanket. There was a little round table in the middle of the room, on which stood a kerosene lamp with a round flowered shade on it, and the light in the room was warm and soft.

The inner door, which led to the passage, which in turn led to the storm door, was beside the stove.

In a cushioned old rocking-chair beside the table Molly Morden sat alone. She was unravelling the wool from an old blue sweater and winding the yarn on a ball. She had quite a large ball of it. And on the table beside her was her knitting with the needles sticking in it, and a large pair of scissors. Her glasses lay on the table beside her, for she did not need them for knitting. She was pretty and young and neat. Her golden hair was done up on the top of her head and a blue bow was in her hair. Her hands worked quickly with the ravelling. As she worked, she glanced now and then at the door to the passage. The wind whistled in the chimney softly, but it was a quiet night, muffled with snow.

Suddenly she stopped her work. Her hands were still. She looked towards the door and listened. The tramping feet of the patrol went by in the street and the sound of their voices could be heard faintly. The sound faded away. Molly ripped out new yarn and wound it on the ball. And again she stopped. There was a rustle at the door and then three short knocks. Molly put down her work and went to the door.

"Yes?" she called.

She unlocked the door and opened it and a heavily cloaked figure came in. It was Annie, the cook, red-eyed and wrapped in mufflers. She slipped in quickly, as though practised at getting speedily through doors and getting them closed again behind her. She stood there red-nosed, sniffling and glancing quickly around the room.

Molly said, "Good evening, Annie. I didn't expect you to-night. Take your things off and get warm. It's cold out."

Annie said, "The soldiers brought winter early. My father always said a war brought bad weather, or bad weather brought a war. I don't remember which."

"Take off your things and come to the stove."

"I can't," said Annie importantly. "They're coming."

"Who are coming?" Molly said.

"His Excellency," said Annie, "and the doctor and the two Anders boys."

"Here?" Molly asked. "What for?"

Annie held out her hand and there was a little package in it. "Take it," she said. "I stole it from the colonel's plate. It's meat."

And Molly unwrapped the little cake of meat and put it in her mouth and she spoke around her chewing. "Did you get some?"

Annie said, "I cook it, don't I? I always get some."

"When are they coming?"

Annie sniffled. "The Anders boys are sailing for England. They've got to go. They're hiding now."

"Are they?" Molly asked. "What for?"

"Well, it was their brother, Jack, was shot to-day for wrecking that little car. The soldiers are looking for the rest of the family. You know how they do."

"Yes," Molly said, "I know how they do. Sit down, Annie."

"No time," said Annie. "I've got to get back and tell His Excellency it's all right here."

Molly said, "Did anybody see you come?"

Annie smiled proudly. "No, I'm awful good at sneaking."

"How will the Mayor get out?"

Annie laughed. "Joseph is going to be in his bed in case they look in, right in his night-shirt, right next to Madame!" And she laughed again. She said, "Joseph better lie pretty quiet."

Molly said, "It's an awful night to be sailing."

"It's better than being shot."

"Yes, so it is. Why is the Mayor coming here?"

"I don't know. He wants to talk to the Anders boys. I've got to go now, but I came to tell you."

Molly said, "How soon are they coming?"

"Oh, maybe half, maybe three-quarters of an hour," Annie said. "I'll come in first. Nobody bothers with old cooks." She started for the door and she turned midway, and as though accusing Molly of saying the last words she said truculently, "I'm not so old!" And she slipped out of the door and closed it behind her.

Molly went on knitting for a moment and then she got up and went to the stove and lifted the lid. The glow of the fire lighted her face. She stirred the fire and added a few lumps of coal and closed the stove again. Before she could get to her chair, there was a knocking on the outer door. She crossed the room and said to herself, "I wonder what she forgot." She went into the passage and she said, "What do you want?"

A man's voice answered her. She opened the door and a man's voice said, "I don't mean any harm. I don't mean any harm."

Molly backed into the room and Lieutenant Tonder followed her in. Molly said, "Who are you? What do you want? You can't come in here. What do you want?"

Lieutenant Tonder was dressed in his great grey overcoat. He entered the room and took off his helmet and he spoke pleadingly. "I don't mean any harm. Please let me come in."

Molly said, "What do you want?"

She shut the door behind him and he said, "Miss, I only want to talk, that's all. I want to hear you talk. That's all I want."

"Are you forcing yourself on me?" Molly asked.

"No, miss, just let me stay a little while and then I'll go."

"What is it you want?"

Tonder tried to explain. "Can you understand this—can you believe this? Just for a little while, can't we forget this war? Just for a little while. Just for a little while, can't we talk together like people—together?"

Molly looked at him for a long time and then a smile came to her lips. "You don't know who I am, do you?"

Tonder said, "I've seen you in the town. I know you're lovely. I know I want to talk to you."

And Molly still smiled. She said softly. "You don't know who I am." She sat in her chair and Tonder stood like a child, looking very clumsy. Molly continued, speaking quietly: "Why, you're lonely. It's as simple as that, isn't it?"

Tonder licked his lips and he spoke eagerly. "That's it," he said. "You understand. I knew you would. I knew you'd have to." His words came tumbling out. "I'm lonely to the point of illness. I'm lonely in the quiet and the hatred." And he said pleadingly, "Can't we talk, just a little bit?"

Molly picked up her knitting. She looked quickly at the front door. "You can stay not more than fifteen minutes. Sit down a little, Lieutenant."

She looked at the door again. The house creaked. Tonder became tense and he said, "Is someone here?"

"No, the snow is heavy on the roof. I have no man any more to push it down."

Tonder said gently, "Who did it? Was it something we did?"

And Molly nodded, looking far off. "Yes."

He sat down. "I'm sorry." After a moment he said, "I wish I could do something. I'll have the snow pushed off the roof."

"No," said Molly, "no."

"Why not?"

"Because the people would think I had joined with you. They would expel me. I don't want to be expelled."

Tonder said, "Yes, I see how that would be. You all hate us. But I'll take care of you if you'll let me."

Now Molly knew she was in control, and her eyes narrowed a little cruelly and she said, "Why do you ask? You are the conqueror. Your men don't have to ask. They take what they want."

"That's not what I want," Tonder said. "That's not the way I want it."

And Molly laughed, still a little cruelly. "You want me to like you, don't you, Lieutenant?"

He said simply, "Yes," and he raised his head and he said, "You are so beautiful, so warm. Your hair is bright. Oh, I've seen no kindness in a woman's face for so long!"

"Do you see any in mine?" she asked.

He looked closely at her. "I want to."

She dropped her eyes at last. "You're making love to me, aren't you, Lieutenant?"

He said clumsily, "I want you to like me. Surely I want you to like me. Surely I want to see that in your eyes. I have seen you in the streets. I have watched you pass by. I've given orders that you mustn't be molested. Have you been molested?"

And Molly said quietly, "Thank you; no, I've not been molested."

His words rushed on. "Why, I've even written a poem for you. Would you like to see my poem?"

And she said sardonically, "Is it a long poem? You have to go very soon."

He said, "No, it's a little tiny poem. It's a little bit of a poem." He reached inside his tunic and brought out a folded paper and handed it to her. She leaned close to the lamp and put on her glasses, and she read quietly:

Your eyes in their deep heavens
Possess me and will not depart;
A sea of blue thoughts rushing
And pouring over my heart.

She folded the paper and put it in her lap. "Did you write this, Lieutenant?"

"Yes."

She said a little tauntingly, "To me?"

And Tonder answered uneasily, "Yes."

She looked at him steadily, smiling. "You didn't write it, Lieutenant, did you?"

He smiled back like a child caught in a lie. "No."

Molly asked him, "Do you know who did?"

Tonder said, "Yes, Heine wrote it. It's '*Mit deinen blauen Augen.*' I've always loved it." He laughed embarrassedly and Molly laughed with him, and suddenly they were laughing together. He stopped laughing just as suddenly and a bleakness came into his eyes. "I haven't laughed like this since forever." He said, "They told us the people would like us, would admire us. They do not. They only hate us." And then he changed the subject as though he worked against time. "You are so beautiful. You are as beautiful as the laughter."

Molly said, "You're beginning to make love to me, Lieutenant. You must go in a moment."

And Tonder said, "Maybe I want to make love to you. A man needs love. A man dies without love. His insides shrivel and his chest feels like a dry chip. I'm lonely."

Molly got up from her chair. She looked nervously at the door and she walked to the stove and, coming back, her face grew hard and her eyes grew punishing and she said, "Do you want to go to bed with me, Lieutenant?"

"I didn't say that! Why do you talk that way?"

Molly said cruelly, "Maybe I'm trying to disgust you. I was married once. My husband is dead. You see, I'm not a virgin." Her voice was bitter.

Tonder said, "I only want you to like me."

And Molly said, "I know. You are a civilized man. You know that love-making is more full and whole and delightful if there is liking, too."

Tonder said, "Don't talk that way! Please don't talk that way!"

Molly glanced quickly at the door. She said, "We are a conquered people, Lieutenant. You have taken the food away. I'm hungry. I'll like you better if you feed me."

Tonder said, "What are you saying?"

"Do I disgust you, Lieutenant? Maybe I'm trying to. My price is two sausages."

Tonder said, "You can't talk this way!"

"What about your own girls, Lieutenant, after the last war? A man could choose among your girls for an egg or a slice of bread. Do you want me for nothing, Lieutenant? Is the price too high?"

He said, "You fooled me for a moment. But you hate me, too, don't you? I thought maybe you wouldn't."

"No, I don't hate you," she said. "I'm hungry and—I hate you!"

Tonder said, "I'll give you anything you need, but——"

And she interrupted him. "You want to call it something else? You don't want a whore. Is that what you mean?"

Tonder said, "I don't know what I mean. You make it sound full of hatred."

Molly laughed. She said, "It's not nice to be hungry. Two sausages, two fine, fat sausages can be the most precious things in the world."

"Don't say those things," he said. "Please don't!"

"Why not? They're true."

"They aren't true! This can't be true!"

She looked at him for a moment and then she sat down and her eyes fell to her lap and she said, "No, it's not true. I don't hate you. I'm lonely too. And the snow is heavy on the roof."

Tonder got up and moved near to her. He took one of her hands in both of his and he said softly, "Please don't hate me. I'm only a lieutenant. I didn't ask to come here. You didn't ask to be my enemy. I'm only a man, not a conquering man."

Molly's fingers encircled his hands for a moment and she said, softly, "I know; yes, I know."

And Tonder said, "We have some right to life in all this death."

She put her hand to his cheek for a moment and she said, "Yes."

"I'll take care of you," he said. "We have some right to life in all the killing." His hand rested on her shoulder. Suddenly she grew rigid and her eyes were wide and staring as though she saw a vision. His hand released her and he asked, "What's the matter? What is it?" Her eyes stared straight ahead and he repeated, "What is it?"

Molly spoke in a haunted voice. "I dressed him like a little boy for his first day in school. And he was afraid, I buttoned his shirt and tried to comfort him, but he was beyond comfort. And he was afraid."

Tonder said, "What are you saying?"

And Molly seemed to see what she described. "I don't know why they let him come home. He was confused. He didn't know what was happening. He didn't even kiss me when he went away. He was afraid, and very brave, like a little boy on his first day of school."

Tonder stood up. "That was your husband."

Molly said, "Yes, my husband. I went to the Mayor, but he was helpless. And then he marched away—not very well nor steadily—and you took him out and you shot him. It was more strange than terrible then. I didn't quite believe it then."

Tonder said, "Your husband!"

"Yes; and now, in the quiet house, I believe it. Now, with the heavy snow on the roof, I believe it. And in the loneliness before daybreak, in the half-warmed bed, I know it then."

Tonder stood in front of her. His face was full of misery. "Good night," he said. "God keep you. May I come back?"

And Molly looked at the wall and at the memory; "I don't know," she said.

"I'll come back."

"I don't know."

He looked at her and then he quietly went out of the door, and Molly still stared at the wall. "God keep me." She stayed for a moment staring at the wall. The door opened silently and Annie came in. Molly did not even see her.

Annie said disapprovingly, "The door was open."

Molly looked slowly towards her, her eyes still wide open. "Yes. Oh yes, Annie."

"The door was open. There was a man came out. I saw him. He looked like a soldier."

And Molly said, "Yes, Annie."

"Was it a soldier here?"

"Yes, it was a soldier."

And Annie asked suspiciously, "What was he doing here?"

"He came to make love to me."

Annie said, "Miss, what are you doing? You haven't joined them, have you? You aren't with them, like that Corell?"

"No, I'm not with them, Annie."

Annie said, "If the Mayor's here and they come back, it'll be your fault if anything happens; it'll be your fault!"

"He won't come back. I won't let him come back."

But the suspicion stayed with Annie. She said, "Shall I tell them to come in now? Do you say it's safe?"

"Yes, it's safe. Where are they?"

"They're out behind the fence," said Annie.

"Tell them to come in."

And while Annie went out, Molly got up and smoothed her hair and she shook her head, trying to be alive again. There was a little sound in the passage. Two tall, blond young men entered. They were dressed in pea-jackets and dark turtle-neck sweaters. They wore stocking caps perched on their heads. They were wind-burned and strong and they looked almost like twins. Will Anders and Tom Anders, the fishermen.

"Good evening, Molly. You've heard?"

"Annie told me. It's a bad night to go."

Tom said, "It's better than a clear night. The planes see you on a clear night. What's the Mayor want, Molly?"

"I don't know. I heard about your brother. I'm sorry."

The two were silent and they looked embarrassed. Tom said, "You know how it is, better than most."

"Yes; I know."

Annie came in the door again and she said in a hoarse whisper,

"They're here!" And Mayor Orden and Doctor Winter came in. They took off their coats and caps and laid them on the couch. Orden went to Molly and kissed her on the forehead.

"Good evening, dear."

He turned to Annie. "Stand in the passage, Annie. Give us one knock for the patrol, one when it's gone, and two for danger. You can leave the outer door open a crack so that you can hear if anyone comes."

Annie said, "Yes, sir." She went into the passage and shut the door behind her.

Doctor Winter was at the stove, warming his hands. "We got word you boys were going to-night."

"We've got to go," Tom said.

Orden nodded. "Yes, I know. We heard you were going to take Mr. Corell with you."

Tom laughed bitterly. "We thought it would be only right. We're taking his boat. We can't leave him around. It isn't good to see him in the streets."

Orden said sadly, "I wish he had gone away. It's just a danger to you, taking him."

"It isn't good to see him in the streets." Will echoed his brother. "It isn't good for the people to see him here."

Winter asked, "Can you take him? Isn't he cautious at all?"

"Oh, yes, he's cautious, in a way. At twelve o'clock, though, he walks to his house usually. We'll be behind the wall. I think we can get him through his lower garden to the water. His boat's tied up there. We were on her to-day getting her ready."

Orden repeated, "I wish you didn't have to. It's just an added danger. If he makes a noise, the patrol might come."

Tom said, "He won't make a noise, and it's better if he disappears at sea. Some of the town people might get him and then there would be too much killing. No, it's better if he goes to sea."

Molly took up her knitting again. She said, "Will you throw him overboard?"

Will blushed. "He'll go to sea, ma'am." He turned to the Mayor. "You wanted to see us, sir?"

"Why, yes, I want to talk to you. Doctor Winter and I have tried to think—there's so much talk about justice, injustice, conquest. Our people are invaded, but I don't think they're conquered."

There was a sharp knock on the door and the room was silent. Molly's needles stopped, and the Mayor's outstretched hand remained in the air. Tom, scratching his ear, left his hand there and stopped scratching. Everyone in the room was motionless. Every eye was turned towards the door. Then first faintly and then growing louder, there came the tramp of the patrol, the squeak of their boots in the snow, and the sound of their talking as they went by. They passed the door and their footsteps disappeared in the distance. There was a second tap on the door. And in the room the people relaxed.

Orden said, "It must be cold out there for Annie." He took up his coat from the couch and opened the inner door and handed his coat through. "Put this around your shoulders, Annie," he said and closed the door.

"I don't know what I'd do without her," he said. "She gets everywhere, she sees and hears everything."

Tom said, "We should be going pretty soon, sir."

And Winter said, "I wish you'd forget about Mr. Corell."

"We can't. It isn't good to see him in the streets." He looked inquiringly at Mayor Orden.

Orden began slowly. "I want to speak simply. This is a little town. Justice and injustice are in terms of little things. Your brother's shot and Alex Morden's shot. Revenge against a traitor. The people are angry and they have no way to fight back. But it's all in little terms. It's people against people, not idea against idea."

Winter said, "It's funny for a doctor to think of destruction, but I think all invaded people want to resist. We are disarmed; our spirits and bodies aren't enough. The spirit of a disarmed man sinks."

Will Anders asked, "What's all this for, sir? What do you want of us?"

"We want to fight them and we can't," Orden said. "They're using hunger on the people now. Hunger brings weakness. You boys are sailing for England. Maybe nobody will listen to you but tell them from us—from a small town—to give us weapons."

Tom asked, "You want guns?"

Again there was a quick knock on the door and the people froze where they were, and from outside there came the sound of the patrol, but at double step, running. Will moved quickly towards the door. The running steps came abreast of the house. There were muffled orders and the patrol ran by, and there was a second tap at the door.

Molly said, "They must be after somebody. I wonder who, this time."

"We should be going," Tom said uneasily. "Do you want guns, sir? Shall we ask for guns?"

"No, tell them how it is. We are watched. Any move we make calls for reprisals. If we could have simple, secret weapons, weapons of stealth, explosives, dynamite to blow up rails, grenades, if possible, even poison." He spoke angrily. "This is no honourable war. This is a war of treachery and murder. Let us use the methods that have been used on us! Let the British bombers drop their big bombs on the works, but let them also drop us little bombs to use, to hide, to slip under the rails, under tanks. Then we will be armed, secretly armed. Then the invader will never know which of us is armed. Let the bombers bring us simple weapons. We will know how to use them!"

Winter broke in. "They'll never know where it will strike. The soldiers, the patrol, will never know which of us is armed."

Tom wiped his forehead. "If we get through, we'll tell them, sir, but—well, I've heard it said that in England there are still men in power who do not care to put weapons in the hands of common people."

Orden stared at him. "Oh! I hadn't thought of that. Well, we can only see. If such people still govern England and America, the world is lost, anyway. Tell them what we say, if they will listen. We must have help, but if we get it"—his face grew very hard—"if we get it, we will help ourselves."

Winter said, "If they will even give us dynamite to hide, to bury in the ground to be ready against need, then the invader can never rest again, never! We will blow up his supplies."

The room grew excited. Molly said fiercely, "Yes, we could fight his rest, then. We could fight his sleep. We could fight his nerves and his certainties."

Will asked quietly, "Is that all, sir?"

"Yes." Orden nodded. "That's the core of it."

"What if they won't listen?"

"You can only try, as you are trying the sea to-night."

"Is that all, sir?"

The door opened and Annie came quietly in. Orden went on, "That's all. If you have to go now, let me send Annie out to see that the way is clear." He looked up and saw that Annie had come in. Annie said, "There's a soldier coming up the path. He looks like the soldier that was here before. There was a soldier here with Molly before."

The others looked at Molly. Annie said, "I locked the door."

"What does he want?" Molly asked. "Why does he come back?"

There was a gentle knocking at the outside door. Orden went to Molly. "What is this, Molly? Are you in trouble?"

"No," she said, "no! Go out the back way. You can get out through the back. Hurry, hurry out!"

The knocking continued on the front door. A man's voice called softly. Molly opened the door to the kitchen. She said, "Hurry, hurry!"

The Mayor stood in front of her. "Are you in trouble, Molly? You haven't done anything?"

Annie said coldly, "It looks like the same soldier. There was a soldier here before."

"Yes," Molly said to the Mayor. "Yes, there was a soldier here before."

The Mayor said, "What did he want?"

"He wanted to make love to me."

"But he didn't?" Orden said.

"No," she said, "he didn't. Go now, and I'll take care."

Orden said, "Molly, if you're in trouble, let us help you."

"The trouble I'm in no one can help me with," she said. "Go now," and she pushed them out of the door.

Annie remained behind. She looked at Molly. "Miss, what does this soldier want?"

"I don't know what he wants."

"Are you going to tell him anything?"

"No." Wonderingly, Molly repeated, "No." And then sharply she said. "No, Annie, I'm not!"

Annie scowled at her. "Miss, you'd better not tell him anything!" And she went out and closed the door behind her.

The tapping continued on the front door and a man's voice could be heard through the door.

Molly went to the centre lamp, and her burden was heavy on her. She looked down at the lamp. She looked at the table, and she saw the big scissors lying beside her knitting. She picked them up wonderingly by the blades. The blades slipped through her fingers until she held the long shears and she was holding them like a knife, and her eyes were horrified. She looked down into the lamp and the light flooded up in her face. Slowly she raised the shears and placed them inside her dress.

The tapping continued on the door. She heard the voice calling to her. She leaned over the lamp for a moment and then suddenly she blew out the light. The room was dark except for a spot of red that came from the coal stove. She opened the door. Her voice was strained and sweet. She called, "I'm coming, Lieutenant, I'm coming!"

CHAPTER VII

In the dark, clear night, a white, half-withered moon brought little light. The wind was dry and singing over the snow, a quiet wind that blew steadily, evenly from the cold point of the Pole. Over the land the snow lay very deep and dry as sand. The houses snuggled down in the hollows of banked snow, and their windows were dark and shuttered against the cold, and only a little smoke rose from the banked fires.

In the town the footpaths were frozen hard and packed hard. And the streets were silent, too, except when the miserable, cold patrol came by. The houses were dark against the night, and a little lingering warmth remained in the houses against the morning. Near the mine entrance the guards watched the sky and trained their instruments on the sky and turned their listening-instruments against the sky, for it was a clear night for bombing. On nights like this the feathered steel spindles came whistling down and roared to splinters. The land would be visible from the sky to-night, even though the moon seemed to throw little light.

Down towards one end of the village, among the small houses, a dog complained about the cold and the loneliness. He raised his nose to his god and gave a long and fulsome account of the state of the world as it applied to him. He was a practised singer with a full bell throat and great versatility of range and control. The six men of the patrol slogging dejectedly up and down the streets heard the singing of the dog, and one of the muffled soldiers said, "Seems to me he's getting worse every night. I suppose we ought to shoot him."

And another answered, "Why? Let him howl. He sounds good to me. I used to have a dog at home that howled. I never could break him. Yellow dog. I don't mind the howl. They took my dog when they took the others," he said factually, in a dull voice.

And the corporal said, "Couldn't have dogs eating up food that was needed."

"Oh, I'm not complaining. I know it was necessary. I can't plan the way the leaders do. It seems funny to me, though, that some people here have dogs, and they don't have even as much food as we have. They're pretty gaunt, though, dogs and people."

"They're fools," said the corporal. "That's why they lost so quickly. They can't plan the way we can."

"I wonder if we'll have dogs again after it's over," said the soldier. "I suppose we could get them from America or some place and start the breeds again. What kind of dogs do you suppose they have in America?"

"I don't know," said the corporal. "Probably dogs as crazy as everything else they have." And he went on, "Maybe dogs are no good, anyway. It might be just as well if we never bothered with them, except for police work."

"It might be," said the soldier. "I've heard the Leader doesn't like dogs. I've heard they make him itch and sneeze."

"You hear all kinds of things," the corporal said. "Listen!" The patrol stopped and from a great distance came the bee hum of planes.

"There they come," the corporal said. "Well, there aren't any lights. It's been two weeks, hasn't it, since they came before?"

"Twelve days," said the soldier.

The guards at the mine heard the high drone of the planes. "They're flying high," a sergeant said. And Captain Loft tilted his head back so that he could see under the rim of his helmet. "I judge over 20,000 feet," he said. "Maybe they're going on over."

"Aren't very many." The sergeant listened. "I don't think there are more than three of them. Shall I call the battery?"

"Just see they're alert, and then call Colonel Lanser—no, don't call him. Maybe they aren't coming here. They're nearly over and they haven't started to dive yet."

"Sounds to me like they're circling. I don't think there are more than two," the sergeant said.

In their beds the people heard the planes and they squirmed deep into their feather-beds and listened. In the palace of the Mayor the little sound awakened Colonel Lanser, and he turned over on his back and looked at the dark ceiling with wide-open eyes, and he held his breath to listen better and then his heart beat so that he could not hear as well as he could when he was breathing. Mayor Orden heard the planes in his sleep and they made a dream for him and he moved and whispered in his sleep.

High in the air the two bombers circled, mud-coloured planes. They cut their throttles and soared, circling. And from the belly of each one tiny little objects dropped, hundreds of them, one after another. They plummeted a few feet and then little parachutes opened and drifted small packages silently and slowly downward towards the earth, and the planes raised their throttles and gained altitude, and then cut their throttles and circled again, and more of the little objects plummeted down, and then the planes turned and flew back in the direction from which they had come.

The tiny parachutes floated like thistledown and the breeze spread them out and distributed them as seeds on the ends of thistle-down are distributed. They drifted so slowly and landed so gently that sometimes the ten-inch packages of dynamite stood upright in the snow, and the little parachutes folded gently down around them. They looked black against the snow. They landed in the white fields and among the woods of the hills and they landed in trees and hung down from the branches. Some of them landed on the house-tops of the little town, some in the small front yards, and one landed and stood upright in the snow crown on top of the head of the village statue of St. Albert the Missionary.

One of the little parachutes came down in the street ahead o the patrol and the sergeant said: "Careful! It's a time bomb."

"It ain't big enough," a soldier said.

"Well, don't go near it." The sergeant had his flashlight out and he turned it on the object, a little parachute no bigger than a handkerchief, coloured light blue, and hanging from it a package wrapped in blue paper.

"Now don't anybody touch it," the sergeant said. "Harry, you go down to the mine and get the captain. We'll keep an eye on this damn thing."

The late dawn came and the people moving out of their houses in the country saw the spots of blue against the snow. They went to them and picked them up. They unwrapped the paper and read the printed words. They saw the gift and suddenly each finder grew furtive, and he concealed the long tube under his coat and went to some secret place and hid the tube.

And word got to the children about the gift and they combed the countryside in a terrible Easter-egg hunt, and when some lucky child saw the blue colour, he rushed to the prize and opened it and then he hid the tube and told his parents about it. There were some people who were frightened, who turned the tubes over to the military, but they were not very many. And the soldiers scurried about the town in another Easter-egg hunt, but they were not so good at it as the children were.

In the drawing-room of the palace of the Mayor the dining-table remained with the chairs about as it had been placed the day Alex Morden was shot. The room had not the grace it had when it was still the palace of the Mayor. The walls, bare of standing chairs, looked very blank. The table with a few papers scattered about on it made the room look like a business office. The clock on the mantel struck nine. It was a dark day now, overcast with clouds, for the dawn had brought the heavy snow-clouds.

Annie came out of the Mayor's room: she swooped by the table and glanced at the papers that lay there. Captain Loft came in. He stopped in the doorway, seeing Annie.

"What are you doing here?" he demanded.

And Annie said sullenly, "Yes, sir."

"I said, what are you doing here?"

"I thought to clean up, sir."

"Let things alone, and go along."

And Annie said, "Yes, sir," and she waited until he was clear of the door, and she scuttled out.

Captain Loft turned back through the doorway and he said, "All right, bring it in." A soldier came through the door behind him, his rifle hung over his shoulder by a strap, and in his arms he held a number of the blue packages, and from the ends of the packages there dangled the little strings and pieces of blue cloth.

Loft said, "Put them on the table." The soldier gingerly laid the packages down. "Now go upstairs and report to Colonel Lanser that I'm here with the—things," and the soldier wheeled about and left the room.

Loft went to the table and picked up one of the packages, and his face wore a look of distaste. He held up the little blue cloth parachute, held it above his head and dropped it, and the cloth opened and the package floated to the floor. He picked up the package again and examined it.

Now Colonel Lanser came quickly into the room followed by Major Hunter. Hunter was carrying a square of yellow paper in his hand. Lanser said, "Good morning, Captain," and he went to the head of the table and sat down. For a moment he looked at the little pile of tubes, and then he picked up one and held it in his hand. "Sit down, Hunter," he said. "Have you examined these?"

Hunter pulled out a chair and sat down. He looked at the yellow paper in his hand. "Not very carefully," he said. "There are three breaks in the railroad all within ten miles."

"Well, take a look at them and see what you think," Lanser said.

Hunter reached for a tube and stripped off the outer covering, and inside was a small package next to the tube. Hunter took out a knife and cut into the tube. Captain Loft looked over his shoulder. Then Hunter smelled the cut and rubbed his fingers together, and he said, "It's silly. It's commercial dynamite. I don't know what per cent. of nitroglycerine until I test it." He looked at the end. "It has a regular dynamite cap, fulminate of mercury, and a fuse—about a minute, I suppose." He tossed the tube back on to the table. "It's very cheap and very simple," he said.

The colonel looked at Loft. "How many do you think were dropped?"

"I don't know, sir," said Loft. "We picked up about fifty of them, and about ninety parachutes they came in. For some reason the people leave the parachutes when they take the tubes, and then there are probably a lot we haven't found yet."

Lanser waved his hand. "It doesn't really matter," he said. "They can drop as many as they want. We can't stop it, and we can't use it against them, either. They haven't conquered anybody."

Loft said fiercely, "We can beat them off the face of the earth!"

Hunter was prising the copper cap out of the top of one of the sticks, and Lanser said, "Yes—we can do that. Have you looked at this wrapper, Hunter?"

"Not yet, I haven't had time."

"It's kind of devilish, this thing," said Colonel Lanser. "The wrapper is blue, so that it's easy to see. Unwrap the outer paper and here"—he picked up the small package—"here is a piece of chocolate. Everybody will be looking for it. I'll bet our own soldiers steal the chocolate. Why, the kids will be looking for them, like Easter eggs."

A soldier came in and laid a square of yellow paper in front of the colonel and retired, and Lanser glanced at it and laughed harshly. "Here's something for you, Hunter. Two more breaks in your line."

Hunter looked up from the copper cap he was examining, and he asked, "How general is this? Did they drop them everywhere?"

Lanser was puzzled. "Now, that's the funny thing. I've talked to the capital. This is the only place they've dropped them."

"What do you make of that?" Hunter asked.

"Well, it's hard to say. I think this is a test place. I suppose if it works here they'll use it everywhere, and if it doesn't work here they won't bother."

"What are you going to do?" Hunter asked.

"The capital orders me to stamp this out so ruthlessly that they won't drop it anywhere else."

Hunter said plaintively, "How am I going to mend five breaks in the railroad? I haven't rails now for five breaks."

"You'll have to rip out some of the old sidings, I guess," said Lanser.

Hunter said, "That'll make a hell of a road-bed."

"Well, anyway, it will make a road-bed."

Major Hunter tossed the tube he had torn apart on to the pile, and Loft broke in, "We must stop this thing at once, sir. We must arrest and punish people who pick these things up, before they use them. We have to get busy so these people won't think we are weak."

Lanser was smiling at him, and he said, "Take it easy, Captain. Let's see what we have first, and then we'll think of remedies."

He took a new package from the pile and unwrapped it. He took the little piece of chocolate, tasted it, and he said, "This is a devilish thing. It's good chocolate, too. I can't even resist it myself. The prize in the grab-bag." Then he picked up the dynamite. "What do you think of this really, Hunter?"

"What I told you. It's very cheap and very effective for small jobs, dynamite with a cap and a one-minute fuse. It's good if you know how to use it. It's no good if you don't."

Lanser studied the print on the inside of the wrapper. "Have you read this?"

"Glanced at it," said Hunter.

"Well, I have read it, and I want you to listen to it carefully," said Lanser. He read from the paper: "'To the unconquered people: Hide this. Do not expose yourself. You will need this later. It is a present from your friends to you and from you to the invader of your country. Do not try to do large things with it.'" He began to skip through the bill. "Now, here, 'rails in the country.' And, 'work at night.' And, 'tie up transportation.' Now here, 'Instructions: rails. Place stick under rail close to the joint, and tight against a tie. Pack mud or hard-beaten snow around it so that it is firm. When the fuse is lighted you have a slow count of sixty before it explodes.' "

He looked up at Hunter, and Hunter said simply, "It works." Lanser looked back at his paper and he skipped through. " 'Bridges: Weaken, do not destroy.' And here, 'transmission poles,' and here, 'culverts, trucks.' " He laid the blue handbill down. "Well, there it is."

Loft said angrily, "We must do something! There must be a way to control this. What does headquarters say?"

Lanser pursed his lips and his fingers played with one of the tubes. "I could have told you what they'd say before they said it. I have the orders. 'Set booby-traps and poison the chocolate.' " He paused for a moment and then he said, "Hunter, I'm a good, loyal man, but sometimes when I hear the brilliant ideas of headquarters I wish I were a civilian, an old, crippled civilian. They always think they are dealing with stupid people. I don't say that this is a measure of their intelligence, do I?"

Hunter looked amused. "Do you?"

Lanser said sharply, "No, I don't. But what will happen? One man will pick up one of these and get blown to bits by our booby trap. One kid will eat chocolate and die of strychnine poisoning. And then?" He looked down at his hands. "They will poke them with poles, or lasso them, before they touch them. They will try the chocolate on the cat. God damn it, Major, these are intelligent people. Stupid traps won't catch them twice."

Loft cleared his throat. "Sir, this is defeatist talk," he said. "We must do something. Why do you suppose it was only dropped here, sir?"

And Lanser said, "For one of two reasons: either this town was picked at random or else there is communication between this town and the outside. We knew that some of the young men have got away."

Loft repeated dully, "We must do something, sir."

Now Lanser turned on him. "Loft, I think I'll recommend you for the General Staff. You want to get to work before you even know what the problem is. This is a new kind of conquest. Always before, it was possible to disarm a people and keep them in ignorance. Now they listen to their radios and we can't stop them. We can't even find their radios."

A soldier looked in through the doorway. "Mr. Corell to see you, sir."

Lanser replied, "Tell him to wait." He continued to talk to Loft. "They read the handbills, weapons drop from the sky for them. Now it's dynamite, Captain. Pretty soon it may be grenades, and then poison."

Loft said anxiously, "They haven't dropped poison yet."

"No, but they will. Can you think what will happen to the morale of our men or even to you if the people had some of those little game darts, you know, those silly little things you throw at a target, the points coated perhaps with cyanide, silent, deadly little things that you couldn't hear coming, that would pierce the uniform and make no noise? And what if our men knew that arsenic was about? Would you or they drink or eat comfortably?"

Hunter said dryly, "Are you writing the enemy's campaign, Colonel?"

"No, I'm trying to anticipate it."

Loft said, "Sir, we sit here talking when we should be searching for this dynamite. If there is organization among these people, we have to find it, we have to stamp it out."

"Yes," said Lanser, "we have to stamp it out, ferociously I suppose. You take a detail, Loft. Get Prackle to take one. I wish we had more junior officers. Tonder's getting killed didn't help us a bit. Why couldn't he let women alone?"

Loft said, "I don't like the way Lieutenant Prackle is acting, sir."

"What's he doing?"

"He isn't doing anything, but he's jumpy and he's gloomy."

"Yes," Lanser said, "I know. It's a thing I've talked about so much. You know," he said, "I might be a major-general if I hadn't talked about it so much. We trained our young men for victory and you've got to admit they're glorious in victory, but they don't quite know how to act in defeat. We told them they were brighter and braver than other young men. It was a kind of shock to them to find out that they aren't a bit braver or brighter than other young men."

Loft said harshly, "What do you mean by defeat? We are not defeated."

And Lanser looked coldly up at him for a long moment and did not speak, and finally Loft's eyes wavered, and he said, "Sir."

"Thank you," said Lanser.

"You don't demand it of the others, sir."

"They don't think about it, so it isn't an insult. When you leave it out, it's insulting."

"Yes, sir," said Loft.

"Go on, now, try to keep Prackle in hand. Start your search. I don't want any shooting unless there's an overt act, do you understand?"

"Yes, sir," said Loft, and he saluted formally and went out of the room.

Hunter regarded Colonel Lanser amusedly. "Weren't you rough on him?"

"I had to be. He's frightened. I know his kind. He has to be disciplined when he's afraid or he'll go to pieces. He relies on discipline the way other men rely on sympathy. I suppose you'd better get to your rails. You might as well expect that to-night is the time when they'll really blow them, though."

Hunter stood up and he said, "Yes. I suppose the orders are coming in from the capital?"

"Yes."

"Are they——?"

"You know what they are," Lanser interrupted. "You know what they'd have to be. Take the leaders, shoot the leaders, take hostages, shoot the hostages, take more hostages, shoot them"—his voice had risen but now it sank almost to a whisper—"and the hatred growing and the hurt between us deeper and deeper."

Hunter hesitated. "Have they condemned any from the list of names?" and he motioned slightly towards the Mayor's bedroom.

Lanser shook his head. "No, not yet. They are just arrested, so far."

Hunter said quietly, "Colonel, do you want me to recommend—maybe you're overtired, Colonel? Could I—you know—could I report that you're overtired?"

For a moment Lanser covered his eyes with his hand, and then his shoulders straightened and his face grew hard. "I'm not a civilian, Hunter. We're short enough of officers already. You know that. Get to your work, Major. I have to see Corell."

Hunter smiled. He went to the door and opened it, and he said out of the door, "Yes, he's here," and over his shoulder he said to Lanser, "It's Prackle. He wants to see you."

"Send him in," said Lanser.

Prackle came in, his face sullen, belligerent. "Colonel Lanser, sir, I wish to——"

"Sit down," said Lanser. "Sit down and rest a moment. Be a good soldier, Lieutenant."

The stiffness went out of Prackle quickly. He sat down beside the table and rested his elbows on it. "I wish——"

And Lanser said, "Don't talk for a moment. I know what it is. You didn't think it would be this way, did you? You thought it would be rather nice."

"They hate us," Prackle said. "They hate us so much."

Lanser smiled. "I wonder if I know what it is. It takes young men to make good soldiers, and young men need young women, is that it?"

"Yes, that's it."

"Well," Lanser said kindly, "does she hate you?"

Prackle looked at him in amazement. "I don't know, sir. Sometimes I think she's only sorry."

"And you're pretty miserable?"

"I don't like it here, sir."

"No, you thought it would be fun, didn't you? Lieutenant Tonder went to pieces and then he went out and they got a knife in him. I could send you home. Do you want to be sent home, knowing we need you here?"

Prackle said uneasily, "No, sir, I don't."

"Good. Now I'll tell you, and I hope you'll understand it. You're not a man any more. You are a soldier. Your comfort is of no importance and, Lieutenant, your life isn't of much importance. If you live, you will have memories. That's about all you will have. Meanwhile you must take orders and carry them out. Most of the orders will be unpleasant, but that's not your business. I will not lie to you, Lieutenant. They should have trained you for this, and not for flower-strewn streets. They should have built your soul with truth, not led it along with lies." His voice grew hard. "But you took the job, Lieutenant. Will you stay with it or quit it? We can't take care of your soul."

Prackle stood up. "Thank you, sir."

"And the girl," Lanser continued, "the girl, Lieutenant, you may rape her, or protect her, or marry her—that is of no importance so long as you shoot her when it is ordered."

Prackle said wearily, "Yes, sir, thank you, sir."

"I assure you it is better to know. I assure you of that. It is better to know. Go now, Lieutenant, and if Corell is still waiting, send him in." And he watched Lieutenant Prackle out of the doorway.

When Mr. Corell came in, he was a changed man. His left arm was in a cast, and he was no longer the jovial, friendly, smiling Corell. His face was sharp and bitter, and his eyes squinted down like little dead pig's eyes.

"I should have come before, Colonel," he said, "but your lack of co-operation made me hesitant."

Lanser said, "You were waiting for a reply to your report, I remember."

"I was waiting for much more than that. You refused me a position of authority. You said I was valueless. You did not realize that I was in this town long before you were. You left the Mayor in his office, contrary to my advice."

Lanser said, "Without him here we might have had more disorder than we have."

"That is a matter of opinion," Corell said. "This man is a leader of a rebellious people."

"Nonsense," said Lanser; "he's just a simple man."

With his good hand Corell took a black note-book from his right pocket and opened it with his fingers. "You forgot, Colonel, that I had my sources, that I had been here a long time before you. I have to report to you that Mayor Orden has been in constant contact with every happening in this community. On the night when Lieutenant Tonder was murdered, he was in the house where the murder was committed. When the girl escaped to the hills, she stayed with one of his relatives. I traced her there, but she was gone. Whenever men have escaped, Orden has known about it and has helped them. And I even strongly suspect that he is somewhere in the picture of these little parachutes."

Lanser said eagerly, "But you can't prove it."

"No," Corell said, "I can't prove it. The first thing I know; the last I only suspect. Perhaps now you will be willing to listen to me."

Lanser said quietly, "What do you suggest?"

"These suggestions, Colonel, are a little stronger than suggestions. Orden must now be a hostage and his life must depend on the peacefulness of this community. His life must depend on the lighting of a single fuse on one single stick of dynamite."

He reached into his pocket again and brought out a little folding book, and he flipped it open and laid it in front of the colonel. "This sir, was the answer to my report from headquarters. You will notice that it gives me certain authority."

Lanser looked at the little book and he spoke quietly: "You really did go over my head, didn't you?" He looked up at Corell with frank dislike in his eyes. "I heard you'd been injured. How did it happen?"

Corell said, "On the night when your lieutenant was murdered I was waylaid. The patrol saved me. Some of the townsmen escaped in my boat that night. Now, Colonel, must I express more strongly than I have that Mayor Orden must be held hostage?"

Lanser said, "He is here, he hasn't escaped. How can we hold him more hostage than we are?"

Suddenly in the distance there was a sound of an explosion, and both men looked around in the direction from which it came. Corell said, "There it is, Colonel, and you know perfectly well that if this experiment succeeds there will be dynamite in every invaded country."

Lanser repeated quietly, "What do you suggest?"

"Just what I have said. Orden must be held against rebellion."

"And if they rebel and we shoot Orden?"

"Then that little doctor is next; although he holds no position, he's next in authority in the town."

"But he holds no office."

"He has the confidence of the people."

"And when we shoot him, what then?"

"Then we have authority. Then rebellion will be broken. When we have killed the leaders, the rebellion will be broken."

Lanser asked quizzically, "Do you really think so?"

"It must be so."

Lanser shook his head slowly and then he called, "Sentry!" The door opened and a soldier appeared in the doorway. "Sergeant," said Lanser, "I have placed Mayor Orden under arrest, and I have placed Doctor Winter under arrest. You will see to it that Orden is guarded and you will bring Winter here immediately."

The sentry said, "Yes, sir."

Lanser looked up at Corell and he said, "You know, I hope you know what you're doing. I do hope you know what you're doing."

CHAPTER VIII

In the little town the news ran quickly. It was communicated by whispers in doorways, by quick, meaningful looks—"The Mayor's been arrested"—and through the town a little quiet jubilance ran, a fierce little jubilance, and people talked quietly together and went apart, and people going in to buy food leaned close to the shopmen for a moment and a word passed between them.

The people went into the country, into the woods, searching for dynamite. And children playing in the snow found the dynamite, and by now even the children had their instructions. They opened the packages and ate the chocolate, and then they buried the dynamite in the snow and told their parents where it was.

Far out in the country a man picked up a tube and read the instructions and he said to himself, "I wonder if this works." He stood the tube up in the snow and lighted the fuse, and he ran back from it and counted, but his count was fast. It was sixty-eight before the dynamite exploded. He said, "It does work," and he went hurriedly about looking for more tubes.

Almost as though at a signal the people went into their houses and the doors were closed, the streets were quiet. At the mine the soldiers carefully searched every miner who went into the shaft, searched and re-searched, and the soldiers were nervous and rough and they spoke harshly to the miners. The miners looked coldly at them, and behind their eyes was a little fierce jubilance.

In the drawing-room of the palace of the Mayor the table had been cleaned up, and a soldier stood guard at Mayor Orden's bedroom door. Annie was on her knees in front of the coal grate, putting little pieces of coal on the fire. She looked up at the sentry standing in front of Mayor Orden's door and she said truculently, "Well, what are you going to do to him?" The soldier did not answer.

The outside door opened and another soldier came in, holding Doctor Winter by the arm. He closed the door behind Doctor Winter and stood against the door inside the room. Doctor Winter said, "Hello, Annie, how's His Excellency?"

And Annie pointed at the bedroom and said, "He's in there."

"He isn't ill?" Doctor Winter said.

"No, he didn't seem to be," said Annie. "I'll see if I can tell him you're here." She went to the sentry and spoke imperiously. "Tell His Excellency that Doctor Winter is here, do you hear me?"

The sentry did not answer and did not move, but behind him the door opened and Mayor Orden stood in the doorway. He ignored the sentry and brushed past him and stepped into the room. For a moment the sentry considered taking him back, and then he returned to his place beside the door. Orden said: "Thank you, Annie. Don't go too far away, will you? I might need you."

Annie said, "No, sir, I won't. Is Madame all right?"

"She's doing her hair. Do you want to see her, Annie?"

"Yes, sir," said Annie, and she brushed past the sentry too, and went into the bedroom and shut the door.

Orden said, "Is there something you want, Doctor?"

Winter grinned sardonically and pointed over his shoulder to his guard. "Well, I guess I'm under arrest. My friend here brought me."

Orden said, "I suppose it was bound to come. What will they do now, I wonder?" And the two men looked at each other for a long time and each one knew what the other one was thinking.

And then Orden continued as though he had been talking. "You know, I couldn't stop it if I wanted to."

"I know," said Winter, "but they don't know." And he went on with a thought he had been having. "A time-minded people," he said, "and the time is nearly up. They think that just because they have only one leader and one head, we are all like that. They know that ten heads lopped off will destroy them, but we are a free people; we have as many heads as we have people, and in a time of need leaders pop up among us like mushrooms."

Orden put his hand on Winter's shoulder and he said, "Thank you. I knew it, but it's good to hear you say it. The little people won't go under, will they?" He searched Winter's face anxiously.

And the doctor reassured him. "Why, no, they won't. As a matter of fact, they will grow stronger with outside help."

The room was silent for a moment. The sentry shifted his position a little and his rifle clinked on a button.

Orden said, "I can talk to you, Doctor, and I probably won't be able to talk again. There are little shameful things in my mind." He coughed and glanced at the rigid soldier, but the soldier gave no sign of having heard. "I have been thinking of my own death. If they follow the usual course, they must kill me, and then they must kill you." And when Winter was silent, he said, "Mustn't they?"

"Yes, I guess so." Winter walked to one of the gilt chairs, and as he was about to sit down he noticed that its tapestry was torn, and he petted the seat with his fingers as though that would mend it. And he sat down gently because it was torn.

And Orden went on, "You know, I'm afraid, I have been thinking of ways to escape, to get out of it. I have been thinking of running away. I have been thinking of pleading for my life, and it makes me ashamed."

And Winter, looking up, said, "But you haven't done it."

"No, I haven't."

"And you won't do it."

Orden hesitated. "No, I won't. But I have thought of it."

And Winter said, gently, "How do you know everyone doesn't think of it? How do you know I haven't thought of it?"

"I wonder why they arrested you too," Orden said. "I guess they will have to kill you too."

"I guess so," said Winter. He rolled his thumbs and watched them tumble over and over.

"You know so." Orden was silent for a moment and then he said, "You know, Doctor, I am a little man and this is a little town, but there must be a spark in little men that can burst into flame. I am afraid, I am terribly afraid, and I thought of all the things I might do to save my own life, and then that went away, and sometimes now I feel a kind of exultation, as though I were bigger and better than I am, and do you know what I have been thinking, Doctor?" He smiled, remembering. "Do you remember in school, in the *Apology*? Do you remember Socrates says: 'Someone will say, "And are you not ashamed, Socrates, of a course of life which is likely to bring you to an untimely end?" To him I may fairly answer, "There you are mistaken: a man who is good for anything ought not to calculate the chance of living or dying; he ought only to consider whether he is doing right or wrong." ' " Orden paused, trying to remember.

Doctor Winter sat tensely forward now, and he went on with it: " 'Acting the part of a good man or of a bad.' I don't think you have it quite right. You never were a good scholar. You were wrong in the denunciation, too."

Orden chuckled. "Do you remember that?"

"Yes," said Winter, eagerly, "I remember it well. You forgot a line or a word. It was graduation, and you were so excited you forgot to tuck in your shirt-tail and your shirt-tail was out. You wondered why they laughed."

Orden smiled to himself, and his hand went secretly behind him and patrolled for a loose shirt-tail. "I was Socrates," he said, "and I denounced the School Board. How I denounced them! I bellowed it, and I could see them grow red."

Winter said, "They were holding their breaths to keep from laughing. Your shirt-tail was out."

Mayor Orden laughed. "How long ago? Forty years."

"Forty-six."

The sentry by the bedroom door moved quietly over to the sentry by the outside door. They spoke softly out of the corners of their mouths like children whispering in school. "How long you been on duty?"

"All night. Can't hardly keep my eyes open."

"Me too. Hear from your wife on the boat yesterday?"

"Yes! She said say hello to you. Said she heard you was wounded. She don't write much."

"Tell her I'm all right."

"Sure—when I write."

The Mayor raised his head and looked at the ceiling and he muttered, "Um—um—um. I wonder if I can remember—how does it go?"

And Winter prompted him, " 'And now, O men——' "

And Orden said softly, " 'And now, O men who have condemned me——' "

Colonel Lanser came quietly into the room; the sentries stiffened. Hearing the words, the colonel stopped and listened.

Orden looked at the ceiling, lost in trying to remember the old words. " 'And now, O men who have condemned me,' " he said, " 'I would fain prophesy to you—for I am about to die—and—in the hour of death—men are gifted with prophetic power. And I—prophesy to you who are my murderers—that immediately after my—my death——' "

And Winter stood up, saying, "Departure."

Orden looked at him. "What?"

And Winter said, "The word is 'departure', not 'death'. You made the same mistake before. You made that mistake forty-six years ago."

"No, it is death. It is death." Orden looked around and saw Colonel Lanser watching him. He asked, "Isn't it 'death'?"

Colonel Lanser said, " 'Departure.' It is 'immediately after my departure.' "

Doctor Winter insisted, "You see, that's two against one. 'Departure' is the word. It is the same mistake you made before."

Then Orden looked straight ahead and his eyes were in his memory, seeing nothing outward. And he went on: " 'I prophesy to you who are my murderers that immediately after my—departure punishment far heavier than you have inflicted on me will surely await you.' "

Winter nodded encouragingly, and Colonel Lanser nodded, and they seemed to be trying to help him to remember. And Orden went on: " 'Me you have killed because you wanted to escape the accuser, and not to give an account of your lives——' "

Lieutenant Prackle entered excitedly, crying, "Colonel Lanser!"

Colonel Lanser said, "Shh——" and he held out his hand to restrain him.

And Orden went on softly, " 'But that will not be as you suppose; far otherwise.' " His voice grew stronger. " 'For I say that there will be more accusers of you than there are now' "—he made a little gesture with his hand, a speech-making gesture—" 'accusers whom hitherto I have restrained; and as they are younger they will be more inconsiderate with you, and you will be more offended at them.' " He frowned, trying to remember.

And Lieutenant Prackle said, "Colonel Lanser, we have found some men with dynamite."

And Lanser said, "Hush."

Orden continued. " 'If you think that by killing men you can prevent someone from censuring your evil lives you are mistaken.' " He frowned and thought and he looked at the ceiling, and he smiled embarrassedly and he said, "That's all I can remember. It is gone away from me."

And Doctor Winter said, "It's very good after forty-six years, and you weren't very good at it forty-six years ago."

Lieutenant Prackle broke in, "The men have dynamite, Colonel Lanser."

"Did you arrest them?"

"Yes, sir. Captain Loft and——"

Lanser said, "Tell Captain Loft to guard them." He recaptured himself and he advanced into the room and he said, "Orden, these things must stop."

And the Mayor smiled helplessly at him. "They cannot stop, sir."

Colonel Lanser said harshly, "I arrested you as a hostage for the good behaviour of your people. Those are my orders."

"But that won't stop it," Orden said simply. "You don't understand. When I have become a hindrance to the people, they will do without me."

Lanser said, "Tell me truly what you think. If the people know that you will be shot if they light another fuse, what will they do?"

The Mayor looked helplessly at Doctor Winter. And then the

bedroom door opened and Madame came out, carrying the Mayor's chain of office in her hand. She said, "You forgot this."

Orden said, "What? Oh, yes," and he stooped his head and Madame slipped the chain of office over his head, and he said, "Thank you, my dear."

Madame complained, "You always forget it. You forget it all the time."

The Mayor looked at the end of the chain he held in his hand—the gold medallion with the insignia of his office carved on it. Lanser pressed him: "What will they do?"

"I don't know," said the Mayor. "I think they will light the fuse."

"Suppose you ask them not to?"

Winter said, "Colonel, this morning I saw a little boy building a snow man, while three grown soldiers watched to see that he did not caricature your leader. He made a pretty good likeness, too, before they destroyed it."

Lanser ignored the doctor. "Suppose you ask them not to?" he repeated.

Orden seemed half asleep; his eyes were drooped, and he tried to think. He said, "I am not a very brave man, sir. I think they will light it, anyway." He struggled with his speech. "I hope they will, but if I ask them not to, they will be sorry."

Madame said, "What is this all about?"

"Be quiet a moment, dear," the Mayor said.

"But you think they will light it?" Lanser insisted.

The Mayor spoke proudly, "Yes, they will light it. I have no choice of living or dying, you see, sir, but—I do have a choice of how I do it. If I tell them not to fight, they will be sorry, but they will fight. If I tell them to fight, they will be glad, and I who am not a very brave man will have made them a little braver." He smiled apologetically. "You see, it is an easy thing to do, since the end for me is the same."

Lanser said, "If you say yes, we can tell them you said no. We can tell them you begged for your life."

And Winter broke in angrily, "They would know. You do not keep secrets. One of your men got out of hand one night and he said the flies had conquered the flypaper, and now the whole nation knows his words. They have made a song of it. The flies have conquered the flypaper. You do not keep secrets, Colonel."

From the direction of the mine a whistle tooted shrilly. And a quick gust of wind sifted dry snow against the windows.

Orden fingered his gold medallion. He said quietly, "You see, sir, nothing can change it. You will be destroyed and driven out." His voice was very soft. "The people don't like to be conquered, sir, and so they will not be. Free men cannot start a war, but once it is started, they can fight on in defeat. Herd men, followers of a leader, cannot do that, and so it is always the herd men who win battles and the free men who win wars. You will find that is so, sir."

Lanser was erect and stiff. "My orders are clear. Eleven o'clock was the deadline. I have taken hostages. If there is violence, the hostages will be executed."

And Doctor Winter said to the colonel, "Will you carry out the orders, knowing they will fail?"

Lanser's face was tight. "I will carry out my orders no matter what they are, but I do think, sir, a proclamation from you might save many lives."

Madame broke in plaintively, "I wish you would tell me what all this nonsense is."

"It is nonsense, dear."

"But they can't arrest the Mayor," she explained to him.

Orden smiled at her. "No," he said, "they can't arrest the Mayor. The Mayor is an idea conceived by free men. It will escape arrest."

From the distance there was a sound of an explosion, and the echo of it rolled to the hills and back again. The whistle at the coal-mine tooted a shrill, sharp warning. Orden stood very tensely for a moment and then he smiled. A second explosion roared—nearer this time and heavier—and its echo rolled back from the mountains. Orden looked at his watch and then he took his watch and chain and put them in Doctor Winter's hand. "How did it go about the flies?" he asked.

"The flies have conquered the flypaper," Winter said.

Orden called, "Annie!" The bedroom door opened instantly and the Mayor said, "Were you listening?"

"Yes, sir." Annie was embarrassed.

And now an explosion roared near by and there was a sound of splintering wood and breaking glass, and the door behind the sentries puffed open. And Orden said, "Annie, I want you to stay with Madame as long as she needs you. Don't leave her alone." He put his arm around Madame and he kissed her on the forehead and then he moved slowly towards the door where Lieutenant Prackle stood. In the doorway he turned back to Doctor Winter. "Crito, I owe a cock to Asclepius," he said tenderly. "Will you remember to pay the debt?"

Winter closed his eyes for a moment before he answered, "The debt shall be paid."

Orden chuckled then. "I remembered that one. I didn't forget that one." He put his hand on Prackle's arm, and the lieutenant flinched away from him.

And Winter nodded slowly. "Yes, you remembered. The debt shall be paid."

CANNERY ROW

For Ed Ricketts

who knows why or should

CANNERY Row in Monterey in California is a poem, a stink, a grating noise, a quality of light, a tone, a habit, a nostalgia, a dream. Cannery Row is the gathered and scattered, tin and iron and rust and splintered wood, chipped pavement and weedy lots and junk-heaps, sardine canneries of corrugated iron, honky-tonks, restaurants and whore-houses, and little crowded groceries, and laboratories and flop-houses. Its inhabitants are, as the man once said, "Whores, pimps, gamblers, and sons of bitches," by which he meant Everybody. Had the man looked through another peep-hole he might have said, "Saints and angels and martyrs and holy men," and he would have meant the same thing.

In the morning when the sardine fleet has made a catch, the purse-seiners waddle heavily into the bay blowing their whistles. The deep-laden boats pull in against the coast where the canneries dip their tails into the bay. The figure is advisedly chosen, for if the canneries dipped their mouths into the bay the canned sardines which merged from the other end would be, metaphorically at least, even more horrifying. Then cannery whistles scream and all over the town men and women scramble into their clothes and come running down to the Row to go to work. Then shining cars bring the upper classes down: superintendents, accountants, owners, who disappear into offices. Then from the town pour Wops and Chinamen and Polaks, men and women in trousers and rubber coats and oilcloth aprons. They come running to clean and cut and pack and cook and can the fish. The whole street rumbles and groans and screams and rattles while the silver rivers of fish pour in out of the boats and the boats rise higher and higher in the water until they are empty. The canneries rumble and rattle and squeak until the last fish is cleaned and cut and cooked and canned, and then the whistles scream again and the dripping, smelly, tired Wops and Chinamen and Polaks, men and women, struggle out and droop their ways up the hill into the town and Cannery Row becomes itself again—quiet and magical. Its normal life returns. The bums who retired in disgust under the black cypress tree come out to sit on the rusty pipes in the vacant lot. The girls from Dora's emerge for a bit of sun if there is any. Doc strolls from the Western Biological Laboratory and crosses the street to Lee Chong's grocery for two quarts of beer. Henri the painter noses like an Airedale through the junk in the grass-grown lot for some part or piece of wood or metal he needs for the boat he is building. Then the darkness edges in and the street light comes on in front of Dora's—the lamp which makes perpetual moonlight in Cannery Row. Callers arrive at Western Biological to see Doc, and he crosses the street to Lee Chong's for five quarts of beer.

How can the poem and the stink and the grating noise—the quality of light, the tone, the habit and the dream—be set down alive? When you collect marine animals there are certain flat worms so delicate that they are almost impossible to capture whole, for they break and tatter under the touch. You must let them ooze and crawl of their own will on to a knife blade and then lift them gently into your bottle of sea water. And perhaps that might be the way to write this book—to open the page and to let the stories crawl in by themselves.

CHAPTER I

LEE CHONG's grocery, while not a model of neatness, was a miracle of supply. It was small and crowded, but within its single room a man could find everything he needed or wanted to live and to be happy—clothes, food, both fresh and canned, liquor, tobacco, fishing equipment, machinery, boats, cordage, caps, pork chops. You could buy at Lee Chong's a pair of slippers, a silk kimono, a quarter-pint of whisky and a cigar. You could work out combinations to fit almost any mood. The one commodity Lee Chong did not keep could be had across the lot at Dora's.

The grocery opened at dawn and did not close until the last wandering vagrant dime had been spent or retired for the night. Not that Lee Chong was avaricious. He wasn't, but if one wanted to spend money, he was available. Lee's position in the community surprised him as much as he could be surprised. Over the course of the years everyone in Cannery Row owed him money. He never pressed his clients, but when the bill became too large, Lee cut off credit. Rather than walk into the town up the hill, the client usually paid or tried to.

Lee was round-faced and courteous. He spoke a stately English without ever using the letter R. When the tong wars were going on in California, it happened now and then that Lee found a price on his head. Then he would go secretly to San Francisco and enter a hospital until the trouble blew over. What he did with his money, no one ever knew. Perhaps he didn't get it. Maybe his wealth was entirely in unpaid bills. But he lived well and he had the respect of all his neighbours. He trusted his clients until further trust became ridiculous. Sometimes he made business errors, but even these he turned to advantage in good-will if in no other way. It was that way with the Palace Flop-house and Grill. Anyone but Lee Chong would have considered the transaction a total loss.

Lee Chong's station in the grocery was behind the cigar counter. The cash register was then on his left and the abacus on his right. Inside the glass case were the brown cigars, the cigarettes, the Bull Durham, the Duke's mixture, the Five Brothers, while behind him in racks on the wall were the pints, half-pints and quarters of Old Green River, Old Town House, Old Colonel, and the favourite—Old Tennessee, a blended whisky guaranteed four months old, very cheap and known in the neighbourhood as Old Tennis Shoes. Lee Chong did not stand between the whisky and the customer without reason. Some very practical minds had on occasion tried to divert his attention to another part of the store. Cousins, nephews, sons and daughters-in-law waited on the rest of the store, but Lee never left the cigar counter. The top of the glass was his desk. His fat delicate hands rested on the glass, the fingers moving like small, restless sausages. A broad golden wedding-ring on the middle finger of his left hand was his only jewellery and with it he silently tapped on the rubber change mat from which the little rubber tits had long been worn. Lee's mouth was full and benevolent and the flash of gold when he smiled was rich and warm. He wore half-glasses and since he looked at everything through them, he had to tilt his head back to see in the distance. Interest and discounts, addition, subtraction he worked out on the abacus with his little restless sausage fingers, and his brown, friendly eyes roved over the grocery and his teeth flashed at the customers.

On an evening when he stood in his place on a pad of newspaper to keep his feet warm, he contemplated with humour and sadness a business deal that had been consummated that afternoon and re-consummated later that same afternoon. When you leave the grocery, if you walk catty-cornered across the grass-grown lot, threading your way among the great rusty pipes thrown out of the canneries, you will see a path worn in the weeds. Follow it past the cypress tree, across the railroad track, up a chicken-walk with cleats, and you will come to a long, low building which for a long time was used as a storage place for fish-meal. It was just a great big roofed room and it belonged to a worried gentleman named Horace Abbeville. Horace had two wives and six children, and over a period of years he had managed through pleading and persuasion to build a grocery debt second to none in Monterey. That afternoon he had come into the grocery and his sensitive, tired face had flinched at the shadow of sternness that crossed Lee's face. Lee's fat finger tapped the rubber mat. Horace laid his hands palm up on the cigar counter. "I guess I owe you plenty dough," he said simply.

Lee's teeth flashed up in appreciation of an approach so different from any he had ever heard. He nodded gravely, but he waited for the trick to develop.

Horace wet his lips with his tongue, a good job from corner to corner. "I hate to have my kids with that hanging over them," he said. "Why, I bet you wouldn't let them have a pack of spearmint now."

Lee Chong's face agreed with this conclusion. "Plenty dough," he said.

Horace continued, "You know that place of mine across the track up there where the fish-meal is."

Lee Chong nodded. It was his fish-meal.

Horace said earnestly, "If I was to give you that place—would it clear me up with you?"

Lee Chong tilted his head back and stared at Horace through his half-glasses while his mind flicked among accounts and his right hand moved restlessly to the abacus. He considered the construction, which was flimsy, and the lot, which might be valuable if a cannery ever wanted to expand. "Shu," said Lee Chong.

"Well, get out the accounts and I'll make you a bill of sale on that place." Horace seemed in a hurry.

"No need papers," said Lee. "I make paid-in-full paper."

They finished the deal with dignity and Lee Chong threw in a quarter-pint of Old Tennis Shoes. And then Horace Abbeville, walking very straight, went across the lot and past the cypress tree and across the track and up the chicken-walk and into the building that had been his, and he shot himself on a heap of fish-meal. And although it has nothing to do with this story, no Abbeville child, no matter who its mother was, knew the lack of a stick of spearmint ever afterward.

But to get back to the evening. Horace was on the trestles with the embalming needles in him, and his two wives were sitting on the steps of his house with their arms about each other (they were good friends until after the funeral, and then they divided up the children and never spoke to each other again). Lee Chong stood behind the cigar counter and his nice brown eyes were turned inward on a calm and eternal Chinese sorrow. He knew he could not have helped it, but he wished he might have known and perhaps tried to help. It was deeply a part of Lee's kindness and understanding that man's right to kill himself is inviolable, but sometimes a friend can make it unnecessary. Lee had already underwritten the funeral and sent a wash-basket of groceries to the stricken families.

Now Lee Chong owned the Abbeville building—a good roof, a good floor, two windows and a door. True it was piled high with fish-meal and the smell of it was delicate and penetrating. Lee

Chong considered it as a storehouse for groceries, as a kind of warehouse, but he gave that up on second thought. It was too far away and anyone can go in through a window. He was tapping the rubber mat with his gold ring and considering the problem when the door opened and Mack came in. Mack was the elder, leader, mentor, and to a small extent the exploiter of a little group of men who had in common no families, no money, and no ambitions beyond food, drink and contentment. But whereas most men in their search for contentment destroy themselves and fall wearily short of their targets, Mack and his friends approached contentment casually, quietly, and absorbed it gently. Mack and Hazel, a young man of great strength, Eddie, who filled in as a bar-tender at "La Ida", Hughie and Jones, who occasionally collected frogs and cats for Western Biological, were currently living in those large rusty pipes in the lot next to Lee Chong's. That is, they lived in the pipes when it was damp, but in fine weather they lived in the shadow of the black cypress tree at the top of the lot. The limbs folded down and made a canopy under which a man could lie and look out at the flow and vitality of Cannery Row.

Lee Chong stiffened ever so slightly when Mack came in and his eyes glanced quickly about the store to make sure that Eddie or Hazel or Hughie or Jones had not come in too and drifted away among the groceries.

Mack laid out his cards with a winning honesty. "Lee," he said, "I and Eddie and the rest heard you own the Abbeville place."

Lee Chong nodded and waited.

"I and my friends thought we'd ast you if we could move in there. We'll keep up the property," he added quickly. "Wouldn't let anybody break in or hurt anything. Kids might knock out the windows, you know——" Mack suggested. "Place might burn down if somebody don't keep an eye on it."

Lee tilted his head back and looked into Mack's eyes through the half-glasses and Lee's tapping finger slowed its tempo as he thought deeply. In Mack's eyes there was good-will and good-fellowship and a desire to make everyone happy. Why then did Lee Chong feel slightly surrounded? Why did his mind pick its way as delicately as a cat through cactus? It had been sweetly done, almost in a spirit of philanthropy. Lee's mind leaped ahead at the possibilities—no, they were probabilities, and his finger-tapping slowed still further. He saw himself refusing Mack's request and he saw the broken glass from the windows. Then Mack would offer a second time to watch over and preserve Lee's property—and at the second refusal, Lee could smell the smoke, could see the little flames creeping up the walls. Mack and his friends would try to help to put it out. Lee's finger came to a gentle rest on the change-mat. He was beaten. He knew that. There was left to him only the possibility of saving face, and Mack was likely to be very generous about that. Lee said, "You like pay lent my place? You like live there same hotel?"

Mack smiled broadly and he was generous. "Say——" he cried. "That's an idear. Sure. How much?"

Lee considered. He knew it didn't matter what he charged. He wasn't going to get it, anyway. He might just as well make it a really sturdy face-saving sum. "Fi' dolla' week," said Lee.

Mack played it through to the end. "I'll have to talk to the boys about it," he said dubiously. "Couldn't you make that four dollars a week?"

"Fi' dolla'," said Lee firmly.

"Well, I'll see what the boys say," said Mack.

And that was the way it was. Everyone was happy about it. And if it be thought that Lee Chong suffered a total loss, at least his mind did not work that way. The windows were not broken. Fire did not break out, and while no rent was ever paid, if the tenants ever had any money, and quite often they did have, it never occurred to them to spend it anywhere except at Lee Chong's grocery. What he had was a little group of active and potential customers under wraps. But it went further than that. If a drunk caused trouble in the grocery, if the kids swarmed down from New Monterey intent on plunder, Lee Chong had only to call and his tenants rushed to his aid. One further bond is established—you cannot steal from your benefactor. The saving to Lee Chong in cans of beans and tomatoes and milk and water-melons more than paid the rent. And if there was a sudden and increased leakage among the groceries in New Monterey, that was none of Lee Chong's affair.

The boys moved in and the fish-meal moved out. No one knows who named the house that has been known ever after as the Palace Flop-house Grill. In the pipes and under the cypress tree there had been no room for furniture and the little niceties which are not only the diagnoses but the boundaries of our civilization. Once in the Palace Flop-house, the boys set about furnishing it. A chair appeared and a cot and another chair. A hardware store supplied a can of red paint not reluctantly, because it never knew about it, and as a new table or footstool appeared it was painted, which not only made it very pretty but also disguised it to a certain extent in case a former owner looked in. And the Palace Flop-house and Grill began to function. The boys could sit in front of their door and look down across the track and across the lot and across the street right into the front windows of Western Biological. They could hear the music from the laboratory at night. And their eyes followed Doc across the street when he went to Lee Chong's for beer. And Mack said, "That Doc is a fine fellow. We ought to do something for him."

CHAPTER II

THE WORD is a symbol and a delight which sucks up men and scenes, trees, plants, factories, and Pekingese. Then the Thing becomes the Word and back to Thing again, but warped and woven into a fantastic pattern. The Word sucks up Cannery Row, digests it and spews it out, and the Row has taken the shimmer of the green world and the sky-reflecting seas. Lee Chong is more than a Chinese grocer. He must be. Perhaps he is evil balanced and held suspended by good—an Asiatic planet held to its orbit by the pull of Lao Tze and held away from Lao Tze by the centrifugality of abacus and cash register—Lee Chong suspended, spinning, whirling among groceries and ghosts. A hard man with a can of beans—a soft man with the bones of his grandfather. For Lee Chong dug into the grave on China Point and found the yellow bones, the skull with grey ropy hair still sticking to it. And Lee carefully packed the bones, femurs, and tibias really straight, skull in the middle, with pelvis and clavicle surrounding it and ribs curving on either side. Then Lee Chong sent his boxed and brittle grandfather over the western sea to lie at last in ground made holy by his ancestors.

Mack and the boys, too, spinning in their orbits. They are the Virtues, the Graces, the Beauties of the hurried mangled craziness of Monterey and the cosmic Monterey where men in fear and hunger destroy their stomachs in the fight to secure certain food, where men hungering for love destroy everything lovable about them. Mack and the boys are the Beauties, the Virtues, the Graces. In the world ruled by tigers with ulcers, rutted by strictured bulls, scavenged by blind jackals, Mack and the boys dine delicately with the tigers, fondle the frantic heifers, and wrap up the crumbs to feed the seagulls of Cannery Row. What can it profit a man to gain the whole world and to come to his property with a gastric ulcer, a blown prostate, and bifocals? Mack and the boys avoid the trap, walk around the poison, step over the noose, while a generation of trapped, poisoned, and trussed-up men scream at them and call them no-goods, come-to-bad-ends, blots-on-the-town, thieves, rascals, bums. Our Father who art in nature, who has given the gift of survival to the coyote, the common brown rat, the English sparrow, the house-fly and the moth, must have a great and overwhelming love for no-goods and blots-on-the-town and bums, and Mack and the boys. Virtues and graces and laziness and zest. Our Father who art in nature.

CHAPTER III

Lee Chong's is to the right of the vacant lot (although why it is called vacant when it is piled high with old boilers, with rusting pipes, with great square timbers, and stacks of five-gallon cans, no one can say). In the rear of the vacant lot is the railroad track and the Palace Flop-house. But on the left-hand boundary of the lot is the stern and stately whore-house of Dora Flood; a decent, clean, honest, old-fashioned sporting house where a man can take a glass of beer among friends. This is no fly-by-night cheap clip-joint, but a sturdy, virtuous club, built, maintained, and disciplined by Dora, who, madam and girl for fifty years, has through the exercise of special gifts of tact and honesty, charity and a certain realism, made herself respected by the intelligent, the learned, and the kind. And by the same token she is hated by the twisted and lascivious sisterhood of married spinsters whose husbands respect the home but don't like it very much.

Dora is a great woman, a great big woman with flaming orange hair and a taste for Nile-green evening dresses. She keeps an honest, one-price house, sells no hard liquor, and permits no loud or vulgar talk in her house. Of her girls some are fairly inactive, due to age and infirmities, but Dora never puts them aside, although, as she says, some of them don't turn three tricks a month, but they go right on eating three meals a day. In a moment of local love, Dora named her place the Bear Flag Restaurant and the stories are many of people who have gone in for a sandwich. There are normally twelve girls in the house, counting the old ones, a Greek cook, and a man who is known as a watchman, but who undertakes all manner of delicate and dangerous tasks. He stops fights, ejects drunks, soothes hysteria and cures headaches, and tends bar. He bandages cuts and bruises, passes the time of day with cops, and, since a good half of the girls are Christian Scientists, reads aloud his share of *Science and Health* on a Sunday morning. His predecessor, being a less well-balanced man, came to an evil end, as shall be reported, but Alfred has triumphed over his environment and has brought his environment up with him. He knows what men should be there and what men shouldn't be there. He knows more about the home life of Monterey citizens than anyone in town.

As for Dora—she leads a ticklish existence. Being against the law, at least against its letter, she must be twice as law-abiding as anyone else. There must be no drunks, no fighting, no vulgarity, or they close Dora up. Also, being illegal, Dora must be especially philanthropic. Everyone puts the bite on her. If the police give a dance for their pension fund and everyone else gives a dollar, Dora has to give fifty dollars. When the Chamber of Commerce improved its gardens, the merchants each gave five dollars, but Dora was asked for and gave a hundred. With everything else it is the same—Red Cross, Community Chest, Boy Scouts—Dora's unsung, unpublicized, shameless dirty wages of sin lead the list of donations. But during the depression she was hardest hit. In addition to the usual charities, Dora saw the hungry children of Cannery Row and the jobless fathers and the worried women, and Dora paid grocery bills right and left for two years and very nearly went broke in the process. Dora's girls are well trained and pleasant. They never speak to a man on the street although he may have been in the night before.

Before Alfy, the present watchman, took over, there was a tragedy in the Bear Flag Restaurant which saddened everyone. The previous watchman was named William, and he was a dark and lonesome-looking man. In the day-time when his duties were few he would grow tired of female company. Through the windows he could see Mack and the boys sitting on the pipes in the vacant lot, dangling their feet in the mallow weeds and taking the sun while they discoursed slowly and philosophically of matters of interest but of no importance. Now and then as he watched them he saw them take out a pint of Old Tennis Shoes and, wiping the neck of the bottle on a sleeve, raise the pint one after another. And William began to wish he could join that good group. He walked out one day and sat on the pipe. Conversation stopped and an uneasy and hostile silence fell on the group. After a while William went disconsolately back to the Bear Flag, and through the window he saw the conversation spring up again, and it saddened him. He had a dark and ugly face and a mouth twisted with brooding.

The next day he went again and this time he took a pint of whisky. Mack and the boys drank the whisky—after all they weren't crazy, but all the talking they did was "Good luck", and "Lookin' at you."

After a while William went back to the Bear Flag and he watched them through the window, and he heard Mack raise his voice saying, "But God damn it, I hate a pimp!" Now this was obviously untrue, although William didn't know that. Mack and the boys just didn't like William.

Now William's heart broke. The bums would not receive him socially. They felt that he was too far beneath them. William had always been introspective and self-accusing. He put on his hat and walked out along the sea, clear out to the Lighthouse. And he stood in the pretty little cemetery where you can hear the waves drumming always. William thought dark and broody thoughts. No one loved him. No one cared about him. They might call him a watchman, but he was a pimp—a dirty pimp, the lowest thing in the world. And then he thought how he had a right to live and be happy just like anyone else, by God he had. He walked back angrily, but his anger went away when he came to the Bear Flag and climbed the steps. It was evening and the juke-box was playing "Harvest Moon" and William remembered that the first hooker who ever gaffed for him used to like that song before she ran away and got married and disappeared. The song made him awfully sad. Dora was in the back parlour having a cup of tea when William came in. She said, "What's the matter, you sick?"

"No," said William. "But what's the percentage? I feel lousy. I think I'll bump myself off."

Dora had handled plenty of neurotics in her time. Kid 'em out of it was her motto. "Well, do it on your own time and don't mess up the rugs," she said.

A grey, damp cloud folded over William's heart and he walked slowly out and down the hall and knocked on Eva Flanagan's door. She had red hair and went to confession every week. Eva was quite a spiritual girl with a big family of brothers and sisters, but she was an unpredictable drunk. She was painting her nails and messing them pretty badly when William went in, and he knew she was bagged and Dora wouldn't let a bagged girl work. Her fingers were nail-polish to the first joint and she was angry. "What's eating you?" she said. William grew angry too. "I'm going to bump myself off," he said fiercely.

Eva screeched at him. "That's a dirty, lousy, stinking sin," she cried, and then, "Wouldn't it be like you to get the joint pinched just when I got almost enough kick to take a trip to East St. Louis. You're a no-good bastard." She was still screaming at him when William shut her door after him and went to the kitchen. He was very tired of women. The Greek would be restful after women.

The Greek, big apron, sleeves rolled up, was frying pork chops in two big skillets, turning them over with an ice-pick. "Hello, Kits. How is going things?" The pork chops hissed and swished in the pan.

"I don't know, Lou," said William. "Sometimes I think the best thing to do would be—kluck!" He drew his finger across his throat.

The Greek laid the ice-pick on the stove and rolled his sleeves higher. "I tell you what I hear, Kits," he said. "I hear like the fella talks about it don't never do it." William's hand went out for the ice-pick and he held it easily in his hand. His eyes looked deeply into the Greek's dark eyes, and he saw disbelief and amusement, and then as he stared the Greek's eyes grew troubled and then worried. And William saw the change, saw first how the Greek knew he could do it and then the Greek knew he would do it. As soon as he saw that in the Greek's eyes William knew he had to do it. He was sad because now it seemed silly. His hand rose and the ice-pick snapped into his heart. It was amazing how easily it went in. William was the watchman before Alfred came. Everyone liked Alfred. He could sit on the pipes with Mack and the boys any time. He could even visit up at the Palace Flop-house.

CHAPTER IV

IN THE evening just at dusk, a curious thing happened on Cannery Row. It happened in the time between sunset and the lighting of the street light. There is a small, quiet, grey period then. Down the hill, past the Palace Flop-house, down the chicken-walk and through the vacant lot came an old Chinaman. He wore an ancient flat straw hat, blue jeans, both coat and trousers, and heavy shoes of which one sole was loose so that it slapped the ground when he walked. In his hand he carried a covered wicker basket. His face was lean and brown and corded and jerky and his old eyes were brown, even the whites were brown and deep-set so that they looked out of holes. He came by just at dusk and crossed the street and went through the opening between Western Biological and the Hediondo Cannery. Then he crossed the little beach and disappeared among the piles and steel posts which support the piers. No one saw him again until dawn.

But in the dawn, during the time when the street light has been turned off and the daylight has not come, the old Chinaman crept out from among the piles, crossed the beach and the street. His wicker basket was heavy and wet and dripping now. His loose sole flap-flapped on the street. He went up the hill to the second street, went through a gate in a high board fence and was not seen again until evening. People, sleeping, heard his flapping shoe go by and they awakened for a moment. It had been happening for years, but no one ever got used to him. Some people thought he was God and very old people thought he was Death and children thought he was a very funny old Chinaman, as children always think anything old and strange is funny. But the children did not taunt him or shout at him as they should, for he carried a little cloud of fear about with him.

Only one brave and beautiful boy of ten named Andy from Salinas ever crossed the old Chinaman. Andy was visiting in Monterey, and he saw the old man and knew he must shout at him if only to keep his self-respect, but even Andy, brave as he was, felt the little cloud of fear. Andy watched him go by evening after evening, while his duty and his terror wrestled. And then one evening Andy braced himself and marched behind the old man singing in a shrill falsetto: "Ching-Chong Chinaman sitting on a rail—'Long came a white man an' chopped off his tail."

The old man stopped and turned. Andy stopped. The deep-brown eyes looked at Andy and the thin corded lips moved. What happened then Andy was never able either to explain or to forget. For the eyes spread out until there was no Chinaman. And then it was one eye—one huge brown eye as big as a church door. Andy looked through the shiny transparent brown door and through it he saw a lonely countryside, flat for miles but ending against a row of fantastic mountains shaped like cows' and dogs' heads and tents and mushrooms. There was low, coarse grass on the plain and here and there a little mound. And a small animal like a woodchuck sat on each mound. And the loneliness—the desolate cold aloneness of the landscape made Andy whimper because there wasn't anybody at all in the world and he was left. Andy shut his eyes so he wouldn't have to see it any more and when he opened them, he was in Cannery Row and the old Chinaman was just flip-flapping between Western Biological and the Hediondo Cannery. Andy was the only boy who ever did that, and he never did it again.

CHAPTER V

Western Biological was right across the street and facing the vacant lot. Lee Chong's grocery was on its catty-corner right and Dora's Bear Flag Restaurant was on its catty-corner left. Western Biological deals in strange and beautiful wares. It sells the lovely animals of the sea, the sponges, tunicates, anemones, the stars and buttle-stars, the sun-stars, the bivalves, barnacles, the worm and shells, the fabulous and multiform little brothers, the living, moving flowers of the sea, nudibranchs and tectibranchs, the spiked and nobbed and needly urchins, the crabs and demi-crabs, the little dragons, the snapping shrimps, and ghost shrimps so transparent that they hardly throw a shadow. And Western Biological sells bugs and snails and spiders, and rattlesnakes, and rats, and honey bees, and gila monsters. These are all for sale. Then there are little unborn humans, some whole and others sliced thin and mounted on slides. And for students there are sharks with the blood drained out and yellow and blue colour substituted in veins and arteries, so that you may follow the systems with a scalpel. And there are cats with coloured veins and arteries, and frogs the same. You can order anything living from Western Biological and sooner or later you will get it.

It is a low building facing the street. The basement is the storeroom with shelves, shelves clear to the ceiling, loaded with jars o preserved animals. And in the basement is a sink and instrument for embalming and for injecting. Then you go through the backyard to a covered shed on piles over the ocean and here are the tanks for the larger animals, the sharks and rays and octopi, each in their concrete tanks. There is a stairway up the front of the building and a door that opens into an office where there is a desk piled high with unopened mail, filing cabinets, and a safe with the door propped open. Once the safe got locked by mistake and no one knew the combination. And in the safe was an open can of sardines and a piece of Roquefort cheese. Before the combination could be sent by the maker of the lock, there was trouble in the safe. It was then that Doc devised a method for getting revenge on a bank if anyone should ever want to. "Rent a safety-deposit box," he said, "then deposit in it one whole fresh salmon and go away for six months." After the trouble with the safe, it was not permitted to keep food there any more. It is kept in the filing cabinets. Behind the office is a room where in aquaria are many living animals; there are also the microscopes and the slides and the drug cabinets, the cases of laboratory glass, the work-benches and little motor, the chemicals. From this room come smells—formalin, and dry starfish, and sea water and menthol, carbolic acid and acetic acid, smell of brown wrapping-paper and straw and rope, smell of chloroform and ether, smell of ozone from the motors, smell of fine steel and thin lubricant from the microscopes, smell of banana oil and rubber tubing, smell of drying wool socks, and boots, sharp pungent smell of rattlesnakes, and musty, frightening smell of rats. And through the back door comes the smell of kelp and barnacles when the tide is out and the smell of salt and spray when the tide is in.

To the left the office opens into a library. The walls are bookcases to the ceiling, boxes of pamphlets and separates, books of all kinds, dictionaries, encyclopaedias, poetry, plays. A great phonograph stands against the wall with hundreds of records lined up beside it. Under the window is a redwood bed and on the walls and to the bookcases are pinned reproductions of Daumiers, and Graham, Titian, and Leonardo and Picasso, Dali and George Grosz, pinned here and there at eye-level, so that you can look at them if you want to. There are chairs and benches in this little room and of course the bed. As many as forty people have been here at one time.

Behind this library or music-room, or whatever you want to call it, is the kitchen, a narrow chamber with a gas-stove, a water-heater, and a sink. But whereas some food is kept in the filing cabinets in the office, dishes and cooking fat and vegetables are kept in glass-fronted sectional bookcases in the kitchen. No whimsy dictated this. It just happened. From the ceiling of the kitchen hang pieces of bacon, and salami, and black bêche-de-mer. Behind the kitchen is a toilet and a shower. The toilet leaked for five years until a clever and handsome guest fixed it with a piece of chewing gum.

Doc is the owner and operator of the Western Biological Laboratory. Doc is rather small, deceptively small, for he is wiry and very strong and when passionate anger comes on him he can be very fierce. He wears a beard and his face is half Christ and half satyr and his face tells the truth. It is said he has helped many a girl out of one trouble and into another. Doc has the hands of a brain surgeon, and a cool warm mind. Doc tips his hat to dogs as he drives by and the dogs look up and smile at him. He can kill anything for need, but he could not even hurt a feeling for pleasure. He has one great fear—that of getting his head wet, so that, summer or winter, he ordinarily wears a rain hat. He will wade in a tide pool up to the chest without feeling damp, but a drop of rain-water on his head makes him panicky.

Over a period of years Doc dug himself into Cannery Row to an extent not even he suspected. He became the fountain of philosophy and science and art. In the laboratory the girls from Dora's heard the Plain Songs and Gregorian music for the first time. Lee Chong listened while Li Po was read to him in English. Henri the painter heard for the first time the Book of the Dead and was so moved that he changed his medium. Henri had been painting with glue, iron rust, and coloured chicken-feathers, but he changed and his next four paintings were done entirely with different kinds of nutshells. Doc would listen to any kind of nonsense and change it for you to a kind of wisdom. His mind had no horizon—and his sympathy had no warp. He could talk to children, telling them very profound things so that they understood. He lived in a world of wonders, of excitement. He was concupiscent as a rabbit and gentle as hell. Everyone who knew him was indebted to him. And everyone who thought of him thought next, "I really must do something nice for Doc."

CHAPTER VI

Doc was collecting marine animals in the Great Tide Pool on the tip of the Peninsula. It is a fabulous place; when the tide is in, a wave-churned basin, creamy with foam, whipped by the combers that roll in from the whistling buoy on the reef. But when the tide goes out the little water world becomes quiet and lovely. The sea is very clear and the bottom becomes fantastic with hurrying, fighting, feeding, breeding animals. Crabs rush from frond to frond of the waving algae. Starfish squat over mussels and limpets, attach their million little suckers and then slowly lift with incredible power until the prey is broken from the rock. And then the starfish stomach comes out and envelops its food. Orange and speckled and fluted nudibranchs slide gracefully over the rocks, their skirts waving like the dresses of Spanish dancers. And black eels poke their heads out of crevices and wait for prey. The snapping shrimps with their trigger claws pop loudly. The lovely, coloured world is glassed over. Hermit crabs like frantic children scamper on the bottom sand. And now one, finding an empty snail shell he likes better than his own, creeps out, exposing his soft body to the enemy for a moment, and then pops into the new shell. A wave breaks over the barrier, and churns the glassy water for a moment and mixes bubbles into the pool, and then it clears and is tranquil and lovely and murderous again. Here a crab tears a leg from his brother. The anemones expand like soft and brilliant flowers, inviting any tired and perplexed animal to lie for a moment in their arms and when some small crab or little tide-pool Johnnie accepts the green and purple invitation, the petals whip in, the stinging cells shoot tiny narcotic needles into the prey and it grows weak and perhaps sleepy while the searing caustic digestive acids melt its body down.

Then the creeping murderer, the octopus, steals out, slowly, softly, moving like a grey mist, pretending now to be a bit of weed, now a rock, now a lump of decaying meat, while its evil goat eyes watch coldly. It oozes and flows toward a feeding crab, and as it comes close its yellow eyes burn and its body turns rosy with the pulsing colour of anticipation and rage. Then suddenly it runs lightly on the tip of its arms, as ferociously as a charging cat. It leaps savagely on the crab, there is a puff of black fluid, and the struggling mass is obscured in the sepia cloud while the octopus murders the crab. On the exposed rock out of water the barnacles bubble behind their closed doors and the limpets dry out. And down to the rocks come the black flies to eat anything they can find. The sharp smell of iodine from the algae, and the lime smell of calcareous bodies and the smell of powerful protean, smell of sperm and ova fill the air. On the exposed rocks the starfish emit semen and eggs from between their rays. The smells of life and richness, of death and digestion, of decay, and birth, burden the air. And salt spray blows in from the barrier where the ocean waits for its rising-tide strength to permit it back into the Great Tide Pool again. And on the reef the whistling buoy bellows like a sad and patient bull.

In the pool Doc and Hazel worked together. Hazel lived in the Palace Flop-house with Mack and the boys. Hazel got his name in as haphazard a way as his life was ever afterward. His worried mother had had seven children in eight years. Hazel was the eighth, and his mother became confused about his sex when he was born. She was tired and run down anyway from trying to feed and clothe seven children and their father. She had tried every possible way of making money—paper flowers, mushrooms at home, rabbits for meat and fur—while her husband from a canvas chair gave her every help his advice and reasoning and criticism could offer. She had a great-aunt named Hazel who was reputed to carry life insurance. The eighth child was named Hazel before the mother got it through her head that Hazel was a boy, and by that time she was used to the name and never bothered to change it. Hazel grew up—did four years in grammar school, four years in reform school, and didn't learn anything in either place. Reform schools are supposed to teach viciousness and criminality, but Hazel didn't pay enough attention. He came out of reform school as innocent of viciousness as he was of fractions and long division. Hazel loved to hear conversation but he didn't listen to words—just to the tone of conversation. He asked questions, not to hear the answers but simply to continue the flow. He was twenty-six—dark-haired and pleasant, strong, willing, and loyal. Quite often he went collecting with Doc and he was very good at it once he knew what was wanted. His fingers could creep like an octopus, could grab and hold like an anemone. He was sure-footed on the slippery rocks and he loved the hunt. Doc wore his rain hat and high rubber boots as he worked, but Hazel sloshed about in tennis-shoes and blue jeans. They were collecting starfish. Doc had an order for three hundred.

Hazel picked a nobby, purplish starfish from the bottom of the pool and popped it into his nearly-full gunny sack. "I wonder what they do with them," he said.

"Do with what?" Doc asked.

"The starfish," said Hazel. "You sell 'em. You'll send out a barrel of 'em. What do the guys do with 'em? You can't eat 'em."

"They study them," said Doc patiently and he remembered that he had answered this question for Hazel dozens of times before. But Doc had one mental habit he could not get over. When anyone asked a question, Doc thought he wanted to know the answer. That was the way with Doc. *He* never asked unless he wanted to know and he could not conceive of the brain that would ask without wanting to know. But Hazel, who simply wanted to hear talk, had developed a system of making the answer to one question the basis of another. It kept conversation going.

"What do they find to study?" Hazel continued. "They're just starfish. There's millions of 'em around. I could get you a million of 'em."

"They're complicated and interesting animals," Doc said a little defensively. "Besides, these are going to the Middle West to Northwestern University."

Hazel used his trick. "They got no starfish there?"

"They got no ocean there," said Doc.

"Oh!" said Hazel and he cast frantically for a peg to hang a new question on. He hated to have a conversation die out like this. He wasn't quick enough. While he was looking for a question Doc asked one. Hazel hated that, it meant casting about in his mind for an answer, and casting about in Hazel's mind was like wandering alone in a deserted museum. Hazel's mind was choked with uncatalogued exhibits. He never forgot anything, but he never bothered to arrange his memories. Everything was thrown together like fishing-tackle in the bottom of a rowboat, hooks and sinkers and line and lures and gaffs all snarled up.

Doc asked, "How are things going up at the Palace?"

Hazel ran his fingers through his dark hair and he peered into the clutter of his mind. "Pretty good," he said. "That fellow Gay is moving in with us, I guess. His wife hits him pretty bad. He don't mind that when he's awake, but she waits till he gets to sleep and then hits him. He hates that. He has to wake up and beat her up and then when he goes to sleep she hits him again. He don't get any rest, so he's moving in with us."

"That's a new one," said Doc. "She used to swear out a warrant and put him in jail."

"Yeah!" said Hazel. "But that was before they built the new jail in Salinas. Used to be thirty days and Gay was pretty hot to get out, but this new jail—radio in the tank and good bunks and the sheriff's a nice fellow. Gay gets in there and he don't want to come out. He likes it so much his wife won't get him arrested any more. So she figured out this hitting him while he's asleep. It's nerve-racking, he says. And you know as good as me—Gay never did take any pleasure in beating her up. He only done it to keep his self-respect. But he gets tired of it. I guess he'll be with us now."

Doc straightened up. The waves were beginning to break over the barrier of the Great Tide Pool. The tide was coming in and little rivers from the sea had begun to flow over the rocks. The wind blew freshly in from the whistling buoy and the barking sea-lions came from around the point. Doc pushed his rain hat on the back of his head. "We've got enough starfish," he said and then went on, "Look, Hazel, I know you've got six or seven undersized abalone in the bottom of your sack. If we get stopped by a game warden, you're going to say they're mine, on my permit—aren't you?"

"Well—hell," said Hazel.

"Look," Doc said kindly. "Suppose I get an order for abalones and maybe the game warden thinks I'm using my collecting permit too often. Suppose he thinks I'm eating them."

"Well—hell," said Hazel.

"It's like the industrial alcohol board. They've got suspicious minds. They always think I'm drinking the alcohol. They think that about everyone."

"Well, ain't you?"

"Not much of it," said Doc. "That stuff they put in it tastes terrible, and it's a big job to re-distil it."

"That stuff ain't so bad," said Hazel. "Me and Mack had a snort at it the other day. What is it they put in?"

Doc was about to answer when he saw it was Hazel's trick again. "Let's get moving," he said. He hoisted his sack of starfish on his shoulder. And he had forgotten the illegal abalones in the bottom of Hazel's sack.

Hazel followed him up out of the tide pool and up the slippery trail to solid ground. The little crabs scampered and skittered out of their way. Hazel felt that he had better cement the grave over the topic of the abalones.

"That painter guy came back to the Palace," he offered.

"Yes?" said Doc.

"Yeah! You see, he done all our pictures in chicken-feathers and now he says he got to do them all over again with nutshells. He says he's changed his—his med—medium."

Doc chuckled. "He still building his boat?"

"Sure," said Hazel. "He's got it all changed around. New kind of a boat. I guess he'll take it apart and change it. Doc—is he nuts?"

Doc swung his heavy sack of starfish to the ground and stood panting a little. "Nuts?" he asked. "Oh, yes, I guess so. Nuts about the same amount we are, only in a different way."

Such a thing had never occurred to Hazel. He looked upon himself as a crystal pool of clarity and on his life as a troubled glass of misunderstood virtue. Doc's last statement had outraged him a little. "But the boat——" he cried. "He's been building that boat for seven years that I know of. The blocks rotted out and he made concrete blocks. Every time he gets it nearly finished he changes it and starts over again. I think he's nuts. Seven years on a boat."

Doc was sitting on the ground pulling off his rubber boots. "You don't understand," he said gently. "Henri loves boats, but he's afraid of the ocean."

"What's he want a boat for, then?" Hazel demanded.

"He likes boats," said Doc. "But suppose he finishes his boat. Once it's finished people will say, 'Why don't you put it in the water?' Then if he puts it in the water, he'll have to go out in it, and he hates the water. So you see, he never finishes the boat—so he doesn't ever have to launch it."

Hazel had followed this reasoning to a certain point, but he abandoned it before it was resolved, not only abandoned it but searched for some way to change the subject. "I think he's nuts," he said lamely.

On the black earth on which the ice-plants bloomed, hundreds of black stink bugs crawled. And many of them stuck their tails up in the air. "Look at all them stink bugs," Hazel remarked, grateful to the bugs for being there.

"They're interesting," said Doc.

"Well, what they got their arses up in the air for?"

Doc rolled up his wool socks and put them in the rubber boots and from his pocket he brought out dry socks and a pair of thin moccasins. "I don't know why," he said. "I looked them up recently—they're very common animals and one of the commonest things they do is put their tails up in the air. And in all the books there isn't one mention of the fact that they put their tails up in the air or why."

Hazel turned one of the stink bugs over with the toe of his wet tennis-shoes and the shining black beetle strove madly with floundering legs to get upright again. "Well, why do *you* think they do it?"

"I think they're praying," said Doc.

"What!" Hazel was shocked.

"The remarkable thing," said Doc, "isn't that they put their tails up in the air—the really incredibly remarkable thing is that we find it remarkable. We can only use ourselves as yardsticks. If we did something as inexplicable and strange we'd probably be praying—so maybe they're praying."

"Let's get the hell out of here," said Hazel.

CHAPTER VII

THE PALACE FLOP-HOUSE was no sudden development. Indeed when Mack and Hazel and Eddie and Hughie and Jones moved into it, they looked upon it as little more than shelter from the wind and the rain, as a place to go when everything else had closed or when their welcome was thin and sere with over-use. Then the Palace was only a long bare room, lit dimly by two small windows, walled with unpainted wood smelling strongly of fish-meal. They had not loved it then. But Mack knew that some kind of organization was necessary, particularly among such a group of ravening individualists.

A training army which has not been equipped with guns and artillery and tanks uses artificial guns and masquerading trucks to simulate its destructive panoply—and its toughening soldiers get used to field-guns by handling logs on wheels.

Mack, with a piece of chalk, drew five oblongs on the floor, each seven feet long and four feet wide, and in each square he wrote a name. These were the simulated beds. Each man had property rights inviolable in his space. He could legally fight a man who encroached on his square. The rest of the room was property common to all. That was in the first days when Mack and the boys sat on the floor, played cards hunkered down, and slept on the hard boards. Perhaps, save for an accident of weather, they might always have lived that way. However, an unprecedented rainfall which went on for over a month changed all that. House-ridden, the boys grew tired of squatting on the floor. Their eyes became outraged by the bare board walls. Because it sheltered them the house grew dear to them. And it had the charm of never knowing the entrance of an outraged landlord. For Lee Chong never came near it. Then one afternoon Hughie came in with an army cot which had a torn canvas. He spent two hours sewing up the rip with fishing-line. And that night the others lying on the floor in their squares watched Hughie ooze gracefully into his cot—they heard him sigh with abysmal comfort and he was asleep and snoring before anyone else.

The next day Mack puffed up the hill carrying a rusty set of springs he had found on a scrap-iron dump. The apathy was broken then. The boys outdid one another in beautifying the Palace Flophouse until after a few months it was, if anything, over-furnished. There were old carpets on the floor, chairs with and without seats. Mack had a wicker chaise-longue painted bright red. There were tables, a grandfather clock without dial face or works. The walls were whitewashed, which made it almost light and airy. Pictures began to appear—mostly calendars showing improbable luscious blondes holding bottles of Coca-Cola. Henri had contributed two pieces from his chicken-feather period. A bundle of gilded cat-tails stood in one corner and a sheaf of peacock-feathers was nailed to the wall beside the grandfather clock.

They were some time acquiring a stove and when they did find what they wanted, a silver-scrolled monster with floriated warming ovens and a front like a nickel-plated tulip garden, they had trouble getting it. It was too big to steal and its owner refused to part with it to the sick widow with eight children whom Mack invented and patronized in the same moment. The owner wanted a dollar and a half and didn't come down to eighty cents for three days. The boys closed at eighty cents and gave him an IOU, which he probably still has. This transaction took place in Seaside and the stove weighed three hundred pounds. Mack and Hughie exhausted every possibility of haulage for ten days and only when they realized that no one was going to take this stove home for them did they begin to carry it. It took them three days to carry it to Cannery Row, a distance of five miles, and they camped beside it at night. But once installed in the Palace Flop-house, it was the glory and the hearth and the centre. Its nickel flowers and foliage shone with a cheery light. It was the gold tooth of the Palace. Fired up, it warmed the big room. Its oven was wonderful and you could fry an egg on its shiny black lids.

With the great stove came pride, and with pride, the Palace became home. Eddie planted morning glories to run over the door and Hazel acquired some rather rare fuchsia bushes planted in five-gallon cans which made the entrance formal and a little cluttered. Mack and the boys loved the Palace and they even cleaned it a little sometimes. In their minds they sneered at unsettled people who had no house to go to and occasionally in their pride they brought a guest home for a day or two.

Eddie was understudy bartender at 'La Ida'. He filled in when Whitey the regular bartender was sick, which was as often as Whitey could get away with it. Every time Eddie filled in, a few bottles disappeared, so he couldn't fill in too often. But Whitey liked to have Eddie take his place because he was convinced, and correctly, that Eddie was one man who wouldn't try to keep his job permanently. Almost anyone could have trusted Eddie to this extent. Eddie didn't have to remove much liquor. He kept a gallon jug under the bar and in the mouth of the jug there was a funnel. Anything left in the glasses Eddie poured into the funnel before he washed the glasses. If an argument or a song were going on at 'La Ida', or late at night when good-fellowship had reached its logical conclusion, Eddie poured glasses half- or two-thirds-full into the funnel. The resulting punch which he took back to the Palace was always interesting and sometimes surprising. The mixture of rye, beer, bourbon, Scotch, wine, rum and gin was fairly constant, but now and then some effete customer would order a stinger or an anisette or a curaçao and these little touches gave a distinct character to the punch. It was Eddie's habit always to shake a little Angostura into the jug before he left. On a good night Eddie got three-quarters of a gallon. It was a source of satisfaction to him that nobody was out anything. He had observed that a man got just as drunk on half a glass as on a whole one, that is, if he was in the mood to get drunk at all.

Eddie was a very desirable inhabitant of the Palace Flop-house. The others never asked him to help with the house-cleaning and once Hazel washed four pairs of Eddie's socks.

Now on the afternoon when Hazel was out collecting with Doc in the Great Tide Pool, the boys were sitting around in the Palace sipping the result of Eddie's latest contribution. Gay was there too, the latest member of the group. Eddie sipped speculatively from his glass and smacked his lips. "It's funny how you get a run," he said. "Take last night. There was at least ten guys ordered Manhattans. Sometimes maybe you don't get two calls for a Manhattan in a month. It's the grenadine gives the stuff that taste."

Mack tasted his—a big taste—and refilled his glass. "Yes," he said sombrely, "it's little things make the difference." He looked about to see how this gem had set with the others.

Only Gay got the full impact. "Sure is," he said. "Does——"

"Where's Hazel to-day?" Mack asked.

Jones said, "Hazel went out with Doc to get some starfish."

Mack nodded his head soberly. "That Doc is a hell of a nice fella," he said. "He'll give you a quarter any time. When I cut myself he put on a new bandage every day. A hell of a nice fella."

The others nodded in profound agreement.

"I been wondering for a long time," Mack continued, "what we could do for him—something nice. Something he'd like."

"He'd like a dame," said Hughie.

"He's got three-four dames," said Jones. "You can always tell—when he pulls them front curtains closed, and when he plays that kind of church music on the phonograph."

Mack said reprovingly to Hughie, "Just because he doesn't run no dame naked through the streets in the day-time, you think Doc's celebrate."

"What's celebrate?" Eddie asked.

"That's when you can't get no dame," said Mack.

"I thought it was a kind of a party," said Jones.

A silence fell on the room. Mack shifted in his chaise-longue. Hughie let the front legs of his chair down on the floor. They looked into space and then they all looked at Mack. Mack said, "Hum!"

Eddie said, "What kind of a party you think Doc'd like?"

"What other kind is there?" said Jones.

Mack mused, "Doc wouldn't like this stuff from the winin' jug."

"How do you know?" Hughie demanded. "You never offered him none."

"Oh, I know," said Mack. "He's been to college. Once I seen a dame in a fur coat go in there. Never did see her come out. It was two o'clock the last I looked—and that church music goin'. No—you couldn't offer him none of this." He filled his glass again.

"This tastes pretty nice after the third glass," Hughie said loyally.

"No," said Mack. "Not for Doc. Have to be whisky—the real thing."

"He likes beer," said Jones. "He's all the time going over to Lee's for beer—sometimes in the middle of the night."

Mack said, "I figure when you buy beer, you're buying too much tare. Take eight per cent. beer—why you're spending your dough for 92 per cent. water and colour and hops and stuff like that. Eddie," he added, "you think you could get four-five bottles of whisky at 'La Ida' next time Whitey's sick?"

"Sure," said Eddie. "Sure I could get it, but that'd be the end—no more golden eggs. I think Johnnie's suspicious anyways. Other day he says, 'I smell a mouse named Eddie.' I was gonna lay low and only bring the jug for a while."

"Yeah!" said Jones. "Don't you lose that job. If something happened to Whitey, you could fall right in there for a week or so till they got somebody else. I guess if we're goin' to give a party for Doc, we got to buy the whisky. How much is whisky a gallon?"

"I don't know," said Hughie. "I never get more than a half-pint at a time myself—at one time, that is. I figure you get a quart and right away you got friends. But you get a half-pint and you can drink it in the lot before—well before you got a lot of folks around."

"It's going to take dough to give Doc a party," said Mack. "If we're going to give him a party at all it ought to be a good one. Should have a big cake. I wonder when is his birthday?"

"Don't need a birthday for a party," said Jones.

"No—but it's nice," said Mack. "I figure it would take ten or twelve bucks to give Doc a party you wouldn't be ashamed of."

They looked at one another speculatively. Hughie suggested, "The Hediondo Cannery is hiring guys."

"No," said Mack quickly. "We got good reputations and we don't want to spoil them. Every one of us keeps a job for a month or more when we take one. That's why we can always get a job when we need one. S'pose we take a job for a day or so—why, we'll lose our reputation for sticking. Then if we needed a job there wouldn't be nobody have us." The rest nodded quick agreement.

"I figure I'm gonna work a couple of months—November and part of December," said Jones. "Makes it nice to have money around Christmas. We could cook a turkey this year."

"By God, we could," said Mack. "I know a place up Carmel Valley where there's fifteen hundred in one flock."

"Valley," said Hughie. "You know, I used to collect stuff up the Valley for Doc, turtles and crayfish and frogs. Got a nickel apiece for frogs."

"Me, too," said Gay. "I got five hundred frogs one time."

"If Doc needs frogs it's a set-up," said Mack. "We could go up the Carmel River and have a little outing and we wouldn't tell Doc what it was for and then we'd give him one hell of a party."

A quiet excitement grew in the Palace Flop-house. "Gay," said Mack, "take a look out the door and see if Doc's car is in front of his place."

Gay set down his glass and looked out. "Not yet," he said.

"Well, he ought to be back any minute," said Mack. "Now here's how we'll go about it. . . ."

CHAPTER VIII

In April, 1932, the boiler at the Hediondo Cannery blew a tube for the third time in two weeks and the board of directors, consisting of Mr. Randolph and a stenographer, decided that it would be cheaper to buy a new boiler than to have to shut down so often. In time the new boiler arrived and the old one was moved into the vacant lot between Lee Chong's and the Bear Flag Restaurant, where it was set on blocks to await an inspiration on Mr. Randolph's part on how to make some money out of it. Gradually, the plant engineer removed the tubing to use to patch other outworn equipment at the Hediondo. The boiler looked like an old-fashioned locomotive without wheels. It had a big door in the centre of its nose and a low fire door. Gradually it became red and soft with rust and gradually the mallow weeds grew up around it and the flaking rust fed the weeds. Flowering myrtle crept up its sides and the wild anise perfumed the air about it. Then someone threw out a datura root and the thick, fleshy tree grew up and the great white bells hung down over the boiler door and at night the flowers smelled of love and excitement, an incredibly sweet and moving odour.

In 1935 Mr. and Mrs. Sam Malloy moved into the boiler. The tubing was all gone now and it was a roomy, dry and safe apartment. True, if you came in through the fire door you had to get down on your hands and knees, but once in there was head room in the middle and you couldn't want a dryer, warmer place to stay. They shagged a mattress through the fire door and settled down. Mr. Malloy was happy and contented there and for quite a long time so was Mrs. Malloy.

Below the boiler on the hill there were numbers of large pipes also abandoned by the Hediondo. Toward the end of 1937 there was a great catch of fish and the canneries were working full-time and a housing shortage occurred. Then it was that Mr. Malloy took to renting the larger pipes as sleeping quarters for single men at a very nominal fee. With a piece of tar paper over one end and a square of carpet over the other, they made comfortable bedrooms, although men used to sleeping curled up had to change their habits or move out. There were those, too, who claimed that their snores echoing back from the pipes woke them up. But on the whole Mr. Malloy did a steady small business and was happy.

Mrs. Malloy had been contented until her husband became a landlord and then she began to change. First it was a rug, then a wash-tub, then a lamp with a coloured silk shade. Finally, she came into the boiler on her hands and knees one day and she stood up and said a little breathlessly, "Holman's are having a sale of curtains. Real lace curtains and edges of blue and pink—$1.98 a set with curtain rods thrown in."

Mr. Malloy sat up on the mattress. "Curtains?" he demanded. "What in God's name do you want curtains for?"

"I like things nice," said Mrs. Malloy. "I always did like to have things nice for you," and her lower lip began to tremble.

"But, darling," Sam Malloy cried, "I got nothing against curtains. I like curtains."

"Only $1.98," Mrs. Malloy quavered, "and you begrutch me $1.98," and she sniffled and her chest heaved.

"I don't begrutch you," said Mr. Malloy. "But, darling—for Christ's sake what are we going to do with curtains? We got no windows."

Mrs. Malloy cried and cried and Sam held her in his arms and comforted her.

"Men just don't understand how a woman feels," she sobbed. "Men just never try to put themselves in a woman's place."

And Sam lay beside her and rubbed her back for a long time before she went to sleep.

CHAPTER IX

When Doc's car came back to the laboratory, Mack and the boys secretly watched Hazel help to carry in the sacks of starfish. In a few minutes Hazel came damply up the chicken-walk to the Palace. His jeans were wet with sea water to the thighs and where it was drying the white salt rings were forming. He sat heavily in the patient rocker that was his and shucked off his wet tennis-shoes.

Mack asked, "How is Doc feeling?"

"Fine," said Hazel. "You can't understand a word he says. Know what he said about stink bugs? No—I better not tell you."

"He seems in a nice friendly mood?" Mack asked.

"Sure," said Hazel. "We got two-three hundred starfish. He's all right."

"I wonder if we better all go over?" Mack asked himself and he answered himself, "No, I guess it would be better if one went alone. It might get him mixed up if we all went."

"What is this?" Hazel asked.

"We got plans," said Mack. "I'll go myself so as not to startle him. You guys stay here and wait. I'll come back in a few minutes."

Mack went out and he teetered down the chicken-walk and across the track. Mr. Malloy was sitting on a brick in front of his boiler.

"How are you, Sam?" Mack asked.

"Pretty good."

"How's the missus?"

"Pretty good," said Mr. Malloy. "You know any kind of glue that you can stick cloth to iron?"

Ordinarily, Mack would have thrown himself headlong into this problem, but now he was not to be deflected. "No," he said.

He went across the vacant lot, crossed the street and entered the basement of the laboratory.

Doc had his hat off now, since there was practically no chance of getting his head wet unless a pipe broke. He was busy removing the starfish from the wet sacks and arranging them on the cool concrete floor. The starfish were twisted and knotted up, for a starfish loves to hang on to something and for an hour these had found only each other. Doc arranged them in long lines and very slowly they straightened out until they lay in symmetrical stars on the concrete floor. Doc's pointed brown beard was damp with perspiration as he worked. He looked up a little nervously as Mack entered. It was not that trouble always came in with Mack, but something always entered with him.

"Hiya, Doc?" said Mack.

"All right," said Doc uneasily.

"Hear about Phyllis Mae over at the Bear Flag? She hit a drunk and got his tooth in her fist and it's infected clear to the elbow. She showed me the tooth. It was out of a plate. Is a false tooth poison, Doc?"

"I guess everything that comes out of the human mouth is poison," said Doc warningfully. "Has she got a doctor?"

"The bouncer fixed her up," said Mack.

"I'll take her some sulfa," said Doc, and he waited for the storm to break. He knew Mack had come for something and Mack knew he knew it.

Mack said, "Doc, you got any need for any kind of animals now?"

Doc sighed with relief. "Why?" he asked guardedly.

Mack became open and confidential. "I'll tell you, Doc. I and the boys got to get some dough—we simply got to. It's for a good purpose, you might say a worthy cause."

"Phyllis Mae's arm?"

Mack saw the chance, weighed it and gave it up. "Well—no," he said. "It's more important than that. You can't kill a whore. No—this is different. I and the boys thought if you needed something, why, we'd get it for you and that way we could make a little piece of change."

It seemed simple and innocent. Doc laid down four more starfish in lines. "I could use three or four hundred frogs," he said. "I'd get them myself, but I've got to go down to La Jolla to-night. There's a good tide to-morrow and I have to get some octopi."

"Same price for frogs?" Mack asked. "Five cents apiece?"

"Same price," said Doc.

Mack was jovial. "Don't you worry about frogs, Doc," he said. "We'll get you all the frogs you want. You just rest easy about frogs. Why, we can get them right up Carmel River. I know a place."

"Good," said Doc. "I'll take all you get, but I need about three hundred."

"Just you rest easy, Doc. Don't you lose no sleep about it. You'll get your frogs, maybe seven-eight hundred." He put the Doc at ease about frogs and then a little cloud crossed Mack's face. "Doc," he said, "any chance of using your car to go up the Valley?"

"No," said Doc. "I told you. I have to drive to La Jolla to-night to make to-morrow's tide."

"Oh," said Mack dispiritedly. "Oh. Well, don't you worry about it, Doc. Maybe we can get Lee Chong's old truck." And then his face fell a little further. "Doc," he said, "on a business deal like this, would you advance two or three bucks for petrol? I know Lee Chong won't give us petrol."

"No," said Doc. He had fallen into this before. Once he had financed Gay to go for turtles. He financed him for two weeks and at the end of that time Gay was in jail on his wife's charge and he never did go for turtles.

"Well, maybe we can't go, then," said Mack sadly.

Now, Doc really needed the frogs. He tried to work out some method which was business and not philanthropy. "I'll tell you what I'll do," he said. "I'll give you a note to my petrol station so you can get ten gallons of petrol. How will that be?"

Mack smiled. "Fine," he said. "That will work out just fine. I and the boys will get an early start to-morrow. Time you get back from the south, we'll have more damn frogs than you ever seen in your life."

Doc went to the labelling desk and wrote a note to Red Williams at the petrol station, authorizing the issue of ten gallons of petrol to Mack. "Here you are," he said.

Mack was smiling broadly. "Doc," he said, "you can get to sleep to-night and not even give frogs a thought. We'll have piss-pots full of them by the time you get back."

Doc watched him go a little uneasily. Doc's dealings with Mack and the boys had always been interesting, but rarely had they been profitable to Doc. He remembered ruefully the time Mack sold him fifteen tom-cats and by night the owners came and got every one. "Mack," he had asked, "why all tom-cats?"

Mack said, "Doc, it's my own invention, but I'll tell you because you're a good friend. You make a big wire trap and then you don't use bait. You use—well—you use a lady cat. Catch every damn tom-cat in the country that way."

From the laboratory Mack crossed the street and went through the swinging screen doors into Lee Chong's grocery. Mrs. Lee was cutting bacon on the big butcher's block. A Lee cousin primped up slightly wilted heads of lettuce the way a girl primps a loose finger wave. A cat lay asleep on a big pile of oranges. Lee Chong stood in his usual place behind the cigar counter and in front of the liquor shelves. His tapping finger on the change mat speeded up a little when Mack came in.

Mack wasted no time in sparring. "Lee," he said, "Doc over there's got a problem. He's got a big order for frogs from the New York Museum. Means a lot to Doc. Besides the dough there's a lot of credit getting an order like that. Doc's got to go south and I and the boys said we'd help him out. I think a guy's friends ought to help him out of a hole when they can, especially a nice guy like Doc. Why, I bet he spends sixty-seventy dollars a month with you."

Lee Chong remained silent and watchful. His fat finger barely moved on the change mat, but it flicked slightly like a tense cat's tail.

Mack plunged into his thesis. "Will you let us take your old truck to go up Carmel Valley for frogs for Doc—for good old Doc?"

Lee Chong smiled in triumph. "Tluck no good," he said. "Bloke down."

This staggered Mack for a moment, but he recovered. He spread the order for petrol on the cigar counter. "Look!" he said. "Doc needs them frogs. He give me this order for petrol to get them. I can't let Doc down. Now Gay is a good mechanic. If he fixes your truck and puts it in good shape, will you let us take it?"

Lee put back his head so that he could see Mack through his half-glasses. There didn't seem to be anything wrong with the proposition. The truck really wouldn't run. Gay really was a good mechanic and the order for petrol was definite evidence of good faith.

"How long you be gone?" Lee asked.

"Maybe half a day, maybe a whole day. Just till we get the frogs."

Lee was worried, but he couldn't see any way out. The dangers were all there and Lee knew all of them. "Okay," said Lee.

"Good," said Mack. "I knew Doc could depend on you. I'll get Gay right to work on that truck." He turned about to leave. "By the way," he said. "Doc's paying us five cents apiece for those frogs. We're going to get seven or eight hundred. How about taking a pint of Old Tennis Shoes just till we can get back with the frogs?"

"No!" said Lee Chong.

CHAPTER X

FRANKIE BEGAN coming to Western Biological when he was eleven years old. For a week or so he just stood outside the basement door and looked in. Then one day he stood inside the door. Ten days later he was in the basement. He had very large eyes and his hair was a dark, wiry, dirty shock. His hands were filthy. He picked up a piece of excelsior and put it in the garbage can and then he looked at Doc where he worked labelling specimen bottles containing purple Velella. Finally Frankie got to the work-bench and he put his dirty fingers on the bench. It took Frankie three weeks to get that far, and he was ready to bolt every instant of the time.

Finally one day Doc spoke to him. "What's your name, son?"

"Frankie."

"Where do you live?"

"Up there," a gesture up the hill.

"Why aren't you in school?"

"I don't go to school."

"Why not?"

"They don't want me there."

"Your hands are dirty. Don't you ever wash?"

Frankie looked stricken and then he went to the sink and scrubbed his hands almost raw every day.

And he came to the laboratory every day. It was an association without much talk. Doc by a telephone call established that what Frankie said was true. They didn't want him in school. He couldn't learn and there was something a little wrong with his co-ordination. There was no place for him. He wasn't an idiot, he wasn't dangerous, his parents, or parent, would not pay for his keep in an institution. Frankie didn't often sleep at the laboratory, but he spent his days there. And sometimes he crawled in the excelsior crate and slept. That was probably when there was a crisis at home.

Doc asked, "Why do you come here?"

"You don't hit me or give me a nickel," said Frankie.

"Do they hit you at home?"

"There's uncles around all the time at home. Some of them hit me and tell me to get out and some of them give me a nickel and tell me to get out."

"Where's your father?"

"Dead," said Frankie vaguely.

"Where's your mother?"

"With the uncles."

Doc clipped Frankie's hair and got rid of the lice. At Lee Chong's he got him a new pair of overalls and a striped sweater and Frankie became his slave.

"I love you," he said one afternoon. "Oh, I love you."

He wanted to work in the laboratory. He swept out every day, but there was something a little wrong. He couldn't get a floor quite clean. He tried to help with grading crayfish for size. There they were in a bucket, all sizes. They were to be grouped in the big pans —laid out—all the three-inch ones together and all the four-inch ones, and so forth. Frankie tried and the perspiration stood on his forehead, but he couldn't do it. Size relationships just didn't get through to him.

"No," Doc would say. "Look, Frankie. Put them beside your finger like this so you'll know which ones are this long. See? This one goes from the tip of your finger to the base of your thumb. Now you just pick out another one that goes from the tip of your finger down to the same place and it will be all right." Frankie tried and he couldn't do it. When Doc went upstairs Frankie crawled in the excelsior box and didn't come out all afternoon.

But Frankie was a nice, good, kind boy. He learned to light Doc's cigars and he wanted Doc to smoke all the time so he could light the cigars.

Better than anything else Frankie loved it when there were parties upstairs in the laboratory. When girls and men gathered to sit and talk, when the great phonograph played music that throbbed in his stomach and made beautiful and huge pictures form vaguely in his head, Frankie loved it. Then he crouched down in a corner behind a chair where he was hidden and could watch and listen. When there was laughter at a joke he didn't understand Frankie laughed delightedly behind his chair, and when the conversation dealt with abstractions his brow furrowed and he became intent and serious.

One afternoon he did a desperate thing. There was a small party in the laboratory. Doc was in the kitchen pouring beer when Frankie appeared beside him. Frankie grabbed a glass of beer and rushed it through the door and gave it to a girl sitting in a big chair.

She took the glass and said, "Why, thank you," and she smiled at him.

And Doc coming through the door said, "Yes, Frankie is a great help to me."

Frankie couldn't forget that. He did the thing in his mind over and over, just how he had taken the glass and just how the girl sat and then her voice—"Why, thank you," and Doc—"a great help to me—Frankie," and Oh, my God!

He knew a big party was coming because Doc bought steaks and a great deal of beer and Doc let him help clean out all the upstairs. But that was nothing, for a great plan had formed in Frankie's mind and he could see just how it would be. He went over it again and again. It was beautiful. It was perfect.

Then the party started and people came and sat in the front room, girls and young women and men.

Frankie had to wait until he had the kitchen to himself and the door closed. And it was some time before he had it so. But at last he was alone and the door was shut. He could hear the chatter of conversation and the music from the great phonograph. He worked very quietly—first the tray—then get out the glasses without breaking any. Now fill them with beer and let the foam settle a little and then fill again.

Now he was ready. He took a great breath and opened the door. The music and the talk roared around him. Frankie picked up the tray of beer and walked through the door. He knew how. He went straight toward the same young woman who had thanked him before. And then, right in front of her, the thing happened, the co-ordination failed, the hands trembled, the muscles panicked, the nerves telegraphed to a dead operator, the responses did not come back. Tray and beer collapsed forward into the young woman's lap. For a moment Frankie stood still. And then he turned and ran.

The room was quiet. They could hear him run downstairs and go into the cellar. They heard a hollow scrabbling sound—and then silence.

Doc walked quietly down the stairs and into the cellar. Frankie was in the excelsior box burrowed down clear to the bottom, with the pile of excelsior on top of him. Doc could hear him whimpering there. Doc waited for a moment and then he went quietly back upstairs.

There wasn't a thing in the world he could do.

CHAPTER XI

The Model T Ford truck of Lee Chong had a dignified history. In 1923 it had been a passenger car belonging to Dr. W. T. Waters. He used it for five years and sold it to an insurance man named Rattle. Mr. Rattle was not a careful man. The car he got in clean, nice condition he drove like fury. Mr. Rattle drank on Saturday nights and the car suffered. The fenders were broken and bent. He was a pedal rider too and the bands had to be changed often. When Mr.

Rattle embezzled a client's money and ran away to San José, he was caught with a high-hair blonde and sent up within ten days.

The body of the car was so battered that its next owner cut it in two and added a little truck bed.

The next owner took off the front of the cab and the windshield. He used it to haul squids and he liked a fresh breeze to blow in his face. His name was Francis Almones, and he had a sad life, for he always made just a fraction less than he needed to live. His father had left him a little money, but year by year and month by month, no matter how hard Francis worked or how careful he was, his money grew less until he just dried up and blew away.

Lee Chong got the truck in payment of a grocery bill.

By this time the truck was little more than four wheels and an engine, and the engine was so crochety and sullen and senile that it required expert care and consideration. Lee Chong did not give it these things, with the result that the truck stood in the tall grass behind the grocery most of the time with the mallows growing between its spokes. It had solid tyres on its back wheels and blocks held its front wheels off the ground.

Probably any one of the boys from the Palace Flop-house could have made the truck run, for they were all competent practical mechanics, but Gay was an inspired mechanic. There is no term comparable to green thumbs to apply to such a mechanic, but there should be. For there are men who can look, listen, tap, make an adjustment, and a machine works. Indeed there are men near whom a car runs better. And such a one was Gay. His fingers on a timer or a carburettor adjustment screw were gentle and wise and sure. He could fix the delicate electric motors in the laboratory. He could have worked in the canneries all the time had he wished, for in that industry, which complains bitterly when it does not make back its total investment every year in profits, the machinery is much less important than the fiscal statement. Indeed, if you could can sardines with ledgers, the owners would have been very happy. As it was, they used decrepit, struggling old horrors of machines that needed the constant attention of a man like Gay.

Mack got the boys up early. They had their coffee and immediately moved over to the truck where it lay among the weeds. Gay was in charge. He kicked the blocked-up front wheels. "Go borrow a pump and get those pumped up," he said. Then he put a stick in the petrol-tank under the board which served as a seat. By some miracle there was a half-inch of petrol in the tank. Now Gay went over the most probable difficulties. He took out the coil boxes, scraped the points, adjusted the gap, and put them back. He opened the carburettor to see that petrol came through. He pushed on the crank to see that the whole shaft wasn't frozen and the pistons rusted in their cylinders.

Meanwhile the pump arrived and Eddie and Jones spelled each other on the tyres.

Gay hummed, "Dum tiddy—dum tiddy," as he worked. He removed the spark-plugs and scraped the points and bored the carbon out. Then Gay drained a little petrol into a can and poured some into each cylinder before he put the spark-plugs back. He straightened up. "We're going to need a couple of dry cells," he said. "See if Lee Chong will let us have a couple."

Mack departed and returned almost immediately with a universal No which was designed by Lee Chong to cover all future requests.

Gay thought deeply. "I know where's a couple—pretty good ones too, but I won't go get them."

"Where?" asked Mack.

"Down cellar at my house," said Gay. "They run the front door-bell. If one of you fellas wants to kind of edge into my cellar without my wife seeing you, they're on top of the side stringer on the left-hand side as you go in. But for God's sake don't let my wife catch you."

A conference elected Eddie to go, and he departed.

"If you get caught don't mention me," Gay called out after him. Meanwhile Gay tested the bands. The low-high pedal didn't quite touch the floor, so he knew there was a little band left. The brake pedal did touch the floor, so there was no brake, but the reverse pedal had lots of band left. On a Model T Ford the reverse is your margin of safety. When your brake is gone, you can use reverse as a brake. And when the low-gear band is worn too thin to pull up a steep hill, why, you can turn round and back up it. Gay found there was plenty of reverse and he knew everything was all right.

It was a good omen that Eddie came back with the dry cells without trouble. Mrs. Gay had been in the kitchen. Eddie could hear her walking about, but she didn't hear Eddie. He was very good at such things.

Gay connected the dry cells and he advanced the petrol and retarded the spark-lever. "Twist her tail," he said.

He was such a wonder, Gay was—the little mechanic of God, the St. Francis of all things that turn and twist and explode, the St. Francis of coils and armatures and gears. And if at some time all the heaps of cars—cut-down Dusenbergs, Buicks, De Sotos and Plymouths, American Austins and Isotta-Fraschinis—praise God in a great chorus, it will be largely due to Gay and his brotherhood.

One twist—one little twist—and the engine caught and laboured and faltered and caught again. Gay advanced the spark and reduced the petrol. He switched over to the magneto and the Ford of Lee Chong chuckled and jiggled and clattered happily as though it knew it was working for a man who loved and understood it.

There were two small technical legal difficulties with the truck—it had no recent licence plates and it had no lights. But the boys hung a rag permanently and accidentally on the rear plate to conceal its vintage and they dabbed the front plate with good thick mud. The equipment of the expedition was slight: some long-handled frog-nets and some gunny sacks. City hunters going out for sport load themselves with food and liquor, but not Mack. He presumed rightly that the country was where food came from. Two loaves of bread and what was left of Eddie's wining jug was all the supply. The party clambered on the truck. Gay drove and Mack sat beside him; they bumped round the corner of Lee Chong's and down through the lot, threading among the pipes. Mr. Malloy waved at them from his seat by the boiler. Gay eased across the pavement and down off the kerb gently because the front tyres showed fabric all the way around. With all their alacrity, it was afternoon when they got started.

The truck eased into Red Williams' service station. Mack got out and gave his paper to Red. He said, "Doc was a little short of change. So if you'll put five gallons in and just give us a buck instead of the other five gallons, why, that's what Doc wants. He had to go south, you know. Had a big deal down there."

Red smiled good-naturedly. "You know, Mack," he said, "Doc got to figuring if there was some kind of loop-hole, and he put his finger on the same one you did. Doc's a pretty bright fellow. So he phoned me last night."

"Put in the whole ten gallons," said Mack. "No—wait. It'll slop around and spill. Put in five and give us five in a can—one of them sealed cans."

Red smiled happily. "Doc kind of figured that one too," he said.

"Put in ten gallons," said Mack. "And don't go leaving none in the hose."

The little expedition did not go through the centre of Monterey. A delicacy about the licence plates and the lights made Gay choose back streets. There would be the time when they would go up Carmel Hill and down into the Valley, a good four miles on a main highway, exposed to any passing cop until they turned up the fairly unfrequented Carmel Valley road. Gay chose a back street that brought them out on the main highway at Peter's Gate just before the steep Carmel Hill starts. Gay took a good noisy clattering run at the hill and in fifty yards he put the pedal down to low. He knew it wouldn't work, the band was worn too thin. On the level it was all right, but not on a hill. He stopped, let the truck back round and aimed it down the hill. Then he gave it the petrol and the reverse pedal. And the reverse was not worn. The truck crawled steadily and slowly but backward up Carmel Hill.

And they very nearly made it. The radiator boiled, of course, but most Model T experts believed that it wasn't working well if it wasn't boiling.

Someone should write an erudite essay on the moral, physical, and æsthetic effect of the Model T Ford on the American nation. Two generations of Americans know more about the Ford coil than the clitoris, about the planetary system of gears than the solar system of stars. With the Model T, part of the concept of private property disappeared. Pliers ceased to be privately owned and a tyre-pump belonged to the last man who had picked it up. Most of the babies of the period were conceived in Model T Fords and not a few were born in them. The theory of the Anglo-Saxon home became so warped that it never quite recovered.

The truck backed sturdily up Carmel Hill and it got past the Jack's Peak road and was just going into the last and steepest pull when the motor's breathing thickened, gulped, and strangled. It seemed very quiet when the motor was still. Gay, who was heading down-hill anyway, ran down the hill fifty feet and turned into the Jack's Peak road entrance.

"What is it?" Mack asked.

"Carburettor, I think," said Gay. The engine sizzled and creaked with heat and the jet of steam that blew down the overflow-pipe sounded like the hiss of an alligator.

The carburettor of a Model T is not complicated, but it needs all of its parts to function. There is a needle valve, and the point must be on the needle and must sit in its hole or the carburettor does not work.

Gay held the needle in his hand and the point was broken off. "How in hell you s'pose that happened?" he asked.

"Magic," said Mack, "just pure magic. Can you fix it?"

"Hell, no," said Gay. "Got to get another one."

"How much they cost?"

"About a buck if you buy one new—quarter at a wrecker's."

"You got a buck?" Mack asked.

"Yeah, but I won't need it."

"Well, get back as soon as you can, will you? We'll just stay right here."

"Anyways, you won't go running off without a needle valve," said Gay. He stepped out to the road. He thumbed three cars before one stopped for him. The boys watched him climb in and start down the hill. They didn't see him again for one hundred and eighty days.

Oh, the infinity of possibility! How could it happen that the car that picked up Gay broke down before it got into Monterey? If Gay had not been a mechanic, he would not have fixed the car. If he had not fixed it the owner wouldn't have taken him to Jimmy Brucia's for a drink. And why was it Jimmy's birthday? Out of all the possibilities in the world—the millions of them—only events occurred that lead to the Salinas jail. Sparky Enea and Tiny Colletti had made up a quarrel and were helping Jimmy to celebrate his birthday. The blonde came in. The musical argument in front of the juke-box. Gay's new friend who knew a judo hold and tried to show it to Sparky and got his wrist broken when the hold went wrong. The policeman with a bad stomach—all unrelated, irrevelant details and yet all running in one direction. Fate just didn't intend Gay to go on that frog-hunt, and Fate took a hell of a lot of trouble and people and accidents to keep him from it. When the final climax came with the front of Holman's bootery broken out and the party trying on shoes in the display window, only Gay didn't hear the fire whistle. Only Gay didn't go to the fire, and when the police came they found him sitting all alone in Holman's window wearing one brown Oxford and one patent leather dress shoe with a grey cloth top.

Back at the truck the boys built a little fire when it got dark and the chill crept up from the ocean. The pines above them soughed in the fresh sea wind. The boys lay in the pine-needles and looked at the lonely sky through the pine branches. For a while they spoke of the difficulties Gay must be having getting a needle valve, and then gradually as the time passed they didn't mention him any more.

"Somebody should of gone with him," said Mack.

About ten o'clock Eddie got up. "There's a construction camp a piece up the hill," he said. "I think I'll go up and see if they got any Model T's."

CHAPTER XII

Monterey is a city with a long and brilliant literary tradition. It remembers with pleasure and some glory that Robert Louis Stevenson lived there. Treasure Island certainly had the topography and the coastal plan of Pt. Lobos. More recently in Carmel there have been a great number of literary men about, but there is not the old flavour, the old dignity of the true *belles-lettres*. Once the town was greatly outraged over what the citizens considered a slight to an author. It had to do with the death of Josh Billings, the great humorist.

Where the new post office is, there used to be a deep gulch with water flowing in it and a little foot-bridge over it. On one side of the gulch was a fine old adobe and on the other the house of the doctor who handled all the sickness, birth, and death in the town. He worked with animals too and, having studied in France, he even dabbled in the new practice of embalming bodies before they were buried. Some of the old-timers considered this sentimental and some thought it wasteful, and to some it was sacrilegious since there was no provision for it in any sacred volume. But the better and richer families were coming to it, and it looked to become a fad.

One morning elderly Mr. Carriaga was walking from his house on the hill down toward Alvarado Street. He was just crossing the foot-bridge when his attention was drawn to a small boy and a dog struggling up out of the gulch. The boy carried a liver while the dog dragged yards of intestine at the end of which a stomach dangled. Mr. Carriaga paused and addressed the little boy politely: "Good morning."

In those days little boys were courteous. "Good morning, sir."

"Where are you going with the liver?"

"I'm going to make some chum and catch some mackerel."

Mr. Carriaga smiled. "And the dog, will he catch mackerel, too?"

"The dog found that. It's his, sir. We found them in the gulch."

Mr. Carriaga smiled and strolled on, and then his mind began to work. That isn't a beef liver, it's too small. And it isn't a calf's liver, it's too red. It isn't a sheep's liver——Now his mind was alert. At the corner he met Mr. Ryan.

"Anyone die in Monterey last night?" he asked.

"Not that I know of," said Mr. Ryan.

"Anyone killed?"

"No."

They walked on together and Mr. Carriaga told about the little boy and the dog.

At the "Adobe Bar" a number of citizens were gathered for their morning conversation. There Mr. Carriaga told his story again, and he had just finished when the constable came into the "Adobe". He should know if anyone had died. "No one died in Monterey," he said. "But Josh Billings died out at the Hotel del Monte."

The men in the bar were silent. And the same thought went through all their minds. Josh Billings was a great man, a great writer. He had honoured Monterey by dying there and he had been degraded. Without much discussion a committee formed, made up of everyone there. The stern men walked quickly to the gulch and across the foot-bridge and they hammered on the door of the doctor who had studied in France.

He had worked late. The knocking got him out of bed and brought him, tousled of hair and beard, to the door in his night-gown. Mr. Carriaga addressed him sternly: "Did you embalm Josh Billings?"

"Why—yes."

"What did you do with his 'innards'?"

"Why—I threw them in the gulch where I always do."

They made him dress quickly then and they hurried down to the beach. If the little boy had gone quickly about his business, it would have been too late. He was just getting into a boat when the committee arrived. The intestine was in the sand where the dog had abandoned it.

Then the French doctor was made to collect the parts. He was forced to wash them reverently and pick out as much sand as possible. The doctor himself had to stand the expense of the leaden box which went into the coffin of Josh Billings. For Monterey was not a town to let dishonour come to a literary man.

CHAPTER XIII

MACK AND the boys slept peacefully on the pine-needles. Some time before dawn Eddie came back. He had gone a long way before he found a Model T. And then when he did, he wondered whether or not it would be a good idea to take the needle out of its seat. It might not fit. So he took the whole carburettor. The boys didn't wake up when he got back. He lay down beside them and slept under the pine-trees. There was one nice thing about Model T's. The parts were not only interchangeable, they were unidentifiable.

There is a beautiful view from the Carmel grade: the curving bay with the waves creaming on the sand, the dune country around Seaside, and right at the bottom of the hill the warm intimacy of the town.

Mack got up in the dawn and hustled his pants where they bound him and he stood looking down on the bay. He could see some of the purse-seiners coming in. A tanker stood over against Seaside, taking on oil. Behind him the rabbits stirred in the bush. Then the sun came up and shook the night chill out of the air the way you'd shake a rug. When he felt the first sun warmth, Mack shivered.

The boys ate a little bread while Eddie installed the new carburettor. And when it was ready, they didn't bother to crank it. They pushed it out to the highway and coasted in gear until it started. And then, Eddie driving, they backed up over the rise, over the top, and turned and headed forward and down past Hatton Fields. In Carmel Valley the artichoke plants stood grey-green and the willows were lush along the river. They turned left up the valley. Luck blossomed from the first. A dusty Rhode Island Red rooster who had wandered too far from his own farmyard crossed the road and Eddie hit him without running too far off the road. Sitting in the back of the truck, Hazel picked him as they went and let the feathers fly from his hand, the most widely distributed evidence on record, for there was a little breeze in the morning blowing down from Jamesburg and some of the red chicken-feathers were deposited on Pt. Lobos and some even blew out to sea.

The Carmel is a lovely little river. It isn't very long, but in its course it has everything a river should have. It rises in the mountains, and tumbles down a while, runs through shallows, is dammed to make a lake, spills over the dam, crackles among round boulders, wanders lazily under sycamore, spills into pools where trout live, drops in against banks where crayfish live. In the winter it becomes a torrent, a mean little fierce river, and in the summer it is a place for children to wade in and for fishermen to wander in. Frogs blink from its banks and the deep ferns grow beside it. Deer and foxes come to drink from it secretly in the morning and evening, and now and then a mountain lion, crouched flat, laps its water. The farms of the rich little valley back up the river and take its water for the orchards and the vegetables. The quail call beside it and the wild doves come whistling in at dusk. Raccoons pace its edges looking for frogs. It's everything a river should be.

A few miles up the valley the river cuts in under a high cliff from which vines and ferns hang down. At the base of this cliff there is a pool, green and deep, and on the other side of the pool there is a little sandy place where it is good to sit and cook your dinner.

Mack and the boys came down to this place happily. It was perfect. If frogs were available, they would be here. It was a place to relax, a place to be happy. On the way out they had thriven. In addition to the big red chicken there was a sack of carrots which had fallen from a vegetable truck, half a dozen onions which had not. Mack had a bag of coffee in his pocket. In the truck there was a five-gallon can with the top cut off. The wining-jug was nearly half full. Such things as salt and pepper had been brought. Mack and the boys would have thought anyone who travelled without salt, pepper and coffee very silly indeed.

Without effort, confusion, or much thought, four round stones were rolled together on the little beach. The rooster who had challenged the sunrise of this very day lay dismembered and clean in water in the five-gallon can with peeled onions about him, while a little fire of dead willow sticks sputtered between the stones, a very little fire. Only fools build big fires. It would take a long time to cook this rooster, for it had taken him a long time to achieve his size and muscularity. But as the water began to boil gently about him, he smelled good from the beginning.

Mack gave them a pep talk. "The best time for frogs is at night," he said, "so I guess we'll just lay around till it gets dark." They sat in the shade and gradually one by one they stretched out and slept.

Mack was right. Frogs do not move around much in the daytime; they hide under ferns and they look secretly out of holes under rocks. The way to catch frogs is with a flashlight at night. The men slept, knowing they might have a very active night. Only

Hazel stayed awake to replenish the little fire under the cooking chicken.

There is no golden afternoon next to the cliff. When the sun went over it at about two o'clock a whispering shade came to the beach. The sycamores rustled in the afternoon breeze. Little water-snakes slipped down to the rocks and then gently entered the water and swam along through the pool, their heads held up like little periscopes and a tiny wake spreading behind them. A big trout jumped in the pool. The gnats and mosquitoes which avoid the sun came out and buzzed over the water. All of the sun bugs, the flies, the dragonflies, the wasps, the hornets, went home. And as the shadow came to the beach, as the first quail began to call, Mack and the boys awakened. The smell of the chicken stew was heart-breaking. Hazel had picked a fresh bay-leaf from a tree by the river and he had dropped it in. The carrots were in now. Coffee in its own can was simmering on its own rock, far enough from the flame so that it did not boil too hard. Mack awakened, started up, stretched, staggered to the pool, washed his face with cupped hands, hacked, spat, washed out his mouth, broke wind, tightened his belt, scratched his legs, combed his wet hair with his fingers, drank from the jug, belched and sat down by the fire. "By God, that smells good," he said.

Men all do about the same things when they wake up. Mack's process was loosely the one all of them followed. And soon they had all come to the fire and complimented Hazel. Hazel stuck his pocket-knife into the muscles of the chicken.

"He ain't going to be what you'd call tender," said Hazel. "You'd have to cook him about two weeks to get him tender. How old about do you judge he was, Mack?"

"I'm forty-eight and I ain't as tough as he is," said Mack.

Eddie said, "How old can a chicken get, do you think—that's if nobody pushes him around or he don't get sick?"

"That's something nobody isn't ever going to find out," said Jones.

It was a pleasant time. The jug went around and warmed them.

Jones said, "Eddie, I don't mean to complain none. I was just thinkin'. S'pose you had two or three jugs back of the bar. S'pose you put all the whisky in one and all the wine in another——"

A slightly shocked silence followed this suggestion. "I didn't mean nothing," said Jones quickly. "I like it this way——" Jones talked too much then because he knew he had made a social blunder and he wasn't able to stop. "What I like about it this way is you never know what kind of a drunk you're going to get out of it," he said. "You take whisky," he said hurriedly. "You more or less know what you'll do. A fightin' guy fights and a cryin' guy cries, but this"—he said magnanimously—"why, you don't know whether it'll run you up a pine-tree or start you swimming to Santa Cruz. It's more fun that way," he said weakly.

"Speaking of swimming," said Mack to fill in the indelicate place in the conversation and to shut Jones up. "I wonder whatever happened to that guy McKinley Moran. Remember that deep-sea diver?"

"I remember him," said Hughie. "I and him used to hang around together. He just didn't get much work and then he got to drinking. It's kind of tough on you divin' and drinkin'. Got to worryin' too. Finally he sold his suit and helmet and pump and went on a hell of a drunk and then he left town. I don't know where he went. He wasn't no good after he went down after that Wop that got took down with the anchor from the *Twelve Brothers*. McKinley just dove down. Bust his ear-drums, and he wasn't any good after that. Didn't hurt the Wop a bit."

Mack sampled the jug again. "He used to make a lot of dough during Prohibition," Mack said. "Used to get twenty-five bucks a day from the government to dive lookin' for liquor on the bottom and he got three dollars a case from Louie for not findin' it. Had it worked out so he brought up one case a day to keep the government happy. Louie didn't mind that none. Made it so they didn't get in no new divers. McKinley made a lot of dough."

"Yeah," said Hughie. "But he's like everybody else—gets some dough and he wants to get married. He got married three times before his dough run out. I could always tell. He'd buy a white fox piece and bang!—next thing you'd know, he's married."

"I wonder what happened to Gay," Eddie asked. It was the first time they had spoken of him.

"Same thing, I guess," said Mack. "You just can't trust a married guy. No matter how much he hates his old lady, why, he'll go back to her. Get to thinkin' and broodin' and back he'll go. You can't trust him no more. Take Gay," said Mack. "His old lady hits him. But I bet you when Gay's away from her three days, he gets it figured out that it's his fault and he goes back to make it up to her."

They ate long and daintily, spearing out pieces of chicken, holding the dripping pieces until they cooled and then gnawing the muscled meat from the bone. They speared the carrots on pointed willow switches and finally they passed the can and drank the juice. And around them the evening crept in as delicately as music. The quail called each other down to the water. The trout jumped in the pool. And the moths came down and fluttered about the pool as the daylight mixed into the darkness. They passed the coffee-can about and they were warm and fed and silent. At last Mack said, "God damn it. I hate a liar."

"Who's been lyin' to you?" Eddie asked.

"Oh, I don't mind a guy that tells a little one to get along or to hop up a conversation, but I hate a guy that lies to himself."

"Who done that?" Eddie asked.

"Me," said Mack. "And maybe you guys. Here we are," he said earnestly, "the whole god-damned shabby lot of us. We worked it out that we wanted to give Doc a party. So we come out here and have a hell of a lot of fun. Then we'll go back and get the dough from Doc. There's five of us, so we'll drink five times as much liquor as he will. And I ain't sure we're doin' it for Doc. I ain't sure we ain't doin' it for ourselves. And Doc's too nice a fella to do that to. Doc is the nicest fella I ever knew. I don't want to be the kind of guy that would take advantage of him. You know one time I put the bee on him for a buck. I give him a hell of a story. Right in the middle I seen he knew god-damn well the story was so much malarky. So right in the middle I says, 'Doc, that's a fuggin' lie!' And he put his hand in his pocket and brought out a buck. 'Mack,' he said, 'I figure a guy that needs it bad enough to make up a lie to get it, really needs it,' and he give me the buck. I paid him that buck back the next day. I never did spend it. Just kept it overnight and then give it back to him."

Hazel said, "There ain't nobody likes a party better than Doc. We're givin' him the party. What the hell is the beef?"

"I don't know," said Mack. "I'd just like to give him something when I didn't get most of it back."

"How about a present?" Hughie suggested. "S'pose we just bought the whisky and give it to him and let him do what he wants."

"Now you're talkin'," said Mack. "That's just what we'll do. We'll give him the whisky and fade out."

"You know what'll happen," said Eddie. "Henri and them people from Carmel will smell that whisky out and then instead of only five of us there'll be twenty. Doc told me one time himself they can smell him fryin' a steak from Cannery Row clear down to Point Sur. I don't see the percentage. He'd come out better if we gave him the party ourselves."

Mack considered this reasoning. "Maybe you're right," he said at last. "But s'pose we give him something except whisky, maybe cuff-links with his initials."

"Oh, horse shit," said Hazel. "Doc don't want stuff like that."

The night was in by now and the stars were white in the sky. Hazel fed the fire and it put a little room of light on the beach. Over the hill a fox was barking sharply. And now in the night the smell of sage came down from the hills. The water chuckled over the stones where it went out of the deep pool.

Mack was mulling over the last piece of reasoning when the sound of footsteps on the ground made them turn. A man dark and large stalked near and he had a shotgun over his arm and a pointer walked shyly and delicately at his heel.

"What the hell are you doing here?" he asked.

"Nothing," said Mack.

"The land's posted. No fishing, hunting, fires, camping. Now you just pack up and put that fire out and get off this land."

Mack stood up humbly. "I didn't know, Captain," he said. "Honest, we never seen the sign, Captain."

"There's signs all over. You couldn't have missed them."

"Look, Captain, we made a mistake and we're sorry," said Mack. He paused and looked closely at the slouching figure. "You are a military man, aren't you, sir? I can always tell. Military men don't carry his shoulders the same as ordinary people. I was in the army so long, I can always tell."

Imperceptibly the shoulders of the man straightened, nothing obvious, but he held himself differently.

"I don't allow fires on my place," he said.

"Well, we're sorry," said Mack. "We'll get right out, Captain. You see, we're working for some scientists. We're tryin' to get some frogs. They're working on cancer and we're helpin' out getting some frogs."

The man hesitated for a moment. "What do they do with the frogs?" he asked.

"Well, sir," said Mack, "they give cancer to the frogs and then they can study and experiment and they got it nearly licked if they can just get some frogs. But if you don't want us on your land, Captain, we'll get right out. Never would of come in if we knew." Suddenly Mack seemed to see the pointer for the first time. "By God, that's a fine-lookin' bitch," he said enthusiastically. "She looks like Nola that win the field trials in Virginia last year. She a Virginia dog, Captain?"

The captain hesitated and then he lied. "Yes," he said shortly. "She's lame. Tick got her right on her shoulder."

Mack was instantly solicitous. "Mind if I look, Captain? Come, girl. Come on, girl." The pointer looked up at her master and then sidled up to Mack. "Pile on some twigs so I can see," he said to Hazel.

"It's up where she can't lick it," said the captain, and he leaned over Mack's shoulder to look.

Mack pressed some pus out of the evil-looking crater on the dog's shoulder. "I had a dog once had a thing like this and it went right in an killed him. She just had pups, didn't she?"

"Yes," said the captain, "six. I put iodine on that place."

"No," said Mack, "that won't draw. You got any Epsom salts up at your place?"

"Yes—there's a big bottle."

"Well, you make a hot poultice of Epsom salts and put it on there. She's weak, you know, from the pups. Be a shame if she got sick now. You'd lose the pups too." The pointer looked deep into Mack's eyes and then she licked his hand.

"Tell you what I'll do, Captain. I'll look after her myself. Epsom salt'll do the trick. That's the best thing."

The captain stroked the dog's head. "You know, I've got a pond up by the house that's so full of frogs I can't sleep nights. Why don't you look up there? They bellow all night. I'd be glad to get rid of them."

"That's mighty nice of you," said Mack. "I'll bet those docs would thank you for that. But I'd like to get a poultice on this dog." He turned to the others. "You put out this fire," he said. "Make sure there ain't a spark left and clean up around. You don't want to leave no mess. I and the captain will go and take care of Nola here. You fellows follow along when you get cleared up." Mack and the captain walked away together.

Hazel kicked sand on the fire. "I bet Mack could of been President of the U.S. if he wanted," he said.

"What could he do with it if he had it?" Jones asked. "There wouldn't be no fun in that."

CHAPTER XIV

EARLY MORNING is a time of magic in Cannery Row. In the grey time after the light has come and before the sun has risen, the Row seems to hang suspended out of time in a silvery light. The street lights go out, and the weeds are a brilliant green. The corrugated iron of the canneries glows with the pearly lucence of platinum or old pewter. No automobiles are running then. The street is silent of progress and business. And the rush and drag of the waves can be heard as they splash in among the piles of the canneries. It is a time of great peace, a deserted time, a little era of rest. Cats drip over the fences and slither like syrup over the ground to look for fish-heads. Silent early-morning dogs parade majestically, picking and choosing judiciously whereon to pee. The seagulls come flapping in to sit on the cannery roofs, to await the day of refuse. They sit on the roof peaks shoulder to shoulder. From the rocks near the Hopkins Marine Station comes the barking of sea-lions like the baying of hounds. The air is cool and fresh. In the back gardens the gophers push up the morning mounds of fresh damp earth and they creep out and drag flowers into their holes. Very few people are about, just enough to make it seem more deserted than it is. One of Dora's girls comes home from a call on a patron too wealthy or too sick to visit the Bear Flag. Her make-up is a little sticky and her feet are tired. Lee Chong brings the garbage cans out and stands them on the kerb. The old Chinaman comes out of the sea and flap-flaps across the street and up past the Palace. The cannery watchmen look out and blink at the morning light. The bouncer at the Bear Flag steps out on the porch in his shirt-sleeves and stretches and yawns and scratches his stomach. The snores of Mr. Malloy's tenants in the pipes have a deep tunnelly quality. It is the hour of the pearl—the interval between day and night when time stops and examines itself.

On such a morning and in such a light two soldiers and two girls strolled easily along the street. They had come out of "La Ida" and they were very tired and very happy. The girls were hefty, big-breasted and strong and their blonde hair was in slight disarray. They wore printed rayon party dresses, wrinkled now and clinging to their convexities. And each girl wore a soldier's cap, one far back on her head and the other with the visor down almost on her nose. They were full-lipped, broad-nosed, hippy girls and they were very tired.

The soldiers' tunics were unbuttoned and their belts were threaded through their epaulettes. The ties were pulled down a little so the shirt-collars could be unbuttoned. And the soldiers wore the girls' hats, one a tiny yellow straw boater with a bunch of daisies on the crown, the other a white knitted half-hat, to which medallions of blue cellophane adhered. They walked holding hands, swinging their hands rhythmically. The soldier on the outside had a large brown-paper bag filled with cold canned beer. They strolled softly in the pearly light. They had had a hell of a time and they felt good. They smiled delicately like weary children remembering a party. They looked at one another and smiled and they swung their hands. Past the Bear Flag they went and said "Hiya" to the bouncer who was scratching his stomach. They listened to the snores from the pipes and laughed a little. At Lee Chong's they stopped and looked into the messy display window where tools and clothes and food crowded for attention. Swinging their hands and scuffing their feet, they came to the end of Cannery Row and turned up to the railroad-track. The girls climbed up on the rails and walked along on them and the soldiers put their arms around the plump waists to keep them from falling. They went past the boat-works and turned down into the park-like property of the Hopkins Marine Station. There is a tiny curved beach in front of the station, a miniature beach between little reefs. The gentle morning waves licked up the beach and whispered softly. The fine smell of seaweed came from the exposed rocks. As the four came to the beach a sliver of the sun broke over Tom Work's land across the head of the bay and it gilded the water and made the rocks yellow. The girls sat formally down in the sand and straightened their skirts over their knees. One of the soldiers punched holes in four cans of beer and handed them round. And then the men lay down and put their heads in the girls' laps and looked up into their faces. And they smiled at each other, a tired and peaceful and wonderful secret.

From up near the station came the barking of a dog—the watchman, a dark and surly man, had seen them and his black and surly cocker spaniel had seen them. He shouted at them, and when they did not move he came down on the beach and his dog barked monotonously. "Don't you know you can't lay around here? You got to get off. This is private property!"

The soldiers did not even seem to hear him. They smiled on and the girls were stroking their hair over the temples. At last in slow motion one of the soldiers turned his head so that his cheek was cradled between the girl's legs. He smiled benevolently at the caretaker. "Why don't you take a flying fuggut at the moon?" he said kindly, and he turned back to look at the girl.

The sun lighted her blonde hair and she scratched him over one ear. They didn't even see the caretaker go back to his house.

CHAPTER XV

By the time the boys got up to the farmhouse Mack was in the kitchen. The pointer bitch lay on her side, and Mack held a cloth saturated with Epsom salts against her tick-bite. Among her legs the big fat wiener pups nuzzled and bumped for milk and the bitch looked patiently up into Mack's face, saying, "You see how it is? I try to tell him, but he doesn't understand."

The captain held a lamp and looked down on Mack.

"I'm glad to know about that," he said.

Mack said, "I don't want to tell you about your business, sir, but these pups ought to be weaned. She ain't got a hell of a lot of milk left and them pups are chewin' her to pieces."

"I know," said the captain. "I s'pose I should have drowned them all but one. I've been so busy trying to keep the place going. People don't take the interest in bird dogs they used to. It's all poodles and boxers and Dobermans."

"I know," said Mack. "And there ain't no dog like a pointer for a man. I don't know what's come over people. But you wouldn't of drowned them, would you, sir?"

"Well," said the captain, "since my wife went into politics, I'm 'ust running crazy. She got elected to the Assembly for this district, and when the Legislature isn't in session she's off making speeches. And when she's home she's studying all the time and writing bills."

"Must be lousy in—I mean it must be pretty lonely," said Mack. "Now if I had a pup like this"—he picked up a squirming puzz-faced pup—"why, I bet I'd have a real bird dog in three years. I'd take a bitch every time."

"Would you like to have one?" the captain asked.

Mack looked up. "You mean you'd let me have one? Oh! Jesus Christ, yes."

"Take your pick," said the captain. "Nobody seems to understand bird dogs any more."

The boys stood in the kitchen and gathered quick impressions. It was obvious that the wife was away—the opened cans, the frying-pan with lace from fried eggs still sticking to it, the crumbs on the kitchen table, the open box of shotgun shells on the bread-box, all shrieked of the lack of a woman, while the white curtains and the papers on the dish shelves and the too small towels on the rack told them a woman had been there. And they were unconsciously glad she wasn't there. The kind of women who put papers on shelves and had little towels like that instinctively distrusted and disliked Mack and the boys. Such women knew that they were the worst threats to a home, for they offered ease and thought and companionship as opposed to neatness, order, and properness. They were very glad she was away.

Now the captain seemed to feel that they were doing him a favour. He didn't want them to leave. He said hesitantly, "S'pose you boys would like a little something to warm you up before you go out for the frogs?"

The others looked at Mack. Mack was frowning as though he was thinking it through. "When we're out doin' scientific stuff, we make it a kind of a rule not to touch nothin'," he said, and then quickly, as though he might have gone too far: "But seein' as how you been so nice to us—well, I wouldn't mind a short one myself. I don't know about the boys."

The boys agreed that they wouldn't mind a short one either. The captain got a flashlight and went down in the cellar. They could hear him moving lumber and boxes about, and he came back upstairs with a five-gallon oak keg in his arms. He set it on the table. "During Prohibition I got some corn whisky and laid it away. I just got to thinking I'd like to see how it is. It's pretty old now. I'd almost forgot it. You see—my wife——" he let it go at that because it was apparent that they understood. The captain knocked out the oak plug from the end of the keg and got glasses down from the shelf that had scallop-edged paper laid on it. It is a hard job to pour a small drink from a five-gallon keg. Each of them got half a water-glass of the clear brown liquor. They waited ceremoniously for the captain and then they said, "Over the river," and tossed it back. They swallowed, tasted their tongues, sucked their lips, and there was a faraway look in their eyes.

Mack peered into his empty glass as though some holy message was written in the bottom. And then he raised his eyes. "You can't say nothin' about that," he said. "They don't put that in bottles." He breathed in deeply and sucked his breath as it came out. "I don't think I ever tasted nothin' as good as that," he said.

The captain looked pleased. His glance wandered back to the keg. "It is good," he said. "You think we might have another little one?"

Mack stared into his glass again. "Maybe a short one," he agreed. "Wouldn't it be easier to pour out some in a pitcher? You're liable to spill it that way."

Two hours later they recalled what they had come for.

The frog pool was square—fifty feet wide and seventy feet long and four feet deep. Lush soft grass grew about its edge, and a little ditch brought the water from the river to it and from it little ditches went out to the orchards. There were frogs there all right, thousands of them. Their voices beat the night, they boomed and barked and croaked and rattled. They sang to the stars, to the waning moon, to the waving grasses. They bellowed love songs and challenges. The men crept through the darkness toward the pool. The captain carried a nearly-filled pitcher of whisky and every man had his own glass. The captain had found them flashlights that worked. Hughie and Jones carried gunny sacks. As they drew quietly near, the frogs heard them coming. The night had been roaring with frog song and then suddenly it was silent. Mack and the boys and the captain sat down on the ground to have one last short one and to map their campaign. And the plan was bold.

During the millennia that frogs and men have lived in the same world, it is probable that men have hunted frogs. And during that time a pattern of hunt and parry has developed. The man with net or bow or lance or gun creeps noiselessly, as he thinks, toward the frog. The pattern requires that the frog sit still, sit very still and wait. The rules of the game require the frog to wait until the final flicker of a second, when the net is descending, when the lance is in the air, when the finger squeezes the trigger—then the frog jumps, plops into the water, swims to the bottom and waits until the man goes away. That is the way it is done, the way it has always been done. Frogs have every right to expect it will always be done that way. Now and then the net is too quick, the lance pierces, the gun flicks and that frog is gone, but it is all fair and in the frame-work. Frogs don't resent that. But how could they have anticipated Mack's new method? How could they have foreseen the horror that followed? The sudden flashing of lights, the shouting and squealing of men, the rush of feet. Every frog leaped, plopped into the pool, and swam frantically to the bottom. Then into the pool plunged the line of men, stamping, churning, moving in a crazy line up the pool, flinging their feet about. Hysterically the frogs, displaced from their placid spots, swam ahead of the crazy thrashing feet, and the feet came on. Frogs are good swimmers, but they haven't much endurance. Down the pool they went until finally they were bunched and crowded against the ends. And the feet and wildly-plunging bodies followed them. A few frogs lost their heads and floundered among the feet and got through, and these were saved. But the majority decided to leave this pool for ever, to find a new home in a new country where this kind of thing didn't happen. A wave of frantic, frustrated frogs, big ones, little ones, brown ones, green ones, men frogs and women frogs, a wave of them broke over the bank, crawled, leaped, scrambled. They clambered up the grass, they clutched at each other, little ones rode on big ones. And then—horror on horror—the flashlights found them. Two men gathered them like berries. The line came out of the water and closed in on their rear and gathered them like potatoes. Tens and fifties of them were flung into the gunny sacks, and the sacks filled with tired, frightened, and disillusioned frogs, with dripping, whimpering frogs. Some got away, of course, and some had been saved in the pool. But never in frog history had such an execution taken place. Frogs by the pound, by the fifty pounds. They weren't counted, but there must have been six or seven hundred. Then happily Mack tied up the necks of the sacks. They were soaking, dripping wet and the air was cool. They had a short one in the grass before they went back to the house, so they wouldn't catch cold.

It is doubtful whether the captain had ever had so much fun. He was indebted to Mack and the boys. Later when the curtains caught fire and were put out with the little towels, the captain told the boys not to mind it. He felt it was an honour to have them burn his house clear down, if they wanted to. "My wife is a wonderful woman," he said in a kind of peroration. "Most wonderful woman. Ought to have been a man. If she was a man I wouldn' of married her." He laughed a long time over that and repeated it three or four times, and resolved to remember it so he could tell it to a lot of other people. He filled a jug with whisky and gave it to Mack. He wanted to go to live with them in the Palace Flop-house. He decided that his wife would like Mack and the boys if she only knew them. Finally he went to sleep on the floor with his head among the puppies. Mack and the boys poured themselves a short one and regarded him seriously.

Mack said, "He give me that jug of whisky, didn't he? You heard him?"

"Sure he did," said Eddie. "I heard him."

"And he give me a pup?"
"Sure, pick of the litter. We all heard him. Why?"
"I never did roll a drunk and I ain't gonna start now," said Mack. "We got to get out of here. He's gonna wake up feelin' lousy and it's goin' to be all our fault. I just don't want to be here." Mack glanced at the burned curtains, at the floor glistening with whisky and puppy dirt, at the bacon grease that was coagulating on the stove front. He went to the pups, looked them over carefully, felt bone and frame, looked in eyes and regarded jaws, and he picked out a beautifully-spotted bitch with a liver-coloured nose and a fine dark-yellow eye. "Come on, darling," he said.

They blew out the lamp because of the danger of fire. It was just turning dawn as they left the house.

"I don't think I ever had such a fine trip," said Mack. "But I got to thinkin' about his wife comin' back and it gave me the shivers." The pup whined in his arms and he put it under his coat. "He's a real nice fella," said Mack. "After you get him feelin' easy, that is." He strode on toward the place where they had parked the Ford. "We shouldn't go forgettin' we're doin' all this for Doc," he said. "From the way things are pannin' out, it looks like Doc is a pretty lucky guy."

CHAPTER XVI

PROBABLY THE busiest time the girls of the Bear Flag ever had was the March of the big sardine catch. It wasn't only that the fish ran in silvery billions and money ran almost as freely. A new regiment moved into the Presidio and a new bunch of soldiers always shop around a good deal before they settle down. Dora was short-handed just at that time, too, for Eva Flanagan had gone to East St. Louis on a vacation, Phyllis Mae had broken her leg getting out of the roller-coaster in Santa Cruz, and Elsie Doublebottom had made a novena and wasn't much good for anything else. The men from the sardine fleet, loaded with dough, were in and out all afternoon. They sail at dark and fish all night, so they must play in the afternoon. In the evening the soldiers of the new regiment came down and stood around playing the musical box and drinking Coca-Cola and sizing up the girls for the time when they would be paid. Dora was having trouble with her income-tax, for she was entangled in that curious enigma which said the business was illegal and then taxed her for it. In addition to everything else there were the regulars—the steady customers who had been coming down for years, the labourers from the gravel-pits, the riders from the ranches, the railroad men who came in the front door, and the city officials and prominent business men who came in the rear entrance by the tracks and who had little chintz sitting-rooms assigned to them.

All in all it was a terrific month and right in the middle of it the influenza epidemic had to break out. It came to the whole town. Mrs. Talbot and her daughter of the San Carlos Hotel had it. Tom Work had it. Benjamin Peabody and his wife had it. Excelentisima Maria Antonia Field had it. The whole Gross family came down with it.

The doctors of Monterey—and there were enough of them to take care of the ordinary diseases, accidents and neuroses—were running crazy. They had more business than they could do among clients who, if they didn't pay their bills, at least had the money to pay them. Cannery Row, which produces a tougher breed than the rest of the town, was late in contracting it, but finally it got them too. The schools were closed. There wasn't a house that hadn't feverish children and sick parents. It was not a deadly disease, as it was in 1917, but with children it had a tendency to go into the mastoids. The medical profession was very busy, and besides, Cannery Row was not considered a very good financial risk.

Now Doc of the Western Biological Laboratory had no right to practise medicine. It was not his fault that everyone in the Row came to him for medical advice. Before he knew it he found himself running from shanty to shanty taking temperatures, giving physics, borrowing and delivering blankets and even taking food from house to house where mothers looked at him with inflamed eyes from their beds, and thanked him and put the full responsibility for their children's recovery on him. When a case got really out of hand he phoned a local doctor and sometimes one came, if it seemed to be an emergency. But to the families it was all emergency. Doc didn't get much sleep. He lived on beer and canned sardines. In Lee Chong's, where he went to get beer, he met Dora, who was there to buy a pair of nail-clippers.

"You look done in," Dora said.

"I am," Doc admitted. "I haven't had any sleep for about a week."

"I know," said Dora. "I hear it's bad. Comes at a bad time too."

"Well, we haven't lost anybody yet," said Doc. "But there are some awful sick kids. The Ransel kids have all developed mastoiditis."

"Is there anything I can do?" Dora asked.

Doc said, "You know, there is. People get so scared and helpless. Take the Ransels—they're scared to death and they're scared to be alone. If you, or some of the girls, could just sit with them."

Dora, who was soft as a mouse's belly, could be as hard as carborundum. She went back to the Bear Flag and organized it for service. It was a bad time for her, but she did it. The Greek cook made a ten-gallon cauldron of strong soup and kept it full and kept it strong. The girls tried to keep up their business, but they went in shifts to sit with the families, and they carried pots of soup when they went. Doc was in almost constant demand. Dora consulted him and detailed the girls where he suggested. And all the time the business at the Bear Flag was booming. The musical-box never stopped playing. The men of the fishing fleet and the soldiers stood in line. And the girls did their work and then they took their pots of soup and went to sit with the Ransels, with the McCarthys, with the Ferrias. The girls slipped out the back door, and sometimes staying with the sleeping children the girls dropped to sleep in their chairs. They didn't use make-up for work any more. They didn't have to. Dora herself said she could have used the total membership of the old ladies' home. It was the busiest time the girls at the Bear Flag could remember. Everyone was glad when it was over.

CHAPTER XVII

In spite of his friendliness and his friends Doc was a lonely and set-apart man. Mack probably noticed it more than anybody. In a group, Doc seemed always alone. When the lights were on and the curtains drawn, and the Gregorian music played on the great phonograph, Mack used to look down on the laboratory from the Palace Flop-house. He knew Doc had a girl in there, but Mack used to get a dreadful feeling of loneliness out of it. Even in the dear close contact with a girl Mack felt that Doc would be lonely. Doc was a night crawler. The lights were on in the lab all night and yet he seemed to be up in the daytime too. And the great shrouds of music came out of the lab at any time of the day or night. Sometimes when it was all dark and when it seemed that sleep had come at last, the diamond-true child voices of the Sistine Choir would come from the windows of the laboratory.

Doc had to keep up his collecting. He tried to get to the good tides along the coast. The sea rocks and the beaches were his stock-pile. He knew where everything was when he wanted it. All the articles of his trade were filed away on the coast, sea cradles here, octopi here, tub worms in another place, sea pansies in another. He knew where to get them, but he could not go for them exactly when he wanted. For Nature locked up the items and only released them occasionally. Doc had to know not only the tides, but when a particular low tide was good in a particular place. When such a low tide occurred, he packed his collecting tools in his car, he packed his jars, his bottles, his plates and preservatives, and he went to the beach or reef or rock ledge where the animals he needed were stored.

Now he had an order for small octopi and the nearest place to get them was the boulder-strewn inter-tidal zone at La Jolla, between Los Angeles and San Diego. It meant a five-hundred-mile drive each way and his arrival had to coincide with the retreating waters.

The little octopi live among the boulders embedded in sand. Being timid and young, they prefer a bottom on which there are many caves and little crevices and lumps of mud where they may hide from predators and protect themselves from the waves. But on the same flat there are millions of sea cradles. While filling a definite order for octopi, Doc could replenish his stock of the cradles.

Low tide was 5.17 a.m. on a Thursday. If Doc left Monterey on Wednesday morning he could be there easily in time for the tide on Thursday. He would have taken someone with him for company, but quite by accident everyone was away or was busy. Mack and the boys were up Carmel Valley collecting frogs. Three young women he knew and would have enjoyed as companions had jobs and couldn't get away in the middle of the week. Henri the painter was occupied, for Holman's Department Store had employed not a flag-pole sitter, but a flag-pole skater. On a tall mast on top of the store he had a little round platform and there he was on skates going round and round. He had been there three days and three nights. He was out to set a new record for being on skates on a platform. The previous record was 127 hours, so he had some time to go. Henri had taken up his post across the street at Red Williams' petrol station. Henri was fascinated. He thought of doing a huge abstraction called Substratum Dream of a Flag-pole Skater. Henri couldn't leave town while the skater was up there. He protested that there were philosophic implications in flag-pole skating that no one had touched. Henri sat in a chair, leaned back against the lattice which concealed the door of the men's toilet at Red Williams'. He kept his eye on the eyrie skating-platform and obviously he couldn't go with Doc to La Jolla. Doc had to go alone, because the tide would not wait.

Early in the morning he got his things together. Personal things went in a small satchel. Another satchel held instruments and syringes. Having packed, he combed and trimmed his brown beard, saw that his pencils were in his shirt pocket, and his magnifying-glass attached to his lapel. He packed the trays, bottles, glass plates, preservatives, rubber boots and a blanket into the back of his car. He worked through the pearly time, washed three days' dishes, put the garbage into the surf. He closed the doors but did not lock them, and by nine o'clock was on his way.

It took Doc longer to go places than other people. He didn't drive fast and he stopped and ate hamburgers very often. Driving up to Lighthouse Avenue he waved at a dog that looked round and smiled at him. In Monterey, before he even started, he felt hungry and stopped at Herman's for a hamburger and beer. While he ate his sandwich and sipped his beer, a lot of conversation came back to him. Blaisedell, the poet, had said to him, "You love beer so much. I'll bet some day you'll go in and order a beer milk-shake." It was a simple piece of foolery, but it had bothered Doc ever since. He wondered what a beer milk-shake would taste like. The idea gagged him, but he couldn't let it alone. It cropped up every time he had a glass of beer. Would it curdle the milk? Would you add sugar? It was like a shrimp ice-cream. Once the thing got into your head you couldn't forget it. He finished his sandwich and paid Herman. He purposely didn't look at the milk-shake machines lined up so shiny against the back wall. If a man ordered a beer milk-shake, he thought, he'd better do it in a town where he wasn't known. But then, a man with a beard, ordering a beer milk-shake in a town where he wasn't known—they might call the police. A man with a beard was always a little suspect anyway. You couldn't say you wore a beard because you like a beard. People didn't like you for telling the truth. You had to say you had a scar, so you couldn't shave. Once when Doc was at the University of Chicago he had love trouble and he had worked too hard. He thought it would be nice to take a very long walk. He put on a little knapsack and he walked through Indiana and Kentucky and North Carolina and Georgia, clear to Florida. He walked among farmers and mountain people, among the swamp people and fishermen. And everywhere people asked him why he was walking through the country.

Because he loved true things he tried to explain. He said he was nervous and besides he wanted to see the country, smell the ground and look at grass and birds and trees, to savour the country, and there was no other way to do it save on foot. And people didn't like him for telling the truth. They scowled, or shook and tapped their heads, they laughed as though they knew it was a lie and they appreciated a liar. And some, afraid for their daughters or their pigs, told him to move on, to get going, just not to stop near their place if he knew what was good for him.

And so he stopped trying to tell the truth. He said he was doing it on a bet—that he stood to win a hundred dollars. Everyone liked him then and believed him. They asked him in to dinner and gave him a bed and they put lunches up for him and wished him good luck and thought he was a hell of a fine fellow. Doc still loved true things, but he knew it was not a general love and it could be a very dangerous mistress.

Doc didn't stop in Salinas for a hamburger. But he stopped in

Gonzales, in King City, and in Paso Robles. He had hamburger and beer at Santa Maria—two in Santa Maria, because it was a long pull from there to Santa Barbara. In Santa Barbara he had soup, lettuce and string-bean salad, pot roast and mashed potatoes, pineapple-pie and blue cheese and coffee, and after that he filled the petrol tank and went to the toilet. While the service station checked his oil and tyres, Doc washed his face and combed his beard and when he came back to the car a number of potential hitch-hikers were waiting.

"Going south, Mister?"

Doc travelled on the highways a good deal. He was an old hand. You have to pick your hitch-hikers very carefully. It's best to get an experienced one, for he relapses into silence. But the new ones try to pay for their ride by being interesting. Doc had had a leg talked off by some of these. Then after you have made up your mind about the one you want to take, you protect yourself by saying you aren't going far. If your man turns out too much for you, you can drop him. On the other hand, you may be just lucky and get a man very much worth knowing. Doc made a quick survey of the line and chose his company, a thin-faced salesman-like man in a blue suit. He had deep lines beside his mouth and dark brooding eyes.

He looked at Doc with dislike. "Going south, Mister?"

"Yes," said Doc, "a little way."

"Mind taking me along?"

"Get in!" said Doc.

When they got to Ventura it was pretty soon after the heavy dinner, so Doc only stopped for beer. The hitch-hiker hadn't spoken once. Doc pulled up at a roadside stand.

"Want some beer?"

"No," said the hitch-hiker. "And I don't mind saying I think it's not a very good idea to drive under the influence of alcohol. It's none of my business what you do with your own life, but in this case you've got an automobile, and that can be a murderous weapon in the hands of a drunken driver."

At the beginning Doc had been slightly startled. "Get out of the car," he said softly.

"What?"

"I'm going to punch you on the nose," said Doc. "If you aren't out of this car before I count ten. One—two—three——"

The man fumbled at the door catch and backed hurriedly out of the car. But once outside he howled, "I'm going to find an officer. I'm going to have you arrested."

Doc opened the box on the dashboard and took out a monkey-wrench. His guest saw the gesture and walked hurriedly away.

Doc walked angrily to the counter of the stand.

The waitress, a blonde beauty with just the hint of a goitre, smiled at him. "What'll it be?"

"Beer milk-shake," said Doc.

"What?"

Well, here it was and what the hell! Might just as well get it over with now as some time later.

The blonde asked, "Are you kidding?"

Doc knew wearily that he couldn't explain, couldn't tell the truth. "I've got a bladder complaint," he said. "Bipalychaetsonectomy, the doctors call it. I'm supposed to drink a *beer milk-shake*. Doctor's orders."

The blonde smiled reassuringly. "Oh! I thought you was kidding," she said archly. "You tell me how to make it. I didn't know you was sick."

"Very sick," said Doc, "and due to be sicker. Put in some milk, and add half a bottle of beer. Give me the other half in a glass—no sugar in the milk-shake." When she served it, he tasted it wryly. And it wasn't so bad—it just tasted like stale beer and milk.

"It sounds awful," said the blonde.

"It's not so bad when you get used to it," said Doc. "I've been drinking it for seventeen years."

CHAPTER XVIII

DOC HAD driven slowly. It was late afternoon when he stopped in Ventura, so late in fact that when he stopped in Carpenteria he only had a cheese sandwich and went to the toilet. Besides, he intended to get a good dinner in Los Angeles, and it was dark when he got there. He drove on through and stopped at a big Chicken-in-the-Rough place he knew about. And there he had fried chicken, julienne potatoes, hot biscuits and honey, and a piece of pineapple-pie and blue cheese. And here he filled his thermos-bottle with hot coffee, had them make up six ham sandwiches and bought two quarts of beer for breakfast.

It was not so interesting driving at night. No dogs to see, only the highway lighted with his headlights. Doc speeded up to finish the trip. It was about two o'clock when he got to La Jolla. He drove through the town and down to the cliff below which his tidal flat lay. There he stopped the car, ate a sandwich, drank some beer, turned out the lights and curled up in the seat to sleep.

He didn't need a clock. He had been working in a tidal pattern so long that he could feel a tide change in his sleep. In the dawn he awakened, looked out through the windshield and saw that the water was already retreating down the bouldery flat. He drank some hot coffee, ate three sandwiches and had a quart of beer.

The tide goes out imperceptibly. The boulders show and seem to rise up and the ocean recedes, leaving little pools, leaving wet weed and moss and sponge, iridescence and brown and blue and China-red. On the bottoms lie the incredible refuse of the sea, shells broken and chipped and bits of skeleton, claws, the whole sea bottom a fantastic cemetery on which the living scamper and scramble.

Doc pulled on his rubber boots and set his rain hat fussily. He took his buckets and jars and his crowbar, and put his sandwiches in one pocket and his thermos-bottle in another pocket, and he went down the cliff to the tidal flat. Then he worked down the flat after the retreating sea. He turned over the boulders with his crowbar and now and then his hand darted quickly into the standing-water and brought out a little angry squirming octopus, which blushed with rage and spat ink on his hand. Then he dropped it into a jar of sea water with the others, and usually the newcomer was so angry that it attacked its fellows.

It was good hunting that day. He got twenty-two little octopi. And he picked off several hundred sea cradles and put them in his wooden bucket. As the tide moved out he followed it, while the morning came and the sun arose. The flat extended out two hundred yards and then there was a line of heavy weed-crusted rocks before it dropped off to deep water. Doc worked out to the barrier-edge. He had about what he wanted now, and the rest of the time he looked under stones, leaned down and peered into the tide pools, with their brilliant mosaics and their scuttling, bubbling life. And he came at last to the outer barrier, where the long leathery brown algæ hung down into the water. Red starfish clustered on the rocks, and the sea pulsed up and down against the barrier, waiting to get in again. Between two weeded rocks on the barrier Doc saw a flash of white under water and then the floating weed covered it. He climbed to the place over the slippery rocks, held himself firmly, and gently reached down and parted the brown algæ. Then he grew rigid. A girl's face looked up at him, a pretty, pale girl with dark hair. The eyes were open and clear and the face was firm and the hair washed gently about her head. The body was out of sight, caught in the crevice. The lips were slightly parted and the teeth showed, and on the face was only comfort and rest. Just under water it was and the clear water made it very beautiful. It seemed to Doc that he looked at it for many minutes, and the face burned into his picture memory.

Very slowly he raised his hand and let the brown weed float back and cover the face. Doc's heart pounded deeply and his throat felt tight. He picked up his bucket and his jars and his crowbar and went slowly over the slippery rocks back toward the beach.

And the girl's face went ahead of him. He sat down on the beach in the coarse dry sand and pulled off his boots. In the jar the little octopi were huddled up, each keeping as far as possible from the others. Music sounded in Doc's ears, a high thin piercingly sweet flute carrying a melody he could never remember, and, against this, a pounding surf-like wood-wind section. The flute went up into regions beyond the hearing range and even there it carried its unbelievable melody. Goose pimples came out on Doc's arms. He shivered and his eyes were wet the way they get in the focus of great beauty. The girl's eyes had been grey and clear and the dark hair floated, drifting lightly over the face. The picture was set for all time. He sat there while the first little spout of water came over the reef, bringing the returning tide. He sat there hearing the music, while the sea crept in again over the bouldery flat. His hand tapped out the rhythm, and the terrifying flute played in his brain. The eyes were grey and the mouth smiled a little or seemed to catch its breath in ecstasy.

A voice seemed to awaken him. A man stood over him. "Been fishing?"

"No, collecting."

"Well—what are them things?"

"Baby octopi."

"You mean devil-fish? I didn't know there was any there. I've lived here all my life."

"You've got to look for them," said Doc listlessly.

"Say," said the man, "aren't you feeling well? You look sick."

The flute climbed again and plucked cellos sounded below and the sea crept in and in toward the beach. Doc shook off the music, shook off the face, shook the chill out of his body. "Is there a police station near?"

"Up in town. Why, what's wrong?"

"There's a body out on the reef."

"Where?"

"Right out there—wedged between two rocks. A girl."

"Say——" said the man. "You get a bounty for finding a body. I forget how much."

Doc stood up and gathered his equipment. "Will you report it? I'm not feeling well."

"Give you a shock, did it? Is it—bad? Rotten or eat up?"

Doc turned away. "You take the bounty," he said. "I don't want it." He started toward the car. Only the tiniest piping of the flute sounded in his head.

CHAPTER XIX

Probably nothing in the way of promotion Holman's Department Store ever did attracted so much favourable comment as the engagement of the flag-pole skater. Day after day, there he was up on his little round platform skating round and round, and at night he could be seen up there too, dark against the sky, so that everybody knew he didn't come down. It was generally agreed, however, that a steel rod came up through the centre of the platform at night and he strapped himself to it. But he didn't sit down and no one minded the steel rod. People came from Jamesburg to see him and from down the coast as far as Grimes Point. Salinas people came over in droves and the Farmers Mercantile of that town put in a bid for the next appearance, when the skater could attempt to break his own record and thus give the new world's record to Salinas. Since there weren't many flag-pole skaters and since this one was by far the best, he had for the past year gone about breaking his own world's record.

Holman's was delighted about the venture. They had a white sale, a remnant sale, an aluminium sale, and a crockery sale all going at the same time. Crowds of people stood in the street watching the lone man on his platform.

His second day up, he sent down word that someone was shooting at him with an air-gun. The display department used its head. It figured the angles and located the offender. It was old Doctor Merrivale, hiding behind the curtains of his office, plugging away with a Daisy air-rifle. They didn't denounce him and he promised to stop. He was very prominent in the Masonic Lodge.

Henri the painter kept his chair at Red Williams' service station. He worked out every possible philosophic approach to the situation and came to the conclusion that he would have to build a platform at home and try it himself. Everyone in the town was more or less affected by the skater. Trade fell off out of sight of him and got better the nearer you came to Holman's. Mack and the boys went up and looked for a moment and then went back to the Palace. They couldn't see that it made much sense.

Holman's set up a double bed in their window. When the skater broke the world's record he was going to come down and sleep right in the window without taking off his skates. The trade name of the mattress was on a little card at the foot of the bed.

Now in the whole town there was interest and discussion about this sporting event, but the most interesting question of all and the one that bothered the whole town was never spoken of. No one mentioned it, and yet it was there haunting everyone. Mrs. Trolat wondered about it as she came out of the Scotch bakery with a bag of sweet buns. Mr. Hall in men's furnishings wondered about it. The three Willoughby girls giggled whenever they thought of it. But no one had the courage to bring it into the open.

Richard Frost, a high-strung and brilliant young man, worried about it more than anyone else. It haunted him. Wednesday night he worried and Thursday night he fidgeted. Friday night he got drunk and had a fight with his wife. She cried for a while and then pretended to be asleep. She heard him slip from bed and go into the kitchen. He was getting another drink. And then she heard him dress quietly and go out. She cried some more then. It was very late. Mrs. Frost was sure he was going down to Dora's Bear Flag.

Richard walked sturdily down the hill through the pines until he came to Lighthouse Avenue. He turned left and went up toward Holman's. He had the bottle in his pocket and just before he came to the store he took one more slug of it. The street lights were turned down low. The town was deserted. Not a soul moved. Richard stood in the middle of the street and looked up.

Dimly on top of the high mast he could see the lonely figure of the skater. He took another drink. He cupped his hand and called huskily, "Hey!" There was no answer. "Hey!" he called louder, and looked around to see if the cops had come out of their place beside the bank.

Down from the sky came a surly reply, "What do you want?"

Richard cupped his hands again. "How—how do you—go to the toilet?"

"I've got a can up here," said the voice.

Richard turned and walked back the way he had come. He walked along Lighthouse and up through the pines and he came to his house and let himself in. As he undressed he knew his wife was awake. She bubbled a little when she was asleep. He got into bed and she made room for him.

"He's got a can up there," Richard said.

CHAPTER XX

In mid-morning the Model T truck rolled triumphantly home to Cannery Row and hopped the gutter and creaked up through the weeds to its place behind Lee Chong's. The boys blocked up the front wheels, drained what petrol was left into a five-gallon can, took their frogs and went wearily home to the Palace Flop-house. Then

Mack made a ceremonious visit to Lee Chong while the boys got a fire going in the big stove. Mack thanked Lee with dignity for lending the truck. He spoke of the great success of the trip, of the hundreds of frogs taken. Lee smiled shyly and waited for the inevitable.

"We're in the chips," Mack said enthusiastically. "Doc pays us a nickel a frog and we got about a thousand."

Lee nodded. The price was standard. Everybody knew that.

"Doc's away," said Mack. "Jesus, is he gonna be happy when he sees all them frogs!"

Lee nodded again. He knew Doc was away and he also knew where the conversation was going.

"Say, by the way," said Mack as though he had just thought of it. "We're a little bit short right now——" He managed to make it sound like a very unusual situation.

"No whisky," said Lee Chong, and he smiled.

Mack was outraged. "What would we want whisky for? Why, we got a gallon of the finest whisky you ever laid a lip over—a whole full god-damned-running-over gallon. By the way," he continued, "I and the boys would like to have you just step up for a snort with us. They told me to ask you."

In spite of himself Lee smiled with pleasure. They wouldn't offer it if they didn't have it.

"No," said Mack. "I'll lay it on the line. I and the boys are pretty short and we're pretty hungry. You know the price of frogs is twenty for a buck. Now Doc is away and we're hungry. So what we thought is this. We don't want to see you lose nothing, so we'll make over to you twenty-five frogs for a buck. You got a five-frog profit there and nobody loses his shirt."

"No," said Lee. "No money."

"Well, hell, Lee, all we need is a little groceries. I'll tell you what—we want to give Doc a little party when he gets back. We got plenty of liquor, but we'd like to get maybe some steaks, and stuff like that. He's such a nice guy. Hell, when your wife had that bad tooth, who give her the laudanum?"

Mack had him. Lee was indebted to Doc—deeply indebted. What Lee was having trouble comprehending was how his indebtedness to Doc made it necessary that he give credit to Mack.

"We don't want you to have like a mortgage on frogs," Mack went on. "We will actually deliver right into your hands twenty-five frogs for every buck of groceries you let us have and you can come to the party too."

Lee's mind nosed over the proposition like a mouse in a cheese cupboard. He could find nothing wrong with it. The whole thing was legitimate. Frogs *were* cash as far as Doc was concerned, the price was standard and Lee had a double profit. He had his five-frog margin and also he had the grocery mark-up. The whole thing hinged on whether they actually had any frogs.

"We go see flog," Lee said at last.

In front of the Palace he had a drink of the whisky, inspected the damp sacks of frogs, and agreed to the transaction. He stipulated, however, that he would take no dead frogs. Now Mack counted fifty frogs into a can and walked back to the grocery with Lee and got two dollars' worth of bacon and eggs and bread.

Lee, anticipating a brisk business, brought a big packing-case out and put it into the vegetable department. He emptied the fifty frogs into it and covered it with a wet gunny sack to keep his charges happy.

And business was brisk. Eddie sauntered down and bought two frogs' worth of Bull Durham. Jones was outraged a little later when the price of Coca-Cola went up from one to two frogs. In fact bitterness arose as the day wore on and prices went up. Steak, for instance—the very best steak shouldn't have been more than ten frogs a pound, but Lee set it at twelve and a half. Canned peaches were sky-high, eight frogs for a No. 2 can. Lee had a stranglehold on the consumers. He was pretty sure that the Thrift Market or Holman's would not approve of this new monetary system. If the boys wanted steak, they knew they had to pay Lee's prices. Feeling ran high when Hazel, who had coveted a pair of yellow silk arm-bands for a long time, was told that if he didn't want to pay thirty-five frogs for them he could go somewhere else. The poison of greed was already creeping into the innocent and laudable merchandising agreement. Bitterness was piling up. But in Lee's packing-case the frogs were piling up too.

Financial bitterness could not eat too deeply into Mack and the boys, for they were not mercantile men. They did not measure their joy in goods sold, their egos in bank balances, nor their loves in what they cost. While they were mildly irritated that Lee was taking them for an economic ride, or perhaps hop, two dollars' worth of bacon and eggs was in their stomachs lying right on top of a fine slug of whisky and right on top of the breakfast was another slug of whisky. And they sat in their own chairs in their own house and watched Darling learning to drink canned milk out of a sardine can. Darling was, and was destined to remain, a very happy dog, for in the group of five men there were five distinct theories of dog training, theories which clashed so that Darling never got any training at all. From the first she was a precocious bitch. She slept on the bed of the man who had given her the last bribe. They really stole for her sometimes. They wooed her away from one another. Occasionally all five agreed that things had to change and that Darling must be disciplined, but in the discussion of method the intention invariably drifted away. They were in love with her. They found the little puddles she left on the floor charming. They bored all their acquaintances with her cuteness and they would have killed her with food if in the end she hadn't had better sense than they.

Jones made her a bed in the bottom of the grandfather clock, but Darling never used it. She slept with one or another of them as the fancy moved her. She chewed the blankets, tore the mattresses, sprayed the feathers out of the pillows. She coquetted and played her owners against one another. They thought she was wonderful. Mack intended to teach her tricks and go in vaudeville, and he didn't even house-break her.

They sat in the afternoon smoking, digesting, considering, and now and then having a delicate drink from the jug. And each time they warned that they must not take too much, for it was to be for Doc. They must not forget that for a minute.

"What time you figure he'll be back?" Eddie asked.

"Usually gets in about eight or nine o'clock," said Mack. "Now we got to figure when we're going to give it. I think we ought to give it to-night."

"Sure," the others agreed.

"Maybe he might be tired," Hazel suggested. "That's a long drive."

"Hell," said Jones, "nothing rests you like a good party. I've been so dog-tired my pants were draggin', and then I've went to a party and felt fine."

"We got to do some real thinkin'," said Mack. "Where we going to give it—here?"

"Well, Doc, he likes his music. He's always got his phonograph going at a party. Maybe he'd be more happy if we give it over at his place."

"You got something there," said Mack. "But I figure it ought to be like a surprise party. And how we going to make like it's a party and not just us bringin' over a jug of whisky?"

"How about decorations?" Hughie suggested. "Like Fourth of July or Halloween."

Mack's eyes looked off into space and his lips were parted. He could see it all. "Hughie," he said, "I think you got something there. I never would have thought you could do it, but by God you really rang a duck that time." His voice grew mellow and his eyes looked into the future. "I can just see it," he said. "Doc comes home. He's tired. He drives up. The place is all lit up. He thinks somebody's broke in. He goes up the stairs, and by God the place has got the hell decorated out of it. There's crêpe paper and there's favours and a big cake. Jesus, he'd know it was a party then. And it wouldn't be no little mouse-fart party neither. And we're kind of hiding so for a minute he don't know who done it. And then we come out yelling. Can't you see his face? By God, Hughie, I don't know how you thought of it."

Hughie blushed. His conception had been much more conservative, based in fact on the New Year's party at "La Ida", but if it was going to be like that, why, Hughie was willing to take credit. "I just thought it would be nice," he said.

"Well, it's a pretty nice thing," said Mack, "and I don't mind saying when the surprise kind of wears off I'm going to tell Doc who thought it up." They leaned back and considered the thing. And in their minds the decorated laboratory looked like the conservatory at the Hotel del Monte. They had a couple more drinks, just to savour the plan.

Lee Chong kept a very remarkable store. For instance, most stores buy yellow-and-black crêpe paper and black paper caps, masks and papier-mâché pumpkins in October. There is a brisk business for Halloween and then these items disappear. Maybe they are sold or thrown out, but you can't buy them, say, in June. The same is true of Fourth of July equipment, flags and bunting and sky-rockets. Where are they in January? Gone—no one knows where. This was not Lee Chong's way. You could buy Valentines in November at Lee Chong's, shamrocks, hatchets and paper cherry trees in August. He had fire-crackers he had laid up in 1920. One of the mysteries was where he kept his stock, since his was not a very large store. He had bathing-suits he had bought when long skirts and black stockings and head bandanas were in style. He had bicycle clips and ratting shuttles and mah-jong sets. He had badges that said "Remember the Maine" and felt pennants commemorating "Fighting Bob". He had mementos of the Panama Pacific International Exposition of 1915—little towers of jewels. And there was one other unorthodoxy in Lee's way of doing business. He never had a sale, never reduced a price and never remaindered. An article that cost thirty cents in 1912 still was thirty cents, although mice and moths might seem to some to have reduced its value. But there was no question about it. If you wanted to decorate a laboratory in a general way, not being specific about the season but giving the impression of a cross between Saturnalia and a pageant of the Flags of all Nations, Lee Chong's was the place to go for your stuff.

Mack and the boys knew that, but Mack said, "Where we going to get a big cake? Lee hasn't got nothing but them little bakery cakes."

Hughie had been so successful before, he tried again. "Why'n't Eddie bake a cake?" he suggested. "Eddie used to be fry cook at the San Carlos for a while."

The instant enthusiasm for the idea drove from Eddie's brain the admission that he had never baked a cake.

Mack put it on a sentimental basis besides. "It would mean more to Doc," he said. "It wouldn't be like no god-damned old soggy bought cake. It would have some heart in it."

As the afternoon and the whisky went down the enthusiasm rose. There were endless trips to Lee Chong's. The frogs were gone from one sack and Lee's packing-case was getting crowded. By six o'clock they had finished the gallon of whisky and were buying half-pints of Old Tennis Shoes at fifteen frogs a crack, but the pile of decorating materials was heaped on the floor of the Palace Flop-house—miles of crêpe paper commemorating every holiday in vogue and some that had been abandoned.

Eddie watched his stove like a mother hen. He was baking a cake in the wash-basin. The recipe was guaranteed not to fail by the company which made the shortening. But from the first the cake had acted strangely. When the batter was completed it writhed and panted as though animals were squirming and crawling inside it. Once in the oven it put up a bubble like a baseball which grew tight and shiny and then collapsed with a hissing sound. This left such a crater that Eddie made a new batch of batter and filled in the hole. And now the cake was behaving very curiously, for while the bottom was burning and sending out a black smoke the top was rising and falling glueyly with a series of little explosions.

When Eddie finally put it out to cool, it looked like one of Bel Geddes's miniatures of a battlefield on a lava bed.

This cake was not fortunate, for while the boys were decorating the laboratory Darling ate what she could of it, was sick on it, and finally curled up in its still warm dough and went to sleep.

But Mack and the boys had taken the crêpe paper, the masks, the broomsticks and paper pumpkins, the red, white, and blue bunting, and moved over the lot and across the street to the laboratory. They disposed of the last of the frogs for a quart of Old Tennis Shoes and two gallons of 49-cent wine.

"Doc is very fond of wine," said Mack. "I think he likes it even better than whisky."

Doc never locked the laboratory. He went on the theory that anyone who really wanted to break in could easily do it, that people were essentially honest and that, finally, there wasn't much the average person would want to steal there, anyway. The valuable things were books and records, surgical instruments and optical glass and such things that a practical working burglar wouldn't look at twice. His theory had been sound as far as burglars, snatch thieves, and kleptomaniacs were concerned, but it had been completely ineffective regarding his friends. Books were often "borrowed". No can of beans ever survived his absence, and on several occasions, returning late, he had found guests in his bed.

The boys piled the decorations in the ante-room and then Mack stopped them. "What's going to make Doc happiest?" he asked.

"The party!" said Hazel.

"No," said Mack.

"The decorations?" Hughie suggested. He felt responsible for the decorations.

"No," said Mack, "the frogs. That's going to make him feel best of all. And maybe by the time he gets here, Lee Chong might be closed and he can't even see his frogs until to-morrow. No, sir," Mack cried. "Them frogs ought to be right here, right in the middle of the room with a piece of bunting on it and a sign that says: 'Welcome Home, Doc'."

The committee which visited Lee met with stern opposition. All sorts of possibilities suggested themselves to his suspicious brain. It was explained that he was going to be at the party so he could watch his property, that no one questioned that they were his. Mack wrote out a paper transferring the frogs to Lee in case there should be any question.

When his protests weakened a little they carried the packing-case over to the laboratory, tacked red, white, and blue bunting over it, lettered the big sign with iodine on a card, and they started the decorating from there. They had finished the whisky by now and they really felt in a party mood. They criss-crossed the crêpe paper, and put the pumpkins up. Passers-by in the street joined the party and rushed over to Lee's to get more to drink. Lee Chong joined the party for a while, but his stomach was notoriously weak and he got sick and had to go home. At eleven o'clock they fried the steaks and ate them. Someone digging through the records found an album of Count Basie and the great phonograph roared out. The noise could be heard from the boat-works to "La Ida". A group of customers from the Bear Flag mistook Western Biological for a rival house and charged up the stairs whooping with joy. They were evicted by the outraged hosts, but only after a long, happy, and bloody battle that took out the front door and broke two windows. The crashing of jars was unpleasant. Hazel going through the kitchen to the toilet tipped the frying-pan of hot grease on himself and the floor and was badly burned.

At one-thirty a drunk wandered in and passed a remark which was considered insulting to Doc. Mack hit him a clip which is still remembered and discussed. The man rose off his feet, described a small arc, and crashed through the packing-case in among the frogs. Someone trying to change a record dropped the tone down and broke the crystal.

No one has studied the psychology of a dying party. It may be raging, howling, boiling, and then a fever sets in and a little silence and then quickly, quickly it is gone, the guests go home or go to sleep or wander away to some other affair and they leave a dead body.

The lights blazed in the laboratory. The front door hung sideways by one hinge. The floor was littered with broken glass. Phonograph records, some broken, some only nicked, were strewn about. The plates with pieces of steak ends and coagulating grease were on the floor, on top of the bookcases, under the bed. Whisky-glasses lay sadly on their sides. Someone trying to climb the bookcases had pulled out a whole section of books and spilled them in broken-backed confusion on the floor. And it was empty, it was over.

Through the broken end of the packing-case a frog hopped and sat feeling the air for danger, and then another joined him. They could smell the fine, damp, cool air coming in the door and in through the broken windows. One of them sat on the fallen card which said: "Welcome Home, Doc". And then the two hopped timidly toward the door.

For quite a while a little river of frogs hopped down the steps, a swirling, moving river. For quite a while Cannery Row crawled with frogs—was overrun with frogs. A taxi which brought a very late customer to the Bear Flag squashed five frogs in the street. But well before dawn they had all gone. Some found the sewer and some worked their way up the hill to the reservoir and some went into culverts and some only hid among the weeds in the vacant lot.

And the lights blazed in the quiet empty laboratory.

CHAPTER XXI

In the back room of the laboratory the white rats in their cages ran and skittered and squeaked. In the corner of a separate cage a mother rat lay over her litter of blind, naked children and let them suckle and the mother stared about nervously and fiercely.

In the rattlesnake cage the snakes lay with their chins resting on their own coils and they stared straight ahead out of their scowling dusty black eyes. In another cage a Gila monster with a skin like a beaded bag reared slowly up and clawed heavily and sluggishly at the wire. The anemones in the aquaria blossomed open, with green and purple tentacles and pale green stomachs. The little sea-water pump whirred softly and the needles of driven water hissed into the tanks, forcing lines of bubbles under the surface.

It was the hour of the pearl. Lee Chong brought his garbage cans out to the kerb. The bouncer stood on the porch of the Bear Flag and scratched his stomach. Sam Malloy crawled out of the boiler and sat on his wood block and looked at the lightening east.

Over on the rocks near Hopkins Marine Station the sea-lions barked monotonously. The old Chinaman came up out of the sea with his dripping basket and flip-flapped up the hill.

Then a car turned into Cannery Row and Doc drove up to the front of the laboratory. His eyes were red-rimmed with fatigue. He moved slowly with tiredness. When the car had stopped, he sat still for a moment to let the road jumps get out of his nerves. Then he climbed out of the car. At his step on the stairs, the rattlesnakes ran out their tongues and listened with their waving forked tongues. The rats scampered madly about the cages. Doc climbed the stairs. He looked in wonder at the sagging door and at the broken window. The weariness seemed to go out of him. He stepped quickly inside. Then he went quickly from room to room, stepping round the broken glass. He bent down quickly and picked up a smashed phonograph record and looked at its title.

In the kitchen the spilled grease had turned white on the floor. Doc's eyes flamed red with anger. He sat down on his couch and his head settled between his shoulders and his body weaved a little in his rage. Suddenly he jumped up and turned on the power in his great phonograph. He put on a record and put down the arm. Only a hissing roar came from the loudspeaker. He lifted the arm, stopped the turn-table, and sat down on the couch again.

On the stairs there were bumbling uncertain footsteps and through the door came Mack. His face was red. He stood uncertainly in the middle of the room. "Doc"—he said—"I and the boys——"

For the moment Doc hadn't seemed to see him. Now he leaped to his feet. Mack shuffled backward. "Did you do this?"

"Well, I and the boys——" Doc's small hard fist whipped out and splashed against Mack's mouth. Doc's eyes shone with a red animal rage. Mack sat down heavily on the floor. Doc's fist was hard and sharp. Mack's lips were split against his teeth and one front tooth bent sharply inward. "Get up!" said Doc.

Mack lumbered to his feet. His hands were at his sides. Doc hit him again, a cold, calculated, punishing punch in the mouth. The blood spurted from Mack's lips and ran down his chin. He tried to lick his lips.

"Put up your hands. Fight, you son-of-a-bitch," Doc cried, and he hit him again and heard the crunch of breaking teeth.

Mack's head jolted, but he was braced now so he wouldn't fall. And his hands stayed at his side. "Go ahead, Doc," he said thickly through his broken lips. "I got it coming."

Doc's shoulders sagged with defeat. "You son-of-a-bitch," he said bitterly. "Oh, you dirty son-of-a-bitch." He sat down on the couch and looked at his cut knuckles.

Mack sat down in a chair and looked at him. Mack's eyes were wide and full of pain. He didn't even wipe away the blood that flowed down his chin. In Doc's head the monotonal opening of Monteverdi's *Hor ch' el Ciel e la Terra* began to form, the infinitely sad and resigned mourning of Petrarch for Laura. Doc saw Mack's broken mouth through the music, the music that was in his head and in the air. Mack sat perfectly still, almost as though he could hear the music too. Doc glanced at the place where the Monteverdi album was and then he remembered that the phonograph was broken.

He got to his feet. "Go wash your face," he said, and he went out and down the stairs and across the street to Lee Chong's. Lee wouldn't look at him as he got two quarts of beer out of the ice-box. He took the money without saying anything. Doc walked back across the street.

Mack was in the toilet cleaning his bloody face with wet paper towels. Doc opened a bottle and poured gently into a glass, holding it at an angle so that very little collar rose to the top. He filled a second tall glass and carried the two into the front room. Mack came back dabbing at his mouth with wet towelling. Doc indicated the beer with his head. Now Mack opened his throat and poured down half the glass without swallowing. He sighed explosively and stared into the beer. Doc had already finished his glass. He brought the bottle in and filled both glasses again. He sat down on his couch.

"What happened?" he asked.

Mack looked at the floor and a drop of blood fell from his lips to his beer. He mopped his split lips again. "I and the boys wanted to give you a party. We thought you'd be home last night."

Doc nodded his head, "I see."

"She got out of hand," said Mack. "It don't do no good to say I'm sorry. I been sorry all my life. This ain't no new thing. It's always like this." He swallowed deeply from his glass. "I had a wife," Mack said. "Same thing. Ever'thing I done turned sour. She couldn't stand it any more. If I done a good thing it got poisoned up some way. If I give her a present they was something wrong with it. She only got hurt from me. She couldn't stand it no more. Same thing ever' place 'til I just got to clowning. I don't do nothin' but clown no more. Try to make the boys laugh."

Doc nodded again. The music was sounding in his head again, complaint and resignation all in one. "I know," he said.

"I was glad when you hit me," Mack went on. "I thought to myself, 'Maybe this will teach me. Maybe I'll remember this.' But, hell, I won't remember nothin'. I won't learn nothin'. Doc," Mack cried, "the way I seen it, we was all happy and havin' a good time. You was glad because we was givin' you a party. And we was glad. The way I seen it, it was a good party." He waved his hand at the wreckage on the floor. "Same thing when I was married. I'd think her out and then—but it never come off that way."

"I know," said Doc. He opened the second quart of beer and poured the glasses full.

"Doc," said Mack. "I and the boys will clean up here—and we'll pay for the stuff that's broke. If it takes us five years we'll pay for it."

Doc shook his head slowly and wiped the beer foam from his moustache. "No," he said, "I'll clean it up. I know where everything goes."

"We'll pay for it, Doc."

"No you won't, Mack," said Doc. "You'll think about it and it'll worry you for quite a long time, but you won't pay for it. There's maybe three hundred dollars in broken museum glass. Don't say you'll pay for it. That will just keep you uneasy. It might be two or three years before you forgot about it and felt entirely easy again. And you wouldn't pay it, anyway."

"I guess you're right," said Mack. "God damn it, I *know* you're right. What can we do?"

"I'm over it," said Doc. "Those socks in the mouth got it out of my system. Let's forget it."

Mack finished his beer and stood up. "So long, Doc," he said.

"So long. Say, Mack—what happened to your wife?"

"I don't know," said Mack. "She went away." He walked clumsily down the stairs and crossed over and walked up the lot and up the chicken-walk to the Palace Flop-house. Doc watched his progress through the window. And then wearily he got a broom from behind the water-heater. It took him all day to clean up the mess.

CHAPTER XXII

Henri the painter was not French and his name was not Henri. Also he was not really a painter. Henri had so steeped himself in stories of the Left Bank in Paris that he lived there although he had never been there. Feverishly he followed in periodicals the Dadaist movements and schisms, the strangely feminine jealousies and religiousness, the obscurantisms of the forming and breaking schools. Regularly he revolted against outworn techniques and materials. One season he threw out perspective. Another year he abandoned red, even as the mother of purple. Finally he gave up paint entirely. It is not known whether Henri was a good painter or not, for he threw himself so violently into movements that he had very little time left for painting of any kind.

About his painting there is some question. You couldn't judge very much from his productions in different-coloured chicken-feathers and nutshells. But as a boat-builder he was superb. Henri was a wonderful craftsman. He had lived in a tent years ago when he started his boat and until galley and cabin were complete enough to move into. But once he was housed and dry he had taken his time on the boat. The boat was sculptured rather than built. It was thirty-five feet long and its lines were in a constant state of flux. For a while it had a clipper bow and a fan-tail like a destroyer. Another time it had looked vaguely like a caravel. Since Henri had no money, it sometimes took him months to find a plank or a piece of iron or a dozen brass screws. That was the way he wanted it, for Henri never wanted to finish his boat.

It sat among the pine trees on a lot Henri rented for five dollars a year. This paid the taxes and satisfied the owner. The boat rested in a cradle on concrete foundations. A rope ladder hung over the side except when Henri was at home. Then he pulled up the rope ladder and only put it down when guests arrived. His little cabin had a wide padded seat that ran round three sides of the room. On this he slept and on this his guests sat. A table folded down when it was needed and a brass lamp hung from the ceiling. His galley was a marvel of compactness, but every item in it had been the result of months of thought and work.

Henri was swarthy and morose. He wore a beret long after other people abandoned them, he smoked a calabash pipe and his dark hair fell about his face. Henri had many friends whom he loosely classified as those who could feed him and those whom he had to feed. His boat had no name. Henri said he would name it when it was finished.

Henri had been living in and building his boat for ten years. During that time he had been married twice and had promoted a number of semi-permanent liaisons. And all of these young women had left him for the same reason. The seven-foot cabin was too small for two people. They resented bumping their heads when they stood up and they definitely felt the need for a toilet. Marine toilets obviously would not work in a shore-bound boat, and Henri refused to compromise with a spurious landsman's toilet. He and his friends of the moment had to stroll away among the pines. And one after another his loves left him.

Just after the girl he had called Alice left him, a very curious thing happened to Henri. Each time he was left alone, he mourned formally for a while, but actually he felt a sense of relief. He could stretch out in his little cabin. He could eat what he wanted. He was glad to be free of the endless female biologic functions for a while.

It had become his custom, each time he was deserted, to buy a gallon of wine, to stretch out on the comfortably hard bunk and get drunk. Sometimes he cried a little all by himself, but it was luxurious stuff and he usually had a wonderful feeling of well-being from it. He would read Rimbaud aloud with a very bad accent, marvelling the while at his fluid speech.

It was during one of his ritualistic mournings for the lost Alice that the strange thing began to happen. It was night and his lamp was burning and he had just barely begun to get drunk when suddenly he knew he was no longer alone. He let his eye wander cautiously up and across the cabin, and there on the other side sat a devilish young man, a dark, handsome young man. His eyes gleamed with cleverness and spirit and energy and his teeth flashed. There was something very dear and yet very terrible in his face. And beside him sat a golden-haired little boy, hardly more than a baby. The man looked down at the baby and the baby looked back and laughed delightedly as though something wonderful were about to happen. Then the man looked over at Henri and smiled and he glanced back at the baby. From his upper left vest pocket he took an old-fashioned straight-edged razor. He opened it and indicated the child with a gesture of his head. He put a hand among the curls and the baby laughed gleefully, and then the man tilted the chin and cut the baby's throat and the baby went right on laughing. But Henri was howling with terror. It took him a long time to realize that neither the man nor the baby was still there.

Henri, when his shaking had subsided a little, rushed out of his cabin, leaped over the side of the boat and hurried away down the hill through the pines. He walked for several hours and at last he walked down to Cannery Row.

Doc was in the basement working on cats when Henri burst in. Doc went on working while Henri told about it, and when it was over Doc looked closely at him to see how much actual fear and how much theatre was there. And it was mostly fear.

"Is it a ghost, do you think?" Henri demanded. "Is it some reflection of something that has happened or is it some Freudian horror out of me, or am I completely nuts? I saw it, I tell you. It happened right in front of me as plainly as I see you."

"I don't know," said Doc.

"Well, will you come up with me, and see if it comes back?"

"No," said Doc. "If I saw it, it might be a ghost and it would scare me badly because I don't believe in ghosts. And if you saw it again and I didn't it would be a hallucination and you would be frightened."

"But what am I going to do?" Henri asked. "If I see it again I'll know what's going to happen and I'm sure I'll die. You see, he doesn't look like a murderer. He looks nice and the kid looks nice and neither of them give a damn. But he cut that baby's throat. I saw it."

"I don't know," said Doc. "I'm not a psychiatrist or a witch-hunter and I'm not going to start now."

A girl's voice called into the basement. "Hi, Doc, can I come in?"

"Come along," said Doc.

Doc introduced her to Henri.

"He's got a problem," said Doc. "He either has a ghost or a terrible conscience and he doesn't know which. Tell her about it, Henri."

Henri went over the story again and the girl's eyes sparkled.

"But that's horrible," she said when he finished. "I've never in my life even caught the smell of a ghost. Let's go back up and see if he comes again."

Doc watched them go a little sourly. After all, it had been his date.

The girl never did see the ghost, but she was fond of Henri, and it was five months before the cramped cabin and the lack of a toilet drove her out.

CHAPTER XXIII

A BLACK gloom settled over the Palace Flop-house. All the joy went out of it. Mack came back from the laboratory with his mouth torn and his teeth broken. As a kind of penance, he did not wash his face. He went to his bed and pulled his blanket over his head and he didn't get up all day. His heart was as bruised as his mouth. He went over all the bad things he had done in his life and everything he had ever done seemed bad. He was very sad.

Hughie and Jones sat for a while staring into space and then morosely they went over to the Hediondo Cannery and applied for jobs and got them.

Hazel felt so bad that he walked to Monterey and picked a fight with a soldier and lost it on purpose. That made him feel a little better, to be utterly beaten by a man Hazel could have licked without half trying.

Darling was the only happy one of the whole club. She spent the day under Mack's bed happily eating up his shoes. She was a clever dog and her teeth were very sharp. Twice, in his black despair, Mack reached under the bed and caught her and put her in bed with him for company, but she squirmed out and went back to eating his shoes.

Eddie mooned on down to "La Ida" and talked to his friend the bartender. He got a few drinks and borrowed some nickels with which he played *Melancholy Baby* five times on the musical-box.

Mack and the boys were under a cloud and they knew it, and they knew they deserved it. They had become social outcasts. All of their good intentions were forgotten now. The fact that the party was given for Doc, if it was known, was never mentioned or taken into consideration. The story ran through the Bear Flag. It was told in the canneries. At "La Ida" drunks discussed it virtuously. Lee Chong refused to comment. He was feeling financially bruised. And the story as it grew went this way: They had stolen liquor and money. They had maliciously broken into the laboratory and systematically destroyed it out of pure malice and evil. People who really knew better took this view. Some of the drunks at "La Ida" considered going over and beating the hell out of the whole lot of them to show them they couldn't do a thing like that to Doc.

Only a sense of the solidarity and fighting ability of Mack and the boys saved them from some kind of reprisal. There were people who felt virtuous about the affair who hadn't had the material of virtue for a long time. The fiercest of the whole lot was Tom Sheligan, who would have been at the party if he had known about it.

Socially Mack and the boys were beyond the pale. Sam Malloy didn't speak to them as they went by the boiler. They drew into themselves and no one could foresee how they would come out of the cloud. For there are two possible reactions to social ostracism—either a man emerges determined to be better, purer, and kindlier, or he goes bad, challenges the world and does even worse things. This last is by far the commonest reaction to stigma.

Mack and the boys balanced on the scales of good and evil. They were kind and sweet to Darling; they were forbearing and patient with one another. When the first reaction was over they gave the Palace Flop-house a cleaning such as it had never had. They polished the bright work on the stove and they washed all their clothes and blankets. Financially they had become dull and solvent. Hughie and Jones were working and bringing home their pay. They bought groceries up the hill at the Thrift Market because they could not stand the reproving eyes of Lee Chong.

It was during this time that Doc made an observation which may have been true, but since there was one factor missing in his reasoning it is not known whether he was correct. It was the Fourth of July. Doc was sitting in the laboratory with Richard Frost. They drank beer and listened to a new album of Scarlatti and looked out the window. In front of the Palace Flop-house there was a large log of wood where Mack and the boys were sitting in the mid-morning sun. They faced down the hill toward the laboratory.

Doc said, "Look at them. There are your true philosophers. I think," he went on, "that Mack and the boys know everything that has ever happened in the world and possibly everything that will happen. I think they survive in this particular world better than other people. In a time when people tear themselves to pieces with ambition and nervousness and covetousness, they are relaxed. All of our so-called successful men are sick men, with bad stomachs, and bad souls, but Mack and the boys are healthy and curiously clean. They can do what they want. They can satisfy their appetites without calling them something else." This speech so dried out Doc's throat that he drained his beer glass. He waved two fingers in the air and smiled. "There's nothing like that first taste of beer," he said.

Richard Frost said, "I think they're just like anyone else. They just haven't any money."

"They could get it," Doc said. "They could ruin their lives and get money. Mack has qualities of genius. They're all very clever if they want something. They just know the nature of things too well to be caught in that wanting."

If Doc had known of the sadness of Mack and the boys he would not have made the next statement, but no one had told him about the social pressure that was exerted against the inmates of the Palace.

He poured beer slowly into his glass. "I think I can show you proof," he said. "You see how they are sitting facing this way? Well—in about half an hour the Fourth of July Parade is going to pass on Lighthouse Avenue. By just turning their heads they can see it, by standing up they can watch it, and by walking two short blocks they can be right beside it. Now I'll bet you a quart of beer they won't even turn their heads."

"Suppose they don't?" said Richard Frost. "What will that prove?"

"What will it prove?" cried Doc. "Why, just that they know what will be in the parade. They will know that the Mayor will ride first in an automobile with bunting streaming back from the hood. Next will come Long Bob on his white horse with the flag. Then the city council, then two companies of soldiers from the Presidio, next the Elks with purple umbrellas, then the Knights Templars in white ostrich-feathers and carrying swords. Next the Knights of Columbus with red ostrich-feathers and carrying swords. Mack and the boys know that. The band will play. They've seen it all. They don't have to look again."

"The man doesn't live who doesn't have to look at a parade," said Richard Frost.

"Is it a bet, then?"

"It's a bet."

"It has always seemed strange to me," said Doc. "The things we admire in men—kindness and generosity, openness, honesty, understanding and feeling—are the concomitants of failure in our system. And those traits we detest—sharpness, greed, acquisitiveness, meanness, egotism and self-interest—are the traits of success. And while men admire the quality of the first they love the produce of the second."

"Who wants to be good if he has to be hungry too?" said Richard Frost.

"Oh, it isn't a matter of hunger. It's something quite different. The sale of souls to gain the whole world is completely voluntary and almost unanimous—but not quite. Everywhere in the world there are Mack and the boys. I've seen them in an ice-cream seller in Mexico and in an Aleut in Alaska. You know how they tried to give me a party and something went wrong. But they wanted to give me a party. That was their impulse. Listen," said Doc. "Isn't that the band I hear?" Quickly he filled two glasses with beer and the two of them stepped close to the window.

Mack and the boys sat dejectedly on their log and faced the laboratory. The sound of the band came from Lighthouse Avenue, the drums echoing back from the buildings. And suddenly the Mayor's car crossed and it sprayed bunting from the radiator—then Long Bob on his white horse carrying the flag, then the band, then the soldiers, the Elks, the Knights Templar, the Knights of Columbus. Richard and the Doc leaned forward tensely, but they were watching the line of men sitting on the log.

And not a head turned, not a neck straightened up. The parade filed past and they did not move. And the parade was gone. Doc drained his glass and waved two fingers gently in the air and he said, "Hah! There's nothing in the world like that first taste of beer."

Richard started for the door. "What kind of beer do you want?"

"The same kind," said Doc gently. He was smiling up the hill at Mack and the boys.

It's all fine to say, "Time will heal everything, this too shall pass away. People will forget"—and things like that when you are not involved, but when you are there is no passage of time, people do not forget and you are in the middle of something that does not change. Doc didn't know the pain and self-destructive criticism in the Palace Flop-house or he might have tried to do something about it. And Mack and the boys did not know how he felt or they would have held up their heads again.

It was a bad time. Evil stalked darkly in the vacant lot. Sam Malloy had a number of fights with his wife and she cried all the time. The echoes inside the boiler made it sound as though she were crying under water. Mack and the boys seemed to be the node of trouble. The nice bouncer at the Bear Flag threw out a drunk, but threw him too hard and too far and broke his back. Alfred had to go over to Salinas three times before it was cleared up, and that didn't make Alfred feel very well. Ordinarily he was too good a bouncer to hurt anyone. His A and C was a miracle of rhythm and grace.

On top of that a group of high-minded ladies in the town demanded that the dens of vice must close to protect young American manhood. This happened about once a year in the dead period between the Fourth of July and the County Fair. Dora usually closed the Bear Flag for a week when it happened. It wasn't so bad. Everyone got a vacation and little repairs to the plumbing and the walls could be made. But this year the ladies went on a real crusade. They wanted somebody's scalp. It had been a dull summer and they were restless. It got so bad that they had to be told who actually owned the property where vice was practised, what the rents were and what little hardships might be the result of their closing. That was how close they were to being a serious menace.

Dora was closed a full two weeks and there were three conventions in Monterey while the Bear Flag was closed. Word got around and Monterey lost five conventions for the following year. Things were bad all over. Doc had to get a loan at the bank to pay for the glass that was broken at the party. Elmer Rechati went to sleep on the Southern Pacific track and lost both legs. A sudden and completely unexpected storm tore a purse-seiner and three lampara boats loose from their moorings and tossed them broken and sad on Del Monte beach.

There is no explaining a series of misfortunes like that. Every man blames himself. People in their black minds remember sins committed secretly and wonder whether they have caused the evil sequence. One man may put it down to sun-spots while another invoking the law of probabilities doesn't believe it. Not even the doctors had a good time of it, for while many people were sick none of it was good-paying sickness. It was nothing a good physic or a patent medicine wouldn't take care of.

And to cap it all, Darling got sick. She was a very fat and lively puppy when she was struck down, but five days of fever reduced her to a little skin-covered skeleton. Her liver-coloured nose was pink and her gums were white. Her eyes glazed with illness and her whole body was hot, although she trembled sometimes with cold. She wouldn't eat and she wouldn't drink and her fat little belly shrivelled up against her spine, and even her tail showed the articulations through the skin. It was obviously distemper.

Now a genuine panic came over the Palace Flop-house. Darling had come to be vastly important to them. Hughie and Jones instantly quit their jobs so they could be near to help. They sat up in shifts. They kept a cool, damp cloth on her forehead and she got weaker and sicker. Finally, although they didn't want to, Hazel and

Jones were chosen to call on Doc. They found him working over a tide-chart while he ate a chicken stew of which the principal ingredient was not chicken but sea cucumber. They thought he looked at them a little coldly.

"It's Darling," they said. "She's sick."

"What's the matter with her?"

"Mack says it's distemper."

"I'm not a veterinarian," said Doc. "I don't know how to treat these things."

Hazel said, "Well, couldn't you just take a look at her? She's sick as hell."

They stood in a circle while Doc examined Darling. He looked at her eyeballs and her gums and felt in her ear for fever. He ran his finger over the ribs that stuck out like spokes and at the poor spine. "She won't eat?" he asked.

"Not a thing," said Mack.

"You'll have to force-feed her—strong soups and eggs and cod liver oil."

They thought he was cold and professional. He went back to his tide-charts and his stew.

But Mack and the boys had something to do now. They boiled meat until it was as strong as whisky. They put cod liver oil far back on her tongue so that some of it got down her. They held up her head and made a little funnel of her chops and poured the cool soup in. She had to swallow or drown. Every two hours they fed her and gave her water. Before they had slept in shifts—now no one slept. They sat silently and waited for Darling's crisis.

It came early in the morning. The boys sat in their chairs half asleep, but Mack was awake and his eyes were on the puppy. He saw her ears flip twice, and her chest heave. With infinite weakness she climbed slowly to her spindly legs, dragged herself to the door, took four laps of water and collapsed on the floor.

Mack shouted the others awake. He danced heavily. All the boys shouted at one another. Lee Chong heard them and snorted to himself as he carried out the garbage cans. Alfred the bouncer heard them and thought they were having a party.

By nine o'clock Darling had eaten a raw egg and half a pint of whipped cream by herself. By noon she was visibly putting on weight. In a day she romped a little; by the end of the week she was a well dog.

At last a crack had developed in the wall of evil. There were evidences of it everywhere. The purse-seiner was hauled back into the water and floated. Word came down to Dora that it was all right to open up the Bear Flag. Earl Wakefield caught a sculpin with two heads and sold it to the museum for eight dollars. The wall of evil and of waiting was broken. It broke away in chunks. The curtains were drawn at the laboratory that night and Gregorian music played until two o'clock, and then the music stopped and no one came out. Some force wrought with Lee Chong's heart and all in an Oriental moment he forgave Mack and the boys and wrote off the frog debt, which had been a momentary headache from the beginning. And to prove to the boys that he had forgiven them he took a pint of Old Tennis Shoes up and presented it to them. Their trading at the Thrift Market had hurt his feelings, but it was all over now. Lee's visit coincided with the first destructive healthy impulse Darling had since her illness. She was completely spoiled now and no one thought of house-breaking her. When Lee Chong came in with his gift, Darling was deliberately and happily destroying Hazel's only pair of rubber boots, while her happy masters applauded her.

Mack never visited the Bear Flag professionally. It would have seemed a little like incest to him. There was a house out by the baseball park he patronized. Thus, when he went into the front bar, everyone thought he wanted a beer. He stepped up to Alfred. "Dora around?" he asked.

"What do you want with her?" Alfred asked.

"I got something I want to ask her."

"What about?"

"That's none of your god-damn business," said Mack.

"Okay. Have it your way. I'll see if she wants to talk to you."

A moment later he led Mack into the sanctum. Dora sat at a roll-top desk. Her orange hair was piled in ringlets on her head and she wore a green eyeshade. With a stub pen she was bringing her books up-to-date, a fine old double-entry ledger. She was dressed in a magnificent pink silk wrapper with lace at the wrists and throat. When Mack came in she whirled her pivot-chair about and faced him. Alfred stood in the door and waited. Mack stood until Alfred closed the door and left.

Dora scrutinized him suspiciously. "Well—what can I do for you?" she demanded at last.

"You see, ma'am," said Mack. "Well, I guess you heard what we done over at Doc's some time back."

Dora pushed the eyeshade back up on her head and she put the pen in an old-fashioned coil-spring holder. "Yeah!" she said. "I heard."

"Well, ma'am, we did it for Doc. You may not believe it, but we wanted to give him a party. Only he didn't get home in time and—well, she got out of hand."

"So I heard," said Dora. "Well, what do you want me to do?"

"Well," said Mack, "I and the boys thought we'd ask you. You know what we think of Doc. We wanted to ask you what you thought we could do for him that would kind of show him."

Dora said, "Hum," and she flopped back in her pivot-chair and crossed her legs and smoothed her wrapper over her knees. She shook out a cigarette, lighted it and studied. "You gave him a party he didn't get to. Why don't you give him a party he does get to?" she said.

"Jesus," said Mack afterwards talking to the boys. "It was just as simple as that. Now there is one hell of a woman. No wonder she got to be madam. There is one hell of a woman."

CHAPTER XXIV

MARY TALBOT, Mrs. Tom Talbot, that is, was lovely. She had red hair with green lights in it. Her skin was golden, with a green undercast, and her eyes were green, with little golden spots. Her face was triangular, with wide cheek-bones, wide-set eyes, and her chin was pointed. She had long dancer's legs and dancer's feet, and she seemed never to touch the ground when she walked. When she was excited, and she was excited a good deal of the time, her face flushed with gold. Her great-great-great-great-great-grandmother had been burned as a witch.

More than anything in the world Mary Talbot loved parties. She loved to give parties and she loved to go to parties. Since Tom didn't make much money Mary couldn't give parties all the time, so she tricked people into giving them. Sometimes she telephoned a friend and said bluntly, "Isn't it about time you gave a party?"

Regularly, Mary had six birthdays a year, and she organized costume parties, surprise parties, holiday parties. Christmas Eve at her house was a very exciting thing. For Mary glowed with parties. She carried her husband along on the wave of her excitement.

In the afternoons when Tom was at work Mary sometimes gave tea-parties for the neighbourhood cats. She set a footstool with doll cups and saucers. She gathered the cats, and there were plenty of them, and then she held long and detailed conversations with them. It was a kind of play she enjoyed very much—a kind of satiric game, and it covered and concealed from Mary the fact that she didn't have very nice clothes and the Talbots didn't have any money. They were pretty near absolute bottom most of the time, and when they really scraped, Mary managed to give some kind of a party.

She could do that. She could infect a whole house with gaiety and she used her gift as a weapon against the despondency that lurked always around outside the house waiting to get in at Tom. That was Mary's job as she saw it—to keep the despondency away from Tom because everyone knew he was going to be a great success some time. Mostly she was successful in keeping the dark things out of the house, but sometimes they got in at Tom and laid him out. Then he would sit and brood for hours, while Mary frantically built up a back-fire of gaiety.

One time when it was the first of the month and there were curt notes from the water company and the rent wasn't paid and a manuscript had come back from *Collier's* and the cartoons had come back from *The New Yorker* and pleurisy was hurting Tom pretty badly, he went into the bedroom and lay down on the bed.

Mary came softly in, for the blue-grey colour of his gloom had seeped out under the door and through the keyhole. She had a little bouquet of candytuft in a collar of paper lace.

"Smell," she said and held the bouquet to his nose. He smelled the flowers and said nothing. "Do you know what day this is?" she asked and thought wildly for something to make it a bright day.

Tom said, "Why don't we face it for once? We're down. We're going under. What's the good kidding ourselves?"

"No we're not," said Mary. "We're magic people. We always have been. Remember that ten dollars you found in a book—remember when your cousin sent you five dollars? Nothing can happen to us."

"Well, it has happened," said Tom. "I'm sorry," he said. "I just can't talk myself out of it this time. I'm sick of pretending everything. For once I'd like to have it real—just for once."

"I thought of giving a little party to-night," said Mary.

"On what? You're not going to cut out the baked ham picture from a magazine again and serve it on a platter, are you? I'm sick of that kind of kidding. It isn't funny any more. It's sad."

"I could give a little party," she insisted. "Just a small affair. Nobody will dress. It's the anniversary of the founding of the Bloomer League—you didn't even remember that."

"It's no use," said Tom. "I know it's mean, but I just can't rise to it. Why don't you just go out and shut the door and leave me alone? I'll get you down if you don't."

She looked at him closely and saw that he meant it. Mary walked quietly out and shut the door, and Tom turned over on the bed and put his face down between his arms. He could hear her rustling about in the other room.

She decorated the door with old Christmas things, glass balls, and tinsel, and she made a placard that said: "Welcome Tom, our

Hero." She listened at the door and couldn't get anything. A little disconsolately she got out the footstool and spread a napkin over it. She put her bouquet in a glass in the middle of the foot-stool and set out four little cups and saucers. She went into the kitchen, put the tea in the teapot and set the kettle to boil. Then she went out into the yard.

Kitty Randolph was sunning herself by the front fence. Mary said, "Miss Randolph—I'm having a few friends in to tea if you would care to come." Kitty Randolph rolled over languorously on her back and stretched in the warm sun. "Don't be later than four o'clock," said Mary. "My husband and I are going to the Bloomer League Centennial Reception at the Hotel."

She strolled round the house to the backyard where the blackberry vines clambered over the fence. Kitty Casini was squatting on the ground growling to herself and flicking her tail fiercely. "Mrs. Casini," Mary began, and then she stopped, for she saw what the cat was doing. Kitty Casini had a mouse. She patted it gently with her unarmed paw and the mouse squirmed horribly away, drawing its paralysed legs behind it. The cat let it get nearly to the cover of the blackberry vines and then she reached delicately out and white thorns had sprouted on her paw. Daintily she stabbed the mouse through the back and drew it wriggling to her and her tail flicked with tense delight.

Tom must have been at least half asleep when he heard his name called over and over. He jumped up, shouting, "What is it? Where are you?" He could hear Mary crying. He ran into the yard and saw what was happening. "Turn your head," he shouted and he killed the mouse. Kitty Casini had leaped to the top of the fence, where she watched him angrily. Tom picked up a rock and hit her in the stomach and knocked her off the fence.

In the house Mary was still crying a little. She poured the water into the teapot and brought it to the table. "Sit there," she told Tom and he squatted down on the floor in front of the footstool.

"Can't I have a big cup?" he asked.

"I can't blame Kitty Casini," said Mary. "I know how cats are. It isn't her fault. But—Oh, Tom! I'm going to have trouble inviting her again. I'm just not going to like her for a while, no matter how much I want to." She looked closely at Tom and saw that the lines were gone from his forehead and that he was not blinking badly. "But then I'm so busy with the Bloomer League these days," she said. "I just don't know how I'm going to get everything done."

Mary Talbot gave a pregnancy party that year. And everyone said, "God! A kid of hers is going to have fun."

CHAPTER XXV

CERTAINLY ALL of Cannery Row and probably all of Monterey felt that a change had come. It's all right not to believe in luck and omens. Nobody believes in them. But it doesn't do any good to take chances with them and no one takes chances. Cannery Row, like every other place else, is not superstitious, but will not walk under a ladder or open an umbrella in the house. Doc was a pure scientist and incapable of superstition, and yet when he came in late one night and found a line of white flowers across the door-sill he had a bad time of it. But most people in Cannery Row simply do not believe in such things and then live by them.

There was no doubt in Mack's mind that a dark cloud had hung on the Palace Flop-house. He had analysed the abortive party and found that a misfortune had crept into every crevice, that bad luck had come up like hives on the evening. And once you got into a routine like that the best thing to do was just to go to bed until it was over. You couldn't buck it. Not that Mack was superstitious.

Now a kind of gladness began to penetrate into the Row and to spread out from there. Doc was almost supernaturally successful with a series of lady visitors. He didn't half try. The puppy at the Palace was growing like a pole bean, and having a thousand generations of training behind her, she began to train herself. She got disgusted with wetting on the floor and took to going outside. It was obvious that Darling was going to grow up a good and charming dog. And she had developed no chorea from her distemper.

The benignant influence crept like gas through the Row. It got as far as Herman's hamburger stand, it spread to the San Carlos Hotel. Jimmy Brucia felt it, and Johnny, his singing bartender. Sparky Evea felt it and joyously joined battle with three new out of town cops. It even got as far as the County Jail in Salinas, where Gay, who had lived a good life by letting the sheriff beat him at draughts, suddenly grew cocky and never lost another game. He lost his privileges that way, but he felt a whole man again.

The sea-lions felt it and their barking took on a tone and a cadence that would have gladdened the heart of St. Francis. Little girls studying their catechism suddenly looked up and giggled for no reason at all. Perhaps some electrical finder could have been developed so delicate that it would have located the source of all this spreading joy and fortune. And triangulation might possibly have located it in the Palace Flop-house and Grill. Certainly the Palace was lousy with it. Mack and the boys were charged. Jones was seen to leap from his chair only to do a quick tap dance and sit down again. Hazel smiled vaguely at nothing at all. The joy was so general and so suffused that Mack had a hard time keeping it centred and aimed at its objective. Eddie, who had worked at "La Ida" pretty regularly, was accumulating a cellar of some promise. He no longer added beer to the wining jug. It gave a flat taste to the mixture, he said.

Sam Malloy had planted morning glories to grow over the boiler. He had put out a little awning and under it he and his wife often sat in the evening. She was crocheting a bedspread.

The joy even got into the Bear Flag. Business was good. Phyllis Mae's leg was knitting nicely and she was nearly ready to go to work again. Eva Flanagan got back from East St. Louis very glad to be back. It had been hot in East St. Louis and it hadn't been as fine as she remembered it. But then she had been younger when she had had so much fun there.

The knowledge or conviction about the party for Doc was no sudden thing. It didn't burst out full-blown. People knew about it, but let it grow gradually, like a pupa in the cocoons of their imaginations.

Mack was realistic about it. "Last time we forced her," he told the boys. "You can't never give a good party that way. You got to let her creep up on you."

"Well, when's it going to be?" Jones asked impatiently.

"I don't know," said Mack.

"Is it gonna be a surprise party?" Hazel asked.

"It ought to, that's the best kind," said Mack.

Darling brought him a tennis-ball she had found and he threw it out the door into the weeds. She bounced away after it.

Hazel said, "If we knew when was Doc's birthday, we could give him a birthday-party."

Mack's mouth was open. Hazel constantly surprised him. "By God, Hazel, you got something," he cried. "Yes, sir, if it was his birthday there'd be presents. That's just the thing. All we got to find out is when it is."

"That ought to be easy," said Hughie. "Why don't we ask him?"

"Hell," said Mack. "Then he'd catch on. You ask a guy when is his birthday, and especially if you've already give him a party like we done, and he'll know what you want to know for. Maybe I'll just go over and smell around a little and not let on."

"I'll go with you," said Hazel.

"No—if two of us went, he might figure we were up to something."

"Well, hell, it was my idear," said Hazel.

"I know," said Mack. "And when it comes off, why, I'll tell Doc it was your idea. But I think I better go over alone."

"How is he—friendly?" Eddie asked.

"Sure, he's all right."

Mack found Doc way back in the downstairs part of the laboratory. He was dressed in a long rubber apron and he wore rubber gloves to protect his hands from the formaldehyde. He was injecting the veins and arteries of small dog-fish with colour mass. His little ball mill rolled over and over, mixing the blue mass. The red fluid was already in the pressure-gun. Doc's fine hands worked precisely, slipping the needle into place and pressing the compressed-air trigger that forced the colour into the veins. He laid the finished fish in a neat pile. He would have to go over these again to put the blue mass in the arteries. The dog-fish made good dissection specimens.

"Hi, Doc," said Mack. "Keepin' pretty busy?"

"Busy as I want," said Doc. "How's the pup?"

"Doin' just fine. She would of died if it hadn't been for you."

For a moment a wave of caution went over Doc and then slipped off. Ordinarily a compliment made him wary. He had been dealing with Mack for a long time. But the tone had nothing but gratefulness in it. He knew how Mack felt about the pup. "How are things going up at the Palace?"

"Fine, Doc, just fine. We got two new chairs. I wish you'd come up and see us. It's pretty nice up there now."

"I will," said Doc. "Eddie still bring back the jug?"

"Sure," said Mack. "He ain't puttin' beer in it no more and I think the stuff is better. It's got more zip."

"It had plenty of zip before," said Doc.

Mack waited patiently. Sooner or later Doc was going to wade into it and he was waiting. If Doc seemed to open the subject himself it would be less suspicious. This was always Mack's method.

"Haven't seen Hazel for some time. He isn't sick, is he?"

"No," said Mack and he opened the campaign. "Hazel is all right. Him and Hughie are havin' one hell of a battle. Been goin' on for a week," he chuckled. "An' the funny thing is it's about somethin' they don't neither of them know nothin' about. I stayed out of it because I don't know nothin' about it neither, but not them. They've even got a little mad at each other."

"What's it about?" Doc asked.

"Well, sir," said Mack, "Hazel's all the time buyin' these here charts and lookin' up lucky days and stars and stuff like that. And Hughie says it's all a bunch of malarky. Hughie, he says if you know when a guy is born you can tell about him and Hughie says they're just sellin' Hazel them charts for two bits apiece. Me, I don't know nothin' about it. What do you think, Doc?"

"I'd kind of side with Hughie," said Doc. He stopped the ball mill, washed out the colour-gun and filled it with blue mass.

"They got goin' hot the other night," said Mack. "They ask me when I'm born so I tell 'em April 12 and Hazel he goes and buys one of them charts and read all about me. Well, it did seem to hit in some places. But it was nearly all good stuff and a guy will believe good stuff about himself. It said I'm brave and smart and kind to my friends. But Hazel says it's all true. When's your birthday, Doc?" At the end of the long discussion it sounded perfectly casual. You couldn't put your finger on it. But it must be remembered that Doc had known Mack a very long time. If he had not he would have said December 18, which was his birthday, instead of October 27, which was not. "October 27," said Doc. "Ask Hazel what that makes me."

"It's probably so much malarky," said Mack, "but Hazel he takes it serious. I'll ask him to look you up, Doc."

When Mack left, Doc wondered casually what the build-up was. For he had recognized it as a lead. He knew Mack's technique, his method. He recognized his style. And he wondered to what purpose Mack could put the information. It was only later, when rumours began to creep in, that Doc added the whole thing up. Now he felt slightly relieved, for he had expected Mack to put the bite on him.

CHAPTER XXVI

THE TWO little boys played in the boat works yard until a cat climbed the fence. Instantly they gave chase, drove it across the tracks and there filled their pockets with granite stones from the road-bed. The cat got away from them in the tall weeds, but they kept the stones because they were perfect in weight, shape and size for throwing. You can't ever tell when you're going to need a stone like that. They turned down Cannery Row and whanged a stone at the corrugated-iron front of Morden's Cannery. A startled man looked out the office window and then rushed for the door, but the boys were too quick for him. They were lying behind a wooden stringer in the lot before he even got near the door. He couldn't have found them in a hundred years.

"I bet he could look all his life and he couldn't find us," said Joey.

They got tired of hiding after a while with no one looking for them. They got up and strolled on down Cannery Row. They looked a long time in Lee's window, coveting the pliers, the hacksaws, the engineers' caps and the bananas. Then they crossed the street and sat down on the lower step of the stairs that went to the second storey of the laboratory.

Joey said, "You know, this guy in here got babies in bottles."

"What kind of babies?" Willard asked.

"Regular babies, only before they're borned."

"I don't believe it," said Willard.

"Well, it's true. The Sprague kid seen them and he says they ain't no bigger than this and they got little hands and feet and eyes."

"And hair?" Willard demanded.

"Well, the Sprague kid didn't say about hair."

"You should of asked him. I think he's a liar."

"You better not let him hear you say that," said Joey.

"Well, you can tell him I said it. I ain't afraid of him and I ain't afraid of you. I ain't afraid of anybody. You want to make something of it?" Joey didn't answer. "Well, do you?"

"No," said Joey. "I was thinkin', why don't we just go up and ask the guy if he's got babies in bottles? Maybe he'd show them to us, that is if he's got any."

"He ain't there," said Willard. "When he's here, his car's here. He's away someplace. I think it's a lie. I think the Sprague kid is a liar. I think you're a liar. You want to make something of that?"

It was a lazy day. Willard was going to have to work hard to get up any excitement. "I think you're a coward, too. You want to make something of that?" Joey didn't answer. Willard changed his tactics. "Where's your old man now?" he asked in a conversational tone.

"He's dead," said Joey.

"Oh yeah? I didn't hear. What'd he die of?"

For a moment Joey was silent. He knew Willard knew, but he couldn't let on he knew, not without fighting Willard, and Joey was afraid of Willard.

"He committed—he killed himself."

"Yeah?" Willard put on a long face. "How'd he do it?"

"He took rat poison."

Willard's voice shrieked with laughter. "What'd he think he was, a rat?"

Joey chuckled a little at the joke, just enough, that is.

"He must of thought he was a rat," Willard cried. "Did he go crawling around like this—look, Joey—like this? Did he wrinkle up his nose like this? Did he have a big old long tail?" Willard was helpless with laughter. "Why'n't he just get a rat-trap and put his head in it?" They laughed themselves out on that one, Willard really wore it out. Then he probed for another joke. "What'd he look like when he took it—like this?" He crossed his eyes and opened his mouth and stuck out his tongue.

"He was sick all day," said Joey. "He didn't die till the middle of the night. It hurt him."

Willard said, "What'd he do it for?"

"He couldn't get a job," said Joey. "Nearly a year he couldn't get a job. And you know a funny thing? The next morning a guy come around to give him a job."

Willard tried to recapture his joke. "I guess he just figured he was a rat," he said, but it fell through even for Willard.

Joey stood up and put his hands in his pockets. He saw a little coppery shine in the gutter and walked toward it, but just as he reached it Willard shoved him aside and picked up the penny.

"I saw it first," Joey cried. "It's mine."

"You want to try and make something of it?" said Willard. "Why'n't you go and take rat poison?"

CHAPTER XXVII

Mack and the boys—the Virtues, the Beatitudes, the Beauties. They sat in the Palace Flop-house and they were the stone dropped in the pool, the impulse which sent out ripples to all of Cannery Row and beyond, to Pacific Grove, to Monterey, even over the hill to Carmel.

"This time," said Mack, "we got to be sure he gets to the party. If he don't get there, we don't give it."

"Where we going to give it this time?" Jones asked.

Mack tipped his chair back against the wall and hooked his feet around the front legs. "I've give that a lot of thought," he said. "Of course we could give it here, but it would be pretty hard to surprise him here. And Doc likes his own place. He's got his music there." Mack scowled around the room. "I don't know who broke his phonograph last time," he said. "But if anybody so much as lays a finger on it next time I personally will kick the hell out of him."

"I guess we'll just have to give it at his place," said Hughie.

People didn't get the news of the party—the knowledge of it just slowly grew up in them. And no one was invited. Everyone was going. October 27 had a mental red circle around it. And since it was to be a birthday party there were presents to be considered.

Take the girls at Dora's. All of them had at one time or another gone over to the laboratory for advice or medicine or simply for unprofessional company. And they had seen Doc's bed. It was covered with an old faded red blanket full of fox tails and burrs and sand, for he took it on all his collecting trips. If money came in he bought laboratory equipment. It never occurred to him to buy a new blanket for himself. Dora's girls were making a patchwork quilt, a beautiful thing of silk. And since most of the silks available came from underclothing and evening dresses, the quilt was glorious in strips of flesh pink and orchid and pale yellow and cerise. They worked on it in the late mornings and in the afternoons before the boys from the sardine fleet came in. Under the community of effort, those fights and ill-feelings that always are present in a whore-house completely disappeared.

Lee Chong got out and inspected a twenty-five-foot string of fire-crackers and a big bag of China lily bulbs. These, to his way of thinking, were the finest things you could have for a party.

Sam Malloy had long had a theory of antiques. He knew that old furniture and glass and crockery which had not been very valuable in its day had, when time went by, taken on desirability and cash value out of all proportion to its beauty or utility. He knew of one chair that had brought five hundred dollars. Sam collected pieces of historic automobiles and he was convinced that some day his collection, after making him very rich, would repose on black velvet in the best museums. Sam gave the party a good deal of thought and then he went over his treasures, which he kept in a big locked box behind the boiler. He decided to give Doc one of his finest pieces—the connecting-rod and piston from a 1916 Chalmers. He rubbed and polished this beauty until it gleamed like a piece of ancient armour. He made a little box for it and lined it with black cloth.

Mack and the boys gave the problem considerable thought and came to the conclusion that Doc always wanted cats and had some trouble getting them. Mack brought out his double cage. They borrowed a female in an interesting condition and set their trap under the cypress tree at the top of the vacant lot. In the corner of the Palace they built a wire cage and in it their collection of angry tom-cats grew every night. Jones had to make two trips a day to the canneries for fish heads to feed their charges. Mack considered, and correctly, that twenty-five tom-cats would be as nice a present as they could give Doc.

"No decorations this time," said Mack. "Just a good solid party with lots of liquor."

Gay heard about the party clear over in the Salinas jail, and he made a deal with the sheriff to get off that night, and borrowed two dollars from him for a round-trip bus ticket. Gay had been very nice to the sheriff, who wasn't a man to forget it, particularly because election was coming up and Gay could, or said he could, swing quite a few votes. Besides, Gay could give the Salinas jail a bad name if he wanted to.

Henri had suddenly decided that the old-fashioned pin-cushion was an art form which had flowered and reached its peak in the 'nineties and had since been neglected. He revived the form and was delighted to see what could be done with coloured pins. The picture was never completed—you could change it by rearranging the pins. He was preparing a group of these pieces for a one-man show when he heard about the party, and he finally abandoned his own work and began a giant pin-cushion for Doc. It was to be an intricate and provocative design in green, yellow, and blue pins, all cool colours, and its title was Pre-Cambrian Memory.

Henri's friend Eric, a learned barber who collected the first editions of writers who never had a second edition or a second book, decided to give Doc a rowing-machine he had got at the bankruptcy proceedings of a client with a three-year barber bill. The rowing-machine was in fine condition. No one had rowed it much. No one ever uses a rowing-machine.

The conspiracy grew and there were endless visits back and forth, discussions of presents, liquor, of what time will we start and nobody must tell Doc.

Doc didn't know when he first became aware that something was going on that concerned him. In Lee Chong's conversation stopped when he entered. At first it seemed to him that people were cold to him. When at least half a dozen people asked him what he was doing October 27 he was puzzled, for he had forgotten he had given this date as his birthday. Actually he had been interested in the horoscope for a spurious birth date, but Mack had never mentioned it again and so Doc forgot it.

One evening he stopped in at the Halfway House because they had a draught beer he liked and kept it at the right temperature. He gulped his first glass and then settled down to enjoy his second when he heard a drunk talking to the bartender. "You goin' to the party?"

"What party?"

"Well," said the drunk confidentially, "you know Doc, down in Cannery Row."

The bartender looked up the bar and then back.

"Well," said the drunk, "they're givin' him a hell of a party on his birthday."

"Who is?"

"Everybody."

Doc mulled this over. He did not know the drunk at all.

His reaction to the idea was not simple. He felt a great warmth that they should want to give him a party and at the same time he quaked inwardly, remembering the last one they had given.

Now everything fell into place—Mack's question and the silences when he was about. He thought of it a lot that night, sitting beside his desk. He glanced about, considering what things would have to be locked up. He knew the party was going to cost him plenty.

The next day he began making his own preparations for the party. His best records he carried into the back room, where they could be locked away. He moved every bit of equipment that was breakable back there too. He knew how it would be—his guests would be hungry and they wouldn't bring anything to eat. They would run out of liquor early, they always did. A little wearily he went up to the Thrift Market, where there was a fine and understanding butcher. They discussed meat for some time. Doc ordered fifteen pounds of steaks, ten pounds of tomatoes, twelve heads of lettuces, six loaves of bread, a big jar of peanut butter, and one of strawberry jam, five gallons of wine and four quarts of good substantial, but not distinguished, whisky. He knew he would have trouble at the bank the first of the month. Three or four such parties, he thought, and he would lose the laboratory.

Meanwhile, on the Row the planning reached a crescendo. Doc was right, no one thought of food, but there were odd pints and quarts put away all over. The collection of presents was growing and the guest list, if there had been one, was a little like a census. At the Bear Flag a constant discussion went on about what to wear. Since they would not be working, the girls did not want to wear the long, beautiful dresses which were their uniforms. They decided to wear street clothes. It wasn't as simple as it sounded. Dora insisted that a skeleton crew remain on duty to take care of the regulars. The girls divided up into shifts, some to stay until they were relieved by others. They had to flip for who would go to the party first. The first ones would see Doc's face when they gave him the beautiful quilt. They had it on a frame in the dining-room and it was nearly finished. Mrs. Malloy had put aside her bedspread for a while. She was crocheting six doilies for Doc's beer glasses. The first excitement was gone from the Row now and its place was taken by a deadly cumulative earnestness. There were fifteen tom-cats in the cage at the Palace Flop-house and their yowling made Darling nervous at night.

CHAPTER XXVIII

Sooner or later Frankie was bound to hear about the party. For Frankie drifted about like a small cloud. He was always on the edge of groups. No one noticed him or paid any attention to him. You couldn't tell whether he was listening or not. But Frankie did hear about the party and he heard about the presents and a feeling of fullness swelled in him and a feeling of sick longing.

In the window of Jacob's Jewellery Store was the most beautiful thing in the world. It had been there a long time. It was a black onyx clock with a gold face, but on top of it was the real beauty. On top was a bronze group—St. George killing the dragon. The dragon was on his back with his claws in the air and in his breast was St. George's spear. The Saint was in full armour, with the visor raised, and he rode a fat, big-buttocked horse. With his spear he pinned the dragon to the ground. But the wonderful thing was that he wore a pointed beard and he looked a little like Doc.

Frankie walked to Alvarado Street several times a week to stand in front of the window and look at this beauty. He dreamed about it too, dreamed of running his fingers over the rich, smooth bronze. He had known about it for months when he heard of the party and the presents.

Frankie stood on the pavement for an hour before he went inside.

"Well?" said Mr. Jacobs. He had given Frankie a visual searching as he came in and he knew there wasn't seventy-five cents on him.

"How much is that?" Frankie asked huskily.

"What?"

"That."

"You mean the clock? Fifty dollars—with the group seventy-five dollars."

Frankie walked out without replying. He went down to the beach and crawled under an overturned rowboat and peeked out at the little waves. The bronze beauty was so strong in his head that it seemed to stand out in front of him. And a frantic trapped feeling came over him. He had to get the beauty. His eyes were fierce when he thought of it.

He stayed under the boat all day and at night he emerged and went back to Alvarado Street. While people went to the movies and came out and went to the Golden Poppy, he walked up and down the block. And he didn't get tired or sleepy, for the beauty burned in him like fire.

At last the people thinned out and gradually disappeared from the streets and the parked cars drove away and the town settled to sleep.

A policeman looked closely at Frankie. "What you doing out?" he asked.

Frankie took to his heels and fled around the corner and hid behind a barrel in the alley. At two-thirty he crept to the door of Jacob's and tried the knob. It was locked. Frankie went back to the alley and sat behind the barrel and thought. He saw a broken piece of concrete lying beside the barrel and he picked it up.

The policeman reported that he heard the crash and ran to it. Jacob's window was broken. He saw the prisoner walking rapidly away and chased him. He didn't know how the boy could run that far and that fast carrying fifty pounds of clock and bronze, but the prisoner nearly got away. If he had not blundered into a blind street he would have got away.

The chief called Doc the next day. "Come on down, will you? I want to talk to you."

They brought Frankie in very dirty and frowsy. His eyes were red, but he held his mouth firm and he even smiled a little welcome when he saw Doc.

"What's the matter, Frankie?" Doc asked.

"He broke into Jacob's last night," the chief said. "Stole some stuff. We got in touch with his mother. She says it's not her fault, because he hangs around your place all the time."

"Frankie—you shouldn't have done it," said Doc. The heavy stone of inevitability was on his heart. "Can't you parole him to me?" Doc asked.

"I don't think the judge will do it," said the chief. "We've got a mental report. You know what's wrong with him?"

"Yes," said Doc. "I know."

"And you know what's likely to happen when he comes into puberty?"

"Yes," said Doc, "I know," and the stone weighed terribly on his heart.

"The doctor thinks we better put him away. We couldn't before, but now he's got a felony on him, I think we better."

As Frankie listened the welcome died in his eyes.

"What did he take?" Doc asked.

"A great big clock and a bronze statue."

"I'll pay for it."

"Oh, we got it back. I don't think the judge will hear of it. It'll just happen again. You know that."

"Yes," said Doc softly, "I know. But maybe he had a reason. Frankie," he said, "why did you take it?"

Frankie looked a long time at him. "I love you," he said.

Doc ran out and got in his car and went collecting in the caves below Pt. Lobos.

CHAPTER XXIX

At four o'clock on October 27, Doc finished bottling the last of a lot of jelly-fish. He washed out the formalin jug, cleaned his forceps, powdered and took off his rubber gloves. He went upstairs, fed the rats, and put some of his best records and his microscopes in the back room. Then he locked it. Sometimes an illuminated guest wanted to play with the rattlesnakes. By making careful preparations, by foreseeing possibilities, Doc hoped to make this party as non-lethal as possible without making it dull.

He put on a pot of coffee, started the *Great Fugue* on the phonograph, and took a shower. He was very quick about it, for he was dressed in clean clothes and was having his cup of coffee before the music was completed.

He looked out through the window at the lot and up at the Palace, but no one was moving. Doc didn't know who or how many were coming to his party. But he knew he was watched. He had been conscious of it all day. Not that he had seen anyone, but someone or several people had kept him in sight. So it was to be a surprise party. He might as well be surprised. He would follow his usual routine, as though nothing were happening. He crossed to Lee Chong's and bought two quarts of beer. There seemed to be a suppressed Oriental excitement at Lee's. So they were coming too. Doc went back to the laboratory and poured out a glass of beer. He drank the first off for thirst and poured a second one to taste. The lot and the street were still deserted.

Mack and the boys were in the Palace and the door was closed. All afternoon the stove had roared, heating water for baths. Even Darling had been bathed and she wore a red bow around her neck.

"What time you think we should go over?" Hazel asked.

"I don't think before eight o'clock," said Mack. "But I don't see nothin' against us havin' a short one to kind of get warmed up."

"How about Doc getting warmed up?" Hughie said. "Maybe I ought just to take him a bottle like it was just nothing."

"No," said Mack. "Doc just went over to Lee's for some beer."

"You think he suspects anything?" Jones asked.

"How could he?" asked Mack.

In the corner cage two tom-cats started an argument and the whole cageful commented with growls and arched backs. There were only twenty-one cats. They had fallen short of their mark.

"I wonder how they'll get them cats over there?" Hazel began. "We can't carry that big cage through the door."

"We won't," said Mack. "Remember how it was with the frogs. No, we'll just tell Doc about them. He can come over and get them." Mack got up and opened one of Eddie's wining jugs. "We might as well get warmed up," he said.

At five-thirty the old Chinaman flap-flapped down the hill, past the Palace. He crossed the lot, crossed the street, and disappeared between Western Biological and the Hediondo.

At the Bear Flag the girls were getting ready. A kind of anchor watch had been chosen by straws. The ones who stayed were to be relieved every hour.

Dora was splendid. Her hair freshly dyed orange was curled and piled on her head. She wore her wedding ring and a big diamond brooch on her breast. Her dress was white silk, with a black bamboo pattern. In the bedrooms the reverse of ordinary procedure was in practice.

Those who were staying wore long evening dresses, while those who were going had on short print dresses and looked very pretty. The quilt, finished and backed, was in a big cardboard box in the bar. The bouncer grumbled a little, for it had been decided that he couldn't go to the party. Someone had to look after the house. Contrary to orders, each girl had a pint hidden and each girl watched for the signal to fortify herself a little for the party.

Dora strode magnificently into her office and closed the door. She unlocked the top drawer of the roll-top desk, took out a bottle and a glass and poured herself a snort. And the bottle clinked softly on the glass. A girl listening outside the door heard the clink and spread the word. Dora would not be able to smell breaths now. And the girls rushed for their rooms and got out their pints. Dusk had come to Cannery Row, the grey time between daylight and street light. Phyllis Mae peeked round the curtain in the front parlour.

"Can you see him?" Doris asked.

"Yeah. He's got the lights on. He's sitting there like he's reading. Jesus, how that guy does read! You'd think he'd ruin his eyes. He's got a glass of beer in his hand."

"Well," said Doris, "we might as well have a little one, I guess."

Phyllis Mae was still limping a little, but she was as good as new. She could, she said, lick her weight in City Councilmen. "Seems kind of funny," she said. "There he is, sitting over there and he don't know what's going to happen."

"He never comes in here for a trick," Doris said a little sadly.

"Lots of guys don't want to pay," said Phyllis Mae. "Costs them more, but they figure it different."

"Well, hell, maybe he likes them."

"Likes who?"

"Them girls that go over there."

"Oh, yeah—maybe he does. I been over there. He never made a pass at me."

"He wouldn't," said Doris. "But that don't mean if you didn't work here you wouldn't have to fight your way out."

"You mean he don't like our profession?"

"No, I don't mean that at all. He probably figures a girl that's workin' has got a different attitude."

They had another small snort.

In her office, Dora poured herself one more, swallowed it and locked the drawer again. She fixed her perfect hair in the wall mirror, inspected her shining red nails, and went out to the bar. Alfred the bouncer was sulking. It wasn't anything he said nor was his expression unpleasant, but he was sulking just the same. Dora looked him over coldly. "I guess you figure you're getting the blocks, don't you?"

"No," said Alfred. "No, it's quite all right."

That quite threw Dora. "Quite all right, is it? You got a job, Mister. Do you want to keep it or not?"

"It's quite all right," Alfred said frostily. "I ain't putting out no beef." He put his elbows on the bar and studied himself in the mirror. "You just go and enjoy yourself," he said. "I'll take care of everything here. You don't need to worry."

Dora melted under his pain. "Look," she said. "I don't like to have the place without a man. Some lush might get smart and the kids couldn't handle him. But a little later you can come over and you could kind of keep your eye on the place out of the window. How would that be? You could see if anything happened."

"Well," said Alfred, "I would like to come." He was mollified by her permission. "Later I might drop over for just a minute or two. They was a mean drunk in last night. An' I don't know, Dora—I kind of lost my nerve since I bust that guy's back. I just ain't sure of myself no more. I'm gonna pull a punch some night and get took."

"You need a rest," said Dora. "Maybe I'll get Mack to fill in and you can take a couple of weeks off." She was a wonderful madam, Dora was.

Over at the laboratory, Doc had a little whisky after his beer. He was feeling a little mellow. It seemed a nice thing to him that they would give him a party. He played the *Pavane to a Dead Princess* and felt sentimental and a little sad. And because of his feeling he went on with *Daphnis and Chloe*. There was a passage in it that reminded him of something else. The observers in Athens before Marathon reported seeing a great line of dust crossing the Plain, and they heard the clash of arms and they heard the Eleusinian Chant. There was part of the music that reminded him of that picture.

When it was done he got another whisky and he debated in his mind about the *Brandenburg*. That would snap him out of the sweet and sickly mood he was getting into. But what was wrong with the sweet and sickly mood? It was rather pleasant. "I can play anything I want," he said aloud. "I can play *Clair de Lune* or *The Maiden with Flaxen Hair*. I'm a free man."

He poured a whisky and drank it. And he compromised with the *Moonlight Sonata*. He could see the neon light of "La Ida" blinking on and off. And then the street light in front of the Bear Flag came on.

A squadron of huge brown beetles hurled themselves against the light and then fell to the ground and moved their legs and felt around with their antennæ. A lady cat strolled lonesomely along the gutter looking for adventure. She wondered what had happened to all the tom-cats who had made life interesting and the nights hideous.

Mr. Malloy on his hands and knees peered out of the boiler door to see if anyone had gone to the party yet. In the Palace the boys sat restlessly watching the black hands of the alarm clock.

CHAPTER XXX

THE NATURE of parties has been imperfectly studied. It is, however generally understood that a party has a pathology, that it is a kind of an individual and that it is likely to be a very perverse individual. And it is also generally understood that a party hardly ever goes the way it is planned or intended. This last, of course, excludes those dismal slave parties, whipped and controlled and dominated, given by ogreish professional hostesses. These are not parties at all, but acts and demonstrations, about as spontaneous as peristalsis and as interesting as its end product.

Probably everyone in Cannery Row had projected his imagination to how the party would be—the shouts of greeting, the congratulation, the noise and good feeling. And it didn't start that way at all. Promptly at eight o'clock Mack and the boys, combed and clean, picked up their jugs and marched down the chicken-walk, over the railroad track, through the lot across the street and up the steps of Western Biological. Everyone was embarrassed. Doc held the door open and Mack made a little speech. "Being as how it's your birthday, I and the boys thought we would wish you happy birthday and we got twenty-one cats for you as a present."

He stopped and they stood forlornly on the stairs.

"Come on in," said Doc. "Why—I'm—I'm surprised. I didn't even know you knew it was my birthday."

"All tom-cats," said Hazel. "We didn't bring 'em down."

They sat down formally in the room on the left. There was a long silence. "Well," said Doc, "now you're here, how about a little drink?"

Mack said: "We brought a little snort," and he indicated the three jugs Eddie had been accumulating. "They ain't no beer in it," said Eddie.

Doc covered his early evening reluctance. "No," he said. "You've got to have a drink with me. It just happens I laid in some whisky."

They were just seated formally, sipping delicately at the whisky, when Dora and the girls came in. They presented the quilt. Doc laid it over his bed and it was beautiful. And they accepted a little drink. Mr. and Mrs. Malloy followed with their presents.

"Lots of folks don't know what this stuff's going to be worth," said Sam Malloy as he brought out the Chalmers 1916 piston and connecting-rod. "There probably isn't three of these here left in the world."

And now people began to arrive in droves. Henri came in with a pin-cushion three by four feet. He wanted to give a lecture on his new art form, but by this time the formality was broken. Mr. and Mrs. Gay came in. Lee Chong presented the great string of fire-crackers and the China lily bulbs. Someone ate the lily bulbs by eleven o'clock, but the fire-crackers lasted longer. A group of comparative strangers came in from "La Ida". The stiffness was going out of the party quickly. Dora sat in a kind of throne, her orange hair flaming. She held her whisky-glass daintily, with her little finger extended. And she kept an eye on the girls to see that they conducted themselves properly. Doc put dance music on the phonograph and he went to the kitchen and began to fry the steaks.

The first fight was not a bad one. One of the group from "La Ida" made an immoral proposal to one of Dora's girls. She protested and Mack and the boys, outraged at this breach of propriety, threw him out quickly and without breaking anything. They felt good then, for they knew they were contributing.

Out in the kitchen Doc was frying steaks in three skillets, and he cut up tomatoes and piled up sliced bread. He felt very good. Mack was personally taking care of the phonograph. He had found an album of Benny Goodman's trios. Dancing had started, indeed the party was beginning to take on depth and vigour. Eddie went into the office and did a tap-dance. Doc had taken a pint with him to the kitchen and he helped himself from the bottle. He was feeling better and better. Everyone was surprised when he served the meat. Nobody was really hungry and they cleaned it up instantly. Now the food set the party into a kind of rich digestive sadness. The whisky was gone and Doc brought out the gallons of wine.

Dora, sitting enthroned, said, "Doc, play some of that nice music. I get Christ awful sick of that musical box over home."

Then Doc played *Ardo* and the *Amor* from an album of Monteverdi. And the guests sat quietly and their eyes were inward. Dora breathed beauty. Two newcomers crept up the stairs and entered quietly. Doc was feeling a golden pleasant sadness. The guests were silent when the music stopped. Doc brought out a book and he read in a clear, deep voice:

Even now
If I see my soul the citron-breasted fair one
Still gold-tinted, her face like our night stars,
Drawing unto her; her body beaten about with flame,
Wounded by the flaring spear of love,
My first of all by reason of her fresh years,
Then is my heart buried alive in snow.

Even now
If my girl with lotus eyes came to me again
Weary with the dear weight of young love,
Again I would give her to these starved twins of arms
And from her mouth drink down the heavy wine,
As a reeling pirate bee in fluttered ease
Steals up the honey from the nunephar.

Even now
If I saw her lying all wide eyes
And with collyrium the indent of her cheek
Lengthened to the bright ear and her pale side
So suffering the fever of my distance,
Then would my love for her be ropes of flowers, and night
A black-haired lover on the breasts of day.

Even now
My eyes that hurry to see no more are painting, painting
Faces of my lost girl. O golden rings
That tap against cheeks of small magnolia-leaves,
O whitest so soft parchment where
My poor divorced lips have written excellent
Stanzas of kisses, and will write no more.

Even now
Death sends me the flickering of powdery lids
Over wild eyes and the pity of her slim body
All broken up with the weariness of joy;
The little red flowers of her breasts to be my comfort
Moving above scarves, and for my sorrow
Wet crimson lips that once I marked as mine.

Even now
They chatter her weakness through the two bazaars
Who was so strong to love me. And small men
That buy and sell for silver being slaves
Crinkle the fat about their eyes; and yet

No Prince of the Cities of the Sea has taken her,
Leading to his grim bed. Little lonely one,
You cling to me as a garment clings; my girl.

Even now
I love long black eyes that caress like silk,
Ever and ever sad and laughing eyes,
Whose lids make such sweet shadow when they close
It seems another beautiful look of hers.
I love a fresh mouth, ah, a scented mouth,
And curving hair, subtle as a smoke,
And light fingers, and laughter of green gems.

Even now
I remember that you made answer very softly,
We being one soul, your hand on my hair,
The burning memory rounding your near lips;
I have seen the priestesses of Rati make love at moon fall
And then in a carpeted hall with a bright gold lamp
*Lie down carelessly anywhere to sleep.**

Phyllis Mae was openly weeping when he stopped and Dora herself dabbed at her eyes. Hazel was so taken by the sound of the words that he had not listened to their meaning. But a little world sadness had slipped over all of them. Everyone was remembering a lost love, everyone a call.

Mack said, "Jesus, that's pretty. Reminds me of a dame——" and he let it pass. They filled the wine-glasses and became quiet. The party was slipping away in sweet sadness. Eddie went out in the office and did a little tap-dance and came back and sat down again. The party was about to recline and go to sleep when there was a tramp of feet on the stairs. A great voice shouted, "Where's the girls?"

Mack got up almost happily and crossed quickly to the door. And a smile of joy illuminated the faces of Hughie and Jones. "What girls you got in mind?" Mack asked softly.

"Ain't this a whore-house? Cab-driver said they was one down here."

"You made a mistake, Mister." Mack's voice was gay.

"Well, what's them dames in there?"

They joined battle then. They were the crew of a San Pedro tuna-boat, good, hard, happy, fight-wise men. With the first rush they burst through to the party. Dora's girls had each one slipped

* "Black Marigolds," translated from the Sanskrit by E. Powys Mathers

off a shoe and held it by the toe. As the fight raged by they would clip a man on the head with the spike heel. Dora leaped for the kitchen and came roaring out with a meat grinder. Even Doc was happy. He flailed about with the Chalmers 1916 piston and connecting-rod.

It was a good fight. Hazel tripped and got kicked in the face twice before he could get to his feet again. The Franklin stove went over with a crash. Driven to a corner the newcomers defended themselves with heavy books from the bookcases. But gradually they were driven back. The two front windows were broken out. Suddenly Alfred, who had heard the trouble from across the street, attacked from the rear with his favourite weapon, an indoor ball bat. The fight raged down the steps and into the street and across into the lot. The front door was hanging limply from one hinge again. Doc's shirt was torn off and his slight strong shoulder dripped blood from a scratch. The enemy was driven half-way up the lot when the sirens sounded. Doc's birthday party had barely time to get inside the laboratory and wedge the broken door closed and turn out the lights before the police car cruised up. The cops didn't find anything. But the party was sitting in the dark giggling happily and drinking wine. The shift changed at the Bear Flag. The fresh contingent raged in full of hell. And then the party really got going. The cops came back, looked in, clicked their tongues and joined in. Mack and the boys used the squad car to go to Jimmy Brucia's for more wine, and Jimmy came back with them. You could hear the roar of the party from end to end of Cannery Row. The party had all the best qualities of a riot and a night on the barricades. The crew from the San Pedro tuna-boat crept humbly back and joined the party. They were embraced and admired. A woman five blocks away called the police to complain about the noise and couldn't get anyone. The cops reported their own car stolen and later found it on the beach. Doc sitting cross-legged on the table smiled and tapped his fingers gently on his knee. Mack and Phyllis Mae were doing Indian wrestling on the floor. And the cool bay wind blew in through the broken windows. It was then that someone lighted the twenty-five-foot string of fire-crackers.

CHAPTER XXXI

A WELL-GROWN gopher took up residence in a thicket of mallow weeds in the vacant lot on Cannery Row. It was a perfect place. The deep green luscious mallows towered up crisp and rich, and as they matured their little cheeses hung down provocatively. The earth was perfect for a gopher-hole, too, black and soft and yet with a little clay in it so that it didn't crumble and the tunnels didn't cave in. The gopher was fat and sleek and he had always plenty of food in his cheek pouches. His little ears were clean and well set and his eyes were as black as old-fashioned pin-heads and just about the same size. His digging hands were strong and the fur on his back was glossy brown and the fawn-coloured fur on his chest was incredibly soft and rich. He had long curving yellow teeth and a little short tail. Altogether he was a beautiful gopher and in the prime of his life.

He came to the place over-land and found it good and he began his burrow on a little eminence where he could look out among the mallow weeds and see the trucks go by on Cannery Row. He could watch the feet of Mack and the boys as they crossed the lot to the Palace Flop-house. As he dug down into the coal-black earth he found it even more perfect, for there were great rocks under the soil. When he made his great chamber for the storing of food it was under a rock so that it could never cave in, no matter how hard it rained. It was a place where he could settle down and raise any number of families and the burrow could increase in all directions.

It was beautiful in the early morning when he first poked his head out of the burrow. The mallows filtered green light down on him and the first rays of the rising sun shone into his hole and warmed it so that he lay there content and very comfortable.

When he had dug his great chamber and his four emergency exits and his waterproof deluge room, the gopher began to store food. He cut down only the perfect mallow stems and trimmed them to the exact length he needed and he took them down the hole and stacked them neatly in his great chamber, and arranged them so they wouldn't ferment or get sour. He had found the perfect place to live. There were no gardens about, so no one would think of setting a trap for him. Cats there were, many of them, but they were so bloated with fish-heads and guts from the canneries that they had long ago given up hunting. The soil was sandy enough so that water never stood about or filled a hole for long. The gopher worked and worked until he had his great chamber crammed with food. Then he made little side chambers for the babies who would inhabit them. In a few years there might be thousands of his progeny spreading out from the original hearthstone.

But as time went on the gopher began to be a little impatient, for no female appeared. He sat in the entrance of his hole in the morning and made penetrating squeaks that are inaudible to the human ear but can be heard deep in the earth by other gophers. And still no female appeared. Finally in a sweat of impatience he went up across the track until he found another gopher-hole. He squeaked provocatively in the entrance. He heard a rustling and smelled female, and then out of the hole came an old battle-torn bull gopher who mauled and bit him so badly that he crept home and lay in his great chamber for three days recovering, and he lost two toes from one front paw from that fight.

Again he waited and squeaked beside his beautiful burrow in the beautiful place, but no female ever came, and after a while he had to move away. He had to move two blocks up the hill to a dahlia garden where they put out traps every night.

CHAPTER XXXII

Doc awakened very slowly and clumsily like a fat man getting out of a swimming-pool. His mind broke the surface and fell back several times. There was red lipstick on his beard. He opened one eye, saw the brilliant colours of the quilt and closed his eye quickly. But after a while he looked again. His eye went past the quilt to the floor, to the broken plate in the corner, to the glasses standing on the table turned over on the floor, to the spilled wine and the books like heavy fallen butterflies. There were little bits of curled red paper all over the place and the sharp smell of fire-crackers. He could see through the kitchen door to the steak plates stacked high and the skillets deep in grease. Hundreds of cigarette butts were stamped out on the floor. And under the fire-cracker smell was a fine combination of wine and whisky and perfume. His eye stopped for a moment on a little pile of hairpins in the middle of the floor.

He rolled over slowly and supporting himself on one elbow he looked out the broken window. Cannery Row was quiet and sunny. The boiler door was open. The door of the Palace Flop-house was closed. A man slept peacefully among the weeds in the vacant lot. The Bear Flag was shut up tight.

Doc got up and went into the kitchen and lighted the gas water-heater on his way to the toilet. Then he came back and sat on the edge of his bed and worked his toes together while he surveyed the wreckage. From up the hill he could hear the church bells ringing. When the gas heater began rumbling he went back to the bathroom and took a shower and he put on blue jeans and a flannel shirt. Lee Chong was closed, but he saw who was at the door and opened it. He went to the refrigerator and brought out a quart of beer without being asked. Doc paid him.

"Good time?" Lee asked. His brown eyes were a little inflamed in their pouches.

"Good time!" said Doc, and he went back to the laboratory with his cold beer. He made a peanut butter sandwich to eat with his beer. It was very quiet in the street. No one went by at all. Doc heard music in his head—violas and 'cellos, he thought. And they played cool, soft, soothing music with nothing much to distinguish it. He ate his sandwich and sipped his beer and listened to the music. When he had finished his beer, Doc went into the kitchen and cleared the dirty dishes out of the sink. He ran hot water in it and poured soap chips under the running water so that the foam stood high and white. Then he moved about collecting all the glasses that weren't broken. He put them in the soapy hot water. The steak-plates were piled high on the stove with their brown juice and their white grease sticking them together. Doc cleared a place on the table for the clean glasses as he washed them. Then he unlocked the door of the back room and brought out one of his albums of Gregorian music and he put a Paternoster and Agnus Dei on the turn-table and started it going. The angelic, disembodied voices filled the laboratory. They were incredibly pure and sweet. Doc worked carefully, washing the glasses so that they would not clash together and spoil the music. The boys' voices carried the melody up and down, simply but with the richness that is in no other singing. When the record had finished, Doc wiped his hands and turned it off. He saw a book lying half under his bed and picked it up and he sat down on the bed. For a moment he read to himself, but then his lips began to move and in a moment he read aloud—slowly, pausing at the end of each line.

Even now
I mind the coming and talking of wise men from towers
Where they thought away their youth. And I, listening,
Found not the salt of the whispers of my girl,
Murmur of confused colours, as we lay near sleep;
Little wise words and little witty words,
Wanton as water, honied with eagerness.

In the sink the high white foam cooled and ticked as the bubbles burst. Under the piers it was very high tide, and the waves splashed on rocks they had not reached in a long time.

Even now
I mind that I loved cypress and roses, clear,
The great blue mountains and the small grey hills,
The sounding of the sea. Upon a day
I saw strange eyes and hands like butterflies;
For me at morning larks flew from the thyme
And children came to bathe in little streams.

Doc closed the book. He could hear the waves beat under the piles and he could hear the scampering of white rats against the wire. He went into the kitchen and felt the cooling water in the sink. He ran hot water into it. He spoke aloud to the sink and the white rats, and to himself:

Even now
I know that I have savoured the hot taste of life
Lifting green cups and gold at the great feast.
Just for a small and forgotten time
I have had full in my eyes from off my girl
The whitest pouring of eternal light——

He wiped his eyes with the back of his hand. And the white rats scampered and scrambled in their cages. And behind the glass the rattlesnakes lay still and stared into space with their dusty, frowning eyes.

THE PEARL

"In the town they tell the story of the great pearl—how it was found and how it was lost again. They tell of Kino, the fisherman, and of his wife, Juana, and of the baby, Coyotito. And because the story has been told so often, it has taken root in every man's mind. And, as with all retold tales that are in people's hearts, there are only good and bad things and black and white things and good and evil things and no in-between anywhere.

"If this story is a parable, perhaps everyone takes his own meaning from it and reads his own life into it. In any case, they say in the town that . . ."

CHAPTER I

Kino awakened in the near dark. The stars still shone and the day had drawn only a pale wash of light in the lower sky to the east. The roosters had been crowing for some time, and the early pigs were already beginning their ceaseless turning of twigs and bits of wood to see whether anything to eat had been overlooked. Outside the brush house in the tuna clump, a covey of little birds chittered and flurried with their wings.

Kino's eyes opened, and he looked first at the lightening square which was the door and then he looked at the hanging box where Coyotito slept. And last he turned his head to Juana, his wife, who lay beside him on the mat, her blue head-shawl over her nose and over her breasts and around the small of her back. Juana's eyes were open too. Kino could never remember seeing them closed when he awakened. Her dark eyes made little reflected stars. She was looking at him as she was always looking at him when he awakened.

Kino heard the little splash of morning waves on the beach. It was very good—Kino closed his eyes again to listen to his music. Perhaps he alone did this and perhaps all of his people did it. His people had once been great makers of songs so that everything they saw or thought or did or heard became a song. That was very long ago. The songs remained; Kino knew them, but no new songs were added. That does not mean that there were no personal songs. In Kino's head there was a song now, clear and soft, and if he had been able to speak of it, he would have called it the Song of the Family.

His blanket was over his nose to protect him from the dank air. His eyes flicked to a rustle beside him. It was Juana arising, almost soundlessly. On her hard bare feet she went to the hanging box where Coyotito slept, and she leaned over and said a little reassuring word. Coyotito looked up for a moment, and closed his eyes and slept again.

Juana went to the fire pit and uncovered a coal and fanned it alive while she broke little pieces of brush over it.

Now Kino got up and wrapped his blanket about his head and nose and shoulders. He slipped his feet into his sandals and went outside to watch the dawn.

Outside the door he squatted down and gathered the blanket ends about his knees. He saw the specks of Gulf clouds flame high in the air. And a goat came near and sniffed at him and stared with its cold yellow eyes. Behind him, Juana's fire leaped into flame and threw spears of light through the chinks of the brush-house wall and threw a wavering square of light out the door. A late moth blustered in to find the fire. The Song of the Family came now from behind Kino. And the rhythm of the family song was the grinding-stone where Juana worked the corn for the morning cakes.

The dawn came quickly now, a wash, a glow, a lightness, and then an explosion of fire as the sun arose out of the Gulf. Kino looked down to cover his eyes from the glare. He could hear the pat of the corn-cakes in the house and the rich smell of them on the cooking plate. The ants were busy on the ground, big black ones with shiny bodies and little dusty quick ants. Kino watched with the detachment of God while a dusty ant frantically tried to escape the sand trap an ant lion had dug for him. A thin, timid dog came close and, at a soft word from Kino, curled up, arranged its tail nearly over its feet, and laid its chin delicately on the pile. It was a black dog with yellow-gold spots where its eyebrows should have been. It was a morning like other mornings and yet perfect among mornings.

Kino heard the creak of the rope when Juana took Coyotito out of his hanging box and cleaned him and hammocked him in her shawl in a loop that placed him close to her breast. Kino could see these things without looking at them. Juana sang softly an ancient song that had only three notes and yet endless variety of interval. And this was part of the family song, too. It was all part. Sometimes it rose to an aching chord that caught the throat saying this is safety, this is warmth, this is the *Whole*.

Across the brush fence were other brush houses, and the smoke came from them too, and the sound of breakfast, but those were other songs, their pigs were other pigs, their wives were not Juana. Kino was young and strong and his black hair hung over his brown forehead. His eyes were warm and fierce and bright and his moustache was thin and coarse. He lowered his blanket from his nose now, for the dark poisonous air was gone and the yellow sunlight fell on the house. Near the brush fence two roosters bowed and feinted at each other with squared wings and neck feathers ruffed out. It would be a clumsy fight. They were not game chickens. Kino watched them for a moment, and then his eyes went up to a flight of wild doves twinkling inland to the hills. The world was awake now, and Kino arose and went into his brush house.

As he came through the door, Juana stood up from the glowing fire pit. She put Coyotito back in his hanging box and then she combed her black hair and braided it in two braids and tied the ends with thin green ribbon. Kino squatted by the fire pit and rolled a hot corn-cake and dipped it in sauce and ate it, and he drank a little pulque; and that was breakfast. That was the only breakfast he had ever known outside of feast days and one incredible fiesta on cookies that had nearly killed him. When Kino had finished, Juana came back to the fire and ate her breakfast. They had spoken once, but there is not need for speech if it is only a habit anyway. Kino sighed with satisfaction—and that was conversation.

The sun was warming the brush house, breaking through its crevices in long streaks. And one of the streaks fell on the hanging box where Coyotito lay, and on the ropes that held it.

It was a tiny movement that drew their eyes to the hanging box. Kino and Juana froze in their positions. Down the rope that hung the baby's box from the roof support a scorpion moved slowly. His stinging tail was straight out behind him, but he could whip it up in a flash of time.

Kino's breath whistled in his nostrils and he opened his mouth to stop it. And then the startled look was gone from him and the rigidity from his body. In his mind a new song had come, the Song of Evil, the music of the enemy, of any foe of the family, a savage, secret, dangerous melody, and, underneath, the Song of the Family cried plaintively.

The scorpion moved delicately down the rope towards the box. Under her breath Juana repeated an ancient magic to guard against such evil, and on top of that she muttered a Hail Mary between clenched teeth. But Kino was in motion. His body glided quietly across the room, noiselessly and smoothly. His hands were in front of him, palms down, and his eyes were on the scorpion. Beneath it in the hanging box Coyotito laughed and reached up his hand towards it. It sensed danger when Kino was almost within reach of it. It stopped, and its tail rose up over its back in little jerks and the curved thorn on the tail's end glistened.

Kino stood perfectly still. He could hear Juana whispering the old magic again, and he could hear the evil music of the enemy. He could not move until the scorpion moved, and it felt for the source of the death that was coming to it. Kino's hand went forward very slowly, very smoothly. The thorned tail jerked upright. And at that moment the laughing Coyotito shook the rope and the scorpion fell.

Kino's hand leaped to catch it, but it fell past his fingers, fell on the baby's shoulder, landed and struck. Then, snarling, Kino had it, had it in his fingers, rubbing it to a paste in his hands. He threw it down and beat it into the earth floor with his fist, and Coyotito screamed with pain in his box. But Kino beat and stamped the enemy until it was only a fragment and a moist place in the dirt. His teeth were bared and fury flared in his eyes and the Song of the Enemy roared in his ears.

But Juana had the baby in her arms now. She found the puncture with redness starting from it already. She put her lips down over the puncture and sucked hard and spat and sucked again while Coyotito screamed.

Kino hovered; he was helpless, he was in the way.

The screams of the baby brought the neighbours. Out of their brush houses they poured—Kino's brother Juan Tomás and his fat wife Apolonia and their four children crowded in the door and blocked the entrance, while behind them others tried to look in, and one small boy crawled among legs to have a look. And those in front passed the word back to those behind—"Scorpion. The baby has been stung."

Juana stopped sucking the puncture for a moment. The little hole was slightly enlarged and its edges whitened from the sucking, but the red swelling extended farther around it in a hard lymphatic mound. And all of these people knew about the scorpion. An adult might be very ill from the sting, but a baby could easily die from the poison. First, they knew, would come swelling and fever and tightened throat, and then cramps in the stomach, and then Coyotito might die if enough of the poison had gone in. But the stinging pain of the bite was going away. Coyotito's screams turned to moans.

Kino had wondered often at the iron in his patient, fragile wife. She, who was obedient and respectful and cheerful and patient, could arch her back in child pain with hardly a cry. She could stand fatigue and hunger almost better than Kino himself. In the canoe she was like a strong man. And now she did a most surprising thing.

"The doctor," she said. "Go to get the doctor."

The word was passed out among the neighbours where they stood close-packed in the little yard behind the brush fence. And they repeated among themselves, "Juana wants the doctor." A wonderful thing, a memorable thing, to want the doctor. To get him would be a remarkable thing. The doctor never came to the cluster of brush houses. Why should he, when he had more than he could do to take care of the rich people who lived in the stone and plaster houses of the town?

"He would not come," the people in the yard said.

"He would not come," the people in the door said, and the thought got into Kino.

"The doctor would not come," Kino said to Juana.

She looked up at him, her eyes as cold as the eyes of a lioness. This was Juana's first baby—this was nearly everything there was in Juana's world. And Kino saw her determination and the music of the family sounded in his head with a steely tone.

"Then we will go to him," Juana said, and with one hand she arranged her dark-blue shawl over her head and made of one end of it a sling to hold the moaning baby and made of the other end of it a shade over his eyes to protect him from the light. The people in the door pushed against those behind to let her through. Kino followed her. They went out of the gate to the rutted path and the neighbours followed them.

The thing had become a neighbourhood affair. They made a quick soft-footed procession into the centre of the town, first Juana and Kino, and behind them Juan Tomás and Apolonia, her big stomach jiggling with the strenuous pace, then all the neighbours with the children trotting on the flanks. And the yellow sun threw their black shadows ahead of them so that they walked on their own shadows.

They came to the place where the brush houses stopped and the city of stone and plaster began, the city of harsh outer walls and inner cool gardens where a little water played and the bougainvillaea crusted the walls with purple and brick-red and white. They heard from the secret gardens the singing of caged birds and heard the splash of cooling water on hot flagstones. The procession crossed the blinding plaza and passed in front of the church. It had grown now, and on the outskirts the hurrying newcomers were being softly informed how the baby had been stung by a scorpion, how the father and mother were taking it to the doctor.

And the newcomers, particularly the beggars from the front of the church, who were great experts in financial analysis, looked quickly at Juana's old blue skirt, saw the tears in her shawl, appraised the green ribbon on her braids, read the age of Kino's blanket and the thousand washings of his clothes, and set them down as poverty people and went along to see what kind of drama might develop. The four beggars in front of the church knew everything in the town. They were students of the expressions of young women as they went in to confession, and they saw them as they came out and read the nature of the sin. They knew every little scandal and some very big crimes. They slept at their posts in the shadow of the church so that no one crept in for consolation without their knowledge. And they knew the doctor. They knew his ignorance, his cruelty, his avarice, his appetites, his sins. They knew his clumsy abortions and the little brown pennies he gave sparingly for alms. They had seen his corpses go into the church. And, since early mass was over and business was slow, they followed the procession, these endless searchers after perfect knowledge of their fellow men, to see what the fat, lazy doctor would do about an indigent baby with a scorpion bite.

The scurrying procession came at last to the big gate in the wall of the doctor's house. They could hear the splashing water and the singing of caged birds and the sweep of the long brooms on the flagstones. And they could smell the frying of good bacon from the doctor's house.

Kino hesitated a moment. This doctor was not of his people. This doctor was of a race which for nearly four hundred years had beaten and starved and robbed and despised Kino's race, and frightened it too, so that the indigene came humbly to the door. And, as always when he came near to one of this race, Kino felt weak and afraid and angry at the same time. Rage and terror went together. He could kill the doctor more easily than he could talk to him, for all of the doctor's race spoke to all of Kino's race as though they were simple animals. And as Kino raised his right hand to the iron ring knocker in the gate, rage swelled in him, and the pounding music of the enemy beat in his ears, and his lips drew tight against his teeth—but with his left hand he reached to take off his hat. The iron ring pounded against the gate. Kino took off his hat and stood waiting. Coyotito moaned a little in Juana's arms, and she spoke softly to him. The procession crowded close, the better to see and hear.

After a moment the big gate opened a few inches. Kino could see the green coolness of the garden and little splashing fountain through the opening. The man who looked out at him was one of his own race. Kino spoke to him in the old language. "The little one —the first-born—has been poisoned by the scorpion," Kino said. "He requires the skill of the healer."

The gate closed a little, and the servant refused to speak in the old language. "A little moment," he said. "I go to inform myself," and he closed the gate and slid the bolt home. The glaring sun threw the bunched shadows of the people blackly on the white wall.

In his chamber the doctor sat up in his high bed. He had on his dressing-gown of red watered silk that had come from Paris, a little tight over the chest now if it was buttoned. On his lap was a silver tray with a silver chocolate pot and a tiny cup of egg-shell china, so delicate that it looked silly when he lifted it with his big hand, lifted it with the tips of thumb and forefinger and spread the other three fingers wide to get them out of the way. His eyes rested in puffy little hammocks of flesh and his mouth drooped with discontent. He was growing very stout, and his voice was hoarse with the fat that pressed on his throat. Beside him on a table was a small Oriental gong and a bowl of cigarettes. The furnishings of the room were heavy and dark and gloomy. The pictures were religious, even the large tinted photograph of his dead wife, who, if masses willed and paid for out of her own estate could do it, was in Heaven. The doctor had once for a short time been a part of the great world and his whole subsequent life was memory and longing for France. "That," he said, "was civilized living"—by which he meant that on a small income he had been able to keep a mistress and eat in restaurants. He poured his second cup of chocolate and crumbled a sweet biscuit in his fingers. The servant from the gate came to the open door and stood waiting to be noticed.

"Yes?" the doctor asked.

"It is a little Indian with a baby. He says a scorpion stung it."

The doctor put his cup down gently before he let his anger rise. "Have I nothing better to do than cure insect bites for 'little Indians'? I am a doctor, not a veterinary."

"Yes, Patron," said the servant.

"Has he any money?" the doctor demanded. "No, they never have any money. I, I alone in the world am supposed to work for nothing—and I am tired of it. See if he has any money!"

At the gate the servant opened the door a trifle and looked out at the waiting people. And this time he spoke in the old language.

"Have you money to pay for the treatment?"

Now Kino reached into a secret place somewhere under his blanket. He brought out a paper folded many times. Crease by crease he unfolded it, until at last there came to view eight small misshapen seed pearls, as ugly and grey as little ulcers, flattened and almost valueless. The servant took the paper and closed the gate again, but this time he was not gone long. He opened the gate just wide enough to pass the paper back.

"The doctor has gone out," he said. "He was called to a serious case." And he shut the gate quickly out of shame.

And now a wave of shame went over the whole procession. They melted away. The beggars went back to the church steps, the stragglers moved off, and the neighbours departed so that the public shaming of Kino would not be in their eyes.

For a long time Kino stood in front of the gate with Juana beside him. Slowly he put his suppliant hat on his head. Then, without warning, he struck the gate a crushing blow with his fist. He looked down in wonder at his split knuckles and at the blood that flowed down between his fingers.

CHAPTER II

THE TOWN lay on a broad estuary, its old yellow plastered buildings hugging the beach. And on the beach the white and blue canoes that came from Nayarit were drawn up, canoes preserved for generations by a hard shell-like waterproof plaster whose making was a secret of the fishing people. They were high and graceful canoes with curving bow and stern and a braced section midships where a mast could be stepped to carry a small lateen sail.

The beach was yellow sand, but at the water's edge a rubble of shell and algæ took its place. Fiddler crabs bubbled and sputtered in their holes in the sand, and in the shallows little lobsters popped in and out of their tiny homes in the rubble and sand. The sea bottom was rich with crawling and swimming and growing things. The brown algæ waved in the gentle currents and the green eel grass swayed and little sea horses clung to its stems. Spotted botete, the poison fish, lay on the bottom in the eel-grass beds, and the bright-coloured swimming crabs scampered over them.

On the beach the hungry dogs and the hungry pigs of the town searched endlessly for any dead fish or sea bird that might have floated in on a rising tide.

Although the morning was young, the hazy mirage was up. The uncertain air that magnified some things and blotted out others hung over the whole Gulf so that all sights were unreal and vision could not be trusted; so that sea and land had the sharp clarities and the vagueness of a dream. Thus it might be that the people of the Gulf trust things of the spirit and things of the imagination, but they do not trust their eyes to show them distance or clear outline or any optical exactness. Across the estuary from the town one section of mangroves stood clear and telescopically defined, while another mangrove clump was a hazy black-green blob. Part of the far shore disappeared into a shimmer that looked like water. There was no certainty in seeing, no proof that what you saw was there or was not there. And the people of the Gulf expected all places were that way, and it was not strange to them. A copper haze hung over the water, and the hot morning sun beat on it and made it vibrate blindingly.

The brush houses of the fishing people were back from the beach on the right-hand side of the town, and the canoes were drawn up in front of this area.

Kino and Juana came slowly down to the beach and to Kino's canoe, which was the one thing of value he owned in the world. It was very old. Kino's grandfather had brought it from Nayarit, and he had given it to Kino's father, and so it had come to Kino. It was at once property and source of food, for a man with a boat can guarantee a woman that she will eat something. It is the bulwark against starvation. And every year Kino refinished his canoe with the hard shell-like plaster by the secret method that had also come to him from his father. Now he came to the canoe and touched the bow tenderly as he always did. He laid his diving rock and his basket and the two ropes in the sand by the canoe. And he folded his blanket and laid it in the bow.

Juana laid Coyotito on the blanket, and she placed her shawl over him so that the hot sun could not shine on him. He was quiet now, but the swelling on his shoulder had continued up his neck and under his ear and his face was puffed and feverish. Juana went to the water and waded in. She gathered some brown seaweed and made a flat damp poultice of it, and this she applied to the baby's swollen shoulder, which was as good a remedy as any and probably better than the doctor could have done. But the remedy lacked his authority because it was simple and didn't cost anything. The stomach cramps had not come to Coyotito. Perhaps Juana had sucked out the poison in time, but she had not sucked out her worry over her first-born. She had not prayed directly for the recovery of the baby—she had prayed that they might find a pearl with which to hire the doctor to cure the baby, for the minds of people are as unsubstantial as the mirage of the Gulf.

Now Kino and Juana slid the canoe down the beach to the water, and when the bow floated, Juana climbed in, while Kino pushed the stern in and waded beside it until it floated lightly and trembled on the little breaking waves. Then in co-ordination Juana and Kino drove their double-bladed paddles into the sea, and the canoe creased the water and hissed with speed. The other pearlers were gone out long since. In a few moments Kino could see them clustered in the haze, riding over the oyster bed.

Light filtered down through the water to the bed where the frilly pearl oysters lay fastened to the rubbly bottom, a bottom strewn with shells of broken, opened oysters. This was the bed that had raised the King of Spain to be a great power in Europe in past years, had helped to pay for his wars, and had decorated the churches for his soul's sake. The grey oysters with ruffles like skirts on the shells, the barnacle-crusted oysters with little bits of weed clinging to the skirts and small crabs climbing over them. An accident could happen to these oysters, a grain of sand could lie in the folds of muscle and irritate the flesh until in self-protection the flesh coated the grain with a layer of smooth cement. But once started, the flesh continued to coat the foreign body until it fell free in some tidal flurry or until the oyster was destroyed. For centuries men had dived down and torn the oysters from their beds and ripped them open, looking for the coated grains of sand. Swarms of fish lived near the bed to live near the oysters thrown back by the searching men and to nibble at the shining inner shells. But the pearls were accidents, and the finding of one was luck, a little pat on the back by God or the gods or both.

Kino had two ropes, one tied to a heavy stone and one to a basket. He stripped off his shirt and trousers and laid his hat in the bottom of the canoe. The water was oily smooth. He took his rock in one hand and his basket in the other, and he slipped feet-first over the side and the rock carried him to the bottom. The bubbles rose behind him until the water cleared and he could see. Above, the surface of the water was an undulating mirror of brightness, and he could see the bottoms of the canoes sticking through it.

Kino moved cautiously so that the water would not be obscured with mud or sand. He hooked his foot in the loop on his rock and his hands worked quickly, tearing the oysters loose, some singly, others in clusters. He laid them in his basket. In some places the oysters clung to one another so that they came free in lumps.

Now, Kino's people had sung of everything that happened or existed. They had made songs to the fishes, to the sea in anger and to the sea in calm, to the light and the dark and the sun and the moon, and the songs were all in Kino and in his people—every song that had ever been made, even the ones forgotten. And as he filled his basket the song was in Kino, and the beat of the song was his pounding heart as it ate the oxygen from his held breath, and the melody of the song was the grey-green water and the little scuttling animals and the clouds of fish that flitted by and were gone. But in the song there was a secret little inner song, hardly perceptible, but always there, sweet and secret and clinging, almost hiding in the counter-melody, and this was the Song of the Pearl That Might Be, for every shell thrown in the basket might contain a pearl. Chance was against it, but luck and the gods might be for it. And in the canoe above him Kino knew that Juana was making the magic of prayer, her face set rigid and her muscles hard to force the luck, to tear the luck out of the gods' hands, for she needed the luck for the swollen shoulder of Coyotito. And because the need was great and the desire was great, the little secret melody of the pearl that might be was stronger this morning. Whole phrases of it came clearly and softly into the Song of the Undersea.

Kino, in his pride and youth and strength, could remain down over two minutes without strain, so that he worked deliberately, selecting the largest shells. Because they were disturbed, the oyster shells were tightly closed. A little to his right a hummock of rubbly rock struck up, covered with young oysters not ready to take. Kino moved next to the hummock, and then, beside it, under a little overhang, he saw a very large oyster lying by itself, not covered with its clinging brothers. The shell was partly open, for the overhang protected this ancient oyster, and in the lip-like muscle Kino saw a ghostly gleam, and then the shell closed down. His heart beat out a heavy rhythm and the melody of the maybe pearl shrilled in his ears. Slowly he forced the oyster loose and held it tightly against his breast. He kicked his foot free from the rock loop, and his body rose to the surface and his black hair gleamed in the sunlight. He reached over the side of the canoe and laid the oyster in the bottom.

Then Juana steadied the boat while he climbed in. His eyes were shining with excitement, but in decency he pulled up his rock, and then he pulled up his basket of oysters and lifted them in. Juana sensed his excitement, and she pretended to look away. It is not good to want a thing too much. It sometimes drives the luck away. You must want it just enough, and you must be very tactful with God or the gods. But Juana stopped breathing. Very deliberately Kino opened his short strong knife. He looked speculatively at the basket. Perhaps it would be better to open *the* oyster last. He took a small oyster from the basket, cut the muscle, searched the folds of flesh, and threw it in the water. Then he seemed to see the great oyster for the first time. He squatted in the bottom of the canoe, picked up the shell and examined it. The flutes were shining black to brown, and only a few small barnacles adhered to the shell. Now Kino was reluctant to open it. What he had seen, he knew, might be a reflection, a piece of flat shell accidentally drifted in or a complete illusion. In this Gulf of uncertain light there were more illusions than realities.

But Juana's eyes were on him and she could not wait. She put her hand on Coyotito's covered head. "Open it," she said softly.

Kino deftly slipped his knife into the edge of the shell. Through the knife he could feel the muscle tighten hard. He worked the blade lever-wise and the closing muscle and the shell fell apart. The lip-like flesh writhed up and then subsided. Kino lifted the flesh, and there it lay, the great pearl, perfect as the moon. It captured the light and refined it and gave it back in silver incandescence. It was as large as a seagull's egg. It was the greatest pearl in the world.

Juana caught her breath and moaned a little. And to Kino the secret melody of the maybe pearl broke clear and beautiful, rich and warm and lovely, glowing and gloating and triumphant. In the surface of the great pearl he could see dream forms. He picked the pearl from the dying flesh and held it in his palm, and he turned it over and saw that its curve was perfect. Juana came near to stare at it in his hand, and it was the hand he had smashed against the doctor's gate, and the torn flesh of the knuckles was turned greyish white by the sea water.

Instinctively Juana went to Coyotito where he lay on his father's blanket. She lifted the poultice of seaweed and looked at the shoulder. "Kino," she cried shrilly.

He looked past his pearl, and he saw that the swelling was going out of the baby's shoulder, the poison was receding from its body. Then Kino's fist closed over the pearl and his emotion broke over him. He put back his head and howled. His eyes rolled up and he screamed and his body was rigid. The men in the other canoes looked up, startled, and then they dug their paddles into the sea and raced towards Kino's canoe.

CHAPTER III

A TOWN is a thing like a colonial animal. A town has a nervous system and a head and shoulders and feet. A town is a thing separate from all other towns, so that there are no two towns alike. And a town has a whole emotion. How news travels through a town is a mystery not easily to be solved. News seems to move faster than small boys can scramble and dart to tell it, faster than women can call it over the fences.

Before Kino and Juana and the other fishers had come to Kino's brush house, the nerves of the town were pulsing and vibrating with the news—Kino had found the Pearl of the World. Before panting little boys could strangle out the words, their mothers knew it. The news swept on past the brush houses, and it washed in a foaming wave into the town of stone and plaster. It came to the priest walking in his garden, and it put a thoughtful look in his eyes and a memory of certain repairs necessary to the church. He wondered what the pearl would be worth. And he wondered whether he had baptized Kino's baby, or married him for that matter. The news came to the shopkeepers, and they looked at men's clothes that had not sold so well.

The news came to the doctor where he sat with a woman whose illness was age, though neither she nor the doctor would admit it. And when it was made plain who Kino was, the doctor grew stern and judicious at the same time. "He is a client of mine," the doctor said. "I am treating his child for a scorpion sting." And the doctor's eyes rolled up a little in their fat hammocks and he thought of Paris. He remembered the room he had lived in there as a great and luxurious place, and he remembered the hard-faced woman who had lived with him as a beautiful and kind girl, although she had been none of these three. The doctor looked past his aged patient and saw himself sitting in a restaurant in Paris and a waiter was just opening a bottle of wine.

The news came early to the beggars in front of the church, and it made them giggle a little with pleasure, for they knew that there is no alms-giver in the world like a poor man who is suddenly lucky.

Kino had found the Pearl of the World. In the town, in little offices, sat the men who bought pearls from the fishers. They waited in their chairs until the pearls came in, and then they cackled and fought and shouted and threatened until they reached the lowest price the fisherman would stand. But there was a price below which they dared not go, for it had happened that a fisherman in despair had given his pearls to the church. And when the buying was over, these buyers sat alone and their fingers played restlessly with the pearls, and they wished they owned the pearls. For there were not many buyers really—there was only one, and he kept these agents in separate offices to give a semblance of competition. The news came to these men, and their eyes squinted and their finger-tips burned a little, and each one thought how the patron could not live for ever and someone had to take his place. And each one thought how with some capital he could get a new start.

All manner of people grew interested in Kino—people with things to sell and people with favours to ask. Kino had found the Pearl of the World. The essence of pearl mixed with essence of men and a curious dark residue was precipitated. Every man suddenly became related to Kino's pearl, and Kino's pearl went into the dreams, the speculations, the schemes, the plans, the futures, the wishes, the needs, the lusts, the hungers, of everyone, and only one person stood in the way and that was Kino, so that he became curiously every man's enemy. The news stirred up something infinitely black and evil in the town; the black distillate was like a scorpion, or like hunger in the smell of food, or like loneliness when love is withheld. The poison sacs of the town began to manufacture venom, and the town swelled and puffed with the pressure of it.

But Kino and Juana did not know these things. Because they were happy and excited they thought everyone shared their joy. Juan Tomás and Apolonia did, and they were the world too. In the afternoon, when the sun had gone over the mountains of the Peninsula to sink in the outward sea, Kino squatted in his house with Juana beside him. And the brush house was crowded with neighbours. Kino held the great pearl in his hand, and it was warm and alive in his hand. And the music of the pearl had merged with the music of the family so that one beautified the other. The neighbours looked at the pearl in Kino's hand and they wondered how such luck could come to any man.

And Juan Tomás, who squatted on Kino's right hand because he was his brother, asked, "What will you do now that you have become a rich man?"

Kino looked into his pearl, and Juana cast her eyelashes down and arranged her shawl to cover her face so that her excitement could not be seen. And in the incandescence of the pearl the pictures formed of the things Kino's mind had considered in the past and had given up as impossible. In the pearl he saw Juana and Coyotito and himself standing and kneeling at the high altar, and they were being married now that they could pay. He spoke softly: "We will be married—in the church."

In the pearl he saw how they were dressed—Juana in a shawl stiff with newness and a new skirt, and from under the long skirt Kino could see that she wore shoes. It was in the pearl—the picture glowing there. He himself was dressed in new white clothes, and he carried a new hat—not of straw but of fine black felt—and he, too, wore shoes—not sandals but shoes that laced. But Coyotito—he was the one—he wore a blue sailor suit from the United States and a little yachting cap such as Kino had seen once when a pleasure-boat put into the estuary. All of these things Kino saw in the lucent pearl, and he said, "We will have new clothes."

And the music of the pearl rose like a chorus of trumpets in his ears.

Then to the lovely grey surface of the pearl came the little things Kino wanted: a harpoon to take the place of one lost a year ago, a new harpoon of iron with a ring in the end of the shaft; and—his mind could hardly make the leap—a rifle—but why not, since he was so rich? And Kino saw Kino in the pearl, Kino holding a Winchester carbine. It was the wildest day-dreaming and very pleasant. His lips moved hesitantly over this——"A rifle," he said. "Perhaps a rifle."

It was the rifle that broke down the barriers. This was an impossibility, and if he could think of having a rifle whole horizons were burst and he could rush on. For it is said that humans are never satisfied, that you give them one thing and they want something more. And this is said in disparagement, whereas it is one of the greatest talents the species has and one that has made it superior to animals that are satisfied with what they have.

The neighbours, close pressed and silent in the house, nodded their heads at his wild imaginings. And a man in the rear murmured, "A rifle. He will have a rifle."

But the music of the pearl was shrilling with triumph in Kino. Juana looked up, and her eyes were wide at Kino's courage and at his imagination. An electric strength had come to him now the horizons were kicked out. In the pearl he saw Coyotito sitting at a little desk in school, just as Kino had once seen it through an open door. And Coyotito was dressed in a jacket, and he had on a white collar and a broad silken tie. Moreover, Coyotito was writing on a big piece of paper. Kino looked at his neighbours fiercely. "My son will go to school," he said, and the neighbours were hushed. Juana caught her breath sharply. Her eyes were bright as she watched him, and she looked quickly down at Coyotito in her arms to see whether this might be possible.

But Kino's face shone with prophecy. "My son will read and open the books, and my son will write and will know writing. And my son will make numbers, and these things will make us free because he will know—he will know and through him we will know." And in the pearl Kino saw himself and Juana squatting by the little fire in the brush hut while Coyotito read from a great book. "This is what the pearl will do," said Kino. And he had never said so many words together in his life. And suddenly he was afraid of his talking. His hand closed down over the pearl and cut the light away from it. Kino was afraid as a man is afraid who says, "I will," without knowing.

Now the neighbours knew they had witnessed a great marvel. They knew that time would now date from Kino's pearl, and that they would discuss this moment for many years to come. If these things came to pass, they would recount how Kino looked and what he said and how his eyes shone, and they would say, "He was a man transfigured. Some power was given to him, and there it started. You see what a great man he has become, starting from that moment. And I myself saw it."

And if Kino's planning came to nothing, those same neighbours would say, "There it started. A foolish madness came over him so that he spoke foolish words. God keep us from such things. Yes, God punished Kino because he rebelled against the way things are. You see what has become of him. And I myself saw the moment when his reason left him."

Kino looked down at his closed hand and the knuckles were scabbed over and tight where he had struck the gate.

Now the dusk was coming. And Juana looped her shawl under the baby so that he hung against her hip, and she went to the fire hole and dug a coal from the ashes and broke a few twigs over it and fanned a flame alive. The little flames danced on the faces of the neighbours. They knew they should go to their own dinners, but they were reluctant to leave.

The dark was almost in, and Juana's fire threw shadows on the brush walls when the whisper came in, passed from mouth to mouth: "The Father is coming—the priest is coming." Then men uncovered their heads and stepped back from the door, and the women gathered their shawls about their faces and cast down their eyes. Kino and Juan Tomás, his brother, stood up. The priest came in—a greying, ageing man with an old skin and a young sharp eye. Children he considered these people, and he treated them like children.

"Kino," he said softly, "thou art named after a great man—and a great Father of the Church." He made it sound like a benediction. "Thy namesake tamed the desert and sweetened the minds of thy people, didst thou know that? It is in the books."

Kino looked quickly down at Coyotito's head, where he hung on Juana's hip. Some day, his mind said, that boy would know what things were in the books and what things were not. The music had gone out of Kino's head, but now, thinly, slowly, the melody of the morning, the music of evil, of the enemy, sounded, but it was faint and weak. And Kino looked at his neighbours to see who might have brought this song in.

But the priest was speaking again. "It has come to me that thou hast found a great fortune, a great pearl."

Kino opened his hand and held it out, and the priest gasped a little at the size and beauty of the pearl. And then he said, "I hope thou wilt remember to give thanks, my son, to Him who has given thee this treasure, and to pray for guidance in the future."

Kino nodded dumbly, and it was Juana who spoke softly. "We will, Father. And we will be married now. Kino has said so." She looked at the neighbours for confirmation, and they nodded their heads solemnly.

The priest said, "It is pleasant to see that your first thoughts are good thoughts. God bless you, my children." He turned and left quietly, and the people let him through.

But Kino's hand had closed tightly on the pearl again, and he was glancing about suspiciously, for the evil song was in his ears, shrilling against the music of the pearl.

The neighbours slipped away to go to their houses, and Juana squatted by the fire and set her clay pot of boiled beans over the little flame. Kino stepped to the doorway and looked out. As always, he could smell the smoke from many fires, and he could see the hazy stars and feel the damp of the night air, so that he covered his nose from it. The thin dog came to him and threshed itself in greeting like a wind-blown flag, and Kino looked down at it and didn't see it. He had broken through the horizons into a cold and lonely outside. He felt alone and unprotected, and scraping crickets and shrilling tree frogs and croaking toads seemed to be carrying the melody of evil. Kino shivered a little and drew his blanket more tightly against his nose. He carried the pearl still in his hand, tightly closed in his palm, and it was warm and smooth against his skin.

Behind him he heard Juana patting the cakes before she put them down on the clay cooking-sheet. Kino felt all the warmth and security of his family behind him, and the Song of the Family came from behind him like the purring of a kitten. But now, by saying what his future was going to be like, he had created it. A plan is a real thing, and things projected are experienced. A plan once made and visualized becomes a reality along with other realities—never to be destroyed but easily to be attacked. Thus Kino's future was real, but having set it up, other forces were set up to destroy it, and this he knew, so that he had to prepare to meet the attack. And this Kino knew also—that the gods do not love men's plans, and the gods do not love success unless it comes by accident. He knew that the gods take their revenge on a man if he be successful through his own efforts. Consequently Kino was afraid of plans, but, having made one, he could never destroy it. And to meet the attack, Kino was already making a hard skin for himself against the world. His eyes and his mind probed for danger before it appeared.

Standing in the door, he saw two men approach; and one of them carried a lantern which lighted the ground and the legs of the men. They turned in through the opening of Kino's brush fence and came to his door. And Kino saw that one was the doctor and the other the servant who had opened the gate in the morning. The split knuckles on Kino's right hand burned when he saw who they were.

The doctor said, "I was not in when you came this morning. But now, at the first chance, I have come to see the baby."

Kino stood in the door, filling it, and hatred raged and flamed in back of his eyes, and fear too, for the hundreds of years of subjugation were cut deep in him.

"The baby is nearly well now," he said curtly.

The doctor smiled, but his eyes in their little lymph-lined hammocks did not smile.

He said, "Sometimes, my friend, the scorpion sting has a curious effect. There will be apparent improvement, and then without warning—pouf!" He pursed his lips and made a little explosion to show how quick it could be, and he shifted his small black doctor's bag about so that the light of the lamp fell upon it, for he knew that Kino's race love the tools of any craft and trust them. "Sometimes," the doctor went on in a liquid tone, "sometimes there will be a withered leg or a blind eye or a crumpled back. Oh, I know the sting of the scorpion, my friend, and I can cure it."

Kino felt the rage and hatred melting towards fear. He did not know, and perhaps the doctor did. And he could not take the chance of putting his certain ignorance against this man's possible knowledge. He was trapped as his people were always trapped, and would be until, as he had said, they could be sure that the things in the books were really in the books. He could not take a chance—not with the life or with the straightness of Coyotito. He stood aside and let the doctor and his man enter the brush hut.

Juana stood up from the fire and backed away as he entered, and she covered the baby's face with the fringe of her shawl. And when the doctor went to her and held out his hand, she clutched the baby tight and looked at Kino where he stood with the fire shadows leaping on his face.

Kino nodded, and only then did she let the doctor take the baby.

"Hold the light," the doctor said, and when the servant held the lantern high, the doctor looked for a moment at the wound on the baby's shoulder. He was thoughtful for a moment and then he rolled back the baby's eyelid and looked at the eyeball. He nodded his head while Coyotito struggled against him.

"It is as I thought," he said. "The poison has gone inwards and it will strike soon. Come, look!" He held the eyelid down. "See—it is blue." And Kino, looking anxiously, saw that indeed it was a little blue. And he didn't know whether or not it was always a little blue. But the trap was set. He couldn't take the chance.

The doctor's eyes watered in their little hammocks. "I will give him something to try to turn the poison aside," he said. And he handed the baby to Kino.

Then from his bag he took a little bottle of white powder and a capsule of gelatine. He filled the capsule with the powder and closed it, and then around the first capsule he fitted a second capsule and closed it. Then he worked very deftly. He took the baby and pinched its lower lip until it opened its mouth. His fat fingers placed the capsule far back on the baby's tongue, beyond the point where he could spit it out, and then from the floor he picked up the little pitcher of pulque and gave Coyotito a drink, and it was done. He looked again at the baby's eyeball and he pursed his lips and seemed to think.

At last he handed the baby back to Juana, and he turned to Kino. "I think the poison will attack within the hour," he said. "The medicine may save the baby from hurt, but I will come back in an hour. Perhaps I am in time to save him." He took a deep breath and went out of the hut, and his servant followed him with the lantern.

Now Juana had the baby under her shawl, and she stared at it with anxiety and fear. Kino came to her, and he lifted the shawl and stared at the baby. He moved his hand to look under the eyelid, and only then saw that the pearl was still in his hand. Then he went to a box by the wall, and from it he brought a piece of rag. He wrapped the pearl in the rag, then went to the corner of the brush house and dug a little hole with his fingers in the dirt floor, and he put the pearl in the hole and covered it up and concealed the place. And then he went to the fire, where Juana was squatting, watching the baby's face.

The doctor, back in his house, settled into his chair and looked at his watch. His people brought him a little supper of chocolate and sweet cakes and fruit, and he stared at the food discontentedly.

In the houses of the neighbours the subject that would lead all conversations for a long time to come was aired for the first time to see how it would go. The neighbours showed one another with their thumbs how big the pearl was, and they made little caressing gestures to show how lovely it was. From now on they would watch

Kino and Juana very closely to see whether riches turned their heads, as riches turn all people's heads. Everyone knew why the doctor had come. He was not good at dissembling and he was very well understood.

Out in the estuary, a tight-woven school of small fishes glittered and broke water to escape a school of great fishes that drove in to eat them. And in the houses the people could hear the swish of the small ones and the bouncing splash of the great ones as the slaughter went on. The dampness arose out of the Gulf and was deposited on bushes and cacti and on little trees in salty drops. And the night mice crept about on the ground and the little night hawks hunted them silently.

The skinny black puppy with flame spots over his eyes came to Kino's door and looked in. He nearly shook his hind quarters loose when Kino glanced up at him, and he subsided when Kino looked away. The puppy did not enter the house, but he watched with frantic interest while Kino ate his beans from the little pottery dish and wiped it clean with a corn-cake and ate the cake and washed the whole down with a drink of pulque.

Kino was finished and was rolling a cigarette when Juana spoke sharply. "Kino." He glanced at her and then got up and went quickly to her, for he saw fright in her eyes. He stood over her, looking down, but the light was very dim. He kicked a pile of twigs into the fire hole to make a blaze, and then he could see the face of Coyotito. The baby's face was flushed and his throat was working and a little thick drool of saliva issued from his lips. The spasm of the stomach muscles began, and the baby was very sick.

Kino knelt beside his wife. "So the doctor knew," he said, but he said it for himself as well as for his wife, for his mind was hard and suspicious and he was remembering the white powder. Juana rocked from side to side and moaned out the little Song of the Family as though it could ward off the danger, and the baby vomited and writhed in her arms. Now uncertainty was in Kino, and the music of evil throbbed in his head and nearly drove out Juana's song.

The doctor finished his chocolate and nibbled the little fallen pieces of sweet cake. He brushed his fingers on a napkin, looked at his watch, arose, and took up his little bag.

The news of the baby's illness travelled quickly among the brush houses, for sickness is second only to hunger as the enemy of poor people. And some said softly, "Luck, you see, brings bitter friends." And they nodded and got up to go to Kino's house. The neighbours scuttled with covered noses through the dark until they crowded into Kino's house again. They stood and gazed, and they made little comments on the sadness that this should happen at a time of joy, and they said, "All things are in God's hands." The old women squatted down beside Juana to try to give her aid if they could and comfort if they could not.

Then the doctor hurried in, followed by his man. He scattered the old women like chickens. He took the baby and examined it and felt its head. "The poison it has worked," he said. "I think I can defeat it. I will try my best." He asked for water, and in the cup of it he put three drops of ammonia, and he prised open the baby's mouth and poured it down. The baby spluttered and screeched under the treatment, and Juana watched him with haunted eyes. The doctor spoke a little as he worked. "It is lucky that I know about the poison of the scorpion, otherwise——" and he shrugged to show what could have happened.

But Kino was suspicious, and he could not take his eyes from the doctor's open bag, and from the bottle of white powder there. Gradually the spasms subsided and the baby relaxed under the doctor's hands. And then Coyotito sighed deeply and went to sleep, for he was very tired with vomiting.

The doctor put the baby in Juana's arms. "He will get well now," he said. "I have won the fight." And Juana looked at him with adoration.

The doctor was closing his bag now. He said, "When do you think you can pay this bill?" He said it even kindly.

"When I have sold my pearl I will pay you," Kino said.

"You have a pearl? A good pearl?" the doctor asked with interest.

And then the chorus of the neighbours broke in. "He has found the Pearl of the World," they cried, and they joined forefinger with thumb to show how great the pearl was.

"Kino will be a rich man," they clamoured. "It is a pearl such as one has never seen."

The doctor looked surprised. "I had not heard of it. Do you keep this pearl in a safe place? Perhaps you would like me to put it in my safe?"

Kino's eyes were hooded now, his cheeks were drawn taut. "I have it secure," he said. "To-morrow I will sell it and then I will pay you."

The doctor shrugged, and his wet eyes never left Kino's eyes. He knew the pearl would be buried in the house, and he thought Kino might look towards the place where it was buried. "It would be a shame to have it stolen before you could sell it," the doctor said, and he saw Kino's eyes flick involuntarily to the floor near the side post of the brush house.

When the doctor had gone and all the neighbours had reluctantly returned to their houses, Kino squatted beside the little glowing coals in the fire hole and listened to the night sound, the soft sweep of the little waves on the shore and the distant barking of dogs, the creeping of the breeze through the brush-house roof and the soft speech of his neighbours in their houses in the village. For these people do not sleep soundly all night; they awaken at intervals and talk a little and then go to sleep again. And after a while Kino got up and went to the door of his house.

He smelled the breeze and he listened for any foreign sound of secrecy or creeping, and his eyes searched the darkness, for the music of evil was sounding in his head and he was fierce and afraid. After he had probed the night with his senses he went to the place by the side post where the pearl was buried, and he dug it up and brought it to his sleeping-mat and under his sleeping-mat he dug another little hole in the dirt floor and buried his pearl and covered it up again.

And Juana, sitting by the fire hole, watched him with questioning eyes, and when he had buried his pearl she asked, "Who do you fear?"

Kino searched for a true answer, and at last he said, "Everyone." And he could feel a shell of hardness drawing over him.

After a while they lay down together on the sleeping-mat, and Juana did not put the baby in his box to-night, but cradled him on her arms and covered his face with her shawl. And the last light went out of the embers in the fire hole.

But Kino's brain burned, even during his sleep, and he dreamed that Coyotito could read, that one of his own people could tell him the truth of things. And in his dream, Coyotito was reading from a book as large as a house, with letters as big as dogs, and the words galloped and played on the book. And then darkness spread over the page, and with the darkness came the music of evil again, and Kino stirred in his sleep; and when he stirred, Juana's eyes opened in the darkness. And then Kino awakened, with the evil music pulsing in him, and he lay in the darkness with his ears alert.

Then from the corner of the house came a sound so soft that it might have been simply a thought, a little furtive movement, a touch of a foot on earth, the almost inaudible purr of controlled breathing. Kino held his breath to listen, and he knew that whatever dark thing was in his house was holding its breath too, to listen. For a time no sound at all came from the corner of the brush house. Then Kino might have thought he had imagined the sound. But Juana's hand came creeping over to him in warning, and then the sound came again!—the whisper of a foot on dry earth and the scratch of fingers in the soil.

And now a wild fear surged in Kino's breast, and on the fear came rage, as it always did. Kino's hand crept into his breast where his knife hung on a string, and then he sprang like an angry cat, leaped striking and spitting for the dark thing he knew was in the corner of the house. He felt cloth, struck at it with his knife and missed, and struck again and felt his knife go through cloth, and then his head crashed with lightning and exploded with pain. There was a soft scurry in the doorway, and running steps for a moment, and then silence.

Kino could feel warm blood running down from his forehead, and he could hear Juana calling to him, "Kino! Kino!" And there was terror in her voice. Then coldness came over him as quickly as the rage had, and he said, "I am all right. The thing has gone."

He groped his way back to the sleeping-mat. Already Juana was working at the fire. She uncovered an ember from the ashes and shredded little pieces of corn-husk over it and blew a little flame into the corn-husks so that a tiny light danced through the hut. And then from a secret place, Juana brought a little piece of consecrated candle and lighted it at the flame and set it upright on a fireplace stone. She worked quickly, crooning as she moved about. She dipped the end of her head-shawl in water and swabbed the blood from Kino's bruised forehead. "It is nothing," Kino said, but his eyes and his voice were hard and cold and a brooding hate was growing in him.

Now the tension which had been growing in Juana boiled up to the surface and her lips were thin. "This thing is evil," she cried harshly. "This pearl is like a sin! It will destroy us," and her voice rose shrilly. "Throw it away, Kino. Let us break it between stones. Let us bury it and forget the place. Let us throw it back into the sea. It has brought evil. Kino, my husband, it will destroy us." And in the firelight her lips and her eyes were alive with her fear.

But Kino's face was set, and his mind and his will were set. "This is our one chance," he said. "Our son must go to school. He must break out of the pot that holds us in."

"It will destroy us all," Juana cried. "Even our son."

"Hush," said Kino. "Do not speak any more. In the morning we will sell the pearl, and then the evil will be gone, and only the good remain. Now hush, my wife." His dark eyes scowled into the little fire, and for the first time he knew that his knife was still in his hands, and he raised the blade and looked at it and saw a little line of blood on the steel. For a moment he seemed about to wipe the blade on his trousers, but then he plunged the knife into the earth and so cleansed it.

The distant roosters began to crow and the air changed and the dawn was coming. The wind of the morning ruffled the water of the estuary and whispered through the mangroves, and the little waves beat on the rubbly beach with an increased tempo. Kino raised the sleeping-mat and dug up his pearl and put it in front of him and stared at it.

And the beauty of the pearl, winking and glimmering in the light of the little candle, cozened his brain with its beauty. So lovely it was, so soft, and its own music came from it—its music of promise and delight, its guarantee of the future, of comfort, of security. Its warm lucence promised a poultice against illness and a wall against insult. It closed a door on hunger. And as he stared at it Kino's eyes softened and his face relaxed. He could see the little image of the consecrated candle reflected in the soft surface of the pearl, and he heard again in his ears the lovely music of the undersea, the tone of the diffused green light of the sea bottom. Juana, glancing secretly at him, saw him smile. And because they were in some way one thing and one purpose, she smiled with him.

And they began this day with hope.

CHAPTER IV

It is wonderful the way a little town keeps track of itself and of all its units. If every single man and woman, child and baby, acts and conducts itself in a known pattern and breaks no walls and differs with no one and experiments in no way and is not sick and does not endanger the ease and peace of mind or steady unbroken flow of the town, then that unit can disappear and never be heard of. But let one man step out of the regular thought or the known and trusted pattern, and the nerves of the townspeople ring with nervousness and communication travels over the nerve lines of the town. Then every unit communicates to the whole.

Thus, in La Paz, it was known in the early morning through the whole town that Kino was going to sell his pearl that day. It was known among the neighbours in the brush huts, among the pearl fishermen; it was known among the Chinese grocery-store owners; it was known in the church, for the altar boys whispered about it. Word of it crept in among the nuns; the beggars in front of the church spoke of it, for they would be there to take the tithe of the first-fruits of the luck. The little boys knew about it with excitement, but most of all the pearl buyers knew about it, and when the day had come, in the offices of the pearl buyers, each man sat alone with his little black velvet tray, and each man rolled the pearls about with his finger-tips and considered his part in the picture.

It was supposed that the pearl buyers were individuals acting alone, bidding against one another for the pearls the fishermen brought in. And once it had been so. But this was a wasteful method, for often, in the excitement of bidding for a pearl, too great a price had been paid to the fishermen. This was extravagant and not to be countenanced. Now there was only one pearl buyer with many hands, and the men who sat in their offices and waited for Kino knew what price they would offer, how high they would bid, and what method each one would use. And although these men would not profit beyond their salaries, there was excitement among the pearl buyers, for there was excitement in the hunt, and if it be a man's function to break down a price, then he must take joy and satisfaction in breaking it as far down as possible. For every man in the world functions to the best of his ability, and no one does less than his best, no matter what he may think about it. Quite apart from any reward they might get, from any word of praise, from any promotion, a pearl buyer was a pearl buyer, and the best and happiest pearl buyer was he who bought for the lowest prices.

The sun was hot yellow that morning, and it drew the moisture from the estuary and from the Gulf and hung it in shimmering scarves in the air so that the air vibrated and vision was unsubstantial. A vision hung in the air to the north of the city—the vision of a mountain that was over two hundred miles away, and the high slopes of this mountain were swaddled with pines and a great stone peak arose above the timber line.

And the morning of this day the canoes lay lined up on the beach; the fishermen did not go out to dive for pearls, for there would be too much happening, too many things to see when Kino went to sell the great pearl.

In the brush houses by the shore, Kino's neighbours sat long over their breakfasts, and they spoke of what they would do if they had found the pearl. And one man said he would give it as a present to the Holy Father in Rome. Another said that he would buy masses for the souls of his family for a thousand years. Another thought he might take the money and distribute it among the poor of La Paz; and a fourth thought of all the good things one could do with the money from the pearl, of all the charities, benefits, of all the rescues one could perform if one had money. All of the neighbours hoped that sudden wealth would not turn Kino's head, would not make a rich man of him, would not graft on to him the evil limbs of greed and hatred and coldness. For Kino was a well-liked man; it would be a shame if the pearl destroyed him. "That good wife, Juana," they said, "and the beautiful baby Coyotito, and the others to come. What a pity it would be if the pearl should destroy them all."

For Kino and Juana this was the morning of mornings of their lives, comparable only to the day when the baby had been born. This was to be the day from which all other days would take their arrangement. Thus they would say, "It was two years before we sold the pearl," or, "It was six weeks after we sold the pearl." Juana, considering the matter, threw caution to the winds, and she dressed

Coyotito in the clothes she had prepared for his baptism, when there would be money for his baptism. And Juana combed and braided her hair and tied the ends with two little bows of red ribbon, and she put on her marriage skirt and waist. The sun was quarter high when they were ready. Kino's ragged white clothes were clean at least, and this was the last day of his raggedness. For to-morrow, or even this afternoon, he would have new clothes.

The neighbours, watching Kino's door through the crevices in their brush houses, were dressed and ready too. There was no self-consciousness about their joining Kino and Juana to go pearl selling It was expected, it was an historic moment, they would be crazy if they didn't go. It would be almost a sign of unfriendship.

Juana put on her head-shawl carefully, and she draped one long end under her right elbow and gathered it with her right hand so that a hammock hung under her arm, and in this little hammock she placed Coyotito, propped up against the head-shawl so that he could see everything and perhaps remember. Kino put on his large straw hat and felt it with his hand to see that it was properly placed, not on the back or side of his head, like a rash, unmarried, irresponsible man, and not flat as an elder would wear it, but tilted a little forward to show aggressiveness and seriousness and vigour. There is a great deal to be seen in the tilt of a hat on a man. Kino slipped his feet into his sandals and pulled the thongs up over his heels. The great pearl was wrapped in an old soft piece of deerskin and placed in a little leather bag, and the leather bag was in a pocket in Kino's shirt. He folded his blanket carefully and draped it in a narrow strip over his left shoulder, and now they were ready.

Kino stepped with dignity out of the house, and Juana followed him, carrying Coyotito. And as they marched up the freshet-washed alley towards the town, the neighbours joined them. The houses belched people; the doorways spewed out children. But because of the seriousness of the occasion, only one man walked with Kino, and that was his brother, Juan Tomás.

Juan Tomás cautioned his brother. "You must be careful to see they do not cheat you," he said.

And, "Very careful," Kino agreed.

"We do not know what prices are paid in other places," said Juan Tomás. "How can we know what is a fair price, if we do not know what the pearl buyer gets for the pearl in another place?"

"That is true," said Kino, "but how can we know? We are here, we are not there."

As they walked up towards the city the crowd grew behind them. and Juan Tomás, in pure nervousness, went on speaking.

"Before you were born, Kino," he said, "the old ones thought of a way to get more money for their pearls. They thought it would be better if they had an agent who took all the pearls to the capital and sold them there and kept only his share of the profit."

Kino nodded his head. "I know," he said. "It was a good thought."

"And so they got such a man," said Juan Tomás, "and they pooled the pearls, and they started him off. And he was never heard of again and the pearls were lost. Then they got another man, and they started him off, and he was never heard of again. And so they gave the whole thing up and went back to the old way."

"I know," said Kino. "I have heard our father tell of it. It was a good idea, but it was against religion, and the Father made that very clear. The loss of the pearls was a punishment visited on those who tried to leave their station. And the Father made it clear that each man and woman is like a soldier sent by God to guard some part of the castle of the Universe. And some are in the ramparts and some far deep in the darkness of the walls. But each one must remain faithful to his post and must not go running about, else the castle is in danger from the assaults of Hell."

"I have heard him make that sermon," said Juan Tomás. "He makes it every year."

The brothers, as they walked along, squinted their eyes a little, as they and their grandfathers and their great-grandfathers had done for four hundred years, since first the strangers came with argument and authority, and gunpowder to back up both. And in the four hundred years Kino's people had learned only one defence—a slight slitting of the eyes and a slight tightening of the lips and a retirement. Nothing could break down this wall, and they could remain whole within the wall.

The gathering procession was solemn, for they sensed the importance of this day, and any children who showed a tendency to scuffle, to scream, to cry out, to steal hats and rumple hair, were hissed to silence by their elders. So important was this day that an old man came to see, riding on the stalwart shoulders of his nephew. The procession left the brush huts and entered the stone and plaster city, where the streets were a little wider and there were narrow pavements beside the buildings. And, as before, the beggars joined them as they passed the church; the grocers looked out at them as they went by; the little saloons lost their customers and the owners closed up shop and went along. And the sun beat down on the streets of the city and even tiny stones threw shadows on the ground.

The news of the approach of the procession ran ahead of it, and in their little dark offices the pearl buyers stiffened and grew alert. They got out papers so that they could be at work when Kino appeared, and they put their pearls in the desks, for it is not good to let an inferior pearl be seen beside a beauty. And word of the loveliness of Kino's pearl had come to them. The pearl buyers' offices were clustered together in one narrow street, and they were barred at the windows, and wooden slats cut out the light so that only a soft gloom entered the offices.

A stout, slow man sat in an office waiting. His face was fatherly and benign, and his eyes twinkled with friendship. He was a caller of good-mornings, a ceremonious shaker of hands, a jolly man who knew all jokes and yet who hovered close to sadness, for in the midst of a laugh he could remember the death of your aunt, and his eyes could become wet with sorrow for your loss. This morning he had placed a flower in a vase on his desk, a single scarlet hibiscus, and the vase sat beside the black velvet-lined pearl tray in front of him. He was shaved close to the blue roots of his beard, and his hands were clean and his nails polished. His door stood open to the morning, and he hummed under his breath while his right hand practised legerdemain. He rolled a coin back and forth over his knuckles and made it appear and disappear, made it spin and sparkle. The coin winked into sight and as quickly slipped out of sight, and the man did not even watch his own performance. The fingers did it all mechanically, precisely, while the man hummed to himself and peered out the door. Then he heard the tramp of feet of the approaching crowd, and the fingers of his right hand worked faster and faster until, as the figure of Kino filled the doorway, the coin flashed and disappeared.

"Good morning, my friend," the stout man said. "What can I do for you?"

Kino stared into the dimness of the little office, for his eyes were squeezed from the outside glare. But the buyer's eyes had become as steady and cruel and unwinking as a hawk's eyes, while the rest of his face smiled in greeting. And secretly, behind his desk, his right hand practised with the coin.

"I have a pearl," said Kino. And Juan Tomás stood beside him and snorted a little at the understatement. The neighbours peered around the doorway, and a line of little boys clambered on the window bars and looked through. Several little boys, on their hands and knees, watched the scene around Kino's legs.

"You have a pearl," the dealer said. "Sometimes a man brings in a dozen. Well, let us see your pearl. We will value it and give you the best price." And his fingers worked furiously with the coin.

Now, Kino instinctively knew his own dramatic effects. Slowly he brought out the leather bag, slowly took from it the soft and dirty piece of deerskin, and then he let the great pearl roll into the black velvet tray, and instantly his eyes went to the buyer's face. But there was no sign, no movement, the face did not change, but the secret hand behind the desk missed in its precision. The coin stumbled over a knuckle and slipped silently into the dealer's lap. And the fingers behind the desk curled into a fist. When the right hand came out of hiding, the forefinger touched the great pearl, rolled it on the black velvet; thumb and forefinger picked it up and brought it near to the dealer's eyes and twirled it in the air.

Kino held his breath and the neighbours held their breath, and the whispering went back through the crowd: "He is inspecting it—No price has been mentioned yet—They have not come to a price."

Now the dealer's hand had become a personality. The hand tossed the great pearl back in the tray, the forefinger poked and insulted it, and on the dealer's face there came a sad and contemptuous smile.

"I am sorry, my friend," he said, and his shoulders rose a little to indicate that the misfortune was no fault of his.

"It is a pearl of great value," Kino said.

The dealer's fingers spurned the pearl so that it bounced and rebounded softly from the side of the velvet tray.

"You have heard of fool's gold," the dealer said. "This pearl is like fool's gold. It is too large. Who would buy it? There is no market for such things. It is a curiosity only. I am sorry. You thought it was a thing of value, and it is only a curiosity."

Now Kino's face was perplexed and worried. "It is the Pearl of the World," he cried. "No one has ever seen such a pearl."

"On the contrary," said the dealer, "it is large and clumsy. As a curiosity it has interest; some museum might perhaps take it in a collection of sea-shells. I can give you, say, a thousand pesos."

Kino's face grew dark and dangerous. "It is worth fifty thousand," he said. "You know it. You want to cheat me."

And the dealer heard a little grumble go through the crowd as they heard his price. And the dealer felt a little tremor of fear.

"Do not blame me," he said quickly. "I am only an appraiser. Ask the others. Go to their offices and show your pearl—or better, let them come here, so that you can see there is no collusion. Boy," he called. And when his servant looked through the rear door, "Boy, go to such a one, and such another and such a third one. Ask them to step in here and do not tell them why. Just say that I will be pleased to see them." And his right hand went behind the desk and pulled another coin from his pocket, and the coin rolled back and forth over the knuckles.

Kino's neighbours whispered together. They had been afraid of something like this. The pearl was large, but it had a strange colour. They had been suspicious of it from the first. And, after all, a thousand pesos was not to be thrown away. It was comparative wealth to a man who was not wealthy. And suppose Kino took a thousand pesos. Only yesterday he had nothing.

But Kino had grown tight and hard. He felt the creeping of fate, the circling of wolves, the hover of vultures. He felt the evil coagulating about him, and he was helpless to protect himself. He heard in his ears the evil music. And on the black velvet the great pearl glistened, so that the dealer could not keep his eyes from it.

The crowd in the doorway wavered and broke and let the three pearl dealers through. The crowd was silent now, fearing to miss a word, to fail to see a gesture or an expression. Kino was silent and watchful. He felt a little tugging at his back, and he turned and looked in Juana's eyes, and when he looked away he had renewed strength.

The dealers did not glance at one another nor at the pearl. The man behind the desk said, "I have put a value on this pearl. The owner here does not think it fair. I will ask you to examine this—this thing, and make an offer. Notice," he said to Kino, "I have not mentioned what I offered."

The first dealer, dry and stringy, seemed now to see the pearl for the first time. He took it up, rolled it quickly between thumb and forefinger, and then cast it contemptuously back into the tray.

"Do not include me in the discussion," he said dryly. "I will make no offer at all. I do not want it. This is not a pearl—it is a monstrosity." His thin lips curled.

Now the second dealer, a little man with a shy soft voice, took up the pearl, and he examined it carefully. He took a glass from his pocket and inspected it under magnification. Then he laughed softly.

"Better pearls are made of paste," he said. "I know these things. This is soft and chalky, it will lose its colour and die in a few months. Look——" He offered the glass to Kino, showed him how to use it, and Kino, who had never seen a pearl's surface magnified, was shocked at the strange-looking surface.

The third dealer took the pearl from Kino's hands. "One of my clients likes such things," he said. "I will offer five hundred pesos, and perhaps I can sell it to my client for six hundred."

Kino reached quickly and snatched the pearl from his hand. He wrapped it in the deerskin and thrust it inside his shirt.

The man behind the desk said, "I'm a fool, I know, but my first offer stands. I still offer one thousand. What are you doing?" he asked, as Kino thrust the pearl out of sight.

"I am cheated," Kino cried fiercely. "My pearl is not for sale here. I will go, perhaps even to the capital."

Now the dealers glanced quickly at one another. They knew they had played too hard; they knew they would be disciplined for their failure, and the man at the desk said quickly, "I might go to fifteen hundred."

But Kino was pushing his way through the crowd. The hum of talk came to him dimly, in his rage blood pounded in his ears, and he burst through and strode away. Juana followed, trotting after him.

When the evening came, the neighbours in the brush houses sat eating their corn-cakes and beans, and they discussed the great theme of the morning. They did not know, it seemed a fine pearl to them, but they had never seen such a pearl before, and surely the dealers knew more about the value of pearls than they. "And mark this," they said. "Those dealers did not discuss these things. Each of the three knew the pearl was valueless."

"But suppose they had arranged it before?"

"If that is so, then all of us have been cheated all of our lives."

Perhaps, some argued, perhaps it would have been better if Kino took the one thousand five hundred pesos. That is a great deal of money, more than he has ever seen. Maybe Kino is being a pig-headed fool. Suppose he should really go to the capital and find no buyer for his pearl. He would never live that down.

And now, said other fearful ones, now that he had defied them, those buyers will not want to deal with him at all. Maybe Kino has cut off his own head and destroyed himself.

And others said, Kino is a brave man, and a fierce man; he is right. From his courage we may all profit. These were proud of Kino.

In his house Kino squatted on his sleeping-mat, brooding. He had buried his pearl under a stone of the fire hole in his house, and he stared at the woven tules of his sleeping-mat until the crossed design danced in his head. He had lost one world and had not gained another. And Kino was afraid. Never in his life had he been far from home. He was afraid of strangers and of strange places. He was terrified of that monster of strangeness they called the capital. It lay over the water and through the mountains, over a thousand miles, and every strange, terrible mile was frightening. But Kino had lost his old world and he must clamber on to a new one. For his dream of the future was real and never to be destroyed, and he had said "I will go", and that made a real thing too. To determine to go and to say it was to be half-way there.

Juana watched him while he buried his pearl, and she watched him while she cleaned Coyotito and nursed him, and Juana made the corn-cakes for supper.

Juan Tomás came in and squatted down beside Kino and remained silent for a long time, until at last Kino demanded, "What else could I do? They are cheats."

Juan Tomás nodded gravely. He was the elder, and Kino looked to him for wisdom. "It is hard to know," he said. "We do know that we are cheated from birth to the overcharge on our coffins. But we survive. You have defied not the pearl buyers, but the whole structure, the whole way of life, and I am afraid for you."

"What have I to fear but starvation?" Kino asked.

But Juan Tomás shook his head slowly. "That we must all fear. But suppose you are correct—suppose your pearl is of great value—do you think then the game is over?"

"What do you mean?"

"I don't know," said Juan Tomás, "but I am afraid for you. It is new ground you are walking on, you do not know the way."

"I will go. I will go soon," said Kino.

"Yes," Juan Tomás agreed. "That you must do. But I wonder if you will find it any different in the capital. Here you have friends and me, your brother. There you will have no one."

"What can I do?" Kino cried. "Some deep outrage is here. My son must have a chance. That is what they are striking at. My friends will protect me."

"Only so long as they are not in danger or discomfort from it," said Juan Tomás. He rose, saying, "Go with God."

And Kino said, "Go with God," and did not even look up, for the words had a strange chill in them.

Long after Juan Tomás had gone Kino sat brooding on his sleeping-mat. A lethargy had settled on him, and a little grey hopelessness. Every road seemed blocked against him. In his head he heard only the dark music of the enemy. His senses were burningly alive, but his mind went back to the deep participation with all things, the gift he had from his people. He heard every little sound of the gathering night, the sleepy complaint of settling birds, the love agony of cats, the strike and withdrawal of little waves on the beach, and the simple hiss of distance. And he could smell the sharp odour of exposed kelp from the receding tide. The little flare of the twig fire made the design on his sleeping-mat jump before his entranced eyes.

Juana watched him with worry, but she knew him and she knew she could help him best by being silent and by being near. And as though she too could hear the Song of Evil, she fought it, singing softly the melody of the family, of the safety and warmth and wholeness of the family. She held Coyotito in her arms and sang the song to him, to keep the evil out, and her voice was brave against the threat of the dark music.

Kino did not move nor ask for his supper. She knew he would ask when he wanted it. His eyes were entranced, and he could sense the wary, watchful evil outside the brush house; he could feel the dark creeping things waiting for him to go out into the night. It was shadowy and dreadful, and yet it called to him and threatened him and challenged him. His right hand went into his shirt and felt his knife; his eyes were wide; he stood up and walked to the doorway.

Juana willed to stop him; she raised her hand to stop him, and her mouth opened with terror. For a long moment Kino looked out into the darkness and then he stepped outside. Juana heard the little rush, the grunting struggle, the blow. She froze with terror for a moment, and then her lips drew back from her teeth like a cat's lips. She set Coyotito down on the ground. She seized a stone from the fireplace and rushed outside, but it was over by then. Kino lay on the ground, struggling to rise, and there was no one near him. Only the shadows and the strike and the rush of waves and the hiss of distance. But the evil was all about, hidden behind the brush fence, crouched beside the house in the shadow, hovering in the air.

Juana dropped her stone, and she put her arms around Kino and helped him to his feet and supported him into the house. Blood oozed down from his scalp and there was a long, deep cut in his cheek from ear to chin, a deep, bleeding slash. And Kino was only half conscious. He shook his head from side to side. His shirt was torn open and his clothes half pulled off. Juana sat him down on his sleeping-mat and she wiped the thickening blood from his face with her skirt. She brought him pulque to drink in a little pitcher, and still he shook his head to clear out the darkness.

"Who?" Juana asked.

"I don't know," Kino said. "I didn't see."

Now Juana brought her clay pot of water and she washed the cut on his face while he stared dazed ahead of him.

"Kino, my husband," she cried, and his eyes stared past her. "Kino, can you hear me?"

"I hear you," he said dully.

"Kino, this pearl is evil. Let us destroy it before it destroys us. Let us crush it between two stones. Let us—let us throw it back in the sea where it belongs. Kino, it is evil, it is evil!"

And as she spoke the light came back in Kino's eyes so that they glowed fiercely and his muscles hardened and his will hardened.

"No," he said. "I will fight this thing. I will win over it. We will have our chance." His fist pounded the sleeping-mat. "No one shall take our good fortune from us," he said. His eyes softened then and he raised a gentle hand to Juana's shoulder. "Believe me," he said. "I am a man." And his face grew crafty.

"In the morning we will take our canoe and we will go over the sea and over the mountains to the capital, you and I. We will not be cheated. I am a man."

"Kino," she said huskily, "I am afraid. A man can be killed. Let us throw the pearl back into the sea."

"Hush," he said fiercely. "I am a man. Hush." And she was silent, for his voice was command. "Let us sleep a little," he said. "In the first light we will start. You are not afraid to go with me?"

"No, my husband."

His eyes were soft and warm on her then, his hand touched her cheek. "Let us sleep a little," he said.

CHAPTER V

THE LATE moon arose before the first rooster crowed. Kino opened his eyes in the darkness, for he sensed movement near him, but he did not move. Only his eyes searched the darkness, and in the pale light of the moon that crept through the holes in the brush house, Kino saw Juana arise silently from beside him. He saw her move towards the fireplace. So carefully did she work that he heard only the lightest sound when she moved the fireplace stone. And then like a shadow she glided towards the door. She paused for a moment beside the hanging box where Coyotito lay, then for a second she was black in the doorway, and then she was gone.

And rage surged in Kino. He rolled up to his feet and followed her as silently as she had gone, and he could hear her quick footsteps going towards the shore. Quietly he tracked her, and his brain was red with anger. She burst clear out of the brush line and stumbled over the little boulders towards the water, and then she heard him coming and she broke into a run. Her arm was up to throw when he leaped at her and caught her arm and wrenched the pearl from her. He struck her in the face with his clenched fist and she fell among the boulders, and he kicked her in the side. In the pale light he could see the little waves break over her, and her skirt floated about and clung to her legs as the water receded.

Kino looked down at her and his teeth were bared. He hissed at her like a snake, and Juana stared at him with wide unfrightened eyes, like a sheep before the butcher. She knew there was murder in him, and it was all right; she had accepted it, and she would not resist or even protest. And then the rage left him and a sick disgust took its place. He turned away from her and walked up the beach and through the brush line. His senses were dulled by his emotion.

He heard the rush, got his knife out and lunged at one dark figure and felt his knife go home, and then he was swept to his knees and swept again to the ground. Greedy fingers went through his clothes, frantic fingers searched him, and the pearl, knocked from his hand, lay winking behind a little stone in the pathway. It glinted in the soft moonlight.

Juana dragged herself up from the rocks on the edge of the water. Her face was a dull pain and her side ached. She steadied herself on her knees for a while and her wet skirt clung to her. There was no anger in her for Kino. He had said, "I am a man," and that meant certain things to Juana. It meant that he was half insane and half god. It meant that Kino would drive his strength against a mountain and plunge his strength against the sea. Juana, in her woman's soul, knew that the mountain would stand while the man broke himself; that the sea would surge while the man drowned in it. And yet it was this thing that made him a man, half insane and half god, and Juana had need of a man; she could not live without a man. Although she might be puzzled by these differences between man and woman, she knew them and accepted them and needed them. Of course she would follow him, there was no question of that. Sometimes the quality of woman, the reason, the caution, the sense of preservation, could cut through Kino's madness and save them all. She climbed painfully to her feet, and she dipped her cupped palms in the little waves and washed her bruised face with the stinging salt water, and then she went creeping up the beach after Kino.

A flight of herring clouds had moved over the sky from the south. The pale moon dipped in and out of the strands of clouds so that Juana walked in darkness for a moment and in light the next. Her back was bent with pain and her head was low. She went through the line of brush when the moon was covered, and when it looked through she saw the glimmer of the great pearl in the path behind the rock. She sank to her knees and picked it up, and the moon went into the darkness of the clouds again. Juana remained on her knees while she considered whether to go back to the sea and finish her job, and as she considered, the light came again, and she saw two dark figures lying in the path ahead of her. She leaped forward and saw that one was Kino and the other a stranger with dark, shiny fluid leaking from his throat.

Kino moved sluggishly, arms and legs stirred like those of a crushed bug, and a thick muttering came from his mouth. Now, in an instant, Juana knew that the old life was gone for ever. A dead man in the path and Kino's knife, dark-bladed beside him, convinced her. All of the time Juana had been trying to rescue something of the old peace, of the time before the pearl. But now it was gone, and there was no retrieving it. And, knowing this, she abandoned the past instantly. There was nothing to do but to save themselves.

Her pain was gone now, her slowness. Quickly she dragged the dead man from the pathway into the shelter of the brush. She went to Kino and sponged his face with her wet skirt. His senses were coming back and he moaned.

"They have taken the pearl. I have lost it. Now it is over," he said. "The pearl is gone."

Juana quieted him as she would quiet a sick child. "Hush," she said. "Here is your pearl. I found it in the path. Can you hear me now? Here is your pearl. Can you understand? You have killed a man. We must go away. They will come for us, can you understand? We must be gone before the daylight comes."

"I was attacked," Kino said uneasily. "I struck to save my life."

"Do you remember yesterday?" Juana asked. "Do you think that will matter? Do you remember the men of the city? Do you think your explanation will help?"

Kino drew a great breath and fought off his weakness. "No," he said. "You are right." And his will hardened and he was a man again.

"Go to our house and bring Coyotito," he said, "and bring all the corn we have. I will drag the canoe into the water and we will go."

He took his knife and left her. He stumbled towards the beach and he came to his canoe. And when the light broke through again he saw that a great hole had been knocked in the bottom. And a searing rage came to him and gave him strength. Now the darkness was closing in on his family; now the evil music filled the night, hung over the mangroves, skirled in the wave-beat. The canoe of his grandfather, plastered over and over, and a splintered hole broken in it. This was an evil beyond thinking. The killing of a man was not so evil as the killing of a boat. For a boat does not have sons and a boat cannot protect itself, and a wounded boat does not heal. There was sorrow in Kino's rage, but this last thing had tightened him beyond breaking. He was an animal now, for hiding, for attacking, and he lived only to preserve himself and his family. He was not conscious of the pain in his head. He leaped up the beach, through the brush line towards his brush house, and it did not occur to him to take one of the canoes of his neighbours. Never once did the thought enter his head, any more than he could have conceived breaking a boat.

The roosters were crowing and the dawn was not far off. Smoke of the first fires seeped out through the walls of the brush houses, and the first smell of cooking corn-cakes was in the air. Already the dawn birds were scampering in the bushes. The weak moon was losing its light and the clouds thickened and curdled to the southward. The wind blew freshly into the estuary, a nervous, restless wind with the smell of storm on its breath, and there was change and uneasiness in the air.

Kino, hurrying towards his house, felt a surge of exhilaration. Now he was not confused, for there was only one thing to do, and

Kino's hand went first to the great pearl in his shirt and then to his knife hanging under his shirt.

He saw a little glow ahead of him, and then without interval a tall flame leaped up in the dark with a crackling roar, and a tall edifice of fire lighted the pathway. Kino broke into a run; it was his brush house, he knew. And he knew that these houses could burn down in a very few moments. And as he ran a scuttling figure ran towards him—Juana, with Coyotito in her arms and Kino's shoulder-blanket clutched in her hand. The baby moaned with fright, and Juana's eyes were wide and terrified. Kino could see the house was gone, and he did not question Juana. He knew, but she said, "It was torn up and the floor dug—even the baby's box turned out, and as I looked they put the fire to the outside."

The fierce light of the burning house lighted Kino's face strongly. "Who?" he demanded.

"I don't know," she said. "The dark ones."

The neighbours were tumbling from their houses now, and they watched the falling sparks and stamped them out to save their own houses. Suddenly Kino was afraid. The light made him afraid. He remembered the man lying dead in the brush beside the path, and he took Juana by the arm and drew her into the shadow of a house away from the light, for light was danger to him. For a moment he considered and then he worked among the shadows until he came to the house of Juan Tomás, his brother, and he slipped into the doorway and drew Juana with him. Outside, he could hear the squeal of children and the shouts of the neighbours, for his friends thought he might be inside the burning house.

The house of Juan Tomás was almost exactly like Kino's house; nearly all the brush houses were alike, and all leaked light and air, so that Juana and Kino, sitting in the corner of the brother's house, could see the leaping flames through the wall. They saw the flames tall and furious, they saw the roof fall and watched the fire die down as quickly as a twig fire dies. They heard the cries of warning of their friends, and the shrill, keening cry of Apolonia, wife of Juan Tomás. She, being the nearest woman relative, raised a formal lament for the dead of the family.

Apolonia realized that she was wearing her second-best head-shawl and she rushed to her house to get her fine new one. As she rummaged in a box by the wall, Kino's voice said quietly, "Apolonia, do not cry out. We are not hurt."

"How do you come here?" she demanded.

"Do not question," he said. "Go now to Juan Tomás and bring him here and tell no one else. This is important to us, Apolonia."

She paused, her hands helpless in front of her, and then, "Yes my brother-in-law," she said.

In a few moments Juan Tomás came back with her. He lighted a candle and came to them where they crouched in a corner, and he said, "Apolonia, see to the door, and do not let anyone enter." He was older, Juan Tomás, and he assumed the authority. "Now, my brother," he said.

"I was attacked in the dark," said Kino. "And in the fight I have killed a man."

"Who?" asked Juan Tomás quickly.

"I do not know. It is all darkness—all darkness and shape of darkness."

"It is the pearl," said Juan Tomás. "There is a devil in this pearl. You should have sold it and passed on the devil. Perhaps you can still sell it and buy peace for yourself."

And Kino said, "Oh, my brother, an insult has been put on me that is deeper than my life. For on the beach my canoe is broken, my house is burned, and in the brush a dead man lies. Every escape is cut off. You must hide us, my brother."

And Kino, looking closely, saw deep worry come into his brother's eyes and he forestalled him in a possible refusal. "Not for long," he said quickly. "Only until a day has passed and the new light has come. Then we will go."

"I will hide you," said Juan Tomás.

"I do not want to bring danger to you," Kino said. "I know I am like a leprosy. I will go to-night and then you will be safe."

"I will protect you," said Juan Tomás, and he called, "Apolonia, close up the door. Do not even whisper that Kino is here."

They sat silently all day in the darkness of the house, and they could hear the neighbours speaking of them. Through the walls of the house they could watch their neighbours raking through the ashes to find the bones. Crouching in the house of Juan Tomás, they heard the shock go into their neighbours' minds at the news of the broken boat. Juan Tomás went out among the neighbours to divert their suspicions, and he gave them theories and ideas of what had happened to Kino and Juana and to the baby. To one he said, "I think they have gone south along the coast to escape the evil that was on them." And to another, "Kino would never leave the sea. Perhaps he has found another boat." And he said, "Apolonia is ill with grief."

And in that day the wind rose up to beat the Gulf and tore the kelps and weeds that lined the shore, and the wind cried through the brush houses and no boat was safe on the water. Then Juan Tomás told among the neighbours: "Kino is gone. If he went to the sea, he is drowned by now." And after each trip among the neighbours Juan Tomás came back with something borrowed. He brought a little woven straw bag of red beans and a gourd full of rice. He borrowed a cup of dried peppers and a block of salt, and he brought in a long working knife, eighteen inches long and heavy as a small axe, a tool and a weapon. And when Kino saw this knife his eyes lighted up, and he fondled the blade and his thumb tested the edge.

The wind screamed over the Gulf and turned the water white, and the mangroves plunged like frightened cattle, and a fine sandy dust arose from the land and hung in a stifling cloud over the sea. The wind drove off the clouds and skimmed the sky clean and drifted the sand of the country like snow.

Then Juan Tomás, when the evening approached, talked long with his brother. "Where will you go?"

"To the north," said Kino. "I have heard that there are cities in the north."

"Avoid the shore," said Juan Tomás. "They are making a party to search the shore. The men in the city will look for you. Do you still have the pearl?"

"I have it," said Kino. "And I will keep it. I might have given it as a gift, but now it is my misfortune and my life and I will keep it." His eyes were hard and cruel and bitter.

Coyotito whimpered and Juana muttered little magics over him to make him silent.

"The wind is good," said Juan Tomás. "There will be no tracks."

They left quietly in the dark before the moon had risen. The family stood formally in the house of Juan Tomás. Juana carried Coyotito on her back, covered and held in by her head-shawl, and the baby slept, cheek turned sideways against her shoulder. The head-shawl covered the baby, and one end of it came across Juana's nose to protect her from the evil night air. Juan Tomás embraced his brother with the double embrace and kissed him on both cheeks. "Go with God," he said, and it was like a death. "You will not give up the pearl?"

"This pearl has become my soul," said Kino. "If I give it up I shall lose my soul. Go thou also with God."

CHAPTER VI

THE WIND blew fierce and strong, and it pelted them with bits of sticks, sand, and little rocks. Juana and Kino gathered their clothing tighter about them and covered their noses and went out into the world. The sky was brushed clean by the wind and the stars were cold in a black sky. The two walked carefully, and they avoided the centre of the town, where some sleeper in a doorway might see them pass. For the town closed itself in against the night, and anyone who moved about in the darkness would be noticeable. Kino threaded his way around the edge of the city and turned north, north by the stars, and found the rutted sandy road that led through the brushy country towards Loreto, where the miraculous Virgin has her station.

Kino could feel the blown sand against his ankles and he was glad, for he knew there would be no tracks. The little light from the stars made out for him the narrow road through the brushy country. And Kino could hear the pad of Juana's feet behind him. He went quickly and quietly, and Juana trotted behind him to keep up.

Some ancient thing stirred in Kino. Through his fear of dark and the devils that haunt the night, there came a rush of exhilaration; some animal thing was moving in him so that he was cautious and wary and dangerous; some ancient thing out of the past of his people was alive in him. The wind was at his back and the stars guided him. The wind cried and whisked in the brush, and the family went on monotonously, hour after hour. They passed no one and saw no one. At last, to their right, the waning moon arose, and when it came up the wind died down, and the land was still.

Now they could see the little road ahead of them, deep cut with sand-drifted wheel tracks. With the wind gone there would be footprints, but they were a good distance from the town and perhaps their tracks might not be noticed. Kino walked carefully in a wheel-rut, and Juana followed in his path. One big cart, going to the town in the morning, could wipe out every trace of their passage.

All night they walked and never changed their pace. Once Coyotito awakened, and Juana shifted him in front of her and soothed him until he went to sleep again. And the evils of the night were about them. The coyotes cried and laughed in the brush, and the owls screeched and hissed over their heads. And once some large animal lumbered away, crackling the undergrowth as it went. And Kino gripped the handle of the big working knife and took a sense of protection from it.

The music of the pearl was triumphant in Kino's head, and the quiet melody of the family underlay it, and they wove themselves into the soft padding of sandalled feet in the dust. All night they walked, and in the first dawn Kino searched the roadside for a covert to lie in during the day. He found his place near to the road, a little clearing where deer might have lain, and it was curtained thickly with the dry, brittle trees that lined the road. And when Juana had seated herself and had settled to nurse the baby, Kino went back to the road. He broke a branch and carefully swept the footprints where they had turned from the roadway. And then, in the first light, he heard the creak of a wagon, and he crouched beside the road and watched a heavy two-wheeled cart go by, drawn by slouching oxen. And when it had passed out of sight, he went back to the roadway and looked at the rut and found that the footprints were gone. And again he swept out his traces and went back to Juana.

She gave him the soft corn-cakes Apolonia had packed for them, and after a while she slept a little. But Kino sat on the ground and stared at the earth in front of him. He watched the ants moving, a little column of them near to his foot, and he put his foot in their path. Then the column climbed over his instep and continued on its way, and Kino left his foot there and watched them move over it.

The sun arose hotly. They were not near the Gulf now, and the air was dry and hot so that the brush cricked with heat and a good resinous smell came from it. And when Juana awakened, when the sun was high, Kino told her things she knew already.

"Beware of that kind of tree there," he said, pointing. "Do not touch it, for if you do and then touch your eyes, it will blind you. And beware of the tree that bleeds. See, that one over there. For if you break it the red blood will flow from it, and it is evil luck." And she nodded and smiled a little at him, for she knew these things.

"Will they follow us?" she asked. "Do you think they will try to find us?"

"They will try," said Kino. "Whoever finds us will take the pearl. Oh, they will try."

And Juana said, "Perhaps the dealers were right and the pearl has no value. Perhaps this has all been an illusion."

Kino reached into his clothes and brought out the pearl. He let the sun play on it until it burned in his eyes. "No," he said, "they would not have tried to steal it if it had been valueless."

"Do you know who attacked you? Was it the dealers?"

"I do not know," he said. "I didn't see them."

He looked into his pearl to find his vision. "When we sell it at last, I will have a rifle," he said, and he looked into the shining surface for his rifle, but he saw only a huddled dark body on the ground with shining blood dripping from its throat. And he said quickly, "We will be married in a great church." And in the pearl he saw Juana with her beaten face crawling home through the night. "Our son must learn to read," he said frantically. And there in the pearl Coyotito's face, thick and feverish from the medicine.

And Kino thrust the pearl back into his clothing, and the music of the pearl had become sinister in his ears, and it was interwoven with the music of evil.

The hot sun beat on the earth so that Kino and Juana moved into the lacy shade of the brush, and small grey birds scampered on the ground in the shade. In the heat of the day Kino relaxed and covered his eyes with his hat and wrapped his blanket about his face to keep the flies off, and he slept.

But Juana did not sleep. She sat quiet as a stone and her face was quiet. Her mouth was still swollen where Kino had struck her, and big flies buzzed around the cut on her chin. But she sat as still as a sentinel, and when Coyotito awakened she placed him on the ground in front of her and watched him wave his arms and kick his feet, and he smiled and gurgled at her until she smiled too. She picked up a little twig from the ground and tickled him, and she gave him water from the gourd she carried in her bundle.

Kino stirred in a dream, and he cried out in a guttural voice, and his hand moved in symbolic fighting. And then he moaned and sat up suddenly, his eyes wide and his nostrils flaring. He listened and heard only the cricking heat and the hiss of distance.

"What is it?" Juana asked.

"Hush," he said.

"You were dreaming."

"Perhaps." But he was restless, and when she gave him a corn-cake from her store he paused in his chewing to listen. He was uneasy and nervous; he glanced over his shoulder; he lifted the big knife and felt its edge. When Coyotito gurgled on the ground, Kino said, "Keep him quiet."

"What is the matter?" Juana asked.

"I don't know."

He listened again, an animal light in his eyes. He stood up then, silently; and, crouched low, he threaded his way through the brush towards the road. But he did not step into the road; he crept into the cover of a thorny tree and peered out along the way he had come.

And then he saw them moving along. His body stiffened and he drew down his head and peeked out from under a fallen branch. In the distance he could see three figures, two on foot and one on horseback. But he knew what they were, and a chill of fear went through him. Even in the distance he could see the two on foot moving slowly along, bent low to the ground. Here one would pause and look at the earth, while the other joined him. They were the trackers, they could follow the trail of a bighorn sheep in the stone mountains. They were as sensitive as hounds. Here he and Juana might have stepped out of the wheel rut, and these people from the inland, these hunters, could follow, could read a broken straw or a little tumbled pile of dust. Behind them, on a horse, was a dark man, his nose covered with a blanket, and across his saddle a rifle gleamed in the sun.

Kino lay as rigid as the tree limb. He barely breathed, and his eyes went to the place where he had swept out the track. Even the sweeping might be a message to the trackers. He knew these inland hunters. In a country where there was little game they managed to live because of their ability to hunt, and they were hunting him. They scuttled over the ground like animals and found a sign and crouched over it while the horseman waited.

The trackers whined a little, like excited dogs on a warming trail. Kino slowly drew his big knife to his hand and made it ready. He knew what he must do. If the trackers found the swept place, he must leap for the horseman, kill him quickly and take the rifle. That was his only chance in the world. And as the three drew nearer on the road, Kino dug little pits with his sandalled toes so that he could leap without warning, so that his feet would not slip. He had only a little vision under the fallen limb.

Now Juana, back in her hidden place, heard the pad of the horse's hoofs and Coyotito gurgled. She took him up quickly and put him under her shawl and gave him her breast and he was silent.

When the trackers came near, Kino could see only their legs and only the legs of the horse from under the fallen branch. He saw the dark horny feet of the men and their ragged white clothes, and he heard the creak of leather of the saddle and the clink of spurs. The trackers stopped at the swept place and studied it, and the horseman stopped. The horse flung his head up against the bit and the bit-roller clicked under his tongue and the horse snorted. Then the dark tracker's turned and studied the horse and watched his ears.

Kino was not breathing, but his back arched a little and the muscles of his arms and legs stood out with tension and a line of sweat formed on his upper lip. For a long moment, the trackers bent over the road, and then they moved on slowly, studying the ground ahead of them, and the horseman moved after them. The trackers scuttled along, stopping, looking, and hurrying on. They would be back, Kino knew. They would be circling and searching, peeping, stooping, and they would come back sooner or later to his covered track.

He slid backwards and did not bother to cover his tracks. He could not; too many little signs were there, too many broken twigs and scuffed places and displaced stones. And there was a panic in Kino now, a panic of flight. The trackers would find his trail, he knew it. There was no escape, except in flight. He edged away from the road and went quickly and silently to the hidden place where Juana was. She looked up at him in question.

"Trackers," he said. "Come!"

And then a helplessness and a hopelessness swept over him, and his face went black and his eyes were sad. "Perhaps I should let them take me."

Instantly Juana was on her feet and her hand lay on his arm.

"You have the pearl," she cried hoarsely. "Do you think they would take you back alive to say they had stolen it?"

His hand strayed limply to the place where the pearl was hidden under his clothes. "They will find it," he said weakly.

"Come," she said. "Come!"

And when he did not respond: "Do you think they would let me live? Do you think they would let the little one here live?"

Her goading struck into his brain; his lips snarled and his eyes were fierce again. "Come," he said. "We will go into the mountains. Maybe we can lose them in the mountains."

Frantically he gathered the gourds and the little bags that were their property. Kino carried a bundle in his left hand, but the big knife swung free in his right hand. He parted the brush for Juana and they hurried to the west, towards the high stone mountains. They trotted quickly through the tangle of the undergrowth. This was panic flight. Kino did not try to conceal his passage; he trotted, kicking the stones, knocking the tell-tale leaves from the little trees. The high sun streamed down on the dry, creaking earth so that even the vegetation ticked in protest. But ahead were the naked granite mountains, rising out of erosion rubble and standing monolithic against the sky. And Kino ran for the high place, as nearly all animals do when they are pursued.

This land was waterless, furred with the cacti which could store water and with the great-rooted brush which could reach deep into the earth for a little moisture and get along on very little. And under-foot was not soil but broken rock, split into small cubes, great slabs, but none of it water-rounded. Little tufts of sad, dry grass grew between the stones, grass that had sprouted with one single rain and headed, dropped its seed, and died. Horned toads watched the family go by and turned their little pivoting dragon heads. And now and then a great jack-rabbit, disturbed in his shape, bumped away and hid behind the nearest rock. The singing heat lay over this desert country, and ahead the stone mountains looked cool and welcoming.

And Kino fled. He knew what would happen. A little way along the road the trackers would become aware that they had missed the path, and they would come back, searching and judging, and in a little while they would find the place where Kino and Juana had rested. From there it would be easy for them—these little stones, the fallen leaves and the whipped branches, the scuffed places where a foot had slipped. Kino could see them in his mind, slipping along the track, whining a little with eagerness, and behind them, dark and half-interested, the horseman with the rifle. His work would come last, for he would not take them back. Oh, the music of evil sang loud in Kino's head now, it sang with the whine of heat and with the dry ringing of snake rattles. It was not large and overwhelming now, but secret and poisonous, and the pounding of his heart gave it undertone and rhythm.

The way began to rise, and as it did the rocks grew larger. But now Kino had put a little distance between his family and the trackers. Now, on the first rise, he rested. He climbed a great boulder and looked back over the shimmering country, but he could not see his enemies, not even the tall horseman riding through the brush. Juana had squatted in the shade of the boulder. She raised her bottle of water to Coyotito's lips; his little dried tongue sucked greedily at it. She looked up at Kino when he came back; she saw him examine her ankles, cut and scratched from the stones and brush, and she covered them quickly with her skirt. Then she handed the bottle to him, but he shook his head. Her eyes were bright in her tired face. Kino moistened his cracked lips with his tongue.

"Juana," he said, "I will go on and you will hide. I will lead them into the mountains, and when they have gone past, you will go north to Loreto or to Santa Rosalia. Then, if I can escape them, I will come to you. It is the only safe way."

She looked full into his eyes for a moment. "No," she said. "We go with you."

"I can go faster alone," he said harshly. "You will put the little one in more danger if you go with me."

"No," said Juana.

"You must. It is the wise thing and it is my wish," he said.

"No," said Juana.

He looked then for weakness in her face, for fear or irresolution, and there was none. Her eyes were very bright. He shrugged his shoulders helplessly then, but he had taken strength from her. When they moved on it was no longer panic flight.

The country, as it rose toward the mountains, changed rapidly. Now there were long outcroppings of granite with deep crevices between, and Kino walked on bare unmarkable stone when he could and leaped from ledge to ledge. He knew that wherever the trackers lost his path they must circle and lose time before they found it again. And so he did not go straight for the mountains any more; he moved in zigzags, and sometimes he cut back to the south and left a sign and then went towards the mountains over bare stone again. And the path rose steeply now, so that he panted a little as he went.

The sun moved downwards towards the bare stone teeth of the mountains, and Kino set his direction for a dark and shadowy cleft in the range. If there were any water at all, it would be there, where he could see, even in the distance, a hint of foliage. And if there were any passage through the smooth stone range, it would be by this same deep cleft. It had its danger, for the trackers would think of it too, but the empty water-bottle did not let that consideration enter. And as the sun lowered, Kino and Juana struggled wearily up the steep slope towards the cleft.

High in the grey stone mountains, under a frowning peak, a little spring bubbled out of a rupture in the stone. It was fed by shade-preserved snow in the summer, and now and then it died completely and bare rocks and dry algæ were on its bottom. But nearly always it gushed out, cold and clean and lovely. In the times when the quick rains fell, it might become a freshet and send its column of white water crashing down the mountain cleft, but nearly always it was a lean little spring. It bubbled out into a pool and then fell a hundred feet to another pool, and this one, overflowing, dropped again, so that it continued, down and down, until it came to the rubble of the upland, and there it disappeared altogether. There wasn't much left of it then anyway, for every time it fell over an escarpment the thirsty air drank it, and it splashed from the pools to the dry vegetation. The animals for miles around came to drink from the little pools, and the wild sheep and the deer, the pumas and raccoons, and the mice—all came to drink. And the birds which spent the day in the brushland came at night to the little pools that were like steps in the mountain cleft. Beside this tiny stream, wherever enough earth collected for root-hold, colonies of plants grew, wild grape and little palms, maidenhair fern, hibiscus, and tall pampas grass with feathery rods raised above the spike leaves. And in the pool lived frogs and water-skaters, and water-worms crawled on the bottom of the pool. Everything that loved water came to these few shallow places. The cats took their prey here, and strewed feathers and lapped water through their bloody teeth. The little pools were places of life because of the water, and places of killing because of the water, too.

The lowest step, where the stream collected before it tumbled down a hundred feet and disappeared into the rubbly desert, was a little platform of stone and sand. Only a pencil of water fell into the pool, but it was enough to keep the pool full and to keep the ferns green in the underhang of the cliff, and wild grape climbed the stone mountain and all manner of little plants found comfort here. The freshets had made a small sandy beach through which the pool flowed, and bright-green watercress grew in the damp sand. The beach was cut and scarred and padded by the feet of animals that had come to drink and to hunt.

The sun had passed over the stone mountains when Kino and Juana struggled up the steep broken slope and came at last to the water. From this step they could look out over the sun-beaten desert to the blue Gulf in the distance. They came utterly weary to the pool, and Juana slumped to her knees and first washed Coyotito's face and then filled her bottle and gave him a drink. And the baby was weary and petulant, and he cried softly until Juana gave him her breasts, and then he gurgled and clucked against her. Kino drank long and thirstily at the pool. For a moment then he stretched out beside the water and relaxed all his muscles and watched Juana feed the baby, and then he got to his feet and went to the edge of the step where the water slipped over, and he searched the distance carefully. His eyes set on a point and he became rigid. Far down the slope he could see the two trackers; they were little more than dots or scurrying ants and behind them a larger ant.

Juana had turned to look at him and she saw his back stiffen.

"How far?" she asked quietly.

"They will be here by evening," said Kino. He looked up the long steep chimney of the cleft where the water came down. "We must go west," he said, and his eyes searched the stone shoulder behind the cleft. And thirty feet up on the grey shoulder he saw a series of little erosion caves. He slipped off his sandals and clambered up to them, gripping the bare stone with his toes, and he looked into the shallow caves. They were only a few feet deep, wind-hollowed scoops, but they sloped slightly downwards and back. Kino crawled into the largest one and lay down and knew that he could not be seen from the outside. Quickly he went back to Juana.

"You must go up there. Perhaps they will not find us there," he said.

Without question she filled her water-bottle to the top, and then Kino helped her up to the shallow cave and brought up the packages of food and passed them to her. And Juana sat in the cave entrance and watched him. She saw that he did not try to erase their tracks in the sand. Instead, he climbed up the brush cliff beside the water, clawing and tearing at the ferns and wild grape as he went. And when he had climbed a hundred feet to the next bench, he came down again. He looked carefully at the smooth rock shoulder towards the cave to see that there was no trace of passage, and last he climbed up and crept into the cave beside Juana.

"When they go up," he said, "we will slip away, down to the lowlands again. I am afraid only that the baby may cry. You must see that he does not cry."

"He will not cry," she said, and she raised the baby's face to her own and looked into his eyes and he stared solemnly back at her.

"He knows," said Juana.

Now Kino lay in the cave entrance, his chin braced on his crossed arms, and he watched the blue shadow of the mountain move out across the brushy desert below until it reached the Gulf, and the long twilight of the shadow was over the land.

The trackers were long in coming, as though they had trouble with the trail Kino had left. It was dusk when they came at last to the little pool. And all three were on foot now, for a horse could not climb the last steep slope. From above they were thin figures in the evening. The two trackers scurried about on the little beach, and they saw Kino's progress up the cliff before they drank. The man with the rifle sat down and rested himself and the trackers squatted near him, and in the evening the points of their cigarettes glowed and receded. And then Kino could see that they were eating, and the soft murmur of their voices came to him.

Then darkness fell, deep and black in the mountain cleft. The animals that used the pool came near and smelled men there and drifted away again into the darkness.

He heard a murmur behind him. Juana was whispering, "Coyotito." She was begging him to be quiet. Kino heard the baby whimper, and he knew from the muffled sounds that Juana had covered his head with her shawl.

Down on the beach a match flared, and in its momentary light Kino saw that two of the men were sleeping, curled up like dogs, while the third watched, and he saw the glint of the rifle in the match light. And then the match died, but it left a picture on Kino's eyes. He could see it, just how each man was, two sleeping curled up and the third squatting in the sand with the rifle between his knees.

Kino moved silently back into the cave. Juana's eyes were two sparks reflecting a low star. Kino crawled quietly close to her and he put his lips near to her cheek.

"There is a way," he said.

"But they will kill you."

"If I get first to the one with the rifle," Kino said, "I must get to him first, then I will be all right. Two are sleeping."

Her hand crept out from under her shawl and gripped his arm. "They will see your white clothes in the starlight."

"No," he said. "And I must go before moonrise."

He searched for a soft word and then gave it up. "If they kill me," he said, "lie quietly. And when they are gone away, go to Loreto."

Her hand shook a little, holding his wrist.

"There is no choice," he said. "It is the only way. They will find us in the morning."

Her voice trembled a little. "Go with God," she said.

He peered close at her and he could see her large eyes. Her hand fumbled out and found the baby, and for a moment his palm lay on Coyotito's head. And then Kino raised his hand and touched Juana's cheek, and she held her breath.

Against the sky in the cave entrance Juana could see that Kino was taking off his white clothes, for dirty and ragged though they were they would show up against the dark night. His own brown skin was a better protection for him. And then she saw how he hooked his amulet neck-string about the horn handle of his great knife, so that it hung down in front of him and left both hands free. He did not come back to her. For a moment his body was black in the cave entrance, crouched and silent, and then he was gone.

Juana moved to the entrance and looked out. She peered like an owl from the hole in the mountain, and the baby slept under the blanket on her back, his face turned sideways against her neck and shoulder. She could feel his warm breath against her skin, and Juana whispered her combination of prayer and magic, her Hail Marys and her ancient intercession against the black unhuman things.

The night seemed a little less dark when she looked out, and to the east there was a lightening in the sky, down near the horizon where the moon would show. And, looking down, she could see the cigarette of the man on watch.

Kino edged like a slow lizard down the smooth rock shoulder. He had turned his neck-string so that the great knife hung down from his back and could not clash against the stone. His spread fingers gripped the mountain, and his bare toes found support through contact, and even his chest lay against the stone so that he would not slip. For any sound, a rolling pebble or a sigh, a little slip of flesh on rock, would rouse the watchers below. Any sound that was not germane to the night would make them alert. But the night was not silent; the little tree frogs that lived near the stream twittered like birds, and the high metallic ringing of the cicadas filled the mountain cleft. And Kino's own music was in his head, the music of the enemy, low and pulsing, nearly asleep. But the Song of the Family had become as fierce and sharp and feline as the snarl of a female puma. The family song was alive now and driving him down on the dark enemy. The harsh cicada seemed to take up its melody, and the twittering tree frogs called little phrases of it.

And Kino crept silently as a shadow down the smooth mountain face. One bare foot moved a few inches and the toes touched the stone and gripped, and the other foot a few inches, and then the palm of one hand a little downwards, and then the other hand, until the whole body, without seeming to move, had moved. Kino's mouth was open so that even his breath would make no sound, for he knew that he was not invisible. If the watcher, sensing movement, looked at the dark place against the stone which was his body, he could see him. Kino must move so slowly he would not draw the watcher's eyes. It took him a long time to reach the bottom and to crouch behind a little dwarf palm. His heart thundered in his chest and his hands and face were wet with sweat. He crouched and took great long breaths to calm himself.

Only twenty feet separated him from the enemy now, and he tried to remember the ground between. Was there any stone which might trip him in his rush? He kneaded his legs against cramp and found that his muscles were jerking after their long tension. And then he looked apprehensively to the east. The moon would rise in a few moments now, and he must attack before it rose. He could see the outline of the watcher, but the sleeping men were below his vision. It was the watcher Kino must find—must find quickly and without hesitation. Silently he drew the amulet string over his shoulder and loosened the loop from the horn-handle of his great knife.

He was too late, for as he rose from his crouch the silver edge of the moon slipped above the eastern horizon, and Kino sank back behind his bush.

It was an old and ragged moon, but it threw hard light and hard shadow into the mountain cleft, and now Kino could see the seated figure of the watcher on the little beach beside the pool. The watcher gazed full at the moon, and then he lighted another cigarette, and the match illumined his dark face for a moment. There could be no waiting now; when the watcher turned his head, Kino must leap. His legs were as tight as wound springs.

And then from above came a little murmuring cry. The watcher turned his head to listen and then he stood up, and one of the sleepers stirred on the ground and awakened and asked quietly, "What is it?"

"I don't know," said the watcher. "It sounded like a cry, almost like a human—like a baby."

The man who had been sleeping said, "You can't tell. Some coyote bitch with a litter. I've heard a coyote pup cry like a baby."

The sweat rolled in drops down Kino's forehead and fell into his eyes and burned them. The little cry came again and the watcher looked up the side of the hill to the dark cave.

"Coyote maybe," he said, and Kino heard the harsh click as he cocked the rifle.

"If it's a coyote, this will stop it," the watcher said as he raised the gun.

Kino was in mid-leap when the gun crashed and the barrel-flash made a picture on his eyes. The great knife swung and crunched hollowly. It bit through neck and deep into chest, and Kino was a terrible machine now. He grasped the rifle even as he wrenched free his knife. His strength and his movement and his speed were a machine. He whirled and struck the head of the seated man like a melon. The third man scrabbled away like a crab, slipped into the pool, and then he began to climb frantically, to climb up the cliff where the water pencilled down. His hands and feet threshed in the tangle of the wild grapevine, and he whimpered and gibbered as he tried to get up. But Kino had become as cold and deadly as steel. Deliberately he threw the lever of the rifle, and then he raised the gun and aimed deliberately and fired. He saw his enemy tumble backwards into the pool, and Kino strode to the water. In the moonlight he could see the frantic frightened eyes, and Kino aimed and fired between the eyes.

And then Kino stood uncertainly. Something was wrong, some signal was trying to get through to his brain. Tree frogs and cicadas were silent now. And then Kino's brain cleared from its red concentration and he knew the sound—the keening, moaning, rising hysterical cry from the little cave in the side of the stone mountain, the cry of death.

Everyone in La Paz remembers the return of the family; there may be some old ones who saw it, but those whose fathers and whose grandfathers told it to them remember it nevertheless. It is an event that happened to everyone.

It was late in the golden afternoon when the first little boys ran hysterically in the town and spread the word that Kino and Juana were coming back. And everyone hurried to see them. The sun was settling towards the western mountains and the shadows on the ground were long. And perhaps that was what left the deep impression on those who saw them.

The two came from the rutted country road into the city, and they were not walking in single file, Kino ahead and Juana behind, as usual, but side by side. The sun was behind them and their long shadows stalked ahead, and they seemed to carry two towers of darkness with them. Kino had a rifle across his arm and Juana carried her shawl like a sack over her shoulder. And in it was a small limp, heavy bundle. The shawl was crusted with dried blood, and the bundle swayed a little as she walked. Her face was hard and lined and leathery with fatigue and with the tightness with which she fought fatigue. And her wide eyes stared inwards on herself. She was as remote and as removed as Heaven. Kino's lips were thin and his jaws tight, and the people say that he carried fear with him, that he was as dangerous as a rising storm. The people say that the two seemed to be removed from human experience; that they had gone through pain and had come out on the other side; that there was almost a magical protection about them. And those people who had rushed to see them crowded back and let them pass and did not speak to them.

Kino and Juana walked through the city as though it were not there. Their eyes glanced neither right nor left nor up nor down, but stared only straight ahead. Their legs moved a little jerkily, like well-made wooden dolls, and they carried pillars of black fear about them. And, as they walked through the stone and plaster city, brokers peered at them from barred windows and servants put one eye to a slitted gate and mothers turned the faces of their youngest children inwards against their skirts. Kino and Juana strode side by side through the stone and plaster city and down among the brush houses, and the neighbours stood back and let them pass. Juan Tomás raised his hand in greeting and did not say the greeting and left his hand in the air for a moment uncertainly.

In Kino's ears the Song of the Family was as fierce as a cry. He was immune and terrible, and his song had become a battle cry. They trudged past the burned square where their house had been without even looking at it. They cleared the brush that edged the beach and picked their way down the shore towards the water. And they did not look towards Kino's broken canoe.

And when they came to the water's edge they stopped and stared out over the Gulf. And then Kino laid the rifle down, and he dug among his clothes, and then he held the great pearl in his hand. He looked into its surface and it was grey and ulcerous. Evil faces peered from it into his eyes, and he saw the light of burning. And in the surface of the pearl he saw the frantic eyes of the man in the pool. And in the surface of the pearl he saw Coyotito lying in the little cave with the top of his head shot away. And the pearl was ugly; it was grey, like a malignant growth. And Kino heard the music of the pearl, distorted and insane. Kino's hand shook a little, and he turned slowly to Juana and held the pearl out to her. She stood beside him, still holding her dead bundle over her shoulder. She looked at the pearl in his hand for a moment and then she looked into Kino's eyes and said softly, "No, you."

And Kino drew back his arm and flung the pearl with all his might. Kino and Juana watched it go, winking and glimmering under the setting sun. They saw the little splash in the distance, and they stood side by side watching the place for a long time.

And the pearl settled into the lovely green water and dropped towards the bottom. The waving branches of the algae called to it and beckoned to it. The lights on its surface were green and lovely. It settled down to the sand bottom among the fern-like plants. Above, the surface of the water was a green mirror. And the pearl lay on the floor of the sea. A crab scampering over the bottom raised a little cloud of sand, and when it settled the pearl was gone.

And the music of the pearl drifted to a whisper and disappeared.

SWEET THURSDAY

For ELIZABETH *with love*

PROLOGUE

One night Mack lay back on his bed in the Palace Flophouse and he said, "I ain't never been satisfied with that book *Cannery Row*. I would of went about it different."

And after a while he rolled over and raised his head on his hand and he said, "I guess I'm just a critic. But if I ever come across the guy that wrote that book I could tell him a few things."

"Like what?" said Whitey No. 1.

"Well," said Mack, "like this here. Suppose there's chapter one, chapter two, chapter three. That's all right, as far as it goes, but I'd like to have a couple of words at the top so it tells me what the chapter's going to be about. Sometimes maybe I want to go back, and chapter five don't mean nothing to me. If there was just a couple of words I'd know that was the chapter I wanted to go back to."

"Go on," said Whitey No. 1.

"Well, I like a lot of talk in a book, and I don't like to have nobody tell me what the guy that's talking looks like. I want to figure out what he looks like from the way he talks. And another thing—I kind of like to figure out what the guy's thinking by what he says. I like some description too," he went on. "I like to know what colour a thing is, how it smells and maybe how it looks, and maybe how a guy feels about it—but not too much of that."

"You sure are a critic," said Whitey No. 2. "Mack, I never give you credit before. Is that all?"

"No," said Mack. "Sometimes I want a book to break loose with a bunch of hooptedoodle. The guy's writing it, give him a chance to do a little hooptedoodle. Spin up some pretty words maybe, or sing a little song with language. That's nice. But I wish it was set aside so I don't have to read it. I don't want hooptedoodle to get mixed up in the story. So if the guy that's writing it wants hooptedoodle, he ought to put it right first. Then I can skip if I want to, or maybe go back to it after I know how the story come out."

Eddie said, "Mack, if the guy that wrote *Cannery Row* comes in, you going to tell him all that?"

Whitey No. 2 said, "Hell, Mack can tell anybody anything. Why, Mack could tell a ghost how to haunt a house."

"You're damn right I could," said Mack, "and there wouldn't be no table-rapping or chains. There hasn't been no improvement in house-haunting in years. You're damn right I could, Whitey!" And he lay back and stared up at the canopy over his bed.

"I can see it now," said Mack.
"Ghosts?" Eddie asked.
"Hell, no," said Mack, "chapters. . . ."

CHAPTER I

WHAT HAPPENED IN BETWEEN

When the war came to Monterey and to Cannery Row everybody fought it more or less, in one way or another. When hostilities ceased everyone had his wounds.

The canneries themselves fought the war by getting the limit taken off fish and catching them all. It was done for patriotic reasons, but that didn't bring the fish back. As with the oysters in *Alice*, "They'd eaten every one." It was the same noble impulse that stripped the forests of the West and right now is pumping water out of California's earth faster than it can rain back in. When the desert comes, people will be sad; just as Cannery Row was sad when all the pilchards were caught and canned and eaten. The pearl-grey canneries of corrugated iron were silent and a pacing watchman was their only life. The street that once roared with trucks was quiet and empty.

Yes, the war got into everybody. Doc was drafted. He put a friend known as Old Jingleballicks in charge of Western Biological Laboratories and served out his time as a tech. sergeant in a V.D. section.

Doc was philosophical about it. He whiled away his free hours with an unlimited supply of government alcohol, made many friends and resisted promotion. When the war was over, Doc was kept on by a grateful government to straighten out certain inventory problems, a job he was fitted for since he had contributed largely to the muck-up. Doc was honourably discharged two years after our victory.

He went back to Western Biological and forced open the water-logged door. Old Jingleballicks hadn't been there for years. Dust and mildew covered everything. There were dirty pots and pans in the sink. Instruments were rusted. The live-animal cages were empty.

Doc sat down in his old chair and a weight descended on him. He cursed old Jingleballicks, savouring his quiet poisonous words, and then automatically he got up and walked across the silent street to Lee Chong's grocery for beer. A well-dressed man of Mexican appearance stood behind the counter, and only then did Doc remember that Lee Chong was gone.

"Beer," said Doc. "Two quarts."
"Coming up," said the Patrón.
"Is Mack around?"
"Sure. I guess so."
"Tell him I want to see him."
"Tell him who wants to see him?"
"Tell him Doc is back."
"Okay, Doc," said the Patrón. "This kind of beer all right?"
"Any kind of beer's all right," said Doc.

Doc and Mack sat late together in the laboratory. The beer lost its edge and a quart of Old Tennis Shoes took its place while Mack filled in the lost years.

Change was everywhere. People were gone, or changed, and that was almost like being gone. Names were mentioned sadly, even the names of the living. Gay was dead, killed by a piece of anti-aircraft fall-back in London. He couldn't keep his nose out of the sky during a bombing. His wife easily remarried on his insurance, but at the Palace Flop-house they kept Gay's bed just as it was before he went—a little shrine to Gay. No one was permitted to sit on Gay's bed.

And Mack told Doc how Whitey No. 1 took a job in a war plant in Oakland and broke his leg the second day and spent three months in luxury. In his white hospital bed he learned to play rhythm harmonica, an accomplishment he enjoyed all the rest of his life.

Then there was the new Whitey, Whitey No. 2, and Mack was proud of him, for Whitey No. 2 had joined First Marines and gone out as a replacement. Someone, not Whitey No. 2, said he had won a Bronze Star, but if he had he'd lost it, so there was no proof. But he never forgave the Marine Corps for taking his prize away from him—a quart jar of ears pickled in brandy. He'd wanted to put that jar on a shelf over his bed, a memento of his service to his country.

Eddie had stayed on his job with Wide Ida at the Café La Ida. The medical examiner, when he looked at his check sheet and saw what was wrong with Eddie, came to the conclusion that Eddie had been technically dead for twelve years. But Eddie got around just the same, and what with the draft taking everybody away he very nearly became a permanent bar-tender for Wide Ida. Out of sentiment he emptied the wining jug into a series of little kegs, and when each keg was full he bunged it and buried it. Right now the Palace is the best-endowed flop-house in Monterey County.

Down about the middle of the first quart of Old Tennis Shoes, Mack told how Dora Flood had died in her sleep, leaving the Bear Flag bereft. Her girls were broken-hearted. They put on a lady-drunk that lasted three days, stuck a "Not Open for Business" sign on the door, but through the walls you could hear them doing honour to Dora in three-part harmony—"Rock of Ages", "Asleep in the Deep", and "St. James Infirmary". Those girls really mourned—they mourned like coyotes.

The Bear Flag was taken over by Dora's next-of-kin, an older sister who came down from San Francisco, where for some years she had been running a Midnight Mission on Howard Street, running it at a profit. She had been a silent partner all along and had dictated its unique practices and policies. For instance, Dora had wanted to name her place the Lone Star, because once in her youth she had spent a wonderful week-end in Fort Worth. But her sister insisted that it be called the Bear Flag, in honour of California. She said if you were hustling a state you should do honour to that state. She didn't find her new profession very different from her old, and she thought of both as a public service. She read horoscopes and continued, after hours at least, to transform the Bear Flag into a kind of finishing school for girls. She was named Flora, but one time in the Mission a gentleman bum finished his soup and said, "Flora, you seem more like a fauna-type to me."

"Say, I like that," she said. "Mind if I keep it?" And she did. She was Fauna ever afterward.

Now all this was sad enough, but there was a greater sadness that Mack kept putting off. He didn't want to get to it. And so he told Doc about Henri the painter.

Mack kind of blamed himself for Henri. Henri had built a boat, a perfect little boat with a nice state-room. But he'd built it up in the woods, because he was afraid of the ocean. His boat sat on concrete blocks and Henri was happy there. One time when there wasn't much else to do, Mack and the boys played a trick on him. They were bored. They went down to the sea rocks and chiselled off a sack of barnacles and took them up and glued them on the bottom of Henri's boat with quick-drying cement. Henri was pretty upset, particularly since he couldn't tell anybody about it. Doc could have reassured him, but Doc was in the Army. Henri scraped the bottom and painted it, but no sooner was the paint dry than the boys did it again, and stuck a little seaweed on too. They were terribly ashamed when they saw what happened. Henri sold his boat and left town within twenty-four hours. He could not shake the persistent and horrifying notion that the boat was going to sea while he was asleep.

And Mack told how Hazel had been in the Army too, although you couldn't get anybody to believe it. Hazel was in the Army long enough to qualify for the G.I. bill, and he enrolled at the University of California for training in astrophysics by making a check mark on an application. Three months later, when some of the confusion had died down, the college authorities discovered him. The Department of Psychology wanted to keep him, but it was against the law.

Hazel often wondered what it was that he had gone to study. He intended to ask Doc, but by the time Doc got back it had slipped his mind.

Doc poured out the last of the first bottle of Old Tennis Shoes, and he said, "You've talked about everything else. What happened to you, Mack?"

Mack said, "I just kind of stayed around and kept things in order."

Well, Mack had kept things in order, and he had discussed war with everybody he'd met. He called his war the Big War. That was the first one. After the war the atom-bomb tests interested him, in a Fourth-of-July kind of way. The huge reward the government offered for the discovery of new uranium deposits set off a chain reaction in Mack, and he bought a second-hand Geiger counter.

At the Monterey bus station the Geiger counter started buzzing and Mack went along with it—first to San Francisco, then to Marysville, Sacramento, Portland. Mack was so scientifically interested that he didn't notice the girl on the same bus. That is, he didn't notice her much. Well, one thing led to another, which was not unique in Mack's experience. The girl was taking the long way to Jacksonville, Florida. Mack would have left her in Tacoma if his Geiger counter hadn't throbbed him eastward. He got clear to Salina, Kansas, with the girl. On a hot muggy day the girl lunged at a fly on the bus and broke her watch, and only then did Mack discover that he had been following a radium dial. Romance alone was not enough for Mack at his age. He arrived back in Monterey on a flat-car, under a tarpaulin that covered a medium-sized tank destined for Fort Ord. Mack was very glad to get home. He had won a few dollars from a guard on the flat-car. He scrubbed out the Palace Flop-house and planted a row of morning glories along the front, and he and Eddie got it ready for the returning heroes. They had quite a time when the heroes straggled back.

Over Doc and Mack a golden melancholy settled like autumn leaves, melancholy concocted equally of Old Tennis Shoes and old times, of friends lost and friends changed. And both of them knew they were avoiding one subject, telling minor stories to avoid a major one. But at last they were dry, and their subject confronted them.

Doc opened with considerable bravery. "What do you think of the new owner over at the grocery?"

"Oh, he's all right," said Mack. "Kind of interesting. The only trouble is he can't never take Lee Chong's place. There was never a friend like Lee Chong," Mack said brokenly.

"Yes, he was wise and good," said Doc.
"And tricky," said Mack.
"And smart," said Doc.
"He took care of a lot of people," said Mack.
"And he took a few," said Doc.

They volleyed Lee Chong back and forth, and their memories built virtues that would have surprised him, and cleverness and beauty too. While one told a fine tale of that mercantile Chinaman the other waited impatiently to top the story. Out of their memories there emerged a being scarcely human, a dragon of goodness and an angel of guile. In such a way are the gods created.

But the bottle was empty now, and its emptiness irritated Mack, and his irritation oozed towards Lee Chong's memory.

"The son-of-a-bitch was sneaky," said Mack. "He should of told us he was going to sell out and go away. It wasn't friendly, doing all that alone without his friends to help."

"Maybe that's what he was afraid of," said Doc. "Lee wrote to me about it. I couldn't advise him—I was too far away—so he was safe."

"You can't never find out what a Chink's got on his mind," said Mack. "Doc, who would of thought he was what you might say—plotting?"

Oh, it had been a shocking thing. Lee Chong had operated his emporium for so long that no one could possibly have foreseen that he would sell out. He was so mixed up in the feeding and clothing of Cannery Row that he was considered permanent. Who could have suspected the secret turnings of his paradoxical Oriental mind, which seems to have paralleled the paradoxical Occidental mind?

It is customary to think of a sea captain sitting in his cabin, planning a future grocery store not subject to wind or bottom-fouling. Lee Chong dreamed while he worked his abacus and passed out pints of Old Tennis Shoes and delicately sliced bacon with his big knife. He dreamed all right—he dreamed of the sea. He did not share his plans or ask advice. He would have got lots of advice.

One day Lee Chong sold out and bought a schooner. He wanted to go trading in the South Seas. He dreamed of palms and Polynesians. In the hold of his schooner he loaded the entire stock of his store—all the canned goods, the rubber boots, the caps and needles and small tools, the fireworks and calendars, even the glass-fronted show-cases where he kept gold-plated collar-buttons and cigarette lighters. He took it all with him. And the last anyone saw of him, he was waving his blue naval cap from the flying bridge of his dream ship as he passed the whistle buoy at Point Pinos into the sunset. And if he didn't go down on the way over, that's where he is now

—probably lying in a hammock under an awning on the rear deck, while beautiful Polynesian girls in very scanty clothes pick over his stock of canned tomatoes and striped mechanics' caps.

"Why do you suppose he done it?" Mack asked.

"Who knows?" said Doc. "Who knows what lies deep in any man's mind? Who knows what any man wants?"

"He won't be happy there," said Mack. "He'll be lonely out among them foreigners. You know, Doc, I figured it out. It was them goddam movies done it. You remember, he used to close up every Thursday night. That's because there was a change of bill at the movie house. He never missed a movie. That's what done it, the movies. I and you, Doc, we know what liars the movies are. He won't be happy out there. He'll just be miserable to come back."

Doc gazed at his run-down laboratory. "I wish I were out there with him."

"Who don't?" said Mack. "Why, them South Sea Island girls will kill him. He ain't as young as he used to be."

"I know," said Doc. "You and I should be out there, Mack, to help protect him from himself. I'm wondering, Mack, should I step across the street and get another pint or should I go to bed?"

"Why don't you flip a coin?"

"You flip the coin," said Doc. "I don't really want to go to bed. If you flip it I'll know how it's going to come out."

Mack flipped, and he was right. Mack said, "I'd just as lief step over for you, Doc. You just set here comfortable—I'll be right back." And he was.

CHAPTER II

THE TROUBLED LIFE OF JOSEPH AND MARY

MACK CAME back with a pint of Old Tennis Shoes and he poured some in Doc's glass and some in his own.

Doc said, "What kind of a fellow is the new owner over there—Mexican, isn't he?"

"Nice fellow," said Mack. "Classy dresser. Name of Joseph and Mary Rivas. Smart as a whip, but kind of unfortunate, Doc—unfortunate and funny. You know how it is, when a pimp falls in love it don't make any difference how much he suffers—it's funny. And Joseph and Mary's kind of like that."

"Tell me about him," said Doc.

"I been studying him," said Mack. "He told me some stuff and I put two and two together. He's smart. You know, Doc, there's a kind of smartness that cuts its own throat. Haven't you knew people that was so busy being smart they never had time to do nothing else? Well, Joseph and Mary is kind of like that."

"Tell me," said Doc.

"I guess you couldn't find no two people oppositer than what you and him is," Mack began. "You're nice, Doc, nice and egg-heady, but a guy would have to be nuts to think you was smart. Everybody takes care of you because you're wide open. Anybody is like to throw a sneak-punch at Joseph and Mary just because he's in there dancing and feinting all the time. And he's nice too, in a way."

"Where'd he come from?" Doc asked.

"Well, I'll tell you," said Mack.

Mack was right. Doc and Joseph and Mary were about as opposite as you can get, but delicately opposite. Their differences balanced like figures of a mobile in a light breeze. Doc was a man whose whole direction and impulse was legal and legitimate. Left to his own devices, he would have obeyed every law, down to pausing at boulevard stop signs. The fact that Doc was constantly jockeyed into illicit practices was the fault of his friends, not of himself—the fault of Wide Ida, whom the liquor laws cramped like a tight girdle, and of the Bear Flag, whose business, while accepted and recognized, was certainly mentioned disparagingly in every conceivable statute book.

Mack and the boys had lived so long in the shadow of the vagrancy laws that they considered them a shield and an umbrella. Their association with larceny, fraud, loitering, illegal congregation, and conspiracy on all levels was not only accepted, but to a certain extent had become a matter of pride to the inhabitants of Cannery Row. But they were lamb-like children of probity and virtue compared to Joseph and Mary. Everything he did naturally turned out to be against the law. This had been true from his earliest childhood. In Los Angeles, where he had been born, he led a gang of pachucos while he was still a child. The charge that he lagged with loaded pennies, if not provable, at least seems reasonable. He rejected the theory of private ownership of removable property almost from birth. At the age of eight he was a pool hustler of such success that Navy officers had been known to put him off limits. When the gang wars started in the Mexican district of Los Angeles, Joseph and Mary rose above pachucos. He set up an ambulatory store, well stocked with switch knives, snap guns, brass knuckles, and, for the very poor, socks loaded with sand, cheap and very effective. At twelve he matriculated at reform school, and two years later emerged with honours. He had learned nearly every criminal technique in existence. This fourteen-year-old handsome boy with sad and innocent eyes could operate the tumblers of a safe with either fingers or stethoscope. He could make second storeys as though he had suction cups on his feet. But no sooner had he mastered these arts than he abandoned them, reasoning that the odds were too great. He was always a smart boy. Joseph and Mary was looking for a profession wherein the victim was a partner of the predator. The badger game, the swinging panel, and the Spanish treasure were nearer to his ideal. But even they fell short. He had never made a police blotter and he wanted to keep it that way. Somewhere he felt there was a profession illegal enough to satisfy him morally and yet safe enough not to outrage his instinctive knowledge of the law of averages. You might have said he was well launched on his career when, suddenly, puberty smote him, and for a number of years his activities took a different direction.

In the fields of larceny and fraud, Joseph and Mary vegetated for a number of years. He was a man when the fog cleared from before his eyes and he could see again. Then just when he was set to go, the Army got him and kept him as long as it could in good conscience. It is said that his final dishonourable discharge is a masterpiece of understatement.

J. and M. never could get set. He started again on his career and took a wrong turning, for he fell under the influence of a young and understanding priest, who drew him into the warm bosom of Mother Church, into which Joseph and Mary had been born anyway. Now Joseph and Mary Rivas approved of confession and forgiveness, and he felt, as perhaps François Villon had, that under the protection of the cloth he might find some outlet for his talent. Father Murphy taught him the theory of honest labour, and when Joseph and Mary had got over the shock of the principle he decided to give it a try. He was still malleable, and he succeeded, where Villon had failed, in keeping his hands off Church property. With the help of Father Murphy, who had influence in the city government, Joseph and Mary found himself the possessor of a city job, a position of dignity, with a monthly cheque to be cashed without fear of finger-printing.

The Plaza in Los Angeles is a pretty square, ornamented with small gardens, palms in great pots, and many, many flowers. It is a landmark, a tourist centre, a city pride, for it preserves a Mexican-ness unknown in Mexico. Joseph and Mary, then, was in charge of watering and cultivating the plants in the Plaza—a job that was not only easy and pleasant but kept him in direct touch with those tourists who might be interested in small packets of art studies. Although Joseph and Mary realized he could never get rich in this job, he took a certain pleasure in being partly legal. It gave him the satisfaction most people find in sin.

At about this time the Los Angeles Police Department had a

puzzle on its hands. Marijuana was being distributed in fairly large quantities and at a greatly reduced price. The narcotics squad conducted raid after raid without finding the source. Every vacant lot was searched from San Pedro to Eagle Rock. And then the countryside was laid out on graph-paper and the search for the pointed leaves of the marijuana went on in ever-widening circles: north past Santa Barbara; east to the Colorado River; south as far as the border. The border was sealed, and it is well known that muggles does not grow in the Pacific Ocean. Six months of intensive search, with the co-operation of all local officials and the state police, got absolutely nowhere. The supply continued unabated, and the narcotics squad was convinced that the pushers did not know the source.

Heaven knows how long the situation might have continued if it had not been for Mildred Bugle, thirteen, head of her class in Beginning Botany, Los Angeles High School. One Saturday afternoon she crossed the Plaza, picked some interesting leaves growing around a potted palm and positively identified them as Cannabis Americana.

Joseph and Mary Rivas might have been in trouble but for the fact that the Los Angeles Police Department was in worse trouble. They could not bring him to book. How would it look if the newspapers got hold of the story that the Plaza was the source of supply? that the product had been planted and nurtured by a city employee, freshened with city water, and fed with city manure?

Joseph and Mary was given a floater so strongly worded that it singed his eyelashes. The police even bought him a bus ticket as far as San Luis Obispo.

Doc chuckled. "You know, Mack," he said, "you're almost building a case for honesty."

"I always put in a good word for it," said Mack.

"How did he get in the wet-back business?" Doc asked.

"Well, he was casing the field for a career," said Mack, "and wet-backs looked like a gold-brick cinch. Joseph and Mary figured the angles and the percentage. You look at it and you see it couldn't flop." He put up his fingers to count facts, then took a quick drink to tide him over the period when his hands would be tied up.

Mack touched the little finger of his left hand with his right forefinger. "Number one," he said. "J. and M. talks Mexican because his old man and his old lady was Mexican before they came to L.A." He touched his third finger. "Number two, the wet-backs come in by theirself. Nobody makes them come. There's a steady supply. Number three, they can't talk English and they don't know a cop from a bucket. They *need* somebody like Joseph and Mary to take care of them and get them jobs and take their pay. If one of them gets mean, all J. and M. got to do is call the federal men, and they deport him without no trouble to J. and M. That's what he was always looking for—a racket with the percentage stacked for the house. He figures he's got three or four crews working in fruit and vegetables and he can kind of lay back and rest, the way he always wanted. That's why he bought out Lee Chong. He figured to make the grocery a kind of labour centre, where he could rest up his men and sell them stuff at the same time. And what he's doing ain't very much against the law."

Doc said, "I can tell, from your tone, it didn't work. What happened?"

"Music," said Mack.

Now it is true that Joseph and Mary did know all the angles, averages, and percentages. His systems couldn't lose, but they did. The odds are against making your point with the dice, and that law holds until magic intervenes and someone makes a run.

There were literally millions of wet-backs in the country—quiet, hard-working, ignorant men, content to bend their backs over the demanding earth. It was a set-up; it couldn't lose. How did it happen, then, that in Joseph and Mary's crew there should be one tenor and one guitar player? Under his horrified eyes an orchestra took shape—two guitars, a guitarón, rhythm and maraca men, a tenor, and two baritones. He would have had the whole lot deported if his nephew, Cacahuete, had not joined them with his hot trumpet.

Joseph and Mary's wet-backs abandoned the carrot and cauliflower fields for the dance floors of the little towns in California. They called themselves the Espaldas Mojadas. They played "Ven á Mi, Mi Chica Dolorosa" and "Mujer de San Luis" and "El Nubito Blanco que Llora".

The Espaldas Mojadas dressed in tight *charro* costumes, wore huge Mexican hats, and played for dances in the Spreckel Fireman's Hall, the Soledad I.O.O.F., the Elks of King City, the Greenfield Garage, the San Ardo Municipal Auditorium. Joseph and Mary stopped fighting them and started booking them. Business was so good he screened new wet-backs for talent. It was Joseph and Mary's first entrance into show business, and its native dishonesty reassured him that his course was well chosen.

"So, you see," said Mack, "it was music done it. You can't trust nothing no more. You take Fauna now—the Bear Flag ain't like any hook-shop on land or sea. She makes them girls take table-manner lessons and posture lessons and she reads the stars. You never seen nothing like it. Everything's changed, Doc, everything."

Doc looked around his mouldy laboratory, and he shivered. "Maybe I'm changed, too," he said.

"Hell, Doc, you can't change. Why, what could we depend on!

Doc, if you change, a lot of people are going to cash in their chips. Why, we was all just waiting around for you to get back so we could go on being normal."

"I don't feel the same, Mack. I'm restless."

"Now you get yourself a girl," said Mack. "You play some of the churchy music to her on your phonograph. And then I'll come in and hustle you for a couple of bucks. Make a try, Doc. You owe it to your friends."

"I'll try," said Doc, "but I have no confidence in it. I'm afraid I've changed."

CHAPTER III
HOOPTEDOODLE (1)

LOOKING BACK, you can usually find the moment of the birth of a new era, whereas, when it happened, it was one day hooked on to the tail of another.

There were prodigies and portents that winter and spring, but you never notice such things until afterwards. On Mount Toro the snow came down as far as Pine Canyon on one side and Jamesburg on the other. A six-legged calf was born in Carmel Valley. A cloud drifting in formed the letters O-N in the sky over Monterey. Mushrooms grew out of the concrete floor of the basement of the Methodist Church. Old Mr. Roletti, at the age of ninety-three, developed senile satyriasis and had to be forcibly restrained from chasing high-school girls. The spring was cold, and the rains came late. Velella in their purple billions sailed into Monterey Bay and were cast up on the beaches, where they died. Killer whales attacked the sea-lions near Seal Rocks and murdered a great number of them. Dr. Wick took a kidney stone out of Mrs. Gaston as big as your hand and shaped like a dog's head, a beagle. The Lions' Club announced a fifty-dollar prize for the best essay on 'Football—Builder of Character.' And last, but far from least, the Sherman rose developed a carnation bud. Perhaps all this meant nothing; you never notice such things until afterwards.

Monterey had changed, and so had Cannery Row and its denizens. As Mack said, "The tum-tum changes, giving place to new. And God tum-tums himself in many ways."

Doc was changing in spite of himself, in spite of the prayers of his friends, in spite of his own knowledge. And why not? Men do change, and change comes like a little wind that ruffles the curtains at dawn, and it comes like the stealthy perfume of wild flowers hidden in the grass. Change may be announced by a small ache, so that you think you're catching cold. Or you may feel a little wind that ruffles the curtains at dawn, and it may even take the form of a hunger that peanuts will not satisfy. Isn't over-eating said to be one of the symptoms of discontent? And isn't discontent the lever of change?

Before the war Doc had lived a benign and pleasant life, which aroused envy in some gnat-bitten men. Doc made a living, as good a living as he needed or wanted, by collecting and preserving various marine animals and selling them to schools, colleges, and museums. He was able to turn affable and uncritical eyes on a world full of excitement. He combined the beauty of the sea with man's loveliest achievement—music. Through his superb gramophone he could hear the angelic voice of the Sistine Choir and could wander half lost in the exquisite masses of William Byrd. He believed there were two human achievements that towered above all others: the *Faust* of Goethe and the *Art of the Fugue* by J. S. Bach. Doc was never bored. He was beloved and preyed on by his friends, and this contented him. For he remembered the words of Diamond Jim Brady who, when told that his friends were making suckers of him, remarked, "It's fun to be a sucker—if you can afford it." Doc could afford it. He had not the vanity which makes men try to be smart.

Doc's natural admiration and desire for women had always been satisfied by women themselves. He had few responsibilities except to be a kindly, generous, and amused man. And these he did not find difficult. All in all, he had always been a fulfilled and contented man. A specimen so rare aroused yearning in other men, for how few men like their work, their lives—how very few men like themselves. Doc liked himself, not in an adulatory sense, but just as he would have liked anyone else. Being at ease with himself put him at ease with the world.

In the Army there had been times when he longed for his music, for his little animals, and for the peace and interest of his laboratory. Coming home, forcing open the water-swollen door, was a pleasure and a pain to him. He sighed as he looked at his bookshelves. It took him ten minutes to decide which record to play first. And then the past was gone and he was faced with the future. Old Jingleballicks had kept the little business going in a manner even more inefficient than Doc had, and then had left it to founder. The stocks of preserved animals were depleted. The business contacts had lapsed. The bank that held his mortgage was no longer checked by patriotism. There was some question whether Doc could ever build back his marginal business. In the old days he would have forgotten such considerations in multiple pleasures and interests. Now discontent nibbled at him—not painfully, but constantly.

Where does discontent start? You are warm enough, but you shiver. You are fed, yet hunger gnaws you. You have been loved, but your yearning wanders in new fields. And to prod all these there's time, the bastard Time. The end of life is now not so terribly far away—you can see it the way you see the finish line when you come into the stretch—and your mind says, "Have I worked enough? Have I eaten enough? Have I loved enough?" All of these, of course, are the foundation of man's greatest curse, and perhaps his greatest glory. "What has my life meant so far, and what can it mean in the time left to me?" And now we're coming to the wicked, poisoned dart: "What have I contributed in the Great Ledger? What am I worth?" And this isn't vanity or ambition. Men seem to be born with a debt they can never pay, no matter how hard they try. It piles up ahead of them. Man owes something to man. If he ignores the debt it poisons him, and if he tries to make payments the debt only increases, and the quality of his gift is the measure of the man.

Doc's greatest talent had been his sense of paying as he went. The finish line had meant nothing to him except that he had wanted to crowd more living into the stretch. Each day ended with its night; each thought with its conclusion; and every morning a new freedom arose over the eastern mountains and lighted the world. There had never been any reason to suppose it would be otherwise. People made pilgrimages to the laboratory to bask in Doc's designed and lovely purposelessness. For what can a man accomplish that has not been done a million times before? What can he say that he will not find in Lao-Tse or the *Bhagavad-gita* or the Prophet Isaiah? It is better to sit in appreciative contemplation of a world in which beauty is eternally supported on a foundation of ugliness; cut out the support, and beauty will sink from sight. It was a good thing Doc had, and many people wished they had it too.

But now the worm of discontent was gnawing at him. Maybe it was the beginning of Doc's middle age that caused it—glands slackening their flow, skin losing its bloom, taste buds weakening, eyes not so penetrating, and hearing dulled a little. Or it might have been the new emptiness of Cannery Row—the silent machines, the rusting metal. Deep in himself Doc felt a failure. But he was a reasonably realistic man. He had his eyes examined, his teeth X-rayed. Dr. Horace Dormody went over him and discovered no secret focus of infection to cause the restlessness. And so Doc threw himself into his work, hoping, the way a man will, to smother the unease with weariness. He collected, preserved, injected, until his stock shelves were crowded again. New generations of cotton rats crawled on the wire netting of the cages, and four new rattlesnakes abandoned themselves to a life of captivity and ease.

But the discontent was still there. The pains that came to Doc were like a stir of uneasiness or the flick of a skipped heart-beat. Whisky lost its sharp delight and the first long pull of beer from a frosty glass was not the joy it had been. He stopped listening in the middle of an extended story. He was not genuinely glad to see a friend. And sometimes, starting to turn over a big rock in the Great Tide Pool—a rock under which he knew there would be a community of frantic animals—he would drop the rock back in place and stand, hands on hips, looking off to sea, where the round clouds piled up white with pink and black edges. And he would be thinking. What am I thinking? What do I want? Where do I want to go? There would be wonder in him, and a little impatience, as though he stood outside and looked in on himself through a glass shell. And he would be conscious of a tone within himself, or several tones, as though he heard music distantly.

Or it might be this way. In the late night Doc might be working at his old and battered microscope, delicately arranging plankton on a slide, moving them with a thread of glass. And there would be three voices singing in him, all singing together. The top voice of his thinking mind would sing, "What lovely little particles, neither plant nor animal, but somehow both—the reservoir of all the life in the world, the base supply of food for everyone. If all of these should die, every other living thing might well die as a consequence." The lower voice of his feeling mind would be singing, "What are you looking for, little man? Is it yourself you're trying to identify? Are you looking at little things to avoid big things?" And the third voice, which came from his marrow, would sing, "Lonesome! Lonesome! What good is it? Who benefits? Thought is the evasion of feeling. You're only walling up the leaking loneliness."

Sometimes he would leave his work and walk out to the lighthouse to watch the white flail of light strike at the horizons. Once there, of course, his mind would go back to the plankton, and he would think: It's a protein food, of course. If I could find a way to release this food directly to humans, why, nobody in the world would have to go hungry again. And the bottom voice would sing, "Lonesome, lonesome! You're trying to buy your way in."

Doc thought he was alone in his discontent, but he was not. Everyone on the Row observed him and worried about him. Mack and the boys worried about him. And Mack said to Fauna, "Doc acts like a guy that needs a dame."

"He can have the courtesy of the house any time," said Fauna.

"I don't mean that," said Mack. "He needs a dame around. He needs a dame to fight with. Why, that can keep a guy so goddam busy defending himself he ain't got no time to blame himself."

Fauna regarded marriage with a benevolent eye. Not only was

it a desirable social condition, but it sent her some of her best customers.

"Well, let's marry him off," said Fauna.

"Oh, no," said Mack. "I wouldn't go that far. My God! Not Doc!"

Doc tried to solve his problem in the ancient way. He took a long, leisurely trip to La Jolla, four hundred miles south. He travelled in the old manner, with lots of beer and a young lady companion whose interest in invertebrate zoology Doc thought might be flexible—and it was.

The whole trip was a success: weather calm and warm, tides low. Under the weed-wreathed boulders of the inter-tidal zone Doc found, by great good fortune, twenty-eight baby octopi with tentacles four or five inches long. It was a little bonanza for him if he could keep them alive. He handled them tenderly, put them in a wooden collecting bucket, and floated seaweed over them for protection. An excitement was growing in him.

His companion began to be a little disappointed. Doc's enthusiasm for the octopi indicated that he was not as flexible as she. And no girl likes to lose centre stage, particularly to an octopus. The four-hundred-mile trip back to Monterey was made in a series of short dashes, for Doc stopped every few miles to dampen the sack that covered the collecting bucket.

"Octopi can't stand heat," he said.

He recited no poetry to her. The subject of her eyes, her feelings, her skin, her thought, did not come up. Instead Doc told her about octopi—a subject that would have fascinated her two days before.

Doc said, "They're wonderful animals, delicate and complicated and shy."

"Ugly brutes," said the girl.

"No, not ugly," said Doc. "But I see why you say it. People have always been repelled and at the same time fascinated by octopi. Their eyes look baleful and cruel. And all kinds of myths have grown up around octopi too. You know the story of the kraken, of course."

"Of course," she said shortly.

"Octopi are timid creatures really," Doc said excitedly. "Most complicated. I'll show you when I get them in the aquarium. Of course there can't be any likeness, but they do have some traits that seem to be almost human. Mostly they hide and avoid trouble, but I've seen one deliberately murder another. They appear to feel terror too, and rage. They change colour when they're disturbed and angry, almost like the rage blush of a man."

"Very interesting," said the girl, and she tucked her skirt in around her knees.

Doc went on, "Sometimes they get so mad they collapse and die of something that parallels apoplexy. They're highly emotional animals. I'm thinking of writing a paper about them."

"You might find out what causes human apoplexy," said the girl, and because he wasn't listening for it, Doc didn't hear the satire in her tone.

There's no need for giving the girl a name. She never came back to Western Biological. Her interest in science blinked out like a candle, but a flame was lighted in Doc.

The flame of conception seems to flare and go out, leaving man shaken, and at once happy and afraid. There's plenty of precedent of course. Everyone knows about Newton's apple. Charles Darwin said his *Origin of Species* flashed complete in one second, and he spent the rest of his life backing it up; and the theory of relativity occurred to Einstein in the time it takes to clap your hands. This is the greatest mystery of the human mind—the inductive leap. Everything falls into place, irrelevancies relate, dissonance becomes harmony, and nonsense wears a crown of meaning. But the clarifying leap springs from the rich soil of confusion, and the leaper is not unfamiliar with pain.

The girl said good-bye and went away, and Doc did not know she was gone. For that matter, he did not know she had been with him.

With infinite care Doc scrubbed out a big aquarium, carpeted it with sea sand, and laid in stones populated with sponges and hydroids and anemones. He planted seaweeds and caught little crabs and eels and tide-pool Johnnys. He carried buckets of sea water from the beach and set up a pump to circulate the water from tank to aquarium and back. He considered every factor within his knowledge—relations of plant and animal life, food, filtering, oxygenation. He built an octopus world within walls of glass, trying to anticipate every octopus need and to eliminate every octopus enemy or danger. He considered light and heat.

Eight of his octopi were dead, but the twenty living ones scuttled to the bottom of their new home and hid themselves, throbbing and blushing with emotion. Doc drew a stool close and peered into the little world he had made, and his mind was filled with cool green thoughts and stately figures. For the moment he was at peace. The pale, expressionless eyes of the octopi seemed to be looking into his eyes.

In the days that followed, Doc's disposition was so unpredictable that Mack exhausted every other possibility before he moved in on Western Biological for the two dollars he thought he needed.

Mack's campaign was probably the most elaborate of his career. It began quietly, and only after a thorough preparation did it begin to take shape. Then spinnerets of emotion laced in and the heavy notes of tragic necessity began to be faintly heard. Drama grew, as it should, out of its inherent earth. Mack's voice was controlled and soft—no trembling yet—just a reasonable, clear, but potentially passionate growth. Mack knew he was doing well. He could hear himself, and he knew that if he were on the receiving end he would find it impossible not to weaken. Why, then, did not Doc turn his eyes from the dimly lit aquarium? He had certainly said "Hello" when Mack came in. A little shakily Mack cut in the *vox angelica*, the *vox dolorosa*, and finally a *bendiga stupenda* so moving that Mack himself was in tears.

Doc did not turn his head.

Mack stood stunned. It is a frightening thing to lay out everything you have, to finish, and have no response. He didn't know what to do next. He said loudly, "Doc!"

"Hello," said Doc.

"Don't you feel good?"

"Sure, Mack. How much do you want?"

"Two dollars."

Doc reached in his hip pocket for his wallet without lifting his eyes. Mack's great performance had been wasted. He might just as well have simply come in and asked for the money. He knew he could never reach such a height again. A sudden anger came over him, and he considered refusing the money, but his natural good sense saved him. He stood there rolling the dollar notes between his fingers. "What's got into you, Doc?" he asked.

Doc turned slowly towards him. "There's going to be one great difficulty," he said. "How am I going to light them? It's always a problem, but in this case it might be insuperable."

"Light what, Doc?"

"We start with two obvious problems," Doc continued. "First, they can't stand heat, and second, they are to a certain extent photophobic. I don't know how I'm going to get enough cold light on them. Would it be possible, do you suppose, to condition them, to light them constantly, so that the photophobia subsides?"

"Oh, sure," said Mack uneasily.

"Don't be too sure," said Doc. "The very process of conditioning might, if it did not kill them, change their normal reactions. It's always difficult to evaluate responses that approximate emotions. If I place them in an abnormal situation, can I trust the response to be normal?"

"No," said Mack.

"You cannot dissect for emotion," Doc went on. "If a human body were found by another species and dissected, there would be no possible way of knowing about its emotions or its thoughts. Now, it occurs to me that the rage, or rather the symptom that seems like rage, must be fairly abnormal in itself. I have seen it happen in aquariums. Does it occur on the sea bottom? Is the observed phenomenon not perhaps limited to the aquarium? No, I can't permit myself to believe that, or my whole thesis fails."

"Doc!" Mack cried. "Look, Doc, it's me—Mack!"

"Hello, Mack," said Doc. "How much did you say?"

"You've already give it to me," said Mack, and he felt like a fool the moment he'd said it.

"I need better equipment," said Doc. "Goddam it, I can't see without better equipment."

"Doc, how's about you and me stepping over and getting a half-pint of Old Tennis Shoes?"

"Fine," said Doc.

"I'll buy," said Mack. "I've got a couple of loose bucks."

Doc said sharply, "I'll have to get some money. Where can I get some money, Mack?"

"I told you, I'll buy, Doc."

"I'll need a wide-angle binocularscope and light. I'll have to find out about light—maybe a pinpoint spot from across the room. No, they'd move out of that. Maybe there are new kinds of lights. I'll have to look into it."

"Come on, Doc."

Doc bought a pint of Old Tennis Shoes and later sent Mack out with money to buy another pint. The two of them sat in the laboratory side by side, staring into the aquarium, resting their elbows on the shelf, and they got to the point where they were mixing a little water with the whisky.

"I got an uncle with an eye like them," said Mack. "Rich old bastard too. I wonder why, when you get rich, you get a cold eye."

"Self-protection," said Doc solemnly. "Conditioned by relatives, I guess."

"Like I was saying, Doc. Everybody in the Row is worried about you. You don't have no fun. You wander around like you was lost."

"I guess it's reorientation," said Doc.

"Well, some people think you need a dame to kind of nudge you out of it. I know a guy that every time he gets feeling low he goes back to his wife. Makes him appreciate what he had. He goes away again and feels just fine."

"Shock therapy," said Doc. "I'm all right, Mack. Don't let anybody get me a wife, though—don't let them give me a wife! I guess a man needs a direction. That's what I've been needing. You can only go in circles so long."

"I kind of like it that way," said Mack.

"I'm going to call my paper 'Symptoms in Some Cephalopods Approximating Apoplexy'."

"Great God Almighty!" said Mack.

CHAPTER IV

THERE WOULD BE NO GAME

As he got to know him, Joseph and Mary regarded Doc with something akin to love—for love feeds on the unknown and unknowable. Doc's honesty was exotic to Joseph and Mary. He found it strange. It attracted him in spite of the fact that he could not understand it. He felt that there was something he had missed, though he could not figure what it was.

One day, sitting in Western Biological, Joseph and Mary saw a chess-board and, finding that it was a game and being good at games, he asked Doc to teach him. J. and M. easily absorbed the characters and qualities of castles and bishops and knights and royalty and pawns. During the first game Doc was called to the telephone, and when he returned he said, "You've moved a pawn of mine and your queen and knight."

"How'd you know?" the Patrón asked.

"I know the game," said Doc. "Look, Joseph and Mary, chess is probably the only game in the world in which it is impossible to cheat."

Joseph and Mary inspected this statement with amazement. "Why not?" he demanded.

"If it were possible to cheat there would be no game," said Doc.

J. and M. carried this away with him. It bothered him at night. He looked at it from all angles. And he went back to ask more about it. He was charmed with the idea, but he couldn't understand it.

Doc explained patiently, "Both players know exactly the same things. The game is played in the mind."

"I don't get it."

"Well, look! You can't cheat in mathematics or poetry or music because they're based on truth. Untruth or cheating is just foreign, it has no place. You can't cheat in arithmetic."

Joseph and Mary shook his head. "I don't get it," he said.

It was a shocking conception, and he was drawn to it because, in a way, its outrageousness seemed to him like a new, strange way of cheating. In the back of his mind an idea stirred. Suppose you took honesty and made a racket of it—it might be the toughest of all to break. It was so new to him that his mind recoiled from it, but still it wouldn't let him alone. His eyes narrowed. "Maybe he's worked out a system," he said to himself.

CHAPTER V

ENTER SUZY

It is popular to picture a small-town constable as dumb and clumsy. In the books he plays the stock bumpkin part. And people retain this attitude even when they know it's not true. We have so many beliefs we know are not true.

A constable, if he has served for a few years, knows more about his town than anyone else and on all levels. He is aware of the delicate political balance between mayor and councilmen, Fire Department and insurance companies. He knows why Mrs. Geltham is giving a big party and who is likely to be there. Usually he knows, when Mabel Andrews reports a burglar, whether it is a rat in the dining-room, a burglar, or just wishful thinking. A constable knows that Mr. Geltham is sleeping with the schoolteacher and how often. He knows when high-school boys have switched from gin to marijuana. He is aware of every ripple on the town's surface. If there is a crime the constable usually knows who didn't do it and often who did. With a good constable on duty a hundred things don't happen that might. Sometimes there's a short discussion in an alley; sometimes a telephone call; sometimes only his shadow under a street light. When he gets a cat down out of a tree he knows all about the owner of the cat. And many weeping, parent-prodded little boys and girls put small things, stolen from the Five-and-Dime, in the constable's hands, and he, if he is a good constable, gives them a sense of mercy-in-justice without injuring the dignity of the law.

A stranger getting off the Del Monte Express in Monterey wouldn't be aware that his arrival was noted, but if something happened that night he would know it all right.

Monterey's Joe Blaikey was a good constable. He wouldn't ever be chief—didn't much want to be. Everybody in town liked Joe and trusted him. He was the only man in town who could stop a husband-and-wife fight. He came by his techniques in both social life and in violence from being the youngest of fifteen nice but violent children. Just getting along at home had been his teacher. Joe knew everyone in Monterey and he could size up a stranger almost instantly.

When a girl named Suzy got off the Greyhound bus, she looked up and down the street, fixed her lipstick, then lifted her beat-up suitcase and headed for the Golden Poppy Restaurant,. Suzy was a pretty girl with a flat nose and a wide mouth. She had a good figure, was twenty-one, five-feet-five, hair probably brown (dyed blonde), brown cloth coat, rabbit-skin collar, cotton print dress, brown calf shoes (heel taps a little run over), scuff on the right toe. She limped slightly on her right foot. Before she picked up her suitcase she opened her brown purse of simulated leather. In it were mirror, comb with two teeth missing, Lucky Strikes, matchbook that said "Hotel Rosaline, San Francisco", half-packet of Peppermint Life Savers, eighty-five cents in silver, no folding money, lipstick but no powder, tin box of aspirin, no keys.

If there had been a murder that night Joe Blaikey could have written all that down, but now he wasn't even aware that he knew it. Joe acted pretty much by instinct. He got into the Golden Poppy just as the waitress was putting a cup of coffee on the counter in front of Suzy.

Joe slipped on to the stool next to her. "Hi, Ella," he said to the waitress. "Cup of coffee."

"Coming up," said Ella. "How's your wife, Joe?"

"Oh, pretty good. Wish she'd get her strength back, though."

"Takes it out of you," said Ella. "Man can't understand that. Give her a tonic and let her rest. I'll have fresh coffee in a minute if you want to wait."

"Yeah," said Joe.

Ella went to the head of the counter, put coffee in the Silex and filled the bowl.

Joe said quietly to Suzy, "What's on your mind, sister?"

"Not a thing," said Suzy. She didn't look at him but she could see him in the shine of a malted machine behind the counter.

"Vacation?"

"Sure."

"How long?"

"Don't know."

"Looking for a job?"

"Maybe."

Ella started towards them, saw what was happening, and got busy at the other end of the counter.

Joe asked, "Know anybody here?"

"I got an aunt here."

"What's her name?"

"That your business?"

"Yep."

"All right, I got no aunt."

Joe smiled at her, and Suzy felt better. She liked a guy who was worried about his wife.

He said to her, "On the bum?"
"Not yet," said Suzy. "You gonna give me trouble, mister?"
"Not if I can help it," said Joe. "You got a Social Security card?"
"Lost it," said Suzy.
Joe said, "It's a tough town. All organized. Don't work the street. The authorities won't have it. If you need a buck to blow town, come to me. My name's Joe Blaikey."
"Thanks, Joe. But I ain't hustling, honest."
"Not yet, you ain't," said Joe. "It's a hell of a town to get a job in since the canneries closed. Take it easy." He stood up and stretched. "I'll get the coffee later, Ella," he said and went out.
Ella's work seemed to be all done. She mopped the counter with a damp cloth. "Swell fella," she said. "More coffee? Fresh is ready."
"Seemed like," said Suzy. "Yeah."
Ella brought a fresh cup. "Where you staying?"
"Don't know yet."
"My sister rents rooms—pretty nice. Four dollars a week. I can give her a ring, see if she's got one vacant."
"I think I'll look around town a little," said Suzy. "Say, mind if I leave my suitcase here? It's kind of heavy."
"Sure. I'll put it back of the counter here."
"Well, s'pose you're off shift when I come back?"
Ella looked levelly at Suzy. "Sister," she said, "I ain't never off shift."
Suzy looked in at the store windows on Alvadoro Street and then she went to the wharf and watched the fishing-boats at their moorings. A school of tiny fish always lay in the shade of the pier and two little boys fished with hand lines and never caught anything. About four o'clock she strolled along deserted Cannery Row, bought a package of Lucky Strikes at the grocery, glanced casually at Western Biological, and knocked on the door of the Bear Flag.
Fauna received her in the combination bedroom and office.
"I'll tell you the truth," said Fauna, "business ain't been good. It may pick up some in June. I wish I could put you on. Ain't you got a hard-luck story that would kind of sway me?"
"Nope," said Suzy.
"You broke?"
"Yep."
"But you don't make nothing of it." Fauna leaned back in her swivel chair and squinted her eyes. "I used to work a Mission," she said. "I know hard-luck stories from both ends. I guess if you laid all the hard luck I've heard end to end, why, the Bible would look short. And some of them stories was true. Now, I could make a guess about you."
Suzy sat silent—posture, hands, face, noncommittal.

"Lousy home," said Fauna. "Fighting all the time. Probably you wasn't more than fifteen or sixteen when you married the guy, maybe he wouldn't. Done it just to get away from the fighting."

Suzy made no reply.

Fauna looked away so that she wouldn't see the hands slowly grip each other. "Got in a family way right off," said Fauna. "That made the guy restless, and he powdered. What did you say?"

"I didn't say nothing," said Suzy.

"Where's the baby?"

"I lost it."

"Do you hate the guy?"

"I got nothing to say," said Suzy.

"Okay with me. I ain't really very interested. There's some dames born for this business. Some are too lazy to work and some hate men. Don't hardly none of them enjoy what they're doing. That would be like a bar-tender that loves to drink. You don't look like a natural-born hustler to me. You ain't lazy. Why don't you get a job?"

"I worked waitress and I worked Five-and-Dime. Only difference is, you get took to a movie instead of three bucks," said Suzy.

"You trying to make a stake?"

"Maybe."

"Got a boy?"

"Nope."

"Hate boys?"

"Nope."

Fauna sighed. "You got me, sister. I can feel myself being got. You're a tough kid. Doing your own time, like an old con. I like that. It works better with me than a hard-luck story. Tell me, you hot?"

"Huh?"

"Under raps, I mean. Anybody got anything on you?"

"Nope."

"Ever done time?"

"Once. Thirty days. Vagrancy."

"Nothing else on the blotter?"

"Nope."

"Can you give off a smile? You'd freeze the customers."

Suzy grinned at Fauna.

"Good God Almighty!" said Fauna. "You look like somebody's sister! I'm afraid you'll cost me. Why do I have to be a push-over? Ever worked a house?"

"Nope."

"Well, it ain't as bad as the street. Doc Wilkins will be in to-morrow."

Suzy asked, "Can I get my suitcase?"

"I guess so." Fauna opened a wallet on her desk. "J. C. Penney's is open till six. Get yourself a dress—fancy but cheap. Get a new toothbrush. And when you come back, for God's sake go to work on your hair. You could be a good-looking kid if you worked it up."

"I been riding a bus," said Suzy.

"That'll do it," said Fauna. "We eat at half-past six. How long since you ate?"

"Yesterday."

"Beef stew to-night, creamed carrots, cherry Jello for dessert."

On her way to the door Suzy paused and her hand patted the door-frame. "Cop worked me over to-day," she said. "Name's Joe Blaikey."

"He's a nice fella. Why, he'd lend you dough," said Fauna.

"That's what he said," Suzy replied. "I love beef stew."

. . . . .

At the Golden Poppy, Ella handed the suitcase over the counter. "You look like a kid with a job," said Ella.

"Looks like. Say, where's J. C. Penney?"

"Turn right and go a block and a half. Yellow front. Be seeing you."

"Sure," said Suzy.

On the sidewalk Joe Blaikey fell in step beside her and took her suitcase from her hand. "That's a good woman," he said. "You just keep your nose clean and you'll be all right."

"How'd you know?" Suzy asked.

"She called me," said Joe. "See you around."

"Okay," said Suzy.

She took her suitcase from him and turned into J. C. Penney's.

"Can I help you?"

"Dress. Not too dear."

"Over here."

"I like that tomatoey one."

"That's a new shade, 'Love Apples'."

"Tomato colour."

"It's rayon. It'll give you good service."

"It better. Size twelve."

"Shoes to match?"

Suzy took a very deep breath. "Yes, by God!" she said.

CHAPTER VI

THE CREATIVE CROSS

FOR DAYS the flame burned in Doc, his phoenix thought. True, he didn't have a proper microscope, but he had eyes, and he had, thank God, an analytic mind that could slough off sensations, emotions, pains. As he stared at the octopi his thesis took form. With a glass needle he stimulated one to fear and rage until it attacked and killed its brother. He removed one passive octopus to a separate jar where he subjected it to mild solutions of menthol, of Epsom salts, sickening it a little and then bringing it back to health again. Then he aroused rage, and when the body colours pulsed and changed he introduced a small amount of cocaine sulphate and saw the emotion disappear into sleep, if you can say an octopus sleeps. Then he aroused it with saline and touched it here and there with the frustrating needle, noted the flush, the growing intensity of colour, the uncertain whipping and groping of the arms, until suddenly it collapsed and died. Doc removed the body and dissected the tissue, trying to find burst vesicles.

"It works!" he said aloud. "I haven't proper equipment to see how it happens, but this animal dies with the appearance of apoplexy. There must be leakage even if I can't see it. I can start my paper with observation."

Doc bought a package of yellow pads and two dozen pencils. He laid them out on his desk, the pencils sharpened to needle points and lined up like yellow soldiers. At the top of a page he printed: OBSERVATIONS AND SPECULATIONS. His pencil point broke. He took up another and drew lace around the O and the B, made a block letter of the S and put fish-hooks on each end. His ankle itched. He rolled down his sock and scratched, and that made his ear itch. "Someone's talking about me," he said and looked at the yellow pad. He wondered whether he had fed the cotton rats. It is easy to forget when you're thinking.

Watching the rats scrabble for the food he gave them, Doc remembered that he had not eaten. When he finished a page or two he would fry some eggs. But wouldn't it be better to eat first so that his flow of thought would not be interrupted later? For some days he had looked forward to this time of peace, of unbroken thought. These were the answer to his restlessness: peace and the life of the mind. It would be better to eat first. He fried two eggs and ate them, staring at the yellow pad under the hanging light. The light was too bright. It reflected painfully on the paper. Doc finished his eggs, got out a sheet of tracing paper, and taped it to the bottom of the shade below the globe. It took time to make it neat. He sat in front of the yellow pad again and drew lace around all the letters of the title, tore off the page, and threw it away. Five pencil points were broken now. He sharpened them and lined them up with their brothers.

A car drove up in front of the Bear Flag. Doc went to the window and looked out. No one he knew, but he saw Mack go into the grocery. He remembered he wanted to ask Mack something.

It's always hard to start to concentrate. The mind darts like a chicken, trying to escape thinking even though thinking is the most rewarding function of man. Doc could take care of this. When you know what you're doing you can handle it. He set his jaw and was starting to turn back to his desk when he saw out of the corners of his eyes the flash of a skirt. He looked out of the window again. A girl had come out of the Bear Flag and was walking along Cannery Row towards Monterey. Doc couldn't see her face, but she had a fine walk, thigh and knee and ankle swinging free and proud, no jerk and totter the way so many women walked as they fell from step to step. No, this girl walked with her shoulders back and her chin up and her arms swinging in rhythm. It's a gay walk, Doc thought. You can tell so much by a walk—discouragement or sickness, determination. There are squinched-up mean walks and blustering walks, shy creeping walks, but this was a gay walk, as though the walker were going happily to a meeting with someone she loved. There was pride in the walk too, but not vanity. Doc hoped she would not turn the corner, but she did. There was a flick of skirt and she was gone. But Doc could see in his mind her swinging limbs, the melody of her lithe, swift movement. Probably ugly as a mud fence, he thought, and then he laughed at himself. "That's full circle," he said. "Mind, I congratulate you. You jumped me to sex, translated it to aesthetics, and ended with sour grapes. How dishonest can I be? And all because I don't want to go to work. I'll work my head off to avoid work. Come, mind. This time you don't get away with it—back to the desk."

He picked up a pencil and wrote, "The observed specimens were twenty small octopi taken in the inter-tidal zone near the town of La Jolla. Specimens were placed in a large aquarium under conditions as nearly approximating their natural habitat as possible. Sea water was continuously filtered and replaced every twenty-four hours. Animals from a typical ecological community were introduced, together with sand, rock, and algæ taken from the collecting point. Small crustaceans were supplied. In spite of precautions, five individuals died within one week. The remaining fifteen seemed to become acclimatized and readily captured and consumed the small grapsoid crabs placed in the aquarium. The lights——" His pencil point broke. He took another, and it broke with a jerk, making a little tear in the paper. He read what he had written; dull, desiccated, he thought. Why should I presume that an animal so far removed from the human—perhaps I'm fooling myself. The middle voice sang subtly, "Looking for yourself in the water—searching, little man, among the hydroids for your soul—looking for contentment in vanity. Are you better than Mack that you should use the secret priestly words of science to cover the fact that you have nothing to say?"

And the bottom voice mourned, "Lonesome! Lonesome! Let me up into the light and warmth. Lonesome!"

Doc jumped up and went to the aquarium and stared into the lighted water. From under a rock an octopus looked out and one of its arms flicked rhythmically, as though it led an orchestra, and the beat was gay and free and fluid—like the swinging thigh and knee and ankle.

Doc put his face in the palm of his hand and pressed blackness on his eyes until specks of green and red light swarmed on his vision. And then he got up and went across the street for beer.

CHAPTER VII

TINDER IS AS TINDER DOES

Joseph and Mary Rivas liked Fauna, even admired her. But he did feel it was a little indecent for a woman to own the Bear Flag, a paying institution with a steady income. Operate it, yes, but not own it. The proprieties told Joseph and Mary there should be a man in the background to drain off the profits. It was his observation that when women had access to money they got nervous. To his mind, a healthy woman was a broke woman. A dame with money was a kind of half-arsed man. She stopped working at being a woman, and, as everybody knows, the finest thing about a woman is that she is a woman.

Joseph and Mary had given some thought to relieving Fauna of the responsibility of the profits: if he owned the Bear Flag and Fauna ran it, there would be a natural and practical balance. Fauna had so far figured her way out from under his philanthropy, but Joseph and Mary did not give up, particularly when it was no trouble not to.

A good stock manipulator reads the financial page and looks for the stock he has, but he also notices other quotations too, just in case. Joseph and Mary kept that kind of eye on the Bear Flag. He felt that some day Fauna might look away from the dealer for a moment. Now that his own affairs ran smoothly, he was able to cast a benevolently rapacious eye about him. He knew about Suzy before she had even got her clothes washed, and he felt Fauna was slipping.

"You got a quail there," he told Fauna. "That's Mary trouble if I ever seen it."

"I guess so," said Fauna.

"Why'd you take her on?"

"I let myself make a mistake once in a while," said Fauna. "She ain't a good hustler, but when I get through with her she might make somebody a damn fine wife."

"She's making a patsy of you," said the Patrón.

"People got to be a patsy now and then," said Fauna. "You never feel real good if you never been a sucker. Once I went missionary down in South America."

"Why?" asked the Patrón.

"Can't remember right off."

"What did you do?"

"Taught them to love one another."

"What did you do?"

"Taught me to shrink heads."

"Savages!" said the Patrón.

"No, they wasn't. Them head-hunters was pretty nice people—honest too. When they sell you a head they give good value. But there's always a wise guy. Like this Athatoolagooloo—a natural-born head-hustler. He'd worked out a way to push monkey heads. Gave them a close shave, didn't have to shrink them much. There's people will buy anything."

"I know," said the Patrón.

"Well, the Bishop come through," said Fauna, "and he give me holy hell for buying up them monkey heads."

"You mean to say *you* bought them?" said the Patrón.

"Sure I bought them. I got a box of them in the wood-shed. Everybody said I was a fool, but it paid off."

"How'd it pay off?"

"Well, look," said Fauna. "My bunch was honest and they shrunk honest heads. S'pose a shipment goes out and this joker Athatoolagooloo slips in a couple of his monkey heads—pretty soon nobody don't trust nobody. Why, people would get to looking arsepants at a real nice head. I bought them up to keep them off the market. I had my reputation to think of."

"Yeah, but this joker——" the Patrón began.

"I know what you're going to say—and he done it too. He had me. He charged me more for them monkey heads than I paid for the real article. He knew he had me."

"That's what I thought. Anybody would," said the Patrón.

"Oh, it all worked out," said Fauna. "If you ever buy a Chungla head you'll know you got the best."

"Yeah, but how about the joker?" said the Patrón.

Fauna opened up her desk drawer and took out a beautiful little item, black as polished ebony and no bigger than a lemon. "He made up real nice, didn't he?" said Fauna.

The Patrón looked nervously away. "I got to get back," he said. "I left my nephew in the store."

"Don't he play trumpet?"

"Drives me crazy," said Joseph and Mary. "Got a new trumpet. Can't get away from it. Made him go practise down on the beach. Figured the waves and the sea-lions would kind of drown him out. The other night he give a passing signal to a Navy tug, and they're still looking for what passed them. But last night was the worst. He was practising down on the beach and he aimed his damn trumpet into that sewer pipe. Got resonance, he said. I don't know if it's true, but I heard that every toilet in the whole neighbourhood give off with 'Stormy Weather'. Old lady Somers was taking an enema. I don't believe what they said happened. I got to get back. That kid can break glass with a high note."

"Come over and visit again," said Fauna.

"You mind what I said about Suzy."

"I will," said Fauna.

It's a funny thing, but you never like to trade at your own place. The store across the street has always got fresher cigarettes than you have. The girls at the Bear Flag never got cigarettes from the slot machine at the Bear Flag. When they wanted Luckies or a 7 Up they went to the Patrón's. For that matter, nearly everyone in Cannery Row went nearly every place in Cannery Row nearly every day.

Joseph and Mary had hardly got back to the grocery before Suzy came in. You wouldn't recommend Joseph and Mary as a celebrator of God's loveliest creation, but if you wanted a quick assay on a babe you couldn't ask for better than Joseph and Mary's. If he was not involved in an emotional way he was good. Between the time Suzy got change and the time she pushed the Lucky Strike button on his cigarette machine, each had gone over the other and registered the result.

Suzy's note: "Greaseball, smart and mean. Look out if he gives you something. A percentage boy. Smiles with his mouth. Eyes like a snake. May trip himself some day by being too smart."

Patrón's note: "Lousy risk for a house. A character. Won't play the rules. Might reverse the field. Too friendly. If she likes a guy she might toss in her roll."

The Patrón would have kicked her out of the Bear Flag. He knew that the only person you can trust is an absolutely selfish person. He always runs true to form. You know everything he'll do. But you take somebody with an underlying kindness, and he might fool you. The only satisfactory sucker is the one who is entirely selfish. Fauna was laying herself wide open.

Joseph and Mary tabulated Suzy the way he might have bought a used car. Pretty good figure, good ankles and legs, too light in the butt and too heavy in the chest. That's a bad sign: a good hustler is flat-chested. Face kind of pretty if she felt like it. Face reflected how she felt. Good-looking if she felt good. A good hustler has a mask, looks the same to everybody, pretty, but you don't remember what she looked like the next morning. Suzy you wouldn't forget. A real bad risk. Suzy liked people or she didn't like them. That in itself was bad.

Cacahuete, the Patrón's nephew, was dusting shelves, and he flashed a gold smile at Suzy.

Suzy lighted up. She didn't smile—she grinned. Her lips were full and her mouth wide, and when she grinned her eyes crinkled and something warm and scary came out of her. That's a bad risk. On top of this was toughness, but not dependable, dull toughness. Suzy might take a poke at Jack Dempsey. She wasn't smart. All in all, Joseph and Mary would've dumped Suzy in a minute. She'd be the kind of dumb dame who'd fall for some guy without finding out his bank balance. She was the kind, he thought, who'd give one guy a helluva lot of trouble but who'd be lousy playing the field. She had something of the same quality Doc had. The Patrón decided to warn Fauna again. This kid could be pure murder in a hook-shop. Such was the Patrón's reasoned opinion, and the Patrón was a professional. If you'd take a doctor's advice about a disease, you'd surely take the Patrón's about a hustler. Both could be wrong, of course.

The appraisals and judgments were almost instantaneous, so that by the time Suzy had opened her cigarettes, put one in her mouth, and lighted it, the judgment was complete.

"How are you?" Joseph and Mary asked.

"Okay," said Suzy. "Fauna wants some yellow pads and a couple of pencils—soft pencils."

The Patrón laid them out. "She does a lot of writing," he said. "She's used six pads in about a month."

"She's doing astrology."

"You believe that stuff?"

"No, but it don't do no harm."

"I knew a guy made a good living with it," said the Patrón.

"Oh, she don't charge nothing," said Suzy.

"I know," said the Patrón. "I can't figure why not. Fauna ain't dumb."

"She sure ain't," said Suzy.

Doc came in with two empty beer bottles. "Get a couple of cold ones back on the ice, will you?" he asked.

Suzy glanced at him, took him in, and looked away. His beard shocked her a little. She didn't stare at him, the way you don't stare at a cripple.

The Patrón said, "Why don't you put in an ice-box? Then you can take a case at a time."

"It's easier to let you keep the ice," said Doc.

"You know Suzy here? She's new at the Bear Flag."

"How do you do," said Doc.

"How do you do," said Suzy. She would have said "Hi" to anyone else.

When Doc had gone the Patrón said, "That's a funny guy."

"It takes all kinds," said Suzy.

"He knows stuff I ain't even heard of." The Patrón was defending Doc the way everyone did.

"Kind of hoity-toity?" asked Suzy.

"Hell no! That's the way he always talks. He don't know no other way."

"Well, I guess it takes all kinds," said Suzy.

"He gets bugs and stuff out of the ocean and sells them."

"Who to?"

"Why, there's people'll buy anything," said the Patrón.

"I guess so. Why don't other people do it?"

"Too much work, and you got to know what to get."

"Say, why does he wear that beard? I used to know a wrestler wore one."

"I don't know why," said the Patrón. "Why'd the wrestler?"

"Thought it made him look tough."

"Well, maybe Doc's the same—but no, he don't want to be tough." The Patrón went on, "In the Army they made a guy with a beard shave it off. Said a guy with a beard wanted to be different, and the best way to not get along in the barracks is to be different."

"Maybe that's it," said Suzy. "I don't mind a different guy if he ain't too different."

"Dames can take it," said the Patrón. "They don't like it but they can take it. What the hell am I doing all this talking for? I got work to do!"

Suzy asked, "You Mexican?"

"American. My old man was Mexican."

"Can you talk that spick talk?"

"Sure."

"Polly-voo?"

"That ain't the same kind," said the Patrón.

"Be seeing you," said Suzy, and she went out and let the screen door slam.

She ain't a bad kid, the Patrón thought, but I'd sure kick her the hell out of the Bear Flag.

Doc looked out of the window of Western Biological. He watched Suzy walk past the vacant lot and up to the front porch of the Bear Flag. Just as she was about to climb the steps she turned and looked around. She thought someone was looking at her. She didn't see Doc.

CHAPTER VIII

THE GREAT ROQUE WAR

Pacific Grove and Monterey sit side by side on a hill bordering the bay. The two towns touch shoulders but they are not alike. Whereas Monterey was founded a long time ago by foreigners, Indians and Spaniards and such, and the town grew up higgledy-piggledy without plan or purpose, Pacific Grove sprang full-blown from the iron heart of a psycho-ideo-legal religion. It was formed as a retreat in the 1880's and came fully equipped with laws, ideals, and customs. On the town's statute books a deed is void if liquor is ever brought on the property. As a result, the sale of iron-and-wine tonic is fantastic. Pacific Grove has a law that requires you to pull your blinds down after sundown, and forbids you to pull them down before. Scorching on bicycles is forbidden, as is sea bathing and boating on Sundays. There is one crime which is not defined but which is definitely against the law. Hijinks are or is forbidden. It must be admitted that most of these laws are not enforced to the hilt. The fence that once surrounded the Pacific Grove retreat is no longer in existence.

Once during its history, Pacific Grove was in trouble, deep trouble. You see, when the town was founded many old people moved to the retreat, people you'd think didn't have anything to retreat from. These old people became grumpy after a while and got to interfering in everything and causing trouble, until a philanthropist named Deems presented the town with two roque courts.

Roque is a complicated kind of croquet, with narrow wickets and short-handled mallets. You play off the side-lines, like billiards. Very complicated, it is. They say it develops character.

In a local sport there must be competition and a prize. In Pacific Grove a cup was given every year for the winning team on the roque courts. You wouldn't think a thing like that would work up much heat, particularly since most of the contestants were over seventy. But it did.

One of the teams was called the Blues and the other the Greens. The old men wore little skull-caps and striped blazers in their team colours.

Well, it wasn't more than two years before all hell broke loose. The Blues would practise in the court right alongside the Greens but they wouldn't speak to them. And then it got into the families of the teams. You were a Blue family or a Green family. Finally the feeling spread outside the family. You were a partisan of the Blues or a partisan of the Greens. It got so that the Greens tried to discourage intermarriage with the Blues, and vice versa. Pretty soon it reached into politics, so that a Green wouldn't think of voting for a Blue. It split the church right down the middle. The Blues and the Greens wouldn't sit on the same side. They made plans to build separate churches.

Of course everything got really hot at tournament time. Things were very touchy. Those old men brought a passion to the game you wouldn't believe. Why, two octogenarians would walk away into the woods and you'd find them locked in mortal combat. They even developed secret languages so that each wouldn't know what the other was talking about.

Well, things got so hot and feeling ran so high that the country had to take notice of it. A Blue got his house burned down and then a Green was found clubbed to death with a roque mallet in the woods. A roque mallet is short-handled and heavy and can be a very deadly weapon. The old men got to carrying mallets tied to their wrists by thongs, like battle-axes. They didn't go any place without them. There wasn't any crime each didn't charge the other with, including things they'd outgrown and couldn't have done if they'd wanted to. The Blues wouldn't trade in Green stores. The whole town was a mess.

The original benefactor, Mr. Deems, was a nice old fellow. He used to smoke a little opium, when it was legal, and this kept him healthy and rested so that he didn't get high blood-pressure or tuberculosis. He was a benevolent man, but he was also a philosopher. When he saw what he had created by giving the roque courts to the Pacific Grove retreat he was saddened, and later horrified. He said he knew how God felt.

The tournament came on July 30, and feeling was so bad that people were carrying pistols. Blue kids and Green kids had gang wars. Mr. Deems, after a period of years, finally figured that as long as he felt like God he might as well act like God. There was too much violence in town.

On the night of July 29, Mr. Deems sent out a bull-dozer. In the morning, where the roque courts had been there was only a deep, ragged hole in the ground. If he'd had time he would have continued God's solution. He'd have filled the hole with water.

They ran Mr. Deems out of Pacific Grove. They would have tarred and feathered him if they could have caught him, but he was safe in Monterey, cooking his yen shi over a peanut-oil lamp.

Every July 30, to this day, the whole town of Pacific Grove gets together and burns Mr. Deems in effigy. They make a celebration of it, dress up a life-size figure, and hang it from a pine tree. Later they burn it. People march underneath with torches, and the poor, helpless figure of Mr. Deems goes up in smoke every year.

There are people who will say that this whole account is a lie, but a thing isn't necessarily a lie even if it didn't necessarily happen.

CHAPTER IX

WHOM THE GODS LOVE THEY DRIVE NUTS

To a casual observer, Cannery Row might have seemed a series of self-contained and selfish units, each functioning alone with no reference to the others. There was little visible connection between La Ida's, the Bear Flag, the grocery (still known as Lee Chong's Heavenly Flower Grocery), the Palace Flop-house, and Western Biological Laboratories. The fact is that each was bound by gossamer threads of steel to all the others—hurt one, and you aroused vengeance in all. Let sadness come to one, and all wept.

Doc was more than first citizen of Cannery Row. He was healer of the wounded soul and the cut finger. Strongly entrenched in legality though he was, he found himself constantly edged into infringements by the needs of his friends, and anyone could hustle him for a buck without half trying. When trouble came to Doc it was everybody's trouble.

What was Doc's trouble? Even he didn't know. He was deeply,

grievingly unhappy. For hours on end he sat at his desk with a yellow pad before him and his needle-sharp pencils lined up. Sometimes his waste-basket was full of crushed, scribbled pages, and at others not even a doodle went down. Then he would move to the aquarium and stare into it. And his voices howled and cried and moaned. "Write!" said his top voice, and "Search!" sang his middle voice, and his lowest voice sighed, "Lonesome! Lonesome!" He did not go down without a struggle. He resurrected old love affairs, he swam deep in music, he read the *Sorrows of Werther*; but the voices would not leave him. The beckoning yellow pages became his enemies. One by one the octopi died in the aquarium. He had worn thin the excuse of his lack of a proper microscope. When the last octopus died, he leaped on this as his excuse. When his friends visited him he would explain. "You see, I can't go on without specimens, and I can't get any more until the spring tides. As soon as I have specimens and a new microscope I can whip the paper right off."

His friends sensed his pain and caught it and carried it away with them. They knew the time was coming when they would have to do something.

In the Palace Flop-house a little meeting occurred—occurred, because no one called it, no one planned it, and yet everyone knew what it was about.

Wide Ida brooded hugely. The Bear Flag was represented by Agnes, Mabel, and Becky. All the boys were accounted for. The meeting began casually and obliquely, as all meetings should.

Hazel said, "Wide Ida throwed out a drunk last night and sprained her shoulder."

"I ain't as young as I used to be," Wide Ida said gloomily.

"The drunk dared her," said Hazel. "He didn't even touch the sidewalk going out. If they was an Olympic event for A. and C., Wide Ida would win it easy."

"Sprained my shoulder up," said Wide Ida.

They kept skirting their problem.

Mack said, "How's Fauna been?"

"Pretty good. She got problems," said Agnes.

Becky was delicately picking off nail polish. "That Fauna," she said, "she's a wonder. She's giving us table-setting lessons. I bet if they was thirty-five forks, she'd know what every one of them was for."

"Ain't they to eat with?" Hazel asked.

"Jesus, what a ignorant!" said Becky. "I bet you don't know a dessert fork from a hole in the ground."

Hazel said belligerently, "You know what a Jackson fork is for?"

"No, what?"

"Just leave it lay and see who's a ignorant," said Hazel.

Wide Ida asked, "Any change with Doc?"

"No," said Mack. "I went over to see him last night. I wisht there was something we could do."

They fell to musing. If the times were hard on Doc, they were equally hard on his friends who loved him. Once he had been infallible. There was nothing he could not do because there was nothing he wanted to do very much. And in spite of themselves a little contempt for him was growing in his friends—a kind and loving contempt that might never have happened if he had not once been so great. People who had once spoken his name with awe now felt better than he because he was no better than they.

"I ain't got an idea's how to proceed," said Mack.

Hazel said, "How's about if we ask Fauna to do his horoscope? She's doing me right now."

"You ain't got no future," said Mack.

"I have too," said Hazel. "I bet Fauna could tell us what to do about Doc."

Mack looked interested. "It's better than nothing," he said. "Hoc sunt. Eddie, you dig up one of them kegs you buried during the war. Hazel, you ask Fauna to come over for a drink. Tell her to bring her star stuff."

"Maybe she's got me finished," said Hazel.

It was a matter of some sorrow to Fauna that she didn't entirely believe in astrology, but she had found that nearly everyone wants to believe that the stars take notice of us. Her science gave her a means for telling people what they ought to do, and Fauna had definite ideas about what everybody ought to do.

In spite of her secret scepticism, every once in a while she turned up a reading that astonished her. Hazel's horoscope had her breathless and baffled. She seriously considered burning it and never telling him.

Hazel led her to the Palace Flop-house and Mack poured her a drink from the keg. She tossed it off, still deep in thought.

"You got my stars wrote down?" Hazel demanded anxiously.

Fauna regarded him sorrowfully. "I don't want to tell you," she said.

"Why not? Is it bad?"

"Awful," said Fauna.

"Come on, tell me. I can take it."

Fauna sighed. "I've checked it over and over," she said. "You sure you give me your true birthday?"

"Sure."

"Then I don't see how it can be wrong." She turned wearily and faced the others. "The stars say Hazel's going to be President of the United States."

There was a shocked silence.

"I don't believe it," said Mack.

"I don't want to be President," Hazel said, and he didn't.

"There is no choice," said Fauna. "The stars have spoke. You will go to Washington."

"I don't want to!" Hazel cried. "I don't know nobody there."

"I wonder where we could all go," said Whitey No. 2. "I seen some islands in the Pacific that was pretty nice. But hell, Hazel would have them too. The U.S. got a mandate."

"I won't take it," said Hazel.

Mack said, "We could kill him."

"His stars don't say it," Fauna said. "He's going to live to seventy-eight and die from a spoiled oyster."

"I don't like oysters," said Hazel.

"Maybe you'll learn in Washington."

Mack said, "Maybe you made a mistake."

"That's what I hoped," said Fauna. "I went over and over it. No, sir! Hazel is going to be President."

"Well, we've weathered some pretty bad ones," Eddie offered forlornly.

"Ain't they no way I can tell them I won't do it? Hell, I'll hide out!" said Hazel desperately.

Fauna shook her head dismally. "I'll check again," she said, "but I don't think you got a prayer. You got nine toes, Hazel?"

"I don't know."

"Well, count."

Hazel took off his shoes and moved his lips. "Nine," he said bitterly.

"That's what the horoscope said. We can only pray it's for the best."

"Lord!" said Whitey No. 2. "That's what I call a nine-to-one prayer. Fauna, now you've went and made a president out of a sow's ear, how about getting Doc's paper wrote?"

"Who's a sow's ear?" Hazel demanded.

"William Henry Harrison."

"Oh!" said Hazel. "Oh yeah!"

Agnes piped up in her hoarse soprano, "Doc just ain't himself. I took him a pint and he didn't hardly pass the time a day. Just set there looking at that yellow paper. Know what was on that paper?"

"Eggs," said Whitey No. 1.

"No. I don't like to tell. It ain't nice."

"Hot damn!" said Mack. "Maybe he's getting well. Go on—what?"

"Well," said Agnes in a shocked voice, "he'd drew a picture of a lady without no clothes on, and right beside that was one of them damn devil-fish, only it was smoking a pipe. Don't hardly seem like the old Doc."

Wide Ida shook herself out of a mountainous lethargy. "He used to be the easygoingest guy in the world. Now he's got a wild hair. Anybody else but Doc, I'd figure it was a dame. But hell! Doc can take dames or let them alone."

Mack said, "He could even takes dames *and* let them alone."

Fauna put her hands on her hips. "You fellas sure there ain't a girl hiding out where he can't get to her?"

"No," said Hazel. "I wisht he'd snap out of it. Go over and talk to him, and he don't say nothing and he don't listen."

"Let's run a few dames past him and see if he picks up," said Whitey No. 2.

Mack said, "I don't believe in it, but I wish Fauna would do a job on Doc. Might give us an idea."

Fauna said, "I never seen nobody that wanted me to do a horoscope that believed in it. I ain't sure I believe in it myself. Sure I'll do Doc. When's his birthday?"

With surprise they realized that no one could remember.

"Seems like it was in autumn," said Eddie.

"Got to have it," Fauna said. "Mack, you think you could find out?"

"I guess so. Say, Fauna, if you ain't got too much integrity, could you maybe rig it a little?"

"How do you mean?"

"Well, kind of tell him to lay off his goddam paper and get back to horsing around."

"What's wrong with his paper if only he gets it wrote?" Hazel demanded.

Mack scratched his stomach. "I guess we got to face it," he said. "Doc wants to write that crazy paper. Driving himself nuts with it. Know what I think? Doc ain't never going to write that paper."

Hazel stood up. "What d'you mean?"

"Well, you know them kind of people they call accident-prone? No matter what they do they get hurt. It's like they *want* accidents. Well, I think Doc don't really want to write that paper."

Whitey No. 1 said, "He sure goes about it the hard way."

"Ever hear of a substitute?" said Mack.

"You mean like on the bench at football?" Eddie asked.

"Hell no!" said Mack. "I mean like a guy is using something to cover up something else—and maybe he don't even know it himself."

Hazel demanded, "You running Doc down?"

"Take it easy," said Mack. "I think Doc's scared to write that paper because he knows it's crazy. Quod erat demonstrandum."

"Huh?" asked Fauna.

"Q.E.D.," said Mack.

"Oh!" said Fauna. "Sure."

CHAPTER X

THERE'S A HOLE IN REALITY THROUGH WHICH WE CAN LOOK IF WE WISH

Doc had made changes. His desk was drawn in front of the window. He sat writing rapidly on his yellow pad. "Colour change," he wrote, "seems to be not only a concentration of fluids to the surface but also a warping of tissue, which, perhaps, refracts the light, giving an impression of colour."

A door slammed. Doc looked out at the street. Fauna was teetering down the chicken walk that led from the Palace Flop-house.

Doc looked back at his pad. There were footsteps on the pavement. He looked up. Wide Ida was going towards her bar. Joseph and Mary came out of the Heavenly Flower and crossed the street, climbed the stairs of Western Biological, and knocked.

"Come in," Doc cried, and there was relief in his voice.

"Thought I'd shovel the dirt a little. That band of mine is practising upstairs. Drives me crazy."

"Well, I'm pretty busy," said Doc.

J. and M. gazed about the room. "Why do you keep snakes?"

"To sell."

"Who'd buy snakes?" said J. and M. "Say, what you looking at?" He craned his neck. "That's the new dame. She's going to give Fauna trouble. Little Mary trouble."

"Who?" Doc asked.

"You wasn't listening, I guess."

"I must get to work," said Doc.

"You know, I still don't get it."

"What?"

"There must be some way to kind of bend the odds in chess."

"There isn't. I've got to go."

"What's the rush?"

"Tide!" said Doc.

Doc walked on the beach beyond the lighthouse. The waves splashed white beside him and sometimes basted his ankles. The sandpipers ran ahead of him as though on little wheels. The golden afternoon moved on toward China, and on the horizon's edge a lumber schooner balanced.

On Doc's left the white sand dunes rounded up, and behind them the dark pine trees seemed to hold a piece of night throughout the day.

Doc thought, Under stimulation there is increased pulsing like a man under physical or emotional strain, something like the release of adrenalin—but no way to prove it. No more specimens until the spring tides.

His middle voice argued, "Maybe you don't believe any of it. Why can't you laugh at yourself? You could once. You're trapped in a cage of self-importance."

"Lonesome!" the low voice cried in his guts. "No one to receive from you or give to you. No one warm enough and dear enough."

Doc wanted desperately to go back to his old life—the hopeless wish of a man wanting to be a little boy, forgetting the pain of little boys. Doc dropped to his knees and dug a hole in the damp sand with a scooped hand. He watched the sea water seep in and crumble the sides of the hole. A sand crab scuttled away from his digging fingers.

From behind him a voice said, "What are you digging for?"

"Nothing," said Doc without looking round.

"There are no clams here."

"I know it," said Doc. And his top voice sang, "I just want to be alone. I don't want to talk or explain or argue or even to listen. Now he'll tell me a theory he's got on oceanography. I won't look round."

The voice behind him said, "There's so much metal in the sea. Why, there's enough magnesium in a cubic mile of sea water to pave the whole country."

I always get them, Doc thought. If there's a bug-houser within miles he's drawn to me.

"I'm a seer," said the voice.

Doc rocked angrily back on his heels. "Okay," he said. "It's just my business but you tell me about it." He didn't remember ever having been discourteous to a stranger before.

This one was a big, bearded stranger with the lively, innocent eyes of a healthy baby. He wore ragged overalls and a blue shirt washed nearly white, and he was barefooted. The straw hat on his head had two large holes cut in the brim, proof that it had once been the property of a horse.

Doc found his interest rising.

"It is my custom to invite a stranger to dinner," said the seer. "Not original, of course. Harun al-Rashid did the same. Please follow me."

Doc stood up from his squatting position. The tendons behind his knees creaked with pain. The seer towered above him, and on closer inspection it was true that his blue eyes had the merry light of a wise baby. But his face was granite—chiselled out of the material of prophets and patriarchs. Doc found himself wondering if some of the saints had not looked like this. From the ragged sleeves of the blue shirt wrists like big grapevines protruded, and hands sheathed in brown calluses criss-crossed with barnacle cuts. The seer carried a pair of ancient basketball shoes in his left hand, and, seeing Doc look at them, he said, "I only wear them in the sea. My feet aren't proof against urchins and barnacles."

In spite of himself, Doc felt surrounded by the man. "Harun," said Doc, "was visited by djinni and the spirits of earth, fire, and water. Do the djinni visit you?" Doc thought, Oh, Lord! Am I going to play along with this nonsense? Why can't I cross my fingers and spit and walk away? I can still walk away.

The seer looked downward at an angle into Doc's face. "I live alone," he said simply. "I live in the open. I hear the waves at night and see the black patterns of the pine boughs against the sky. With sound and silence and colour and solitude, of course I see visions. Anyone would."

"But you don't believe in them?" Doc asked hopefully.

"I don't find it a matter for belief or disbelief," the seer said. "You've seen the sun flatten and take strange shapes just before it sinks in the ocean. Do you have to tell yourself every time that it's an illusion caused by atmospheric dust and light distorted by the sea, or do you simply enjoy the beauty of it? Don't you see visions?"

"No," said Doc.

"From music, don't forms of wishes and forms of memory take shape?"

"That's different," said Doc.

"I don't see any difference," said the seer. "Come along—dinner's ready."

In the dunes there are deep little creases where the wind-crouching pines have made a stand against the moving sand, and in one of these, only a hundred yards back from the beach, the seer had his home. The little valley was protected from the wind. The pine boughs covered it, and the sand was deeply carpeted with sweet pine needles. Once down in the little cup you could hear the wind sweeping the pine tips overhead, and a perpetual dusk hung under the warped trees. The pines survived only by following the suggestions of the stronger forces—crouching low and growing their limbs in the direction of the wind, nourishing the little trailing plants which slow up the pace of the walking dunes. Under the trees a fire was burning, and on a hearth of flat stones blackened tin cans steamed.

"This is my home," the seer said. "You are welcome here. I have a wonderful dinner." He brought a tin box from the fork of a tree, took out a loaf of French bread, and sliced off two thick slices. Then he brought sea urchins from a dripping sack, cracked them on a rock and spread the gonads on the bread. "The males are sweet and the females sour," he said. "I like to mix the two."

"I've tasted them," said Doc. "The Italians eat them. It's about as strong a protein as you can get. Some people think it's aphrodisiac."

There was an iron simplicity in the seer. He was like a monolith of logic standing against waves of angry nonsense.

"Next we'll have steamed limpets," said the seer. "I have a pin here to eat them with. Do you like sea lettuce? It's an acquired taste. And then I have a stew—a kind of universal bouillabaisse—I won't tell you what's in it. You'll see."

"Do you take all your food from the sea?"

The seer smiled at him. "No, not all. I wish I could. It would be simpler. I take all the protein I need, and more, but my human stomach still craves starch. I want a little bread and some potatoes. I love acid with the protein. See—I have a bottle of vinegar and some lemons. And last, I indulge myself with herbs: rosemary and thyme and sage and marjoram."

"How about sugars?" Doc asked. "You won't find sugars in a tide pool."

The seer dropped his eyes and watched a black ant try to climb an avalanche of sand, losing ground all the way. When he spoke his voice was shy and ashamed. "I steal candy bars," he said. "I can't seem to help it."

"The flesh is weak," said Doc.

"Oh, I don't mind that," the seer cried. "Appetites are good things. The more appetites a man has, the richer he is, but I was taught not to steal. I don't believe in stealing. It hurts my feelings when I do, and I don't enjoy the candy bars as much as I would if I didn't steal them, but I love Baby Ruths and Mounds."

They picked the limpets from their shells with pins and dipped them in lemon juice. The stew contained mussels and clams and crabs and little fish seasoned with garlic and rosemary.

"Some people don't like it," said the seer.

After they had finished, Doc lay back in the pine needles, and a fine peacefulness settled on him. The air, the softness of the needles, the odours of kelp and pine and yerba buena, the music of surf against wind-plucking pine needles, the fullness of belly, made a little room of contentment around him.

He said, "I'm surprised they don't lock you up—a reasonable man. It's one of the symptoms of our time to find danger in men like you who don't worry and rush about. Particularly dangerous are men who don't think the world's coming to an end."

"It's coming to an end all right," the seer said. "That started the moment it was born."

"I don't know why they don't put you in jail. It's a crime to be happy without equipment."

"Oh, they do," said the seer, "and they put me under observation every once in a while."

"I forgot," said Doc. "You are crazy, aren't you?"

"I guess so," said the seer, "but not dangerous. And they've never caught me stealing candy bars. I'm very clever at that, and I steal only one at a time."

"Don't ever gather disciples," said Doc. "They'd have you on a cross in no time."

"There's not much danger of that. I don't teach anybody anything."

"I'm not so sure," said Doc. "The doctrine of our time is that man can't get along without a whole hell of a lot of stuff. You may not be preaching it, but you're living treason.

"I'm lazy," said the seer. "Did you ever drink yerba buena tea?"

"No."

"It's strong and aromatic and a mild physic. Can you drink it out of a beer bottle?"

"I don't know why not."

"Look out! The bottle's hot! Here, wrap a twig around it."

After a while the seer asked, "What's aching you, or don't you want to talk about it?"

"I'd just as soon talk about it if I knew what it was," said Doc. "As a matter of fact, it's gone away for the moment."

"Ah, one of those," said the seer. "Do you have a wife or children?"

"No."

"Do you want wife or children?"

"I don't think so."

The seer said, "I saw a mermaid last night. You remember, there was a half moon and a thin drifting mist. There was colour in the night, not like the black and grey and white of an ordinary night. Down at the end of the beach a shelf of rock reaches out, and the tide was low so that there was a smooth bed of kelp. She swam to the edge and then churned her tail, like a salmon leaping a rapid. And then she lay on the kelp bed and made dancing figures with her white arms and hands. She didn't go away until the rising tide covered the kelp bed."

"Was she a dream? Did you imagine her?"

"I don't know. But if I did I'm proud that I could imagine anything so beautiful. What is it you want?"

"I've tried to think," said Doc. "I want to take everything I've seen and thought and learned and reduce them and relate them and refine them until I have something of meaning, something of use. And I can't seem to do it."

"Maybe you aren't ready. And maybe you need help."

"What kind of help?"

"There are some things a man can't do alone. I wouldn't think of trying anything so big without——" He stopped. The heavy waves beat the hard beach, and the yellow light of the setting sun illuminated a cloud to the eastward, a clot of gold.

"Without what?" Doc asked.

"Without love," said the seer. "I have to go to the sunset now. I've come to the point where I don't think it can go down without me. That makes me seem needed." He stood up and brushed the pine needles from his threadbare overalls.

"I'll come to see you again," said Doc.

"I might be gone," the seer replied. "I've got a restlessness in me. I'll probably be gone."

Doc watched him trudge over the brim of the dune and saw the wind flip up the brim of his straw hat and the yellow sun light up his face and glisten in his beard.

CHAPTER XI

HAZEL'S BROODING

After Mack left the Palace Flop-house (and, incidentally, did not find Doc at home), Hazel sat brooding. Things came through slowly to Hazel. He had heard Mack advance this theory about how Doc would never get his paper written, but the impact of the statement did not strike home until he was alone. It is true that all over Cannery Row the feeling was growing that Doc was not infallible, but the news had not seeped through to Hazel. He knew that Doc was in trouble, but the friendly feeling of contempt had not penetrated. If Hazel had wanted to know the day and hour of the world's demise, he would have gone to Doc and Doc's answer would have been final. Alone he brooded, not about Doc's weakness, but about the treachery of Doc's friends who could question him, who would *dare* to question him.

Hazel beat his hand on the arm of his rocking-chair for a while and then he got up and went to Wide Ida's. Eddie was behind the bar, so Hazel had two shots of whisky and paid for a Coke.

He walked between two canneries to the beach. A seagull with a broken wing engaged his kindly interest. He chased it, trying to help it, until it swam to sea and drowned.

Hazel had experienced an earthquake and he searched for the shaker. He walked along the rocks to Pacific Grove Beach, and even the brown young men standing on their hands for the girls did not hold interest. He went up the hill and toured the basement of Holman's Department Store. The floor manager accompanied him, an honour and a precaution few people received. But Hazel didn't even see the shining display of small tools.

You cannot cut the ground from under a man and expect him to act normally. On his way back to Cannery Row, Hazel passed a funeral home where an impressive group was gathering. Ordinarily Hazel would join any kind of celebration with enthusiasm. But now he watched the mounds of gladiolas being carried out and no sense of participation stirred in him. The festive dead would have to be buried without Hazel.

In New Monterey, Hazel walked not around, but right through a dog fight. All the preceding manifestations would have troubled his friends, but if they had known what Hazel was thinking they would have been horrified.

Thinking is always painful, but in Hazel it was heroic. A picture of the process would make you seasick. A grey, whirling furore of images, memories, words, patterns. It was like a traffic jam at a big intersection with Hazel in the middle trying to get something to move somewhere.

He strolled back to Cannery Row but he did not go to the Palace Flop-house. By instinct, he crept under the branches of the black cypress tree in the vacant lot where he had lived for so many years in pre-Palace days. Hazel's thoughts were not complicated. It was just remarkable that he had them at all.

Hazel loved Doc. Doc was in trouble. Somebody was responsible. Who? That it might be a situation rather than a person was beyond his grasp. The person who was hurting Doc must be made to stop it even if he had to be killed. Hazel had nothing against murder. That he hadn't killed anybody was only because he hadn't needed to or wanted to. He tried to recall everything he had heard concerning Doc's frustration, and it was nebulous, all vague, except for one thing: Mack had said Doc couldn't write his paper. That was the only clear statement that had been made. Mack was the one. If Mack knew about it, he must be responsible for it. This was a matter of sorrow to Hazel, because he liked Mack very much. He hoped he wouldn't have to kill him.

It was getting dark under the cypress tree, too dark to read. Hazel always judged light by whether or not you could read by it, in spite of the fact that he never read anything. The front-porch light of the

Bear Flag came on. Western Biological was still dark. Up the hill in the Palace Flop-house the kerosene lantern made a dim glow through the windows. Again and again, Hazel tried to turn to sweet thoughtlessness, but it was no use. Mack was responsible. Mack had to do something about it.

Hazel got up and brushed the cypress dirt from his clothes. He walked up past the rusty pipes and the empty boiler, crossed the railroad track, and went up the chicken walk. Behind him, muffled by the canneries, he could hear Cacahuete playing 'Stormy Weather' on his trumpet and the sea-lions on China Point barking.

In the Palace, Mack and the boys were playing tick-tack-toe with a piece of chalk on the floor. The wining jug was set conveniently near.

"Hi, Hazel," said Mack. "Draw up."

"Mack," Hazel said sadly, "I want you should step outside with me and put up your dukes."

Mack rocked back on his heels. "What!"

"I'm going to beat the holy hell out of you," said Hazel.

"Why?" Mack asked.

This was just the question Hazel was afraid of. He tried to find a quick, tough answer. "You just step out and you'll find out," he said.

"Hazel——" Mack stood up. "Hazel, baby, what's eating you? Tell me. See if I can't make it right."

Hazel felt the whole situation leaving his hands. "You can't treat Doc that way," he said fiercely. "Not Doc!"

"What way am I treating him? I ain't done nothing to Doc, except maybe hustle him a little. But we all done that—even you tried."

"You said he can't write his paper, that's what you done."

"Oh, for God's sake!" said Mack.

"You're yellow, then."

"Okay, I'm yellow. Sometime when I ain't feeling yellow I'll paddywhack you. Sit down. Have a jolt from the jug."

They babied Hazel and pampered him until his eyes were damp with appreciation. But when Hazel's mind dug in, it would not let loose. "You got to help him," he repeated. "He ain't happy, he just mopes. You got to help him."

Mack said, "It ain't entirely our fault. Trouble is, Doc lets concealment like a worm in the bud feed on his damask cheek."

"He sure as hell does," said Whitey No. 2.

"I ain't going to stand for no excuses," said Hazel.

Mack studied the problem from every angle. "Hazel's right," he said at last. "We've been selfish. We never in our lives had such a good friend as Doc, and we're letting him down. Makes me feel ashamed. It's Hazel showed the way. If I was in trouble I wouldn't want Hazel to do no figuring but I sure would like to have him for a friend."

Hazel ducked his head in embarrassment. In his life so few compliments had come his way that he didn't know how to cope with them.

Mack went on, "I make solemn move we all stand up and drink a toast to Hazel—a noble, noble soul!"

"Aw, hell, fellas," said Hazel, and he wiped his eyes on his sleeve.

They stood in a circle around him. Mack and Eddie, Whitey No. 1 and Whitey No. 2, and each one tipped the jug over his elbow and drank to Hazel. Good feeling was running so high they did it again, and were about to do it a third time when Hazel said, "Ain't there something we can drink to so I can get a drink?"

"To Lefty Grove!" said Eddie.

That broke the ice. An era of good feeling set in. They dug up another keg of the private stock Eddie had saved during the war. He started the bung and smelled it delicately.

"I remember this one," he said. "They was some guys up from South America and they brought in a bottle of absinthe."

"Perfumes the whole house," said Mack.

It was like old times, they reminded one another. If Gay were only here—let's drink a toast to good old Gay, our departed friend.

The absinthe had soothed the mixture in the keg and added something sweet and old-fashioned. A courtliness crept into the speech of the dwellers of the Palace Flop-house, an old-world courtesy. Everyone vied to be last, not first, at the refilled jug.

"Next dough we get we'll go up to Woolworth's and get some glasses," said Mack.

"Hell," said Whitey No. 2, "they'll just get broke. But I see what you mean."

Somehow they felt they were living in a moment when history pauses and takes stock and changes course. They knew they would look back on this night as a beginning. At such times men feel the nudge towards oratory.

Mack steadied himself against the stove and begged their attention by rapping on the stovepipe. "Gentlemen," he said, "let us here highly resolve to get Doc's arse out of the sling of despond."

Eddie said, "Remember we done something like that once and damn near ruined him."

Mack's golden mood held. "We were younger then," he said. "This time we're going to think her out and she's going to be foolproof."

Hazel was so far won back into comradeship that he had relaxed into happy incoherence. "To Lefty Grove!" he said.

Mack opened the oven door and sat on it. "I've give it a lot of thought," he said. "Lately I done hardly nothing else."

"You never do hardly nothing else," said Whitey No. 2.

Mack ignored him. "I got a theory——"

"Aw, shut up!" said Eddie.

"Who you talking to?" said Whitey No. 2.

"I don't know," said Eddie innocently, "but if the shoe fits——"

"I got a theory, if you ain't too pie-eyed to listen," said Mack. When he had them quiet he went on, "When you hear my theory you might get kind of violent. I want you to sleep on it before you talk. I think Doc needs a wife."

"*What?*"

"Well, hell, he don't have to marry her," said Mack. "You know what I mean . . ." If the absinthe had not given them tolerance he might have had a series of fights right then. "Kindly do not interrupt," he said. "I will now review the dame situation in the U.S. You take a look at divorces and the reasons for them and you can only think one thing: the only guy that shouldn't have nothing to do with picking out a wife is the guy that's going to marry her. That's a fact. It's a fact that if he's left alone a guy practically always marries the wrong kind of dame."

"Play it safe and don't marry nobody," said Whitey No. 2.

"There's some guys can't operate that way," said Mack.

"Are you suggesting we turn Doc, our true friend, in?"

"I asked you not to shoot off your face until you slept on it," said Mack with dignity.

Hazel tugged at his sleeve. "Ain't you joking, Mack?"

"No," said Mack, "I ain't joking."

"If anything bad come to Doc, you know what I'd do to you?" Hazel asked.

"Yes," said Mack. "I think I do—and I think I'd have it coming."

Hazel's bed was a four-poster on which the bedposts were two-by-fours topped by a quilt. He had built it from memory of a moving picture. When the Palace Flop-house was quiet at last, Hazel lay in his bed and looked up at the log-cabin pattern of his canopy. His mind was whirling. He wished there were some simpler way to help Doc than by the major operation Mack had suggested. Once he got up and looked out of the door and saw that the green-shaded light was on in the laboratory.

"The poor bastard," he whispered.

He didn't sleep well and his dreams were shaped like mushrooms.

CHAPTER XII

FLOWER IN A CRANNIED WALL

Joe Elegant was a pale young man with bangs. He smoked foreign cigarettes in a long ebony holder and he cooked for the Bear Flag. The girls said he made the best popovers in the world, and he could give a massage that would shake the kinks out of a Saturday night when the fleet was in. He sneered most of the time, and except at meal-time kept to himself in his little lean-to behind the Bear Flag, from which the rattle of his typewriter could be heard late at night.

One morning soon after she had come, Suzy was having her coffee while Joe Elegant cleared the table of crumbs from earlier breakfasts.

"You make good coffee," Suzy said.

"Thank you."

"You don't look like a guy would work here."

"It's temporary, I assure you."

"I got a wonderful recipe for gumbo. Want me to give it to you?"

"Fauna designs the meals."

"You ain't very friendly."

"Why should I be?"

He was passing behind her. Suzy reached up, hooked her fingers in his shirt collar, twisted and yanked his face down level with her own. "Listen, you," she began and she scowled into his popping eyes. "Oh, the hell with it," said Suzy and released him.

Joe Elegant stepped back and massaged his throat and smoothed his shirt.

"Sorry," said Suzy.

"It's quite all right."

"What makes you so mean?"

"You said it. I don't belong here."

"Where do you belong?"

"I don't think you'd understand."

"You too good for the place?"

"Let's say I'm different."

"No kidding!" said Suzy.

"I'm writing a novel."

"You are? What about? I love novels."

"You wouldn't like this one."

"Why not?"

"You wouldn't understand it."

"Then what good is it?"

"It isn't intended for the mass."

"I'm the mass, huh? I guess you got something there. I bet you could write a pretty nice hunk of stuff."

Joe Elegant swallowed and his face twitched convulsively. "Sometime I'll read you some of it."

"Say, that would be nice. But you said I couldn't understand it."

"I'll explain it as I go along."

"I'd like that. There's one whole hell of a lot I don't understand."

"Do you like brownies?" he asked.

"I love them."

"I'll make you some. Maybe you'll come to my apartment some afternoon. I could give you a cup of tea."

"Say, you're a nice fella! Got any more coffee?"

"I'll make a fresh pot."

CHAPTER XIII

PARALLELS MUST BE RELATED

Doc spent a restless night. His head was full of yellow pads and seers and octopi. Ordinarily he would have worked or read since he couldn't sleep, but now if he turned on a light he would see the yellow pad and the marshalled pencils.

As the dawn crept over the bay he decided to go for a very long walk, perhaps to follow the shoreline all the way round to Carmel. He arose, and since it was still dusky in the laboratory he turned on the lights to make his coffee.

Wide Ida, from the entrance of "La Ida," saw his lights come on. She put an unlabelled pint bottle of brown liquor in a paper bag and crossed the street to Western Biological.

"Doc," she said, "would you work this stuff over?"

"What is it?"

"They say it's whisky. I just want to know if it'll kill anybody. I got a pretty good buy. They make it up in Pine Canyon."

"That's against the law," said Doc.

"Killing people is against the law too," said Wide Ida.

Doc was torn between bootlegging and murder. He thought sadly that he was always involved in something like this—not good or bad, but bad or less bad. He made a fairly quick analysis. "It's not poison," he said, "but it won't build good healthy stomachs. There's some fusel oil in it. But I guess it's no worse than Old Tennis Shoes."

"Thanks, Doc. What do I owe you?"

"Oh, maybe a quart—but not this stuff."

"I'll send over some Old Taylor."

"You don't have to go off the deep end," said Doc.

"Doc, I hear you got trouble."

"Me? What kind of trouble?"

"I just heard," said Wide Ida,

Doc said angrily, "I've got no trouble. What's all the talk! God Almighty, everybody treats me as though I had a disease. What kind of trouble?"

"If there's anything I can do," she said, and went out quickly, leaving the pint behind.

Doc took a sip of it, made a face, and took a swig. His heart was pounding angrily. He could not admit that the pity of his friends only confirmed his frustration. He knew that pity and contempt are brothers. He set his chin. "I *will* get the spring tides at La Jolla," he said to himself. "I *will* get a new microscope." And the very lowest voice whispered, "Somewhere there's warmth."

He sat down at his desk and wrote viciously, "Parallels must be related." He took another drink from the pint and opened yesterday's mail. There was an order for six sets of slides—starfish, embryonic series, for the Oakland Polytechnic High School. He was almost glad to do the old and practised work. He got his collecting buckets together, threw rubber boots in his old car, and drove out to the Great Tide Pool.

CHAPTER XIV

LOUSY WEDNESDAY

Some days are born ugly. From the very first light they are no damn good whatever the weather, and everybody knows it. No one knows what causes this, but on such a day people resist getting out of bed and set their heels against the day. When they are finally forced out by hunger or job they find that the day is just as lousy as they knew it would be.

On such a day it is impossible to make a good cup of coffee, shoestrings break, cups leap from the shelf by themselves and shatter on the floor, children ordinarily honest tell lies, and children ordinarily good unscrew the tap handles of the gas range and lose the screws and have to be spanked. This is the day the cat chooses to have kittens and house-broken dogs wet on the parlour rug.

Oh, it's awful on such a day! The postman brings overdue bills.

If it's a sunny day it is too damn sunny, and if it is dark who can stand it?

Mack knew it was going to be that kind of a day. He couldn't find his pants. He fell over a box that had crept out in his path. He cursed each brother in the Palace Flop-house, and on his way across the vacant lot he went out of his way to kick a dandelion flower. He was sitting gloomily on a pipe when Eddie came by, and so naturally he walked with Eddie to Wide Ida's to try to do something about it. He hung around waiting for Wide Ida to go so that Eddie could slip him a drink. But Wide Ida was bending over the bar, cursing a letter.

"Taxes," she said. "Every time you get going there's more taxes. You're lucky, Mack. You don't own nothing, and you don't make nothing. Until they start taxing skin you're safe."

"What's the beef?" Mack asked.

"City and county taxes," said Wide Ida.

"On what?"

"On this place. It ain't much, but I was fixed to put a down payment on a new Pontiac."

It was a statement that ordinarily would have aroused a detached compassion in Mack, together with mild self-congratulation that he was not burdened with taxable assets. But now a nagging worry fell on him, and he went back to the Palace Flop-house to worry in greater comfort. He went over the history of the Palace in his mind.

It had belonged to Lee Chong. Long before the war Mack and the boys had rented it from him for five dollars a month, and, naturally enough, they had never paid any rent. Lee Chong would have been shocked if they had. Then Lee Chong sold out to Joseph and Mary. Did the Palace go with the rest? Mack didn't know, but if it did, the Patrón didn't know it. He was no Lee Chong. He would have demanded the rent. But if the Patrón did own the place, he would get a tax bill. If he got a tax bill, he was sure to be on the necks of Mack and the boys. The Patrón was not a man to pay out money without getting more money back, that was certain.

It seemed very unjust. Their home, their security, even their social standing, were cast in the balance. Mack lay on his bed and considered what could be done. Suppose the Patrón demanded back rent—clear back for years. You couldn't trust a man like that. What a lousy day it was! Mack didn't know what to do, so he called a meeting of the boys, even sent Hazel to bring Eddie back from Wide Ida's bar.

It was a grim and shaken assembly. Mack explained all the angles until even Hazel seemed to understand the danger. The boys studied their fingers, looked at the ceiling, blew on their knuckles. Eddie got up and walked round his chair to change his thinking luck.

At last Whitey No 2 said, "We could steal his mail so he won't get no tax bill."

"It ain't practical," said Mack. "Even if it wasn't a crime."

Hazel offered, "We could kill him."

"You ain't heard that's against the law, too?" Mack asked.

"I mean, make it like an accident," said Hazel. "He could fall off Point Lobos."

"Then somebody else inherits the joint and we don't even know who."

The injustice in the theory of private ownership of real estate was descending on them.

"Maybe we could get Doc to talk to him. He likes Doc." This was Whitey No. 1's offering.

"That would only draw it to his attention," said Mack. "Hell, he might even raise the rent."

"He might even try to collect it," said Eddie.

Hazel was going into a slow but luminous burn. He gazed about the whitewashed walls of the Palace Flop-house, at the Coca-Cola calendar girls, at the great and ancient wood-stove, at the grandfather clock, at the framed portrait of Romie Jacks. There were honest unabashed tears in Hazel's eyes. "The son-of-a-bitch," he said. "After all our work he takes away our home—the only place where I ever been happy. How can a guy be so goddam mean?"

"He ain't done it yet," said Mack. "He don't even know about it maybe."

"I wish Doc owned the place," said Eddie. "We wouldn't have no trouble with Doc."

Mack looked at him quickly. "What put that in your head?" he demanded.

"Hell, Doc don't open his mail for weeks on end. Doc would forget to collect the rent and he'd forget to open a tax bill."

Excitement shone in Mack's eyes. "Eddie," he said, "maybe you put your finger in it."

"In what?"

"I got to think it over," said Mack, "but just maybe our darling Eddie here is a genius."

Eddie blushed with pleasure. "What'd I do, Mack?"

"I can't tell you now."

"Hell, Mack, I want to know what I done."

"It was smart," said Mack. "It was a stroke of just pure wonderful. Now let's give the Patrón a going-over. How much guts you think he's got?"

"Plenty," said Hazel. "And he's plenty wise."

Mack spoke slowly, thinking aloud. "Let's see. Joseph and Mary, you might say, is a con man in a general kind of way——"

"He's a nice dresser," said Hazel.

"A con man can't make enemies unless, of course, he wants to get out of town. He got to keep everybody happy and friendly."

"Come on, Mack," Whitey No. 1 demanded. "Tell us!"

"Fellas," said Mack, "if I blowed it now and it wasn't no good, why, you'd kind of lose face in me. I want to think this one out and see if I can't kind of surround him. But if we do her, you'll all have to help."

"Do what?"

"Let me alone now, boys," said Mack, and he went back to his bed and put his head on his crossed hands and studied the rafters of the Palace Flop-house.

Hazel came quietly to his bedside. "You won't let nobody take our home away, will you, Mack?"

"I promise!" said Mack fervently. "Where's Eddie?"

"Went back to Wide Ida's."

"Will you do something for me, Hazel?"

"Sure, Mack."

"Take that lard can over there and see can Eddie fill it full of beer without too much fuss. It'll help me to think better."

"You'll get your beer," said Hazel. "You just keep thinking, Mack. Say, Mack, how do you think Eddie always got a stroke of genius even when he don't know it and I don't never have none?"

"Come again?" said Mack.

"How come—oh, the hell with it!" said Hazel.

CHAPTER XV

THE PLAYING FIELDS OF HARROW

Fauna had made a success of three improbable enterprises. More than likely she could have held her own in steel or chemicals, maybe even in General Electric, for Fauna had the proper ingredients for modern business. She was benevolent and at the same time solvent, public-spirited and privately an individualist, open-handed but with a delicate sense of double-entry book-keeping, sentimental but not soft. She could easily have been chairman of the board of a large corporation. And Fauna took a deep personal interest in her girls.

Shortly after she took over the Bear Flag, Fauna set aside and decorated the Ready Room. It was a large and pleasant apartment with three windows overlooking the vacant lot. Fauna put in deep chairs and couches covered with bright, flower-littered glazed chintz. The curtains matched the furniture, and the pictures were designed to soothe without arousing interest—engravings of cows in ponds, deer in streams, dogs in lakes. Wet animals seem to serve some human need.

For recreation Fauna provided a table-tennis set, a card-table, and a parchesi board. The Ready Room was a place to relax, to read, to gossip, to study, and some of these things were actually done by the girls of the Bear Flag.

One wall was dominated by a large framed board on which were pasted enormous gold stars, and this was Fauna's personal pride. The Ready Room was gay and feminine, it had an exotic, oriental odour from the incense which burned in the blackened lap of a crouching plaster Buddha.

At about a quarter to three, Agnes and Mabel and Becky were relaxing in the Ready Room. It was the time of languor. The vacant lot was washed in clear pale sunshine, which made even the rusty pipes and the old boiler look beautiful. The tall mallow weeds were as sweetly green as a garden. A sleek, grey, lazy Persian cat hunted gophers in the grass and didn't care whether she caught one or not.

Mabel stood at the window. She said, "I heard some people used to live in that old boiler."

Agnes was painting her toe-nails and waving her feet to dry the enamel. "That's before your time," she said. "Mr. and Mrs. Malloy, they had it fixed up nice—awning out front, oriental rug. Once you got inside, through the fire-door, it was real nice. She was a home-maker."

"Why'd they leave?" Becky asked.

"They got to arguing. She kept wanting curtains. He wouldn't let her because there was no windows. When they argued it kind of echoed in there and got on their nerves. He said there wasn't room inside to take a swing at her. He's in the county jail now—trusty. Mrs. Malloy's slinging hash in a grease joint over at Salinas, waiting for him to get out. They was real nice people. He's a high Elk."

Mabel moved away from the window. "You heard the Rattlesnake Club is coming from Salinas to-night? Took the whole house over."

"Yeah," said Becky. "They're having a memorial meeting for dead members. Fauna give them a rate."

Agnes lifted her left leg and blew on her toe-nails. "Like this colour?" she asked.

"It's nice," said Becky. "Looks a little like you was rotting. Say, where the hell is Suzy? She'll find out when Fauna says three o'clock she means three o'clock. Gee, Fauna's a funny name."

Mabel said, "Her name used to be Flora. What is a fauna anyway? I never knew nobody named that."

"Oh, it's like a baby deer," said Becky. "I don't think Suzy'll be here long. She's kind of nuts—got a nuts look in her eye. Goes out walking."

to-morrow aft. to drink a slug of good stuff and talk about something important. Bring the girls. R.S.V.P.' " Fauna paused. "He could of yelled outside the window, but not Mack—he requests the pleasure of our company," She sighed. "What a gent! If he wasn't such a bum I'd aim one of you young ladies at him."

Agnes asked, "What's the matter with Mack's grandma?"

"I don't even know he's got a grandma," said Fauna. "Now when we go over there to-morrow, you young ladies keep your traps shut and just listen." She mused, "Something important—well, it might be like Mack needs twenty bucks, so just keep your heads shut and let me do the thinking."

Suddenly Fauna beat her forehead with the heel of her hand. "I nearly forgot! Joe Elegant baked a great big goddam cake. Suzy, you take four cold cans of beer and that cake and go over and give them to Doc to cheer him up."

"Okay," said Suzy. "But it'll probably moult in his stomach."

"His stomach ain't none of your business," said Fauna.

And when Suzy had gone Fauna said, "I wisht I could stick up a star for that kid. She don't hardly pull her own weight here."

CHAPTER XVI

THE LITTLE FLOWERS OF SAINT MACK

Doc HAD laid ten big starfish out on a shelf, and he set up a line of eight glass dishes half filled with sea water. Although he was inclined to carelessness in his living arrangements his laboratory technique was immaculate. The making of the embryo series gave him pleasure. He had done it hundreds of times before, and felt a safety in the known thing—no speculation here. He did certain things and certain other things followed. There is comfort in routine.

His old life came back to him—a plateau of contentment with small peaks of excitement but none of the jagged pain of original thinking, none of the loneliness of invention. His gramophone played softly, played the safe and certain fugues of Bach, clear as equations. As he worked, a benign feeling came over him. He liked himself again as he once had; liked himself as a person, the way he might like anyone else. The self-hatred which poisons so many people and which had been irritating him was gone for the time. The top voice of his mind sang peacefulness and order, and the raucous middle voice was gentle; it mumbled and snarled but it could not be heard. The lowest voice of all was silent, dreaming of a warm, safe sea.

The rattlesnakes in their wire cages suddenly lifted their heads, felt the air with their forked tongues and then all four set up a dry buzzing rattle. Doc looked up from his work as Mack came in.

Mack glanced at the cage. "Them new snakes ain't got used to me yet," he said.

"Takes a little time," said Doc. "You haven't been here much."

"Didn't feel no welcome here," said Mack.

"I'm sorry, Mack. I guess I've been off my feed, I'll try to do better."

"You going to let up on them devilfish?"

"I don't know."

"They was making you sick."

Doc laughed. "It wasn't the octopi. I guess it was trying to think. I'd got out of the habit."

"I never got the habit," said Mack.

"That's not true," said Doc. "I never knew anyone who devoted more loving thought to minusculæ."

"I never even heard of them," said Mack. "Say, Doc, what do you think of the Patrón—your honest, spit-in-the-lake opinion?"

"I don't think I understand him. We're kind of different."

"You ain't kidding," said Mack. "He ain't honest."

Doc said, "I'd call that expert testimony."

"What do you mean?"

"I mean you bring some experience to bear."

"Oh, I know what you mean," said Mack earnestly. "but you search your heart, Doc, and see if I ain't dishonest in a kind of honest way. I don't really fool nobody—not even myself. And there's another thing—I know when I'm doing it. Joseph and Mary can't tell the difference."

"I think that might be true," said Doc.

"What I'm wondering is—well, I don't think the Patrón wants any trouble around here, do you?"

"Nobody wants any trouble."

"He's got a stake here," Mack went on. "If the whole Row took a skunner to him, why, he just couldn't take that chance, don't you think?"

"If I knew what you were talking about, it might help," said Doc.

"I'm just trying to figure something," said Mack.

"Well, if you mean that the Patrón is in kind of a sensitive position——"

"That's what I do mean," said Mack. "He can't afford to have no enemies."

"Nobody wants enemies," said Doc.

"I know. But he could get his arse in a sling. He got a business and he's got property."

"I see what you mean," said Doc. "You're going to pressure him and you want to know what he'll do. What are you going to try to take away from him, Mack?"

"I'm just thinking."

"I never knew you to think idly. When you think, somebody gets hurt."

"I never hurt nobody, Doc."

"Well, not bad. I will say your bite is not deadly."

Mack was uneasy. He had not intended the conversation to turn to him. He changed the subject.

"Say, Doc, did you hear? The whole country club took a loyalty oath on the eighteenth green. Whitey No. 2 was caddying. Them members all took off their hats and swore they would not destroy the U.S. Government."

"I'm glad," said Doc. "I was worried. Did the caddies take the oath too?"

"Some of them did, but not Whitey. He's kind of an idealist, you might say. He says if he gets an idea to burn down the Capitol he don't want no perjury rap to stand in his way. They won't let him caddy no more."

"Does he want to burn down the Capitol?" Doc asked.

"Well, no. He says he don't want to now, but he don't know what he'll want to do next month. He give us quite a talk about it. Says he was a Marine, went through a lot of fighting for the country, figures he's got a kind of personal interest. He don't want nobody to tell him what to do."

Doc laughed. "So he can't carry golf clubs any more because of his ideals?"

"They say he's a security risk," said Mack. "Whitey claims he ain't got a good enough memory to be a security risk. Besides, they don't talk about nothing out there on the golf course except money and dames."

Doc said, "Heroes always get punished at first."

"Speaking of dames, Doc——"

"Let's," said Doc.

"Whatever happened to that swell-looking babe in the fur coat used to come over?"

"She's not been very well."

"That's too bad," said Mack. "What's she got?"

"Oh, something obscure. Can't seem to track it down."

"I guess with that kind of dough——"

"What do you mean?"

"I seen it happen so many times," said Mack. "You take a dame and she's married to a guy that's making twenty-five bucks a week. You can't kill her with a meat axe. She's got kids and does the washing—may get a little tired, but that's the worse that can happen to her. But let the guy get raised to seventy-five bucks a week and she begins to get colds and take vitamins."

"That's a new theory of medicine," said Doc.

"It ain't new. Hell, just use your eyes. Guy gets up to a hundred a week and this same dame reads *Time* magazine and she's got the newest disease before she even finished the page. I've knew dames that can give doctors cards, spades, and big cassino about medicine. They got stuff called allergy now. Used to call it hay fever—made you sneeze. Guy that figured out allergy should of got a patent. A allergy is, you get sick when there's something you don't want to do. I've knew dames that was allergic to dish-water. Married guy starts making dough—he's got a patient on his hands."

"You sound cynical," said Doc.

"No, I ain't. You just look around and show me one well dame with her old man in the chips."

Doc chuckled. "You think that's what happened to my friend?"

"Oh, hell, no," said Mack. "That's big stuff. When you get dough like that it's different. She got to have something that don't nobody know what it is. She can't have nothing common that you can take salts for. She goes around puzzling doctors. They stand around her and they shake their heads and they scratch and they never seen nothing like her case before."

"I haven't heard you go on like this for a long time," said Doc.

"You ain't been in the mood to listen. You think them doctors is honest?"

"I haven't any reason to doubt it. Why?"

"I bet I could fix rich dames up," said Mack. "At least for a while."

"How would you go about it?"

"Well, sir, first I'd hire me a deaf-and-dumb assistant. His job jest to sit and listen and look worried. Then I'd get me a bottle of Epsom salts and I'd put in a pretty little screw-cap thing and I'd call it Moondust. I'd charge thirty dollars a teaspoonful, and you got to come to my office to get it. Then I'd invent me a machine you strap the dame in. It's all chrome and it lights coloured lights every minute or so. It costs a dame twelve dollars a half-hour and it puts her through the motions she'd do over a scrub-board. I'd cure them! And I'd make a fortune too. Of course they'd get sick right away again, so I'd have something else, like mixed sleeping pills and wake-up pills that keeps you right where you was when you started."

Doc said, "Thank God you haven't got a licence to practise."

"Why?"

"As a matter of fact I don't know why," said Doc. "How about preventive medicine?"

"You mean how to keep them from getting sick?"

"Yes."

"That's easy," said Mack. "Stay broke!"

Doc sat silent for a while. He glanced at the starfish and saw the reproductive fluid beginning to ooze from between their rays. "Say, Mack," he asked, "did you come over to try to get something out of me?"

"I don't think so," said Mack. "If I did I've forgot what it was. I'm sure glad you got over it, Doc."

"Got over what?"

"Oh, them goddam sooplapods."

"Look, Mack!" Sudden anger welled up in Doc. "Don't get any funny ideas. I am going to write that paper. I am going to La Jolla for the spring tides."

"All right, Doc, all right. Have it your own way."

But back in the Palace Flop-house Mack reported to the boys, "Seemed like he was better, but he ain't got over the hump yet. We got to help him not to write that goddam paper."

CHAPTER XVII

SUZY BINDS THE CHEESE

SUZY WAS light on her feet. She was up the stairs and knocking on the door of Western Biological before the snakes rattled. Doc called, "Come in," without looking up from his microscope.

Suzy stood in the doorway. She held a gigantic flop cake on one hand and carried a paper bag of canned beer in the other. "How do you do," she said formally.

Doc looked up. "Oh, hello. For God's sake, what's that?"

"A cake. Joe Elegant made it."

"Why?" Doc asked.

"I think Fauna told him to."

"Well, I hope you like cake," said Doc.

Suzy laughed. "I don't think this is a eating cake. This is a looking cake. Fauna sent you some beer."

"That's more like it," said Doc. "What's Fauna want?"

"Nothing."

"That's funny."

"Where shall I put the cake?" said Suzy.

Now Doc looked at Suzy and Suzy looked at Doc and they both had the same thought and they burst into laughter. Tears streamed from Suzy's eyes. "Oh, Lord!" said Suzy. "Oh, Lord!" She laughed with her mouth wide and her eyes pinched shut. Doc slapped his leg and threw back his head and roared. And the laughter was so pleasant they tried to keep it going after its momentum was spent.

"Oh, Lord," said Suzy, "I got to wipe my eyes." She put the cake down on top of the rattlesnake cage, and hysterical rattling filled the room. Suzy jumped back. "What's that?"

"Rattlesnakes."

"What you got them for?"

"I take their venom and sell it."

"I'd hate to live with a bunch of dirty snakes."

"They're not dirty. They even change their skins. That's more than people do."

"I hate them," said Suzy, and she shuddered.

"You wouldn't, once you knew them."

"Well, I ain't likely to get to know them," said Suzy. "They're dirty."

Doc leaned back in his chair and crossed his legs. He said, "You know, this interests me. Snakes are cleaner than most animals. Wonder why you call them dirty?"

Suzy looked at him levelly. "You want to know why?"

"Sure I do."

"Because you run Fauna down."

"Wait a minute," said Doc. "What's that got—I did not!"

"You said Fauna's trying to get something out of you. She just done it to be nice."

Doc nodded his head slowly. "I see. So you got even by calling snakes dirty."

"You got it, mister. Nobody don't run Fauna down when I'm around."

"It was just a joke," said Doc.

"Didn't sound like no joke to me."

"Why, Fauna's one of my best friends," said Doc. "Let's have a can of beer and make peace."

"Okay," said Suzy. "You make the first move."

Doc said, "Tell Joe Elegant it's an incredible cake."

"Got marshmallow frosting," said Suzy.

"And tell Fauna the beer saved my life."

Suzy's face relaxed. "Okay," she said. "I guess that's okay. Where's the opener?"

"Right in the sink back there."

Suzy brought the two punched cans to Doc's work table. "Say, what you doing?"

"Making slides. When I started I put starfish sperm and ova in each of these glasses. Then every half-hour I kill one glass of the developing embryos, and when I have the whole series, I mount them on slides like this, and one slide shows the whole development."

Suzy bent over the dishes. "I don't see nothing."

"They're too small. I can show you in the glass."

Suzy backed up. "What do you do it for?"

"So students can see how starfish get to be."

"Why do they want to know?"

"Well, I guess because that's the way people get to be."

"Then why don't they study people?"

Doc laughed. "It's a little difficult to kill unborn babies every half-hour. Here, take a look." He pushed a glass dish under the microscope.

Suzy peered in the eyepieces. "God Almighty!" she said. "Did I look like that once?"

"Something like."

"Sometimes I feel like that now. Say, Doc, you got a funny business—bugs and all that."

"There are funnier businesses," he said sharply.

She stiffened. "Meaning my business? You don't like my business, huh?"

"It doesn't matter whether I like it or not. There it is. But it does seem to me a kind of sad substitute for love—a kind of lonesome substitute."

Suzy put her hands on her hips. "And what've you got, mister? Bugs, snakes? Look at this dump! It stinks. Floor ain't been clean in years. You ain't got a decent suit of clothes. You probably can't remember your last hot meal. You sit here breeding bugs—for Chrissake! What do you think that's a substitute for?"

In the old days Doc would have been amused, but now his guard was down and he caught her anger like a disease. "I do what I want," he said. "I live the way I want. I'm free—do you get that? I'm free and I do what I want."

"You ain't got nothing," Suzy said. "Bugs and snakes and a dirty house. I bet some dame threw you over. That's what you're substituting for. Got a wife? No! Got a girl? No!"

Doc found himself shouting, "I don't want a wife. I have all the women I want!"

"Woman and women is two different things," said Suzy. "Guy knows all about women he don't know nothing about a woman."

Doc said, "This guy is happy that way."

"Now you're happy!" said Suzy. "You're a push-over! If no dame's got you it's because no dame wants you. Who the hell would want to live with bugs and snakes in a joint like this?"

"Who'd want to go to bed with anybody that's got three bucks?" said Doc cruelly.

Suzy said icily, "A smart guy. A real smart guy. He's got what he wants. Seems to me I heard you're writing a great big goddam highfalutin paper."

"Who told you that?"

"Everybody knows about it. Everybody's laughing at you behind your back—and you know why? Because everybody knows you're kidding yourself. You ain't never going to write that paper because you can't write that paper. You're just sitting here like a kid playing wish games."

She saw her words go home as surely as though she had watched arrows drive into his chest, and misery and shame overwhelmed her. "I wish I didn't say that," she spoke softly. "I wish to God I never said that."

"It might be true," said Doc quietly. "Maybe you put your finger on the truth. Is everybody laughing at me? Is everybody laughing——?"

"My name's Suzy," she said.

"Are they laughing, Suzy?"

"They got no right to," she said. "I was just fighting back—honest to God I was. I didn't mean any of that stuff I said."

"I love true things," said Doc. "Even when they hurt. Isn't it better to know the truth about oneself?" And he asked it of himself. "Yes, I think it is. I think it is. You're quite right, I've got nothing. That's why I built up the whole story about my paper until I believed it myself—a little man pretending to be a big man, a fool trying to be wise."

"Fauna will kill me," Suzy moaned. "She'll wring my neck. Say, Doc, you got no right to take mad talk from a two-bit hustler—you got no right."

"What's it matter where the truth comes from," he said, "if it's the truth?"

Suzy said, "Doc, I never felt so lousy in my life. Get mad at me, won't you?"

"Why should I get mad? Maybe you've stopped a bunch of nonsense. Perhaps you've nipped a fool in the bud."

"Get mad at me," she begged. "Here! Take a punch at me."

Doc chuckled. "I wish it could be that easy."

Suzy said sadly, "Then I ain't got any choice," and she shrilled at him, "Why, you goddam bum! You lousy stinking fool! Who the hell d'you think you are?"

There was a flutter of footsteps and the door burst open.

It was Becky. "Suzy! You're late. The Rattlesnakes are here. Come on! Get into your tomato dress."

"It's called 'Love Apples'," said Suzy quietly. "So long, Doc," and she followed Becky out.

Doc watched them go. He said aloud, "That's probably the only completely honest human I have ever met." His eyes wandered to the table and suddenly he bellowed, "*Goddam* it! She's made me miss the time. The dirty bitch! I've got to do it all over again." And he dumped the contents of the glass dishes into his slop bucket.

CHAPTER XVIII

A PAUSE IN THE DAY'S OCCUPATION

NOT THE least important and valuable custom Fauna brought to the Bear Flag was the little time of rest and contemplation in the Ready Room after work and before sleep. Grievances were brought out and inspected, quarrels were settled, and all the little matters of interest and despair were turned over and examined for their actual value. Then praise or blame were assigned and plans for improvement were laid out with lore and tact learned in other fields. Fauna warped and nudged and bunted her young ladies towards good nature and kindliness, which are the parents of restful sleep. It was not unusual for light refreshments to be served, and on occasion the young ladies' voices joined in song—"Home Sweet Home", "Old Black Joe", "Down by the Old Mill Stream", "Harvest Moon". Dog watch in the Ready Room was a medicine to weary nerves and frayed bodies.

The Bear Flag was short-handed the night of the memorial meeting for dead members sponsored by the Rattlesnake Club of Salinas. Helen and Wisteria were doing sixty days for a lady fight that is still discussed with admiration in Cannery Row.

When the last Rattlesnake had gone and the big front door was closed, the girls wandered wearily into the Ready Room, sat down, and kicked off their shoes. Becky said, "One of them Rattlesnakes to-night called us an institution and a landmark."

Agnes said acidly, "We get a few more like Suzy and it'll be a institution all right. I got an uncle in a institution. He goes right on fighting the battle of San Juan Hill. Where is Suzy?"

"I'm right here," said Suzy, entering. "I was getting that cracked record out of the juke-box. Am I pooped! Let's put it in the sack."

"Before Fauna gives us good night? You crazy?" Mabel said. "She'd bust a gut."

Becky sighed. "What a night! This is one time the group rate paid off. Them Rattlesnakes ain't turned a trick since midnight, but they sure was active."

"They was going fine until they run out of liquor," said Mabel. "That new stuff Wide Ida sent in must be made of jumping beans."

Suzy said, "I figured if that short one told me once more how his little boy cut a worm in two with a shovel——"

"Oh, you got it too, huh? Know what the little bastard said? Only four years old, too. He said, 'I cut a wum.' Now if he said he cut a camel I could listen to it three or four times."

"That bald one!" said Mabel. "Did *his* wife have an operation! They turned her inside out. Sounded like they was pelting her. He got crying so hard I never did find out what she had."

"A malignant artichoke," said Becky. "I made him say it slow."

Agnes asked, "Say, who is this guy Sigmund Ki they was singing about?"

"Never heard of him," said Becky. "I once knew a dame said she was the original Frankie, though."

"I've personally knew three original Frankies," said Mabel. "Suzy, you got to stop arguing with the customers."

Suzy said, "If that's the live members of the Rattlesnake Club, the dead ones is what I call dead. I can scream twice at a rubber lizard and then the hell with it."

Fauna came out of the bedroom office and stood in the doorway, rubbing lotion into her hands. She had changed to a peach-coloured dressing-gown. She said seriously, "Young ladies, you can make fun of the Rattlesnakes if you want to, but if you ever get in the administration end you will welcome good solid citizens like them. Why, there was some very important people here from Salinas! I give them a good rate, but you notice there's no busted furniture. Them free-spending sailors last Saturday night cost me eighty-five dollars in repairs. That nice boy give Becky a five-dollar tip—but he busted two windows and run off with the deer-antler hall-tree."

Suzy said, "God, I'm sleepy."

Fauna said sharply, "Suzy, I got one rule: never let the sun rise on a cross word or an unbalanced book." She scratched her nose with a pencil. "I just wish there was more Rattlesnakes," she said.

"I wish there was more dead members," Suzy said.

"That's a cross word, Suzy!" said Fauna. "The birds are chirping happily, so why can't we? Now let's relax. Who wants a beer?"

Becky said, "If I say I want it I'll have to get it for everybody. My dogs are tired! You know what I was dancing? A quadrille!"

Fauna said dryly, "I seen you. I'll have to give you some lessons, I guess. You done a kootch quadrille. It ain't your feet should be tired. After all the posture lessons I give you, you still dance like a harlot."

"What's a harlot?" Becky asked.

"A whore," said Mabel.

"Oh, harlot, huh?" said Becky.

Agnes said, "Fauna, I want you should tell Suzy when she goes on errands she should come back. She stayed over Doc's about an hour while the Rattlesnakes was really active."

Suzy asked, "Say, Fauna, what's wrong with Doc?"

"Wrong? Ain't nothing wrong with him," said Fauna. "He's one of the nicest fellas ever lived on Cannery Row. You'd think he'd turn bitter the way everybody hustles him. Wide Ida gets him to analyse her booze, Mack and the boys throw the hook into him for every dime that sticks out, a kid cuts his finger on the Row and he goes to Doc to get it wrapped up. Why, when Becky got in a fight with that Woodman of the World and got bit in the shoulder, she might have lost her arm if it wasn't for Doc. Show her the scar, Becky."

Suzy asked, "Don't Doc never come here?"

"No, he don't. But don't let nothing ever give you the idea he's strange. There's girls goes in there with fur coats and stuff and he plays that churchy kind of music. Doc's all right. He gets what he wants. Dora said every girl made a play for him. I put a stop to that."

"Why'd you do that?" Suzy asked.

"I'm saving him—that's why. You look at them gold stars over there—every star, one of my girls has married well."

Suzy said, "Who marries hustlers?"

"Now that's a bad attitude to take," Fauna said coldly. "That's the kind of attitude I try to discourage. You look at that third star from the end over there. I admit she's kind of snooty, but why shouldn't she be? She's a reader in a big church in San Luis Obispo. I tell you, my girls marry, and marry well!"

Suzy said, "What's that got to do with Doc?"

"I got him staked out for Miss Right," said Fauna. "Some day I'll draw a bead on him."

"Hell," said Suzy, "he said he don't want to marry nobody."

"Watch your language, Suzy," said Fauna. And then with interest she asked, "How'd you get along with him?"

"We got in a hassle," said Suzy. "He made me mad and I made him mad. All them goddam bugs—and a paper about nervous breakdowns in devilfish! Some day a guy in a white coat's going to rap him on the shoulder."

Fauna said, "Don't believe it! Why, some of them bugs he gets as much as ten bucks for."

"Not *apiece*?" said Suzy.

Fauna went on, "Why, he takes an old beat-up cat he paid a quarter for and he shoots red and blue and yellow paint in it and he gets fifteen bucks for it."

"Why, for Chrissake?" Suzy asked.

"Suzy, if you don't watch your language I'll wash out your mouth. Now you just get up and bring the beer for that. You're an ignorant girl, but I'll be goddamned if I'll let you get common."

Suzy went out, and Fauna said, "I wonder if she might be for Doc—she's got an awful big mouth. She'd talk her way out of an apple dumpling."

Suzy came back with a tray of beer bottles.

Becky said, "Fauna, why don't you read Suzy's horoscope?"

"You mean stars and like that?" said Suzy. "What for?"

Becky said, "To see if you're going to marry Doc."

Suzy said angrily, "I like a joke as good as anybody, but don't get rough with me."

Becky said, "Who's rough?"

"I don't believe that crap about stars," said Suzy. "And you lay off talking about Doc. He's been to college—he's read so many books he can't count 'em—and not comic books neither. You lay off talking about him and me."

Fauna said, "That will be enough, miss. You see that chart? Just look at them gold stars. And look particular at that gold star that's got a gold star on it. That young lady is married to a professor at Stanford. He's got about a million books, and she used to take all day Sunday figuring out Jiggs and Maggie. You know what she does? If somebody points to all them books and says, 'Does the little lady read all of them?' she just smiles kind of quiet and mysterious. When they ask her a question, you know what she does? You can learn, Suzy, if you just pay attention. She repeats the last three words anybody says, and first thing you know, they think she said it. Why, her own husband thinks she can read and write! You get smart, Suzy. Doc don't want no dame that knows as much as him. What would he have to talk about? Let him tell you for once. Don't tell him."

Becky said, "She won't. She loves to shoot off her face."

"She damn well better learn to shut up or she won't be no gold star," said Fauna. "That's a good idea about the horoscope. When's your birthday, Suzy?"

"February twenty-third."

"What time was you born?"

"God knows, but I think it was leap year."

Agnes said, "I bet she was born at night. I can always tell."

Fauna went into her room and brought back a chart and pinned it to the wall. And she brought out her schoolroom pointer again. "Now this here's you, Pisces—that's fish."

Suzy said, "You mean I'm fish?"

"You're fish," said Fauna.

"I don't believe a goddam word of it. I don't even like fish," Suzy said. "Why, hell, I break out if I look at a fish!"

"Don't look at them, then," said Fauna. "But if you ain't lied about your birthday you're fish. Now let's see—fish is to Jupiter, carry two in the Saturn, and three left over in the House of Venus——"

"I don't believe none of it," Suzy said.

Fauna looked up from her figuring. "Tell her some of that stuff I done, Mabel."

Mabel said, "I seen her do wonderful stuff. I had a pup one time. Fauna, she done a horoscope on him. It says on that pup's third birthday, ten o'clock, he's going explode."

Suzy asked, "Did he?"

"Well, no. Something went haywire with the chart, I guess. Ten o'clock on that dog's third birthday he caught fire. I was taking a lemon rinse."

"You could use one now," Fauna said.

"What caught him on fire?" Suzy asked.

"He just caught. Spontaneous something or other. He was a pretty good dog, but he wasn't very bright. Never could house-break him. He used to wet on Joe Elegant."

Suzy said, "I bet Joe Elegant set him on fire."

"That's a lie!" said Mabel. "Joe Elegant was in the hospital."

Suddenly Fauna clapped her hands to her brow. "God Almighty!"

"What is it?" said Becky. "What's the matter?"

Fauna said impressively, "Suzy, you know what you're going to marry? You're going to marry a Cancer!"

"Thought you caught it," said Suzy. "I didn't know you had to marry it."

"Don't get funny," said Fauna. "Cancer, that's a crab—and that's also July. Now you just think—who works with crabs and stuff like that?"

Becky said, "Joe Anguro's fish market."

Fauna exploded, "Doc! And if his birthday's in July he's a gone goose. Agnes, when's Doc's birthday?"

"I don't know. Mack's gonna ask him."

"Well, we'll have to find out. Can't let him know why we want to know."

Agnes said, "Mack will find out. Mack's used to hustling Doc."

"Well, I want to know right away. Now you young ladies get some sleep, you hear me? You know what's coming in to-day?" Fauna stuck the pencil in her hair. "A great big fat juicy destroyer! And you know what day it is?"

The girls spoke in a chorus. "Lord-God-Almighty," they said, "pay-day!"

It took Fauna about five minutes to put up her hair and then she was ready to make her final rounds to see that the garbage was out and all the lights turned off. In the dark Ready Room she saw a glowing cigarette.

"Who's there?" she called.

"Me," said Suzy.

"Why ain't you in bed?"

"I was thinking."

"Now I know you'll never make a hustler. What you thinking about, your horoscope?"

"Yeah."

"You like Doc, huh?"

"I put the knife in him. He made me mad."

"Whyn't you let me handle it?" said Fauna. "I think I could maybe get him for you."

"He don't want a wife, and if he did, he don't want nobody like me."

"People don't know what they want," said Fauna. "They got to be pushed. Why would guys in their right mind want to get married? But they do."

"Maybe they fall in love," said Suzy.

"Yeah—and that's the worst that can happen. Know something, Suzy? When a man falls in love it's ninety to one he falls for the dame that's worst for him. That's why I take matters in my own hands."

"How do you mean?" Suzy asked.

"Well, when a guy picks out a dame for himself he's in love with something in himself that hasn't got nothing to do with the dame. She looks like his mother, or she's dark and he's scared of blondes, or maybe he's getting even with somebody, or maybe he ain't quite sure he's a man and has to prove it. Fella that studied stuff like that told me one time—a man don't fall for a dame. He falls for new roses, and he brings his own new roses. The best marriages are the ones pulled off by someone that's smart but not sucked in. I think you'd be good for Doc."

"Why?"

"Because you ain't like him. You want I should try?"

"No," said Suzy. "I wouldn't sandbag no guy. Especially Doc."

"Everybody sandbags everybody," said Fauna.

Suzy said softly, "You know, you was right, Fauna. I was sixteen when it happened. But, you know, he talked to me like I was a girl. I can't even remember how it sounds—talked to like a girl."

Fauna put her hand on Suzy's shoulder. "Maybe you'll find out again," she said. "If I pull this off I'll put a red ring around your gold star. You ready to go to sleep now?"

"I guess so," said Suzy. "Let's don't sandbag Doc."

Suzy waited until Fauna had rustled to her bed and then she crept out of the front door. The light was still burning in Western Biological. She went across the street, past the street light, and up the stairs, and she tapped with her finger-tips. Doc didn't answer. She opened the door and saw him sitting at his table, his eyes red, the glass dishes in front of him. He looked very tired and the skin above his beard was grey.

"You're working late," she said.

"Yes. You made me ruin the first set. I had to do it over. It takes time."

"I'm sorry. Doc, you got to write that paper. I don't know nothing about it, but you got to write it."

"I think you were right the first time," he said. "Maybe I can't."

"Sure you can," said Suzy. "You can do anything you want to."

"Maybe that's it. Maybe I don't want to."

"I want you to."

"What have you got to do with it?"

Suzy blushed and looked at her fingers for an answer. "Everybody wants you to," she said. "You'll let everybody down if you don't do it."

He laughed. "That's not a good reason, Suzy."

She tried another tack. "Everybody hates a coward——"

"If I'm a coward, whose business is it?"

"You got to write it, Doc."

"I won't!"

"I'd help you if I could."

"What in the world could you do?"

Her face flamed. "Maybe give you a kick in the arse. Maybe that's what you need."

"Why can't you leave me alone?" he said. And then, "Goddam it! You've done it again—you made me pass over the time!"

"You done it yourself," said Suzy, "you lousy stiff! You blame everybody else. You done it yourself."

"Get on back to the whore-house!" he shouted. "Go on! Get out!"

In the doorway she stopped and looked back. "God, how I hate a fool!" she said, and she slammed the door behind her.

In a moment there was a tap on the glass.

"Go on home," Doc shouted.

Mack opened the door. "It ain't Suzy, it's me."

"You were listening."

"No, I wasn't. Say, Doc, would you say a piece of property on Cannery Row was a good investment?"

"No," said Doc.

"She's quite a dame," said Mack.

"I thought you said you weren't listening."

"Listen, Doc, nobody in this block was listening—but everybody heard. You know, they say there's three good reasons for marrying a hustler."

"What are you talking about?" said Doc.

Mack counted on his fingers. "Number one, she ain't likely to wander—she's done all her experimenting. Number two, you ain't likely to surprise her or disappoint her. And number three, if a hustler goes for you she ain't got but one reason."

Doc watched him, hypnotized. "What reason?"

"She likes you. Good night, Doc."

"Sit down—have a drink."

"I can't. I got to get some sleep. I got work to do to-morrow. 'Night, Doc."

Doc looked at the door after Mack had closed it. The grain of the unpainted pine seemed to squirm to his weary eyes.

CHAPTER XIX

SWEET THURSDAY (1)

LOOKING BACKWARD in time, you can usually find the day it started, the day of Sarajevo, the day of Munich, the moment of Stalingrad or Valley Forge. You fix the day and hour by some incident that happened to yourself. You remember exactly what you were doing when the Japanese bombed Pearl Harbour.

There is no doubt that forces were in motion on that Thursday in Cannery Row. Some of the causes and directions have been in process for generations. There are always some people who claim they felt it coming. Those who remember it say it felt like earthquake weather.

It was a Thursday, and it was one of those days in Monterey when the air is washed and polished like a lens, so that you can see the houses in Santa Cruz twenty miles across the bay and you can see the redwood trees on a mountain above Watsonville. The stone point of Fremont's Peak, clear the other side of Salinas, stands up nobly against the east. The sunshine had a goldy look and red geraniums burned the air around them. The delphiniums were like little openings in the sky.

There aren't many days like that anyplace. People treasure them. Little kids are likely to give off tin-whistle screams for no reason, and business men find it necessary to take a drive to look at a piece of property. Old people sit looking off into the distance and remember inaccurately that the days of their youth were all like that. Horses roll in the green pastures on such a day and hens make a terrible sunny racket.

Thursday was that magic kind of day. Miss Winch, who took pride in her foul disposition before noon, said good morning to the postman.

Joe Elegant awakened early, intending to work on his novel, on the scene where the young man digs up his grandmother to see if she was as beautiful as he remembered. You will recall his novel, *The Pi Root of Œdipus*. But Joe Elegant saw the golden light on the vacant lot and a dew diamond in the heart of every mallow leaf. He went out in the damp grass in his bare feet and scampered like a kitten until he got to sneezing.

Miss Graves, who sings lead in the butterfly pageant in Pacific Grove, saw her first leprechaun up behind the reservoir—but you can't tell everything that happened every place on that Sweet Thursday.

For Mack and the boys it was the morning of Truth, and since Mack was to bear the brunt of it, his friends cooked him a hot breakfast and Eddie mixed real bourbon whisky in his coffee. Hazel polished Mack's shoes and brushed his best blue jeans. Whitey No. 1 brought out his father's hat for Mack to wear—a narrow-brimmed black hat, the crown peaked up to a point. Whitey No. 1's father had been a switchman on the Southern Pacific, and this hat proved it. He stuffed toilet paper in the back of the sweat-band until it fitted Mack perfectly.

Mack didn't talk. He knew how much depended on him, and he was brave and humble at the same time. The boys put the carefully printed tickets in his hand and saw him off, and then they sat down in the weeds to wait. They knew Mack was quaking inside.

Mack went down the chicken walk and across the railroad track. He passed the old boiler and rapped on the rusty pipes in a wild show of bravado.

In front of the grocery he studied a display of screwdrivers with loving intensity before he went in.

Cacahuete was behind the counter, studying a copy of *Down Beat*. He wore a purple windbreaker with gold piping. A lean and handsome boy, he had the wild and sullen light of genius in his eyes.

"Hi!" said Mack.

"Jar!" said Cacahuete.

"Joseph and Mary around?"

"Upstairs."

"I want to see him personal," said Mack.

Cacahuete gave him a long, surly stare, then went to the back of the store and called, "*Tio mio!*"

"What do you want?"

"Mack wants to see you."

"What about?"

"Who knows?"

Joseph and Mary came down the stairs in a pale blue silk bathrobe. " 'Morning, Mack. These kids have no manners."

Cacahuete shrugged and took his *Down Beat* to the top of the potato bin.

"You're out early," said the Patrón.

Mack began with ceremonial seriousness, "You ain't been here long, Joseph and Mary, but you've made a lot of friends, good friends."

The Patrón inspected this statement and made note of its slight inaccuracy. Still, he had nothing to lose by going along with it. "I like the people around here," he said. "They treat me good." His eyelids lowered sleepily, which meant he was as alert as a radar screen.

Mack said, "In a little town you get kind of hide-bound. But you're a man of the world. You been all over. You know how things is."

The Patrón smiled and acknowledged his wisdom and waited.

"I and the boys want to ask your advice," said Mack. "You ain't likely to get a wild hair."

A vague uneasiness stirred in the Patrón. "What's it about?" he asked tentatively.

Mack drew a deep breath. "A smart business man like you might think it was silly, but maybe you been here long enough to get it. It's a sentimental thing. It's about Doc. I and the boys owe Doc a debt we ain't never going to be able to repay."

"How much?" asked the Patrón. He up-ended a broom and tore out a straw with which to pick his teeth. "Take a powder," he said softly to Cacahuete, and his nephew slithered upstairs.

"It ain't money," said Mack, "it's gratitude. For years Doc's took care of us—get sick, he cures us; get broke, he's there with a buck."

"Everybody says the same," the Patrón observed. He could not put his finger on the attack, and yet he felt there was an attack.

The sound of his own voice had a warming, reassuring effect on Mack. He was the professional practising his profession. "We might of went right on hustling Doc for years," he said, "if only Doc didn't get his arse in a sling."

"He's in trouble?"

"You know he's in trouble," said Mack. "Poor bastard sits there beating his brains out with them sooplapods."

"You told me."

"Well, us boys want to do something about it. We ain't going to see our darling friend crap out if we can help it. I bet he done a couple of nice things for you too."

The Patrón said, "Do you know you can't rig a chess game?"

"We had that out," said Mack impatiently. "Doc's business ain't been good. He can't crack open them sooplapods without he gets a great big goddam microscope—cost about four hundred bucks."

The Patrón said hastily, "If you're passing the hat I'll throw in ten bucks."

"Thanks!" said Mack passionately. "I knew you was a good guy. But that ain't it. I and the boys want to do it ourself. We don't want your ten bucks—we want your advice."

The Patrón went behind the counter, opened the ice-box, took out two cans of beer, speared them open, and slid one up the counter to Mack.

"Thanks," said Mack, and he beered down his dry mouth and throat. "Haaah!" he said. "That's fine. Now here's what we want to know. We got something and we want to raffle it. Then we want to take that raffle money and get that microscope for Doc. We want you should give us a hand with the tickets and stuff like that."

"What you going to raffle?" the Patrón asked.

This was the moment, the horrible moment. Mack's hand shook a little as he poured down the second half of the cool, sharp beer. His insides quaked. "The Palace Flop-house—our home," he said.

The Patrón took a pocket comb out of stock and ran it through his black, shining hair. "It ain't worth four hundred bucks," he said.

Mack nearly cried with relief. He could have kissed the Patrón's hand. He loved Joseph and Mary. A strong and tender tone issued from his throat. "We know that," he said, "but it's our home. Oh, I know it ain't very valuable, but when you got something that ain't worth much—why, you raffle it, don't you? If you got a good cause you can raffle an old pair of socks."

A new respect showed in the Patrón's eyes. "You got something there," he said, and then, "Who's going to win it?"

Mack felt confident now. He knew his man. He was ready to use his knowledge. He said confidentially, "I don't never try to kid a smart hombre. I could tell you we was going to draw honest but you'd know that was double malarky. No, we got an idear."

The Patrón leaned forward. Some of his wariness was lulled. He was still no push-over, but he was softened up. "What's the idear?" he asked.

"Well, we got to have someplace to live, don't we? Now this is between I and the boys and you—okay?"

"Okay," said the Patrón.

"We'll sell Doc a ticket or maybe just put a ticket in his name, and we'll rig the raffle so he wins."

"I don't get it," said the Patrón.

"Look!" said Mack. "Doc gets his microscope, don't he? And we go right on habiting in the Palace Flop-house, but it's Doc's. It's a sap to his old age—a kind of insurance. I and the boys figure that's the least we can do for him."

"S'pose he sells it?" said the Patrón.

"Oh, not Doc! He wouldn't put us out in the street."

A smile spread over the Patrón's large, handsome face. He could find no fault with it. "I guess I never give you proper credit," he said. "You're smart. Maybe we can do some business—I mean, later. You got the raffle tickets?"

"We made them up last night." Mack laid a little pile of cards on the table.

"How much apiece?"

"Says right on them," Mack said. "Two bucks."

"My first offer still stands," said the Patrón. "I'll take five and you can leave me some to sell."

"Think you could use twenty?"

"I could unload nearly fifty," said the Patrón. "I'll put them out with the Espaldas Mojadas."

Mack's knees were weak as he went up the chicken walk. His glazed eyes stared straight ahead. He walked right past the boys and into the Palace Flop-house and sat down heavily on his bed. The boys trooped in behind him and stood around.

"Got him!" said Mack. "He don't know he owns it. He bought five tickets and he's going to sell fifty to his wet-backs!"

There is a point of relief and triumph in which words have no place. Eddie went outside, and they could hear his shovel strike the ground. Mack and the boys knew Eddie was digging up a keg.

And this was only one of the happenings on that Sweet Thursday.

CHAPTER XX

SWEET THURSDAY (2)

Fauna always drew the blinds of her bedroom tight down. Because of the late hours of business, she had to sleep until noon to get her proper rest. On the morning of Sweet Thursday the sun played a trick on her. The window-blind had a hole in it no bigger than the point of a pin. The playful sun picked up the doings of Cannery Row, pushed them through the pin-hole, turned them upside down, and projected them in full colour on the wall of Fauna's bedroom.

Wide Ida waddled across the wall upside down, wearing a print dress strewn with red poppies and on her head a black beret. The Pacific Gas & Electric truck rolled across her wall upside down, its wheels in the air. Mack strode towards the grocery head-down. And a little later, Doc, weary, feet over his head, walked along the wall-paper carrying a quart of beer that would have spilled if it had not been an illusion. At first Fauna tried to go back to sleep, but she was afraid she might miss something. It was the little coloured ghost of upside-down Doc that drew her from her couch.

It is a common experience that a problem difficult at night is resolved in the morning after the committee of sleep has worked on it. And this had happened to Fauna. She was glad when she raised the blind and saw how beautiful was the day. The roof of the Hediondo Cannery where seagulls had perched glowed like a pearl.

Fauna brushed her hair severely back and put on a close-fitting hat of black sequins. She wore her dark-grey knitted suit and carried gloves. In the kitchen she put six bottles of beer in a paper bag, and then, as an afterthought, she rooted out one of the shrunken monkey heads as a present. When she climbed the stairs of Western Biological and stood at the top, puffing a little, you might have thought she was soliciting for the Red Cross instead of for the Bear Flag.

Doc was frying sausages, sprinkling a little chocolate over them. It gave them an odd and oriental flavour, he thought.

"You're up early," he greeted Fauna.

"I figured one quart of beer wouldn't last long."

"It didn't," said Doc. "Have a couple of sausages?"

"Don't mind if I do," said Fauna. For she knew that he who gives to you is in debt to you. "This here's a monkey head that I picked up in my travels."

"Interesting," said Doc.

"You know, there's some folks think they're people's heads," said Fauna.

"Don't see how they could. See the shape of the eyes and ears? Look at the nose."

"Oh, some folks don't look at people very close," said Fauna. "I'll have a bottle of beer with you."

The taste of the chocolate sausages intrigued her. "I never tasted nothing like it," she observed. "Did you ever eat grasshoppers, Doc?"

"Yes," said Doc. "In Mexico. They're kind of peppery."

Fauna was not one to beat around bushes. "You must get sick of everybody wanting something from you," she said.

Doc smiled. "I'd be sicker if they didn't," he said. "What can I do for you? Say, thanks for the cake and the beer last night!"

Fauna asked, "What did you think of the kid?"

"Strange," said Doc. "Somehow I can't see her working at the Bear Flag."

"Neither can I," said Fauna. "She ain't no good at it, but it looks like I'm stuck with her. Trouble with Suzy is, she's got a streak of lady in her and I don't know how to root it out."

Doc munched his sausages and sipped his beer thoughtfully. "I never thought of it, but that could be a drawback," he said.

"She's a nice kid," said Fauna. "I like her fine. But she's a liability in a business way."

"Why don't you kick her out?"

"Oh, I can't," said Fauna. "She's had a tough time. I never had no gift for kicking people out. What I'd like is if she'd pick up and go. She got no future as a floozy."

"She threw the book at me," said Doc.

"You see?" said Fauna. "She's a character. That ain't no good in a house."

"She slapped me in the face with a few basic truths," said Doc. "That's a quick eye she's got."

"And a quicker tongue," said Fauna. "Would you do me a favour?"

"Why, of course," said Doc. "Anything I can."

"I can't go to nobody else," Fauna went on, "they wouldn't understand."

"What is it?"

"Doc," said Fauna, "I knocked around and I seen all kinds. I tell you, if you got a streak of lady in you it spoils you for anything else. Now you never come over to the Bear Flag. You play the field. I personally think that costs more, but I ain't one to mess in the way people want to live."

"I don't think I'm following you," said Doc.

"Okay, I'll lay out the deck. When you're making a play for one of them babes, them amateurs, you got to do quite a lot of talking before you make the sack—ain't that right?"

Doc smiled ruefully. "Right," he said.

"Well, do you always mean every word of it?"

Doc pinched his lower lip. "Why—why—I guess right at the moment I do."

"But afterward?"

"Afterward, if I were to think about it——"

"That's what I mean," said Fauna. "So if you happen to tell a little teensy-beensy bit of baloney you don't blow your brains out."

"You'd do well in the analysis business," said Doc. "What do you want me to do?"

"This kid Suzy's lousy with new roses. She ain't a good hustler because of that streak of lady. I don't know if she'd make a good lady or not. I want her off my neck. Doc, would it do you any harm to make a play for her? I mean, like you do with them dames that come in here."

"What good could that possibly do?" he asked.

"Well, maybe I'm wrong, but the way I figure it, you can use new roses if you want to. If you made a pitch for the kid, like she was a lady, why, she might turn lady on you."

"I still can't see what good it would do," said Doc.

"It would get her the hell out of the Bear Flag," said Fauna. "She wouldn't want to congregate with no more floozies."

"How about me?" said Doc.

"You don't marry them others, do you?"

"No, but——"

"Take a whang at her, will you, Doc?" Fauna begged. "Can't do you no harm. Why, hell, she might scram out of here and take up typewriting or telephone operating. Will you do that for me, Doc?"

He said, "It doesn't seem honest."

Fauna changed her tack. "I was talking to her last night and she said she couldn't remember when a guy had treated her like a girl. What harm would that do?"

"Might make her miserable."

"Might make her fly the coop."

"Maybe she likes it the way it is."

"She don't. I tell you she's a blowed-in-the-glass lady. Look, Doc, you take her out to dinner and I'll buy the dinner. You don't have to make no pass. Just be nice to her."

"I'll have to think about it."

"Think you might do it?"

"I might."

"That's a good kid if you treat her right. You'd be doing me a big favour."

"Suppose she won't go?"

"She will. I won't give her no choice."

Doc looked out of the window and a warmth crept through him, and suddenly he felt better than he could remember feeling.

"I'll think about it," he said.

"I'll throw in three bottles of champagne whenever you say the word," said Fauna.

After lunch Joe Elegant read Fauna his latest chapter. He explained the myth and the symbol. "You see," he said, "the grandmother stands for guilt."

"Ain't she dead and buried?"

"Yes."

"That's a kind of a messy guilt."

"It's the reality beyond reality," said Joe Elegant.

"Balls!" said Fauna. "Listen, Joe, whyn't you write a story about something real?"

"Maybe *you* can tell *me* about the *art* of writing?" he said.

"I sure as hell can," said Fauna. "There's this guy, and he makes love to this dame."

"Very original," said Joe.

"When a man says words he believes them, even if he thinks he's lying."

"For goodness' sake! What are you talking about?"

"I bet I get rid of a certain person and put up a new gold star. You want to take that bet?"

"How did Doc like the cake?" Joe Elegant asked.

"He loved it," said Fauna.

And this was the second event of that Sweet Thursday.

CHAPTER XXI

SWEET THURSDAY WAS ONE HELL OF A DAY

Fission took place in the Palace Flop-house, and from there a chain reaction flared up in all directions. Cannery Row caught fire. Mack and the boys had the energy and the enthusiasm of plutonium. Only very lazy men could have done so much in so short a time. Oh, the meetings, the messages carried, the plans and counter-plans! Mack had to make more and more raffle tickets. What started as a kind of gentle blackmail assumed the nature of an out-pouring of popular love for Doc. People bought tickets, sold tickets, traded tickets. Emissaries covered the Southern Pacific Depot, the Greyhound Bus Station. Joe Blaikey, the constable, carried tickets in his pocket and cancelled parking summonses if the law-breaker bought a two-dollar chance on the Palace Flop-house.

Whitey No. 1 invaded the foreign and fancy purlieus of Pebble Beach and Carmel and the Highlands. Whitey No. 2's method was characteristically direct. The first man to refuse him got a rock through his windscreen, and the news travelled.

To the boys it had become a crusade. And the winning ticket, of course, with Doc's name on it, was in a tomato can, buried in the vacant lot. By tacit agreement no one mentioned the raffle to Doc. To Doc's friends, Mack and the boys mentioned the rigging of the lottery, but to strangers—who cared? It was a perfect example of the collective goodness and generosity of a community.

But if communities have a group Good Fairy they also have an Imp who works parallel with and sometimes in collaboration with the Good Fairy. Cannery Row's Imp saw the Good Fairy stirring to life, and he sprang to action. Into the ears of his clients he whispered a few words, and his constituents grinned with evil pleasure and their thoughts went like this: The Patrón is a wise guy. He's a newcomer, nice clothes, makes his money off poor helpless wetbacks because he's smart. Lee Chong must have sold him the Palace Flop-house and he's forgot it or he never knew it. Once Doc wins it the Patrón won't dare make a move.

It is such fun to outsmart a smart guy. The Imp of the Row had a good professional time and for once his job seemed almost virtuous. People bought more tickets from the Patrón than from anyone else. They wanted to watch his face so they could compare it with his face when he found out.

Now ordinarily Mack and the boys would have strung out the ticket sales over weeks, but time was breathing down their necks. If the Patrón got his tax bill from the county their plan would blow up in their faces. They had to take a chance with Friday—Saturday was the deadline. The boys spread the word that there would be medium-heavy refreshments at the Palace Flop-house on Saturday night and that contributions of any nature would be welcome.

Mack called on Doc the afternoon of Sweet Thursday. "If you ain't doing anything Saturday night," he said, "I and the boys are throwing a little wing-ding. R.S.V.P."

"*Moi, je respond oui.*"

"Come again?"

"I'll be there," said Doc.

Then Mack remembered a mission with which he had been entrusted. "I guess I could squirm it out of you, Doc, like I done once before," he said, "but I'll come right out in the open. When's your birthday?"

A shudder went through Doc. "Please don't give me a party," he begged. "The last one you gave nearly ruined me."

"This hasn't got nothing to do with a party—it's a bet," said Mack. "I stand to win a buck. When is it?" Mack prodded him.

Doc picked the first date that came to him. "July fourth," he said.

"Why, that's like the Fourth of July!"

"A little," said Doc, and he felt greatly relieved.

Later that afternoon Fauna and the girls called formally at the Palace Flop-house in answer to the note Mack had sent asking them to drink a jolt of good stuff. Suzy did not attend. She had been quiet all morning, and then she mooned away on the path that leads along the sea to the lighthouse on Point Pinos. She looked in the tide pools, and she picked a bunch of the tiny flowers that grow as close to the ocean as they can. Suzy was restless and unhappy. She felt excitement and nausea at the same time. She wanted to smile and she wanted to cry, and she was scared and happy and hopeless. Doc had asked her to have dinner with him, at Sonny Boy's on the pier, and Fauna had urged her to go.

Suzy's first reaction had been violent. "I won't do it!" she said.

"Sure you'll go," said Fauna. "I may have to persuade you with a indoor-ball bat—but you'll go."

"You can't make me."

"Want to test that? Why, I've wore my brain down to the knuckles, trying to do something nice for you."

"I ain't got nothing to wear," said Suzy.

"Neither has Doc. If he can go like he does, what right's a chippy to get grand?"

"But hell, Fauna—he's got it inside. People like me got to put on a puff because they got nothing else. I'm afraid I'll turn mean because I don't know how to be nice."

"Suzy," said Fauna, "I'm going to give you a piece of advice, and if you won't take it, I may just call Joe Blaikey and get you floated right out of town. Don't throw the first punch! Wait'll you're hit before you put up your dukes. Most of the time they ain't nobody laid a glove on you."

"Suppose I could wear my suit? It's got a big spot," said Suzy.

"Ask Joe Elegant to spot-clean it and press it. Tell him I said so."

And thus it was that Suzy went walking out lighthouse way on Sweet Thursday.

The meeting in the Palace wasn't really necessary, for word of the raffle had got around and Fauna had bought ten tickets and made each girl buy one.

Eddie had borrowed glasses from Wide Ida's—for once, with her permission. She was invited to the meeting too, and she brought two quarts of Pine Canyon whisky.

"It don't cost hardly nothing," she explained.

Formality took hold of the meeting. Agnes and Mabel kept their knees together when they sat down, and Fauna's look of thunder made Becky snap hers shut so quickly that she spilled her drink.

"She's going to be a wallager," said Mack. "I can't wait to see Doc's face when he wins."

Wide Ida asked, "How you going to explain it to him he wins when he didn't buy no ticket?"

"Why, we'll say a friend did it and don't want his name mentioned. I saw Doc a little while ago. He said he'd sure be here."

Fauna said, "Did you find out when is his birthday?"

"Sure. July fourth."

Fauna exhaled with the sound of escaping gas. "Holy apples! He's a gone goose. He got a born-on Oregon boot. I never seen nothing work out so nice!"

"What're you talking about?" said Mack.

Fauna's eyes were misty. "Mack," she said huskily. "I don't want to horn in on your party, but why couldn't we make it an engagement party too?"

"Who's engaged?"

"Well, they ain't yet—but they will be."

"Who?"

"Doc and Suzy. It's right in their horoscopes."

" S'pose they won't?"

"They will," said Fauna. "You can just depend on that—they will!"

The little group sat in silence, and then Mack said softly, "Did I say it was going to be a wallager? This here's a *tom*-wallager! They ain't been nothing so stupendous since the Second World War! You *sure* Doc'll go for it?"

"You let me take care of that—and don't none of you blab it to him. One time I managed a fighter, Kiss of Death Kelly, welterweight. I'll have Doc in the ring."

Eddie asked, "How about Suzy?"

"Suzy's already in the ring," said Fauna.

They parted quietly, but in their breasts a flame of emotion burned. There never was a day like that Sweet Thursday. And it wasn't over yet.

CHAPTER XXII

THE ARMING

AT FOUR-THIRTY in the afternoon Fauna ordered Suzy to the office bedroom with full field equipment. Suzy dumped her clothes on Fauna's bed.

"That's a hell of a way to keep wrinkles out," Fauna observed. She picked up the grey woollen skirt and jacket, laid them out, inspected them for spots, smelled them for cleaning fluid. "Nice piece of goods," she said.

"Community chest," said Suzy. "I was in the charity ward."

"Well, somebody wasn't." Her eyes noted the brown shoes. She went to the door and yelled, "Joe! Joe Elegant!"

He looked in. "I'm not supposed to be on duty," he said.

"I'm a thorn in the side of the worker," said Fauna. "You run up the street to Wildock's and get new heel-taps on these here. Tell them to fix this scuffed place and give them a nice shine. Wait and bring them back."

Joe complained as he went, but he went.

Fauna said to Suzy, "You got any gloves?"

"No."

"I'll lend you some. Here—these white ones. And here's a handkerchief. I don't want no lipstick marks on it. Now you listen to me, Suzy girl—take care of your shoes, wear clean gloves, carry a white handkerchief, and keep your stocking seams straight. If you do that you can get away with murder. This here's a nice suit—that kind of cloth that the older it gets the better it looks—if your heels ain't run over. Call Becky in!"

When Becky entered Fauna said, "Ain't you got a white piqué dickey and cuffs?"

"I just done them up."

"I want you should lend them to Suzy. Get some thread and sew the cuffs in this here jacket."

"She'll have to wash them."

"She will."

While Becky basted in the cuffs Fauna said, "Turn out your purse, Suzy." She inspected the pile on the bed. "You don't need that aspirin. Here, take my comb—throw that one away. Ain't nothing tackier than a comb missing teeth. Put these here Kleenex in. Here, use my compact and touch up the shine on your nose once in a while. Let's see your nails! Hmmm, pretty good. You washed your hair?"

"Get her a wig," said Becky, and she bit the thread.

"Don't get smart. Come on now—get off your behind and do something with her hair, and not fancy neither." To Suzy she said, "Becky got a light hand with hair. You can't take that coat. Community chest slipped up there." She tapped her teeth with a pencil and then went to her closet and brought out two baum martens that were biting each other's heads off. "Just hang these here bo' martens over your shoulder," Fauna said. "And if you lose them or hurt them I'll cut your tripes out. Now, where are we? No perfume. Douse some of this Florida water on—kind of old-fashioned and young-smelling."

Becky stood behind Suzy's chair, brushing and combing and moulding. "She's got big ears," Becky said. "Maybe I can kind of hide them a little."

"You got a nice hand with hair," Fauna said.

The final briefing took place at six o'clock, with the bedroom door closed.

"Turn around," said Fauna. "Keep your ankles close together. Now, walk! That's good. You got a real nice walk. Like I said, you're a good-looking kid if you work at it a little."

Suzy looked at herself in the mirror and she smiled, for it seemed to her that she really was pretty, and the idea startled her and pleased her too, and when she looked pleased she was even prettier. Then her mouth turned down and blind panic came over her.

"What's the matter?" Fauna demanded.

"What can I talk about? Fauna, I don't want to go! I don't belong with a guy like Doc. Jesus, Fauna, tell him I'm sick. I ain't going."

Fauna let her talk herself out and then she said quietly, "Maybe you'd like to cry now and get your eyes red after all my trouble? Go on, cry!"

"I'm sorry," said Suzy. "You been nice. I ain't no good, Fauna. You're just wasting your time. I know what I'll do—minute he says something I don't understand I'll get mad. I'm scared."

" 'Course you're scared," said Fauna. "But if you didn't care nothing about Doc you wouldn't be scared. You didn't invent it. There ain't never been no dame went out first time with a guy she liked that wasn't scared. Maybe Doc's scared too."

"Oh nuts!" said Suzy.

Fauna said, "If I was your age with your face and shape and what I know, there wouldn't be no man in the world could get away! I got the know-how—but that's all I got. Oh well! I'm going to tell you a few thousand things, Suzy, that if you would listen you'd get anything you want. But hell, you won't listen! Nobody listens, and when they learn the hard way it's too late. Maybe it's a good thing—I don't know."

"I'll listen."

"Sure, but you won't learn. You know, Suzy, they ain't no way in the world to get in trouble by keeping your mouth shut. You look back at every mess you ever got in and you'll find your tongue started it."

"That's true," said Suzy. "But I can't seem to stop."

"You got to learn it like you learn anything else—just practice. Next thing is opinions. You and me is always busting out with opinions. Hell, Suzy, we ain't got no opinions! We just say stuff we heard or seen in the movies. We're scared we'll miss something, like running for a bus. That's the second rule: lay off opinions, because you ain't really got any."

"You got them numbered, huh?" said Suzy.

"I should write a book," said Fauna. " 'If She Could, I Could.' Now take number three. There don't hardly nobody listen, and it's so easy! You don't have to do nothing when you listen. If you do listen it's pretty interesting. If a guy says something that pricks up your interest, why, don't hide it from him. Kind of try to wonder what he's thinking instead of how you're going to answer him back."

"You're sure putting the finger on me," Suzy said softly.

"I only got a little more, but it's the hardest of all, and the easiest."

"What number?"

"I lost track. Don't pretend to be something you ain't and don't make like you know something you don't, or sooner or later you'll sure fall on your arse. And there's one more part to this one, whatever number it is: they ain't nobody was ever insulted by a question. S'pose Doc says something and you don't know what it means. Ask him! The nicest thing in the world you can do for anybody is let them help you."

Suzy was silent, looking down at her hands.

Fauna said, "You got nice nails. How do you keep them so nice?"

Suzy said, "That's easy. My grandma taught me. You keep a old lemon rind, and every time you wash your hands you scrounge your fingernails around in it. And then you shake a little face powder on your hand and you polish your nails on the ham of your hand and you push down the quick with a little piece of lemon wood."

"See what I mean?" said Fauna.

"What?"

"I just asked you a question."

Suzy blushed. "I sure fell into that."

"No, you didn't. I wanted to know. It's best if you ask when you want to know."

"Thanks," said Suzy. "You're a hell of a dame. I wonder if I could learn?"

"You can if you just remember a lot of things: first, you got to remember you're Suzy and you ain't nobody else but Suzy. Then you got to remember that Suzy is a good thing—a real valuable thing—and there ain't nothing like it in the world. It don't do no harm just to say that to yourself. Then, when you got that, remember that there's one hell of a lot Suzy don't know. Only way she can find out is if she sees it, or reads it, or asks it. Most people don't look at nothing but themselves, and that's a rat race."

"What's the fourth thing?" Suzy asked.

"I'm proud of you!" Fauna said. "You listened. The next thing you'll have to do some thinking about. Nobody don't give a particular damn about Suzy one way or the other. It's hard to get them thinking about you because they're too busy thinking about themselves. There's two, three, copper-bottom ways to get their attention:

Talk about them. If you see something nice or good or pretty, tell them. Don't make it a fake, though. Don't fight nobody unless there ain't no other way. Don't never start a fight, and if one starts, let it get going good before you jump in. Best way in the whole world to defend yourself is to keep your dukes down! Now, when you got their attention, first thing they want is to do something for you. Let them. Don't get proud and say you don't need it or want it. That's a slap in the puss. Thing people like most in the world is to give you something and have you like it and need it. That ain't sloppy. That works. You give it a try."

"You think Doc would fall for that stuff?"

"Just give it a try."

Suzy said, "Fauna, didn't you never get married?"

"No."

"Why not?"

Fauna smiled. "Time I learned what I just told you, it was too late."

"I love you," said Suzy.

"Now you see! You got me softened up like butter. I want you should keep them furs."

"But——"

"Watch it!"

"Yeah, I see. I sure do thank you. And would you maybe write down all that stuff so I can get it by heart?"

"Sure I will. Now look, Suzy—to-night, just before you say something, say it first to yourself, and kind of dust it off."

"You mean cussing?"

"I mean cussing, and I mean—well, sometimes if you look at it you don't say it. One whole hell of a lot that passes for talk is just running off at the mouth. I guess you're about ready now."

"Is there anything I can do for you, Fauna?"

"Yes. I want you should repeat after me, 'I'm Suzy and nobody else.' "

" 'I'm Suzy and nobody else.' "

" 'I'm a good thing.' "

" 'I'm a good thing.' "

" 'There ain't nothing like me in the whole world.' "

" 'There ain't nothing'—goddam it, Fauna, now my eyes'll be red!"

"They look pretty that way," said Fauna.

At seven o'clock Doc, dressed in an open-collared shirt, leather jacket and army trousers, rang the bell at the Bear Flag. He looked at Suzy and he said, "I've got to make a telephone call, do you mind?" And he ran back to the laboratory.

Ten minutes later he returned. He had on clean slacks, a tweed jacket, and a tie he hadn't used in years.

Fauna saw him standing under the porch light.

"Honey," she said to Suzy, "you win the first round on points."

CHAPTER XXIII

ONE NIGHT OF LOVE

SONNY BOY is truly the only Greek born in America named Sonny Boy. He operates a restaurant and bar on the wharf in Monterey. Sonny Boy is plump and getting plumper. Although he was born near Sutro Park in San Francisco and went to state schools, Sonny Boy has singlehandedly kept alive the mystery of the Near East. His perfectly round face hints Orient Express and beautiful spies. His bushy voice is congenitally confidential. Sonny Boy can say 'Good evening' and make it sound like an international plot. His restaurant makes friends for him and supports him. Perhaps Sonny Boy, in one sense, wears a long black cape and dines with Balkan countesses where two seas kiss the Golden Horn—but he also runs a good restaurant. He probably knows more secrets than any man in the community, for his martinis are a combination of truth serum and lie detector. *Veritas* is not only *in vino* but regularly batters its way out.

Doc stopped his old car in front of Sonny Boy's, got out, walked round, opened the other door, and helped Suzy out.

She was a little shocked, but she remained silent. The sentence, "You think I'm a cripple, for Crissake!" rose to her throat, but she followed Fauna's advice—whispered it and pushed it back. The fact of his hand on her elbow did a magic thing to her, pushed back her shoulders and raised her chin. The gritty light of resistance went out of her eyes.

Doc opened the door of the bar and stood aside to let Suzy enter. The regulars on the stools turned to look. The eyes crept from pretty face to pretty legs, took in the martens on the way. For one second panic halted her, but she saw no look of recognition in the eyes of the regulars.

Sonny Boy turned sideways to get around the end of the bar. " 'Evening, folks," he said. "Your table is ready. Would you like to have a cocktail here, or shall I send one over?"

"Oh let's sit at the table," said Doc.

Sonny Boy bowed Suzy through the door to the restaurant and she strolled ahead with her nice walk. Sonny Boy, rolling along beside Doc, said in his conspiratorial whisper, "Your secretary called. It's all fixed. You got a secretary, Doc?"

Doc overcame his surprise. "Part-time," he said.

"Who's the lady? She new around here?"

"She's new around here," said Doc. He caught up with Suzy.

"This way," said Sonny Boy. He led them to a round table in front of the stone fireplace. A pine fire crackled and sent out its fragrance. The table had a centrepiece of wild iris. The breadsticks stood like soldiers in their glasses. The napkins were folded to make little crowns. It was the best table in the house, private, but downstage and well lighted.

Suzy's eyes darted around the room. No other table had flowers. Something wonderful happened in Suzy. She didn't walk round the table and sit down. She waited, and when Doc held her chair for her she seated herself, looked smiling up at him, and said, "Thank you."

Sonny Boy hovered over the table. "Good you telephoned," he said. "I had trouble getting pompano, but I got it. How's about a cocktail? The wine's cooling."

Doc said, "One time I had some kind of——"

"I remember!" said Sonny Boy. "The Webster F. Street Lay-Away Plan—a martini made with chartreuse instead of vermouth. Very good."

"Very effective, as I remember it," said Doc. "Two doubles."

"Coming right up," said Sonny Boy. "I told Tony to be right here to play piano like you said, but he's sick."

Doc looked at Suzy to see whether she knew Fauna had made the arrangements. She didn't.

It is probable that if Doc hadn't ordered the Webster F. Street Lay-Away Plans he would have got them anyway. They arrived with a speed that indicated they were already mixed.

The shock of a necktie was leaving Doc. He looked across the table and smiled at Suzy and he wondered, What is beauty in a girl that it can come and go? This Suzy did not faintly resemble the tough hustler who had screamed at him the night before. He raised the cocktail glass. "You're pretty," he said. "I'm glad you came with me. Here's to both of us."

Suzy swallowed a gulp, held back her tears, and waited for the spasm to pass.

"I should have warned you," said Doc, "there's a rumour that this drink is made of rattlesnake venom and raw opium."

Suzy got her breath. "It's good," she said. "But I was watching its right hand and walked into a left hook!"

Her mind cried, "I shouldn't of said that! I forgot already." Then she saw Doc's amusement and it was all right.

Suzy noticed a waiter drifting delicately within earshot. She had discovered something for herself. When in doubt, move slowly. Her head turned towards the waiter and he drifted away. She was delighted with her discovery—everything-in-slow-motion. She lifted her glass slowly, looked at it carefully, then sipped and held it a moment before she put it down. S-l-o-w-ness—it gave meaning to everything. It made everything royal. She remembered how all the unsure and worried people she knew jumped and picked and jittered. Just doing everything slowly, forcing herself, she felt a new kind of security. Don't forget, she told herself. Don't ever forget this. Slow! Slow!

Doc gave her a cigarette and held a match, and she leaned forward so slowly that the flame was touching his fingers before she had lighted it. A lovely warmth stole through her body. She felt bold, not defensively bold, but safe.

She asked, "Do they know—what I am?"

The Lay-Away Plan works equally on all. Doc said, "They know you're with me. That's all they need to know. Shall we have one more?"

It came before he got his finger raised for attention. If this was conspiracy, Sonny Boy wanted to be in on it. If felicity, he liked that too.

"I like a fire," Suzy said. "Once we had a fireplace where I lived."

Doc said, "You're pretty. Yes, by George! You're pretty!"

Suzy swallowed the first words that rose and swallowed the second ones and ended up by dropping her eyes and saying "Thank you" softly.

Sonny Boy personally escorted the waiter, who carried the ice bucket with the chilled Chablis. Then he stood back and surveyed the table. "How is everything, Doc?"

"Just fine," said Doc.

"You ready to eat?"

"Any time," said Doc.

And Suzy's discovery continued to hold good: Take it slow and keep your eyes open and your mouth shut.

The cold cracked crab, the pompano, were new to her, and they required an eating technique she didn't know. She did everything a little behind Doc, and he wasn't conscious that she watched every move he made.

When champagne and fruit and cheese arrived, Suzy knew she had to be alone. A thought so overwhelming had come to her that her knees shook and the blood pounded in her temples. Slow! she warned herself. Take it easy. She looked at the leaping flames and then pivoted her head to Doc. "Will you excuse . . . ?"

"Of course!" He jumped up and drew back her chair. Suzy moved regally towards the Ladies' Room. She could not feel her feet against the floor.

Doc watched her passage. Strange, strange, he thought. What is it? 'Maidenly' is the word. A kind of lonely and terrible modesty. What has made the change? Then he thought, It's an act. Fauna coached her. But he knew that wasn't true. Acting couldn't get into the eyes like that. Coaching couldn't draw the blood to her cheeks. He spun the champagne bottle in its bucket, and he found himself wishing she would hurry back. His eyes found a window that reflected the door to the Ladies' Room.

Behind that door Suzy dampened a paper towel and put it against her forehead. She stared at herself in the mirror and she didn't know the face. She thought of the dinner. "I hate fish," she said out aloud. "It makes me break out. But I ain't broke out." Finally she was ready to inspect the thought that had sent her out: the symbol, the mystery, the signpost with an inexorable pointing finger. It was so plain no one could miss it. Fate was not only pointing the way but booting from behind. She thought of the dishes being taken away: the heaped legs and claws of crabs and—They had eaten their horoscopes! Cancer and Pisces—fish and crab.

"Great God Almighty!" she said, and she was limp in the hands of Fate.

Sonny Boy came to the table. "Everything all right?"

"Fine," said Doc.

"Just like you ordered."

"Huh?"

"Your secretary told me."

"Fine," said Doc, "just the way I wanted it."

When Suzy came back she was dedicated. You can only fight Fate so far, and when you give in to it you're very strong; because all of your force flows in one direction.

Doc held her chair and then he popped the champagne cork and smelled it.

Suzy said, "Can I have it?"

"Of course."

She turned the cork in her fingers and looked at it. It was very beautiful. She put it in her purse and took an iris from the vase.

"Do you like champagne?"

"I love it," she said, and wondered what it would taste like. And she did love it.

Doc said, "You know, out in the sand dunes there are little valleys covered with pines. Sometime, when you can, let's take meat and things out there and cook our supper. It's very nice."

"The fire reminded you," said Suzy.

"That's clever of you—so it did."

She said, "Doc, will you sometime teach me about the stuff you got in your place?"

"Sure I will." A surge of affection filled him. But he was a little afraid too of her terrible modesty. He looked away from her eyes to the wild iris in her hand. "There's an old Welsh story," he said. "It's about a poor knight who made a wife completely out of flowers——"

The wine was strong in Suzy now. She said the sentence twice to herself before she said it aloud to Doc. "I hope she didn't wilt."

The low voice of Doc's guts burst through at last. "I'm lonely," he said. He said it as a simple matter of fact and he said it in wonder. Then he apologized. "I guess I'm a little drunk." He felt very shy. He filled the glasses. "What the hell! Let's have some brandy too."

Suzy turned half away from him so that her face was outlined in leaping pine flames. "You know that place you said—out in the sand dunes?"

"Yes."

"Could we look at it?"

"Whenever you want."

"On our way home?"

"You'll ruin your shoes."

"I know," said Suzy.

"You could take them off."

"I will," said Suzy.

CHAPTER XXIV

WAITING FRIDAY

Not everyone believes that Friday is unlucky, but nearly everybody agrees it is a waiting day. In business, the week is really over. In school, Friday is the half-open gate to freedom. Friday is neither a holiday nor a work-day, but a time of wondering what Saturday will bring. Trade and amusement fall off. Women look through their closets to see what they have to wear. Supper is left-overs from the week.

Joe Elegant ordered sand dabs for supper at the Bear Flag. The Espaldas Mojadas returned from their latest triumph and were ushered with great courtesy to the rooms over the grocery. The Patrón distributed bottles of tequila. Also, he kept a saucer of Seconal at hand. Sometimes a passion of homesickness got into his wet-backs. Sleep, he thought, was better than fighting.

Doc slept late, and when he went to the grocery for his morning beer he found Joseph and Mary alert and gay, and the sound of singing drifted down the stairs.

"Have a good time?" the Patrón asked.

"What do you mean?" Doc demanded.

"Didn't you have a nice party last night?"

"Oh, sure," said Doc. He said it with finality.

"Doc, I'd like you to teach me more of that chess."

"You still think you can cheat at it, do you?"

"No, I just like to figure it out. I got a case of Bohemia beer from Mexico, all cold."

"Wonderful!" said Doc. "That's the best beer in the Western Hemisphere."

"It's a present," said the Patrón.

"Why?"

"I don't know. Maybe I just feel good."

"Thanks," said Doc. He began to feel uneasy.

There were eyes on him. Going back to Western Biological, he felt eyes on him. It's the brandy, he thought. I shouldn't drink brandy. Makes me nervous.

He scrambled two eggs and shook curry powder over them. He consulted the tide chart in Thursday's *Monterey Herald.* There was a fair tide at 2.18 p.m., enough for chitons and brittlestars if the wind wasn't blowing inshore by then. The Bohemia beer settled his nerves without solving his restlessness. And for once the curried eggs didn't taste very good.

Fauna knocked and entered. She flicked her hand at the rattlesnakes. "How do you feel, Doc?"

"All right."

"Get drunk?"

"A little."

"How was the dinner?"

"Wonderful. You know what to order."

"I ought to. Say, you want to box or should we lay it on the line? See what I mean about her?"

"Yes. How does she feel?"

"She ain't up yet."

"I'm going collecting."

"Want me to tell her that?"

"Why should you? Wait—I've got her purse. Want to take it to her?"

"Hell, she ain't crippled. Maybe she'll want to get it herself."

"I won't be here."

"You'll be back."

"Say," he said, "what the hell is this?"

She knew he might turn angry now. "I got a lot to do. You ain't mad at me?"

"Why should I be?"

"Well, if you need anything, let me know."

"Fauna——" he began. "Oh, let it go."

"What do you want?"

"I was going to ask you something—but I don't want to know."

Suzy was hunched over a cup of coffee when Fauna got back.

" 'Morning," said Fauna. And then, "I said good morning."

"Oh, yeah," said Suzy. " 'Morning."

"Look at me!"

"Why not?" Suzy raised her eyes.

"You can look down now," said Fauna.

"You don't know nothing," said Suzy.

"Okay, I don't know nothing. When did I ever get nosey with you? Joe," she called, "bring me a cup of coffee." She slid a tin box of aspirins across the oil-cloth table-cover.

"Thanks." Suzy took three and washed them down with coffee.

"He's going out collecting bugs," said Fauna quietly.

"You went over there?"

"I met him in the street. Have a nice time?"

Suzy looked up at her with eyes so wide that she seemed to be turned inside out. "He didn't make no pass," she said breathlessly. "Went out on the sand dunes and he didn't make no pass."

Fauna smiled. "But he talked nice?"

"Didn't talk much, but he talked nice."

"That's good."

"Maybe I'm nuts, Fauna, but I told him."

"Oh, you ain't nuts."

"I told him everything. He didn't even ask."

Fauna said quietly, "What did he talk about?"

"He said there's a fella in old times made a wife out of flowers."

"What for, for God's sake?"

"Well, I don't know. But it was all right when he said it."

"What else did he say?"

Suzy spoke slowly. "Out in the sand dunes I done most of the talking. But he give me a boost every now and then when I run down."

Fauna said, "He can do that better than anybody."

Suzy's eyes were shining with excitement. "I almost forgot," she said. "I never took no stock in stars and stuff like that, but you know what we had for dinner?"

"Champagne?"

"Fish and crab!" said Suzy. "And I didn't break out."

"Well?"

"Remember what you said, how I'm fish and he's crab?"

Fauna turned her head away. "I got something up my nose," she said. "I wonder if I'm catching cold."

"Do you think that's a sign, Fauna? Do you?"

"Everything's signs," said Fauna. "Everything."

There was a glory in Suzy's eyes. "Right after we ate we was talking, and he said, 'I'm lonely.'"

"Now that ain't like him," Fauna said. "That's a dirty trick!"

"No, ma'am," Suzy contradicted her. "He didn't say it like that. I heard that one before too. He said it like it was pushed out of him. It surprised him, like he didn't know he was going to say it. What do you think, Fauna? Tell me, what do you think?"

"I think there's going to be like a new gold star."

"Well, s'pose—and there ain't no harm in supposing—s'pose I moved over there. It would be—well, it would be right across the street from here. Everybody knows I worked here. Wouldn't that kind of bother him?"

"He knows you work here, don't he? Suzy girl, you got to promise me something. Don't you never try to run away from nothing, because you can't. If you're all right nobody ain't going to tear you down. Guy that runs away, why, he's a fugitive. And a fugitive never gets away."

"How about Doc?" said Suzy.

"Look, if you ain't good enough for him, he ain't good for you."

"I don't want to lay no bear trap for him, Fauna."

Fauna was smiling to herself. She said, "I guess a man is the only kind of varmint sets his own trap, baits it, and then steps into it. You just set still, Suzy girl. Don't do nothing. Nobody can't say you trapped him if you don't do nothing."

"Well, he didn't really say——"

"They never do," said Fauna.

Suzy said weakly, "I can't hardly breathe."

"You know, you ain't cussed once this morning," Fauna said.

"Ain't I?"

"Some of my gold stars was damn good hookers," said Fauna. "But when I put up your gold star, Suzy, the whoring business ain't lost nothing. Like the Patrón says, you're too small in the butt and too big in the bust."

"I don't want nobody to get the idea I'm hustling Doc."

"You're damn right you ain't. I'll see to that." She looked speculatively at Suzy. "You know, I'd like you to get out of town to-night and kind of freshen up."

"Where'll I go?"

"You could go on an errand for me to San Francisco if you

wanted to. I got a little package up there in a safe-deposit box. I'll give you some dough. And I want you should buy some clothes and a hat. Get a nice suit. It'll last you for years. Look! Walk up and down Montgomery Street and see what the nice-looking dames is wearing—you know, the kind of material. They're pretty smart women up there. Before you buy, look around a little—make it nice. Come on back to-morrow."

Suzy said, "You getting me out of the way?"

"Yeah," said Fauna. "You got the idea."

"Why?"

"Suzy girl, that ain't none of your business. There's a two o'clock bus and a four o'clock bus."

"I'll take the four o'clock."

"Why?"

"Well, you said Doc's going out collecting bugs. Maybe while he's gone I could kind of swamp out his joint. It ain't had a scrubbing for years."

"That might make him mad."

"I'll start him a nice stew cooking slow," said Suzy. "I make a real nice stew." She came round the table.

"Get your hands off me!" said Fauna. "Go on now! And don't you ever say that thing again that made a sucker out of me. My best fur!"

"You mean, 'I love you'?"

"That's it. Don't you say it."

"Okay," said Suzy.

CHAPTER XXV

OLD JINGLEBALLICKS

Doc got back from his collecting about four-thirty. He had over a hundred chitons bound with string to little glass plates to keep them from curling, and submerged in sea water in his collecting buckets were hundreds of brittlestars.

Now, killing is one of the delicate operations of a marine zoologist. You want the animal to resemble its living self, but this is impossible. In death the colour changes, just as it does with us. Also, if any violent means of killing is used there is constriction, and in the case of brittlestars the death struggle causes the animal to shed its arms.

In the front room of Western Biological, Doc poured out part of the sea water from his wooden bucket. Then he moved the brittlestars to a large flat-bottomed glass dish and poured some sea water on top of them. The little animals with the snake-like arms whipped about for a moment and then settled down. When they were quite still and resting Doc added a little fresh water to the dish. The arms stirred nervously. He waited a while and then added a little more fresh water. To a sea animal, fresh water is a poison, and if it is slowly introduced it is as subtle as morphine. It relaxes and soothes until the little creature goes to sleep and dies without violence.

Doc sat down to wait for the poison to act. He sensed that there was something wrong. What could it be? Had he forgotten something? He felt all right, the small hangover of the morning was gone. Of course! It was the case of Bohemia beer over at the Patrón's. His subconscious must have been reminding him of the beer. He looked out of the window towards the grocery. And there was something wrong with that too. And finally he saw. His windows were clean. He turned and looked round the laboratory. The records were piled neatly on the shelves, not falling all over themselves. The floor was shining, and that smell—that was soap.

He moved to the kitchen. His dishes were clean, the pans scoured and shining. A delicious odour came from a pot on the gas stove. He lifted the lid. Brown meat juice bubbled up through carrots and onions, and a stick of white celery swam like a fish.

Doc went back to his table and sat down. His cot was made up and smooth and the turned-down sheet was clean. Suddenly a sense of desolation came over him—a great sadness that was like warmth. The toes of his lined-up shoes peeked out at him from under the bed.

The poor kid, he thought. Oh, the poor damn kid! I wonder if she's trying to repay—I hope I haven't done anything bad. My God, I hope she didn't misunderstand anything! What did I say? I know I didn't do anything, but what did I say? I wouldn't hurt Suzy for the world. He glanced around again. She sure does a job of cleaning, he thought. The stew smells wonderful too. He poured a little more fresh water into the glass dish. The arms of the brittle-stars were arranging themselves in small spirals. They hardly moved when the fresh poison was introduced.

The clean laboratory made Doc nervous and apprehensive. And there was something missing from himself, something lost. The lowest voice of all was still. In his black depths he was somehow comforted. He went to the record shelf: not Bach . . . no, not Buxtehude . . . not Palestrina either. His hand strayed to an album not used in a long time. He had opened it before he knew what he was doing. And then he smiled and put the first record on the turntable: Mozart's *Don Giovanni*. It started its overture, and Doc, still smiling, went to the kitchen and stirred the stew. "Don Giovanni," he said. "Is that what I think of myself? No! I do not. But why do I feel so good, and so bad?" He looked at his desk. The yellow pads

were piled neatly and the pencils were sharpened. "I believe I'll try."
And at that point there were fumbling steps on his porch and Old Jingleballicks burst in.

It is madness to write about Old Jingleballicks, but since he came in at this point it is necessary. People coming out of a session with Old Jay felt slightly dizzy, and the wise ones, after a time, just didn't believe it. His name cannot be mentioned, for it occurs on too many bronze plaques that begin, "Donated by——"

Old Jay was born so rich that he didn't know he was rich at all. He thought everybody was that way. He was a scientist, but whether brilliant or a screwball nobody ever knew, and since he had contributed to so many learned foundations and financed so many projects and served on so many boards of trustees, nobody dared openly to wonder. He gave millions away but he was likely to sponge on a friend. His scholastic honours were many, and there were people who thought privately and venomously that they were awarded in hope of a donation, that he was, in fact, like a football player whose grades have little relation to his scholarship.

He was a stubby man with a natural tonsure of yellow hair. His eyes were bright as a bird's eyes, and he was interested in everything. He was so close to reality that he had completely lost touch with realism. Sometimes he amused Doc, and at other times his endless and myopic enthusiasm could drive a man to despair. Old Jingleballicks shouted at everyone under the impression that this made for clarity.

"Did you get my wire?" he cried.

"No."

"Came for your birthday. Always remember it. Same day they burned Giordano Bruno."

"It's not my birthday," said Doc.

"Well, what day is this?"

"Friday."

"Oh! Well, I'll wait over."

"It's in December. I only have one cot."

"All right. I'll sleep on the floor." He wandered to the kitchen, took the lid off the pot, and began eating the stew—blowing on it violently to cool it.

"That's not done," said Doc, and he was irritated to find that he was shouting back.

"Done enough!" cried Old Jay and went on eating.

Doc said, "Hitzler came through. He said you were seen on a lawn in Berkeley, on your knees pulling a worm out of the ground with your teeth."

Old Jay swallowed a half-cooked carrot. "Not so!" he shouted. "Say, this stew's not done."

"That's what I told you."

"Oh! Well, you see I've watched robins getting worms. Little beggars dig in their heels, so to speak. I got to wondering how much actual pull was involved. Had a scale with a clamp in my teeth. Average night crawler resists to the extent of one pound six ounces. I tried forty-eight individuals. Think of it! A three-ounce bird pulls twenty-two ounces, over seven times his own weight. No wonder they eat so much. Just eating keeps them hungry. Like robins?"

"Not particularly," said Doc. "Are you going to eat all my dinner?"

"I guess so," said Old Jingleballicks. "But it's not done. You got anything to drink?"

"I'll get some beer," said Doc.

"Fine! Get a lot."

"Don't you want to contribute a little?"

"I'm short," said Old Jay.

Doc said, "You are not. You're a free-loader."

"Oh!" said Jingleballicks.

"I said, don't you want to contribute!"

"I'm a little short," said Old Jay.

Doc said angrily, "You are not. You're a free-loader. You never pay. You ran the lab while I was in the Army and damn near bankrupted me. I don't say you stole most of the museum glass, I just say it's missing. Did you take those specimen jars?"

"Well, yes," said Old Jingleballicks. And then he said thoughtfully, "I wish you were a charity or an institution."

"What!"

"Then I could endow you," said Old Jingleballicks.

"Well, I'm not an institution. So what do you do? You go to a lot of trouble to keep from paying a couple of dollars for beer." And suddenly despair and humour crashed head-on in Doc and he burst into weary laughter. "Oh Lord," he said, "you're just not possible! You're a ridiculous idea."

"Your stew is burning," said Old Jingleballicks.

Doc leaped to the stove and pulled the pot from the burner. "You ate all the juice," he said bitterly. "Of course it burned!"

"It was very good," said Old Jay.

In the grocery Doc said, "Give me a dozen cans of beer."

"Don't you want the Bohemia?"

"Hell no!" Doc said. "I have a guest who——" And then an evil thought came to him. "A very interesting man," Doc said. "Why don't you come over and have a drink with us? Old—I mean my friend can explain chess to you better than I can."

"Why not?" said the Patrón. "Maybe I better bring a little liquor."

"Why not?" said Doc.

Crossing the street, the Patrón asked, "You going to the party to-morrow?"

"Sure."

"I like you, Doc, but I don't get you. You ain't real," said the Patrón.

"How do you mean?"

"Well, everything you do is—well, you're like that chess. I don't get you at all."

Doc said, "Do you suppose nobody's real to anybody else? You're going to meet a man who can't possibly exist."

"Don't talk like that," said the Patrón nervously.

Old Jay shouted as they went up the stairs, "I bring you tidings of great joy. The human species is going to disappear!"

"This is Joseph and Mary Rivas," said Doc. "Joseph and Mary this is Old Jingleballicks."

"Why can't you rig a chess game?" the Patrón asked.

"Oh, you can, you can! Or at least you can rearrange your opponent. Comes to the same thing. Now, where was I? Oh yes—we are about to join the great reptiles in extinction."

"Good!" said Doc.

"You mean there ain't gonna be no more people?" said the Patrón.

"Right, young man. We have played the final joke on ourselves. Open the beer! Man, in saving himself, has destroyed himself."

"Who's destroyed?" the Patrón demanded.

"There must be chuckling on Olympus," said Old Jingleballicks. "We go not to Armageddon but to the gas chamber, and we generate our own gas——"

Doc said, "I intended to work on my paper."

"Good! I'll help," said Old Jingleballicks.

"Oh God! *No!*" said Doc.

"Man has solved his problems," Old Jay went on. "Predators he has removed from the earth; heat and cold he has turned aside; communicable disease he has practically eliminated. The old live on, the young do not die. The best wards can't even balance the birth rate. There was a time when a small army could cut a population in half in a year. Starvation, typhus, plague, tuberculosis, were trusty weapons. A scratch with a spear-point meant infection and death. Do you know what the incidence of death from battle wounds is to-day? One per cent. A hundred years ago it was eighty per cent. The population grows and the productivity of the earth decreases. In a foreseeable future we shall be smothered by our own numbers. Only birth-control could save us, and that is one thing mankind is never going to practise."

"Broth-er!" said the Patrón. "What makes you so damn happy about it?"

"It is a cosmic joke. Preoccupation with survival has set the stage for extinction."

"I didn't get one goddam word of that," said Joseph and Mary.

Doc's hands were full. In his left he held a small glass of whisky and in his right a can of beer. He sipped from the one and gulped from the other. "Every instinct tells me to stay out of this," he said, "and every impulse makes me want to get into it."

"Good!" said Old Jay. "Is that whisky?"

"Old Tennis Shoes," said Joseph and Mary. "Want some?"

"Perhaps a little later."

"Okay."

"It's a little later now," said Old Jingleballicks.

"I guess you can hustle with anything," said the Patrón. "I got a feeling I'm being took."

"Well, the impulse wins," said Doc. "You have forgotten one thing, Old Jingleballicks. Indeed, there have been species which became extinct through their own miscalculations, but they were species with a small range of variability. Now consider the lemming——"

"That is a very specialised case," said Old Jingleballicks.

"How do you know we aren't? What do lemmings do when their population exceeds the food supply? Whole masses of them swim out to sea and drown, until a balance of food and population is reached."

"I deny your right to use lemmings," said Old Jingleballicks. "Hand me the bottle, will you?"

"Deny and be damned!" Doc said. "Is the lemming migration a disease? Is it a memory? Or is it a psychic manifestation forced on part of the group for the survival of the whole?"

Old Jay howled back at him, "I will not be robbed of extinction! This is a swindle." He turned to the Patrón. "Don't listen to that man. He's a charlatan."

"He sure in hell is," said Joseph and Mary admiringly.

Doc levelled a finger between the eyes of Old Jay, holding his whisky glass like the butt of a pistol. "Disease, you say? Infection? Down almost to non-existence? But tell me, are not neurotic disturbances on the increase? And are they curable or does the cure spread them? Now you wait! Don't you try to talk now. Do you suppose that the tendency toward homo-sexuality might not also have a mathematical progression? And could this not be the human solution?"

"You can't prove it," Old Jingleballicks cried. "It's all talk—over-emphasis. Why, you might as well accuse me of neurotic tendencies and be done with it!" His eyes brimmed with tears. "My friend, my thought-friend, my true friend," he whimpered.

Doc said, "I wouldn't even think of such a thing."

"You wouldn't?"

"Certainly not."

"When are you going to start dinner?" said Old Jingleballicks.

"You've eaten my dinner," said Doc.

"I've got a fine idea," said Old Jay. "While you start dinner, William and Mary can get a fresh bottle of whisky and I'll set up the chessmen."

"It's not William and Mary, it's Joseph and Mary."

"Who is? Oh! My friend, I'm going to teach you the greatest of all games, the ethereal creation of human intelligence. Shall we sugar it up with a little side bet?"

"Why, you dishonest old fraud!" Doc shouted.

"Ten dollars, Mary?"

The Patrón shrugged his shoulders in apology to Doc. "You have to pay to learn things," he said.

"Make it twenty-five," Old Jingleballicks said. "You want to live for ever?"

Doc opened a can of salmon and a can of spaghetti and stirred the two together in a frying pan. He grated nutmeg over it. Sadly he put the burned stewpot to soak in the sink.

A little after dark the Patrón went back to the grocery and sent Cacahuete to deliver a third bottle of whisky. Upstairs he joined the wet-backs as in advancing and retreating lines they danced the sad and stately measures of the Tehuanos. "Sandunga," they sang, "Sandunga mama mia. . . ."

In the darkening laboratory Doc and Old Jay went softly into the third bottle of Old Tennis Shoes.

"You've had the bed long enough," Doc said. "I want it now."

"All right. As I grow older I expect less and less—and get nothing, even from my so-called friends."

"Look here! You've eaten and spoiled my first dinner, stuffed my second, swilled my beer, taken two drinks for one of the whisky, appropriated my bed, broken two phonograph records, and I saw you put my fountain-pen in your pocket. And how you razzle-dazzled the Patrón out of twenty-five dollars I don't know. You shouldn't have told him that under certain circumstances a knight can jump three squares in one direction—that's not honest."

"I know," said Old Jingleballicks. He patted the pillow lovingly. "Now you lie down here and get comfortable. I'll bring you a drink. Feel better now?"

"Oh, I'm all right," said Doc.

"Say, is that place across the street still running?"

A jagged rage whipped Doc upright. "You stay out of there!" he said. "You old fool! Lie down and got to sleep."

"Why should I go? Am I to deny myself the loveliness of women if the price is right? I can hear the tinkle of their sweet voices and see the heaving of their white roundness——"

"Oh, shut up!" Doc said.

"What's the matter, dear friend? I don't remember that you ever starved for love even when it was less near and less reasonable."

"You go to hell," said Doc. "But you go to hell here."

CHAPTER XXVI

THE DEVELOPING STORM

AT THE very moment Doc and Old Jingleballicks were quarrelling over a matter neither of them understood, Mack was sitting, body comfortable but spirit disturbed, in Fauna's office bedroom. In his hand he held a Venetian glass bud vase of whisky. He was pouring out to Fauna a problem that had not come up in his life for many years.

"Don't think that there ain't been parties before at the Palace, and fights," he said. "Why, when the news come that Gay had went to his reward we give a memorial shindig that they don't hardly do no better at the Salinas Rodeo. Gay would of been proud of it—if he could of got in."

Fauna said, "There's talk around that three mourners went to join Gay before nightfall next day."

"Well, you got to expect a certain amount of accidents," said Mack modestly. "That was all fine. But this here's something special. Not only are loyal hearts framing their dear friend for a hunk of charity, but we got a double-header. Right in the Palace Flop-house the holy bounds of matrimony got its spikes dug in on the starting-line. This here's a halcyon brawl. I and the boys got real delicate feelings about it."

"But no clothes," said Fauna.

"Right! We think somebody got to set a standard. If the loyal friends look like mugs, what'll the mugs look like?"

Fauna nodded. "I see what you mean. How far you want to go —monkey-suits?"

"God, no!" Mack said. "Just pants and coats made out of the same stuff and nobody gets in without he's got a necktie on, and none of them bow-ties that light up neither. This is a goddam solemn moment, Fauna."

She scratched her scalp with her pencil.

Mack went on, "I ain't as young as I was. I don't know how many more parties I can take."

"Don't none of us get no younger," said Fauna. She tapped her teeth with the pencil. As it happened, she also had a problem, and she intended to ask Mack's advice. Now, suddenly, the two problems crashed together and a solution for both was born. Into Fauna's eyes came the light of triumph as she murmured, "I got it!"

"Give it to me gentle," said Mack. "I didn't get much sleep to-day."

Fauna got up and found the stick with which she directed astrological traffic or whacked a protruding piece of bad posture. She talked better with the wand in her hand. "This here calls for a drink," she said, and she poured it.

Mack turned the stem of the bud vase in his fingers and sighted through his drink. The red glass made the brown whisky look green.

Fauna said, "There was a queen a long time ago and she was loaded. Didn't think nothing of paying a couple hundred bucks for a house-dress. Got so many bracelets she couldn't bend her arms. You know what she done when she had a birthday or a hanging or something?"

"Overalls," said Mack.

"No, but you're close. Dressed like she's a milkmaid. They'd wash up a cow and the queen'd sit on a gold stool and take a whang at milking. And there's another old dame. Just the top cream of the top cream. Gives them parties can't nobody get in. She wears a head-rag. Done it for years. If you look over the crowd and don't see a head-rag—she ain't there."

Mack's hand shook as he raised the bud vase to his lips. "Is it what I think?"

"Masquerade!" cried Fauna. "There's only two kinds of people in the world gives a masquerade—people who got too much and people who ain't got nothing."

Mack smiled inwardly to himself. "Can I have a freshener?" he asked.

"Help yourself," said Fauna. "Masquerade has got other things too. People get kind of bored with who they are. Makes them something else for a while."

Mack spoke with reverence. "They used to say, if you got something you can't figure out, give it to Mack. Fauna, it's your dice. You're a bull-bitch idear dame. God te-tum-tum His wonders to perform."

"Like it?"

"Like it! Fauna, this here's one *Life* magazine would give its arse for an invite."

"We got to have a theme."

"How do you mean?"

"Well, we can't let people just run wild. You don't know what kind of stuff they'd wear. I don't want no tramp and gunnysack party."

"I guess you're right. You got any idears?"

"How about 'At the court of the Fairy Queen'?"

"No," said Mack. "First place, we got no right to hurt Joe Elegant's feelings; second place, the cops——"

"Well, how about, then, 'Snow White and the Seven Dwarfs'."

"I see the picture," said Mack. "I think you got something. Some of them dwarfs looked like mugs. I can't see Hazel as no fairy, but he'd do fine as a great big over-growed dwarf."

"That's what's nice about it," said Fauna. "Gives you some leeway."

"Do you think this might call for a drink?"

"I sure as hell do! You spread the word, Mack, will you? You come either as a dwarf, a prince or a princess, or you damn well don't get in. Hold that vase steady."

"But not Doc," said Mack.

"You know," said Fauna, "five'll get you seven Doc wears a tie."

CHAPTER XXVII

O FRABJOUS DAY!

THE COMMUNICATIONS system on Cannery Row is mysterious to the point of magic and rapid to the speed of light. Fauna and Mack came to the decision that the party should be a masquerade on Friday evening at 9.11½. By 9.12 the magic had started, and by 9.30 everyone who was not asleep, drunk, or away knew about it. One particularly mean woman who hadn't had a man for a long time commented, "How will you know whether they're in costume or not?"—a statement clearly drawn from her own state of misery. But mainly the news was received with wonder and joy. Mack's tom-wallager had achieved the stature of a bull-bitch tom-wallager.

Consider what was in store for the ticket-holders: a party at the Palace Flop-house; a raffle that amounted to a potlatch; an engagement of exciting proportions unknown in the annals of the Row; and, on top of this, a costume party! Any one of these would have been enough. Together they threatened to be a celebration close to a catastrophe.

Fauna breathed a sigh of relief, for it solved her greatest problem. She wanted to dress Suzy in a certain way, and Suzy, being the tough monkey she was, would have resisted. Now it was easy. There's little difference between the wardrobe of Snow White and that of a lovely young bride.

There will be those who will consider that Fauna took too much upon herself in engineering a marriage without the knowledge or collusion of either party, and such sceptics will be perfectly right. But it was Fauna's conviction, born out of long experience, that most people, one, did not know what they wanted; two, did not know how to go about getting it; and three, didn't know when they had it.

Fauna was one of those rare people who not only have convictions but are quite willing to take responsibility for them. She knew that Doc and Suzy should be together. And since they were too confused, or thoughtless, or shy to bring about that happy state, Fauna was prepared to do it for them. Her critics will cry, "Suppose she is wrong! Maybe this association has no chance of success." And Fauna's answer to this, if she had heard it, would have been, "They ain't doing so good now. It might work. What they got to lose? And when you look at it, what chance has anybody got? Doc put on a tie, didn't he? And if I'm wrong it's my fault. Sure, they'll fight now and then. Who don't? But maybe they'll get something too. What's the odds for anybody?"

And if it was suggested that people should have the right to choose for themselves after thinking it over, she would have replied, "Who thinks? I can think because I ain't part of it."

And if she had been accused of being a busybody she would have said, "Damn right! Done it all my life!" You couldn't win an argument with Fauna because she would agree with you and then go right on as she had planned. She had taken up astrology because she had found that people who won't take advice from a wise and informed friend will blindly follow the orders of planets—which, by all reports, are fairly remote and aloof. Doc would refuse astrology, so he had to be sandbagged. Fauna expected no thanks. She had given that up long ago. Doc could not interpret the black voice of his guts, but it sounded loud in Fauna's ears. She knew his loneliness. When she was with him, that low voice drowned out all the others.

On Saturday morning she made every girl in the house bring out every article of clothing she possessed and lay it on the bed in her office.

Now Mabel was a natural-born, blowed-in-the-glass hustler. In any time, under any system, after a period of orientation, Mabel would have found herself doing exactly what she was doing in Cannery Row. This was not a matter of Fate, but rather a combination of aptitudes and inclinations. Born in a hovel or a castle, Mabel would have gravitated towards hustling.

The heap of finery on Fauna's bed was impressive. Some of those dresses could have got a girl booked for vagrancy just going out to mail a letter.

Mabel took Fauna aside and spoke to her privately. "My grandma came from the old country," she said when the door of her room was closed. Mabel opened the bottom drawer of her bureau and lifted out a brown-paper parcel sealed against air with strips of cellophane tape. "Grandma left it to Mama, and Mama left it to me," she said as she tore the paper. "We ain't none of us needed it." She removed layer after layer of tissue paper and at last spread a dress out on her bed—a wedding dress of sheerest white linen embroidered with sprays of white flowers—stitches so tiny they seemed to grow out of the cloth. The bodice was close-fitting and the skirt very full. Mabel opened a box and laid beside the dress a silver wedding crown. "I guess she wouldn't hurt it none," said Mabel. "Tell her not to spill nothing on it. I'll polish up the crown, it's kind of tarnished—real silver!"

Fauna was speechless for once. Her fingers went to the light and lovely fabric. She was a hard woman to break up, but the dress nearly did it. "Snow White!" she said breathlessly. "I better be careful or I'll get to believing my own pitch. Mabel, I'm going to give you my jet ear-rings."

"I don't want nothing."

"You want my jet ear-rings!"

"Aw shoot!" said Mabel.

"Looks like it might nearly fit her," Fauna observed.

"Well, we can kind of tack it where it don't."

"You know, you're a good girl. You want I should go to work on you?"

"Hell, no!" said Mabel. "I like it here. There's a veil too in this here bag."

"I don't know if we can get away with a veil, but we'll try," said Fauna.

"Oh, hell, she don't know a veil from a hole in the ground," said Mabel.

If only people would give the thought, the care, the judgment to international affairs, to politics, even to their jobs, that they lavish on what to wear to a masquerade, the world would run in greased grooves. On the surface Cannery Row was quieter than usual, but below the surface it seethed. In one corner of the Palace Flop-house, Whitey No. 2 gave careful lessons to little Johnny Carriaga in the art of palming cards. Johnny had been borrowed for the occasion—or, more truthfully, rented—since Alberto Carriaga had received sixty-two cents, the price of a gallon of wine, for the use of his first-born. It was planned that Johnny should be dressed as Cupid, with paper wings, bow and arrow, and quiver. The quiver was added as a hiding-place for the winning raffle ticket. For although nearly everyone on the Row knew the raffle was rigged, a certain pride made it necessary to carry the deception off with dignity. Because of a small distrust of Johnny the arrows in the quiver were tipped with rubber suction cups.

Whitey No. 2 had cut a card the exact size of a raffle ticket. "Now try it again, Johnny," he said. "No, I can see the edge of it. Look! Sort of squeeze the edges in your palm, like this. Now try it again. That's right! That's good. Now let's see you get it out of the quiver. You make a pass with the bow—like this—so they look at your other hand, and you say——"

"I know," said Johnny. " 'I'm Cupid, God of Love, and I draw a bead on unsuspecting hearts.' "

"God! That's beautiful," said Eddie. "I wonder where Mack got that?"

"He made it up," said Whitey No. 2. "Now when you shove up the bow with your right hand, you get the ticket out of the quiver with your left. Try it."

" 'I-am-Cupid-God-of-Love,' " said Johnny, and he brandished the bow.

"That's good," said Whitey No. 2. "It will take a little more practice, though. Don't look at your left hand, Johnny. Look at the bow. Now here's the bowl. Dig around the cards without dropping the ticket. Go on, practise."

"I want thirty-five cents," said Johnny.

"What!"

"If I don't get thirty-five cents I'll tell."

"Mack," said Whitey No. 2, "this here kid's jumped the price."

"Give it to him," said Mack. "I'll flip him double or nothing later."

"Not with that two-headed nickel, you won't," said Johnny.

"Seems like kids got no respect for their elders nowadays," Eddie observed. "If I ever said that, my old man would of clobbered me."

"Maybe your old man wasn't rigging no raffle," said Johnny.

Whitey No. 1 said, "This kid ain't honest. You know where bad kids go, Johnny?"

"I sure do, and I been there," said Johnny.

"Give him the thirty-five cents," said Mack.

What hidden, hoarded longings there are in all of us! Behind the broken nose and baleful eye may be a gentle courtier; behind the postures and symbols and myths of Joe Elegant there may be the hunger to be a man. If one could be, for only an evening, whatever in the world one wished, what would it be? What secret would come out?

To a certain extent the theme of the Palace Flop-house raffle and engagement party was chosen because of Hazel. He was definitely dwarf material. But when he had reviewed the story, asked questions, and got as clear a picture as he ever got of anything, Hazel elected to be Prince Charming. He saw himself in white silk knee breeches and an Eton jacket, his left hand fondling the hilt of a small sword.

They offered him Grumpy, lovable old Grumpy, the prize part of all. They offered him Sweet Pea the Skunk, but Hazel stuck to his dream. It was Prince Charming or he wouldn't attend. Friendships have foundered on less.

"All right," said Mack, "you go ahead. I was going to help you with your costume, but I know when I'm stumped. Hazel, if you're Prince Charming, you're on your own."

"Who cares?" said Hazel. "Who wants your help? I'll bet you're mad because you wanted to be Prince Charming."

"Not me," said Mack. "I'm going as a tree."

"How do you mean?"

"It's a forest, ain't it?" said Mack. "I want a little anenmity. You can't see the tree for the forest."

Hazel went to sit under the cypress tree. He was gloomy and he was frightened because ideas did not come to him, and when he sought them they ran screaming away. But he was determined. He could not let the office down. A man sentenced to be President could not go as a dwarf. It wasn't dignified. Later in the morning he went to the back door of the Bear Flag and called for help from Joe Elegant.

Joe smiled. "I'll help you," he said maliciously.

All over the Row trunks were being opened, and the smell of moth-balls penetrated as far as the middle of the street. And all over the Row the story was being re-written to fit the wardrobe. By unspoken agreement no one planned to be Snow White.

In Western Biological, Doc awakened racked with pain from sleeping on the floor. He lay still for a moment, trying to isolate the part of him that hurt worst. Not the least of his agony was his memory of forcing old Jingleballicks to take his bed. A crazy, alcoholic generosity, probably masochistic in origin, had prompted the sacrifice. He raised up one shattered elbow and looked at the old bastard sleeping so sweetly—his halo of yellow hair surrounding his polished pink pate, his breath puffing in small comfortable snores.

"Wake up!" Doc shouted in fury.

The pale eyes flickered. "What's for breakfast?" said Old Jay.

"Don't you even have the decency to have a hangover?"

"Certainly I do," said Old Jay with dignity. "How's about some beer?"

"Does your head ache?"

"Yes."

"Do your joints ache?"

"Yes."

"Do you have low-blood-pressure depression?"

"Overwhelming."

"Then I've got you," said Doc. "You get the beer."

The pale eyes rolled despairingly. "I'll pay half if you get it."

"No."

"Tell you what I'll do—I'll loan you the money."

"No."

Old Jingleballicks's eyes were bleak. "Reach me my pants," he said, and he fished out a quarter and a dime and held them out.

"No," said Doc.

"God in heaven! What *do* you want?"

"I want two dollars."

"Why, that would be six bottles!"

"Exactly. You're trapped, Old Jingleballicks, and you know it."

Old Jay dug deep and found two one-dollar bills. "Maybe I can write it off to entertainment," he said.

Doc pulled on pants and shirt and went across the street. He took his time. He drank a bottle of beer quickly and then sipped a second while he heard the news of the day from Joseph and Mary.

Back in the laboratory he put the four cold remaining bottles on the table.

"Where's my change?" asked Old Jay.

"I drank your change," said Doc. He was beginning to feel good. He saw the stricken look. "You cheap old fraud," he said happily, "for once you've been had." And he went on, "I wish I could understand you. You must have millions and yet you pinch and squirm and cheat. Why?"

"Please give me beer, I'm dying," said Old Jingleballicks.

"Then die a little longer," said Doc. "I love to see you die!"

"It's not my fault," Old Jay said. "It's a state of mind. You might call it the American state of mind. The tax laws are creating a whole new kind of man—a psyche rather than a psychosis. Two or three generations and we'll maybe set the species. Can I have beer now?"

"No."

"If a man has money he doesn't ask, 'Can I afford this?' but, 'Can I deduct it?' Two men fight over a luncheon bill when both of them are going to deduct it anyway—a whole nation conditioned to dishonesty by its laws, because honesty is penalized. But it's worse than that. If you'll just hand me a bottle I'll tell you."

"Tell me first."

"I didn't write the tax laws," Old Jay said, trembling. "The only creative thing we have is the individual, but the law doesn't permit me to give money to an individual. I must give it to a group, an organization—and the only thing a group has ever created is bookkeeping. To participate in my gift the individual must become part of the group and thus lose his individuality and his creativeness. I didn't write the law. I hate a law that stifles generosity and makes charity good business. Corporations are losing their financial efficiency because waste pays. I deplore it, but I do it. I know you need a microscope, but I can't give it to you because with taxes a four-hundred-dollar microscope costs me twelve hundred dollars—if I give it to you—and nothing if I give it to an institution. Why, if you, through creative work, should win a prize, most of the money would go in taxes. I don't mind taxes. God knows! But I do mind the kind of law that makes of charity not the full warmness of sharing but a stinking expediency. And now, if you don't hand me a beer, I shall be forced——"

"Here's your beer," said Doc.

"What's for breakfast?"

"God knows. The party at the Palace Flop-house to-night is a masquerade. 'Snow White and the Seven Dwarfs.' "

"Why?"

"I don't know."

"I shall go as a red dwarf," said Old Jingleballlicks.

"A dying star," said Doc. "It kinds of fits you with that hair."

When the beer was gone they decided that beer made breakfast redundant. Doc went back for six more bottles, and in a burst of generosity he brought back the Bohemia.

"Now there's beer for you," said Old Jingleballicks. "The Mexicans are a great and noble people. The Pyramid of the Sun and this beer—whole civilizations have produced less. You started to tell me about your paper last night but you got deflected by a girl. I'd like to see that girl."

"I'd like to tell you about my paper. I want to draw some

parallels between emotional responses in cephalopods and in humans, and I'd like to observe the pathological changes that go with these responses. Now the body walls of octopi are semi-transparent. With proper equipment it might be possible to observe these changes as they happen. Sometimes the simpler organisms can give us a key to the more complex. Dementia præcox, for example, was considered purely a psychotic manifestation until it was observed that there were physical symptoms as well."

"Why don't you write your paper?"

"I seem to be afraid to. A kind of terror comes over me when I start."

"What have you got to lose if you fail?"

"Nothing."

"What have you got to gain if you succeed?"

"I don't know."

Old Jingleballicks regarded Doc benignedly. "Have you got enough beer in you so you aren't quarrelsome?"

"I'm never quarrelsome."

"The hell you aren't! Took my head off last night. You hurt my feelings."

"I'm sorry. What did you want to say?"

"Will you let me finish if I start?"

"I'll try."

Old Jay said, "You feel to me like a woman who has never had a baby but knows all the words. There's a lack of fulfilment in you. I think you have violated something or withheld something from yourself—almost as though you were eating plenty but no Vitamin A. You aren't hungry, but you're starving. That's what I think."

"I can't imagine anything I lack. I have freedom, comfort, and the work I like. What have I missed?"

"Well, last night, in every conversation, a girl named Suzy crept in——"

"For God's sake!" said Doc. "Do you know what Suzy is? An illiterate little tramp, a whore! I took her out to dinner because Fauna asked me to. I found her interesting the way I'd find a new species of octopus interesting, that's all. You've always been a goddam fool, Old Jingleballicks, but you've never been a romantic damn fool."

"Who's talking about romance? I was speaking of hunger. Maybe you can't be wholly yourself because you've never given yourself wholly to someone else."

"Of all the esoteric goddam nonsense!" Doc cried. "Why I give floor room to you I don't know."

"Then try to figure out why you get mad," said Old Jay.

"What?"

"Well, aren't you putting a lot of energy into denying something which, if it is not true, deserves no denial?"

"Sometimes I think you're just plain nuts," said Doc.

"Know what I'm going to do?" said Old Jay. "I'm going to buy a bottle of whisky."

"I don't believe it!" said Doc.

CHAPTER XXVIII

WHERE ALFRED THE SACRED RIVER RAN

VERY FEW people know that Hazel had given the Palace Flophouse its name years ago when the boys had first moved in. Inspired by the glory of having a home, Hazel compounded the name of something he knew about and something he didn't, the known and the unknown, the homely and the exotic; and, ever after, the name had stuck, so that it was known by certain people from one end of the state to the other. And the Palace Flop-house had justified its name over the years. It had been shelter and home base to the boys. Also, some surprising events had occurred there.

The building itself was not impressive—redwood board and bat, tarpaper roof, twenty-eight feet long, fourteen feet wide, two square windows, and two doors, one on each side. In this simple box Mack and the boys had moved some remarkable articles, the products of their wits, their work, and sometimes their misfortune. The great cast-iron stove was in excellent condition and bade fair to outlast the Colosseum, which it resembled. The grandfather clock, once the home of a dog, stood empty now—and Eddie wanted to be buried in it. Each of the beds was canopied as a substitute for mending the roof, and Gay's bed was kept just as it was when he went away—patchwork quilt turned down to reveal a grey tennis-flannel sheet. His copy of *Amazing True Desert Stories*, folded open to page 62, lay on top of the apple box just as Gay had left it; and his prize possession, a collector's item, a ring gear and pinions of a 1914 Willys-Knight, lay on a black velvet cloth in the bottom of the box. On the shelf over his head the boys kept some kind of nosegay in a swanky swig glass, for Gay had loved flowers. He ate them—particularly red roses, mustard flowers, wild turnip blossoms, and the petals of one variety of dahlia. No one had ever been allowed to sit or sleep in Gay's bed. He might return one day, the boys thought, even though he was reported dead and his Army insurance paid.

Now there had been tom-wallagers in the Palace Flop-house,

but never such a bull-bitch tom-wallager as was now in the process of exploding. The outside was freshly whitewashed. Beds were pushed together, and the interior was a bower of pine boughs crossed to make a canopy. The great stove was laid out as a bar and the oven was full of cracked ice. In front of the back door a little stage was built, with a painter's drop-cloth for a curtain and the door for an entrance—for certain theatrical effects, not counting the raffle itself, were planned for that area.

This forest bower was lighted by Japanese lanterns, and a string of lanterns led down to the chicken walk above the railroad track. The boys were pleased with their effort.

Mack surveyed the scene and put a name to it that was remembered. "A veritable fairyland," he said.

The Patrón had contributed his prize group of musicians, the original Espaldas Mojadas—two guitars, gourds, bones, castanets, and Haitian drum, and, last, a guitarón, as big as a row-boat. Cacahuete Rivas, the nephew of the Patrón, was scheduled to join his trumpet to the band later, but now he was on the beach, practising his solo softly.

As evening came to Cannery Row the boys were tired but content. Following Mack's lead, they all agreed to be trees. After all, they were the hosts. Their one sorrow was that Hazel had left them. His yearning to be Prince Charming had overcome his love for his friends. In Joe Elegant's tiny bedroom he was being transformed.

"Caught me with my pants down," Mack apologized for the twentieth time. "Hazel's such a mug you forget he's sensitive. Hell, I could of worked out some kind of charming rig if I'd give it some thought. Don't seem right without him here to mess things up."

It is customary at most masquerades for the arriving guests to be shy, ill at ease, and sober, and to stand around uneasily for maybe an hour before the party warms up. In this matter of starting a party Cannery Row is far ahead of some other centres of culture. The party was to start at nine p.m. sharp. The guests would be notified by the trumpet of Cacahuete Rivas, playing "Whistle While You Work".

At least two hours before the signal a series of small earnest parties, at Wide Ida's, the Bear Flag, and in private homes, were practising for the main event. This party was going to begin in full bloom. Of course Mack and the boys were so weighed down with responsibility that they didn't get the best out of their liquor; still, they made progress, and they watched the big hand of the alarm clock on the back of the stove.

In the Bear Flag the pageantry was spread all over the floor.

Snow White was going to have, as ladies of honour, some of the best-known and most respected hookers north of San Luis Obispo. The ladies were dressing in filmy gowns of red, yellow, and green and each one was to carry a bottle of whisky garlanded with ribbons to match her dress. Fauna was going as a witch. It was her own idea. The only costume she really needed was a broom, but she had made a peaked black hat and a black alpaca wrap-around to carry the part off. But Fauna had a pay-off. When the big moment came she was prepared to fling off her black gown, switch broom for wand, and emerge as the fairy god-mother.

Wide Ida's was dwarf country. Eight Happys, four Sneezys, six Dopeys, and nineteen Grumpys clustered about the bar, earnestly singing "Harvest Moon" in one and a half part harmony.

Joseph and Mary had elected to go as Dracula. He hadn't seen Snow White, but to him a moving picture was a moving picture.

At Western Biological, Doc and Old Jingleballicks were hopelessly enmeshed in a discussion of tobacco mosaic. When the dam had burst a flood followed. A garbage can stood in the middle of the floor, and in it nestled, in crushed ice, the six remaining bottles of a case of champagne bought by Old Jay.

Doc and Old Jay had completely forgotten the party. When Cacahuete's trumpet sounded the call to arms they were shouting so loud they didn't hear it. When the youth and beauty of Cannery Row walked gaily up the lantern-lit chicken walk Old Jay and Doc were still screaming at each other.

Suddenly Doc dropped his voice, and it had the effect of a loud noise. "I think I will go away," he said. "I have tried with every sinew and I have failed."

"Nonsense!" said Old Jay. "Young man, you are at the threshold of a great career."

"But what do I care for honours?"

"How do you know? You never got any," said Old Jay.

"Don't try to hold me back, Old Jingle."

"I won't. There's too many of you already. Do you realize you haven't cooked any dinner?"

"I bought a pound of hamburger and you ate it raw before I got it near a pan."

"You shouldn't starve yourself, young friend," said Old Jingleballicks.

Eddie hurled himself up the steps and flung open the door. "Doc!" he cried. "For God's sakes! She's started! They're going to draw!""

Doc picked a bottle from the ice. "Arm yourself, Old Jingleballicks. Forward!"

They had to help Old Jay up the chicken walk.

The drawing was being held for them. Dwarfs, animals, monsters, were drawn up in a half-circle, facing the curtain.

"I guess we're all here," said Mack. He looked behind the curtain. "You all right, Johnny?"

"Goddam cold," said Johnny.

And at that moment Hazel entered proudly, his chin up, his eyes flashing with dignity. Joe Elegant had worked all day to get his revenge on mankind, and Hazel was the result. The basis of his costume was long grey underwear, to which were sewed hearts, diamonds, spades, and clubs in red and black. Hazel's army shoes had yellow pompoms on the toes. An Elizabethan ruff of stiff paper was round his neck, and on his head a Knight Templar's hat with a white ostrich plume. From the belt around his middle hung a long scabbard. His right hand proudly held a cavalry sabre at salute.

Joe Elegant had concentrated his revenge in one area. The drop seat of the costume had been removed and in its place, right on the essential surface of Hazel himself, was painted a bull's eye in concentric circles of red and blue.

Hazel was a breath-taking sight. He did not glance around. He knew he was right—he knew it by the silence. Smartly he turned the sabre to parade rest and crossed his hands on the hilt. His breath caught in his throat.

"I," he said huskily, "I am Prince Charming." And the company could see now that his cheeks were rouged and his eyelashes beaded. "I proteck dam—damsels," he announced. And only then did he turn his proud head for the applause and approval he knew he merited.

There were tears in Mack's eyes. "You done fine, Hazel baby," he said. "Couldn't nobody do better. Who helped you?"

"Joe Elegant," said Hazel. "What a nice guy!"

Whitey No. 2 moved up at Mack's imperceptible signal. "You want I should go now?"

"Right now," said Mack softly. "Kick the bejeezus out of him."

Hazel moved proudly in on their soft talk. "Mr. Joe Elegant presents his compliments," he said. "He is sorry he cannot attend as he had to leave town on business. Let's see—is that all?—yep, that's all."

"We'll thank him when he comes back," said Mack grimly.

The guests looked at Hazel with stricken eyes, and no one laughed. One glance at Mack's jutting chin and doubled fists stopped that impulse.

"Get on with it," Wide Ida growled.

Mack pulled himself together, advanced to the curtain, and turned to face the guests.

"Fellow citizens," he said, "right here in Cannery Row lives a guy that there can't nobody want a better friend. For years we have took his bounty without sharing nothing back at him. Now this guy needs a certain article that runs into dough. Therefore it is the pleasure of I and the boys to raffle off the Palace Flop-house to buy a microscope for Doc. We got three hundred and eighty bucks. Curtain!"

Doc shouted, "Mack! You're crazy!"

"Shut up!" said Mack. "Curtain."

The cloth was pulled aside to reveal Johnny Carriaga dressed in an aluminium supporter and a pair of blue paper wings. Johnny brandished his bow. "I-am-Cupid-God-of-Love!" he shouted. Then the winning ticket slipped from his palm and fluttered to the floor. Johnny scrambled after it, yelling, "I-draw-a-bead-on-unexpected-hearts." He grabbed the ticket and turned to Mack. "What do I do now?" he asked.

Mack gave up. "Oh, what the hell!" Then he shouted, "Is that the ticket you have drawn, Cupid?"

"I have plucked from the many." Johnny hadn't been near the bowl, but he yelled it anyway.

"Give it to me, you little bastard," said Mack quietly. "Friends," he said, "do my eyes deceive me? This *is* a surprise! Well, well! Folks, it gives me great pleasure to announce that the Palace Flop-house has passed into the hands of Doc."

Doc was jarred towards sobriety. He moved close to Mack. "You're crazy!" he said.

"Like a fox," said Mack.

"Who told you you owned it? I didn't tell."

"How do you mean, Doc?"

"I didn't think Chong told anybody but me. He was afraid you'd do something like this."

Mack said, "Let's you and I step outside."

Under the lanterns they faced each other. Doc popped the champagne cork and handed the bottle to Mack who cupped his mouth over the glistening foam.

"What was you saying, Doc?" he asked quietly.

"Chong wanted you and the boys to have a home. He deeded it to you and put up the money for ten years' taxes."

"Well, whyn't he tell us?"

"He was afraid if you knew you owned it you'd mortgage it or sell it and then you wouldn't have a home."

Mack was shaken. "Doc," he said, "would you do me the favour? Don't tell the boys."

"Why, sure."

"Shake on it?"

"Shake! Have a drink."

Suddenly Mack laughed. "Doc," he said, "I and the boys want to ask will you rent the joint to us?"

"Sure I will, Mack."

"I hope they never find out. They'd skin me," said Mack.

"Wouldn't it be simpler if we just forgot the raffle?"

"No, sir!" said Mack. "Chong was right. I wouldn't trust the boys not to sell her sometime when they need a buck. I wouldn't trust myself."

The visit of Old Jingleballicks had put Doc's system to an outrageous test. Meals had been infrequent, sleep fitful, emotions on stilts, and the intake of alcohol enormous. The raffle had jarred him out of a pleasant swimming state into something resembling sobriety, but not very closely. A fog of unreality like a dream feeling was not in him but all around him. He went inside the Palace and saw the dwarfs and monsters and the preposterous Hazel all lighted by the flickering lanterns. None of it seemed the fabric of sweet reality. The music was deafening. Old Jay danced by, clutching a pale brunette to his stomach as though she were a pain—a disgusting sight, and as unreal as the rest.

Anyone untrained in tom-wallagers might well have been startled at this tom-wallager. Eddie waltzed to the rumba music, his arms embracing an invisible partner. Wide Ida lay on the floor Indian-wrestling with Whitey No. 2, at each try displaying acres of pink panties, while a wild conga line of dwarfs and animals milled about. Johnny Carriaga ran wild. Standing on a box, he fired at random but not at unsuspecting hearts. Mrs. Alfred Wong had a rubber-tipped arrow stuck between her shoulder-blades. Then Johnny winged a lantern, and it crashed in flames and set fire to three dwarfs, so that they had to be put out with a punch-bowl.

Mack and Doc were swept into the conga line. To Doc the room began to revolve slowly and then to rise and fall like the deck of a stately ship in a ground-swell. The music roared and tinkled. Hazel beat out rhythm on the stove with his sword until Johnny, aiming carefully, got a bulls-eye on Hazel. Hazel leaped in the air and came down on the oven door, scattering crushed ice all over the floor. One of the guests had got wedged in the grandfather clock. From the outside the Palace Flop-house seemed to swell and subside like rising bread.

Doc cupped his hands close to Mack's ear. "Where's Fauna and the girls?" he shouted.

"Later," Mack cried.

"What?"

"Coming later," and he added, "Better get here pretty soon before the joint burns down."

"What?"

"Skip it," Mack shouted.

At this point Whitey No. 1 fought his way to Mack's side and yelled, "Mack, they're coming!"

Mack rushed to the Espaldas Mojadas and raised both hands at them. Johnny aimed his last arrow at the guitarón and took the fret out clean.

"Hold it!" Mack screamed.

The music stopped, and silence fell on the room. Then the unrealest part of all began to happen.

Very softly the sound of a sweet muted trumpet whispered, and the crazy thing was playing the 'Wedding March' from *Lohengrin*, and even as Doc listened the sly brass began playing with it, slid into minors, took a short rhythm ride, and moaned away at blues. The dancers were very still, almost stuffed. Doc found the source of the music—Cacahuete Rivas in the corner of the room, muting his trumpet with a damp sponge.

Then in this dream the paint-splashed curtain was pulled aside, and Fauna, the witch, came through the door, straddling a broom. Doc thought, God! I'd hate to testify about this. I'd get the booby-hatch!

Fauna barked, "This here's a very happy occasion." She looked around. "Doc, come here."

He moved vaguely towards her.

Four girls from the Bear Flag came through the door, dressed in blinding colours. They ranged themselves two on each side of the door, facing inward, holding the beribboned whisky bottles to make an arch.

Fauna dismounted from her broom and ripped off her black wrapper, displaying a sheath of silver lamé. In her hand miraculously appeared a silver wand tipped with a gold star. She struck a pose, riding on her toes as though prepared for flight. "I am your fairy godmother," she shouted, "I bring you Snow White, the bride!"

Then Suzy appeared in the doorway, a transformed Suzy in a wedding gown. The silver crown was on her head, and from its points a veil was suspended. She looked lovely and young and excited. Her lips were parted.

Fauna yelled, "Doc, come get your girl!"

Doc shook his head to try to wake up. It was a dream, a craziness, the crown, the veil, the virginity. "What in hell is going on?"

It happens that two people standing apart can dip into each other's thoughts. Suzy read his mind on his face. An embarrassed red crept up her neck and darkened her cheeks. She closed her eyes.

And Doc's mind read her pain. His world spun like a top. He heard himself say, "Fairy Godmother, I accept—my—girl."

Suzy opened her eyes and looked in Doc's eyes. Then her jaw muscles tightened and her eyes grew fierce; her sweet mouth hardened to a line. She took off the crown and veil, looked at them a moment, and placed them gently on an apple box.

The crazy trumpet put a samba beat to the "Wedding March" and a guitar took up the throbbing.

"Listen, you mugs," said Suzy over the music, "I could live with a stumblebum in a culvert and be a good wife. I could marry a yellow dog and be nice to him. But, good Christ! Not Doc!" Suddenly she turned and darted out of the door.

Fauna plunged after her. There was no chicken walk out the back way. Suzy slipped and rolled down the embankment and Fauna rolled after her. On the railroad track they gathered themselves together.

"You goddam grandstanding bitch!" said Fauna bitterly. "What do you mean—'not Doc'?"

"I love him," said Suzy.

CHAPTER XXIX

OH, WOE, WOE, WOE!

One of the common reactions to shock is lethargy. If, after an automobile accident, one man is howling and writhing and another sits huietly staring into space, it is usually the quiet man who is badly qurt. A community can go into shock too. Cannery Row did. People drew into themselves, kept their doors closed, and didn't visit. Everyone felt guilty, even those who had not planned the party. Merely to have seen it was enough.

Mack and the boys were doubled up with a sense of unhappy fate. It was their third try at doing something nice for Doc, and it was their third failure. They did not know where to turn to escape their own scorn.

Wide Ida became fiercely taciturn. Her customers drank in silence to escape the guilty rage they knew was just under her muscular surface.

Fauna grieved like a lost setter dog. In a lifetime of preposterous plans she had discovered some failures, but never before a catastrophe.

Even the Patrón experienced little flashes of an emotion new to him. Always before he had managed to swap guilt for blame of circumstance or enemy, but now his accusing finger bent like a comedy pistol and aimed at his own heart. It was an interesting

"You look excited."

"Joe," said Suzy, "you remember once you said if I wanted to blow town you'd lend me the dough?"

"I thought you was staying."

"I am. I wonder could you stake me not to blow town."

"How much?"

"Twenty-five bucks."

"Where you going to live?"

"I'll let you know."

Joe said, "I staked kids before. What the hell have I got to lose?"

"You'll get it back."

"I know I will," said Joe.

The boiler that for many years had rested among the mallow weeds in the vacant lot between the Bear Flag and the grocery was the first boiler the Hediondo Cannery ever had, and the Hediondo was the first cannery Monterey ever had. When it was understood that pilchards could be placed raw in cans, doused with tomato sauce or oil, sealed and then cooked in live steam, a new industry came to Monterey. Hediondo started with small capital and skimped and pioneered its way first to success and finally to oblivion. Its first boiler for producing the cooking-steam was the triumphant improvisation of William Randolph, engineer, fireman, and president. The boiler itself he got for nothing. It was the whole front end of a locomotive of the Pajaro Valley and Coast Railroad. This engine, encountering a split rail one night, leaped a trestle and dived twenty feet into a mud-hole. The railroad company stripped its wheels and valves, whistle and bell, and left the great cylinder standing in the mud.

William Randolph found it, hauled it to Monterey, and set it in concrete at the new Hediondo Cannery. For years it produced low-pressure steam for cooking canned fish, while its tubes blew out at intervals and were replaced.

In 1932, when the cannery was rich and expanding, the old boiler was finally abandoned in the vacant lot to save a moving bill. Old Mr. Randolph was still alive and, although retired, he still hated waste. He stripped out the tubes, leaving only the big cylinder, sixteen feet long and seven feet in diameter. The smoke-stack was still on it, and its fire-door, two feet wide and eighteen inches high, still swung on rusty pins.

Many people had used the boiler for temporary shelter, but Mr. and Mrs. Sam Malloy were the first permanent residents. Mr. Malloy, who was good with his hands, after stripping out the remaining tubes, added a number of little comforts.

A boiler as a home has disadvantages as well as advantages. Some people would baulk at getting down on hands and knees to crawl in through the fire-door. The floor, being rounded, makes for difficulty both in walking and in arranging furniture. The third inconvenience lies in a lack of light.

The advantages of a boiler can be listed as follows: it is absolutely rainproof; it is cosy; and it has wonderful ventilation. By adjusting the damper and fire-door you can have as much draught as you like.

Under the smoke-stack Mr. Malloy had built a little brick fireplace for cold winter nights. In addition to all of these advantages, the boiler was fire-proof, wind-proof, earthquake-proof, and almost bomb-proof. These more than balanced the lack of running water, electricity, and interior plumbing.

There are those, particularly in Carmel-by-the-Sea, who say that Suzy's choice of the boiler as a home was a symbolic retreat to the womb, and, while this may be true, it is also true that this womb had economic factors. At the Golden Poppy, Suzy had her meals free, and in the boiler she had free shelter.

Suzy took the money Joe Blaikey loaned her and went to Holman's Department Store in Pacific Grove. She bought a hammer, saw, assorted nails, two sheets of plywood, a box of pale blue kalsomine and a brush, a tube of Duco cement, a pair of pink cottage curtains with blue flowers, three sheets, two pillow-cases, two towels and a wash-cloth, a tea-kettle, two cups and saucers, and a box of teabags. At Joe's Surplus she bought a used army cot and mattress pad, bowl and pitcher and chamber-pot, two army blankets, a small mirror, and a kerosene lamp. These supplies exhausted her capital, but at the end of her first week of work at the Golden Poppy, Suzy paid Joe back two dollars and a quarter out of tips.

The Row, in its shame, pretended not to see what was going on at the boiler or to hear the sound of hammering late at night. This was good manners rather than a lack of curiosity.

Fauna held out for ten days, and when she did give in to her natural nosiness, she went secretly, late on a Tuesday night, when the Bear Flag was closed for lack of customers. From the window of the Ready Room Fauna could see a little glow of light coming from the fire-door of the boiler. The smoke-stack put out a lazy curl of smoke that smelled of pine pitch. Fauna went silently out of the front door and up through the mallow weeds.

"Suzy," she called softly.

"Who is it?"

"Me, Fauna."

"What do you want?"

"To see if you're all right."

"I'm all right."

Fauna got down on her knees and poked her head through the

fire-door. The transformation was complete. The curving walls were pale blue, and the curtains were stuck to the walls with Duco cement. It was a pleasant feminine apartment. Suzy sat on her cot in the light from the little fireplace. She had built a dressing-table for her mirror and bowl and pitcher, and beside it stood a fruit jar filled with lupins and poppies.

"You sure fixed it up nice," said Fauna. "Ain't you going to invite me in?"

"Come on in, but don't get stuck in the door."

"Give me a hand, will you?"

Suzy pulled and boosted her through the fire-door. "Here," she said, "sit down on the cot. I'm going to get a chair pretty soon."

"We could make you a hook rug," said Fauna. "That would look nice."

"No," said Suzy. "I want to do it myself. Would you like I should make you a cup of tea?"

"Don't mind if I do," said Fauna absently, and then, "You sure you ain't mad?"

"I ain't mad. You know, I never had a place of my own before."

"Well, you've fixed it up real nice," said Fauna. "I can lend you anything you need. You can use the bathroom over at the Bear Flag."

"They got a shower down at the Golden Poppy," said Suzy.

"Now, look," Fauna said. "You got me down and my claws wedged. Don't put the boots to me."

"I ain't."

"This here's a nice cup of tea. I got to tell you one thing, Suzy. I don't care if you want to hear it or not. I been wrong quite a lot, but you're going about this wrong. Don't rub Doc's nose in it. That just makes a man mad."

"What are you talking about?"

"Well, settling here. He can't look out his window without you're in his hair." Fauna braced herself for the explosion, and it did not come.

Suzy looked at her hands. "I got real nice nails," she said. "Down at the Poppy where I got my hands in water all the time I squidge lotion on. Keeps them soft. Fauna, you told me not to run away, and I didn't. I felt like digging a hole in the ground and crawling in and I didn't, because I think what you said was right. I'm going to do it right here in sight."

"That ain't what I said."

"Don't bust in!" said Suzy. "You said about Doc. Now I'm telling you once, and you can tell it all over the Row if you want, then I won't have to tell it to nobody again. You just forget Doc. Doc ain't got nothing to do with me. He come along and I wasn't up to him—wasn't good enough for him. Now maybe it won't never happen again, but if it does—if there's a guy—I'm goddam well going to be good enough for him, inside and outside, public and private; but mostly I'm going to feel good enough. Now, you got that?"

"You better watch that cussing," said Fauna.

"I don't cuss no more."

"You just——"

"Don't try to mix me up," said Suzy. "Did you get what I said?"

"Why, sure, Suzy girl! But I don't see why you won't let your friends give you a hand."

" 'Cause then it wouldn't be me done it. Then I wouldn't be no good."

"You borrowed dough from Joe Blaikey."

"Sure, from a cop. The same cop that was going to float me. He ain't a friend, he's a cop. When I get him paid back maybe he can be a friend."

"You sure make it tough on yourself."

"How else? You can't cut off a leg with a banana."

"You wasn't never no hustler, Suzy. At least you wasn't no good at it."

"I know what I was, and I know what I'm going to be."

"Doc?" Fauna asked.

"That's done, I tell you! Get it through your thick head—that's done!"

"Well, I guess I better be going," Fauna said unhappily. She put the teacup on the little dressing-table, got down on her hands and knees, and crawled to the fire-door. "Give me a boost through, will you, Suzy?"

Suzy stuffed her through the opening the way you'd stuff a sausage. And then she called, "Fauna!"

Fauna put her head in through the door.

"You been the best friend I ever had. If I'm tough, it ain't at you, it's at me. I was always mad at everybody. Turns out it was me I was mad at. When I get friends with myself, maybe I can get friends with somebody without no chip."

Fauna said, "S'pose Doc come a-begging?"

"I ain't no man-trap," said Suzy. "I wouldn't have him if he come walking on his hands. You can't cure a sock in the puss with a sock in the puss. But if ever I like a guy again, and he lays it on the line, why, I'm going to have something to lay on the other side."

"I miss you, Suzy."

"I'll be back when I'm right. I love you."

"Oh, shut up!" said Fauna. And she clanged the fire-door shut.

CHAPTER XXX

A PRESIDENT IS BORN

OF ALL our murky inventions, guilt is at once the most devious, the most comic, the most painful. Was it planted by the group pressure of the tribe to keep the potentially dangerous individual off balance? Is it set in the psycho-tissue, watered and cultivated by ductless glands? Is guilt the unconscious device by which a man cries for attention in an unperceiving world, or can it be that the final human pleasure is pain? Whatever its origin, we scream like cats in copulation, wolf-bay the moon, whip ourselves with the exquisite thorns of contempt, and generally have a hell of a good time at it.

In the pleasures and passions of guilt, Hazel should have been voted the human least likely to succeed. Guilt is a selfish pastime and Hazel had never been aware enough of himself to indulge in it. He watched life as a small boy watches a train go by—mouth open, breathing high and light, pleased, astonished, and a little confused.

Hazel had never amounted to a damn. Mack once described Hazel's education: "He done four years in grammar school and four years in reform school—and he didn't learn nothing either place."

Reform school, you see, where vice and crime are not extra-curricular, failed to have any more effect on Hazel than the fourth grade had. He came out as innocent as he had gone in. Hazel didn't pay enough attention to be evil. If Mack and the boys and Doc hadn't been his friends, there's no telling what might have happened to him. Hazel thought Mack was the world's greatest human, while Doc he didn't consider human at all. Sometimes he said his prayers to Doc.

But Hazel was changing. Imperceptibly he had begun to pay attention. Perhaps Fauna had planted the germ by reading Hazel's horoscope. After his first protest he never mentioned it again, which should in itself have been suspicious.

Hazel did not want to be President of the United States. If there had been any avenue of escape he would have taken it, but his horoscope closed all doors. When a man is finally boxed and he has no choice, he begins to decorate his box. So Hazel, condemned to the presidency, since he could not escape it, began to ornament it. A man can climb high on the steps of responsibility.

Hazel began to prepare himself for the time when his call should come. He read every word of a copy of *Time* magazine, then went back to the beginning and read it again. He thought about it a great deal and came to the conclusion that it was nuts—which proves that Hazel's problem had been inattention, not unintelligence.

He bought a *World Almanac* and read the lives of the Presidents, and he began to wonder what he would do if the British impressed our sailors or the "Fifty-four-Forty" issue ever came up again.

He had accepted his duty and it made him sick. Sometimes in the morning he would awaken happy in the thought that it was a bad dream. Then he would count his toes and relapse into acceptance of his fate and his duty. What made it worst of all was the loneliness. He couldn't discuss it with anyone. He was set apart and above ordinary experience. When he had offered to fight Mack it was not in anger. He was preparing to defend the weak. When he had flown in the face of his friends, and refused to be a dwarf, and insisted on being Prince Charming, Hazel was not being vain. The dignity of his position was greater than himself. He could not let his future down.

In an ordinary time one of the boys would have noticed Hazel's suffering face, the weariness, the pained nobility, and they would have given him two tablespoons of Epsom salts. But in these times all men's souls were being tried, and women's too, and a tried soul doesn't look around much.

Hazel's attempts to figure out what had happened at the masquerade were fruitless. He remembered how he had been dignified and beautiful and then all hell had broken loose. And the aftermath was horrible. The spirit of the Palace Flop-house, tested under the torques and stresses of so many years, was broken, shattered like granite, which withstands so long the hammer blows, then suddenly disintegrates.

Mack, who considered life hardly worse than a bad cold, was sickened to death—his eyes were lack-lustre and his valiant soul was shot. And if Mack was that way, you can imagine what the boys were like—jellyfish washed up on an inhospitable shore.

"What happened?" Hazel asked, and eyes glanced at him and glanced away and no one had the will to explain. For several days Hazel thought it might be the bull-bitch hangover of all time, but it continued into the day of reviving thirst and there was no thirst. Hazel began to be afraid for his friends.

He sat under the cypress tree and he not only kept his mind on the subject, he actually thought about it. It was a time for greatness, and only Hazel had the strength to rise to that bright bait. When he stood up and brushed the cypress dirt from his jeans, he had completed the change. No longer was he Hazel the Innocent, Hazel the Unaware, Hazel the Dope. His shoulders squared to take the weight, and the calm beauty of strength shone from his eyes.

It was dusky in the Palace, mouldy and sad. The boys lay on their beds, listless and ruined. Mack stared up at his canopy, and he was the worst of all, for there was no expression on his face. He had not crashed in flames, he was eroding away.

When Hazel sat down quietly on the side of his bed Mack didn't even take a kick at him, although his shoes were on.

Hazel said, "Mack, Mack darling, you should shake the lead out of your pants now."

Mack did not answer, but he closed his eyes and two tears squeezed out and hung there until they dried.

Hazel said gently, "Mack, you want I should kick the hell out of you?"

Mack moved his head quietly back and forth in negation.

Hazel did not hold back. He threw his trump card in, and the hell with it. "I been over to Doc's," he said. "He's setting there with a pencil in his hand. He ain't wrote nothing. He ain't done nothing. He ain't thought nothing. Get off your behind, Mack, he needs us."

Mack spoke sepulchrally. "He needs us like a mud-dauber's nest up his pants leg. Don't blame me, Hazel. I can't fight back no more. I'm down for the count."

"What's happened, Mack?"

Mack's voice was hollow. "When we done it before we wrecked his joint and busted him, but that was mere chaff."

"How do you mean, mere chaff?"

"Oh, it was things busted—glass, records, dishes, books, stuff like that. But this time we've put a knife in his belly. If you keep trying to pat a guy on the head and instead you knock his brains out, you lost confidence." He sighed and turned over and covered his face with his arms.

"You ain't got the right to give in," Hazel said.

"I got the right to do any goddam thing I want."

"Now that sounds better!"

"Or not do nothing," said Mack.

"Look, Doc got to go to La Jolla, you know that. He got to make the spring tides next week. Then, when his new microscope comes he'll have devilfish and write his paper. We got to help him, Mack."

"Fauna says she used to manage a welterweight name of Kiss of Death Kelly. That's me—Kiss of Death Mack. Everything I touch withers like the sere and yellow leaf."

"Get up!"

"I won't," said Mack.

"Get up, I tell you!"

Mack didn't even respond.

Hazel went outside and looked around. He walked to a broken tar barrel lying in the weeds and pulled out a curved oaken stave. He went back and stood beside Mack's bed.

He judged distance and lift. He hit Mack so hard that his pants split. And only then did Hazel realize how serious it was, for Mack didn't even move. He only groaned.

Hazel fought down panic, and then he remembered his Fate—a sacrifice to Washington, where he would have to eat oysters. "All right, Mack," he said softly. "I'll have to do her myself."

He turned and walked out of the door with quiet dignity.

Mack rolled up on one elbow. "Did you hear what that crazy bastard said? Oh, what the hell! Can't do no worse than I done. Mother, make my bed soon, for I'm sick to the death and I fain would lie down."

"You're already down," said Whitey No. 2.

CHAPTER XXXI

THE THORNY PATH OF GREATNESS

When people change direction it is a rare one who does not spend the first half of his journey looking back over his shoulder. Hazel had chosen, or had been forced to choose, a new path. He had said, "I'll have to do her myself." It had seemed easy. But, sitting under the sheltering branches of the black cypress tree, he had to admit he didn't know who or what in the hell "she" was. He thought with longing of the old time when he was a dope, when he was cared for and thought for and loved. He had paid off, of course, by accepting ridicule, but it had been a lovely time, a warm time.

Doc had said long ago, "I like to have you sit with me, Hazel. You are the well—the original well. A man can give you his deepest secrets. You don't hear or remember. And if you did, it wouldn't make any difference because you don't pay attention. Why, you're better than a well because you listen—but you don't hear. You are a priest without penalties, an analyst without diagnosis."

Those were the good days before Hazel's responsibility. But responsibility required judgment, the choosing between courses, and what was that but thought? Hazel undertook thought, but he did it secretly. No one knew. He was a little ashamed of it. In the sweet old days he would have sat down under the black cypress and then he would have reclined his head on his arm and in less than a minute he would have been asleep. The new Hazel clasped his knees with his arms and mourned into the future. His mind climbed and slipped like an ant in the treacherous crater of an ant lion's trap. He must plan, he must judge, he must choose. No sleep came. He didn't even itch. He had to do her. But what was she? He never knew how his solution came to him. He dropped off to sleep, forehead on knees, then suddenly his muscles leaped as though under a blow. He had a sense of falling—and there was his course laid out before him. It wasn't an honourable course, but it was the only one he had. It almost amounted to treachery.

You will remember that it was Hazel's pleasant social custom to ask questions but not to listen to the answers. People expected that, depended on it. Suppose, he thought, I was to ask and then listen but not let on I'm listening. It was sneaky, but the intention was clean and the end infinitely to be desired.

He would not only listen, he would remember, and he would put all the answers together. Maybe then he would be able to think her and do her. One question would be enough, he thought. Maybe two.

Hazel was weary from his effort. He reclined, put his head on his arm, and slept the good sleep of work well done.

CHAPTER XXXII

HAZEL'S QUEST

Joe Elegant came cautiously back from his journey ready to take another one at a moment's notice. He expected reprisals for Hazel's costume, and there were no reprisals. In gratitude he made popovers at the Bear Flag three evenings in a row—and the girls didn't even know what they were eating. He wanted to know what had happened, but he was afraid to ask. Thus Joe Elegant was glad when Hazel called on him in his little lean-to in the rear of the Bear Flag.

"Sit here," he said. "I'll get you a piece of cake."

While he was gone Hazel regarded the works of Henri the artist on the wall—one from the chicken-feather period and one from the later nutshell time. And he looked at the card-table on which Joe Elegant worked at a portable typewriter. There was a neat pile of manuscript on the table, green paper typed with a green ribbon. A sheet of paper was in the machine. It began: "My dear Anthony West. It was sweet of you——"

Joe came back with a wedge of cake and a glass of milk for Hazel, and while Hazel munched and drank, Joe's large damp eyes bracketed him but never hit him.

"How'd it go?" he asked.

"What?"

"Why, your costume."

"Fine, fine. Everybody was real surprised."

"I'll bet they were. Did Mack say anything?"

"He said I done fine. He almost cried."

Joe Elegant smiled with quiet malice.

Hazel asked vacuously, "Say, what would you think was the matter with Doc?"

Joe crossed his legs professionally and his fingers rippled through the green-typed green pages. "It's the whole and the part and the part is the whole," he said.

"Come again?"

"It's many things and one thing. Doc's libido is driving him one way and his conscience is pulling him another. His myth is the sea, the wind, and the tide, and he relates to it by collecting animals. He carries his treasures to his laboratory. He wants to hide them and perhaps to place the dragon Fafnir on guard."

Hazel nearly said, "He sells them," but that would have given him away as listening. "I knew a dame named Fafnir," he said. "Bertha Fafnir. Third grade. Used to do pitchers of turkeys on the blackboard Thanksgiving. Had starched underskirts, they rustled kind of."

Joe Elegant scowled faintly at the interruption. "Distil the myth and you get the symbol," he went on. "The symbol is the paper he wants to write, but that in itself has impurities, needs distillation. Why? Because it is a substitute, that's why. His symbol is false. That's why he can't write his paper. Frustration! He has taken the wrong path. And so he brings in false solutions. 'I need a microscope,' he says. 'I need to go to La Jolla for the spring tides.' He will not go to La Jolla. He will never write his paper."

"Why not?"

"Wrong symbol. We must go back to the myth, the sea. The sea is his mother. His mother is dead but she is living. He is carrying treasures from his mother's womb and trying to save them. Do you understand?"

"Sure," said Hazel listlessly.

"He needs love. He needs understanding," said Joe Elegant.

"Who don't?" Hazel asked.

"I feel that I could help him if he would let me."

"I kind of thought he'd took a shine to Suzy," said Hazel.

Joe Elegant let a shadow of distaste tighten his mouth. "That would only be a new false path, a new frustration."

Hazel observed, "Some people like one thing, some another."

"Very original!" said Joe Elegant.

It was only a few steps from Joe Elegant's lean-to through the kitchen to the Ready Room. In the Ready Room sat Becky with her feet up, reading her mail. Becky subscribed to " Pen Pals " and had a lively correspondence all over the world. The sheet of rice paper in her hands was from Japan. "Dear Pen Pal," it began, "Your interest missive receipt. How gondola the Goldy State. Japan girl do hair-kink likewise, but not using blitch. My friend, Mitzi Mitzuki very West in minded. Would try if you mailing small little container hydrogen peroxide double pressure."

"Hi!" said Hazel.

Becky laid down her letter. "Ever been to Japan?"

"Nope."

"Me neither. How's Mack?"

"Fine. Say, Becky, what would you say was the matter with Doc?"

"Love," said Becky. "Doc's aching away. Or if he ain't, he ought to be. Nice fella like that."

"He sets like he been pole-axed."

"That'll do it. Poor fella! If it was me, why, I'd go to him and I'd put my cool hand on his brow and I'd say, 'Doc——' "

The door of Fauna's room opened. "I thought I heard voices. Hello, Hazel. Ain't none of the other girls around? Becky's poorly."

"I come to ask you something." said Hazel.

"Well, come on in here. Set down. Want a snort? Is it private? I'll shut the door."

"Yes," said Hazel, and that covered all the questions.

The snort brightened his eye. "What would you say was wrong with Doc?"

"I wouldn't of said it a while ago," said Fauna, "but when he put on that tie—and then, the other night——"

"Hell, he was drunk," said Hazel. "A guy will say anything when he's drunk."

"No, he will not," said Fauna.

"You think it's Suzy?"

"Yes, sir! And if she wasn't nuts, she would go to La Jolla with him and help him work. Why, hell! She'd be in."

"He's trying to write his paper."

"He got himself all bollixed up," said Fauna. "I bet he ain't even thinking about his paper."

"He ain't thinking about nothing."

"That's what I mean. If he could stop not thinking about Suzy, why, he could start thinking about his paper. That's my opinion anyway."

"You think if she went to La Jolla——?"

"I do. But she won't go."

"He wouldn't take her," said Hazel.

"If everybody wasn't such damn fools he wouldn't get asked," said Fauna. "I don't know what we're coming to. Have one more snort?"

"I can't," said Hazel. "I got to see a guy."

It was only a coincidence that Joseph and Mary Rivas was also reading a letter when Hazel entered the grocery. Joseph and Mary was reading and cursing at the same time, cursing in obscure Spanish. The letter was from James Petrillo, and it spoke in no uncertain terms. If the threat in the letter could be carried out, it looked as though what the U.S. Government could not do in keeping wet-backs out, the musicians' union could. The Patrón was in a stew. Ordinarily what he could not eliminate he joined. But Petrillo did not give him that choice. Joseph and Mary's mind strayed towards assassination.

Hazel said, "How're you?"

"Lousy!" said the Patrón.

"Ain't nobody feeling too good," Hazel observed. "Doc's setting over there like he's punch-drunk. What you think's the matter with him?"

"Christ knows!" said the Patrón. "I got troubles of my own. Funny thing," he said, "you know, last night I was coming home from Monterey, late, and there was a shadow up in the vacant lot. It moved into that bright spot the street light throws up by the boiler, and I swear to God it was Doc sneaking around up there."

"No!" said Hazel.

"I say yes." The Patrón looked over the vegetables and the piled canned goods and his eyes dwelt on the cardboard Coca-Cola girl in a swing. "Know something?" he said speculatively. "Before the party I would have said she was just one more tramp. Then she belted loose and moved into the boiler. And then, well—it looks like Doc seen something there. Maybe Suzy's got something I missed. I been thinking I might just take a whack at her."

"You can't," said Hazel. "She's Doc's."

"Hell," said the Patrón, "dames don't belong to nobody. I might just whistle under her window."

"She ain't got no windows," said Hazel.

The Patrón smiled. Petrillo's poison was going out of him. "Yes, sir!" he said. "Maybe I missed something."

"You stay away from her," said Hazel.

Joseph and Mary dropped his eyes, and an Indian looked out for a second. Then he smiled again. "Have it your own way," he said lightly. "I hear she's got a job."

This was the Golden Poppy: long, narrow, high-ceilinged; small octagonal tiles on the floor; dark wood counter with small round stools; units at intervals on the counter—juke-box slot, paper-napkin holder, salt, pepper, sugar, mustard, catsup; rear door to the kitchen with window and service shelf; cash register at the front, cigarette machine beside the door; long mirror behind the counter fronted by the coffee-maker, griddle, toasters, covered cakes and pies, stacked breakfast foods, doughnuts, rack of canned soup and soup heater, fight cards, movie schedule, bus timetable.

There was nothing to be done about the Golden Poppy. It was a dour and gloomy place dedicated to good coffee and sad, soggy food. It could not compete with the gay and phony little restaurants springing up in Monterey, with their checked tablecloths, show-card murals, low ceilings, and candles in cork floats.

The Golden Poppy did not try. There were many people who preferred it to the newcomers—customers who liked cold, damp doughnuts, stringy stews, and canned soup. These diners distrusted fish-nets on the walls and jokes on the menu. To them food was a necessary but solemn sacrament about which there should be no nonsense.

The rush hours were seven to eight-thirty, breakfast; eleven-thirty to one-thirty, lunch; six to eight, dinner. In between these hours there were the coffee customers, the sandwich and doughnut people. In the evening came two rush times: at nine-thirty when the early movie let out, and at eleven-thirty when the second show broke. At twelve-thirty the Golden Poppy curled its petals, except on Saturday nights, when it stayed open until two for the early drunks.

The coming of Suzy to the Golden Poppy had a curious but reasonable effect on Ella. She had, over the years, maintained an iron interdict against weariness and pain. If she had allowed herself to realize how miserable she was she would have cut her throat.

Suzy did more than help, she took over: joked with the salesmen, whistled over the sandwich toaster, remembered that Mr. Garrigas liked cream of celery soup and remembered his name too.

For a day or so Ella had watched Suzy and refused acidly when Suzy suggested that she go home and lie down for a couple of hours. Then her interdict cracked, and the crack widened. Abysmal fatigue, aching legs, and abdominal pains crept through. Ella was an exhausted woman when she came at last to admit it. Going home to lie down for an hour was first a sin, and then a luxury, and finally a drug.

Now when Suzy said after the nine-thirty rush, "Go on home and get a good night's sleep," it seemed perfectly natural. Not only could Suzy hold the fort, but her terse, professional gaiety was drawing in new customers.

At eleven-fifteen Suzy had the four Silexes filled with fresh coffee, the hamburgers between waxed paper in the ice-box, the tomatoes sliced, and the sandwich bread in the drawer below the griddle. At eleven-thirty the customers came in a rush from the second show.

Suzy grew six extra hands: club sandwiches, melted cheese sandwiches, cheeseburgers, and coffee, coffee, coffee! The cash register jangled and the change appeared standing up between the tits of the rubber mat.

"How's about a date Saturday?"

"Sure! Love to."

"Is it a date?"

"Can my husband come?"

"You married?"

"I won't be if I keep that date."

"You're a swell-looking kid."

"You're kind of pretty yourself. Here's your change."

"Keep it."

"Thanks. Cheeseburger coming up. Sorry, eighty-six on the tuna fish sandwiches."

In the seconds between orders, three of her extra hands crashed dishes into the soapy water, rinsed and dried them.

"Hey! Mr. Geltham, you forgot your umbrella!"

"So I did. Thank you." That would be another quarter tip, and the quarter went into a slotted can marked "Joe".

Every morning when Joe Blaikey came in for his coffee a little pile of silver was put before him and checked in the account book. It was amazing how it added up.

At five minutes to twelve Hazel came in and waited against the wall until a stool was vacant.

"Hi, Hazel. What'll it be?"

"Cup of coffee."

"It's on the house, Hazel. How you been?"

"Okay."

Gradually the customers thinned out and then were gone. Suzy's flashing hands put the Golden Poppy to bed: scrubbed the grill, washed down the counter, wiped the necks of the catsup bottles. She looked up to see Hazel sweeping out.

"Say, what the hell are you doing?"

"I figured we're both going the same way. I'll walk with you."

"Why not?" said Suzy. "You can carry my books."

"What?"

"Just a joke."

"Ha, ha!" said Hazel seriously.

They walked down Alvarado Street, all closed up except where the bars splashed neon culture on the sidewalk. At the tip of the Presidio they stopped and leaned their elbows on the iron railing and looked at the fishing-boats in the black water of the bay. They crossed the tracks, went past the Army warehouse, and entered the upper end of Cannery Row. And at last Hazel said, "You're a swell dame."

"Come again?"

"Say, what you think's the matter with Doc?"

"How would I know?"

"You sore at him?"

"How'd you like to mind your own business?"

"It's all right," said Hazel quickly. "I ain't bright. Everybody knows that."

"What's that got to do with keeping out of my hair?"

"Nobody pays no attention to me," said Hazel. He offered this as a recommendation. "Doc says I don't listen. He likes that."

They walked on in silence for a while. Then Hazel said timidly, "He done everything in the world for me. Once he went character witness for me and I ain't got no character. Once I'd of lost a foot, but he opened her up and shook powder on her and I still got her."

Suzy didn't answer. Their footsteps were loud on the pavement and echoed back from the iron fronts of dead canneries.

"Doc's in trouble," Hazel said.

Their footsteps filled the street.

"Anybody in trouble, why, they go to Doc. Nobody goes to him now he's in trouble."

Step, step, step.

"I got to help him," said Hazel. "But I ain't bright."

"What the hell do you want me to do?" said Suzy.

"Well, couldn't you go over and set with him?"

"No."

"If you was in trouble he'd help you."

"I ain't in trouble. How do you know he's in trouble?"

"I'm telling you. I thought you liked him."

"I like him all right. If he was in real trouble like if he was sick or bust his leg, I'd probably take him some soup."

"Jeeze! If he bust his leg he couldn't go to the spring tides," said Hazel.

"Well, he ain't busted his leg."

They passed Wide Ida's. Hazel asked, "You want a beer?"

"No, thanks." Then she said, "Ain't you going up to the Palace?"

"No," said Hazel, "I got to see a guy."

Suzy said, "Once, when I was a kid, I made an ash-tray for my old man and old lady——"

"They like it?"

"They didn't need no ash-tray."
"Didn't they smoke?"
"Yes," said Suzy. "Good night."

Hazel was approaching a state of collapse. In his whole life he had never sustained a thought for more than two minutes. Now his resources reeled under the strain of four hours of concentration. And it was not yet over. He had to make two more visits, and then he had to retire under the black cypress tree to sift his findings. So far he could see no light anywhere. His mental pictures were like those children's kaleidoscopes that change colour and design as they are turned. It seemed to Hazel that a slight zizzing sound came from his brain.

It was a catty night. Big toms crept about, their heads and shoulders flattened to the ground, seeking other toms. Lady cats preened themselves in sweet innocence, unaware of what they hoped was likely to happen to them. On the rocks off Hopkins Marine Station the sea-lions barked with a houndish quaver. The silver canneries were silent under the street lights. And from somewhere on the beach Cacahuete Rivas's trumpet softly mourned the "Memphis Blues".

Hazel had stopped for a moment in appreciation of the secret night. He looked up at the boiler where Suzy had gone, and into the streak of street light he saw a figure move. From the shape and posture he thought it must be the Patrón. In a way it was none of Hazel's business. He walked up the stairs and knocked on the door of Western Biological.

Doc sat on his bed regarding a heap of collecting paraphernalia: nets, buckets and jars, formaldehyde and Epsom salts and menthol, rubber boots and rubber gloves, glass plates and string. On his table stood a small new travelling aquarium with a tiny pump and motor run by two dry cells. Morosely he watched the mist of white air bubbles sift through the sea water.

"Come in," he said to Hazel. "I'm glad to see you."

"Just come to pass the time of day," said Hazel.

"Good. I'm glad. A man feels silly talking to himself, and at the same time it's private. You're the perfect answer, Hazel."

"Say, Doc, I just remembered. What's ass—astrophysic?"

"You don't really want me to tell you, do you?"

"Not very much. I just wondered. I signed up for it."

Doc shuddered. "I don't think I want to hear about that," he said.

"I brang you a pint."

"That's friendly of you. Will you join me?"

"Sure," said Hazel. "You're really going to La Jolla, huh?"

"Well, I guess I have to. That's one of the things I've been trying to figure out. I've made such a stink about it."

"Lot of people think you won't go."

"Well, that's one of the reasons I have to."

"Don't you want to?"

"I don't know," said Doc softly.

He got up from the bed and disengaged the wire from the dry cell. "No point in wasting juice," he said. "I've been tearing myself down like a Model T Ford in a backyard. Got the pieces all laid out. Still don't know why it won't run. Don't even know whether I can get it together again."

"I could help," said Hazel. "I know about Model Ts."

"It might turn out you know about people too," said Doc.

Hazel looked shyly down at his feet. No one had ever accused him of knowing anything before.

Doc chuckled. "That's my good Hazel!"

"Say, Doc, what you think is the matter with you?" Hazel was appalled at his daring, but he had asked. And Doc seemed to find the question reasonable.

"God knows," he said. "Some kind of obscure self-justification, I guess. I wanted to make a contribution to learning. Maybe that was a substitution for fathering children. Right now, my contribution, even if it came off, seems kind of weak. I think maybe I've talked myself into something, and now maybe I have to do it."

Hazel groped among his bits and pieces. "Mack's sorry about what him and Fauna done. He's just sick."

"He shouldn't be," said Doc. "I'm the one who messed it up."

"You mean you would have took Suzy on?"

"I guess so. I've thought about it ever since. For a couple of days there I felt different and better than I ever have in my life. A kind of built-in pain was gone. I felt wide open."

"About Suzy?"

"I guess so. I'm supposed to have this wild free brain without conventional barriers. And what did I do? I balanced a nasty ledger. I weighed education, experience, background, even probable blood lines. Some of the worst people I ever knew had the best of all those. Well, there it is. Saying it has made it even clearer. I guess I've thrown it away."

"Why don't you give it one more try, Doc?"

"How?"

"Why don't you take a candy bar or a bunch of carnations and knock on her door?"

"Right from the beginning, huh? Sounds kind of silly."

"Well, dames is all dame," said Hazel.

"You may have made a discovery. Have you seen her?"

"Yeah. She got that boiler fixed up real pretty. She got a job down at the Golden Poppy."

"How is she? What did she say?"

Hazel cast about again among his broken pieces. Her vehemence came back to him. "When she was a kid she made an ash-tray for her papa and mama——" Hazel let it hang there because it sounded ridiculous.

"Well, what about it?"

"They didn't need no ash-tray," said Hazel.

"She told you that?"

"Yep."

"Let's have a drink."

"I can't, Doc. I got one more—I mean, I got to see a guy."

"This late at night?"

"Yeah." And then Hazel confessed. "You been good to me, Doc. I wouldn't do no bad thing to you."

"Of course you wouldn't."

"But I done it."

"What?"

"Remember you always said you liked me 'cause I didn't listen?"

"Sure I remember."

Hazel's eyes were shy and ashamed. "I listened," he said.

"That's all right."

"Doc——"

"Yes?"

"Joseph and Mary's hanging around the boiler."

Hazel couldn't remember ever having been so tired. He had put his mind to unaccustomed tricks, and it was just as he had been afraid it would be. He had got nothing. He had started out hoping to find some kind of light to guide him. What he had got reminded him of Henri's painting in nutshells. He wanted to sleep a long time, perhaps never to awaken to a world in which he now felt himself a stranger. He had made a mess of it. He wondered if he would make as bad a mess in Washington.

He walked wearily through the vacant lot and up the chicken walk to the Palace Flop-house. He wanted to slip into bed in the dark and hide his failure in sleep.

Mack and the boys were waiting for up him.

"Where the hell you been?" said Mack. "We looked all over for you."

"Just walking around," said Hazel listlessly.

Mack moved and groaned. "Jesus! You hit me a crack," he said. "Damn near killed me."

"I shouldn't of did it," said Hazel. "You want I should rub it?"

"Hell, no! What you been up to? When you get making plans, the sky is falling on my tail, said Henny Penny."

Whitey No. 2 asked, "Who you been with?"

"Everybody. Just walking around."

"Well, who?"

"Oh, Joe Elegant and Fauna and Suzy and Doc."

"You seen Suzy?" Mack demanded.

"Sure. Went down to the Poppy for a cup of coffee."

"Look who's buying coffee!"

"It was on the house," said Hazel.

"Well, what did she say?"

"She says in the third grade she made an ash-tray."

"Oh, Jesus!" said Mack. "Did she say anything about Doc?"

"Yeah, I guess so."

"You guess so!"

"Don't ask me if you're going to be mean to me. That'll just get *me* mean."

Mack shifted painfully to his other buttock.

Hazel felt ringed with hostility. "I guess I'll go outside," he said miserably.

"Wait! What'd she say about Doc?"

"Said she didn't want no part of him, except—I'm going to go on out."

"Except what?"

"Except he got sick or bust a leg."

Mack shook his head. "Sometimes you get me thinking the way you do. God Almighty! I shouldn't of let you out alone."

"I didn't do no harm."

"I bet you didn't do no good neither. I bet right now you're trying to figure out germ warfare—how to get Doc sick."

"I'm tired," said Hazel. "I just want to go to bed."

"Who's stopping you?"

Hazel didn't even take off his clothes before he went to bed, but he didn't sleep either; at least not until the dawn crept out from Salinas. His brain was blistered and his responsibility rode him with surcingle and spurs.

CHAPTER XXXIII

THE DISTANT DRUM

Doc sat for a long time after Hazel had left him. His chest rustled with feeling and his throat was dry. His top mind looked at him—

a scientist, a thinker trained, conditioned to method, to exactness. No single thing could be permitted in unless it could be measured or tasted or heard or seen. The laws of science were Doc's laws, and he sought to obey them. To break these laws was not only sin to him but a danger, for violation would let in anarchy. He was frightened and cold.

His middle mind screamed with joy at his discomfiture. "I told you! All through the years I've told you you were fooling yourself. Let's see you get back to analysis. I dare you!"

And the low-humming mind in his entrails was busy too, aching and yet singing that the ache was necessary and good.

Middle mind had its way. Doc thought, Let's look at this. Here is a man with work to do. The girl—what is she? Let's suppose every good thing should come of a relationship with her. It still would do no good. There is no possible way for this girl and me to be successful—no way under the sun. Not only is she illiterate, but she has a violent temper. She has all the convictions of the uninformed. She is sure of things she has not investigated, not only sure for herself, but sure for everyone. In two months she will become a prude. Then where will freedom go? Your thinking will be like tennis against a bad player. Let's stop this nonsense! Forget it! You can't have it and you don't want it.

Middle mind hooted, "You can't *not* have have it too. Whatever happens, you've got her. Take a feel of your pulse, listen to your pounding heart. Why? You just heard the iron door of the boiler clang, that's why. You haven't even thought what that means yet, but you've got a pain in you because of that clang and because it's three-thirteen in the morning."

Low mind said, "Nothing's bad. It's all part of one thing—the good and bad. Do you know any man and woman—no matter how close—who don't have good and bad? Let me out! Or, by God, I'll set my claws in you and I'll tear at you for all your life! Let me out, I say! Feel this, this red burning? That's rage. Will you let it out or will it fester here until it makes you sick and crazy? Look at the time. You heard that iron door."

Doc looked at his watch—3.17. "Why, that son-of-a-bitch!" he said aloud. He snapped off his light and went to the window and looked out towards the strip of light the street lamp threw on the vacant lot. Then he opened his front door and crept down the stairs. Crossing the street, he followed a broad shadow and hid in it.

The Patrón was sitting on a big rusty pipe trying to work out a puzzle. He had it laid out and the pieces didn't make sense. Here was himself, young, good-looking, snappy dresser, and making dough. And here was a dame, a dime-a-dozen dame, living in a boiler, working for her keep. The Patrón knew methods too, and, if not scientific, they had served him well enough so that he could depend on them. You sweet-talk, you promise, you offer, and in reserve you always hold force. Every dame needs a little force. He felt the swelling knuckles of his right hand. This dame was nuts. She didn't listen to his pitch, and when he brought up force she slammed this iron door and damn near took his fingers off. He was going to lose the nails of all four fingers. The dirty bitch! Thus, musing bitterly, he did not hear Doc's approach.

Doc's fingers locked in the collar of the Patrón's striped shirt and yanked him to his feet. By reflex the Patrón lashed out with his foot and kicked Doc's legs from under him. The two fell together and rolled in the mallow weeds. Joseph and Mary tried for the groin with his knee, while Doc's delicate strong fingers laced around the throat. The Patrón felt the thumbs seeking the hollow below his Adam's apple. He tore at the white face with his fingers and Doc's thumbs went home. Flaring lights whirled in the Patrón's eyes and his brain turned red. He knew that in two seconds his thorax would collapse under the thumbs and he would be dead. He had seen it happen. He knew it and, so knowing, he went limp and in sweating terror felt the thumbs relax.

The Patrón lay still, and his sickened mind figured the chances—the groin or butt of head to chin? But if he missed, the terrible thumbs would come again. He was weak and afraid—afraid even to speak for fear the wrong word might draw the seeking thumbs. "Doc," he whispered, "I give up. You got me."

"Go near that girl again and I'll tear your throat out," Doc whispered back.

"I won't. I swear to God I won't."

In the grocery under the seven-watt light, the Patrón tried to get the cork out of a pint with his mashed fingers, but had to pass the bottle to Doc.

Doc felt the sickness that follows rage—and he also felt silly. He took a gulp of whisky and passed the bottle over the counter. Joseph and Mary drank and then bent over, coughing and spluttering. Doc had to run round the counter to beat him on the back. When he could speak, Joseph and Mary looked at Doc with wonder.

"I can't understand it," he said. "Where'd you learn that trick? What'd you want to do it for? You might of killed me."

"I guess I wanted to," said Doc. "I must have wanted to." He laughed embarrassedly. "I thought you were making a pass at Suzy."

"I was," said Joseph and Mary. "Jesus, Doc, I didn't know you was that way with her."

"I'm not," said Doc. "Give me a drink."

"You wasn't playing tiddlywinks," said Joseph and Mary.

"Now don't get excited. She give me the bum's rush. Hell, she damn near took off my fingers with that door. You ain't got any competition from me, Doc. She's all yours."

"She won't even see me," said Doc.

"Won't? What in hell *is* the matter with her?"

"Who knows?"

They rested their elbows on the counter and faced each other.

"Beats me," said Joseph and Mary. "What you going to do?"

Doc smiled. "Hazel said take her flowers and a candy bar."

"He might have something there. I can't figure her." Gingerly the Patrón let a little whisky dribble down his throat and winced as it passed the bruised place. "I guess she's just nuts," he said. "And if she's nuts, a guy's got to do nuts things. You don't think you could say the hell with her?"

"I have, over and over."

"Don't do no good?"

"Not a bit. I know it's damn foolishness, but there it is."

"I knew guys like that. There ain't nothing to do about it, I guess." His eyes sharpened. "I remember something," he said. "When I was talking to her through that damn fire-door to-night she says, 'When I find a guy that's up to his eyes I'll dive in,' she says. And I says, 'For Doc?' 'Hell, no!' she says. 'He's sliced like package bacon.' "

"I guess she's right," said Doc.

"That ain't what I was thinking. Look, Doc, when you had the hooks in me, if I'd went on—well, would you of?"

"I guess so. I can hardly believe it of myself, but I guess I would have. I never did anything like that before. Why?"

"Well, I just thought—a guy that'll do a killing with his hands ain't sliced too thin. Let's finish the pint, Doc, and then I'll help you."

"Help me what?"

"Flowers," said Joseph and Mary. "We got an hour before daylight. Up above Lighthouse Avenue there's front yards just lousy with flowers."

CHAPTER XXXIV

THE DEEP-DISH SET-DOWN

Joe Elegant was only the cook at the Bear Flat, not the bouncer, with the result that his services were never required late at night. He retired early and set his alarm clock at four. This gave him three or four hours every morning over his portable to tap out green letters on green paper.

The book was going well. His hero had been born in a state of shock and nothing subsequent had reassured him. When a symbol wasn't slapping him in the mouth, a myth was kicking his feet out from under him. It was a book of moods, of dank rooms with cryptic wallpaper, of pale odours, of decaying dreams. There wasn't a character in the whole of *The Pi Root of Œdipus* who wouldn't have made the observation ward. The hero had elderly aunts beside whom the Marquis de Sade was an altar-boy. The pile of green manuscript was three inches thick, and Joe Elegant was beginning to plan his photograph for the back of the dust-cover: open collar, he thought, and a small, wry smile, and one hand relaxed in front of him with an open poison ring on the third finger. He knew which reviewers he could depend on and why. He typed: "A pool scummed with Azolla. In the open water in the middle of the pond a dead fish floated belly up . . ."

Joe Elegant sighed, leaned back, and scratched his stomach. He yawned, went into the Bear Flag's kitchen, and started a pot of coffee. While it was heating he walked out into a glorious morning. The pelicans were drumming in for a run of tom cod, and little pink Kleenex clouds hung over the bay. Joe saw the flowers in front of the boiler door and moved over to inspect them—a huge bouquet of tulips, early roses, jonquils, and iris. They might have been anyone's offering, except that their stems were in a museum jar.

Joe Elegant's life had not been in danger since the engagement and raffle party, but he hadn't felt much friendliness in Cannery Row either. He carried his news into the Bear Flag and served it to Fauna on a tray along with her coffee and crullers. By eight o'clock the news was in the Palace Flop-house, and the early men were ingesting it with their whisky sours at the La Ida.

The best seats were in the Ready Room with its windows overlooking the vacant lot. Mack was there behind a curtain, munching Fauna's crullers. The girls were there in their best kimonos. Becky had put on her mules with the ostrich feathers. At eight-thirty the audience heard the boiler door screech and shushed one another.

Suzy, on her hands and knees, poked her head out of the fire-door and rammed her nose into the giant floral tribute. For a long moment she stared at the flowers, and then she reached out and dragged them inside. The iron door closed after her.

At nine o'clock Suzy re-emerged and walked rapidly towards Monterey. At nine-thirty she was back. She went into the boiler and in a moment came out, pushing her suitcase ahead of her. The audience was filled with dismay, but only for a moment. Suzy climbed the steps and rang the bell at the Bear Flag. Fauna chased the girls to their rooms and Mack out the back way before she answered the door.

Suzy said, "You told me I could use your bathroom."

"Help yourself," said Fauna.

In an hour, when the splashing had ceased, Fauna knocked on the bathroom door. "Want a little toilet water, honey?"

"Thanks," said Suzy.

In a few minutes she emerged, scrubbed and shining.

"Like a cup of coffee?" Fauna asked.

"Wish I could," said Suzy. "I got to run. Thanks for the bath. There ain't nothing like a good deep-dish set-down bath."

Fauna, from behind a curtain, watched her crawl back into the boiler.

In her office bedroom Fauna scribbled a note and sent it by Joe Elegant to Western Biological. It read: "She ain't going to work to-day."

CHAPTER XXXV

IL N'Y A PAS DE MOUCHES SUR LA GRANDMERE

Doc laid his best clothes out on his cot. There were pale acid spots on the washed khaki trousers, the white shirt was yellow with age, and he noticed for the first time that his old tweed jacket was frayed through at both elbows The tie he had worn to the dinner at Sonny Boy's was spotted. He found a black army tie in the bottom of his suitcase. For the first time in his life he was dissatisfied with his clothing. It was silly to feel serious about it, but there was no doubt that he was serious. For a time he sat down and regarded his wardrobe and his life, and he found them both ridiculous. And not less ridiculous was the quaking certainty that he was frightened.

He spoke aloud to the rattlesnakes, and they ran out their forked tongues to listen.

"You are looking at a fool," he said. "I am a reasonable man, a comparatively intelligent man—I.Q. one hundred and eighty-two, University of Chicago, Master's and Ph.D. An informed man in his own field and not ignorant in some other fields. Regard this man!" he said. "He is about to pay a formal call on a girl in a boiler. He has a half-pound box of chocolates for her. This man is scared stiff. Why? I'll tell you why. He is afraid this girl will not approve of him. He is terrified of her. He knows this is funny, but he cannot laugh at it."

The eyes of the snakes looked dustily at him—or seemed to.

Doc went on, "Let me put it this way: there is nothing I can do. They say of an amputee that he remembers his leg. Well, I remember this girl. I am not whole without her. I am not alive without her. When she was with me I was more alive than I have ever been, and not only when she was pleasant either. Even when we were fighting I was whole. At the time I didn't realize how important it was, but I do now. I am not a dope. I know that if I should win her I'll have many horrible times. Over and over, I'll wish I'd never seen her. But I also know that if I fail I'll never be a whole man. I'll live a grey half-life, and I'll mourn for my lost girl every hour of the rest of my life. As thoughtful reptiles you will wonder, 'Why not wait? Look farther! There are better fish in the sea!' But you are not involved. Let me tell you that to me not only are there no better fish, there are no other fish in the sea at all. The sea is lonely without this fish. Put that in your pipe and smoke it!"

He took off his clothes and had a shower and scrubbed himself until his skin was soap-burned and red. He brushed his teeth until his gums bled. His hands were frayed with formalin, but he gouged at his discoloured nails just the same, and he brushed at his overgrown hair and he shaved so close that his face was on fire. At last he was ready—and still he looked for things to do, to put off his departure.

His stomach was crowding up against his chest, forcing him to breathe shallowly. I should take a big slug of whisky, he thought. But it would be on my breath and she would know why I'd taken it. I wonder if she's frightened too? You never know. Women can conceal these things better than men. Oh God, what a fool I am! I can't go this way. I'm falling to pieces. My voice would tremble. Why, the little—no, don't do that. You can't build your courage by running her down. You're going to her, not she to you. Why do I say "you" when it is "I"? Am I afraid of "I"?

And then he knew what to do. He went to his records and he found the *Art of the Fugue*. If I can't get courage from his greatness, he thought, I might as well give up. He sat unmoving while Bach built a world and peopled it and organized it and finally fought his world and was destroyed by it. And when the music stopped, as the man had stopped when death came to him, stopped in the middle of a phrase, Doc had his courage back. "Bach fought savagely," he said. "He was not defeated. If he had lived he would have gone on fighting the impossible fight."

Doc cried to no one, "Give me a little time! I want to think. What did Bach have that I am hungry for to the point of starvation? Wasn't it gallantry? And isn't gallantry the great art of the soul? Is there any more noble quality in the human than gallantry?" He stopped and then suddenly he seemed to be racked with inner tears. "Why didn't I know before?" he asked. "I, who admire it so, didn't even recognize it when I saw it. Old Bach had his talent and his family and his friends. Everyone has something. And what has Suzy got? Absolutely nothing in the world but guts. She's taken on an atomic world with a sling-shot, and, by God, she's going to win! If she doesn't win there's no point in living any more.

"What do I mean, win?" Doc asked himself. "I know. If you are not defeated, you win."

Then he stabbed himself in vengeance for having run Suzy down. "I know what I'm doing. In the face of my own defeat I'm warming myself at her gallantry. Let me face this clearly, please! I need her to save myself. I can be whole only with Suzy."

He stood up and he did not feel silly any more and his mission was not ridiculous. "So long," he said to the rattlesnakes. "Wish me luck!" He took his box of candy and went jauntily down the steps of Western Biological. Crossing the street, he knew he was being observed from every window from which he was visible, and he didn't care. He waved a salute to his unseen audience.

Going through the vacant lot among the mallow weeds, he thought, How do you knock on an iron door? He stooped and picked a rusty tenpenny nail from the ground and he arrived almost gaily at the boiler and tapped a little drum-beat on the iron wall. The fire-door was slightly ajar.

Suzy's voice sounded with a metallic ring. "Who is it?"

"It's I," said Doc. "Or me—somebody like that."

The fire-door opened and Suzy looked out. "Thanks for the flowers," she said.

"I brought you another present."

She looked at the candy box in his hand. Being on her hands and knees, she had to twist her neck to look up at him. Doc couldn't tell whether there was suspicion and doubt on her face or only strained muscles from her position.

"Candy?" she asked.

"Yes."

"I don't——" she began, and then Fauna's words crowded in on her with short punches. "What the hell," she said. "Thanks."

Doc was losing his poise. Suzy had straightened her neck and from her position she couldn't see above his knees. Doc tried for lightness again, and he sounded clumsy to himself. "This is a formal call," he said. "Aren't you going to ask me in?"

"Do you think you can get in?"

"I can try."

"There ain't much room inside."

Doc remained silent.

"Oh, for God's sakes come on in!" said Suzy. She backed her head out of the opening.

Doc got down on his hands and knees. He threw the candy box through the fire-door, then crawled through the opening. He thought with amusement, a man who can do this with dignity need never again fear anything; and at that moment his trouser cuff caught on the door and pulled it closed against his ankle. He was all inside except one foot and he could not free himself. "I seem to be hung up," he said.

"Hold it," said Suzy. She straddled him and worked the cuff loose from the door corner. "I think you tore your pants," she said as she backed off over his shoulders. "Maybe I can mend 'em for you."

Doc's eyes were getting used to the dim interior. A little light came in from the smoke-stack and met a little more that entered from the fire-door.

"It's hard to see at first," said Suzy. "I got a lamp here. Wait, I'll light it up."

"No need," said Doc. He could see now and something in him collapsed with pity at the pretension of the curtains, the painted walls, and the home-built dressing-table with its mirror and bottles. My God, what a brave thing is the human! he thought. And then Suzy brought his rising compassion crashing down.

"There's a welder eats at the Poppy. Know what he's going to do first any day he can? Bring his torch and cut windows in the sides."

Her voice echoed with enthusiasm. "I'll put in little window frames and some flower boxes with red geraniums," she said. " 'Course, I'll have to paint the outside then, white, I think, with green trim. Maybe a trellis like in front. I got a nice hand with roses."

Then she was silent. Constraint and formality sifted in and filled the boiler.

Doc thought in wonder, It's not a boiler at all. Somehow she has managed to make a home of this. He said, "You've done a wonderful job here."

"Thanks."

He spoke his thought. "It's a real home."

"It's comfortable," she said. "I never had no room of my own."

"Well, you have now."

"Sometimes I set in here and think how they'd have to blast to get me out if I didn't want to come."

Doc gathered his courage. "Suzy, I'm sorry for what happened."
"I don't want to talk about it. It wasn't none of your fault."
" Yes, it was."
"I don't think so," she said with finality.
"I would do anything to——"
"Look, Doc," she said, "you won't let it alone, so maybe I got to rub your nose in it a little. It wasn't no fault of yours, but it sure as hell give me a lesson. I had myself a bawl and now it's done. There ain't nothing for you to do. I don't need nothing. Anybody's sorry for me, they're wasting their time. I ain't never had it so good in my life. Got that? Well, don't forget it! There ain't nothing for you nor nobody to do, 'cause I'm doing it all myself. If you can get that through your knocker, okay. If you can't you better take a powder."
He said, "What a conceited fool I've been!"
Then silence hung in the boiler. Suzy broke it when she felt that his nose was sufficiently rubbed in it.
"Know what?" she said brightly. "They got a night class, typing, at the high school. I signed on. Next Saturday I get a rent typewriter. I can learn."
"I'll bet you can too. Maybe you'll type my paper for me."
"You're going to write it after all?"
"I've got to, Suzy. It's all I have. I'm a dead duck without it. I'm going to La Jolla Saturday for the spring tides. I'm glad. Are you?"
"Why not?" she asked. "I don't like to see nobody kicked in the face." She drew up formality like a coverlet. "You want I should make you a nice cup of tea? I got a Sterno stove."
"I'd like it."
She had the situation in hand now, and she talked on easily while she lighted the stove and put her little tea-kettle on to boil.
"I'm making good tips down at the Poppy," she said. "Paid off Joe Blaikey in two weeks. Ella's thinking about taking a week's vacation. She ain't never had a vacation. Hell, I can run the joint easy. 'Scuse that 'hell'. I don't hardly never cuss no more."
"You're doing fine," said Doc. "Could you tell me, without rubbing my nose in it, what you want in a man? Might help me—another time."
"Tea's ready," said Suzy. She passed him the steaming cup. "Leave it steep a little longer," she said. "Sugar's in the cup on the dressing-table."
When he was stirring the sugar in she said, "If I thought it wasn't a pitch you was making I'd tell you."
"I don't think it's a pitch."
"Okay, then. Maybe what I want ain't anywhere in the world,

but I want it. So I think there is such a thing. I want a guy that's wide open. I want him to be a real guy, maybe even a tough guy, but I want a window in him. He can have his dukes up every other place but not with me. And he got to need the hell out of me. He got to be the kind of guy that if he ain't got me he ain't got nothing. And brother, that guy's going to have something!"

"Except for toughness, you're kind of describing me," said Doc.

"You keep out of this! You told me and I was too dumb to listen. You like what you got. You told me straight. I'd spoil it. Took me a long time to wise up, but I sure wised up."

"Maybe what I said wasn't true."

"When you said it with your face it was true all right."

Doc felt beaten. There was no anger in her tone, nothing but acceptance, together with an undertone of excitement. That was it, excitement, almost amounting to gaiety.

He said, "You know, Suzy, you sound happy."

"I am," said Suzy. "And you know who done it for me?"

"Who?"

"Fauna. That's a hunk of dame! She made me proud, and I ain't never been proud before in my life."

"How did she do it?" Doc asked. "I need some of that myself."

"She told me, and made me say it—'There ain't nothing in the world like Suzy'—and she says Suzy is a good thing. And goddam it, it's true! Now let's knock it off, huh?"

"Okay," said Doc. "I guess I ought to be going."

"Yeah," said Suzy, "I got to go to work. Say, remember that guy you told me about that lived out where we went that night?"

"The seer? Sure, what about him?"

"Joe Blaikey had to pick him up."

"What for?"

"Stealing. From the Safeway store. Joe hated to do it."

"I'll see what I can do. So long, Suzy."

"You ain't mad?"

"No, Suzy, but I'm sorry."

"So'm I. But hell, you can't have everything. So long, Doc. Hope you do good at La Jolla."

When Doc crossed the street this time he hoped no one was watching. He went into the laboratory, walked to his cot, and lay down. He was sick with loss. He couldn't think. Only one thing was sure: he had to go to La Jolla. If he didn't he would die, because there would be nothing left in him to believe in, even to defend. He squinched his eyes closed and looked at the bright points of light swimming on his retinas.

There were footsteps on his porch and the snakes whirred their rattles, but not violently.

Hazel opened the door and looked in. He saw Doc's expression and the hope died out of him.

"No soap?" he asked.

"No soap," said Doc.

"There got to be some way."

"There isn't," said Doc.

"Anything I can do?"

"No. Yes, there is too. You know Joe Blaikey?"

"The cop? Sure."

"Well, he picked up a man in the sand dunes. Find Joe and tell him I'm interested in the man. Tell him to be nice to him. I'll be down to see him as soon as I can. Tell Joe the man is harmless." Doc rolled on his side and dug in his pocket. "Here's two dollars. Ask Joe to let you see the man and give him—no, stop at the Safeway and buy a dozen candy bars and take them to the seer and then give him the change."

"Seer?"

"That's the man's name," said Doc wearily.

"I'll do her right now," Hazel said proudly. He went out at a dogtrot.

Doc was arranging himself comfortably in his misery again when there was a knock on the door.

"Come in," he cried.

There was no answer but a second knock and a wild buzzing from the snakes.

"Oh Christ!" said Doc. "I hope not schoolchildren on a culture tour."

It was a telegram, a long one, collect. It said:

EUREKA! GREEK WORD MEANING I HAVE FOUND IT. YOU ARE NOW AN INSTITUTION. HAVE SET UP CEPHALOPOD RESEARCH SECTION AT CALIFORNIA INSTITUTE OF TECHNOLOGY. YOU ARE IN CHARGE. SIX THOUSAND A YEAR AND EXPENSES. GET TO WORK ON YOUR DEVILFISH. AM MAKING ARRANGEMENTS FOR YOU TO READ PAPER CALIFORNIA ACADEMY AT END OF YEAR. ALL CLEARLY DEDUCTIBLE. CONGRATULATIONS. WISH I COULD HEAR YOUR WORDS WHEN YOU HAVE TO PAY FOR THIS WIRE.

Doc laid the telegram beside him on the cot. "The son-of-a-bitch," he said.

CHAPTER XXXVI

LAMA SABACHTHANI?

HAZEL SAT on the end of the steel cot in the Monterey jail and looked with interest at the seer.

"Open up one of them Baby Ruths," he said. "If you're a friend of Doc's, can't nothing bad happen to you."

"I don't know him," said the seer.

"Well, he knows you. That's your good luck."

"I don't know any doctors."

"He ain't that kind. He's a doctor of bugs and stuff like that."

"Oh yes, I do remember. I gave him dinner."

"And he give you candy bars."

"I probably won't eat them."

"Why, for Crissake, not?"

"Tell my friend Doc, that greed poisoned me. I love candy bars. I stole only one at a time and eased my conscience of a little crime. But yesterday an appetite like a whip overcame me. I stole three. The manager of the Safeways says he knew I was stealing one at a time. He let it go. But when I took three he couldn't let it pass. I don't blame him. Who knows what I would have done next? Some other appetite might have driven me. I'll punish myself by smelling these bars and not eating them."

"I think you're nuts!" said Hazel.

"I guess so. I have no basis of comparison so I don't know how other people feel."

"You talk a little like Doc," said Hazel. "I don't get none of it."

"How is he?"

"Not too hot. He got troubles."

"Yes, I could see that. I remember now. He wore loneliness like a shroud. I was afraid for him."

"Jesus, you do talk like him! He got dame trouble."

"That was bound to be. When a man is cold he looks for warmth. When he is lonely there's only one cure. Why doesn't he take the woman?"

"She won't have him unless."

"I see. Sometimes they're that way."

"Who?"

"Women. What do you mean, unless?"

Hazel looked at the seer with level, penetrating eyes. This man talked like Doc. Maybe he could help. But with this thought there came also caution.

"I'd like to ask you something," Hazel said.

"What?"

"Well, this ain't none of it true. It's a kind of a—a whatchamacallit——"

"Hypothetical question?"

"I guess so."

"S'pose there's a guy and he's in trouble."

"Yes?"

"Well, he can't get out of it. But he got a friend maybe he don't know about."

"That's you," said the seer.

"No, it ain't! It's some other guy. I forget his name." He hurried on, "Well, s'pose the guy's in trouble and there's one way he can get out but he can't do it. You think his friend ought to do it?"

"Certainly."

"Even if it hurt like hell?"

"Certainly."

"Even if it might maybe not work?"

"Certainly. I don't know what the situation is with your Doc, but I know how it should be with you. If you love him you must do anything to help him—anything. Even kill him to save him incurable pain. This is the highest and most terrible duty of friendship. I gather that what you must do is violent. You must first make sure it can be successful, and you must, second, make sure within yourself that you know you will be punished. It is quite possible that even if you are successful your friend will never speak to you again. That takes a lot of love—maybe the greatest love. Make sure you love him that much."

Hazel caught his breath. "Hell, there ain't no such guy. It's hypa—it's malarky, a kind of riddle."

"I guess you do love him that much," the seer said.

No one knows how greatness comes to a man. It may lie in his blackness, sleeping, or it may lance into him like those driven fiery particles from outer space. These things, however, are known about greatness: need gives it life and puts it in action; it never comes without pain; it leaves a man changed, chastened, and exalted at the same time—he can never return to simplicity.

Under the black cypress tree Hazel writhed on the ground. From between his clenched teeth came little whimpers. As the night drew on and the moon went down, leaving blackness, so desolation fell on Hazel, so that he cried out against the agony of his greatness as that Other did, feeling forsaken.

Hour after hour the struggle went on, and only about three o'clock in the morning was Hazel saturated. Then he accepted it as he had accepted the poisoned Presidency of the United States. He was calm, for there was no escape. If anyone had seen him it would have been a dull man who did not find him beautiful.

Hazel picked his chosen instrument from the ground—an indoor-ball bat. He crept like a night-coloured cat out of the black shadow of the cypress tree.

In less than three minutes he returned. He lay on his stomach under the tree and wept.

CHAPTER XXXVII
LITTLE CHAPTER

Dr. Horace Dormody hated night calls, like everybody else, but Doc was his friend and he responded to the frenzied voice on the telephone. In the lab he looked at Doc's white face and then at his right arm.

"It's broken all right. I don't know how badly. Think you could get to my car? I want to X-ray."

And later he said, "Well, that's that. It's clean and it will take time. Now, tell me your cock-and-bull story again."

"I was asleep," said Doc. "Only thing I can think is that I must have turned over and it was caught between the cot and the wall."

"You mean you weren't in a fight?"

"I tell you I was asleep. What are you grinning about? What's so funny?"

Dr. Horace said, "Have it your own way. It's none of my business—unless the other fellow shows up. The tissue over the break is smashed. It looks as though it's been hit with a club."

"I can't have it!" Doc cried. "I've got to go to La Jolla tomorrow for the spring tides!"

"And turn over rocks?"

"Sure."

"Try and do it," said Dr. Horace. "Is the cast getting hot?"

"Yes," said Doc despondently.

CHAPTER XXXVIII

HOOPTEDOODLE (2), OR THE PACIFIC GROVE BUTTERFLY FESTIVAL

WHEN THINGS get really bad there are some who seek out others who have it worse, for consolation. It is hard to see how this works, but it seems to. You balance your trouble against another's, and if yours is lighter you feel better.

You would say the situation in Cannery Row was just about hopeless. Consider, then, the plight of the town of Pacific Grove, and you will understand why the lights burned all night in the Masonic Hall and why there was talk of getting rid of the city government. It wasn't a small thing. The whole town was involved. The butterflies had not arrived.

Pacific Grove benefits by one of those happy accidents of nature that gladden the heart, excite the imagination, and instruct the young.

On a certain day in the shouting springtime great clouds of orangey Monarch butterflies, like twinkling aery fields of flowers, sail high in the air on majestic pilgrimage across Monterey Bay and land in the outskirts of Pacific Grove in the pine woods. The butterflies know exactly where they are going. In their millions they land on several pine trees—always the same trees. There they suck the thick, resinous juice which oozes from the twigs, and they get cockeyed. The first-comers suck their fill and then fall drunken to the ground, where they lie like a golden carpet, waving their inebriate legs in the air and giving off butterfly shouts of celebration, while their places on the twigs are taken by new, thirsty millions. After about a week of binge the butterflies sober up and fly away, but not in clouds: they face their Monday morning singly or in pairs.

For a long time Pacific Grove didn't know what it had. Then gradually it was remarked that an increasing number of tourists were drawn to see the butterflies, Where there are tourists there is money, and it is a sin to let it drift away. Pacific Grove had a gravy train right in its lap. And the butterflies came free. It is only natural that the Great Butterfly Festival evolved, and where there is a festival there is bound to be a pageant.

There was ointment trouble at first. Pacific Grove is not only a dry town, but ardently dry. The sale of various tonics of good alcoholic content is the highest in the state, but there is no liquor. The fact that the visiting butterflies came to the dry oasis to get drunk seemed a little unfair, but the town solved this, first, by ignoring it, and then, by hotly denying it. The Butterfly Pageant explains the whole thing: There was once a butterfly princess (sung by Miss Graves), and she wandered away and was lost. Somehow a bunch of Indians (citizens in long brown underwear) got in it. I forget how. Anyway, the loyal subjects searched and searched and at last they found their princess and in their millions came to rescue her. (When they lie flat on their backs their legs are waving greetings to their queen.) It all works out very nicely. The pageant is in the ball park and tourists can buy butterflies made out of every conceivable material from pine cones to platinum. The town makes a very nice thing out of it. Why, the symbol of Pacific Grove on its advertising is the Monarch butterfly.

In all history there has been only one slip-up. In 1924, I think it was, the butterflies did not come, and the frantic town was forced to print hundreds of thousands of paper butterflies in two colours and spread them all over. To-day a wise city government keeps a huge supply of paper Monarchs on hand in case tragedy should strike again.

Now the time of the arrival is set, give one or two days in either direction. The pageant has been practising for months, the Indians are trained, the prince has his tights out of moth-balls, and the princess flowers towards coloratura luxury.

Perhaps it was an omen. Two days before the insects were due, Miss Graves lost her voice. She was a nice young woman, rather pretty and rather tired. She taught fourth grade, which is enough to tire anyone. Sprays and injections had no effect. Perhaps it was psychosomatic pressure that closed her throat and bottled up all but a dry squawk. Her eyes were feverish with despondency.

And then the days went by and the butterflies did not arrive. At first there was panic in Pacific Grove, and then a blind anger set in and the citizens looked about for someone to blame. The city government was a push-over. It was time for a change. Storekeepers whose book-keeping was shaky blamed it on the mayor. Moving-picture attendance had fallen off. The city council took the rap for that. The matter became a growl, and the growl a roar: "Turn the rascals out!"

Then there was a hotel fire in King City, sixty miles away, and guess who came boiling out with an overcoat and a blonde? Mayor Cristy of Pacific Grove didn't even trouble to resign. He left town, and just as well. There was talk of tar and feathers. He must have heard. The town hadn't been so upset since the Great Roque War.

The religious block blamed the whole thing on sin without going into details. The cynics wanted to throw the whole council out, together with the chief of police and the water commissioners. More solid citizens placed the blame where it belonged, on Roosevelt-Truman socialism. And the butterflies did not come.

Then the first grade had its scandal. William Taylor 4th brought his crayons home wrapped in the dust-cover of the Kinsey Report. On being confronted, he panicked and said he got it from the teacher, Miss Bucke. She was questioned, and it developed that her father had signed a petition for the release of Eugene V. Debs in 1918. It had got so nobody could trust anybody.

And Miss Graves went on croaking.

And the butterflies did not come.

So, you see, the trouble on Cannery Row wasn't as horrible as you thought.

CHAPTER XXXIX

SWEET THURSDAY REVISITED

Again it was a Sweet Thursday in the spring. The sun took a leap towards summer and loosed the furled petals of the golden poppies. Before noon you could smell the spice of blue lupins from the fields around Fort Ord.

It was a sweet day for all manner of rattlesnakes. On the parade ground a jack rabbit, crazy with spring, strolled in March Hare madness across the rifle range and drew joyous fire from two companies before he skidded to safety behind a sand dune. That jack rabbit's moment of grandeur cost the government eight hundred and ninety dollars and gladdened the hearts of one hell of a lot of soldiers.

Miss Graves awakened breathless with expectancy. She sang a scale in half-tones and found that her voice was back and all was well with the world. And she was right. At eleven o'clock the Monarch butterflies came boiling in from across the bay and landed in their millions on the pine trees, where they sucked the thick sweet juice and got cock-eyed. The butterfly committee met in emergency session in the fire-house and got out the crowns of fairies and the long brown underwear of Indians. The mayor *pro tem* of Pacific Grove wrote a proclamation for the evening paper.

The tide was very low that morning, preparing for the spring tides, and the warm sun dried the seaweed so that billions of flies came on excursion to feed.

People felt good. Judge Albertson discharged the seer on the recommendation of the Safeway manager.

Dr. Horace Dormody whistled through his mask over an appendectomy and told a political joke to the anaesthetist, but he didn't mention Doc's broken arm. A patient's problems, no matter how funny, were sacred to Dr. Horace. But he couldn't help chuckling discreetly to himself now and then.

How did the word spread about Doc's arm? Who knows? Fauna heard it with her crullers. Alice, Mabel, and Becky got it with their orange juice. The Patrón heard it from Cacahuete, who thereupon rushed to the beach and played three loud and uninhibited choruses of "Sweet Georgia Brown", using six changes of key.

Wide Ida was siphoning Pine Canyon whisky into Old Crow bottles when she heard it.

Mack and the boys had the news early, and it gave them something pressing to do.

Suzy opened up the Poppy that morning. The counter was crowded with breakfasters who dawdled over coffee. It was well into the morning before Suzy heard that Doc had broken his arm. And then she couldn't do anything about it because Ella was getting a permanent. But after she heard it some mid-morning customers got curious service from a Suzy who looked blankly over their heads when they spoke to her. She called Mr. MacMinimin Mr. Gross, and she called Mr. Gross 'you' and served his eggs straight up, which sickened him.

Mack was first on the scene. He didn't even put on his shoes. He regarded the new cast, which still hadn't cooled off, and listened to the only explanation Doc could think of—that he had got his arm caught between the cot and the wall.

"What you going to do?" Mack asked.

"I don't know. I have to get south, I have to!"

Mack was about to make an offer when a thought came to him that made him say, "Maybe something'll turn up." He bolted for the Palace Flop-house.

Once there, he went to Hazel's bed and found it pristine and unwrinkled.

"He ain't been in," said Whitey No. 1.

"Well, what do you think of that?" Mack said with admiration. "Why, the sweet son-of-a-bitch!"

Mack went out to the cypress tree and crawled under its low-hanging limbs, and he dragged Hazel out the way you'd drag a puppy from under a bed and half carried him up to the Palace Flop-house.

Hazel was far gone in emotional fatigue. "I had to," he said hopelessly.

"Anybody seen Suzy?" Mack asked.

"I seen her go to work early," said Eddie.

"Well, you better go break the news to her. Do it off-hand," said Mack. "Now, Hazel, how'd you do it?"

"You mad with me?"

"Hell, no," said Mack. " 'Course we don't know how she'll work out, but it's a step in the right direction." He turned to the two Whiteys. "I want you should notice Hazel didn't bust Doc's leg. That was good judgment. Doc can walk, but he can't work. You, Whitey," he said to Whitey No. 2, "I want you should get over to Doc's and hang around. If anybody offers to drive him down to La Jolla you take care of it. Where's the indoor-ball bat?"

"I throwed it in the bay," said Hazel.

"So that's what it was! Whitey, you get yourself a couple of feet of gas pipe."

Hazel went into collapse. Mack sat on the edge of his bed and placed and replaced cold damp rags on Hazel's feverish brow.

Hazel struggled for speech. "Mack," he said, "I can't do her. I don't care if the stars or even the cops say I got to, I can't do her. I ain't got the poop."

"What you talking about? You already done her."

"I don't mean that. You tell Fauna she got to get somebody else for President of the United States."

Mack stared down at him in amazement. "I'll be damned," he said. "I thought you'd forgot."

"I practised," said Hazel brokenly. "I don't want to let nobody down, Mack, but I just ain't no good at it. Try and get me off, will you, Mack? Please? Pretty goddam please?"

Mack's eyes brimmed with compassion. "Well, you sweet bastard," he said. "You poor little rabbit. Don't you worry. Ain't nobody going to force you. You done noble stuff. Wasn't nobody with guts but you."

"It ain't oysters," Hazel said. "Hell, I could do that. I'd eat old socks if I had to. It's just—the job's too big for me. I'd mess up the whole country."

Mack said, "You just lay there, Hazel baby, Mack's going to take care of it. There ain't nobody brave as you. Whitey," he said to Whitey No. 1, "you set here on Hazel's bed and kind of pet him. Don't let him get up until I get back." And Mack hurried out.

"You got to do something and do it quick," Mack said to Fauna. "S'pose Hazel gets another noble idea—why, hell, he might kill somebody."

"Yeah," said Fauna. "I can see how it is. Just let me get my stuff together. You think he'd like a nice monkey head?"

"He'd love it," said Mack. "He needs it."

Fauna held her chart in front of Hazel's eyes. "Anybody can make a mistake," she said. "They was a fly speck on the chart. Saturn wasn't in the bicuspid at all."

Hazel said suspiciously, "How do I know you ain't malarkying me now just to make me feel good?"

"How many toes you got?"

"I counted them—nine."

"Count them again."

Hazel slipped off his shoes. "Looks like the same as before," he said.

"Look at that little toe kind of bent under. Hell, Hazel, I may of made a mistake with a fly speck, but you miscounted your toes! You got ten. One bent under."

A slow smile began to spread over Hazel's face, a smile of relieved delight. Then for a moment the shadow of worry came back. "Who you think they'll get instead of me?"

"Nobody knows," said Fauna.

"Well, he better be good," said Hazel ominously. And then he abandoned himself to pure relief. " 'I got a little shadow that goes in and out with me,' " he sang.

Fauna rolled up her chart and went home.

Just before noon the express-man picked his unaccustomed way up to the chicken walk to the Palace Flop-house.

"I got a great big crate for you guys," he said. "I ain't got no call to deliver it up a rope ladder. Come on down and get it."

"It's here!" Mack cried. "God works in his tum-te-dum way his tum-tums to perform."

Hazel and Whitey No. 1 and Mack were wrestling the big wooden case up the chicken walk when Eddie joined them.

"Suzy come!" he cried. "I come with her. Seemed like she was about to take off any minute. She's in there with him now."

"Give us a hand," said Mack. "How's she look?"

"Fireball," said Eddie.

They carried the case into the Palace and Mack attacked it with a hand axe.

"There she is," he said when the lid was off.

"She's with Doc. Say, what you got?"

"Look!" said Mack. And he and the boys gazed down on the instrument, the great black tube of an eight-inch reflector, eyepieces socketed beside it, and its tripod cradled.

"Biggest one in the whole damn catalogue," said Mack proudly. "Jesus, Doc'll be happy! Eddie, tell us everything that happened, don't leave nothing out."

What a day it was! A day of purple and gold, the proud colours of the Salinas High School. A squadron of baby angels manoeuvred at twelve hundred feet, holding a pink cloud on which the word J-O-Y flashed on and off. A seagull with a broken wing took off and flew straight up into the air, squawking, "Joy! Joy!"

Suzy was ahead of her racing feet when Eddie intercepted her. She answered yes and no to Eddie's casual comments on the weather, but not only did she not hear the comments, she didn't know Eddie was beside her.

She went up the steps of Western Biological without seeing Whitey No. 2 standing guard with a sash-weight. Her coming relieved him of a duty, but he stuck around to hear.

At the top of the steps Suzy became a breathless, shy girl, and, as anybody knows, there is nothing more indestructible and deadly than a shy young girl. She paused to get her breath and then knocked on the door and went in and forgot to close the door — which was good for Whitey No. 2.

Doc was sitting on his cot gloomily regarding the pile of collecting paraphernalia on the floor.

"I heard you was hurt," Suzy said gently. "I come to see if there was anything I could do."

For a moment Doc's face lightened, then gloom descended. "This shoots the spring tides," he said, staring at the white cast. "I don't know what I'll do."

"Does it hurt much?" Suzy asked.

"Some. It will hurt more later, I guess."

"I'll go down to La Jolla with you."

"And turn over rocks that weigh fifty or a hundred pounds?"

"I ain't put together with spit," said Suzy.

"Can you drive a car?"

"Sure," said Suzy.

"You can't do it," he said. And then, from way down in the deep part of him, there came a bubbling shout, "Sure you can! I need you, Suzy. I need you to go with me. It will be terribly hard work and I'm pretty near helpless."

"You can tell me what to do and what to look for."

"Sure I can. And I'm not entirely helpless. I can use my left hand."

"It's a cinch," said Suzy. "When do we start?"

"I've got to go to-night. If we drive all night we can make the tide at seven-eighteen to-morrow morning. Think you can make it?"

"Cinch," said Suzy. "If you need me."

"I need you all right. I'd be lost without you. But you'll be a tired kid."

"Who cares?" said Suzy.

"I want to ask you something," said Doc. "Old Jingleballicks has set up a foundation for me at Cal. Tech."

"Why not?"

"I don't have to work there."

"Fine."

"I don't know whether I oughtn't to throw it in his face."

"Why don't you?"

"On the other hand, there's all the wonderful equipment."

"Fine," said Suzy.

"I don't like to work for anybody."

"Give it back."

"But there's an invitation to read my paper before the Academy of Science."

"Do it, then."

"I don't know whether I can even write the paper. What shall I do, Suzy?"

"What do you want to do?"

"I don't know."

"What's wrong with that? Say, Doc, I got to do a couple of things. Take me maybe two hours. That too long?"

"Just as long as we start by evening."

"I'll come back soon's I finish."

Doc said, "Suzy, I love you."

She was headed for the door. She whirled and faced him. Her brows were straight and her mouth taut. Then she took a slow breath and her lips became full and turned up at the corners and her eyes shone with incredible excitement.

"Brother," said Suzy, "you got yourself a girl!"

CHAPTER XL

I'M SURE WE SHOULD ALL BE AS HAPPY AS KINGS

In the Palace Flop-house, Suzy sat on a straight chair surrounded by the boys. She wore a look of furious concentration. Her feet were on two bricks and she held a barrel-hoop in her hands. Propped in front of her was a board on which were chalked 'ignition key', 'speedometer', 'choke', and 'gas gauge'. On the floor on her right side stood an apple box with a mop-handle sticking upright out of it.

"Try her again," said Mack. "Turn the key and reach up with your right toe for the starter."

Suzy put her foot on a chalk spot on the floor.

"Chug-a-chug-a-chug," said Hazel happily.

"Push out your clutch."

Suzy pushed her left foot down on a brick.

"Now bring the gear to you and back."

She moved the mop-handle to low gear.

"Ease up the gas and let in the clutch. Now clutch out, away from you and forward. Give it gas. Now clutch out and straight back. There, you done it good. Now do it again."

At the end of an hour and a half Suzy had driven the straight chair roughly a hundred and fifty miles.

"You'll do all right," said Mack. "Take it slow. If you can get two miles out of town without ramming into something, you can tell him the truth. He ain't going to turn back then. He'll tell you what to do. I'll get her started and kind of lined up with the street."

"You're a bunch of nice guys," said Suzy.

"Hell, if Hazel can go to all the trouble to break—oop, sorry!—the least we can do is see he gets some good out of it. Come on now—whang her through the gears again!"

The evening was as lovely as the day had been. The setting sun pinked up the little white caps on the bay and lighted the serious pelicans pounding home to the sea rocks. The metal cannery walls seemed a soft and precious platinum.

Doc's old car stood in front of Western Biological, its back seat loaded with buckets and pans and nets and crow-bars. All Cannery Row was there. The Patrón had set out pints of Old Tennis Shoes along the kerb. Fauna's hair blazed in the setting sun. The girls gave Suzy quick little hugs. Becky was in romantic tears.

Joe Elegant looked out of his lean-to door. He thought he would go to Rome after his book was published.

Doc held a list in his hand and checked equipment.

Only Mack and the boys were missing. And here they came down the chicken walk, balancing among them the tripod and the long black tube. They crossed the track and the lot and they set the tripod down beside the car.

Mack cleared his throat. "Friends," he said, "on behalf of I and the boys it gives me pleasure to present Doc with this here."

Doc looked at the gift—a telescope strong enough to bring the moon to his lap. His mouth fell open. Then he smothered the laughter that rose in him.

"Like it?" said Mack.

"It's beautiful."

"Biggest one in the whole goddam catalogue," said Mack.

Doc's voice was choked. "Thanks," he said. He paused. "After